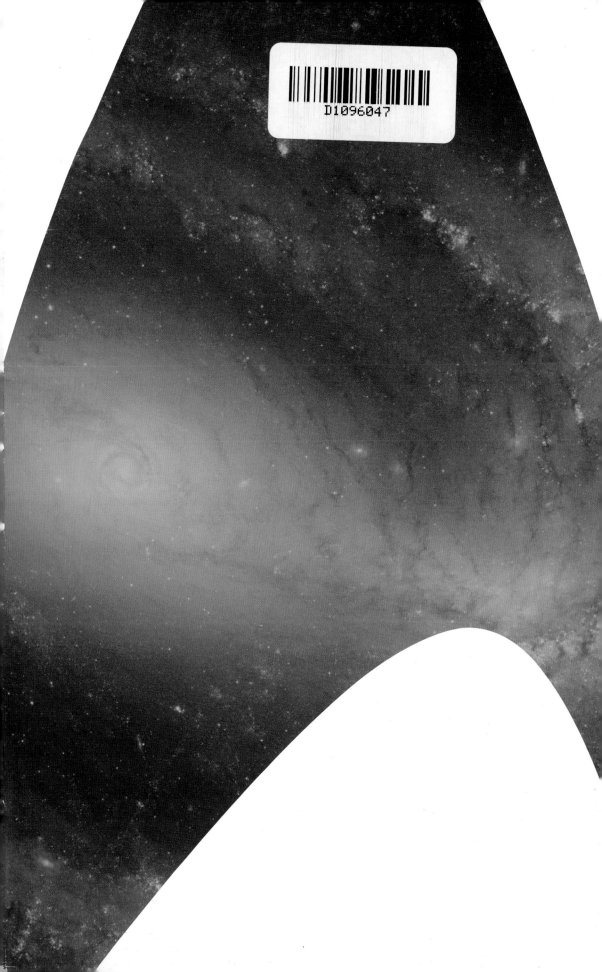

IDW

Facebook: **facebook.com/idwpublishing**
Twitter: **@idwpublishing**
YouTube: **youtube.com/idwpublishing**
Tumblr: **tumblr.idwpublishing.com**
Instagram: **instagram.com/idwpublishing**

COVER ART BY
PAUL SHIPPER

978-1-63140-413-9   20 19 18 17   2 3 4 5

COLLECTION EDITS BY
JUSTIN EISINGER
AND ALONZO SIMON

COLLECTION DESIGN BY
JEFF POWELL

PUBLISHER
TED ADAMS

Originally published as STAR TREK issues #13–24.

Ted Adams, CEO & Publisher
Greg Goldstein, President & COO
Robbie Robbins, EVP/Sr. Graphic Artist
Chris Ryall, Chief Creative Officer/Editor-in-Chief
Matthew Ruzicka, CPA, Chief Financial Officer
Lorelei Bunjes, VP of Digital Services
Jeff Bennington, VP of New Product Development

Special thanks to Risa Kessler and John Van Citters of
CBS Consumer Products for their invaluable assistance.

STAR TREK

THE NEW ADVENTURES
VOLUME 2

WRITTEN BY
MIKE JOHNSON

CREATIVE CONSULTANT
ROBERTO ORCI

HENDORFF

ART BY **STEPHEN MOLNAR**
COLORS BY **JOHN RAUCH**
LETTERS BY **NEIL UYETAKE**

KEENSER'S STORY

ART BY **STEPHEN MOLNAR**
COLORS BY **JOHN RAUCH**
LETTERS BY **NEIL UYETAKE**

MIRRORED

ART BY **ERFAN FAJAR**
ADDITIONAL ART BY
HENDRI PRASETYO AND
MIRALTI FIRMANSYAH
OF **STELLAR LABS**
COLORS BY **IFANSYAH** AND
SAKTI TUWONO OF **STELLAR LABS**
LETTERS BY **NEIL UYETAKE**
Based on the original teleplay
of *Mirror, Mirror* by Jerome Bixby

BONES

WRITTEN BY **MIKE JOHNSON**
AND **F. LEONARD JOHNSON, M.D.**
ART BY **CLAUDIA BALBONI**
INKS BY **ERICA DURANTE**
COLORS BY **CLAUDIA SGC**
LETTERS BY **CHRIS MOWRY**

THE VOICE OF A FALLING STAR

WRITTEN BY **RYAN PARROTT**
ART BY **CLAUDIA BALBONI**
INKS BY **ERICA DURANTE**
COLORS BY **CLAUDIA SGC**
LETTERS BY **SHAWN LEE**

SCOTTY

ART BY **CLAUDIA BALBONI**
INKS BY **ERICA DURANTE**
COLORS BY **ARIANNA FLOREAN**
COLORS SUPERVISOR: **CLAUDIA SGC**
LETTERS BY **NEIL UYETAKE**

RED LEVEL DOWN

WRITTEN BY **RYAN PARROTT**
ART BY **CLAUDIA BALBONI**
AND **LUCA LAMBERTI**
INKS BY **ERICA DURANTE** AND **LUCA LAMBERTI**
COLORS BY **ARIANNA FLOREAN**
COLORS SUPERVISOR: **CLAUDIA SGC**
LETTERS BY **TOM B. LONG**

AFTER DARKNESS

ART BY **ERFAN FAJAR**
ADDITIONAL ART BY **AGRI KARUNIAWAN**
COLORS BY **STELLAR LABS**
LETTERS BY **NEIL UYETAKE**
AND **CHRIS MOWRY**

PREDATORY

PENCILS BY **CLAUDIA BALBONI**
INKS BY **MARINA CASTELVETRO**
COLORS BY **ARIANNA FLOREAN**
COLOR ASSIST BY **AZZURA FLOREAN**
AND **VALENTINA CUOMO**
LETTERS BY **NEIL UYETAKE**

ORIGINAL SERIES EDITS BY **SCOTT DUNBIER**

STAR TREK CREATED BY **GENE RODDENBERRY**

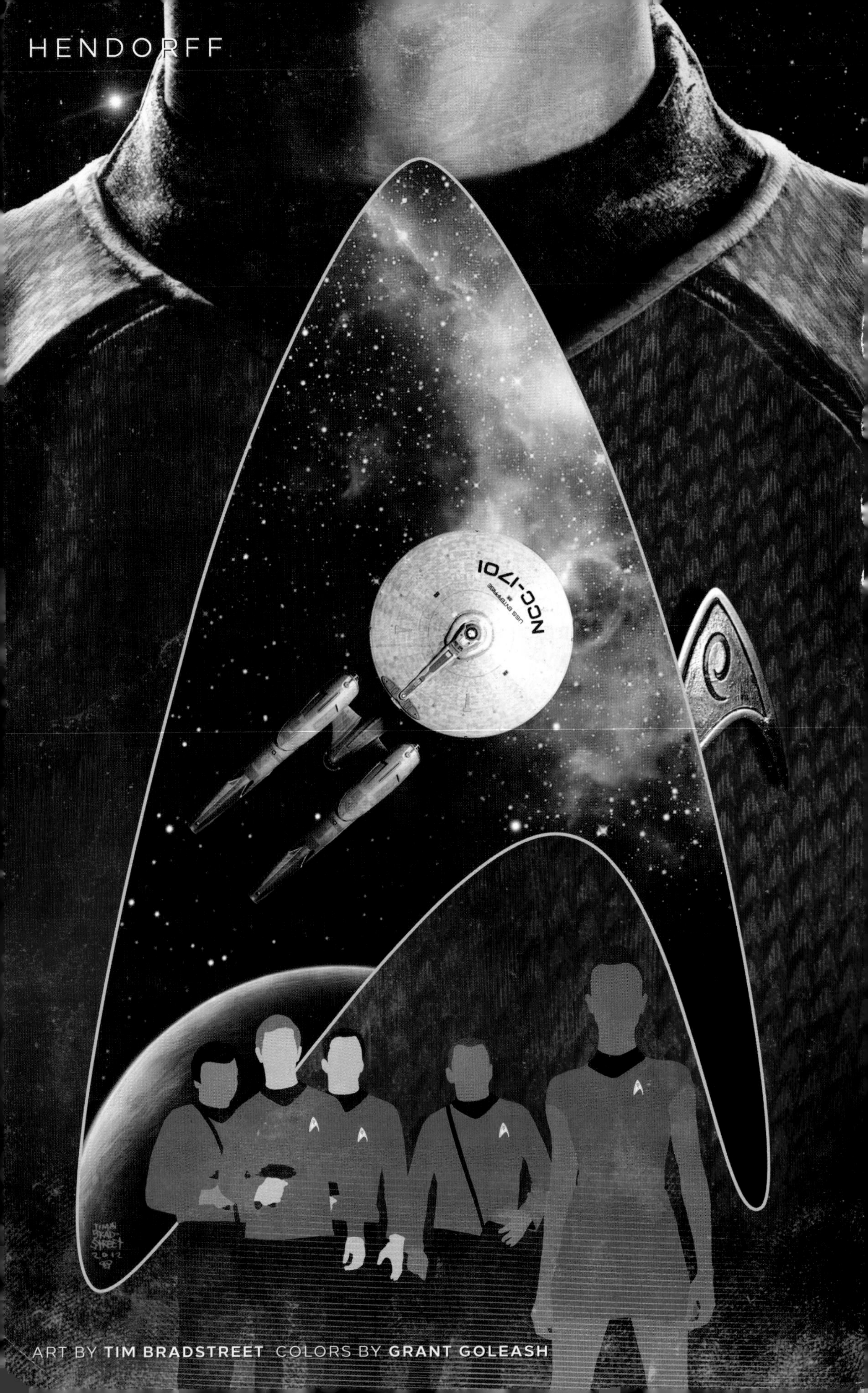
HENDORFF
NCC-1701
USS ENTERPRISE

ART BY **TIM BRADSTREET** COLORS BY **GRANT GOLEASH**

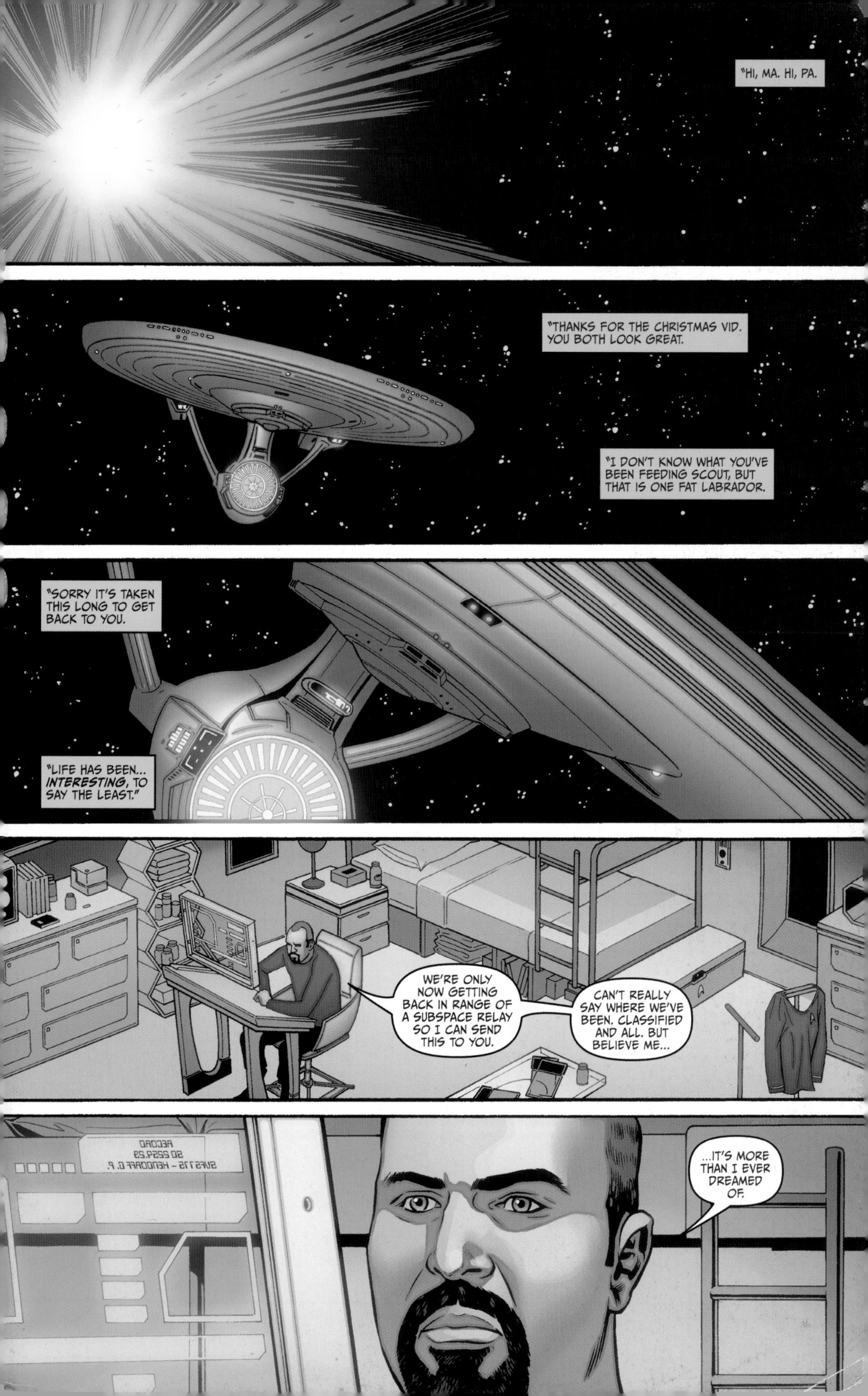
"HI, MA. HI, PA.
"THANKS FOR THE CHRISTMAS VID. YOU BOTH LOOK GREAT.
"I DON'T KNOW WHAT YOU'VE BEEN FEEDING SCOUT, BUT THAT IS ONE FAT LABRADOR.
"SORRY IT'S TAKEN THIS LONG TO GET BACK TO YOU.
"LIFE HAS BEEN... *INTERESTING*, TO SAY THE LEAST."
WE'RE ONLY NOW GETTING BACK IN RANGE OF A SUBSPACE RELAY SO I CAN SEND THIS TO YOU.
CAN'T REALLY SAY WHERE WE'VE BEEN. CLASSIFIED AND ALL. BUT BELIEVE ME...
...IT'S MORE THAN I EVER DREAMED OF.

OFFICIAL MEETING WITH THE CAPTAIN WAS A LITTLE...

"...AWKWARD."

WANTED TO SEE ME, SIR?

HENDORFF!

YES, COME IN, HAVE A SEAT!

I WANTED TO, UH...

...CLEAR THE AIR.

SO TO SPEAK.

CLEAR THE AIR, SIR?

WELL, YEAH, I MEAN...

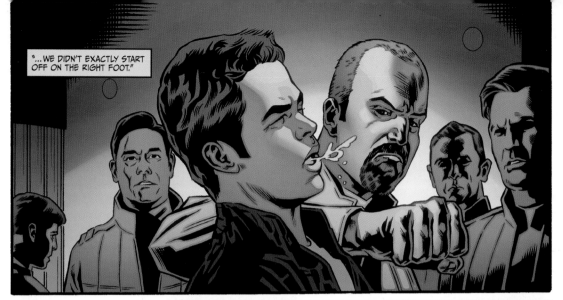

"...WE DIDN'T EXACTLY START OFF ON THE RIGHT FOOT."

ARE YOU REFERRING TO THE INCIDENT IN IOWA A COUPLE OF YEARS BACK, SIR?

THE "INCIDENT"? THAT "INCIDENT" RESET MY JAW.

SIR, IF YOU WANT ME TO APOLOGIZE, I—

NOT YOU, HENDORFF.

ME. I'M THE ONE APOLOGIZING. I WAS WAY OUT OF LINE THAT NIGHT. I DESERVED IT.

I SAW YOU A COUPLE OF TIMES AT THE ACADEMY LATER ON, WANTED TO SAY SOMETHING, BUT... DIDN'T KNOW WHAT.

"AND THEN THERE WAS THE SECOND TIME WE MET, WHEN I WAS AT THE WRONG END OF YOUR PHASER."

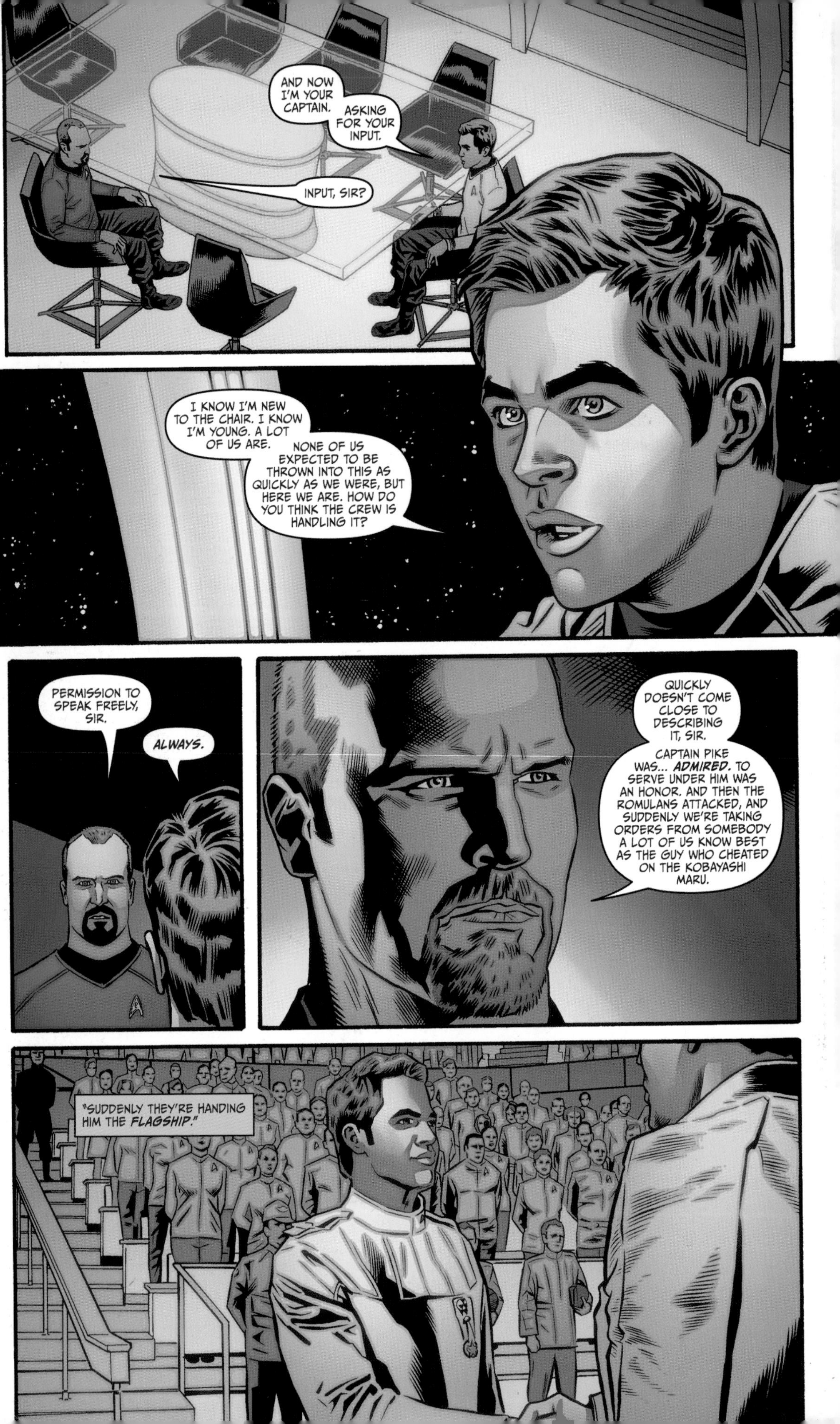
AND NOW I'M YOUR CAPTAIN.
ASKING FOR YOUR INPUT.
INPUT, SIR?
I KNOW I'M NEW TO THE CHAIR. I KNOW I'M YOUNG. A LOT OF US ARE.
NONE OF US EXPECTED TO BE THROWN INTO THIS AS QUICKLY AS WE WERE, BUT HERE WE ARE. HOW DO YOU THINK THE CREW IS HANDLING IT?
PERMISSION TO SPEAK FREELY, SIR.
ALWAYS.
QUICKLY DOESN'T COME CLOSE TO DESCRIBING IT, SIR.
CAPTAIN PIKE WAS... ADMIRED. TO SERVE UNDER HIM WAS AN HONOR. AND THEN THE ROMULANS ATTACKED, AND SUDDENLY WE'RE TAKING ORDERS FROM SOMEBODY A LOT OF US KNOW BEST AS THE GUY WHO CHEATED ON THE KOBAYASHI MARU.
"SUDDENLY THEY'RE HANDING HIM THE FLAGSHIP."

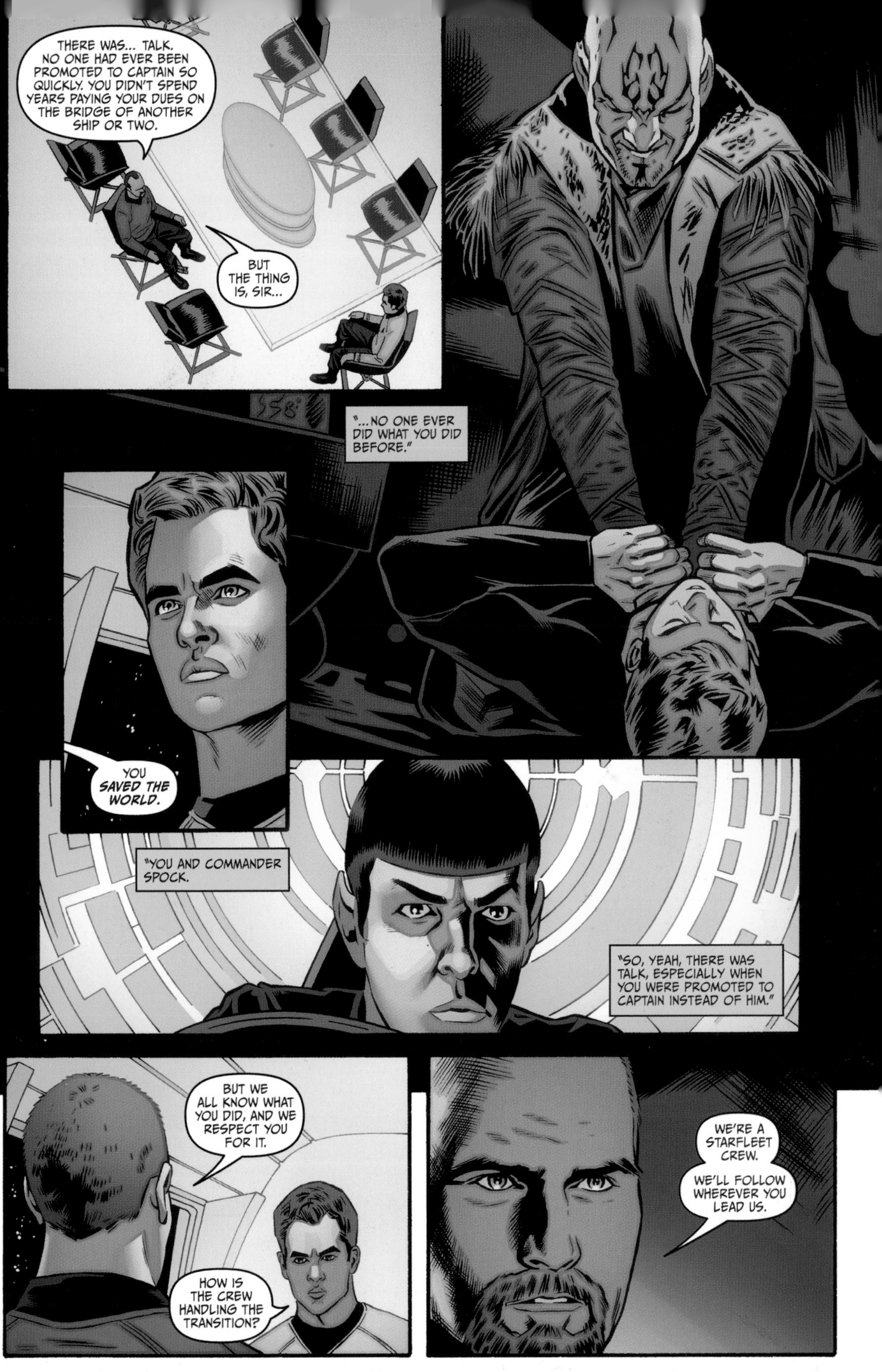
THERE WAS... TALK. NO ONE HAD EVER BEEN PROMOTED TO CAPTAIN SO QUICKLY. YOU DIDN'T SPEND YEARS PAYING YOUR DUES ON THE BRIDGE OF ANOTHER SHIP OR TWO.
BUT THE THING IS, SIR...
"...NO ONE EVER DID WHAT YOU DID BEFORE."
558
YOU *SAVED THE WORLD.*
"YOU AND COMMANDER SPOCK.
"SO, YEAH, THERE WAS TALK, ESPECIALLY WHEN YOU WERE PROMOTED TO CAPTAIN INSTEAD OF HIM."
HOW IS THE CREW HANDLING THE TRANSITION?
BUT WE ALL KNOW WHAT YOU DID, AND WE RESPECT YOU FOR IT.
WE'RE A STARFLEET CREW.
WE'LL FOLLOW WHEREVER YOU LEAD US.

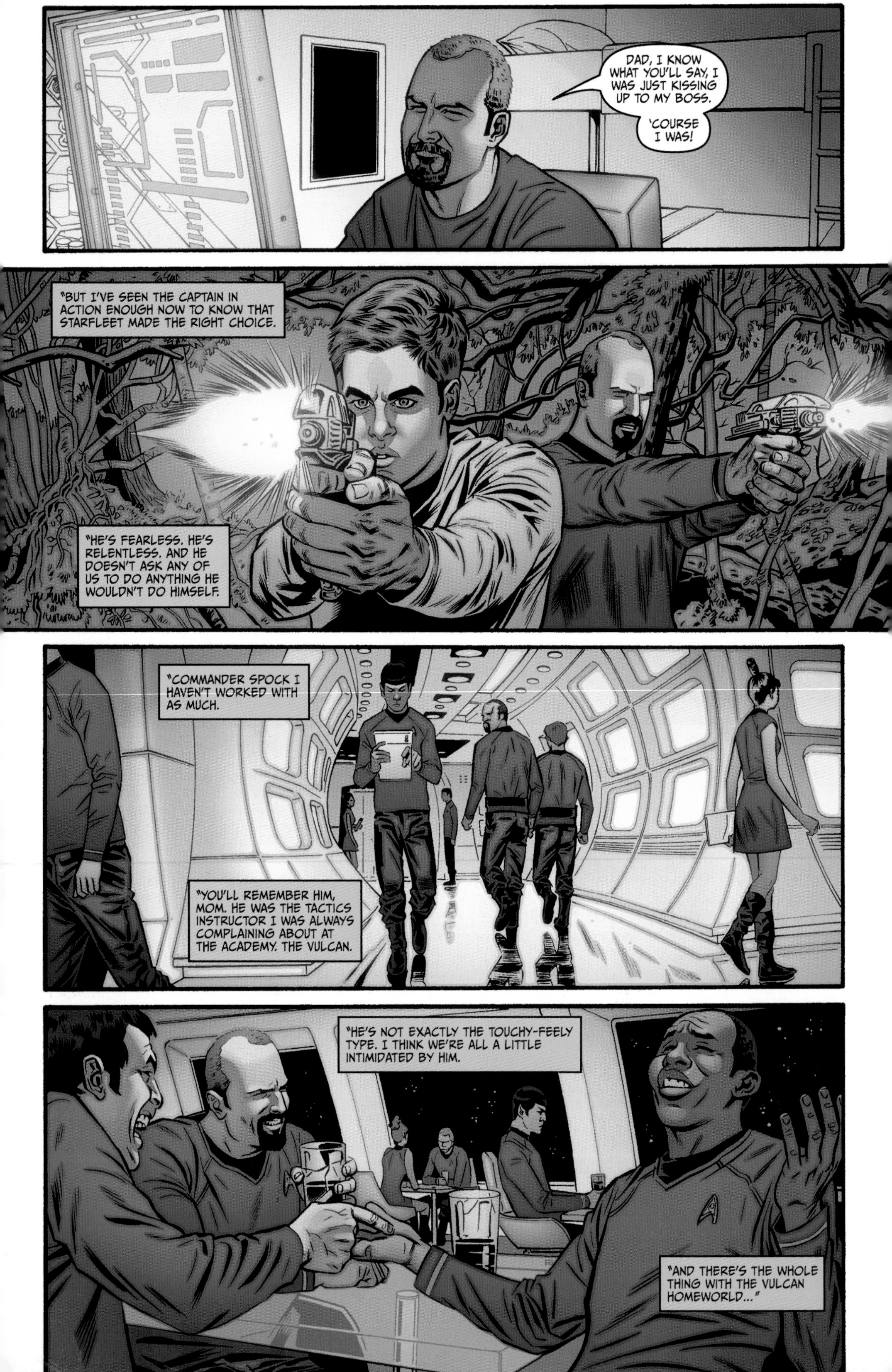
DAD, I KNOW WHAT YOU'LL SAY, I WAS JUST KISSING UP TO MY BOSS.
'COURSE I WAS!
"BUT I'VE SEEN THE CAPTAIN IN ACTION ENOUGH NOW TO KNOW THAT STARFLEET MADE THE RIGHT CHOICE.
"HE'S FEARLESS. HE'S RELENTLESS. AND HE DOESN'T ASK ANY OF US TO DO ANYTHING HE WOULDN'T DO HIMSELF.
"COMMANDER SPOCK I HAVEN'T WORKED WITH AS MUCH.
"YOU'LL REMEMBER HIM, MOM. HE WAS THE TACTICS INSTRUCTOR I WAS ALWAYS COMPLAINING ABOUT AT THE ACADEMY. THE VULCAN.
"HE'S NOT EXACTLY THE TOUCHY-FEELY TYPE. I THINK WE'RE ALL A LITTLE INTIMIDATED BY HIM.
"AND THERE'S THE WHOLE THING WITH THE VULCAN HOMEWORLD..."

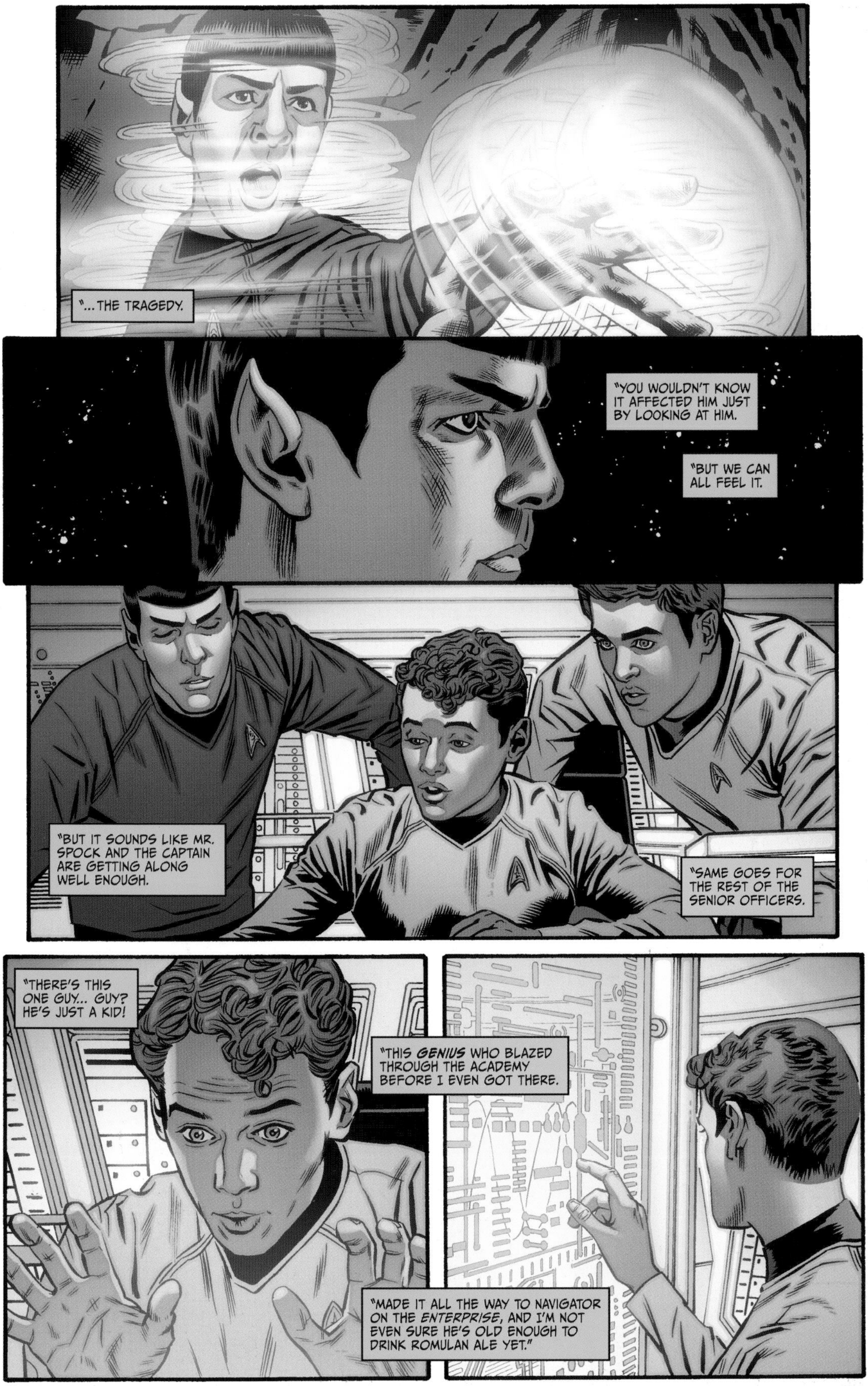
"...THE TRAGEDY.
"YOU WOULDN'T KNOW IT AFFECTED HIM JUST BY LOOKING AT HIM.
"BUT WE CAN ALL FEEL IT.
"BUT IT SOUNDS LIKE MR. SPOCK AND THE CAPTAIN ARE GETTING ALONG WELL ENOUGH.
"SAME GOES FOR THE REST OF THE SENIOR OFFICERS.
"THERE'S THIS ONE GUY... GUY? HE'S JUST A KID!
"THIS *GENIUS* WHO BLAZED THROUGH THE ACADEMY BEFORE I EVEN GOT THERE.
"MADE IT ALL THE WAY TO NAVIGATOR ON THE *ENTERPRISE*, AND I'M NOT EVEN SURE HE'S OLD ENOUGH TO DRINK ROMULAN ALE YET."

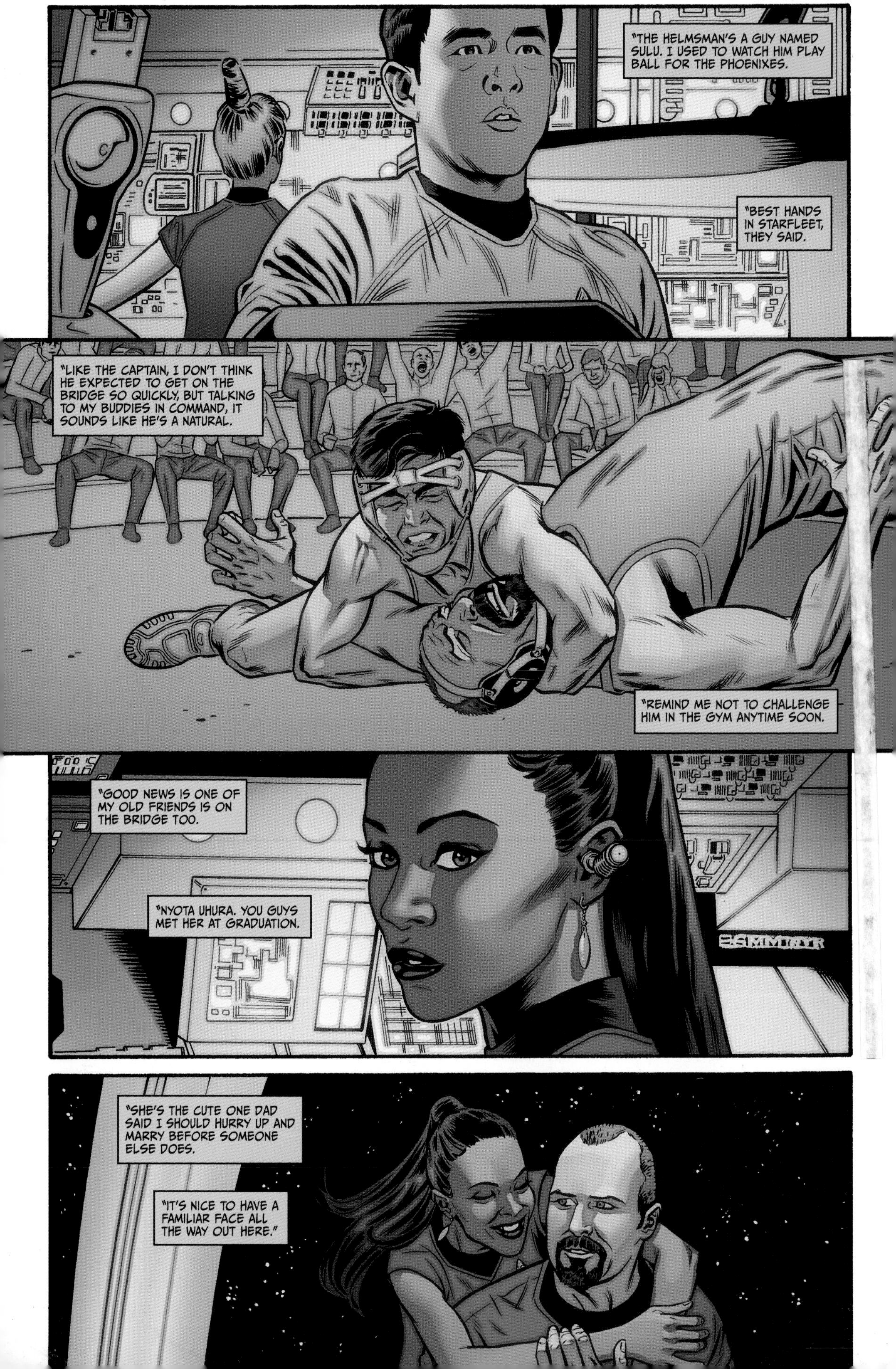
"THE HELMSMAN'S A GUY NAMED SULU. I USED TO WATCH HIM PLAY BALL FOR THE PHOENIXES.
"BEST HANDS IN STARFLEET, THEY SAID.
"LIKE THE CAPTAIN, I DON'T THINK HE EXPECTED TO GET ON THE BRIDGE SO QUICKLY, BUT TALKING TO MY BUDDIES IN COMMAND, IT SOUNDS LIKE HE'S A NATURAL.
"REMIND ME NOT TO CHALLENGE HIM IN THE GYM ANYTIME SOON.
"GOOD NEWS IS ONE OF MY OLD FRIENDS IS ON THE BRIDGE TOO.
"NYOTA UHURA. YOU GUYS MET HER AT GRADUATION.
"SHE'S THE CUTE ONE DAD SAID I SHOULD HURRY UP AND MARRY BEFORE SOMEONE ELSE DOES.
"IT'S NICE TO HAVE A FAMILIAR FACE ALL THE WAY OUT HERE."

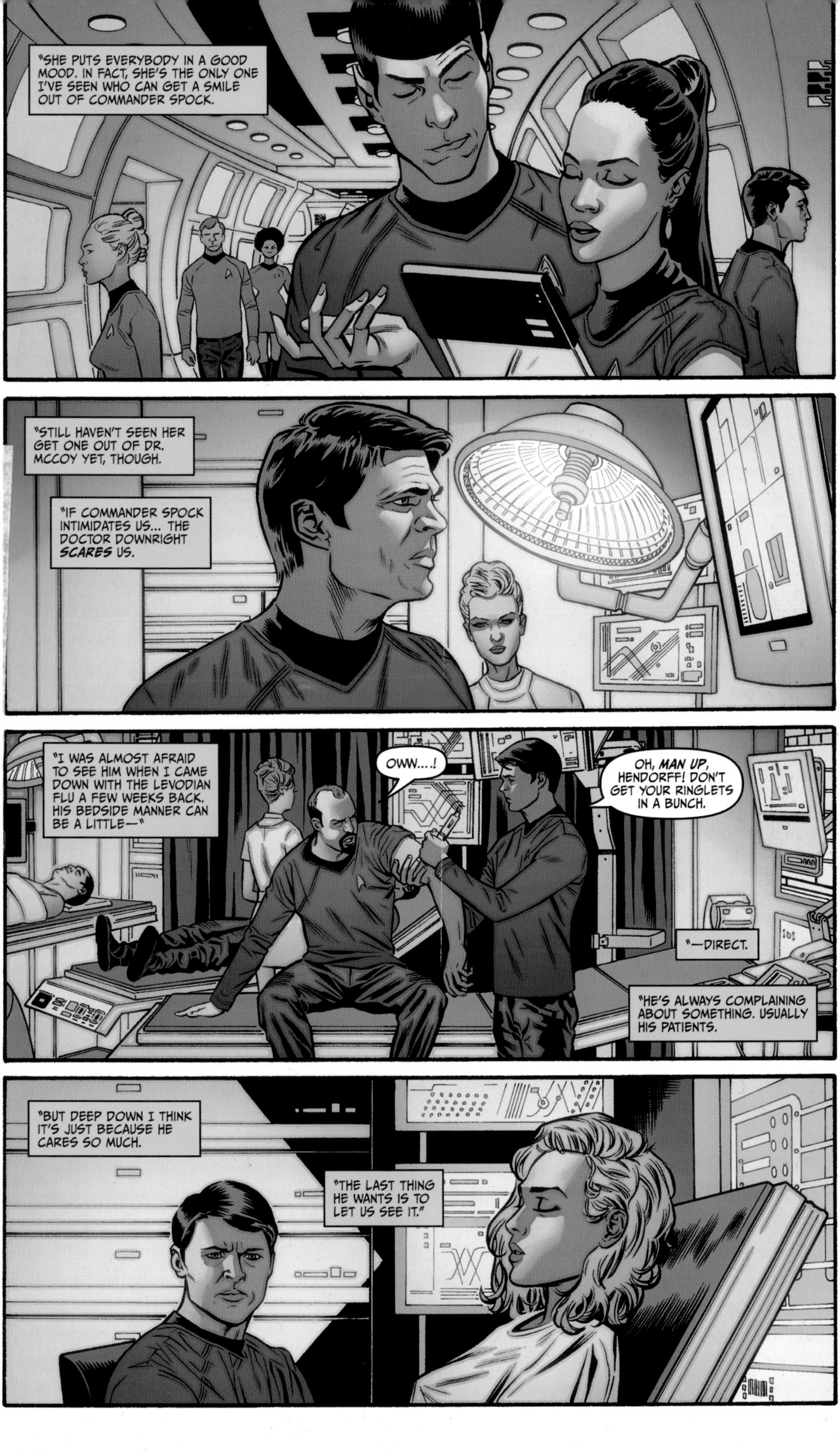
"SHE PUTS EVERYBODY IN A GOOD MOOD. IN FACT, SHE'S THE ONLY ONE I'VE SEEN WHO CAN GET A SMILE OUT OF COMMANDER SPOCK.
"STILL HAVEN'T SEEN HER GET ONE OUT OF DR. MCCOY YET, THOUGH.
"IF COMMANDER SPOCK INTIMIDATES US... THE DOCTOR DOWNRIGHT SCARES US.
"I WAS ALMOST AFRAID TO SEE HIM WHEN I CAME DOWN WITH THE LEVODIAN FLU A FEW WEEKS BACK. HIS BEDSIDE MANNER CAN BE A LITTLE—"
OWW....!
OH, MAN UP, HENDORFF! DON'T GET YOUR RINGLETS IN A BUNCH.
"—DIRECT.
"HE'S ALWAYS COMPLAINING ABOUT SOMETHING. USUALLY HIS PATIENTS.
"BUT DEEP DOWN I THINK IT'S JUST BECAUSE HE CARES SO MUCH.
"THE LAST THING HE WANTS IS TO LET US SEE IT."

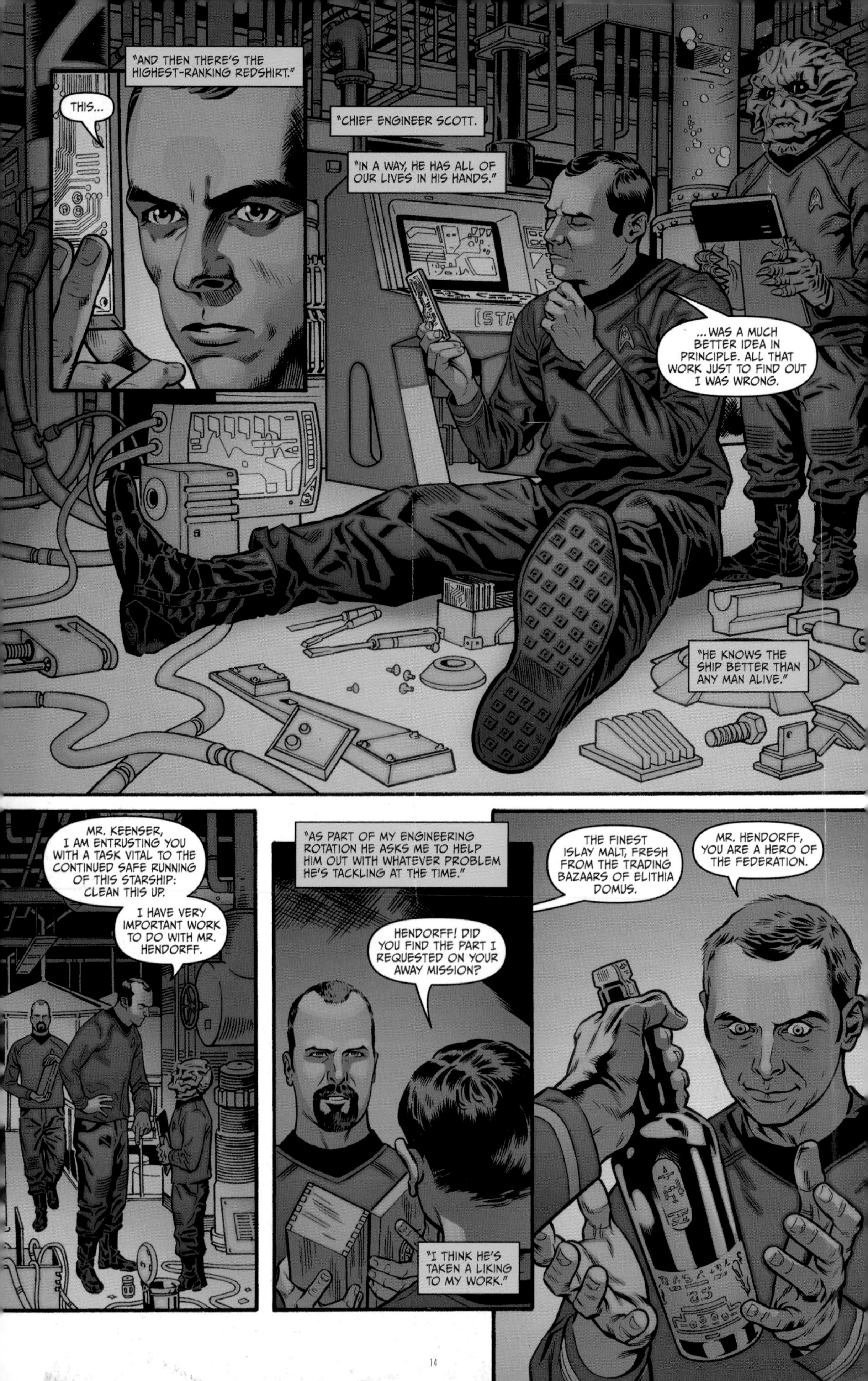

"AND THEN THERE'S THE HIGHEST-RANKING REDSHIRT."
THIS...
"CHIEF ENGINEER SCOTT.
"IN A WAY, HE HAS ALL OF OUR LIVES IN HIS HANDS."
...WAS A MUCH BETTER IDEA IN PRINCIPLE. ALL THAT WORK JUST TO FIND OUT I WAS WRONG.
"HE KNOWS THE SHIP BETTER THAN ANY MAN ALIVE."
MR. KEENSER, I AM ENTRUSTING YOU WITH A TASK VITAL TO THE CONTINUED SAFE RUNNING OF THIS STARSHIP: CLEAN THIS UP.
I HAVE VERY IMPORTANT WORK TO DO WITH MR. HENDORFF.
"AS PART OF MY ENGINEERING ROTATION HE ASKS ME TO HELP HIM OUT WITH WHATEVER PROBLEM HE'S TACKLING AT THE TIME."
HENDORFF! DID YOU FIND THE PART I REQUESTED ON YOUR AWAY MISSION?
"I THINK HE'S TAKEN A LIKING TO MY WORK."
THE FINEST ISLAY MALT, FRESH FROM THE TRADING BAZAARS OF ELITHIA DOMUS.
MR. HENDORFF, YOU ARE A HERO OF THE FEDERATION.

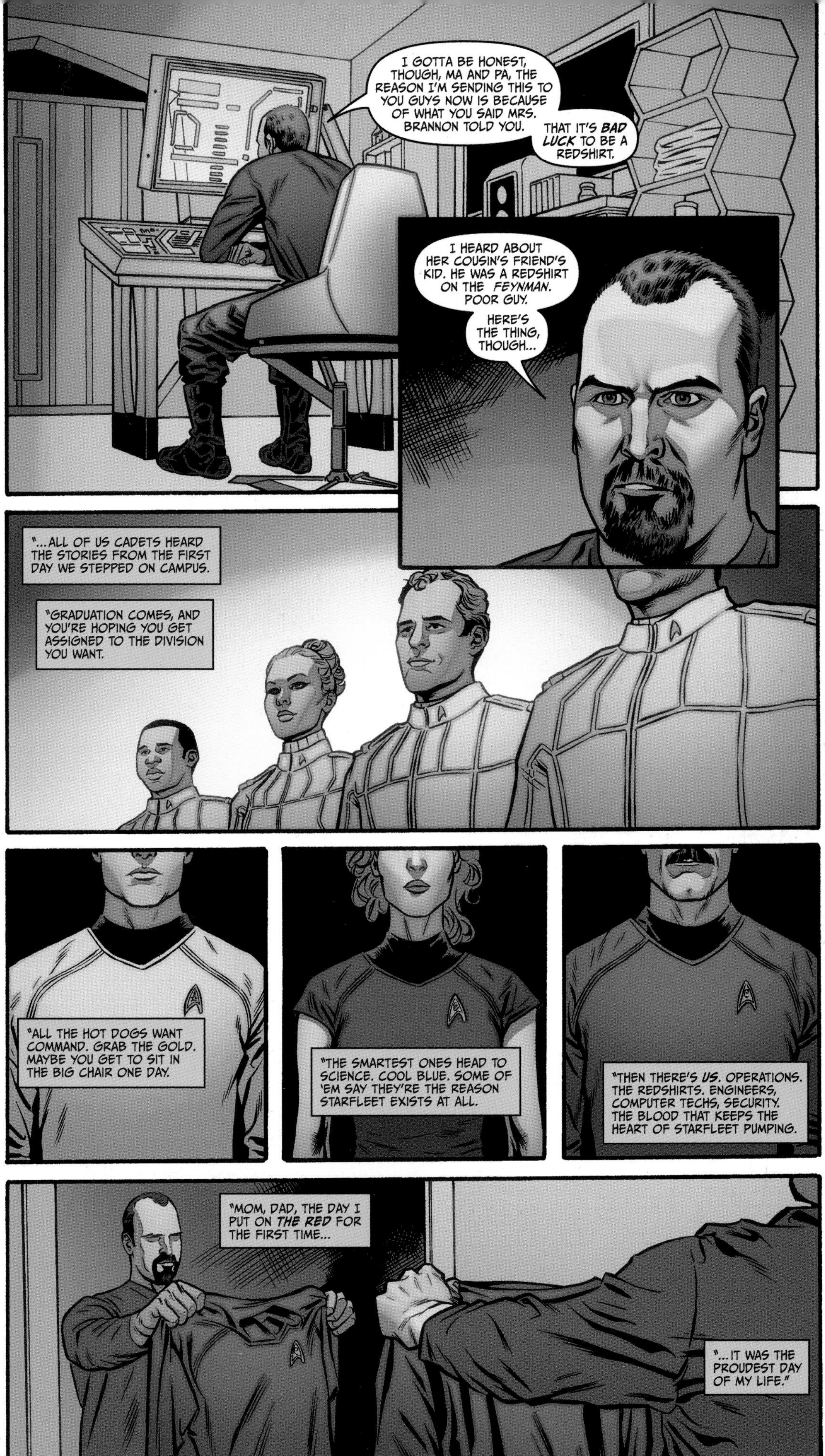
I GOTTA BE HONEST, THOUGH, MA AND PA, THE REASON I'M SENDING THIS TO YOU GUYS NOW IS BECAUSE OF WHAT YOU SAID MRS. BRANNON TOLD YOU.
THAT IT'S BAD LUCK TO BE A REDSHIRT.
I HEARD ABOUT HER COUSIN'S FRIEND'S KID. HE WAS A REDSHIRT ON THE FEYNMAN. POOR GUY.
HERE'S THE THING, THOUGH...
"...ALL OF US CADETS HEARD THE STORIES FROM THE FIRST DAY WE STEPPED ON CAMPUS.
"GRADUATION COMES, AND YOU'RE HOPING YOU GET ASSIGNED TO THE DIVISION YOU WANT.
"ALL THE HOT DOGS WANT COMMAND. GRAB THE GOLD. MAYBE YOU GET TO SIT IN THE BIG CHAIR ONE DAY.
"THE SMARTEST ONES HEAD TO SCIENCE. COOL BLUE. SOME OF 'EM SAY THEY'RE THE REASON STARFLEET EXISTS AT ALL.
"THEN THERE'S US. OPERATIONS. THE REDSHIRTS. ENGINEERS, COMPUTER TECHS, SECURITY. THE BLOOD THAT KEEPS THE HEART OF STARFLEET PUMPING.
"MOM, DAD, THE DAY I PUT ON THE RED FOR THE FIRST TIME...
"...IT WAS THE PROUDEST DAY OF MY LIFE."

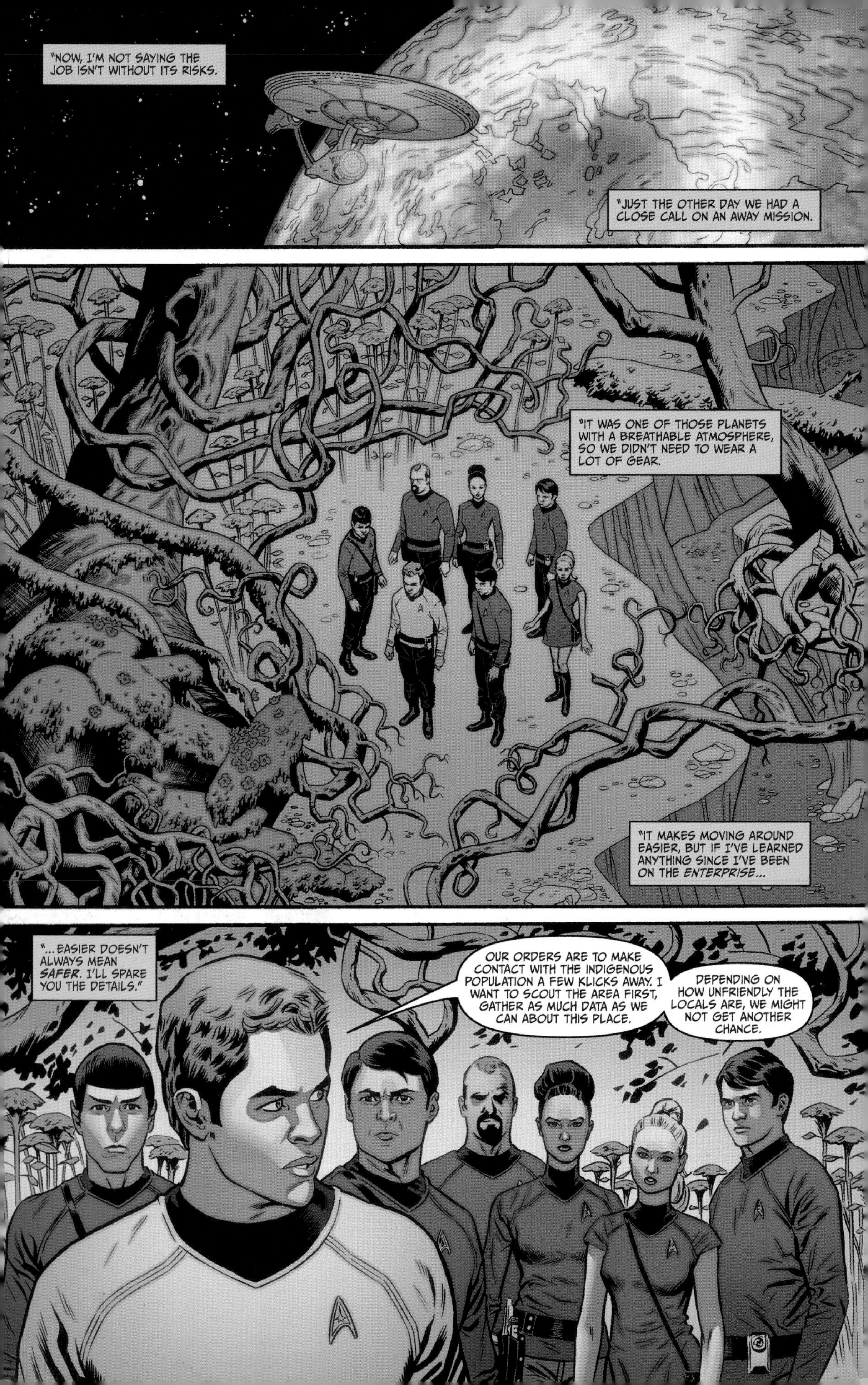
"NOW, I'M NOT SAYING THE JOB ISN'T WITHOUT ITS RISKS.
"JUST THE OTHER DAY WE HAD A CLOSE CALL ON AN AWAY MISSION.
"IT WAS ONE OF THOSE PLANETS WITH A BREATHABLE ATMOSPHERE, SO WE DIDN'T NEED TO WEAR A LOT OF GEAR.
"IT MAKES MOVING AROUND EASIER, BUT IF I'VE LEARNED ANYTHING SINCE I'VE BEEN ON THE *ENTERPRISE*...
"...EASIER DOESN'T ALWAYS MEAN *SAFER*. I'LL SPARE YOU THE DETAILS."
OUR ORDERS ARE TO MAKE CONTACT WITH THE INDIGENOUS POPULATION A FEW KLICKS AWAY. I WANT TO SCOUT THE AREA FIRST, GATHER AS MUCH DATA AS WE CAN ABOUT THIS PLACE.
DEPENDING ON HOW UNFRIENDLY THE LOCALS ARE, WE MIGHT NOT GET ANOTHER CHANCE.

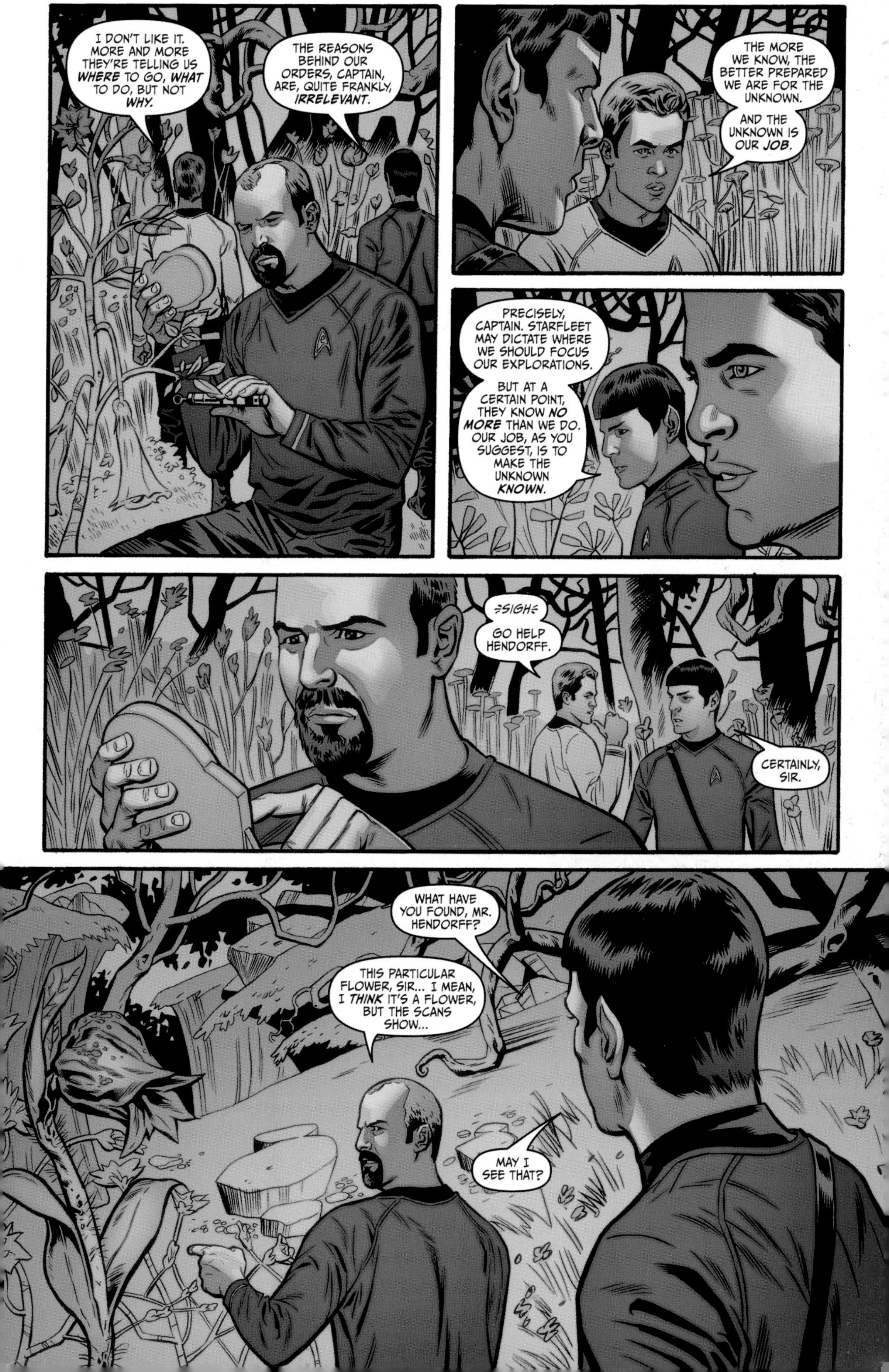
I DON'T LIKE IT. MORE AND MORE THEY'RE TELLING US *WHERE* TO GO, *WHAT* TO DO, BUT NOT *WHY*.
THE REASONS BEHIND OUR ORDERS, CAPTAIN, ARE, QUITE FRANKLY, *IRRELEVANT*.
THE MORE WE KNOW, THE BETTER PREPARED WE ARE FOR THE UNKNOWN.
AND THE UNKNOWN IS OUR *JOB*.
PRECISELY, CAPTAIN. STARFLEET MAY DICTATE WHERE WE SHOULD FOCUS OUR EXPLORATIONS.
BUT AT A CERTAIN POINT, THEY KNOW *NO MORE* THAN WE DO. OUR JOB, AS YOU SUGGEST, IS TO MAKE THE UNKNOWN *KNOWN*.
SIGH
GO HELP HENDORFF.
CERTAINLY, SIR.
WHAT HAVE YOU FOUND, MR. HENDORFF?
THIS PARTICULAR FLOWER, SIR... I MEAN, I *THINK* IT'S A FLOWER, BUT THE SCANS SHOW...
MAY I SEE THAT?

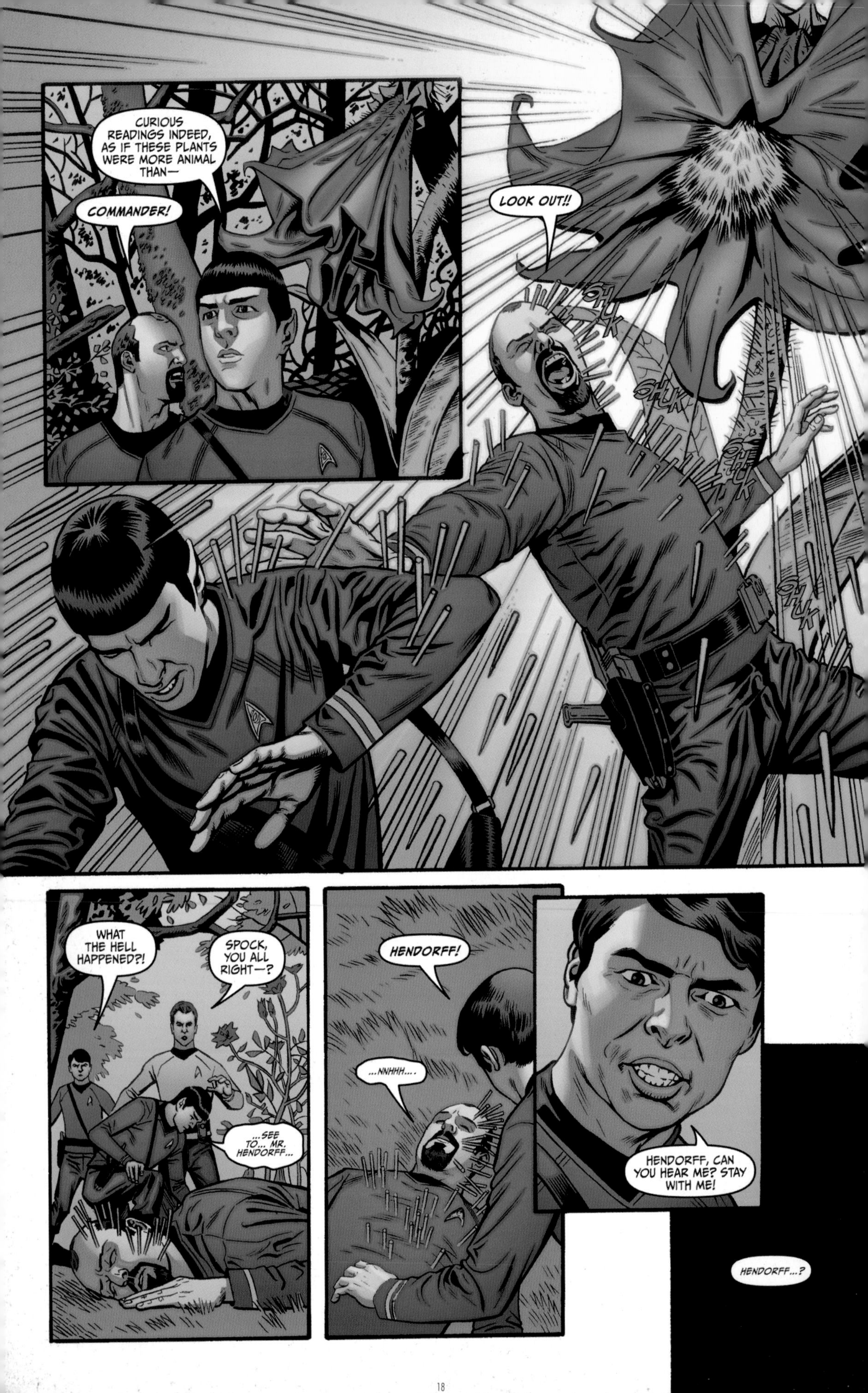

CURIOUS READINGS INDEED, AS IF THESE PLANTS WERE MORE ANIMAL THAN—
COMMANDER!
LOOK OUT!!
CHUK
CHUK
CHUK
CHUK
WHAT THE HELL HAPPENED?!
SPOCK, YOU ALL RIGHT—?
...SEE TO... MR. HENDORFF...
HENDORFF!
...NNHHH....
HENDORFF, CAN YOU HEAR ME? STAY WITH ME!
HENDORFF...?

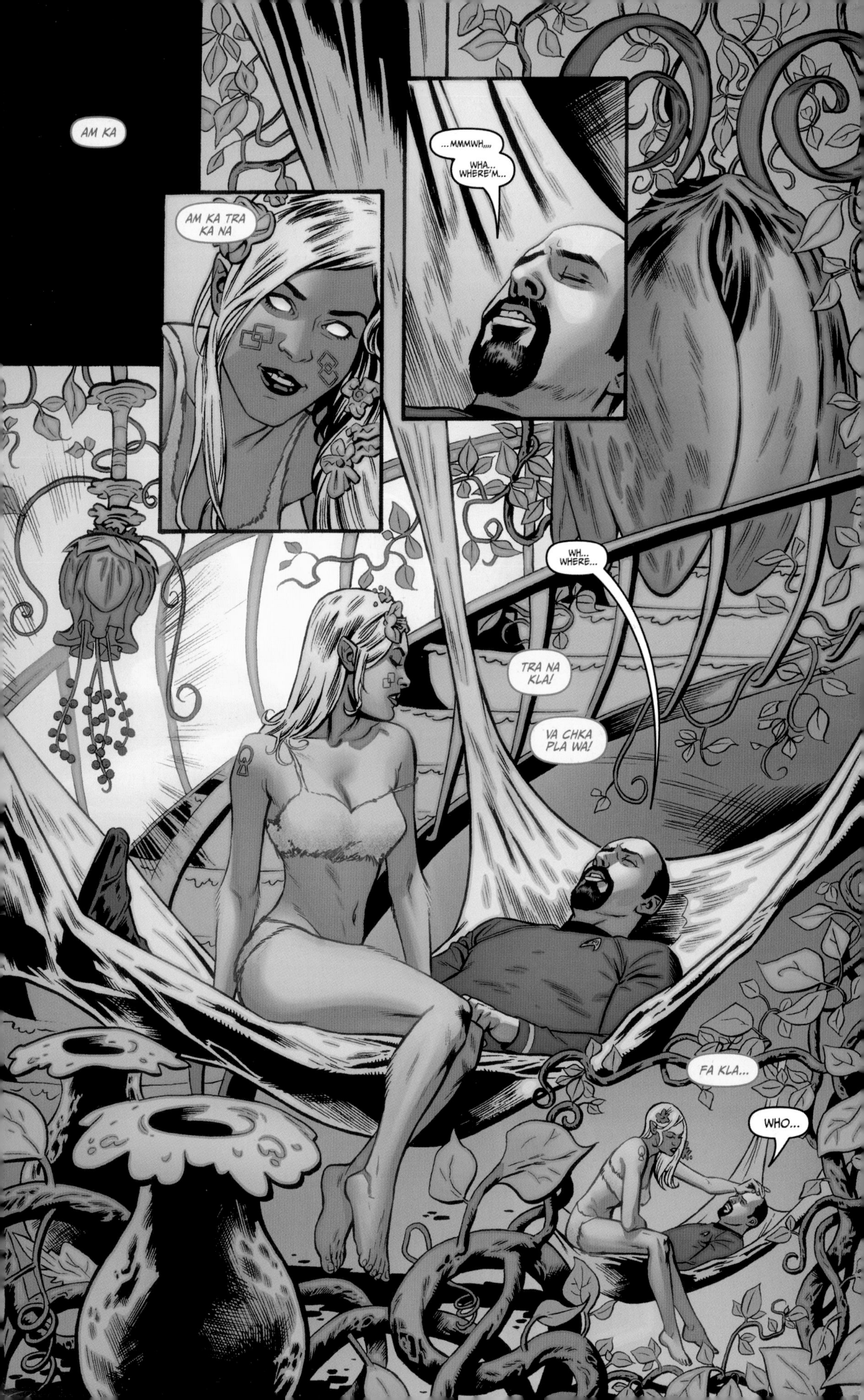
AM KA
AM KA TRA KA NA
...MMMWH....
WHA... WHERE'M...
WH... WHERE...
TRA NA KLA!
VA CHKA PLA WA!
FA KLA...
WHO...

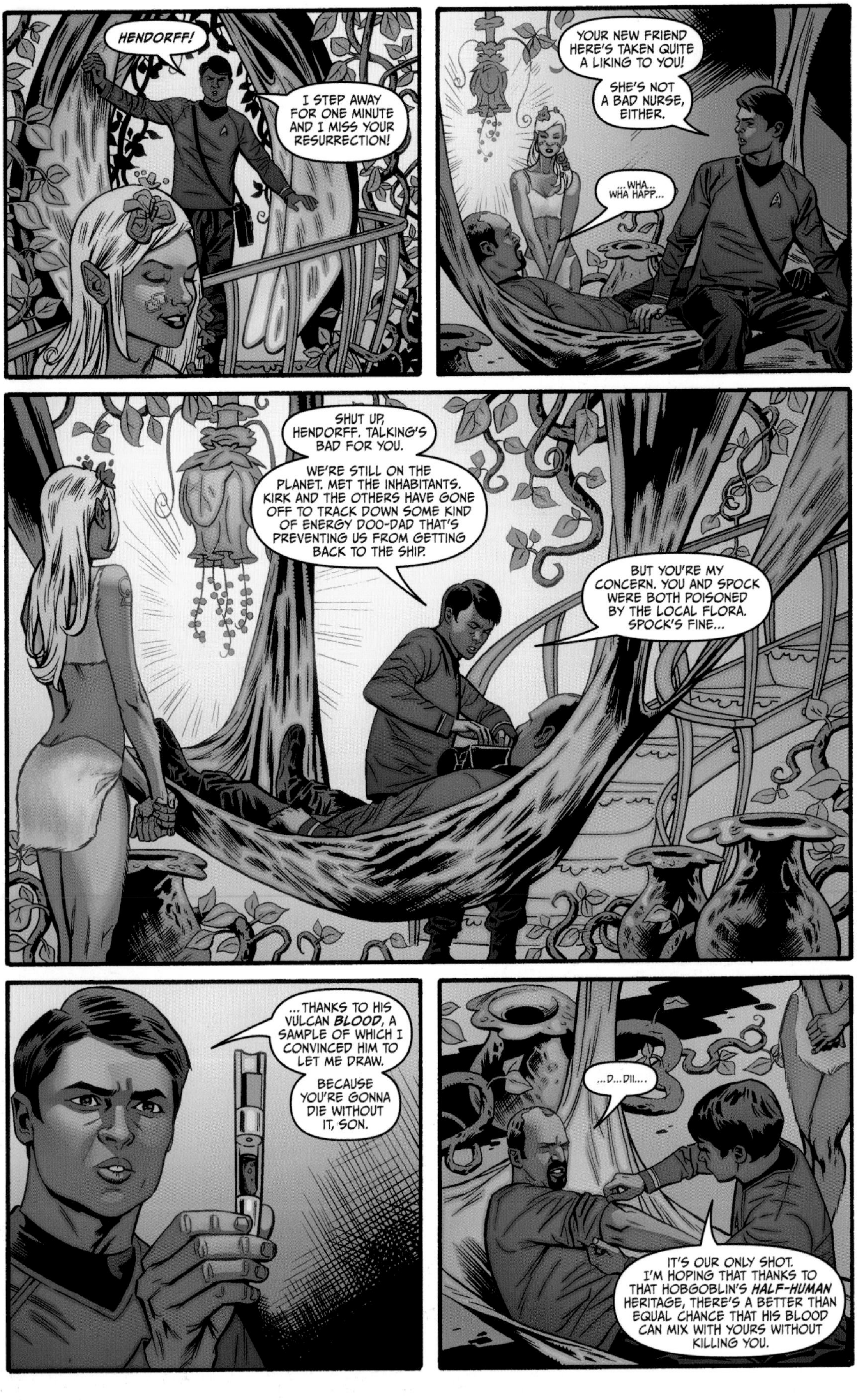
HENDORFF!
I STEP AWAY FOR ONE MINUTE AND I MISS YOUR RESURRECTION!
YOUR NEW FRIEND HERE'S TAKEN QUITE A LIKING TO YOU!
SHE'S NOT A BAD NURSE, EITHER.
...WHA... WHA HAPP...
SHUT UP, HENDORFF. TALKING'S BAD FOR YOU.
WE'RE STILL ON THE PLANET. MET THE INHABITANTS. KIRK AND THE OTHERS HAVE GONE OFF TO TRACK DOWN SOME KIND OF ENERGY DOO-DAD THAT'S PREVENTING US FROM GETTING BACK TO THE SHIP.
BUT YOU'RE MY CONCERN. YOU AND SPOCK WERE BOTH POISONED BY THE LOCAL FLORA. SPOCK'S FINE...
...THANKS TO HIS VULCAN BLOOD, A SAMPLE OF WHICH I CONVINCED HIM TO LET ME DRAW.
BECAUSE YOU'RE GONNA DIE WITHOUT IT, SON.
...D...DII....
IT'S OUR ONLY SHOT. I'M HOPING THAT THANKS TO THAT HOBGOBLIN'S HALF-HUMAN HERITAGE, THERE'S A BETTER THAN EQUAL CHANCE THAT HIS BLOOD CAN MIX WITH YOURS WITHOUT KILLING YOU.

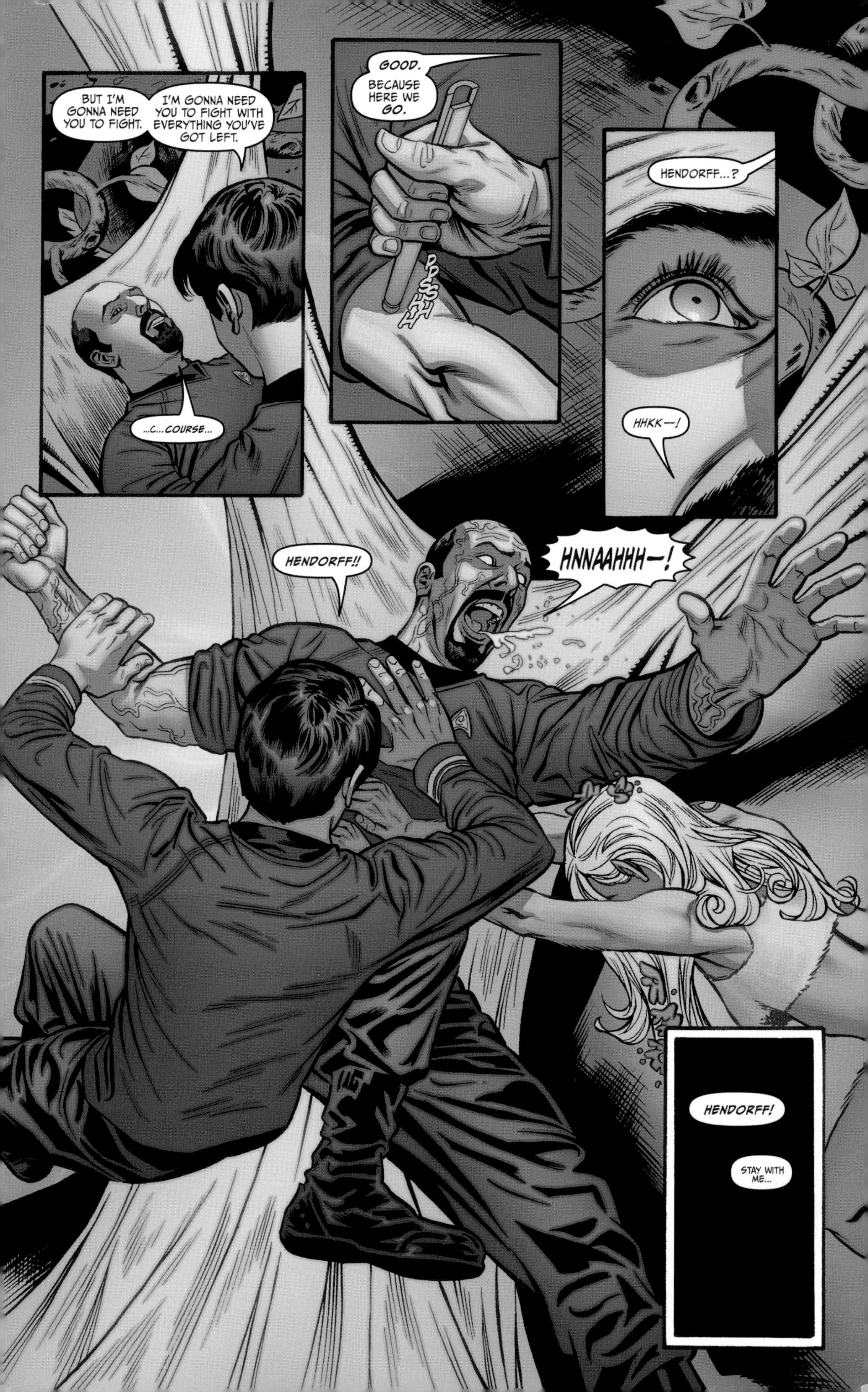
BUT I'M GONNA NEED YOU TO FIGHT.
I'M GONNA NEED YOU TO FIGHT WITH EVERYTHING YOU'VE GOT LEFT.
...C...COURSE...
GOOD. BECAUSE HERE WE GO.
PPSHHH
HENDORFF...?
HHKK—!
HENDORFF!!
HNNAAHHH—!
HENDORFF!
STAY WITH ME...

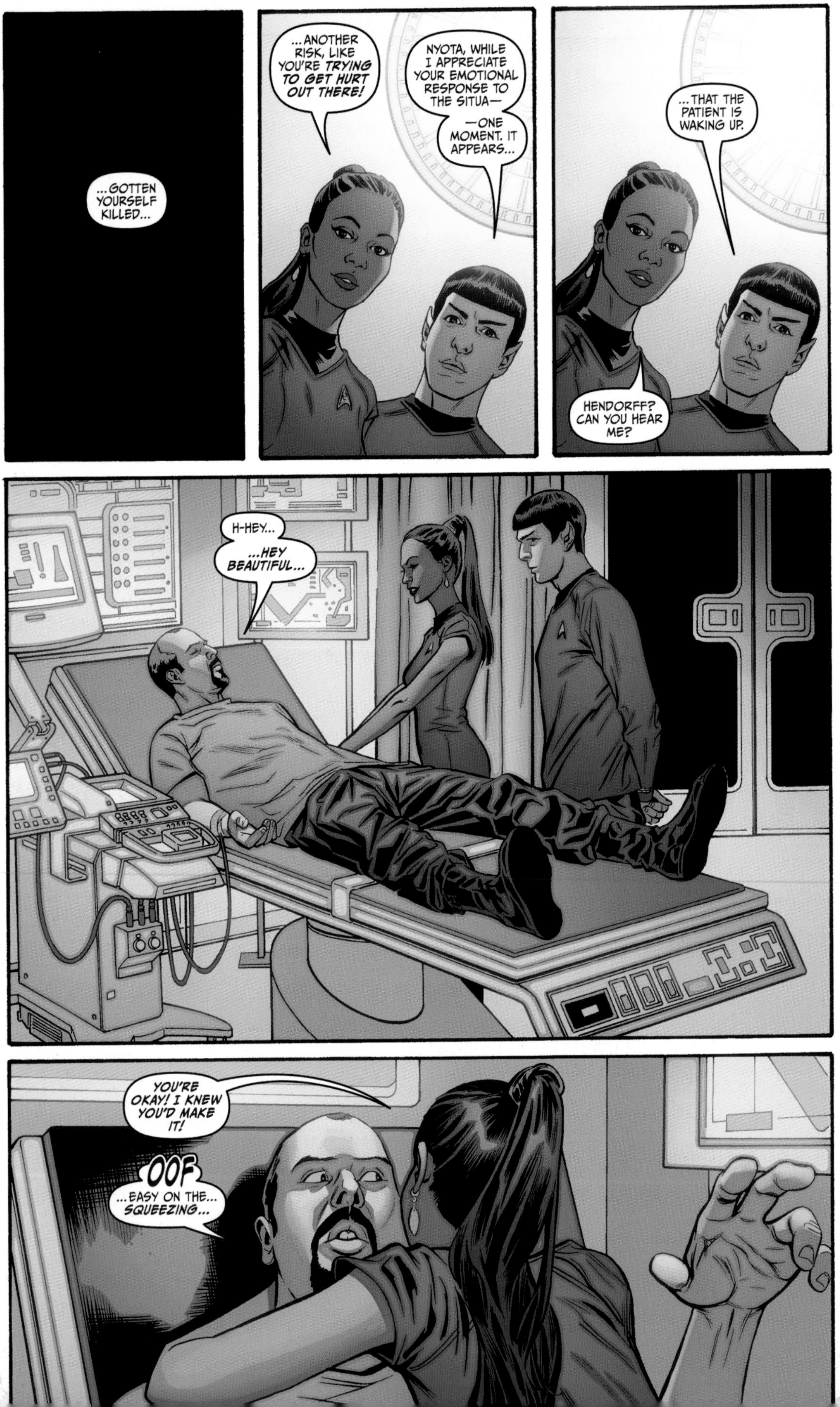
...GOTTEN YOURSELF KILLED...
...ANOTHER RISK, LIKE YOU'RE *TRYING TO GET HURT OUT THERE!*
NYOTA, WHILE I APPRECIATE YOUR EMOTIONAL RESPONSE TO THE SITUA—
—ONE MOMENT. IT APPEARS...
...THAT THE PATIENT IS WAKING UP.
HENDORFF? CAN YOU HEAR ME?
H-HEY...
...HEY BEAUTIFUL...
YOU'RE OKAY! I KNEW YOU'D MAKE IT!
OOF
...EASY ON THE... *SQUEEZING...*

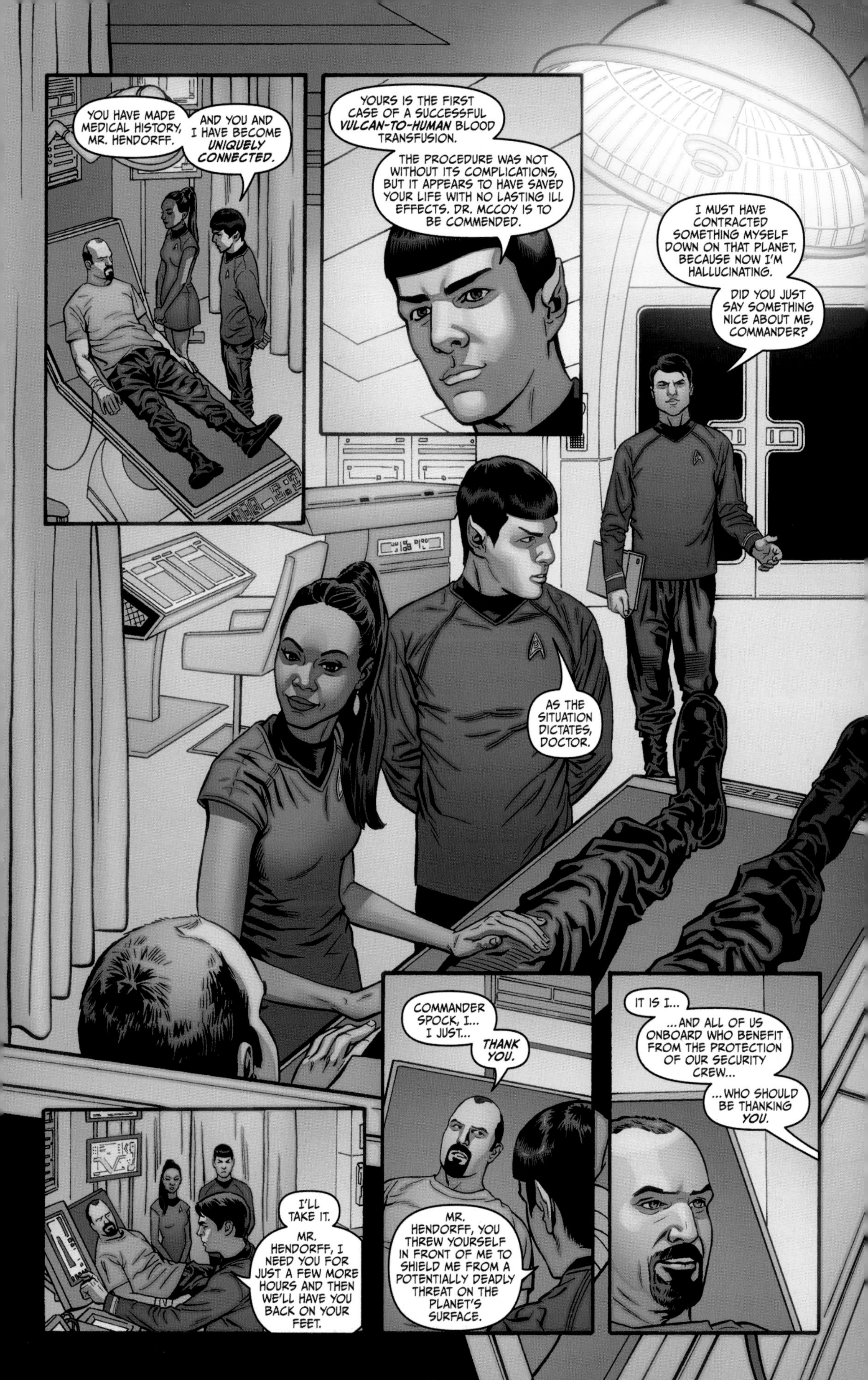

YOU HAVE MADE MEDICAL HISTORY, MR. HENDORFF.
AND YOU AND I HAVE BECOME *UNIQUELY CONNECTED.*
YOURS IS THE FIRST CASE OF A SUCCESSFUL *VULCAN-TO-HUMAN* BLOOD TRANSFUSION.
THE PROCEDURE WAS NOT WITHOUT ITS COMPLICATIONS, BUT IT APPEARS TO HAVE SAVED YOUR LIFE WITH NO LASTING ILL EFFECTS. DR. MCCOY IS TO BE COMMENDED.
I MUST HAVE CONTRACTED SOMETHING MYSELF DOWN ON THAT PLANET, BECAUSE NOW I'M HALLUCINATING.
DID YOU JUST SAY SOMETHING NICE ABOUT ME, COMMANDER?
AS THE SITUATION DICTATES, DOCTOR.
I'LL TAKE IT.
MR. HENDORFF, I NEED YOU FOR JUST A FEW MORE HOURS AND THEN WE'LL HAVE YOU BACK ON YOUR FEET.
COMMANDER SPOCK, I... I JUST... *THANK YOU.*
MR. HENDORFF, YOU THREW YOURSELF IN FRONT OF ME TO SHIELD ME FROM A POTENTIALLY DEADLY THREAT ON THE PLANET'S SURFACE.
IT IS I...
...AND ALL OF US ONBOARD WHO BENEFIT FROM THE PROTECTION OF OUR SECURITY CREW...
...WHO SHOULD BE THANKING *YOU.*

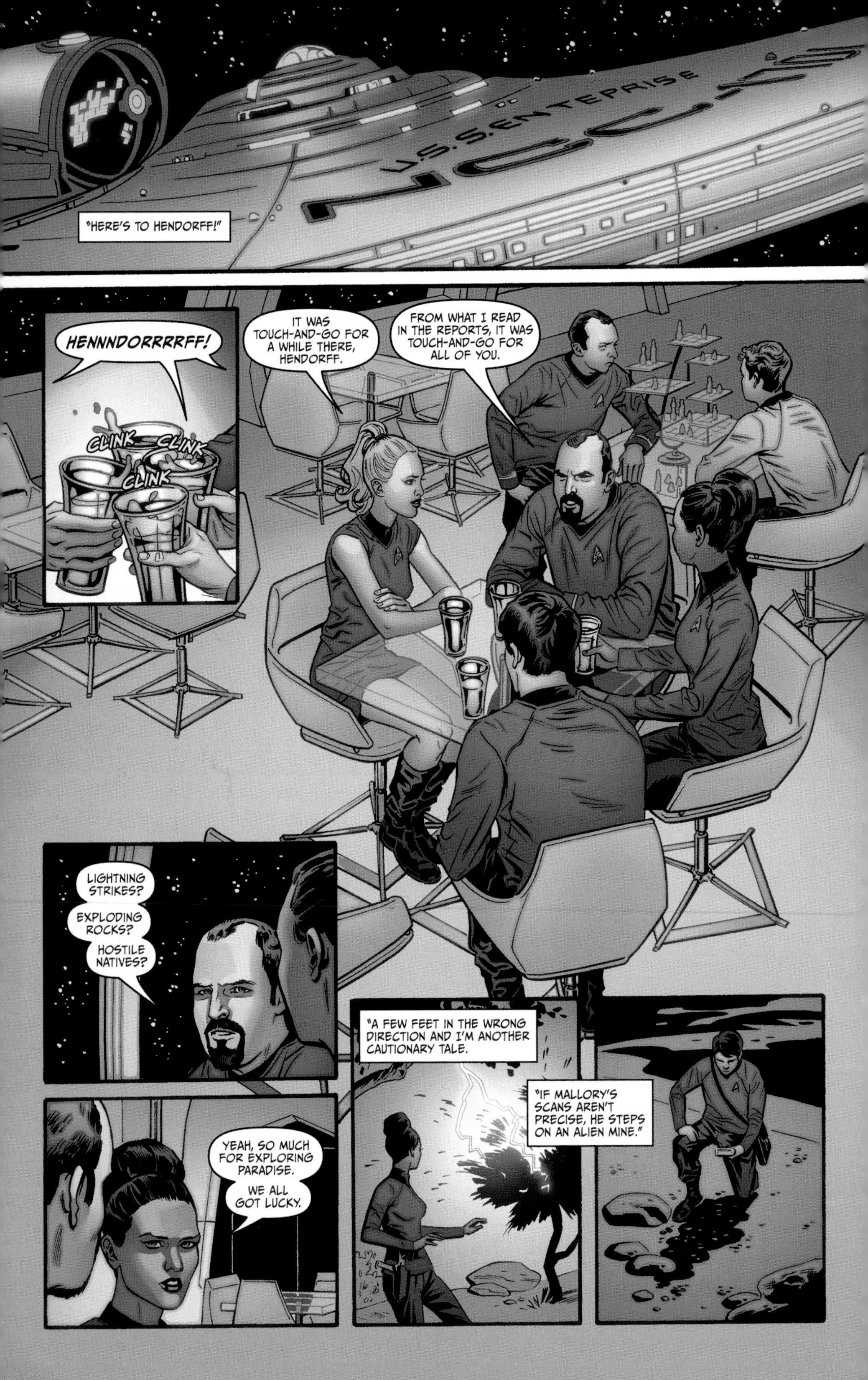

U.S.S. ENTERPRISE
"HERE'S TO HENDORFF!"
HENNNDORRRRFF!
CLINK CLINK
CLINK
IT WAS TOUCH-AND-GO FOR A WHILE THERE, HENDORFF.
FROM WHAT I READ IN THE REPORTS, IT WAS TOUCH-AND-GO FOR ALL OF YOU.
LIGHTNING STRIKES?
EXPLODING ROCKS?
HOSTILE NATIVES?
YEAH, SO MUCH FOR EXPLORING PARADISE.
WE ALL GOT LUCKY.
"A FEW FEET IN THE WRONG DIRECTION AND I'M ANOTHER CAUTIONARY TALE.
"IF MALLORY'S SCANS AREN'T PRECISE, HE STEPS ON AN ALIEN MINE."

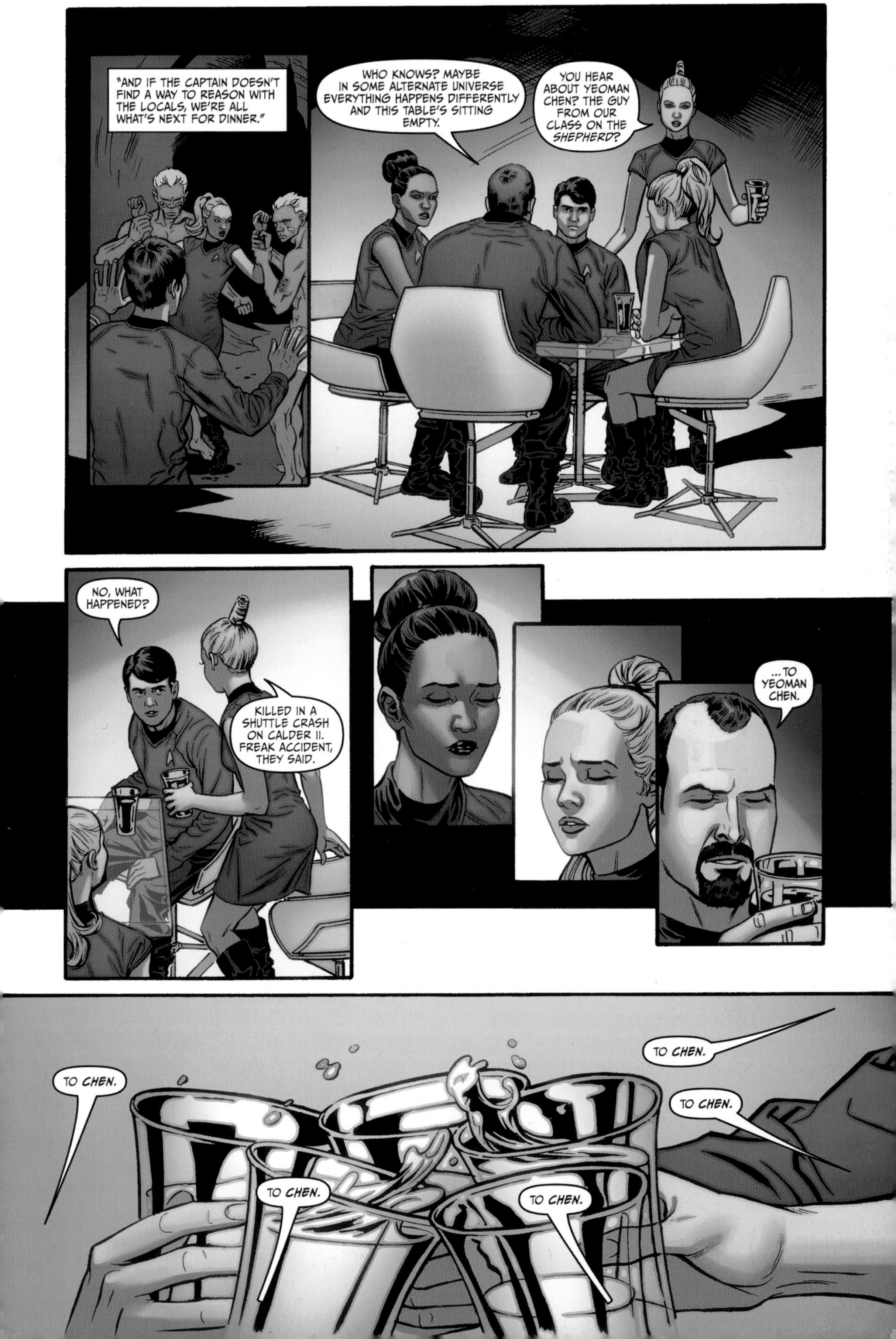
"AND IF THE CAPTAIN DOESN'T FIND A WAY TO REASON WITH THE LOCALS, WE'RE ALL WHAT'S NEXT FOR DINNER."
WHO KNOWS? MAYBE IN SOME ALTERNATE UNIVERSE EVERYTHING HAPPENS DIFFERENTLY AND THIS TABLE'S SITTING EMPTY.
YOU HEAR ABOUT YEOMAN CHEN? THE GUY FROM OUR CLASS ON THE SHEPHERD?
NO, WHAT HAPPENED?
KILLED IN A SHUTTLE CRASH ON CALDER II. FREAK ACCIDENT, THEY SAID.
...TO YEOMAN CHEN.
TO CHEN.
TO CHEN.
TO CHEN.
TO CHEN.
TO CHEN.

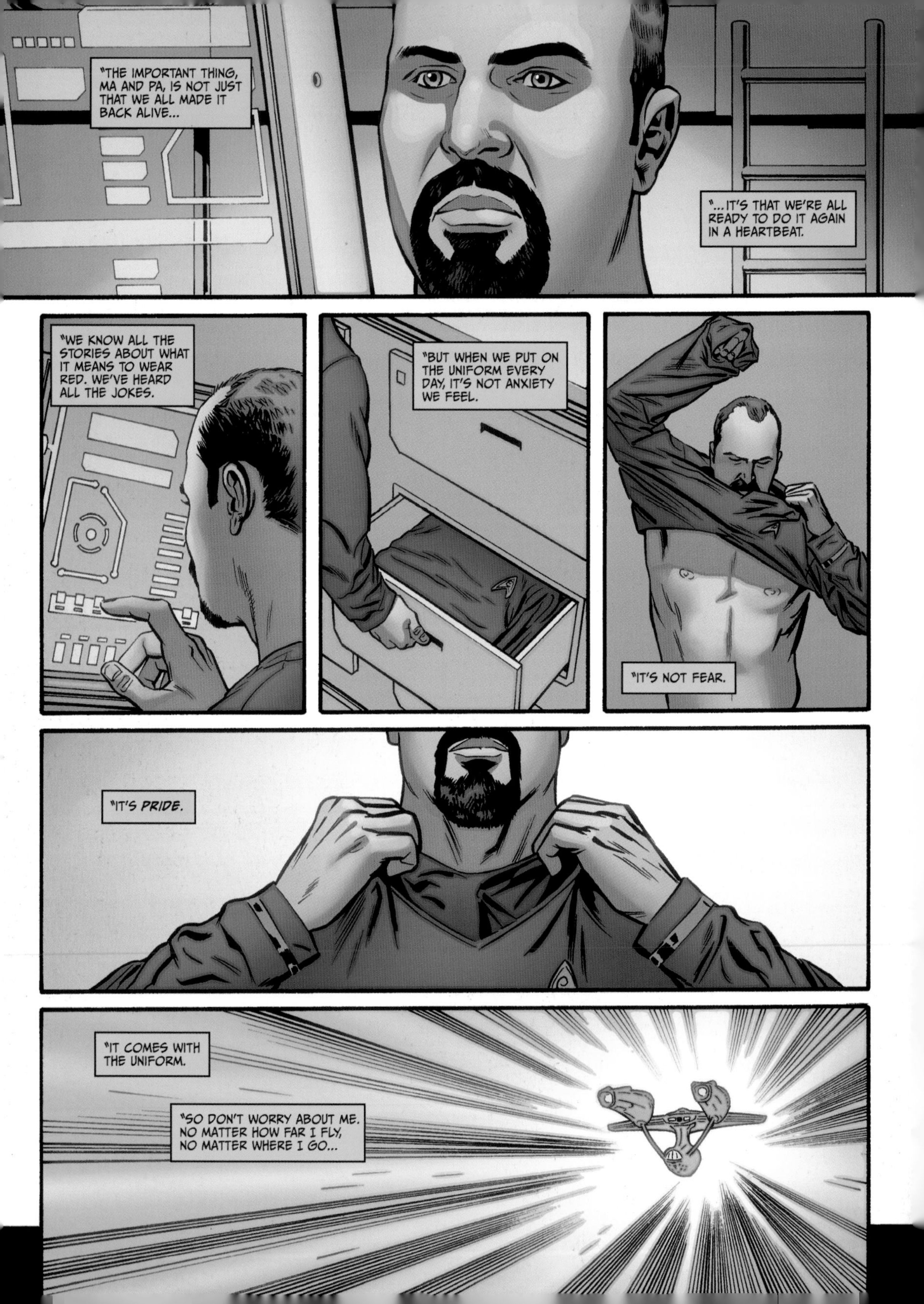
"THE IMPORTANT THING, MA AND PA, IS NOT JUST THAT WE ALL MADE IT BACK ALIVE...
"...IT'S THAT WE'RE ALL READY TO DO IT AGAIN IN A HEARTBEAT.
"WE KNOW ALL THE STORIES ABOUT WHAT IT MEANS TO WEAR RED. WE'VE HEARD ALL THE JOKES.
"BUT WHEN WE PUT ON THE UNIFORM EVERY DAY, IT'S NOT ANXIETY WE FEEL.
"IT'S NOT FEAR.
"IT'S PRIDE.
"IT COMES WITH THE UNIFORM.
"SO DON'T WORRY ABOUT ME. NO MATTER HOW FAR I FLY, NO MATTER WHERE I GO...

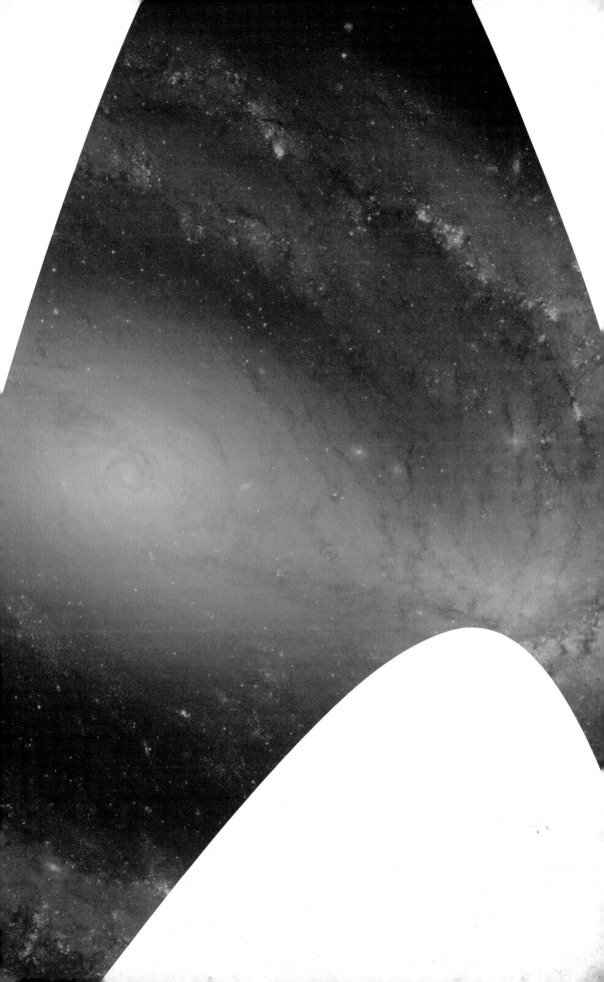

KEENSER'S STORY

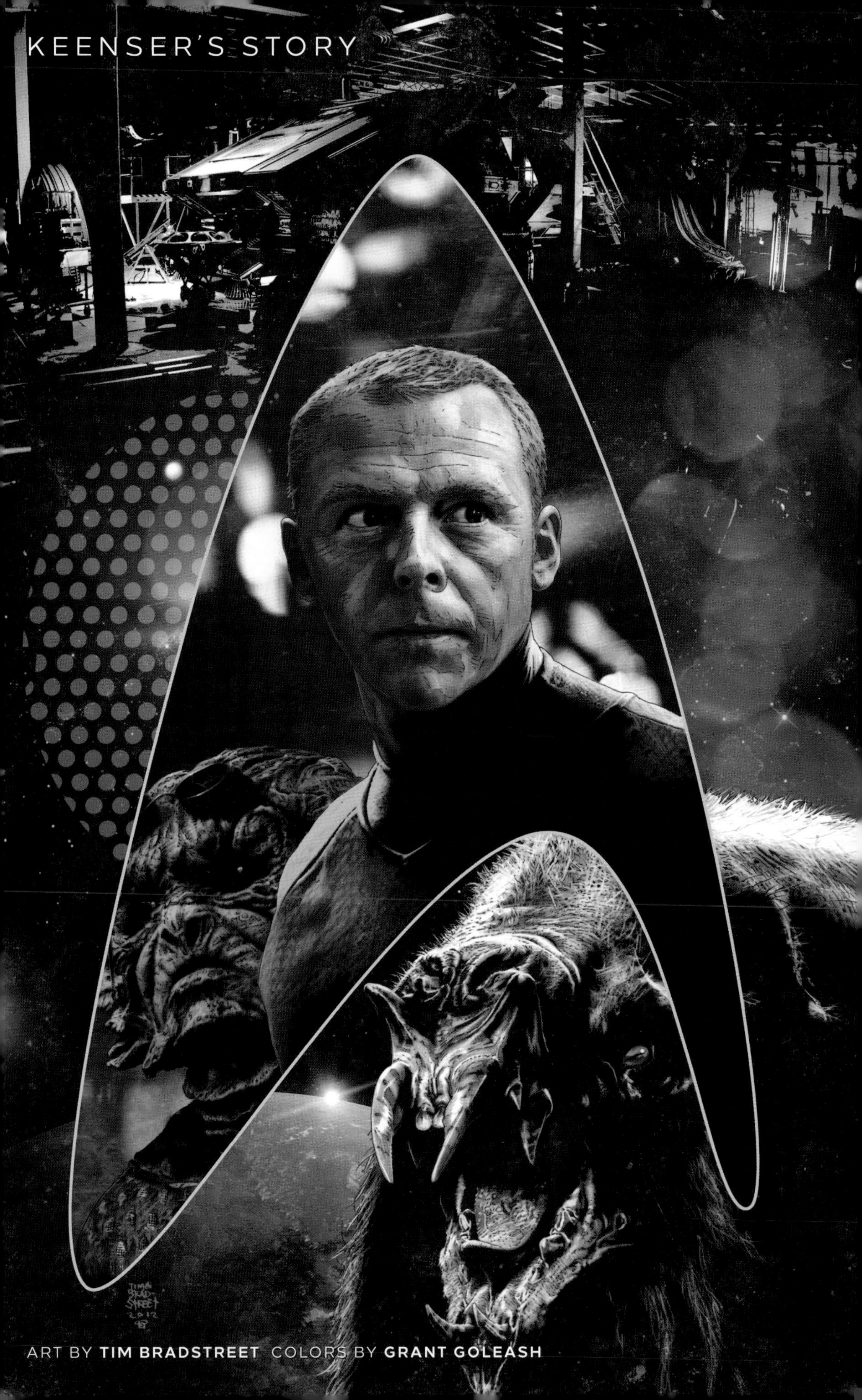

ART BY **TIM BRADSTREET** COLORS BY **GRANT GOLEASH**

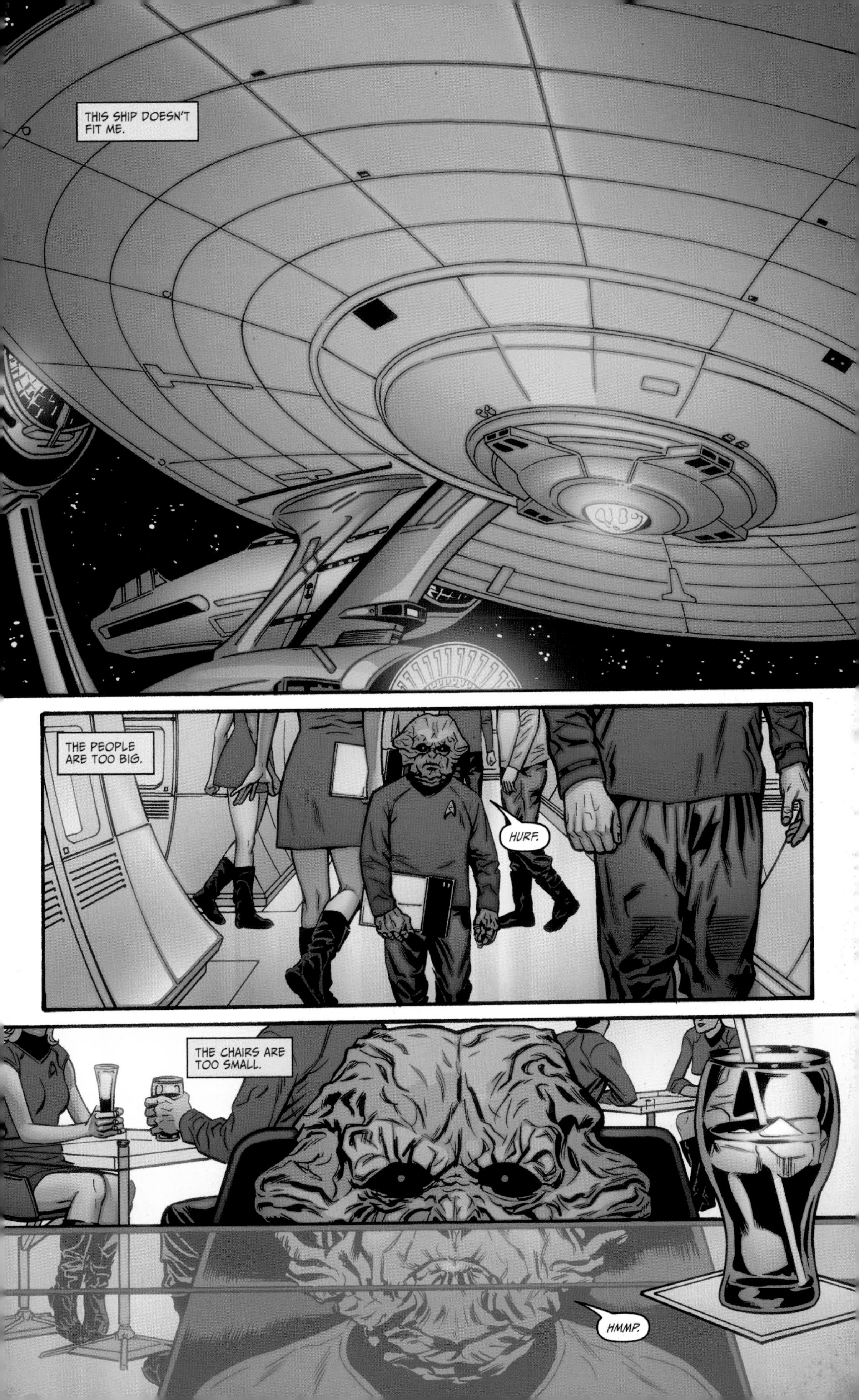
THIS SHIP DOESN'T FIT ME.
THE PEOPLE ARE TOO BIG.
HURF.
THE CHAIRS ARE TOO SMALL.
HMMP.

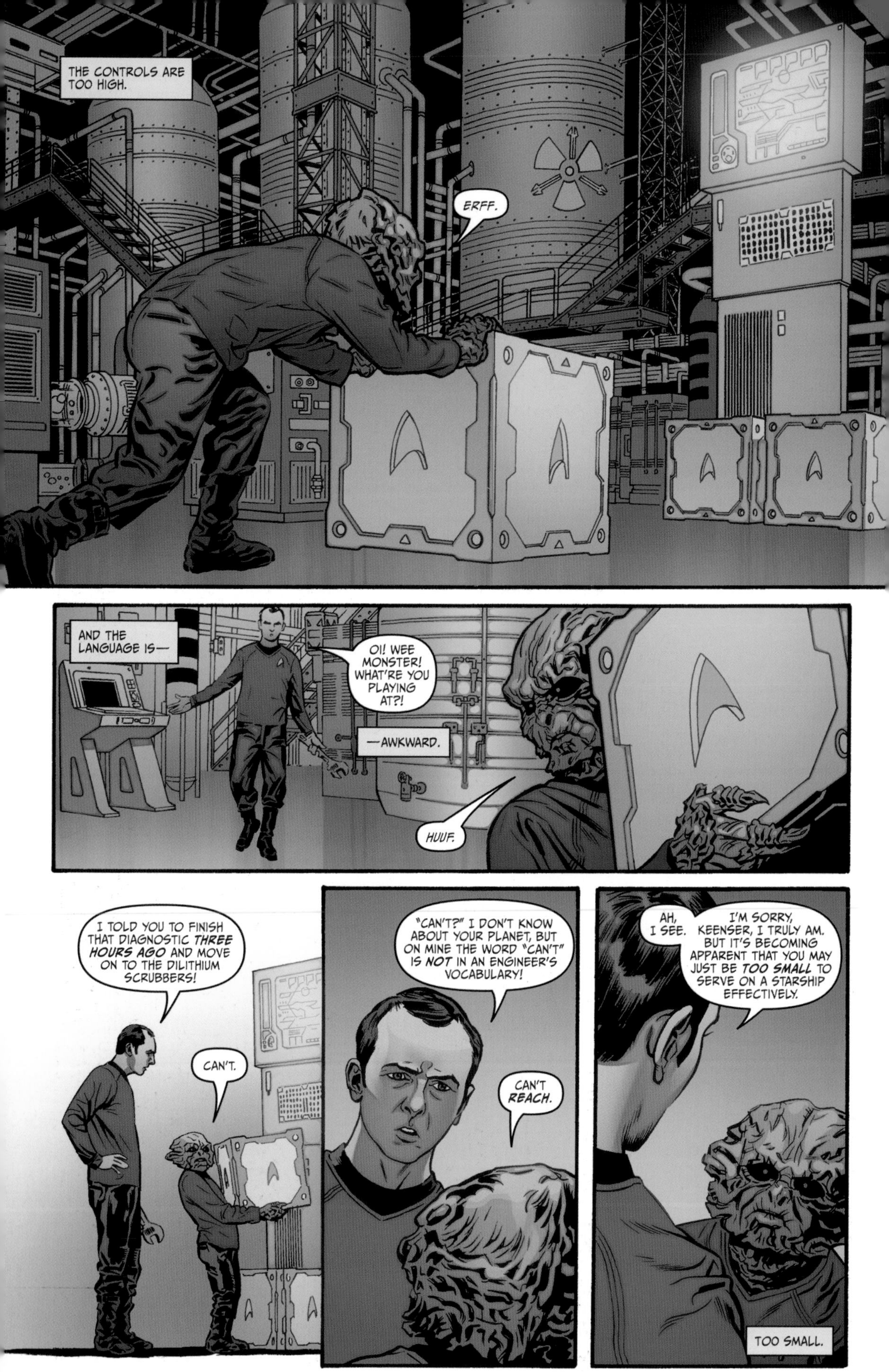
THE CONTROLS ARE TOO HIGH.
ERFF.
AND THE LANGUAGE IS—
OI! WEE MONSTER! WHAT'RE YOU PLAYING AT?!
—AWKWARD.
HUUF.
I TOLD YOU TO FINISH THAT DIAGNOSTIC THREE HOURS AGO AND MOVE ON TO THE DILITHIUM SCRUBBERS!
CAN'T.
"CAN'T?" I DON'T KNOW ABOUT YOUR PLANET, BUT ON MINE THE WORD "CAN'T" IS NOT IN AN ENGINEER'S VOCABULARY!
CAN'T REACH.
AH, I SEE.
I'M SORRY, KEENSER, I TRULY AM. BUT IT'S BECOMING APPARENT THAT YOU MAY JUST BE TOO SMALL TO SERVE ON A STARSHIP EFFECTIVELY.
TOO SMALL.

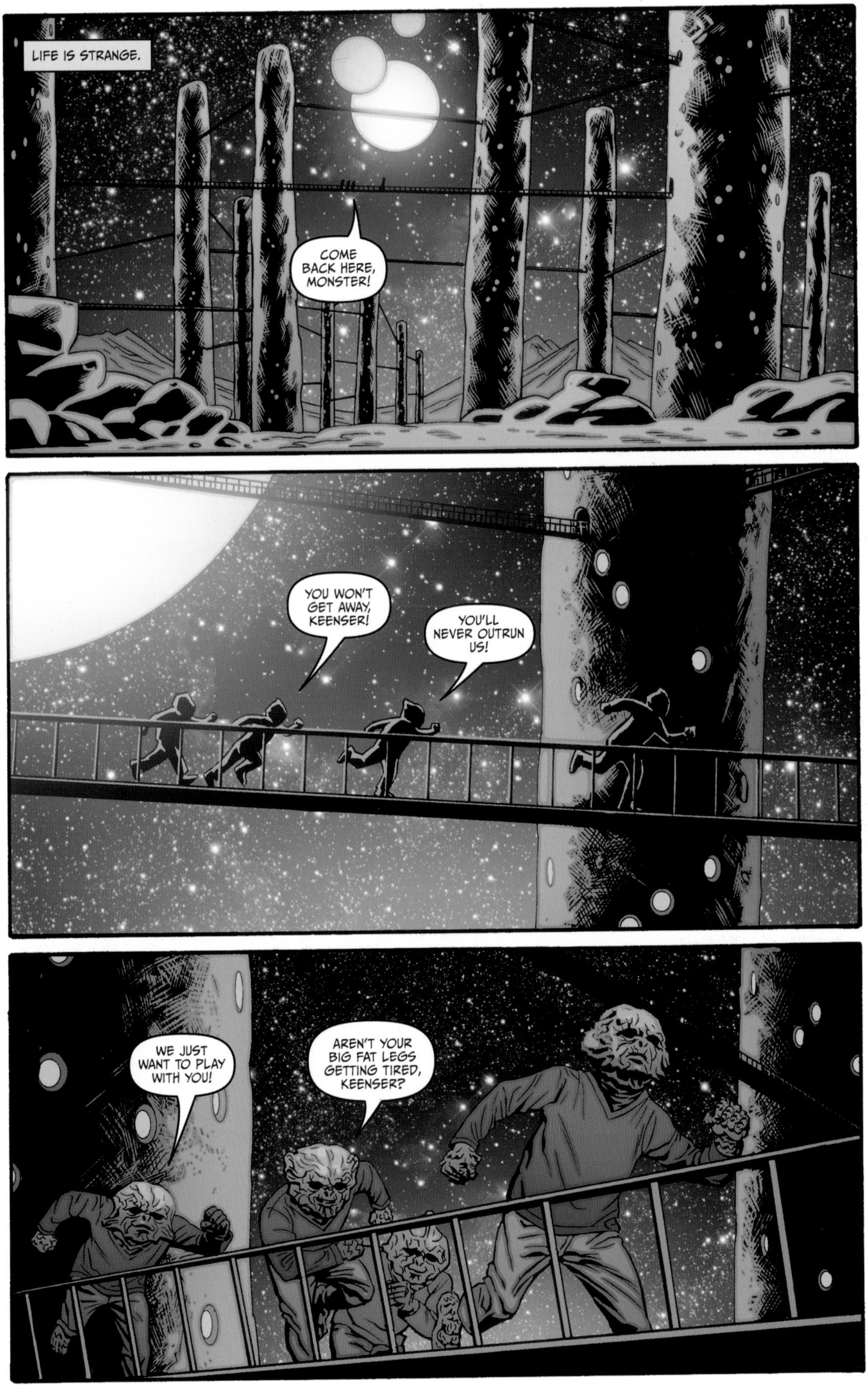
LIFE IS STRANGE.
COME BACK HERE, MONSTER!
YOU WON'T GET AWAY, KEENSER!
YOU'LL NEVER OUTRUN US!
WE JUST WANT TO PLAY WITH YOU!
AREN'T YOUR BIG FAT LEGS GETTING TIRED, KEENSER?

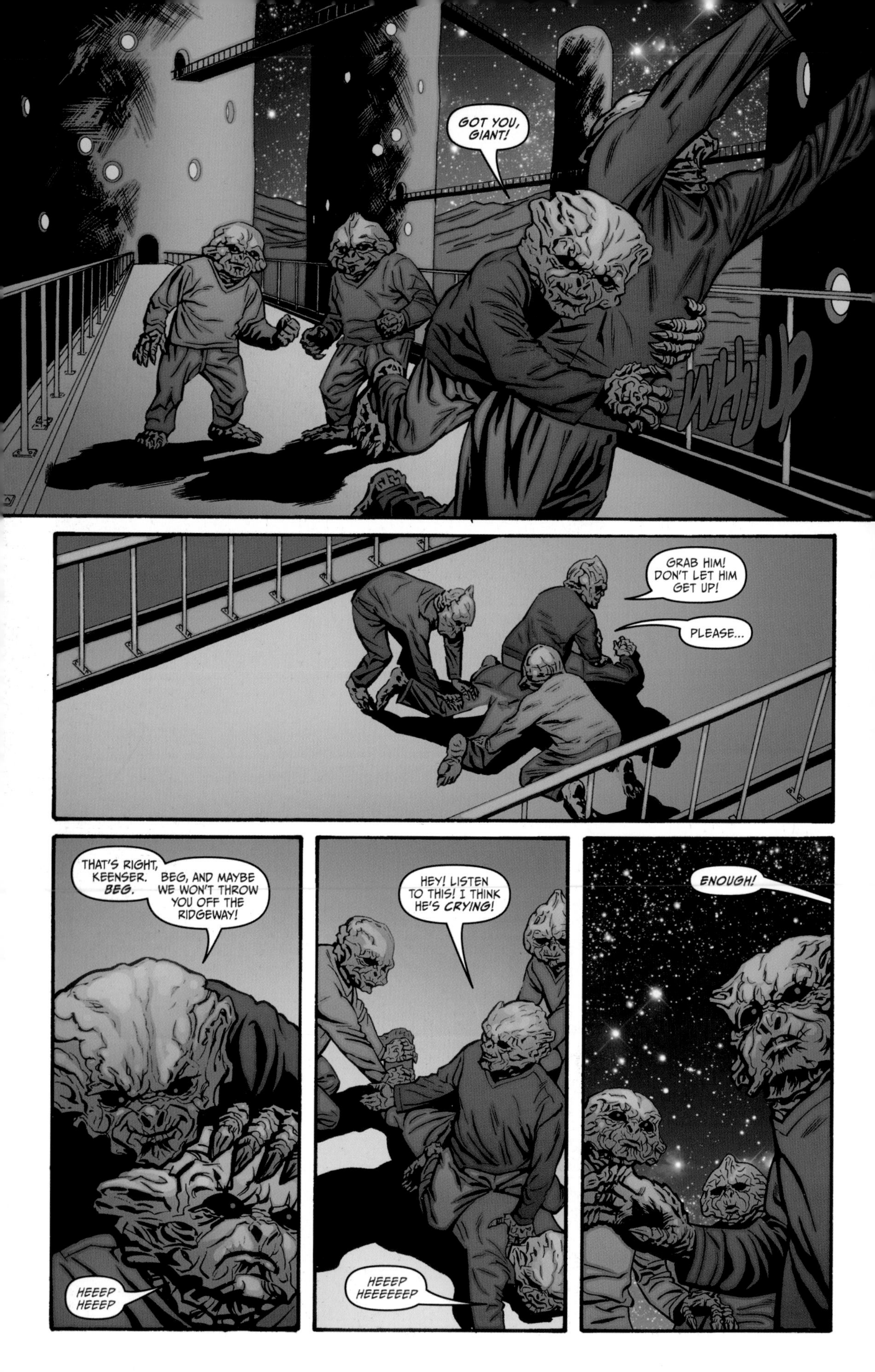
GOT YOU, GIANT!
WHUUP
GRAB HIM! DON'T LET HIM GET UP!
PLEASE...
THAT'S RIGHT, KEENSER. BEG.
BEG, AND MAYBE WE WON'T THROW YOU OFF THE RIDGEWAY!
HEEEP HEEEP
HEY! LISTEN TO THIS! I THINK HE'S CRYING!
HEEEP HEEEEEEP
ENOUGH!

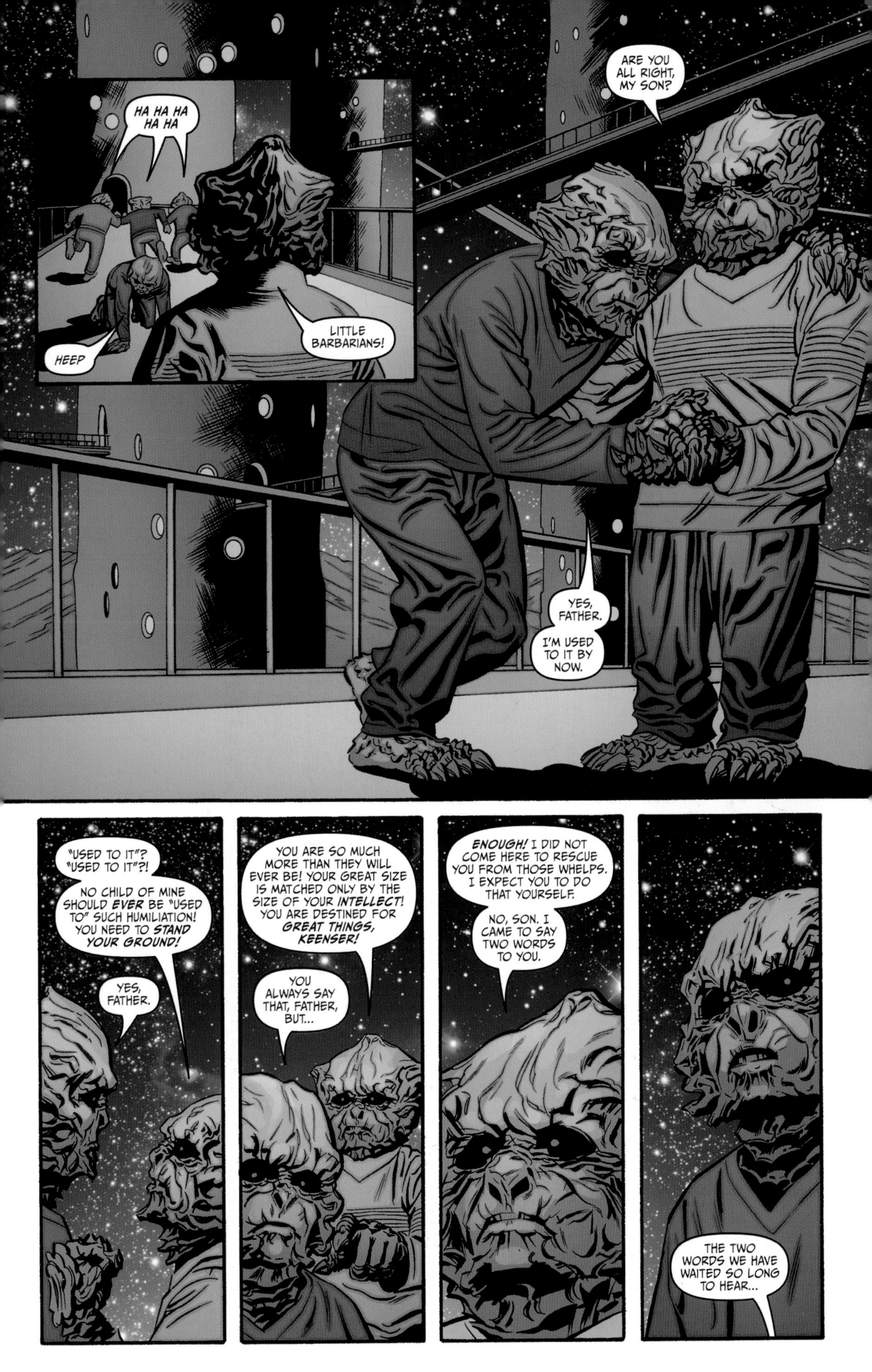
HA HA HA HA HA
HEEP
LITTLE BARBARIANS!
ARE YOU ALL RIGHT, MY SON?
YES, FATHER.
I'M USED TO IT BY NOW.
"USED TO IT"? "USED TO IT"?!
NO CHILD OF MINE SHOULD EVER BE "USED TO" SUCH HUMILIATION! YOU NEED TO STAND YOUR GROUND!
YES, FATHER.
YOU ARE SO MUCH MORE THAN THEY WILL EVER BE! YOUR GREAT SIZE IS MATCHED ONLY BY THE SIZE OF YOUR INTELLECT! YOU ARE DESTINED FOR GREAT THINGS, KEENSER!
YOU ALWAYS SAY THAT, FATHER, BUT...
ENOUGH! I DID NOT COME HERE TO RESCUE YOU FROM THOSE WHELPS. I EXPECT YOU TO DO THAT YOURSELF.
NO, SON. I CAME TO SAY TWO WORDS TO YOU.
THE TWO WORDS WE HAVE WAITED SO LONG TO HEAR...

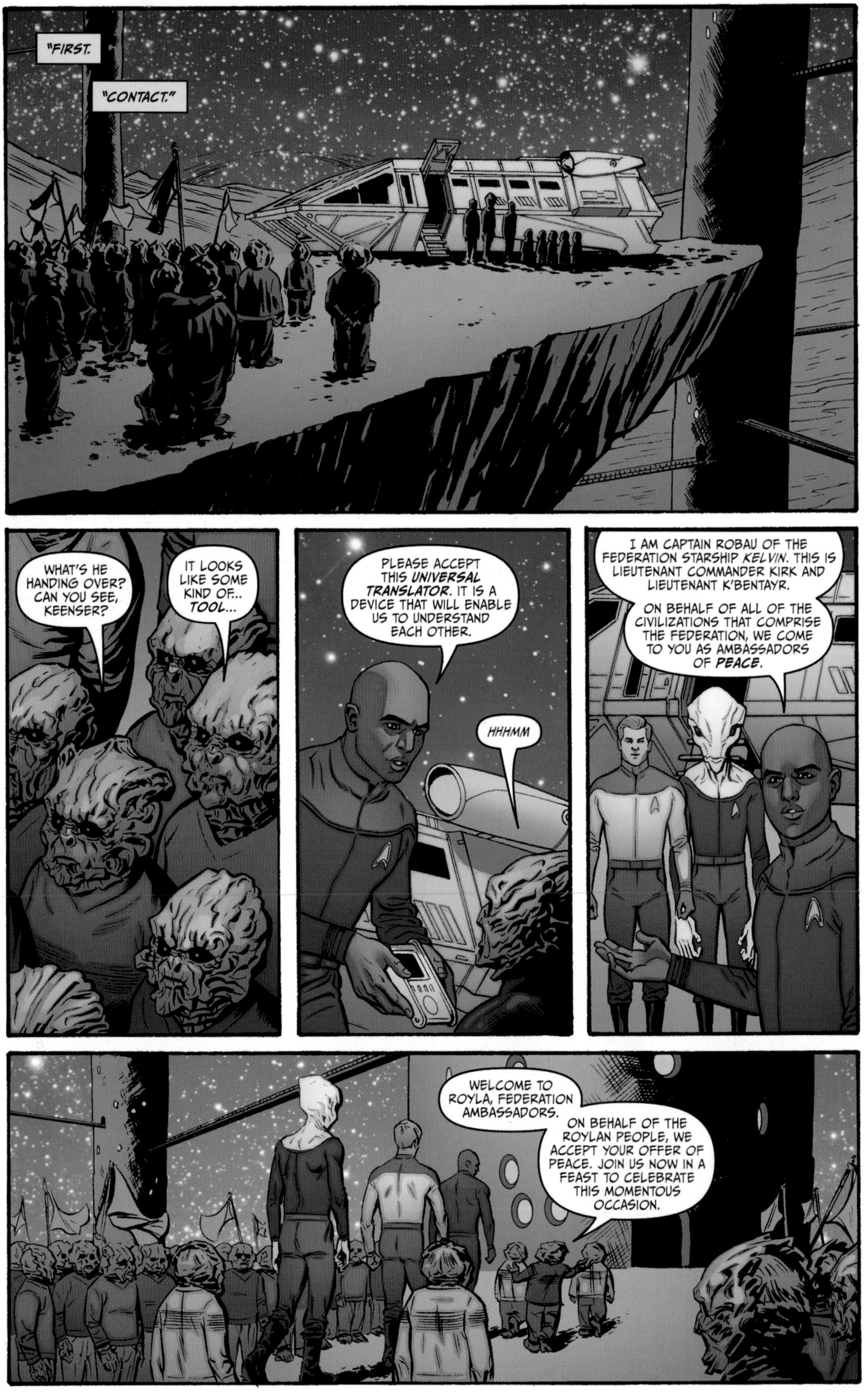
"FIRST.
"CONTACT."
WHAT'S HE HANDING OVER? CAN YOU SEE, KEENSER?
IT LOOKS LIKE SOME KIND OF... TOOL...
PLEASE ACCEPT THIS UNIVERSAL TRANSLATOR. IT IS A DEVICE THAT WILL ENABLE US TO UNDERSTAND EACH OTHER.
HHHMM
I AM CAPTAIN ROBAU OF THE FEDERATION STARSHIP KELVIN. THIS IS LIEUTENANT COMMANDER KIRK AND LIEUTENANT K'BENTAYR.
ON BEHALF OF ALL OF THE CIVILIZATIONS THAT COMPRISE THE FEDERATION, WE COME TO YOU AS AMBASSADORS OF PEACE.
WELCOME TO ROYLA, FEDERATION AMBASSADORS.
ON BEHALF OF THE ROYLAN PEOPLE, WE ACCEPT YOUR OFFER OF PEACE. JOIN US NOW IN A FEAST TO CELEBRATE THIS MOMENTOUS OCCASION.

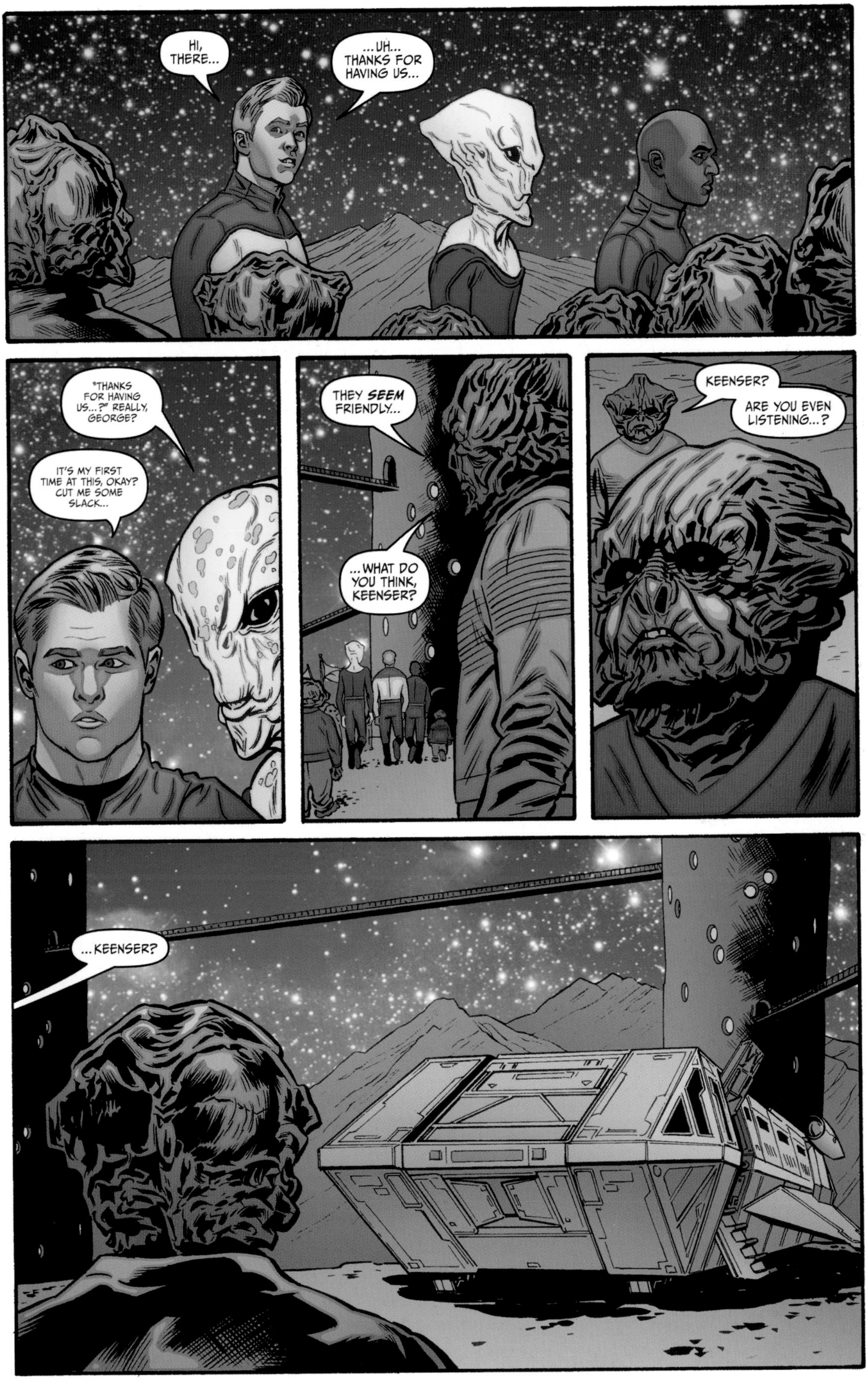
HI, THERE...
...UH... THANKS FOR HAVING US...
"THANKS FOR HAVING US...?" REALLY, GEORGE?
IT'S MY FIRST TIME AT THIS, OKAY? CUT ME SOME SLACK...
THEY SEEM FRIENDLY...
...WHAT DO YOU THINK, KEENSER?
KEENSER?
ARE YOU EVEN LISTENING...?
...KEENSER?

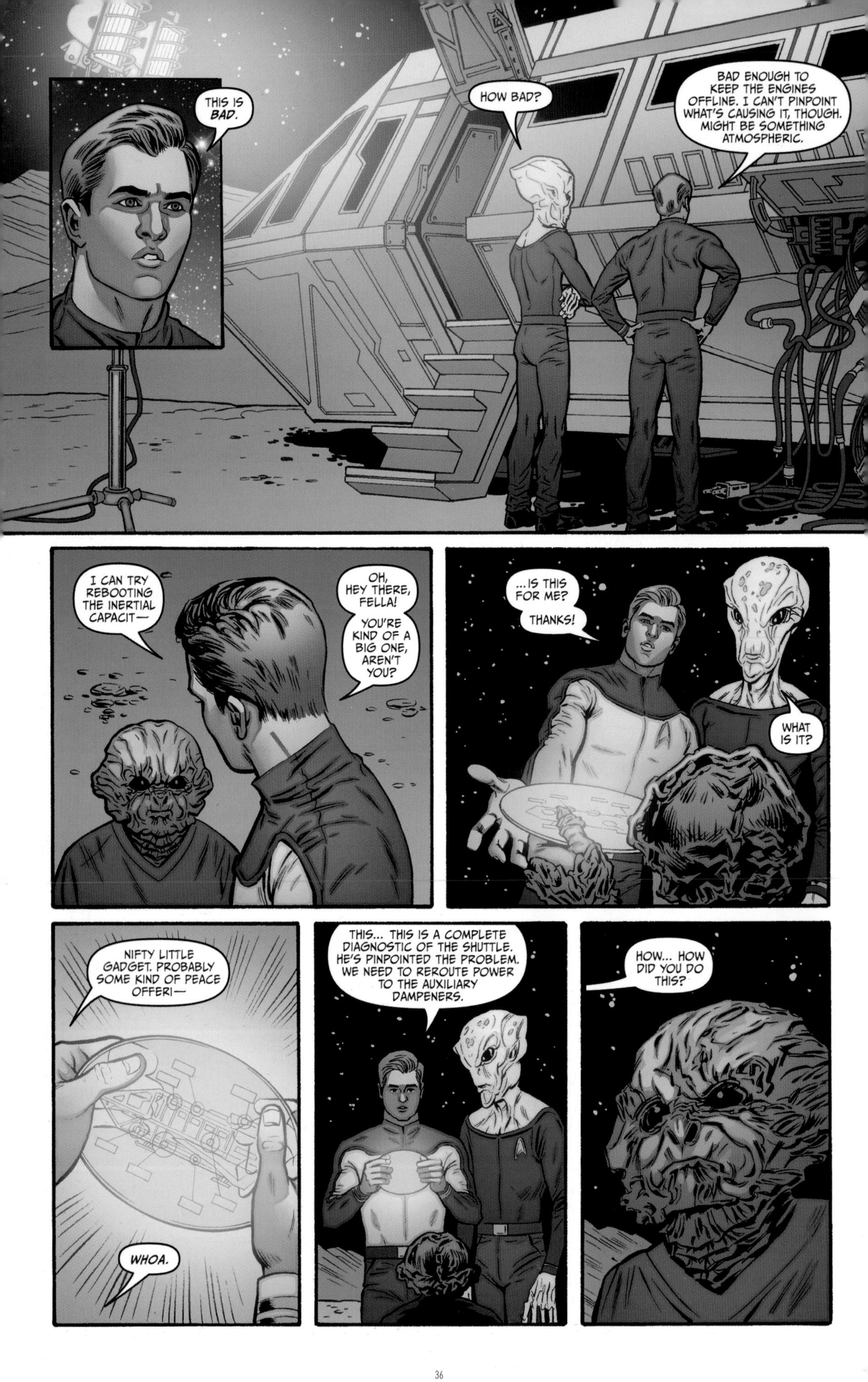
THIS IS BAD.
HOW BAD?
BAD ENOUGH TO KEEP THE ENGINES OFFLINE. I CAN'T PINPOINT WHAT'S CAUSING IT, THOUGH. MIGHT BE SOMETHING ATMOSPHERIC.
I CAN TRY REBOOTING THE INERTIAL CAPACIT—
OH, HEY THERE, FELLA!
YOU'RE KIND OF A BIG ONE, AREN'T YOU?
...IS THIS FOR ME?
THANKS!
WHAT IS IT?
NIFTY LITTLE GADGET. PROBABLY SOME KIND OF PEACE OFFERI—
WHOA.
THIS... THIS IS A COMPLETE DIAGNOSTIC OF THE SHUTTLE. HE'S PINPOINTED THE PROBLEM. WE NEED TO REROUTE POWER TO THE AUXILIARY DAMPENERS.
HOW... HOW DID YOU DO THIS?

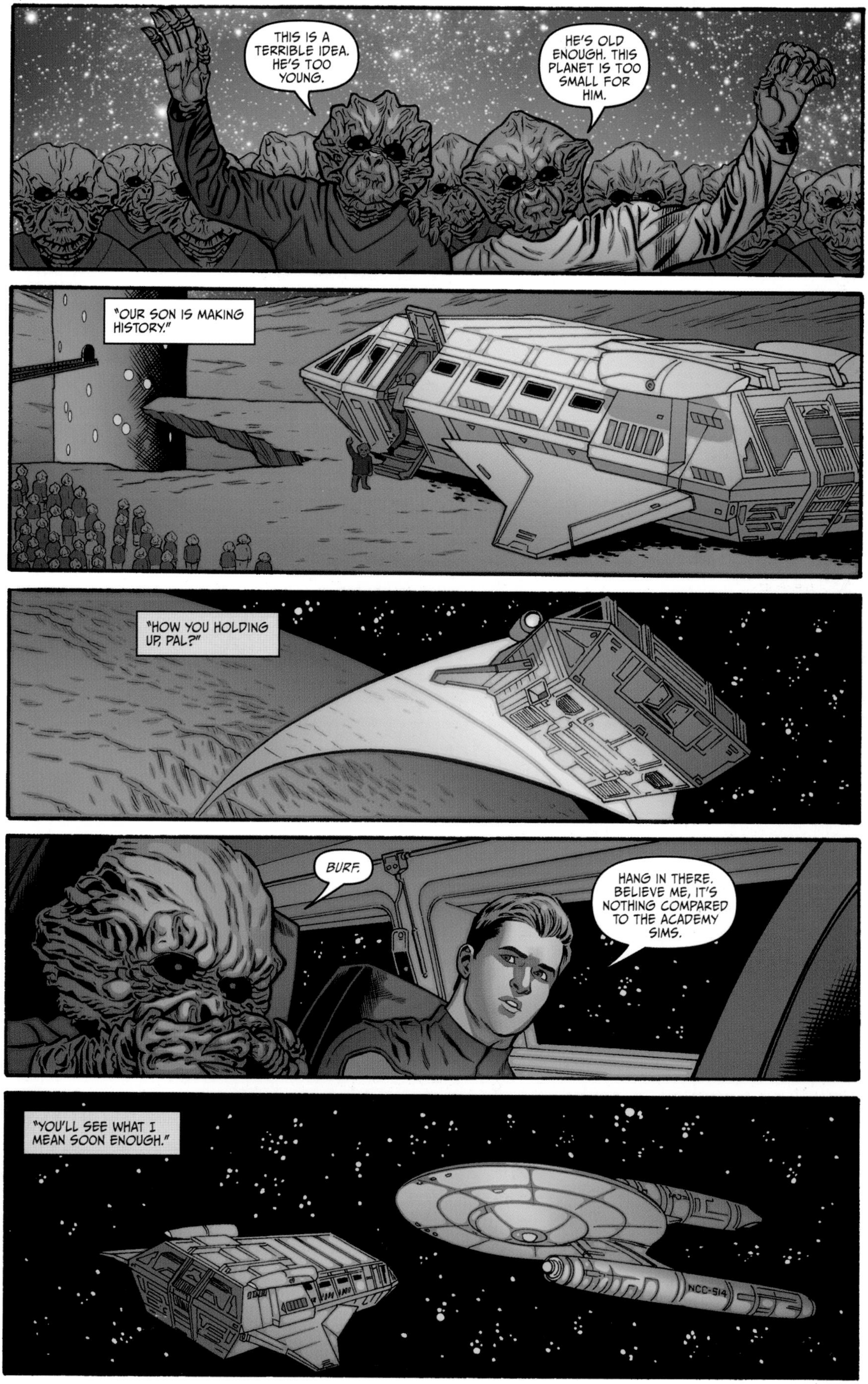
THIS IS A TERRIBLE IDEA. HE'S TOO YOUNG.
HE'S OLD ENOUGH. THIS PLANET IS TOO SMALL FOR HIM.
"OUR SON IS MAKING HISTORY."
"HOW YOU HOLDING UP, PAL?"
BURF.
HANG IN THERE. BELIEVE ME, IT'S NOTHING COMPARED TO THE ACADEMY SIMS.
"YOU'LL SEE WHAT I MEAN SOON ENOUGH."
NCC-514

THREE YEARS LATER.

"CONGRATULATIONS, MR. KEENSER!"

IT IS MY GREAT HONOR TO BESTOW UPON YOU THIS SPECIAL COMMENDATION, MARKING YOUR ACCOMPLISHMENT AS THE FIRST CADET FROM THE ROYLA HOMEWORLD TO EVER GRADUATE FROM THE ACADEMY!

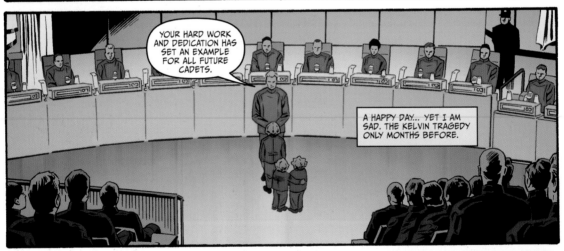

YOUR HARD WORK AND DEDICATION HAS SET AN EXAMPLE FOR ALL FUTURE CADETS.

A HAPPY DAY... YET I AM SAD. THE KELVIN TRAGEDY ONLY MONTHS BEFORE.

MY FRIENDS GONE.

I DEDICATE MY SERVICE TO THEM.

TIME FLIES.

I AM ASSIGNED TO SHIPS.

STARBASES.

STRANGE NEW WORLDS.

AFTER SEVERAL YEARS, A PROMOTION. CHIEF ENGINEER.

ASSIGNED TO A NEW RESEARCH STATION.

DELTA VEGA.

READY TO EXPLORE.

A GOOD CREW.

HERE ARE THE LATEST ESTIMATES, SIR! WE'LL NEED FIVE MORE TURBINES FOR THE EQUATORIAL SUBSTATION, A TWIN-CAP RELAY FOR EACH OF THE POLES, AND STARFLEET COMMAND IS ASKING FOR AN UPDATE ON THE ATMOSPHERICS...

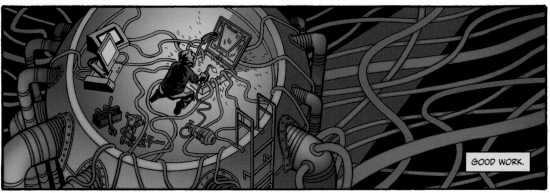

GOOD WORK.

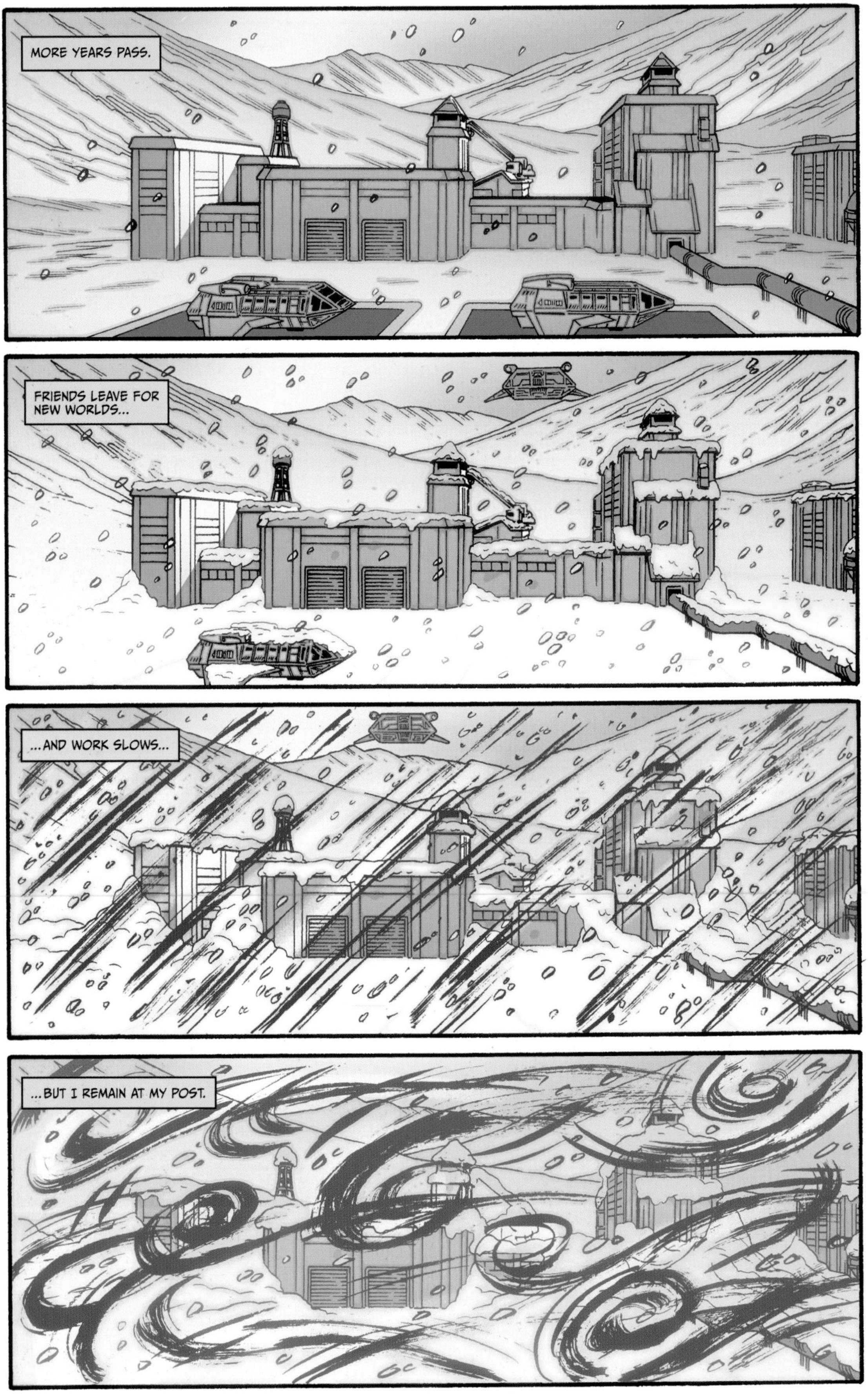
MORE YEARS PASS.
FRIENDS LEAVE FOR NEW WORLDS...
...AND WORK SLOWS...
...BUT I REMAIN AT MY POST.

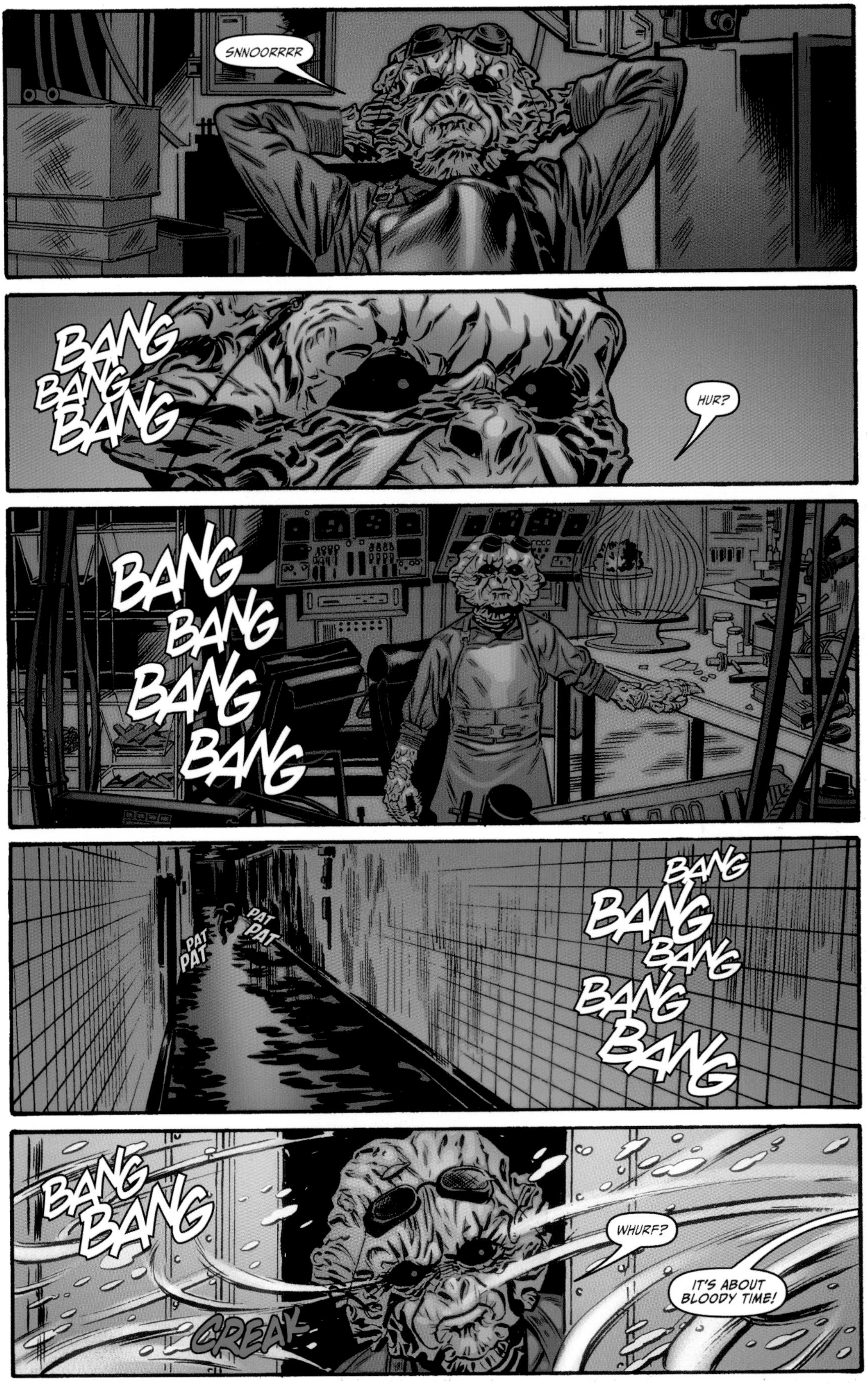
SNNOORRRR
BANG BANG BANG
HUR?
BANG BANG BANG BANG
PAT PAT
PAT PAT
BANG BANG BANG BANG BANG
BANG BANG
CREAK
WHURF?
IT'S ABOUT BLOODY TIME!

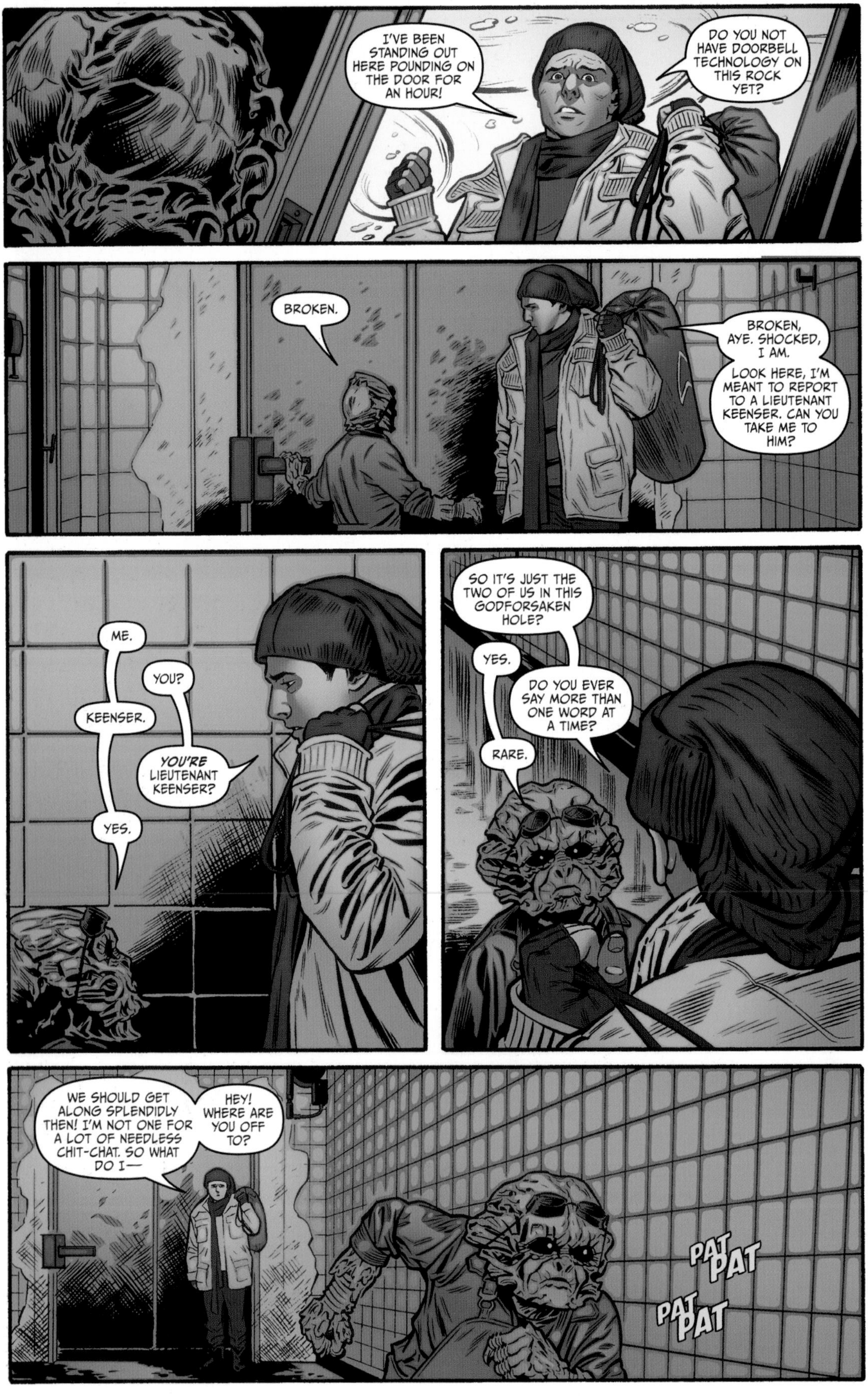
I'VE BEEN STANDING OUT HERE POUNDING ON THE DOOR FOR AN HOUR!
DO YOU NOT HAVE DOORBELL TECHNOLOGY ON THIS ROCK YET?
BROKEN.
BROKEN, AYE. SHOCKED, I AM.
LOOK HERE, I'M MEANT TO REPORT TO A LIEUTENANT KEENSER. CAN YOU TAKE ME TO HIM?
ME.
YOU?
KEENSER.
YOU'RE LIEUTENANT KEENSER?
YES.
SO IT'S JUST THE TWO OF US IN THIS GODFORSAKEN HOLE?
YES.
DO YOU EVER SAY MORE THAN ONE WORD AT A TIME?
RARE.
WE SHOULD GET ALONG SPLENDIDLY THEN! I'M NOT ONE FOR A LOT OF NEEDLESS CHIT-CHAT. SO WHAT DO I—
HEY! WHERE ARE YOU OFF TO?
PAT PAT
PAT PAT

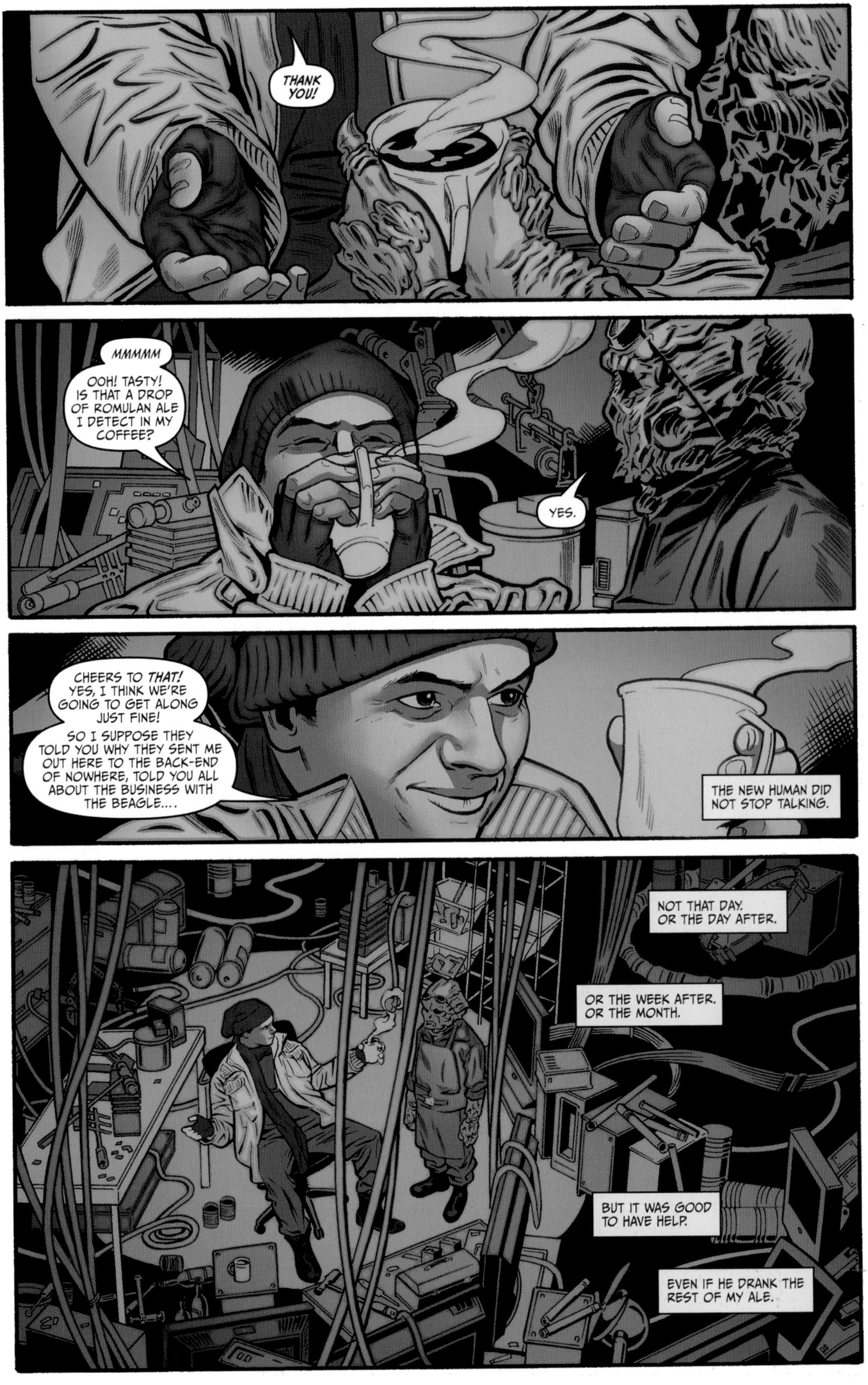
THANK YOU!
MMMMM
OOH! TASTY! IS THAT A DROP OF ROMULAN ALE I DETECT IN MY COFFEE?
YES.
CHEERS TO THAT! YES, I THINK WE'RE GOING TO GET ALONG JUST FINE!
SO I SUPPOSE THEY TOLD YOU WHY THEY SENT ME OUT HERE TO THE BACK-END OF NOWHERE, TOLD YOU ALL ABOUT THE BUSINESS WITH THE BEAGLE....
THE NEW HUMAN DID NOT STOP TALKING.
NOT THAT DAY. OR THE DAY AFTER.
OR THE WEEK AFTER. OR THE MONTH.
BUT IT WAS GOOD TO HAVE HELP.
EVEN IF HE DRANK THE REST OF MY ALE.

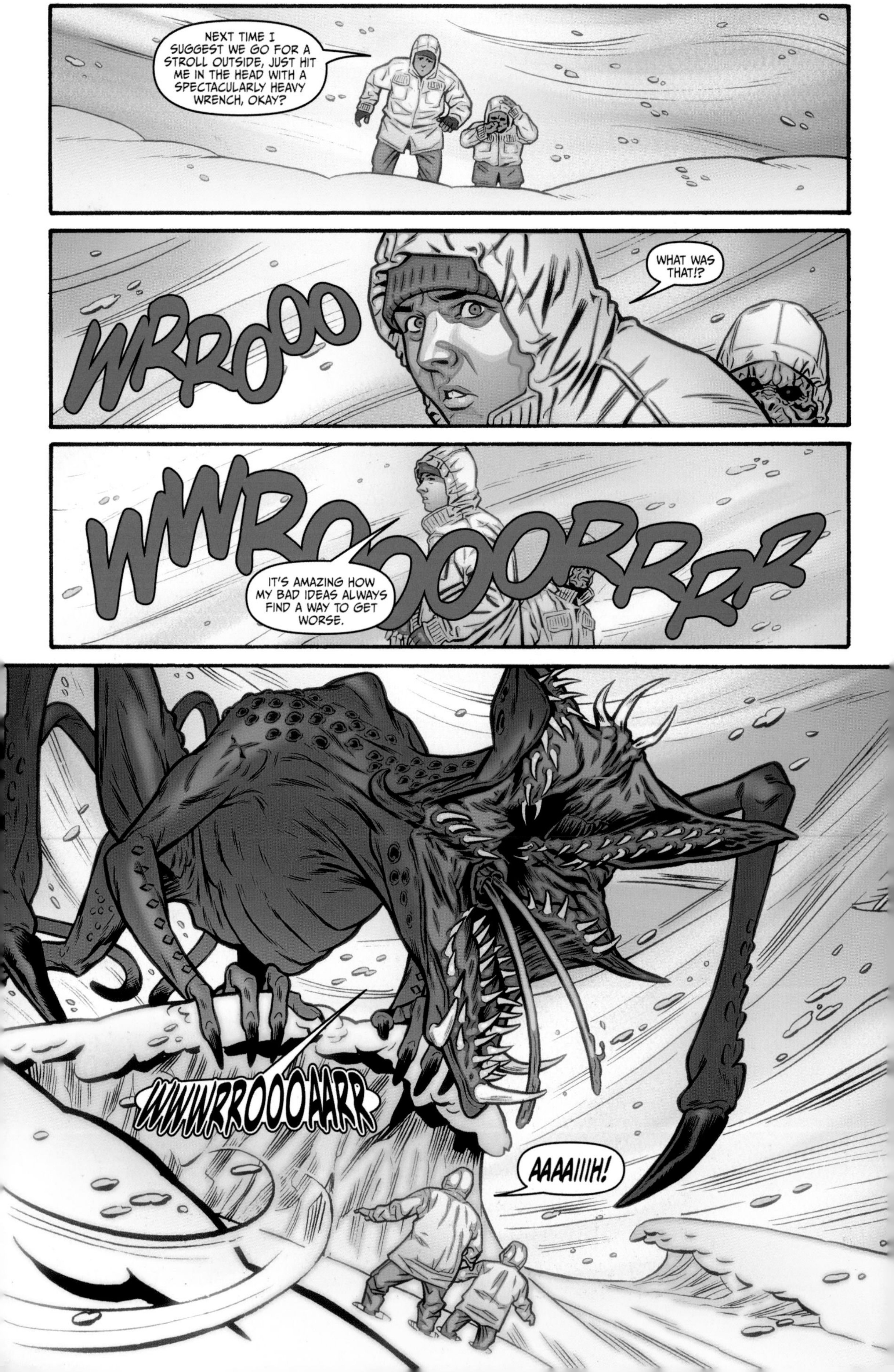
NEXT TIME I SUGGEST WE GO FOR A STROLL OUTSIDE, JUST HIT ME IN THE HEAD WITH A SPECTACULARLY HEAVY WRENCH, OKAY?
WRROOO
WHAT WAS THAT!?
WWROOOORRRR
IT'S AMAZING HOW MY BAD IDEAS ALWAYS FIND A WAY TO GET WORSE.
WWWRROOOAARR
AAAAIIIH!

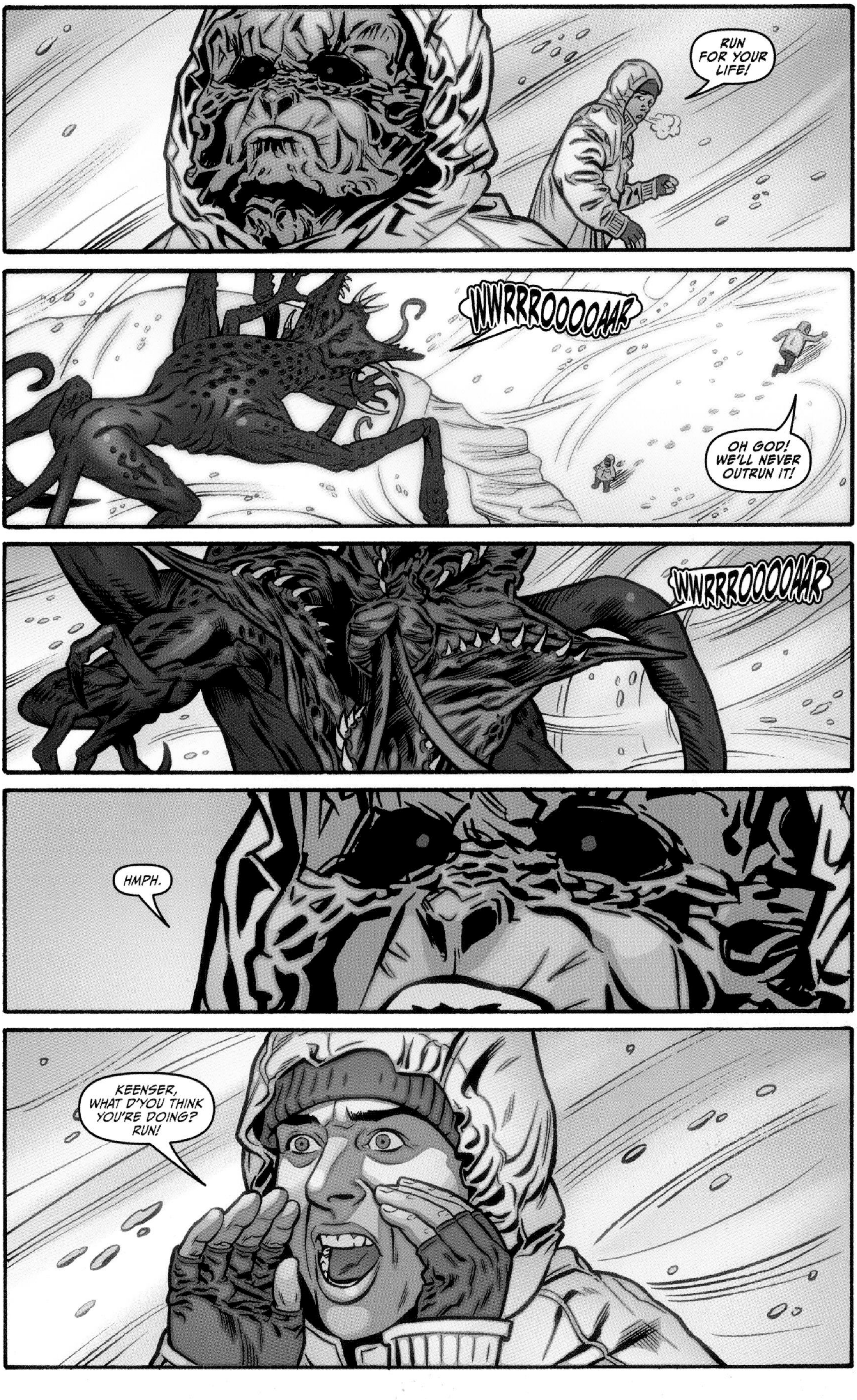
RUN FOR YOUR LIFE!
WWRRROOOOAAR
OH GOD! WE'LL NEVER OUTRUN IT!
WWRRROOOOAAR
HMPH.
KEENSER, WHAT D'YOU THINK YOU'RE DOING? RUN!

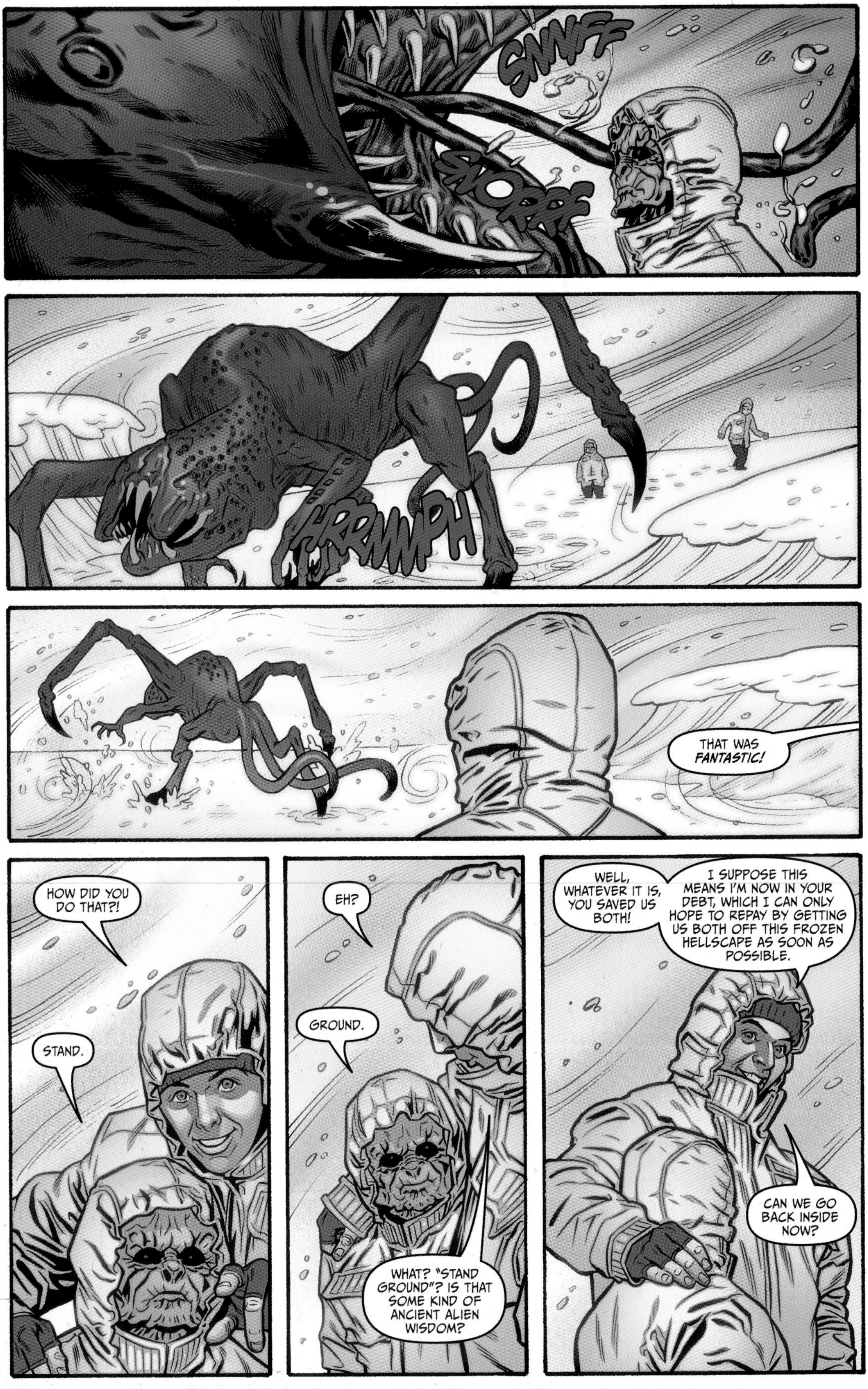
SNNIFF
SNORRF
HRRMMPH
THAT WAS *FANTASTIC!*
HOW DID YOU DO THAT?!
STAND.
EH?
GROUND.
WHAT? "STAND GROUND"? IS THAT SOME KIND OF ANCIENT ALIEN WISDOM?
WELL, WHATEVER IT IS, YOU SAVED US BOTH!
I SUPPOSE THIS MEANS I'M NOW IN YOUR DEBT, WHICH I CAN ONLY HOPE TO REPAY BY GETTING US BOTH OFF THIS FROZEN HELLSCAPE AS SOON AS POSSIBLE.
CAN WE GO BACK INSIDE NOW?

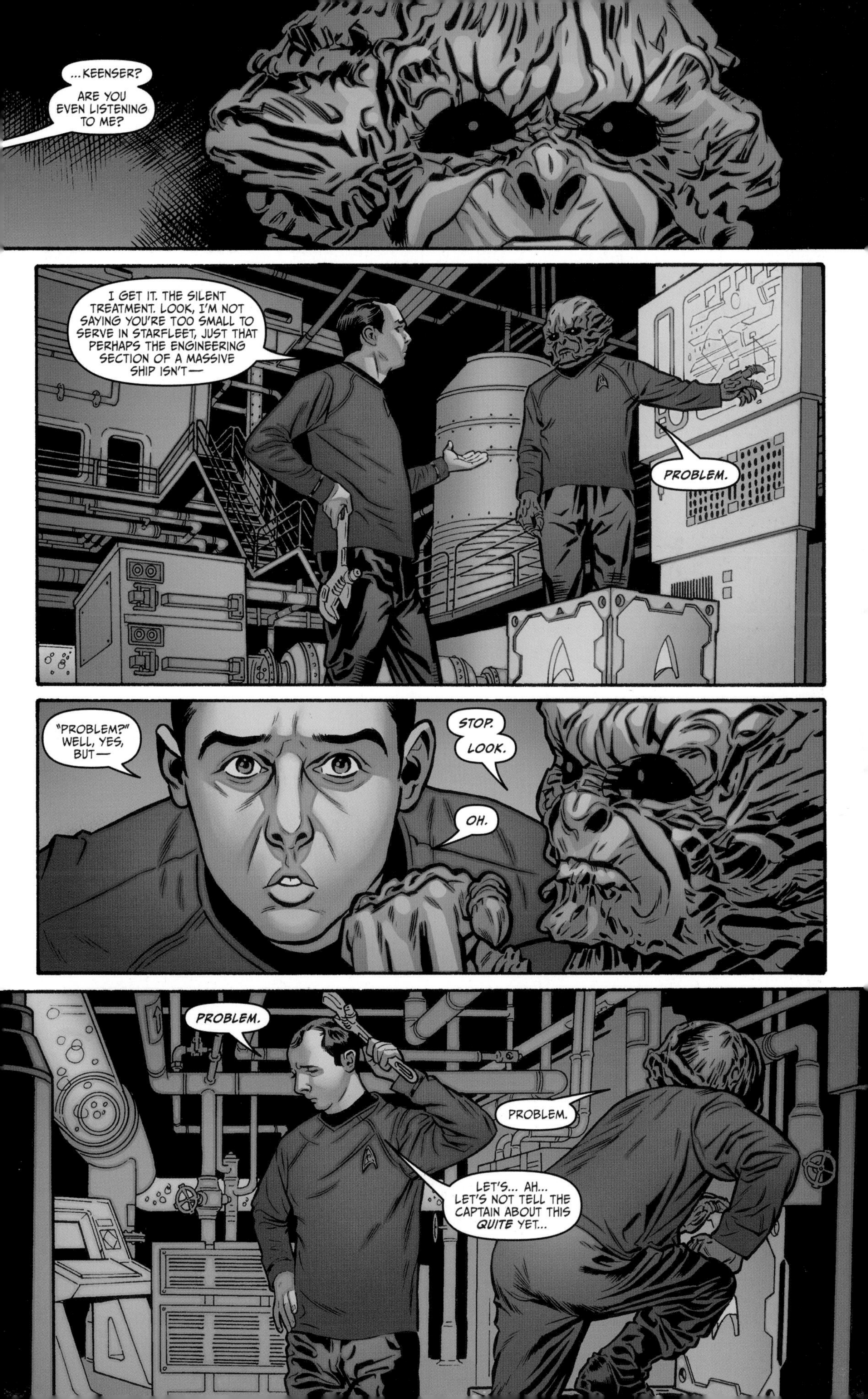
...KEENSER?
ARE YOU EVEN LISTENING TO ME?
I GET IT. THE SILENT TREATMENT. LOOK, I'M NOT SAYING YOU'RE TOO SMALL TO SERVE IN STARFLEET, JUST THAT PERHAPS THE ENGINEERING SECTION OF A MASSIVE SHIP ISN'T—
PROBLEM.
"PROBLEM?" WELL, YES, BUT—
STOP.
LOOK.
OH.
PROBLEM.
PROBLEM.
LET'S... AH... LET'S NOT TELL THE CAPTAIN ABOUT THIS *QUITE* YET...

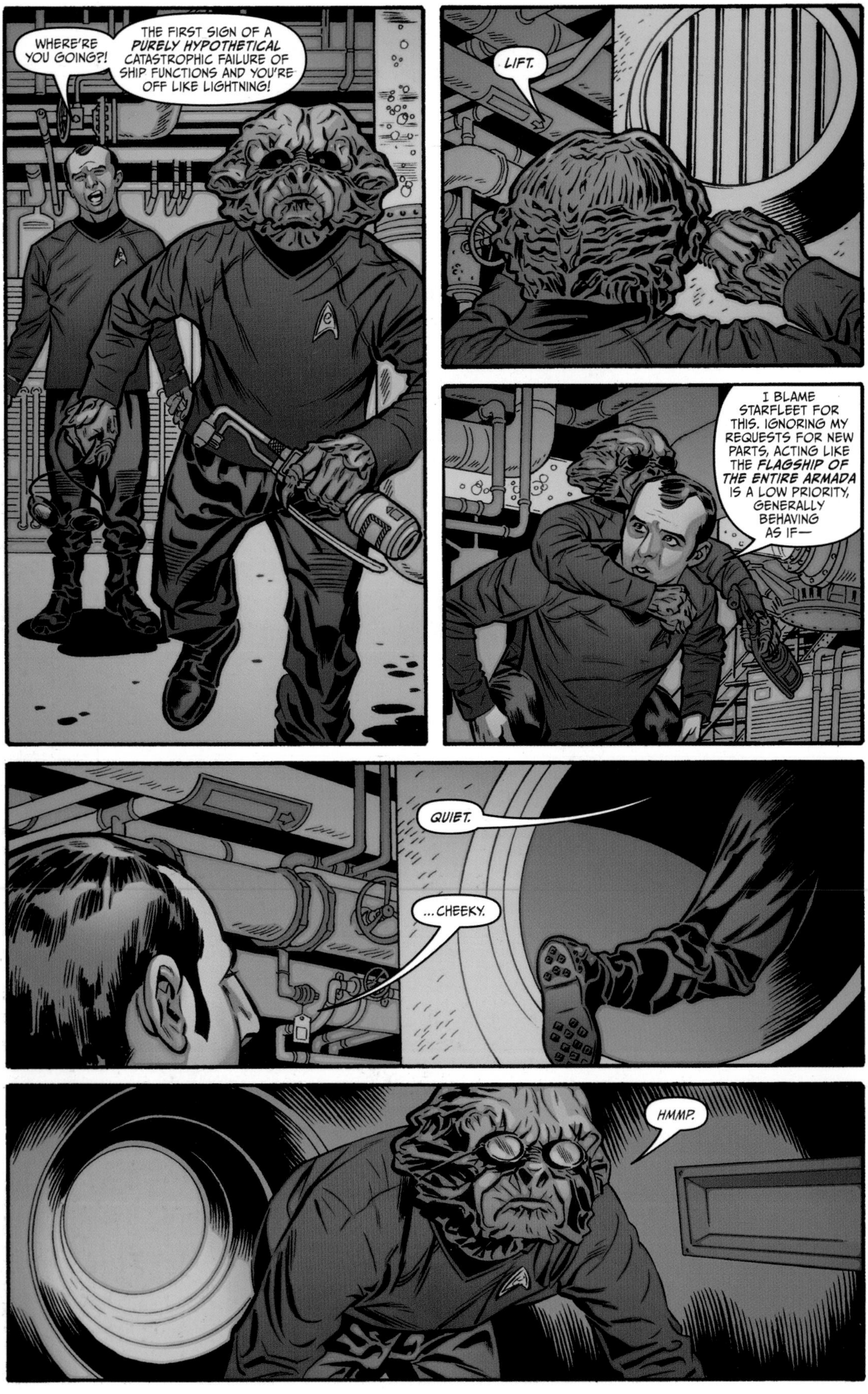
WHERE'RE YOU GOING?!
THE FIRST SIGN OF A *PURELY HYPOTHETICAL* CATASTROPHIC FAILURE OF SHIP FUNCTIONS AND YOU'RE OFF LIKE LIGHTNING!
LIFT.
I BLAME STARFLEET FOR THIS. IGNORING MY REQUESTS FOR NEW PARTS, ACTING LIKE THE *FLAGSHIP OF THE ENTIRE ARMADA* IS A LOW PRIORITY, GENERALLY BEHAVING AS IF—
QUIET.
...CHEEKY.
HMMP.

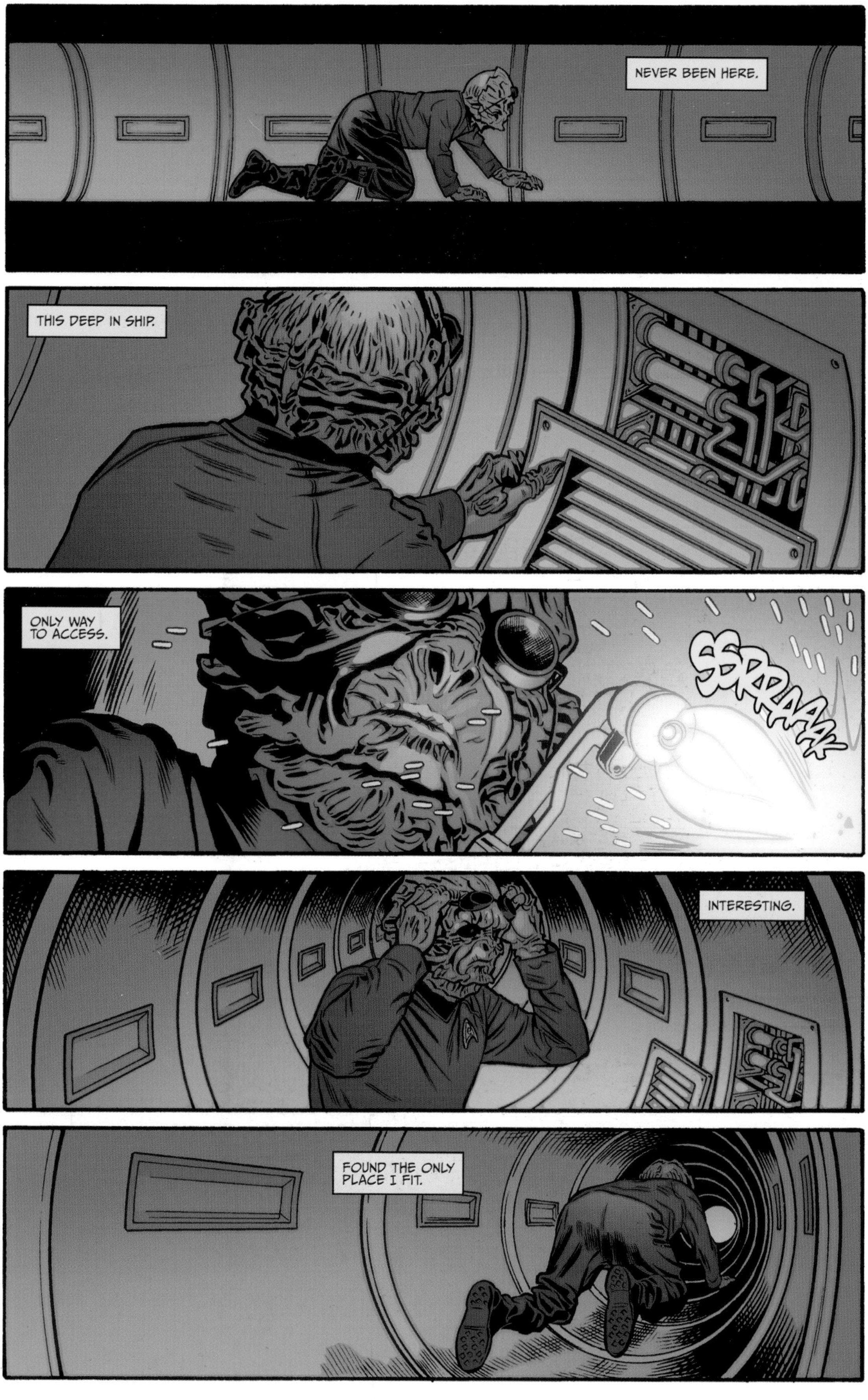
NEVER BEEN HERE.
THIS DEEP IN SHIP.
ONLY WAY TO ACCESS.
SSRRRAAAK
INTERESTING.
FOUND THE ONLY PLACE I FIT.

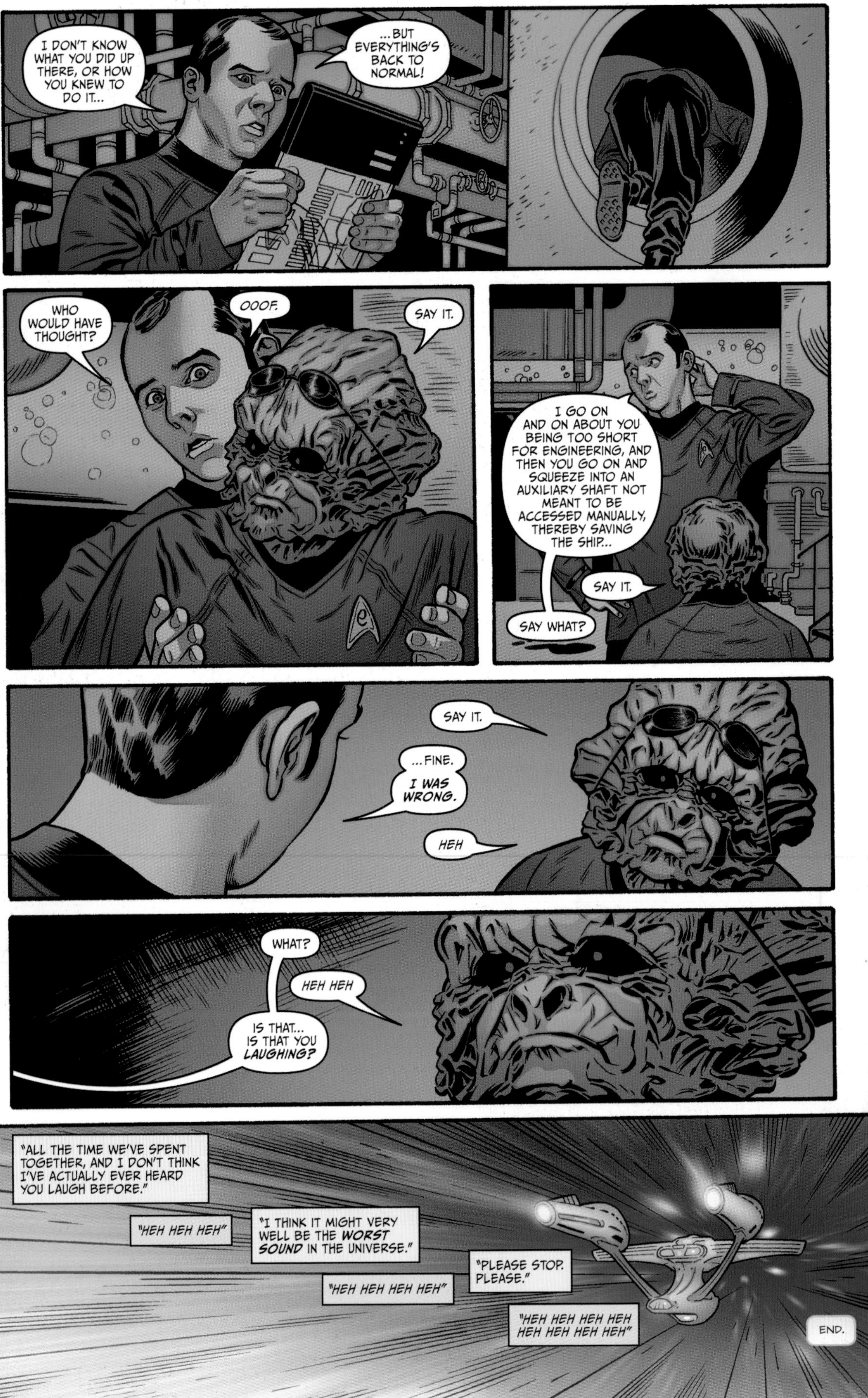

I DON'T KNOW WHAT YOU DID UP THERE, OR HOW YOU KNEW TO DO IT...
...BUT EVERYTHING'S BACK TO NORMAL!
WHO WOULD HAVE THOUGHT?
OOOF.
SAY IT.
I GO ON AND ON ABOUT YOU BEING TOO SHORT FOR ENGINEERING, AND THEN YOU GO ON AND SQUEEZE INTO AN AUXILIARY SHAFT NOT MEANT TO BE ACCESSED MANUALLY, THEREBY SAVING THE SHIP...
SAY IT.
SAY WHAT?
SAY IT.
...FINE. I WAS WRONG.
HEH
WHAT?
HEH HEH
IS THAT... IS THAT YOU LAUGHING?
"ALL THE TIME WE'VE SPENT TOGETHER, AND I DON'T THINK I'VE ACTUALLY EVER HEARD YOU LAUGH BEFORE."
"HEH HEH HEH"
"I THINK IT MIGHT VERY WELL BE THE WORST SOUND IN THE UNIVERSE."
"PLEASE STOP. PLEASE."
"HEH HEH HEH HEH"
"HEH HEH HEH HEH HEH HEH HEH HEH"
END.

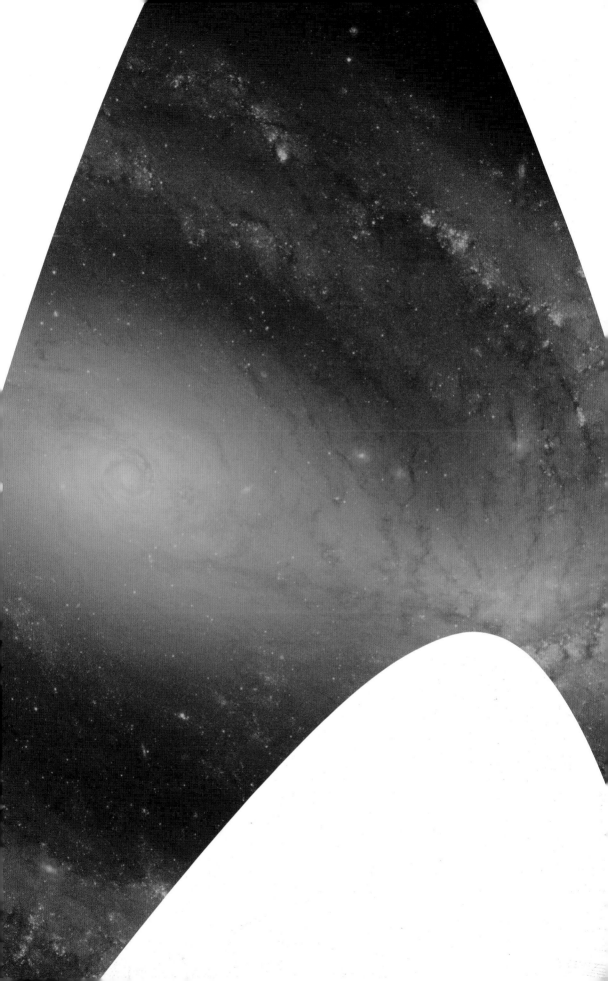

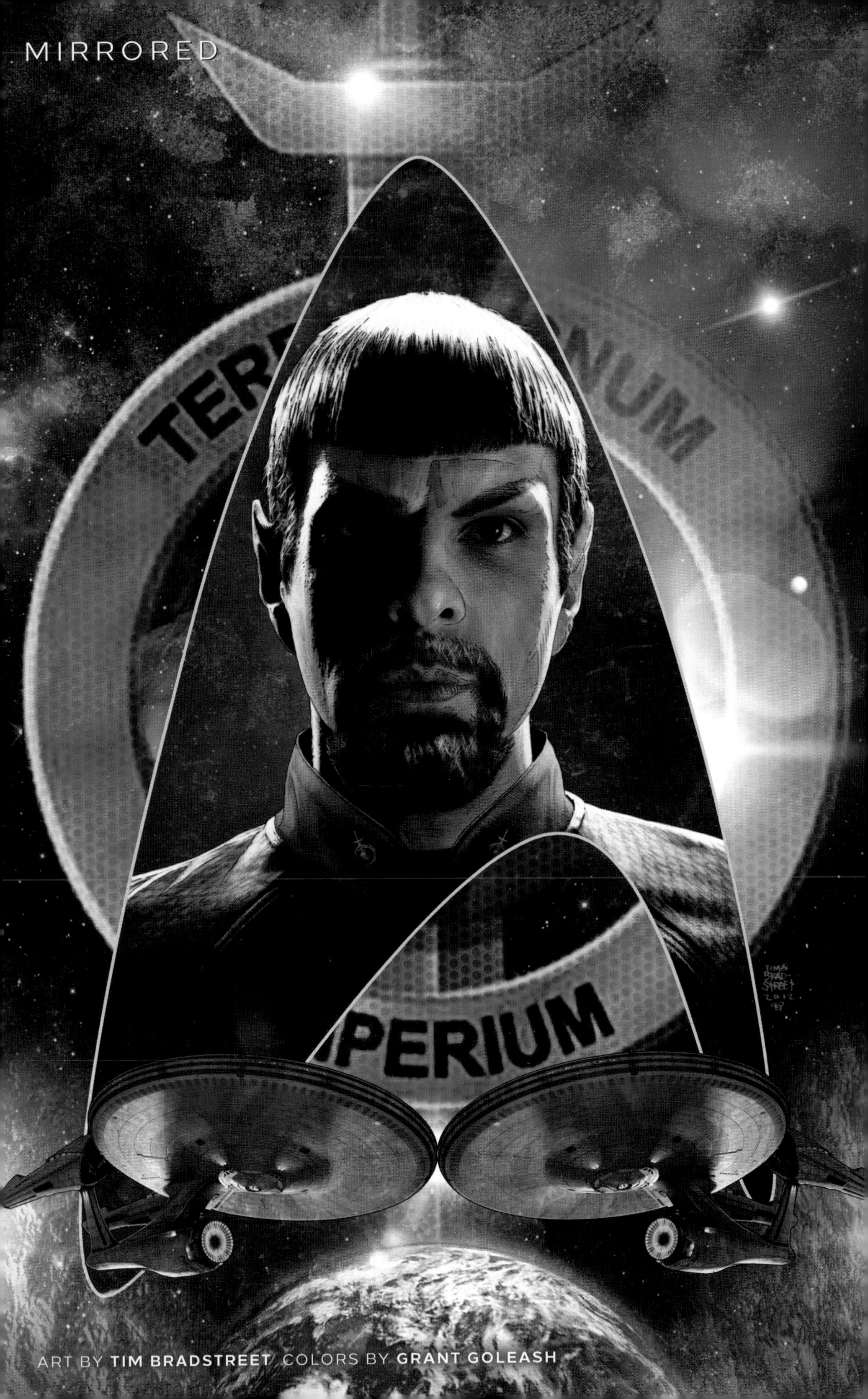

ART BY **TIM BRADSTREET** / COLORS BY **GRANT GOLEASH**

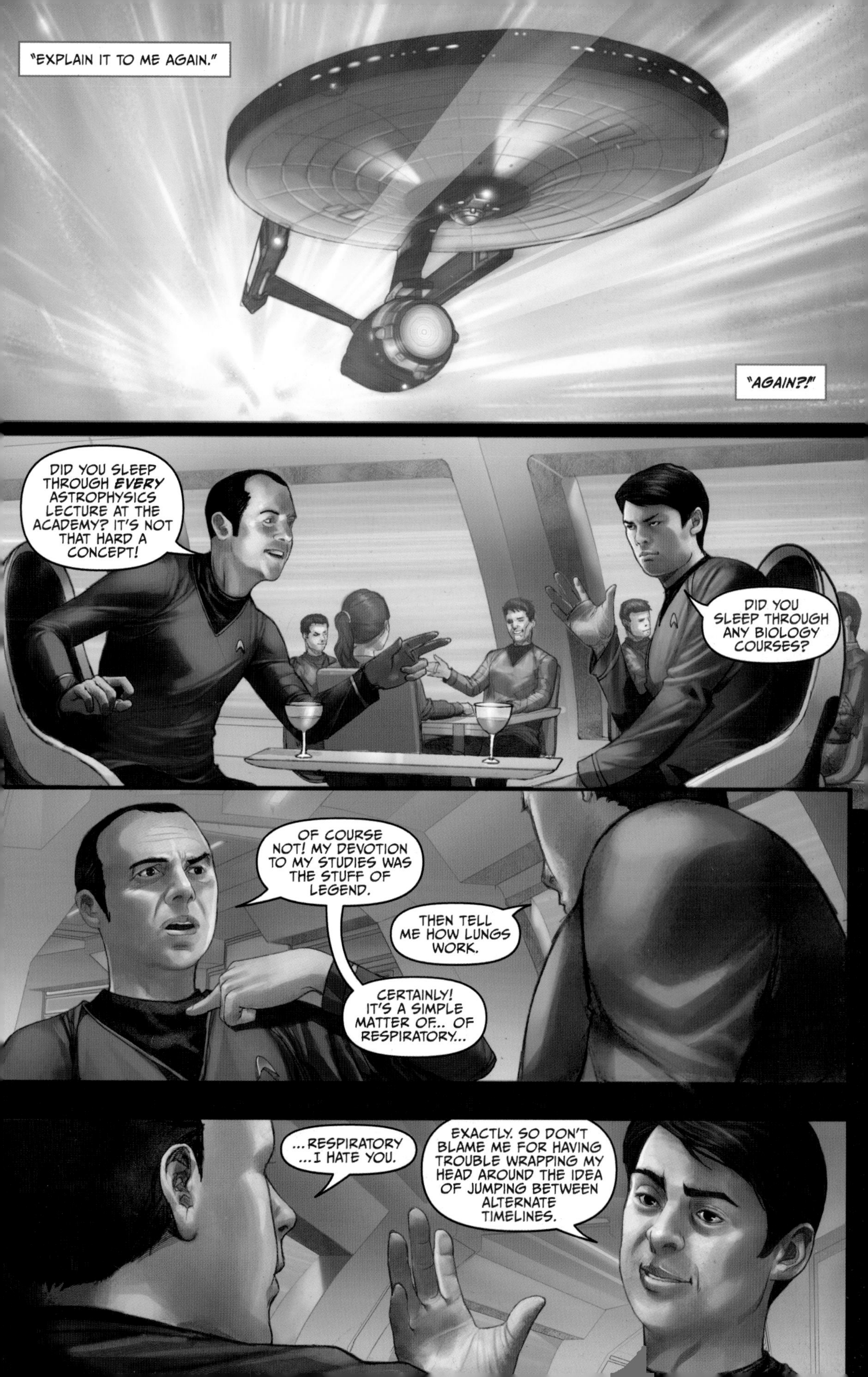
"EXPLAIN IT TO ME AGAIN."
"AGAIN?!"
DID YOU SLEEP THROUGH EVERY ASTROPHYSICS LECTURE AT THE ACADEMY? IT'S NOT THAT HARD A CONCEPT!
DID YOU SLEEP THROUGH ANY BIOLOGY COURSES?
OF COURSE NOT! MY DEVOTION TO MY STUDIES WAS THE STUFF OF LEGEND.
THEN TELL ME HOW LUNGS WORK.
CERTAINLY! IT'S A SIMPLE MATTER OF... OF RESPIRATORY...
...RESPIRATORY ...I HATE YOU.
EXACTLY. SO DON'T BLAME ME FOR HAVING TROUBLE WRAPPING MY HEAD AROUND THE IDEA OF JUMPING BETWEEN ALTERNATE TIMELINES.

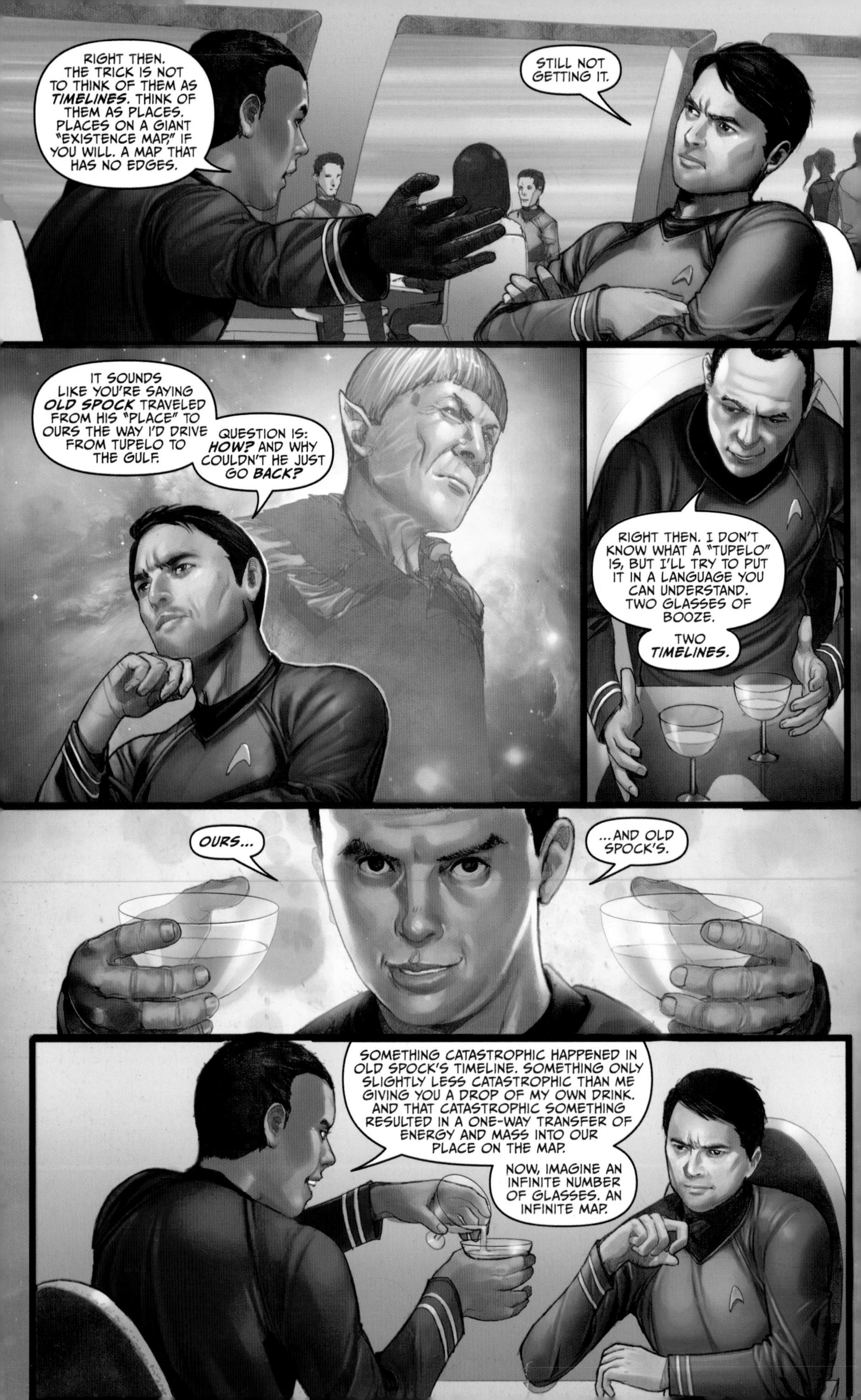
RIGHT THEN. THE TRICK IS NOT TO THINK OF THEM AS *TIMELINES*. THINK OF THEM AS PLACES. PLACES ON A GIANT "EXISTENCE MAP," IF YOU WILL. A MAP THAT HAS NO EDGES.
STILL NOT GETTING IT.
IT SOUNDS LIKE YOU'RE SAYING *OLD SPOCK* TRAVELED FROM HIS "PLACE" TO OURS THE WAY I'D DRIVE FROM TUPELO TO THE GULF.
QUESTION IS: *HOW?* AND WHY COULDN'T HE JUST GO *BACK?*
RIGHT THEN. I DON'T KNOW WHAT A "TUPELO" IS, BUT I'LL TRY TO PUT IT IN A LANGUAGE YOU CAN UNDERSTAND. TWO GLASSES OF BOOZE.
TWO *TIMELINES.*
OURS...
...AND OLD SPOCK'S.
SOMETHING CATASTROPHIC HAPPENED IN OLD SPOCK'S TIMELINE. SOMETHING ONLY SLIGHTLY LESS CATASTROPHIC THAN ME GIVING YOU A DROP OF MY OWN DRINK. AND THAT CATASTROPHIC SOMETHING RESULTED IN A ONE-WAY TRANSFER OF ENERGY AND MASS INTO OUR PLACE ON THE MAP.
NOW, IMAGINE AN INFINITE NUMBER OF GLASSES. AN INFINITE MAP.

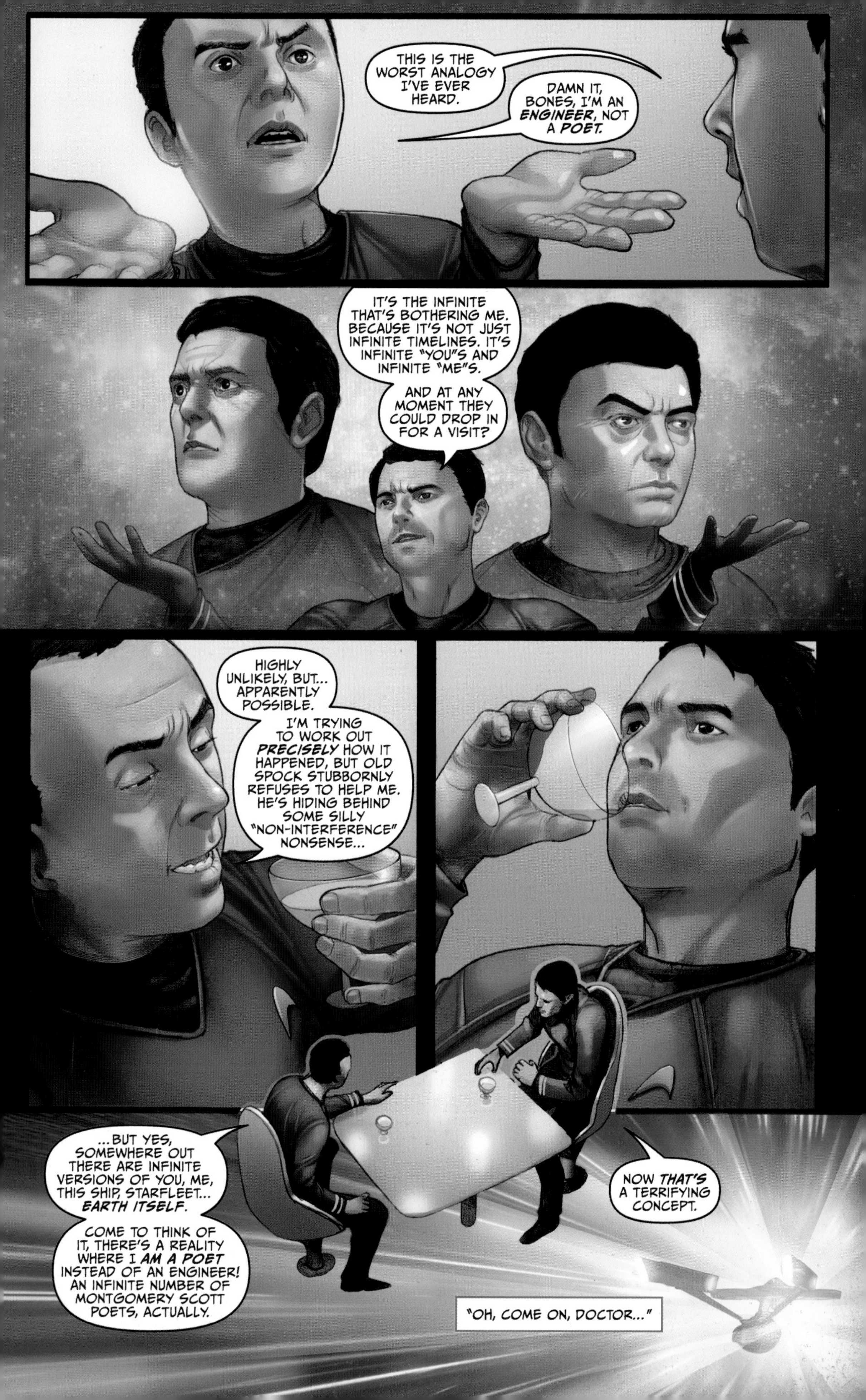
THIS IS THE WORST ANALOGY I'VE EVER HEARD.
DAMN IT, BONES, I'M AN ENGINEER, NOT A POET.
IT'S THE INFINITE THAT'S BOTHERING ME. BECAUSE IT'S NOT JUST INFINITE TIMELINES. IT'S INFINITE "YOU"S AND INFINITE "ME"S.
AND AT ANY MOMENT THEY COULD DROP IN FOR A VISIT?
HIGHLY UNLIKELY, BUT... APPARENTLY POSSIBLE.
I'M TRYING TO WORK OUT PRECISELY HOW IT HAPPENED, BUT OLD SPOCK STUBBORNLY REFUSES TO HELP ME. HE'S HIDING BEHIND SOME SILLY "NON-INTERFERENCE" NONSENSE...
...BUT YES, SOMEWHERE OUT THERE ARE INFINITE VERSIONS OF YOU, ME, THIS SHIP, STARFLEET... EARTH ITSELF.
COME TO THINK OF IT, THERE'S A REALITY WHERE I AM A POET INSTEAD OF AN ENGINEER! AN INFINITE NUMBER OF MONTGOMERY SCOTT POETS, ACTUALLY.
NOW THAT'S A TERRIFYING CONCEPT.
"OH, COME ON, DOCTOR..."

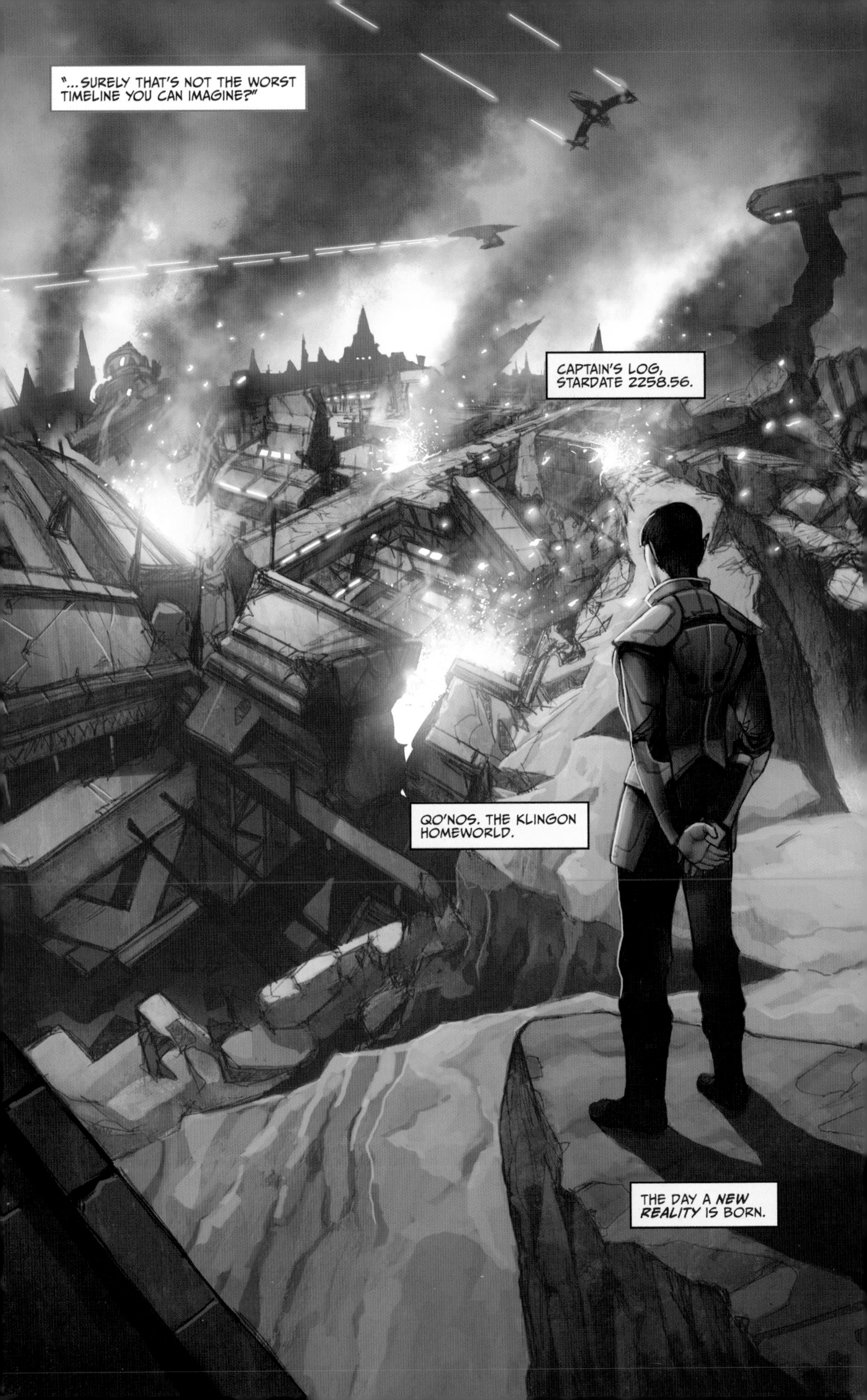
"...SURELY THAT'S NOT THE WORST TIMELINE YOU CAN IMAGINE?"
CAPTAIN'S LOG, STARDATE 2258.56.
QO'NOS. THE KLINGON HOMEWORLD.
THE DAY A *NEW REALITY* IS BORN.

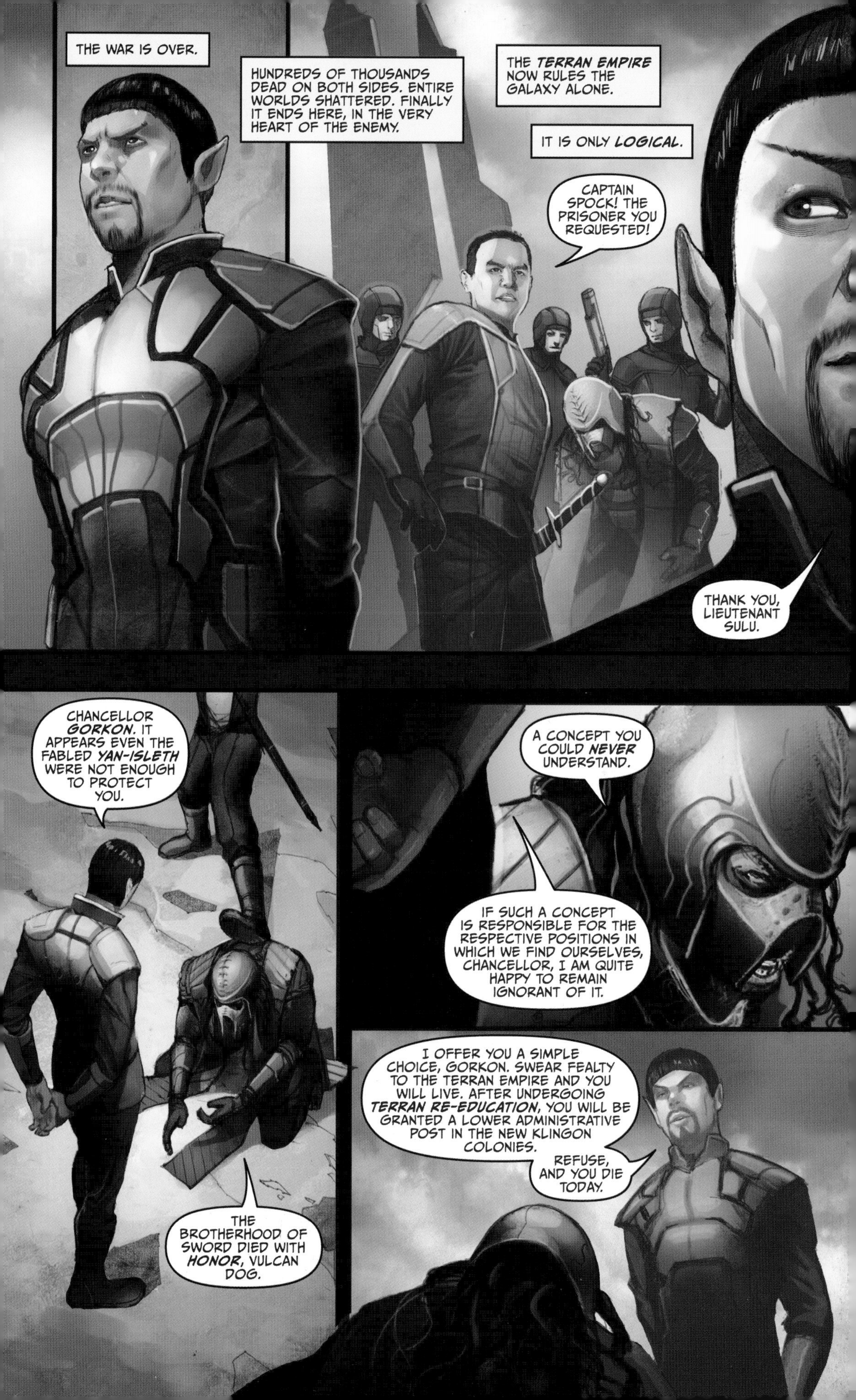
THE WAR IS OVER.
HUNDREDS OF THOUSANDS DEAD ON BOTH SIDES. ENTIRE WORLDS SHATTERED. FINALLY IT ENDS HERE, IN THE VERY HEART OF THE ENEMY.
THE TERRAN EMPIRE NOW RULES THE GALAXY ALONE.
IT IS ONLY LOGICAL.
CAPTAIN SPOCK! THE PRISONER YOU REQUESTED!
THANK YOU, LIEUTENANT SULU.
CHANCELLOR GORKON. IT APPEARS EVEN THE FABLED YAN-ISLETH WERE NOT ENOUGH TO PROTECT YOU.
THE BROTHERHOOD OF SWORD DIED WITH HONOR, VULCAN DOG.
A CONCEPT YOU COULD NEVER UNDERSTAND.
IF SUCH A CONCEPT IS RESPONSIBLE FOR THE RESPECTIVE POSITIONS IN WHICH WE FIND OURSELVES, CHANCELLOR, I AM QUITE HAPPY TO REMAIN IGNORANT OF IT.
I OFFER YOU A SIMPLE CHOICE, GORKON. SWEAR FEALTY TO THE TERRAN EMPIRE AND YOU WILL LIVE. AFTER UNDERGOING TERRAN RE-EDUCATION, YOU WILL BE GRANTED A LOWER ADMINISTRATIVE POST IN THE NEW KLINGON COLONIES.
REFUSE, AND YOU DIE TODAY.

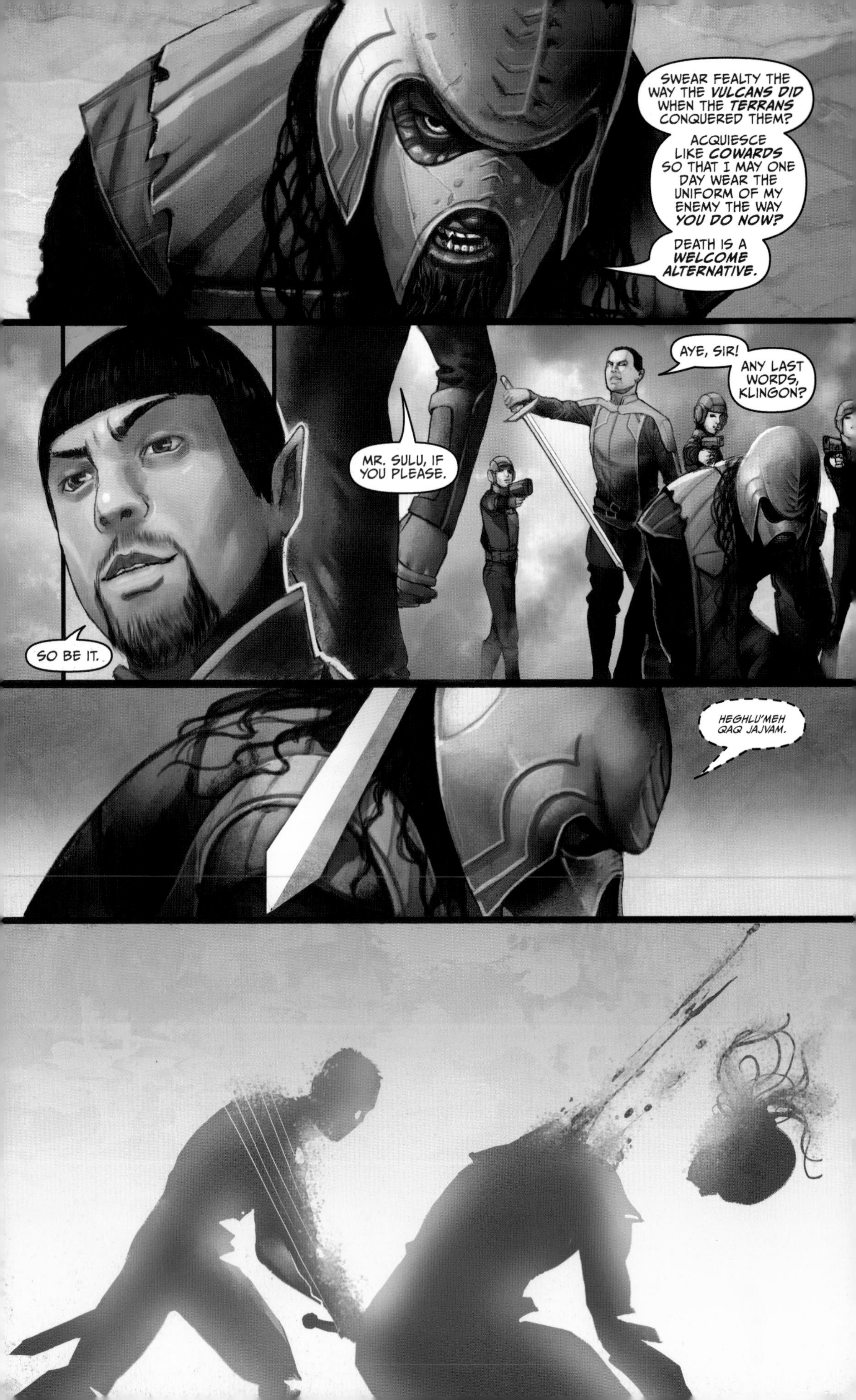

SWEAR FEALTY THE WAY THE ***VULCANS DID*** WHEN THE ***TERRANS*** CONQUERED THEM?
ACQUIESCE LIKE ***COWARDS*** SO THAT I MAY ONE DAY WEAR THE UNIFORM OF MY ENEMY THE WAY ***YOU DO NOW?***
DEATH IS A ***WELCOME ALTERNATIVE.***
SO BE IT.
MR. SULU, IF YOU PLEASE.
AYE, SIR!
ANY LAST WORDS, KLINGON?
HEGHLU'MEH QAQ JAJVAM.

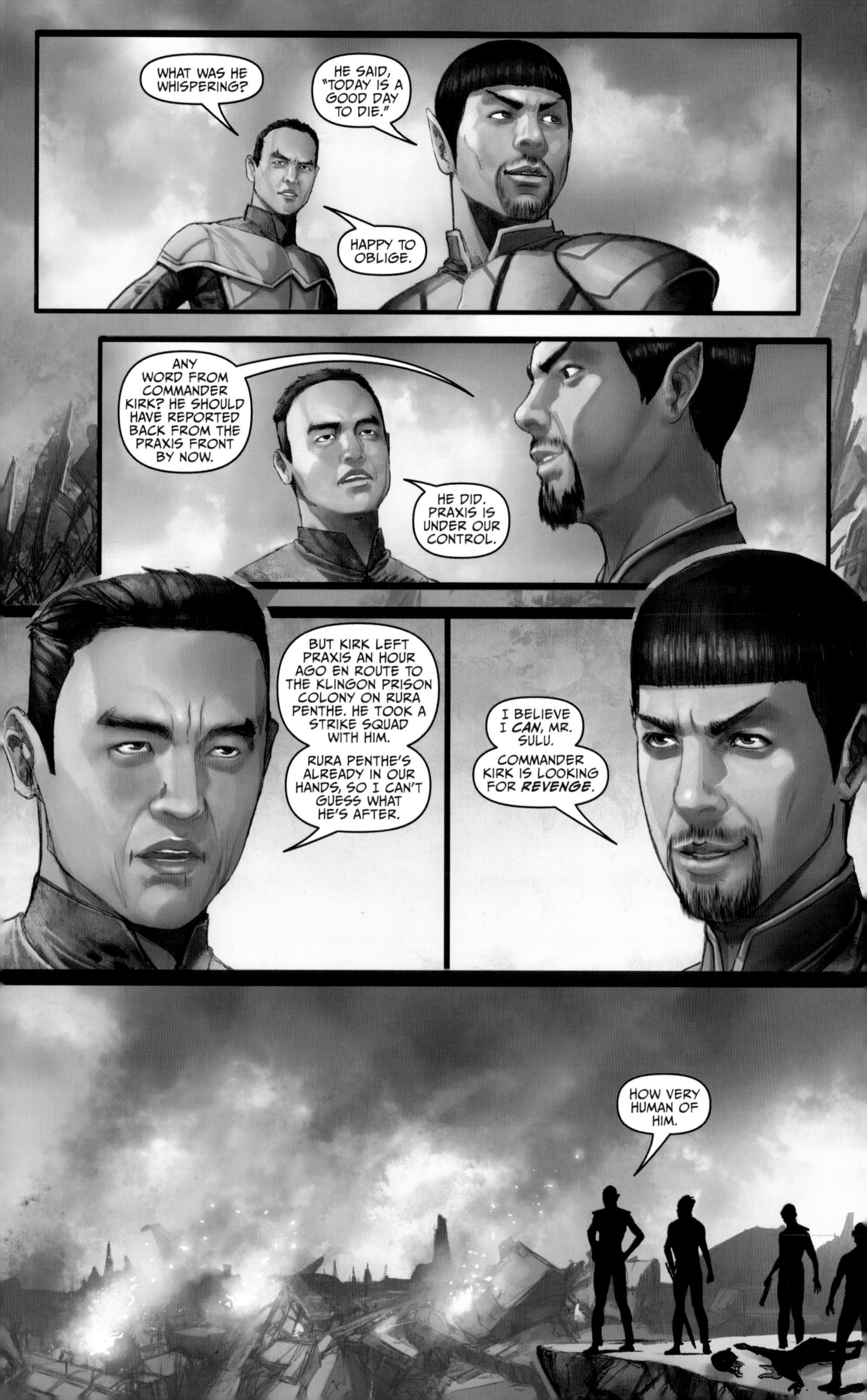
WHAT WAS HE WHISPERING?
HE SAID, "TODAY IS A GOOD DAY TO DIE."
HAPPY TO OBLIGE.
ANY WORD FROM COMMANDER KIRK? HE SHOULD HAVE REPORTED BACK FROM THE PRAXIS FRONT BY NOW.
HE DID. PRAXIS IS UNDER OUR CONTROL.
BUT KIRK LEFT PRAXIS AN HOUR AGO EN ROUTE TO THE KLINGON PRISON COLONY ON RURA PENTHE. HE TOOK A STRIKE SQUAD WITH HIM.
RURA PENTHE'S ALREADY IN OUR HANDS, SO I CAN'T GUESS WHAT HE'S AFTER.
I BELIEVE I *CAN*, MR. SULU.
COMMANDER KIRK IS LOOKING FOR ***REVENGE***.
HOW VERY HUMAN OF HIM.

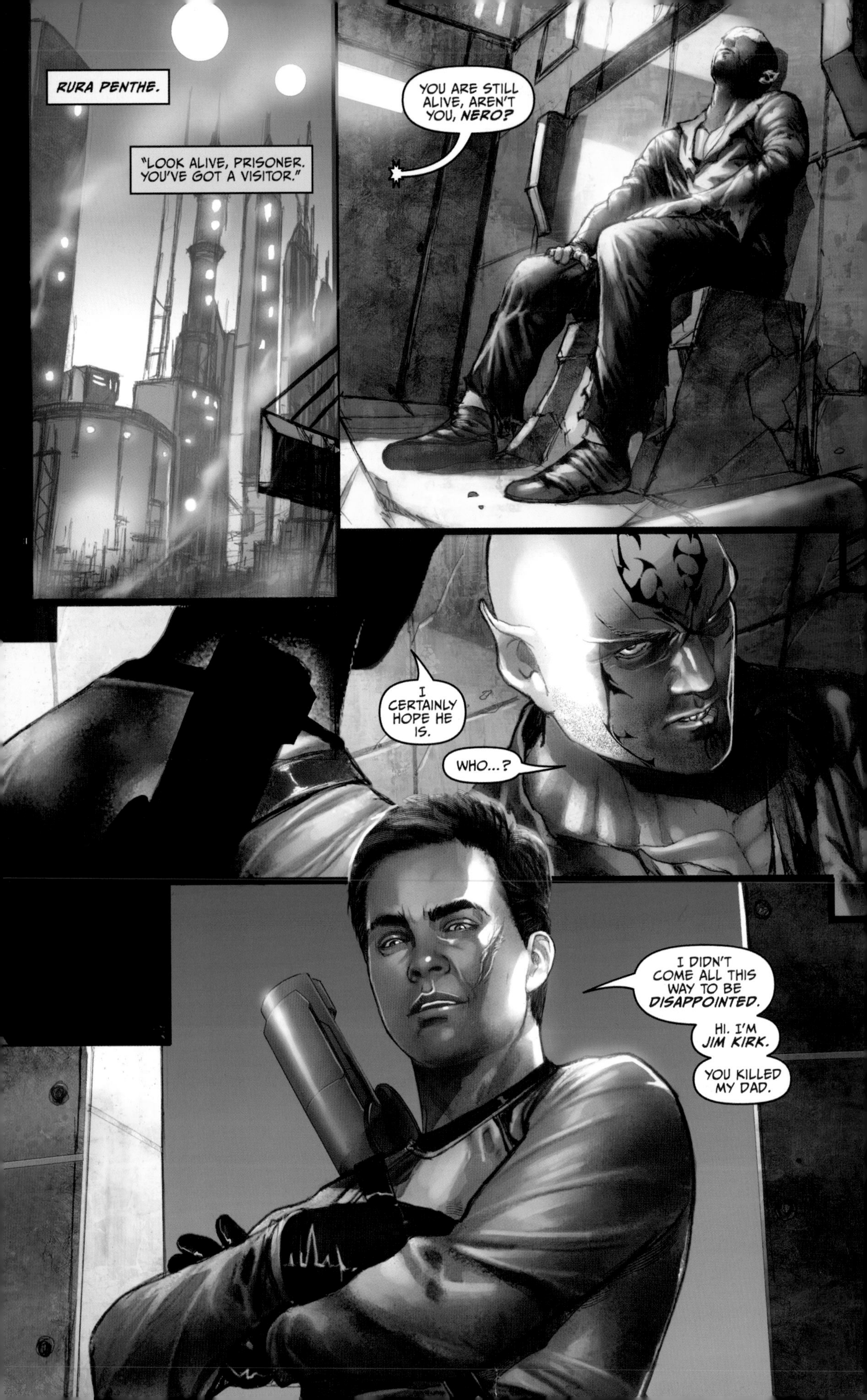
RURA PENTHE.
"LOOK ALIVE, PRISONER. YOU'VE GOT A VISITOR."
YOU ARE STILL ALIVE, AREN'T YOU, NERO?
I CERTAINLY HOPE HE IS.
WHO...?
I DIDN'T COME ALL THIS WAY TO BE DISAPPOINTED.
HI. I'M JIM KIRK.
YOU KILLED MY DAD.

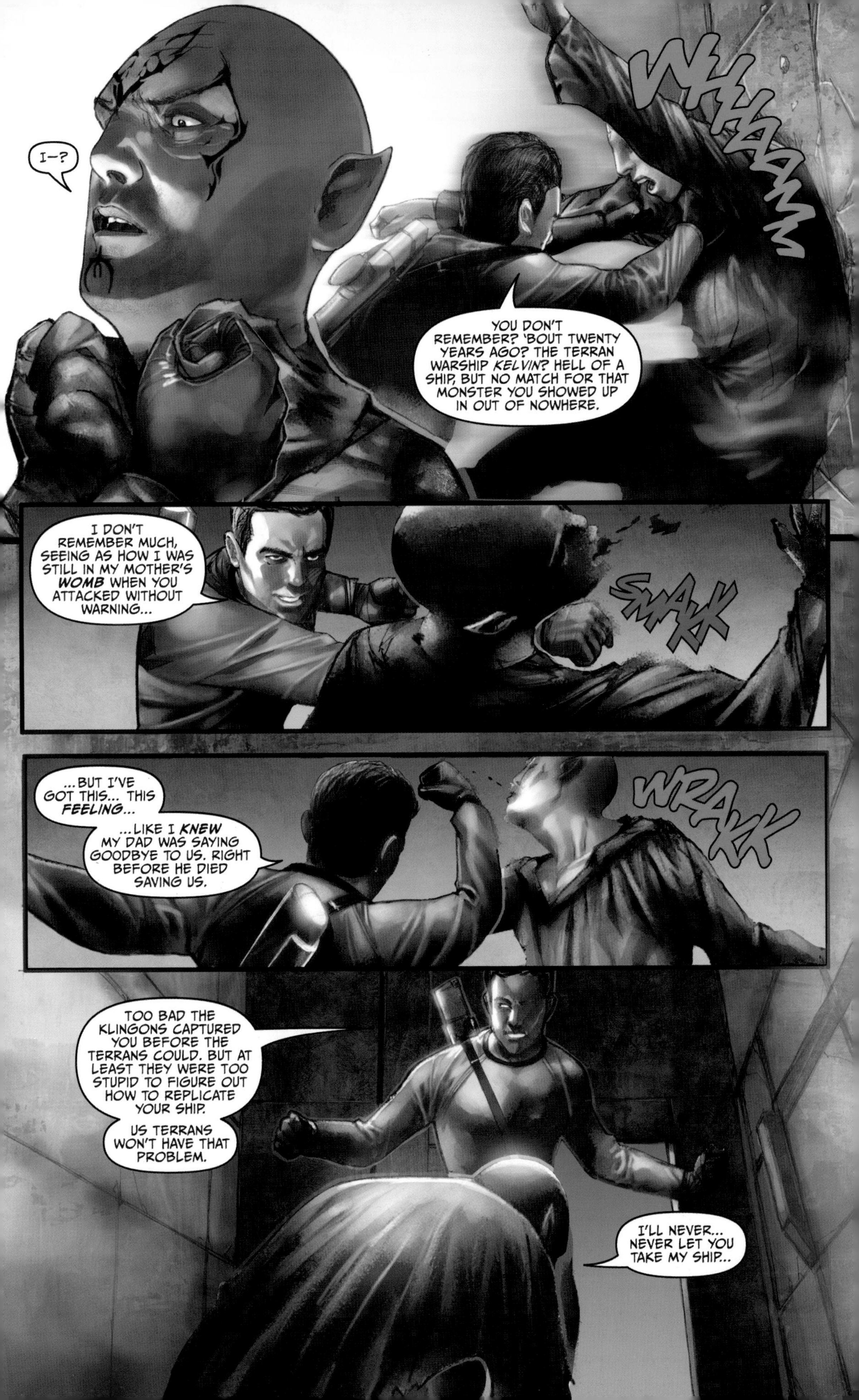
I—?
WHHAAMM
YOU DON'T REMEMBER? 'BOUT TWENTY YEARS AGO? THE TERRAN WARSHIP *KELVIN*? HELL OF A SHIP, BUT NO MATCH FOR THAT MONSTER YOU SHOWED UP IN OUT OF NOWHERE.
I DON'T REMEMBER MUCH, SEEING AS HOW I WAS STILL IN MY MOTHER'S ***WOMB*** WHEN YOU ATTACKED WITHOUT WARNING...
SMAKK
...BUT I'VE GOT THIS... THIS ***FEELING***...
...LIKE I ***KNEW*** MY DAD WAS SAYING GOODBYE TO US. RIGHT BEFORE HE DIED SAVING US.
WRAKK
TOO BAD THE KLINGONS CAPTURED YOU BEFORE THE TERRANS COULD. BUT AT LEAST THEY WERE TOO STUPID TO FIGURE OUT HOW TO REPLICATE YOUR SHIP.
US TERRANS WON'T HAVE THAT PROBLEM.
I'LL NEVER... NEVER LET YOU TAKE MY SHIP...

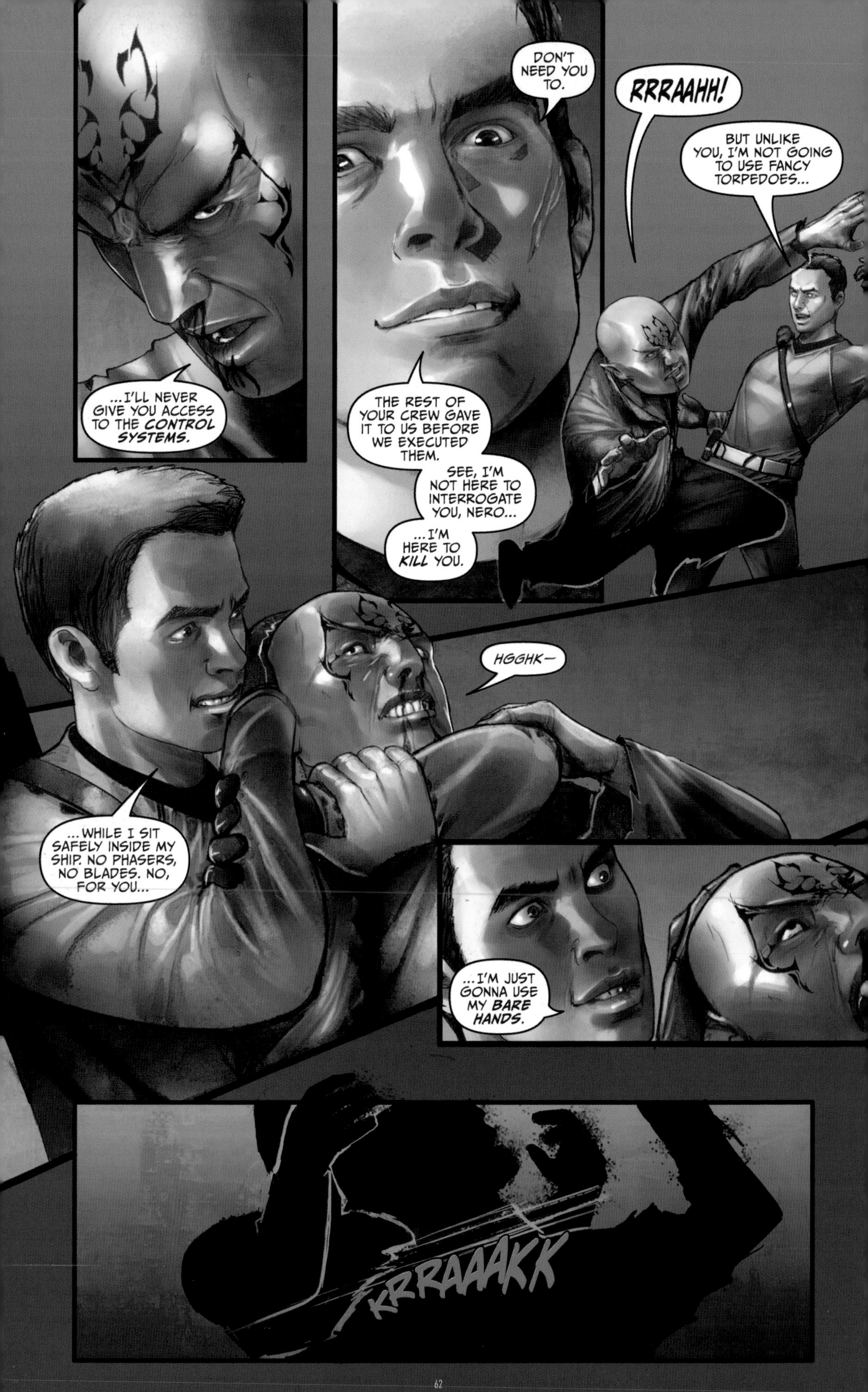
...I'LL NEVER GIVE YOU ACCESS TO THE **CONTROL SYSTEMS.**
DON'T NEED YOU TO.
THE REST OF YOUR CREW GAVE IT TO US BEFORE WE EXECUTED THEM.
SEE, I'M NOT HERE TO INTERROGATE YOU, NERO...
...I'M HERE TO **KILL** YOU.
RRRAAHH!
BUT UNLIKE YOU, I'M NOT GOING TO USE FANCY TORPEDOES...
HGGHK—
...WHILE I SIT SAFELY INSIDE MY SHIP. NO PHASERS, NO BLADES. NO, FOR YOU...
...I'M JUST GONNA USE MY **BARE HANDS.**
KRRAAAKK

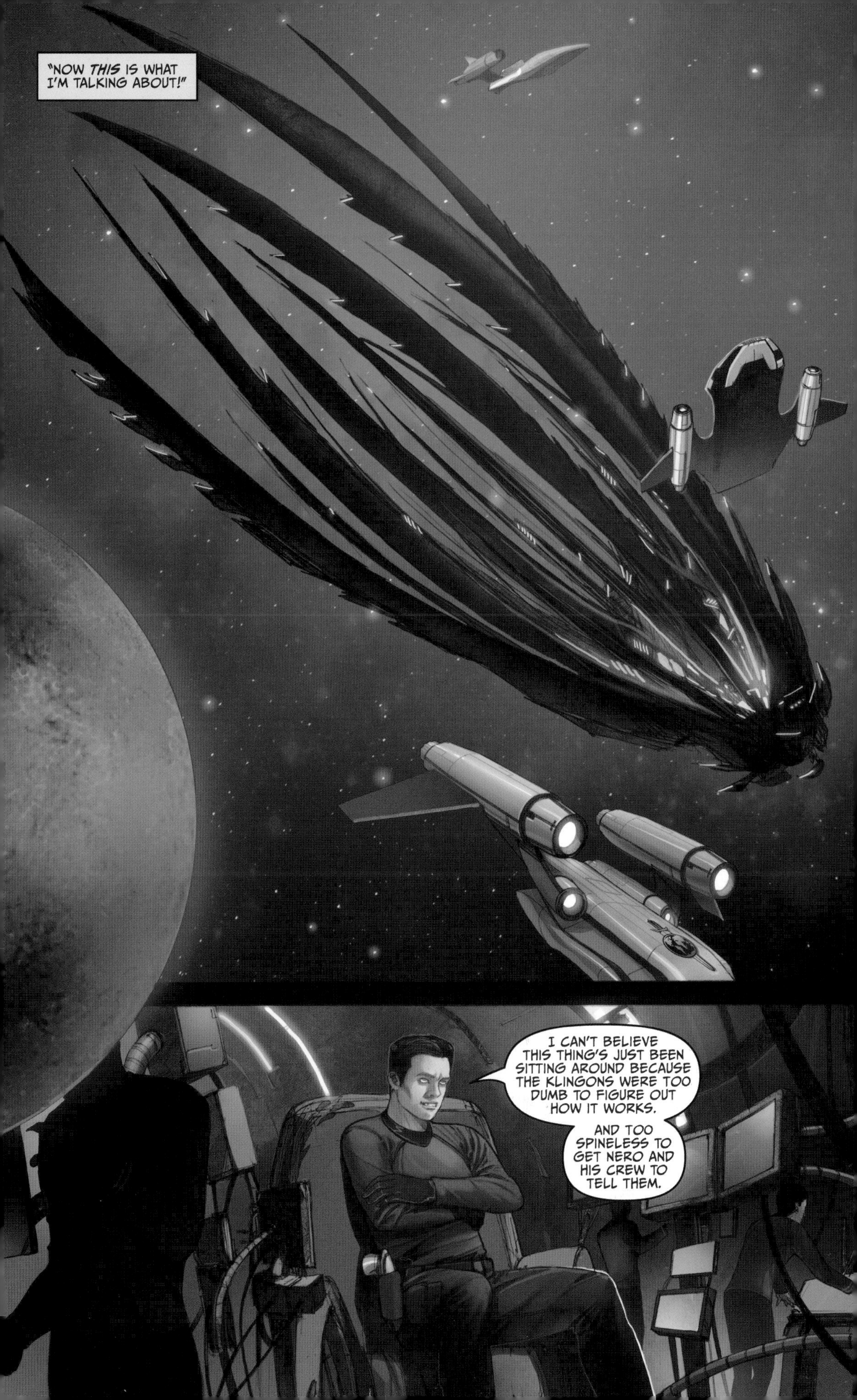
"NOW *THIS* IS WHAT I'M TALKING ABOUT!"
I CAN'T BELIEVE THIS THING'S JUST BEEN SITTING AROUND BECAUSE THE KLINGONS WERE TOO DUMB TO FIGURE OUT HOW IT WORKS.
AND TOO SPINELESS TO GET NERO AND HIS CREW TO TELL THEM.

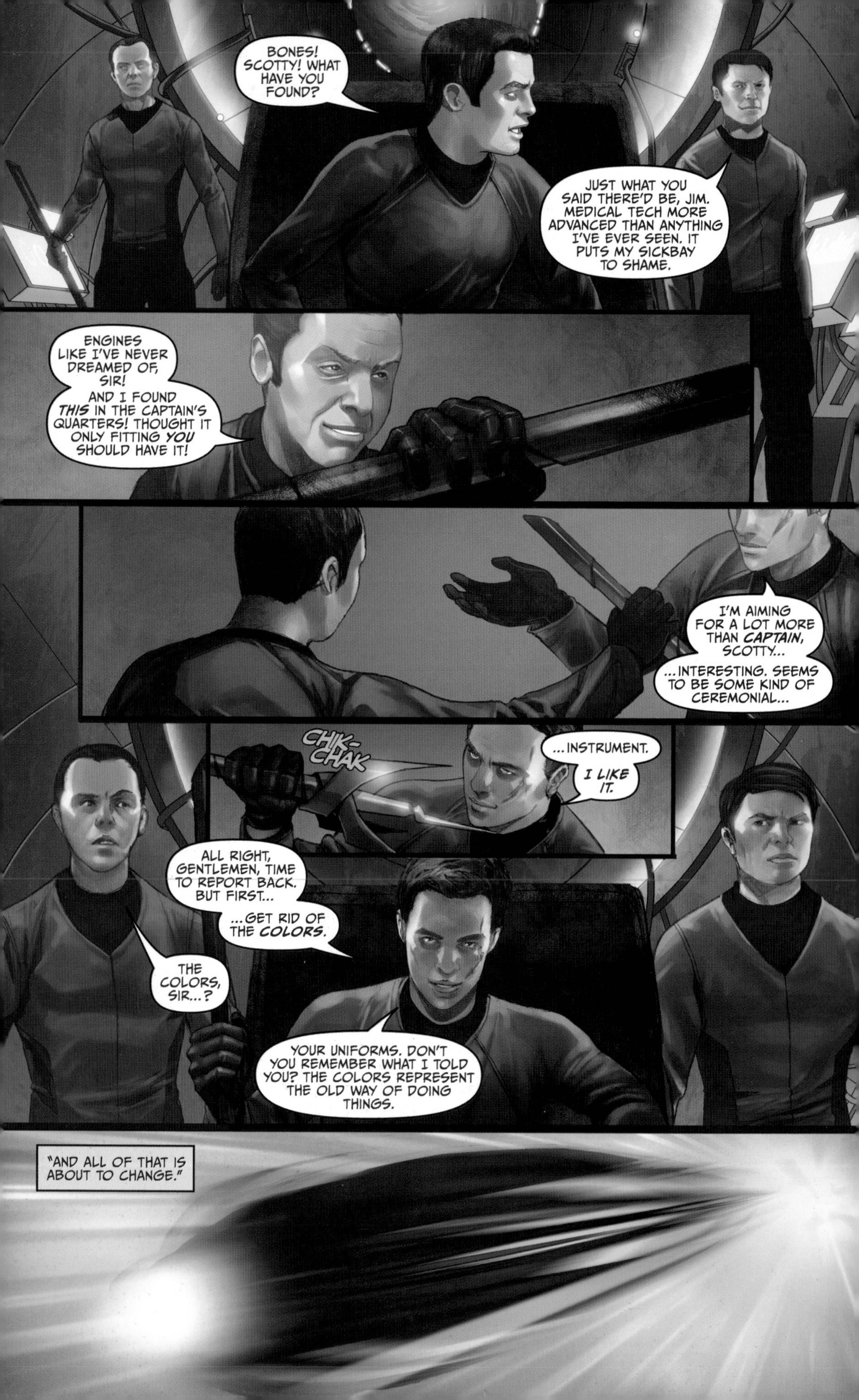

BONES! SCOTTY! WHAT HAVE YOU FOUND?
JUST WHAT YOU SAID THERE'D BE, JIM. MEDICAL TECH MORE ADVANCED THAN ANYTHING I'VE EVER SEEN. IT PUTS MY SICKBAY TO SHAME.
ENGINES LIKE I'VE NEVER DREAMED OF, SIR!
AND I FOUND *THIS* IN THE CAPTAIN'S QUARTERS! THOUGHT IT ONLY FITTING *YOU* SHOULD HAVE IT!
I'M AIMING FOR A LOT MORE THAN *CAPTAIN*, SCOTTY...
...INTERESTING. SEEMS TO BE SOME KIND OF CEREMONIAL...
CHIK-CHAK
...INSTRUMENT.
I LIKE IT.
ALL RIGHT, GENTLEMEN, TIME TO REPORT BACK. BUT FIRST...
...GET RID OF THE *COLORS*.
THE COLORS, SIR...?
YOUR UNIFORMS. DON'T YOU REMEMBER WHAT I TOLD YOU? THE COLORS REPRESENT THE OLD WAY OF DOING THINGS.
"AND ALL OF THAT IS ABOUT TO CHANGE."

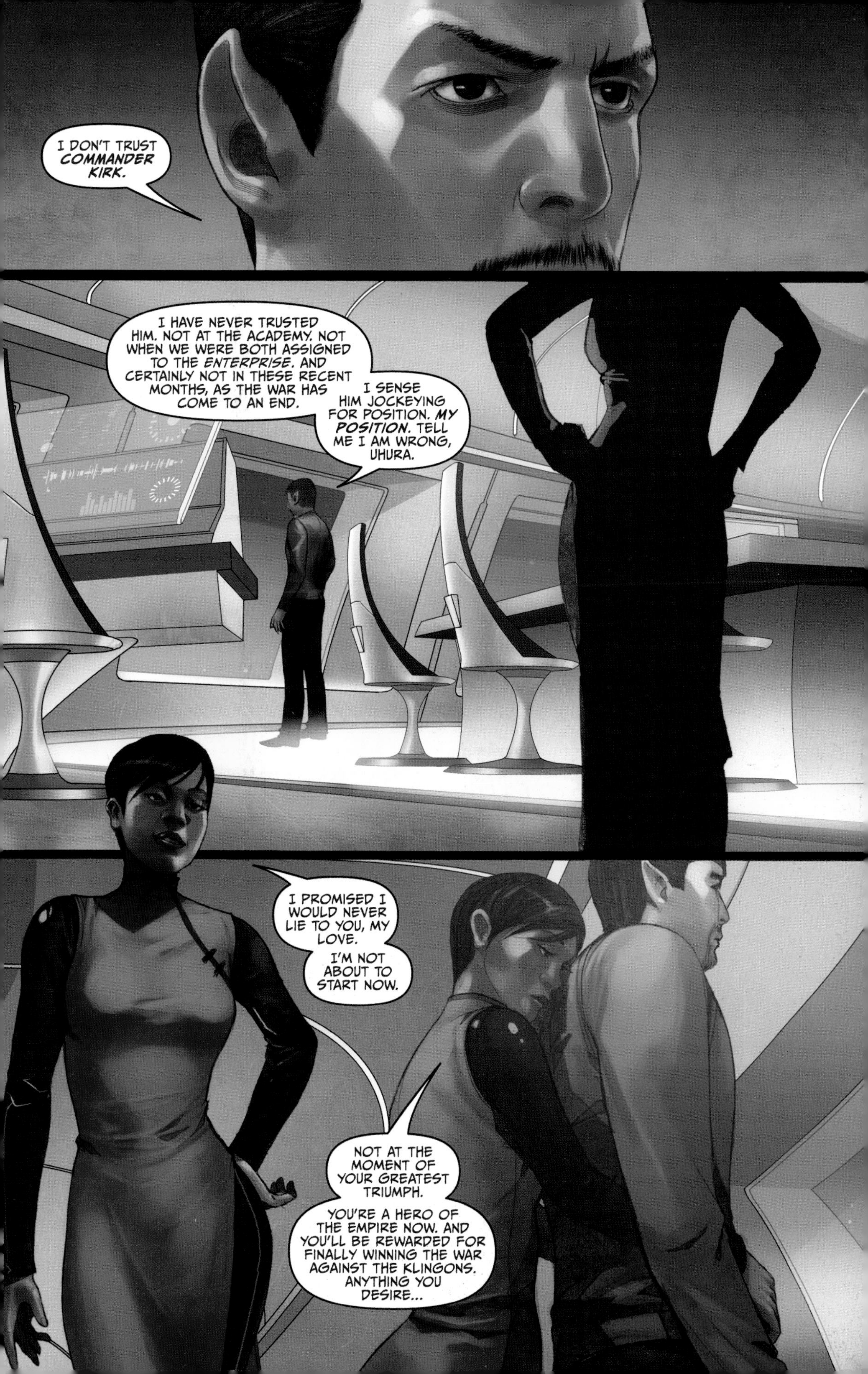
I DON'T TRUST *COMMANDER KIRK.*
I HAVE NEVER TRUSTED HIM. NOT AT THE ACADEMY. NOT WHEN WE WERE BOTH ASSIGNED TO THE *ENTERPRISE.* AND CERTAINLY NOT IN THESE RECENT MONTHS, AS THE WAR HAS COME TO AN END.
I SENSE HIM JOCKEYING FOR POSITION. *MY POSITION.* TELL ME I AM WRONG, UHURA.
I PROMISED I WOULD NEVER LIE TO YOU, MY LOVE.
I'M NOT ABOUT TO START NOW.
NOT AT THE MOMENT OF YOUR GREATEST TRIUMPH.
YOU'RE A HERO OF THE EMPIRE NOW. AND YOU'LL BE REWARDED FOR FINALLY WINNING THE WAR AGAINST THE KLINGONS. ANYTHING YOU DESIRE...

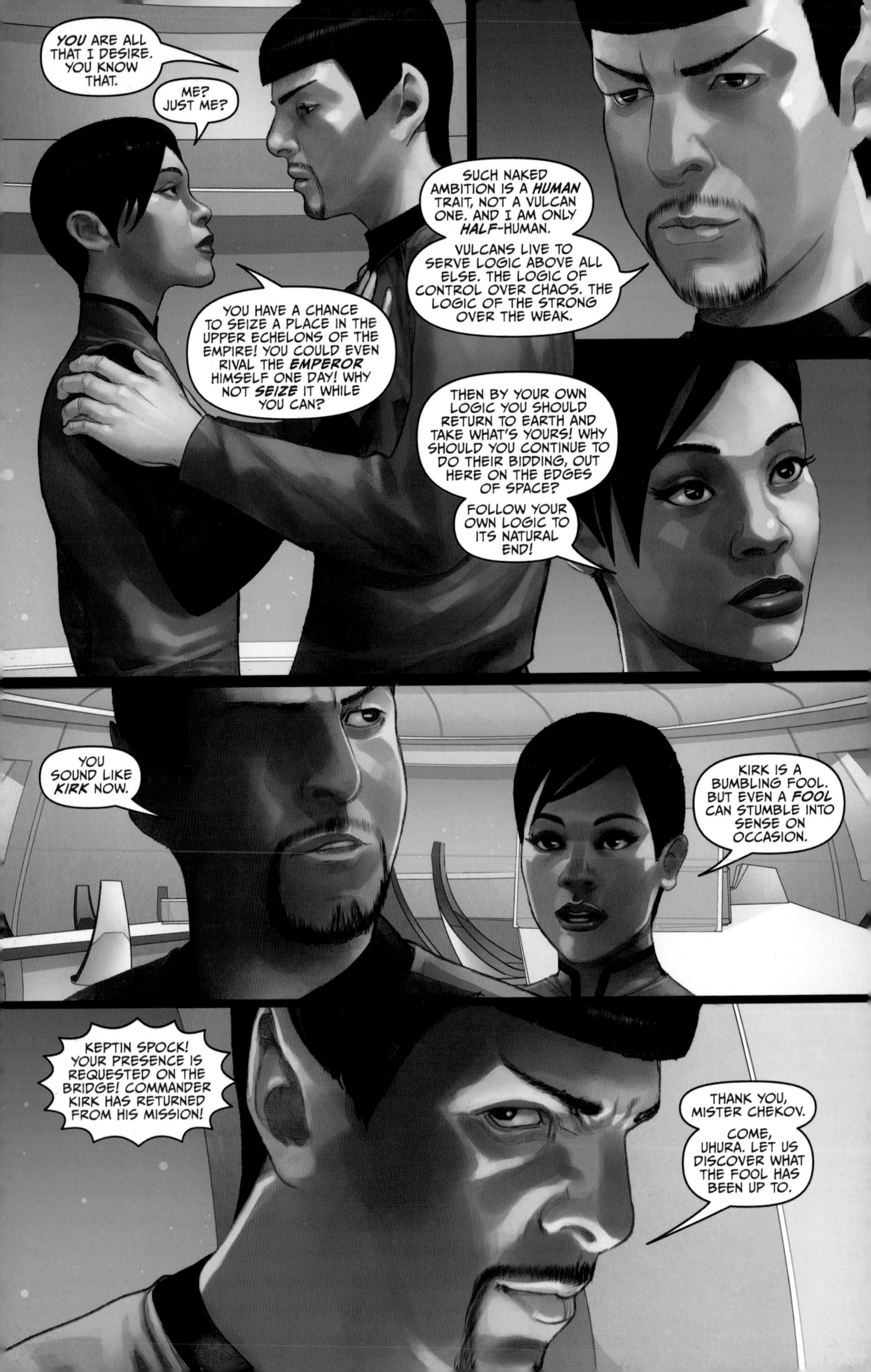
YOU ARE ALL THAT I DESIRE. YOU KNOW THAT.
ME? JUST ME?
SUCH NAKED AMBITION IS A HUMAN TRAIT, NOT A VULCAN ONE. AND I AM ONLY HALF-HUMAN.
VULCANS LIVE TO SERVE LOGIC ABOVE ALL ELSE. THE LOGIC OF CONTROL OVER CHAOS. THE LOGIC OF THE STRONG OVER THE WEAK.
YOU HAVE A CHANCE TO SEIZE A PLACE IN THE UPPER ECHELONS OF THE EMPIRE! YOU COULD EVEN RIVAL THE EMPEROR HIMSELF ONE DAY! WHY NOT SEIZE IT WHILE YOU CAN?
THEN BY YOUR OWN LOGIC YOU SHOULD RETURN TO EARTH AND TAKE WHAT'S YOURS! WHY SHOULD YOU CONTINUE TO DO THEIR BIDDING, OUT HERE ON THE EDGES OF SPACE?
FOLLOW YOUR OWN LOGIC TO ITS NATURAL END!
YOU SOUND LIKE KIRK NOW.
KIRK IS A BUMBLING FOOL. BUT EVEN A FOOL CAN STUMBLE INTO SENSE ON OCCASION.
KEPTIN SPOCK! YOUR PRESENCE IS REQUESTED ON THE BRIDGE! COMMANDER KIRK HAS RETURNED FROM HIS MISSION!
THANK YOU, MISTER CHEKOV.
COME, UHURA. LET US DISCOVER WHAT THE FOOL HAS BEEN UP TO.

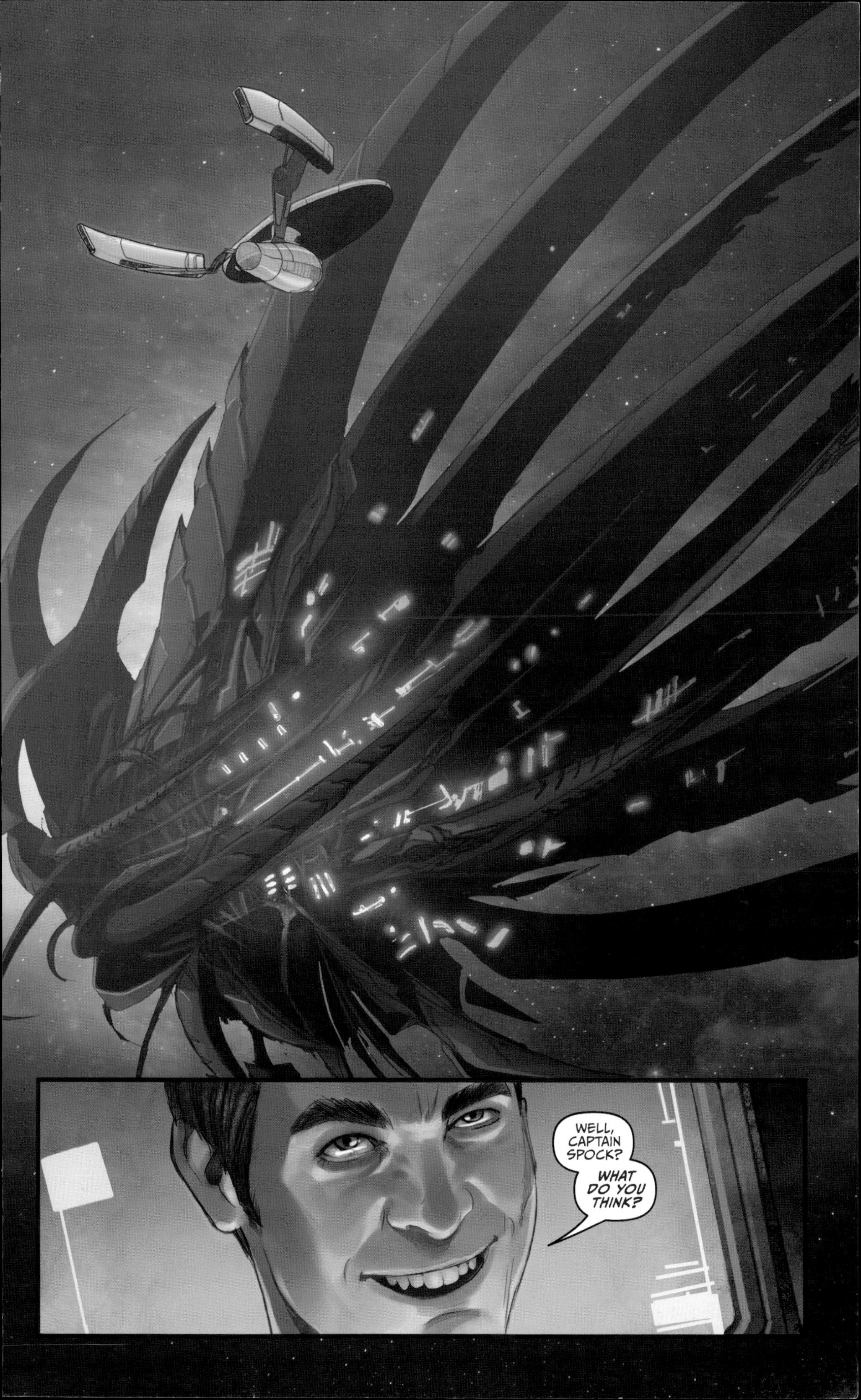
WELL, CAPTAIN SPOCK? WHAT DO YOU THINK?

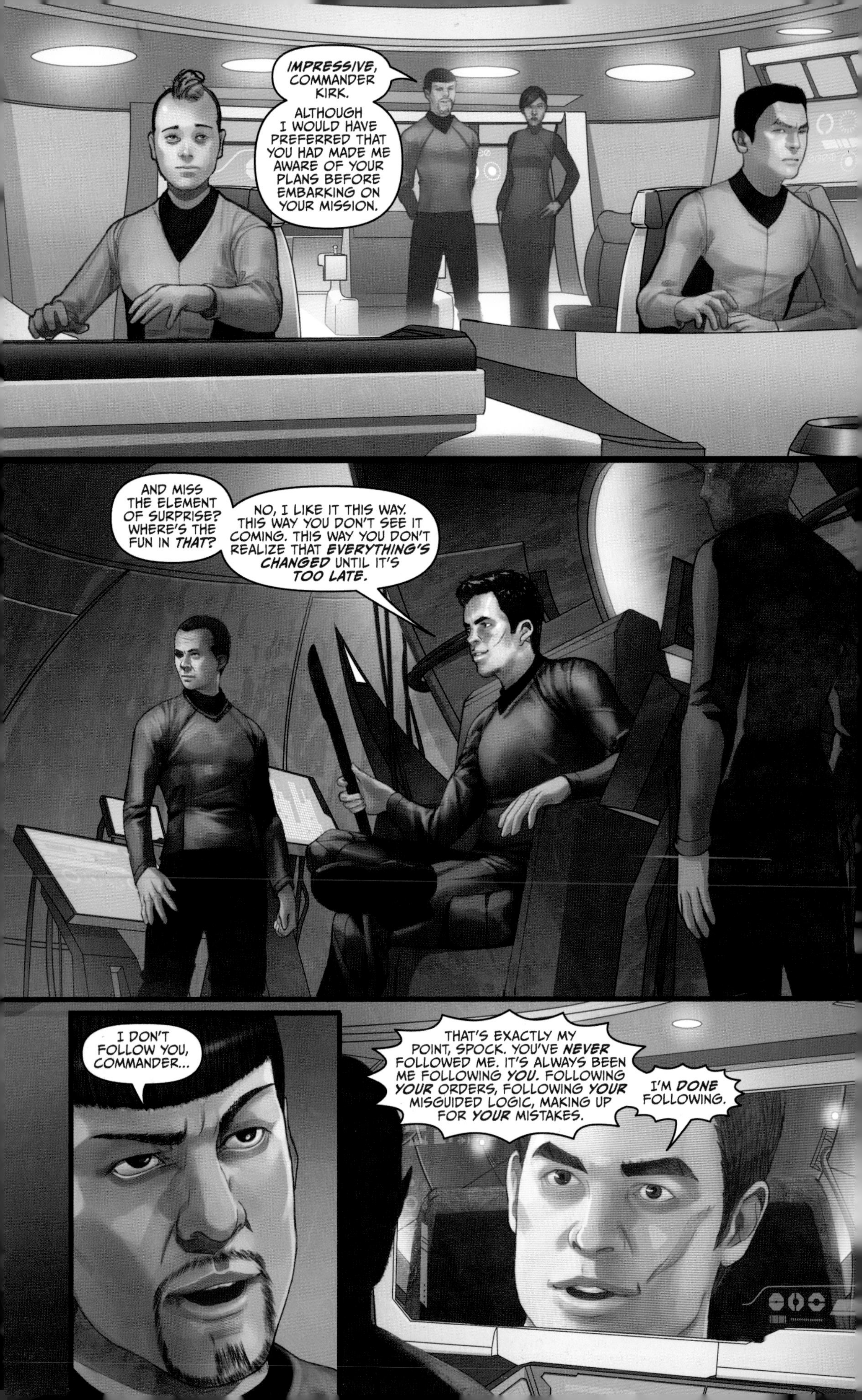
IMPRESSIVE, COMMANDER KIRK.
ALTHOUGH I WOULD HAVE PREFERRED THAT YOU HAD MADE ME AWARE OF YOUR PLANS BEFORE EMBARKING ON YOUR MISSION.
AND MISS THE ELEMENT OF SURPRISE? WHERE'S THE FUN IN THAT?
NO, I LIKE IT THIS WAY. THIS WAY YOU DON'T SEE IT COMING. THIS WAY YOU DON'T REALIZE THAT EVERYTHING'S CHANGED UNTIL IT'S TOO LATE.
I DON'T FOLLOW YOU, COMMANDER...
THAT'S EXACTLY MY POINT, SPOCK. YOU'VE NEVER FOLLOWED ME. IT'S ALWAYS BEEN ME FOLLOWING YOU. FOLLOWING YOUR ORDERS, FOLLOWING YOUR MISGUIDED LOGIC, MAKING UP FOR YOUR MISTAKES.
I'M DONE FOLLOWING.

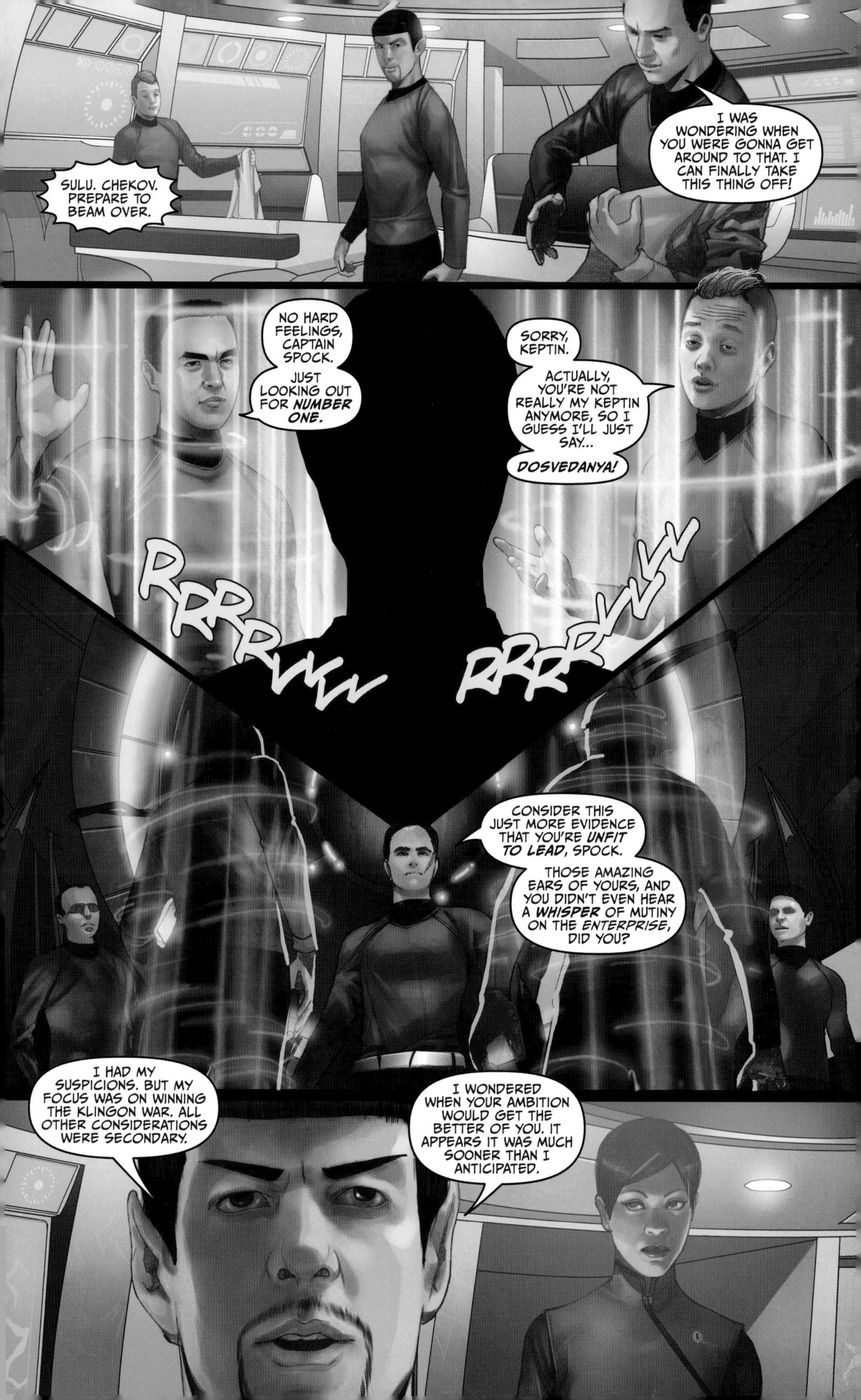
SULU. CHEKOV. PREPARE TO BEAM OVER.
I WAS WONDERING WHEN YOU WERE GONNA GET AROUND TO THAT. I CAN FINALLY TAKE THIS THING OFF!
NO HARD FEELINGS, CAPTAIN SPOCK.
JUST LOOKING OUT FOR NUMBER ONE.
SORRY, KEPTIN.
ACTUALLY, YOU'RE NOT REALLY MY KEPTIN ANYMORE, SO I GUESS I'LL JUST SAY...
DOSVEDANYA!
RRRRVVVN
RRRRVVVN
CONSIDER THIS JUST MORE EVIDENCE THAT YOU'RE UNFIT TO LEAD, SPOCK.
THOSE AMAZING EARS OF YOURS, AND YOU DIDN'T EVEN HEAR A WHISPER OF MUTINY ON THE ENTERPRISE, DID YOU?
I HAD MY SUSPICIONS. BUT MY FOCUS WAS ON WINNING THE KLINGON WAR. ALL OTHER CONSIDERATIONS WERE SECONDARY.
I WONDERED WHEN YOUR AMBITION WOULD GET THE BETTER OF YOU. IT APPEARS IT WAS MUCH SOONER THAN I ANTICIPATED.

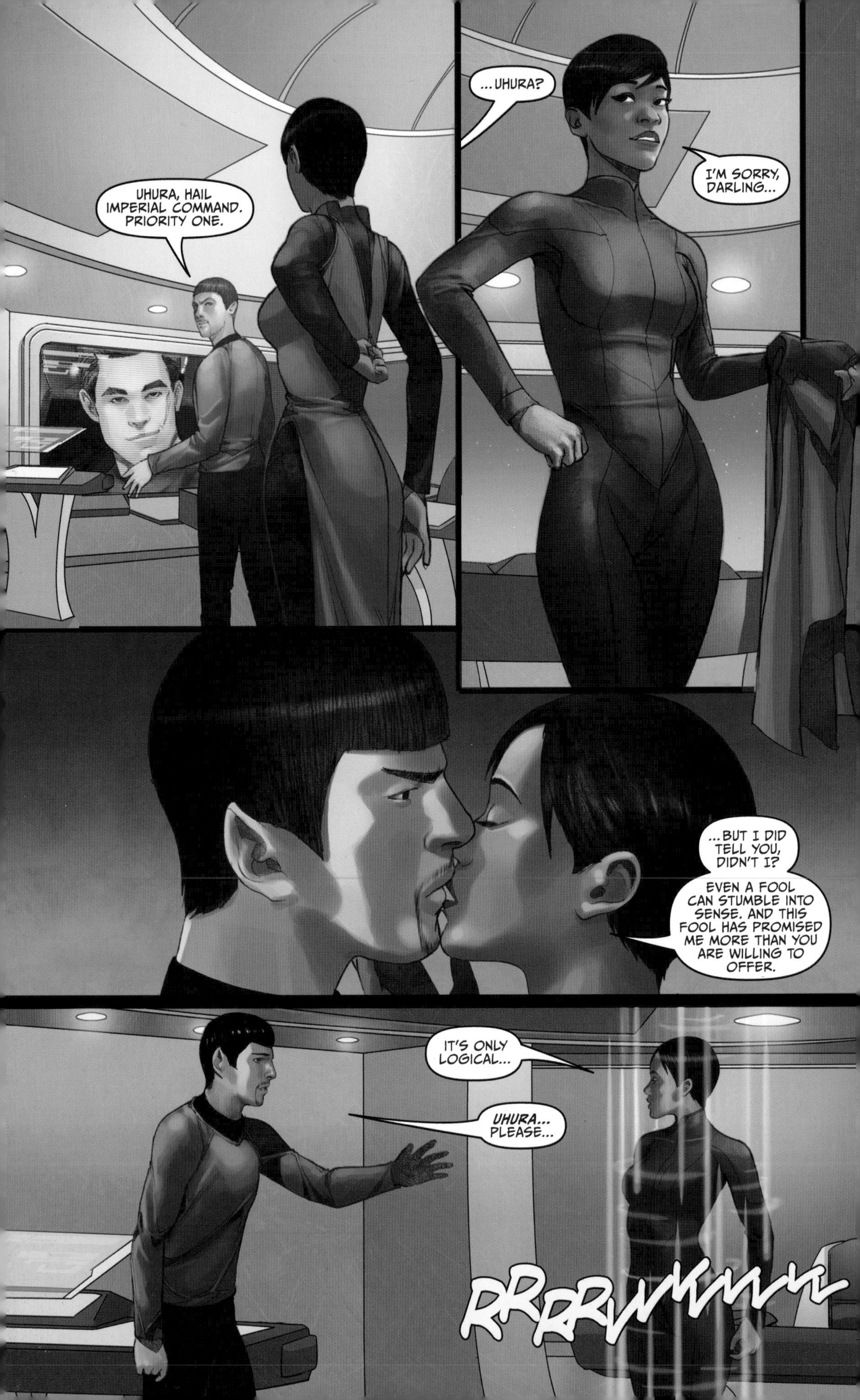
UHURA, HAIL IMPERIAL COMMAND. PRIORITY ONE.
...UHURA?
I'M SORRY, DARLING...
...BUT I DID TELL YOU, DIDN'T I?
EVEN A FOOL CAN STUMBLE INTO SENSE. AND THIS FOOL HAS PROMISED ME MORE THAN YOU ARE WILLING TO OFFER.
IT'S ONLY LOGICAL...
UHURA... PLEASE...
RRRRVVKVVVV

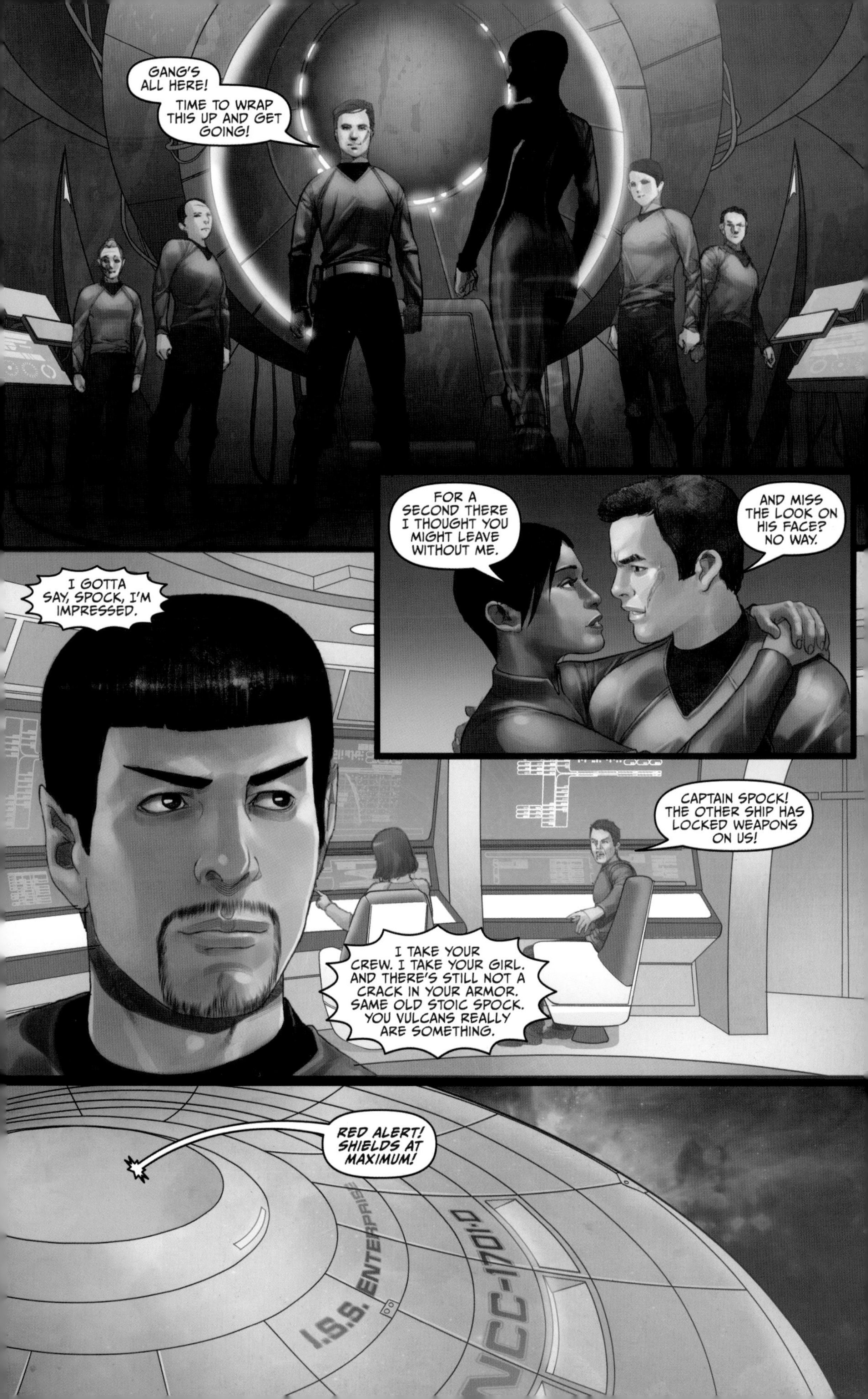
GANG'S ALL HERE!
TIME TO WRAP THIS UP AND GET GOING!
FOR A SECOND THERE I THOUGHT YOU MIGHT LEAVE WITHOUT ME.
AND MISS THE LOOK ON HIS FACE? NO WAY.
I GOTTA SAY, SPOCK, I'M IMPRESSED.
CAPTAIN SPOCK! THE OTHER SHIP HAS LOCKED WEAPONS ON US!
I TAKE YOUR CREW. I TAKE YOUR GIRL. AND THERE'S STILL NOT A CRACK IN YOUR ARMOR. SAME OLD STOIC SPOCK. YOU VULCANS REALLY ARE SOMETHING.
RED ALERT! SHIELDS AT MAXIMUM!
I.S.S. ENTERPRISE
NCC-1701-D

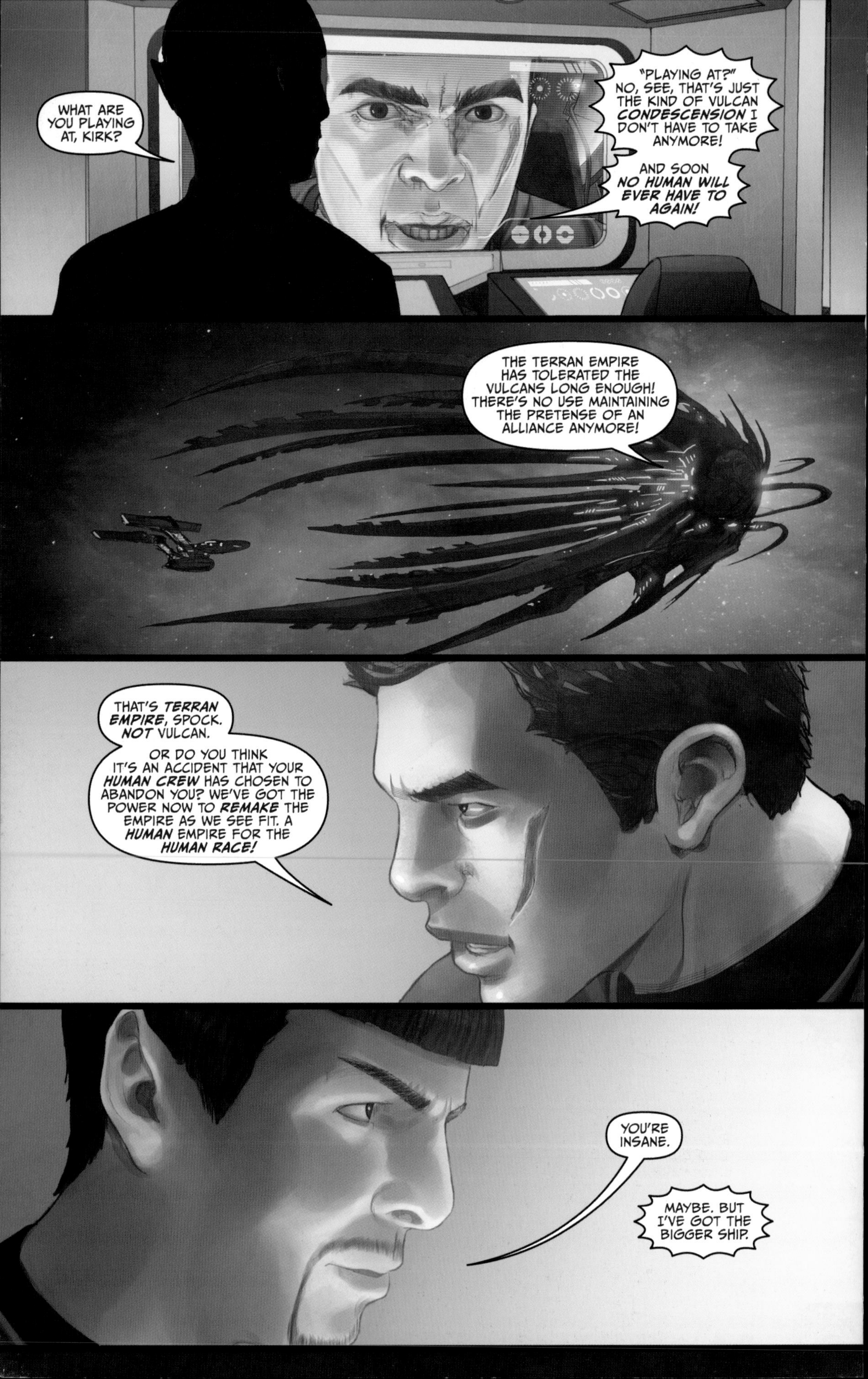

WHAT ARE YOU PLAYING AT, KIRK?
"PLAYING AT?" NO, SEE, THAT'S JUST THE KIND OF VULCAN ***CONDESCENSION*** I DON'T HAVE TO TAKE ANYMORE!
AND SOON ***NO HUMAN WILL EVER HAVE TO AGAIN!***
THE TERRAN EMPIRE HAS TOLERATED THE VULCANS LONG ENOUGH! THERE'S NO USE MAINTAINING THE PRETENSE OF AN ALLIANCE ANYMORE!
THAT'S ***TERRAN EMPIRE***, SPOCK. ***NOT*** VULCAN.
OR DO YOU THINK IT'S AN ACCIDENT THAT YOUR ***HUMAN CREW*** HAS CHOSEN TO ABANDON YOU? WE'VE GOT THE POWER NOW TO ***REMAKE*** THE EMPIRE AS WE SEE FIT. A ***HUMAN*** EMPIRE FOR THE ***HUMAN RACE!***
YOU'RE INSANE.
MAYBE. BUT I'VE GOT THE BIGGER SHIP.

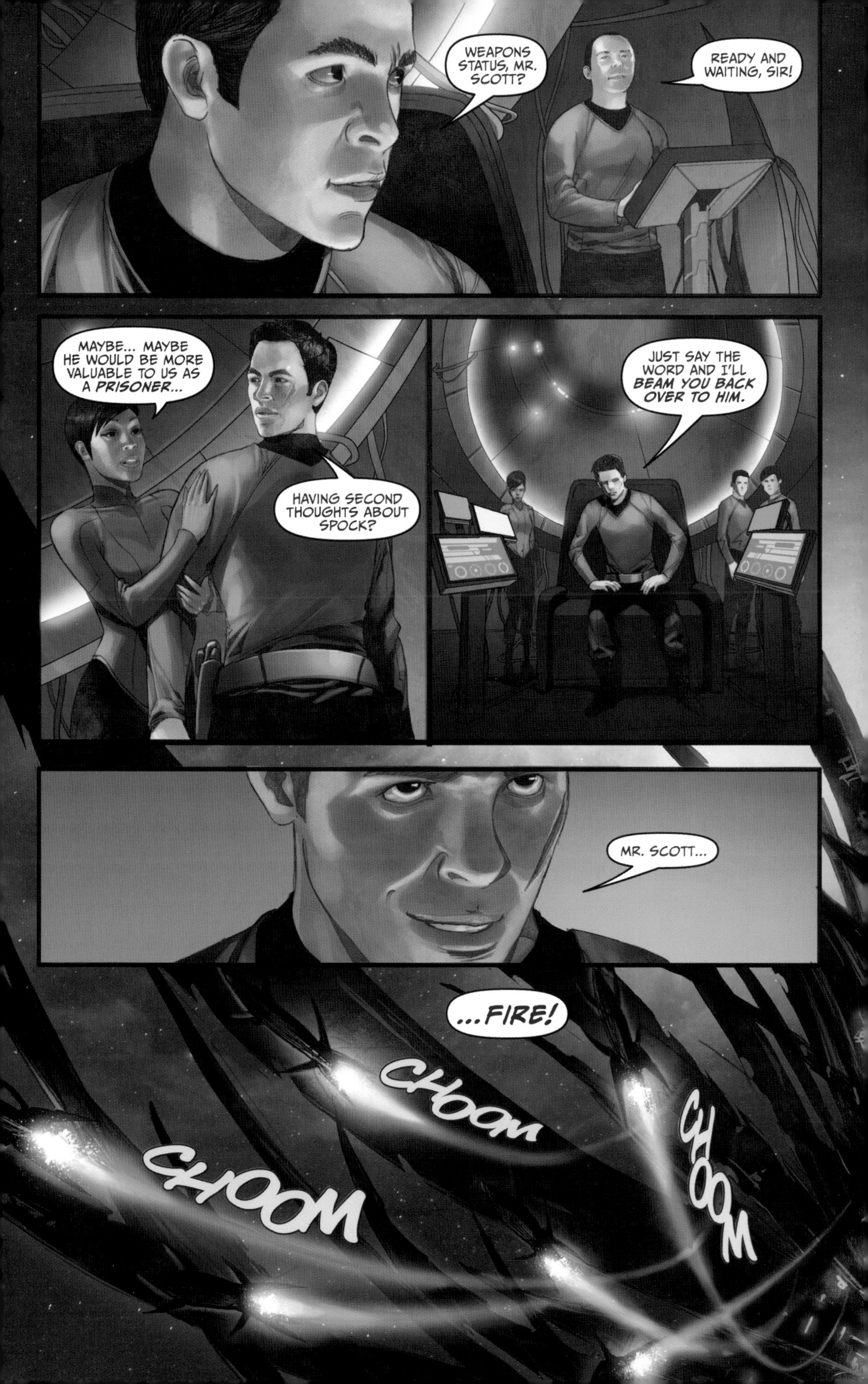
WEAPONS STATUS, MR. SCOTT?
READY AND WAITING, SIR!
MAYBE... MAYBE HE WOULD BE MORE VALUABLE TO US AS A *PRISONER*...
HAVING SECOND THOUGHTS ABOUT SPOCK?
JUST SAY THE WORD AND I'LL *BEAM YOU BACK OVER TO HIM.*
MR. SCOTT...
...*FIRE!*
CHOOM
CHOOM
CHOOM

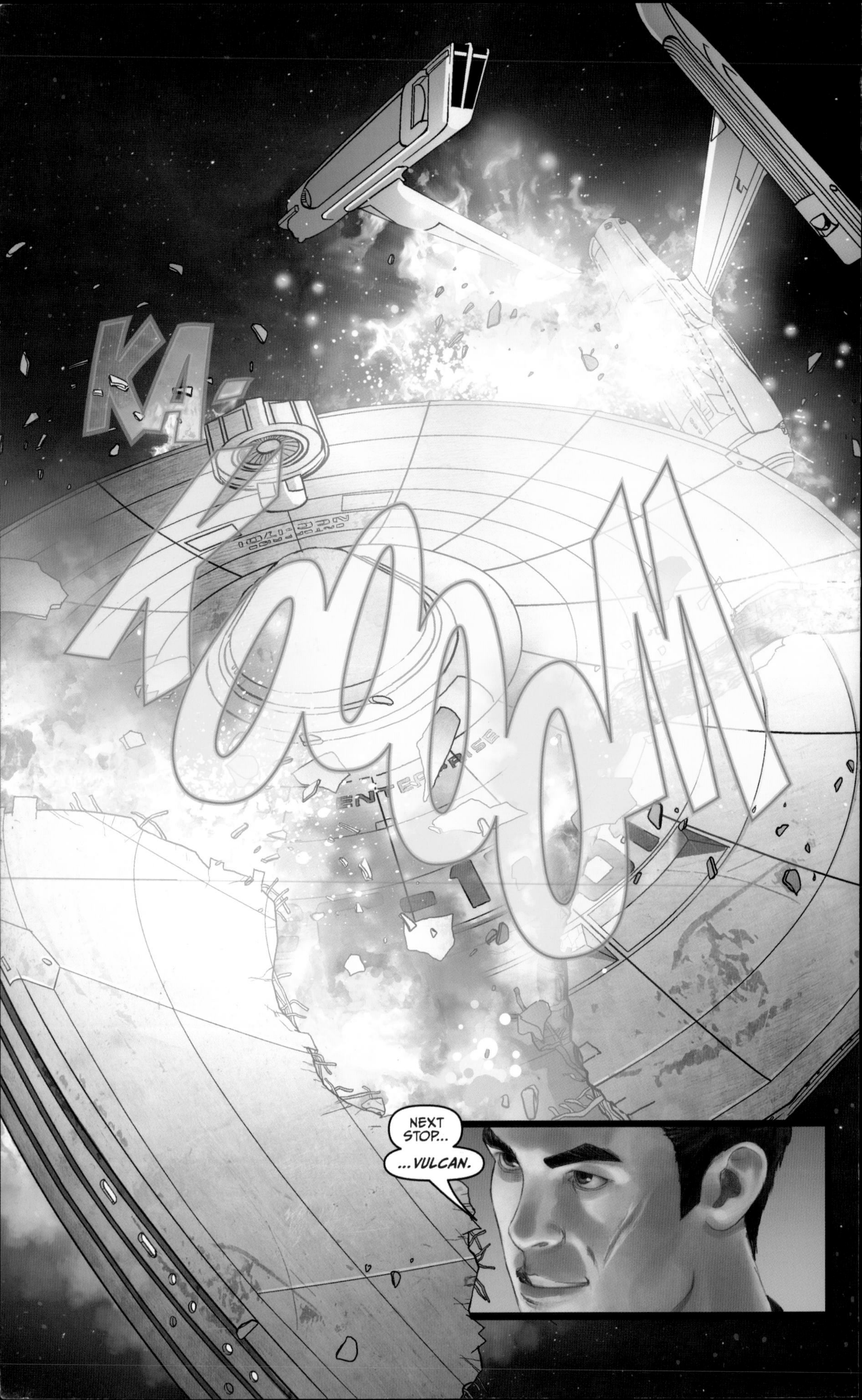
KA-
KOOOOM
NEXT STOP...
...VULCAN.

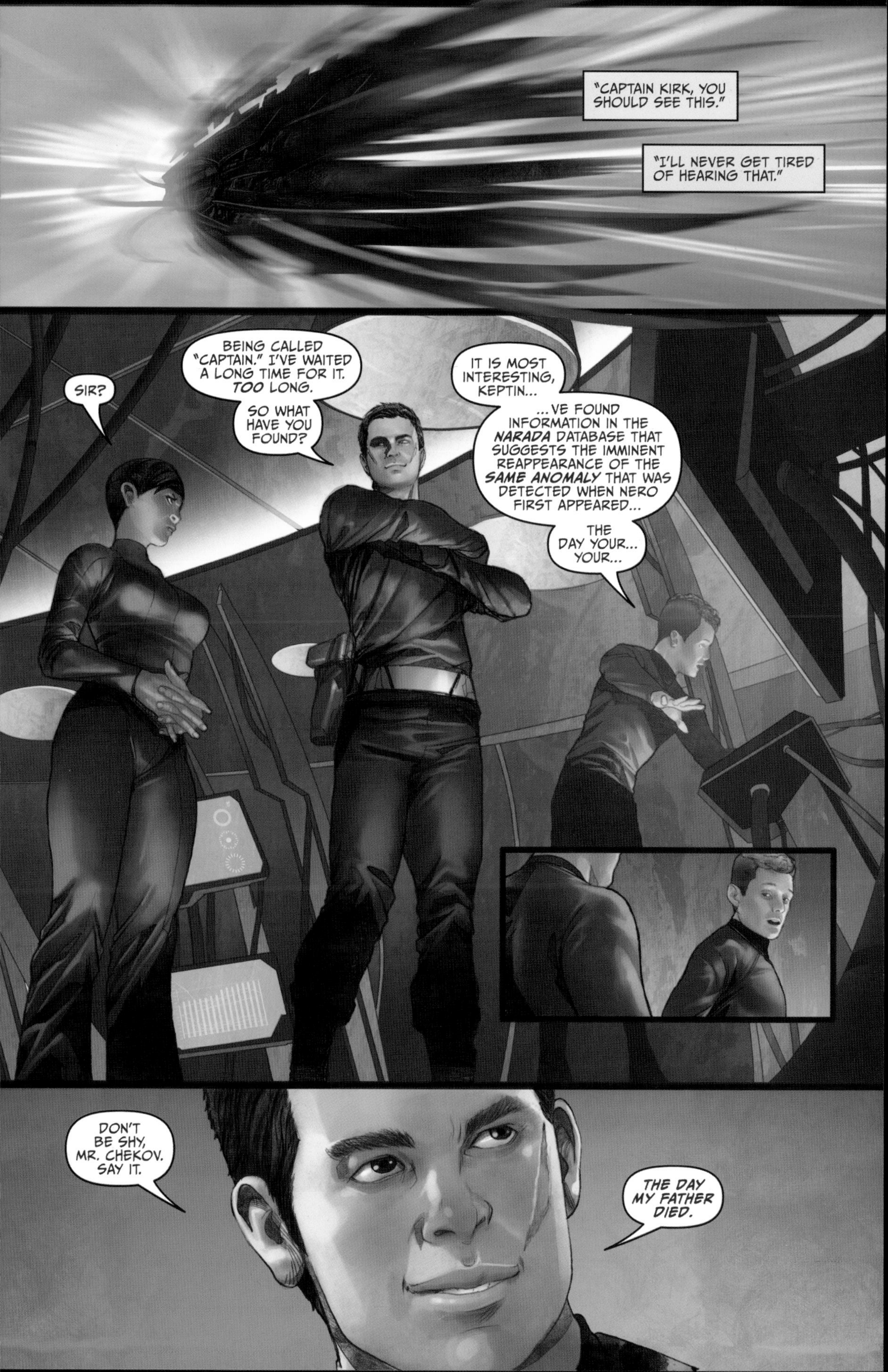
"CAPTAIN KIRK, YOU SHOULD SEE THIS."
"I'LL NEVER GET TIRED OF HEARING THAT."
SIR?
BEING CALLED "CAPTAIN." I'VE WAITED A LONG TIME FOR IT. *TOO* LONG.
SO WHAT HAVE YOU FOUND?
IT IS MOST INTERESTING, KEPTIN...
...VE FOUND INFORMATION IN THE *NARADA* DATABASE THAT SUGGESTS THE IMMINENT REAPPEARANCE OF THE *SAME ANOMALY* THAT WAS DETECTED WHEN NERO FIRST APPEARED...
THE DAY YOUR... YOUR...
DON'T BE SHY, MR. CHEKOV. SAY IT.
THE DAY MY FATHER DIED.

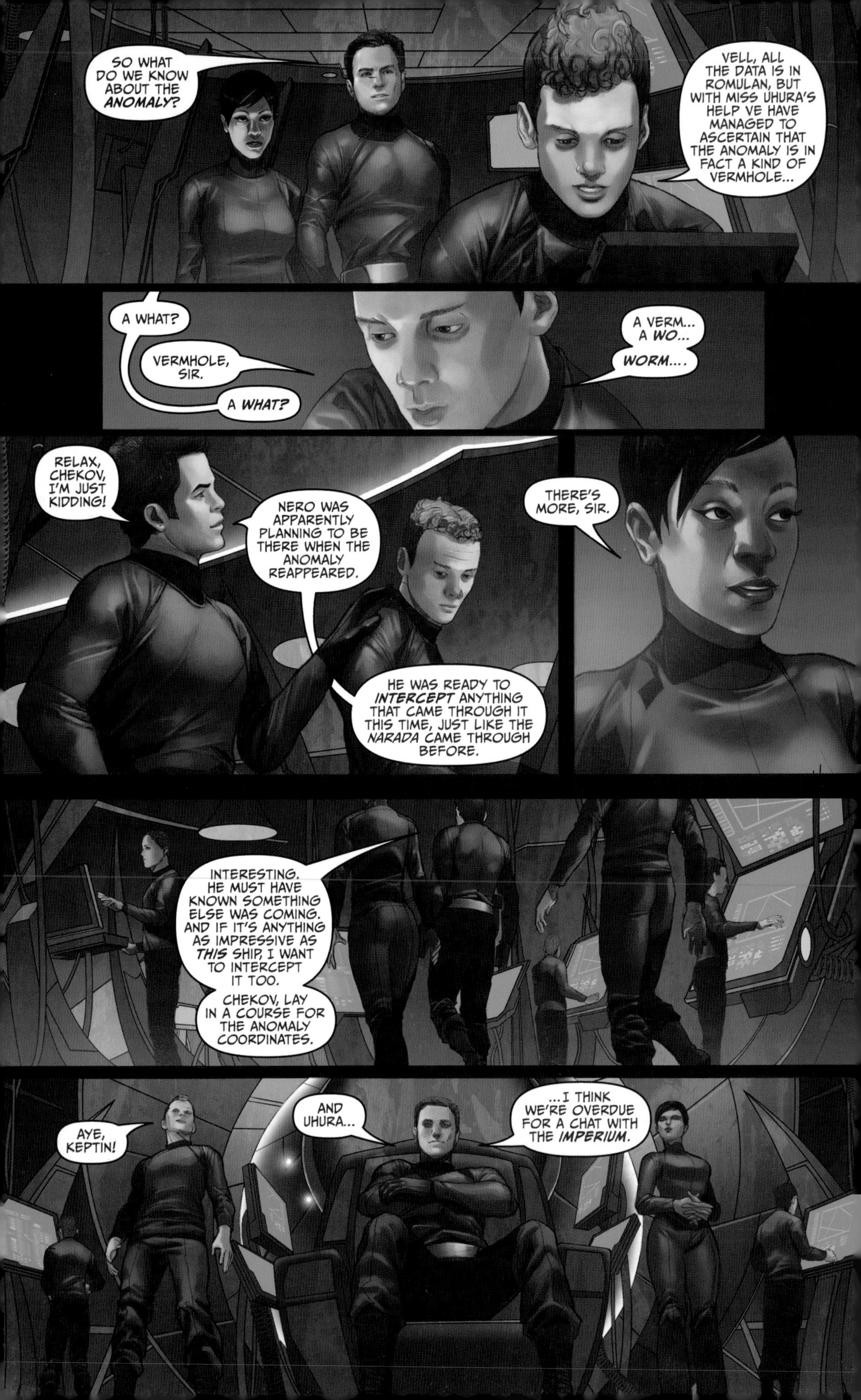
SO WHAT DO WE KNOW ABOUT THE *ANOMALY*?
VELL, ALL THE DATA IS IN ROMULAN, BUT WITH MISS UHURA'S HELP VE HAVE MANAGED TO ASCERTAIN THAT THE ANOMALY IS IN FACT A KIND OF VERMHOLE...
A WHAT?
VERMHOLE, SIR.
A *WHAT?*
A VERM... A *WO*... *WORM*....
RELAX, CHEKOV, I'M JUST KIDDING!
NERO WAS APPARENTLY PLANNING TO BE THERE WHEN THE ANOMALY REAPPEARED.
HE WAS READY TO *INTERCEPT* ANYTHING THAT CAME THROUGH IT THIS TIME, JUST LIKE THE *NARADA* CAME THROUGH BEFORE.
THERE'S MORE, SIR.
INTERESTING. HE MUST HAVE KNOWN SOMETHING ELSE WAS COMING. AND IF IT'S ANYTHING AS IMPRESSIVE AS *THIS* SHIP, I WANT TO INTERCEPT IT TOO.
CHEKOV, LAY IN A COURSE FOR THE ANOMALY COORDINATES.
AYE, KEPTIN!
AND UHURA...
...I THINK WE'RE OVERDUE FOR A CHAT WITH THE *IMPERIUM*.

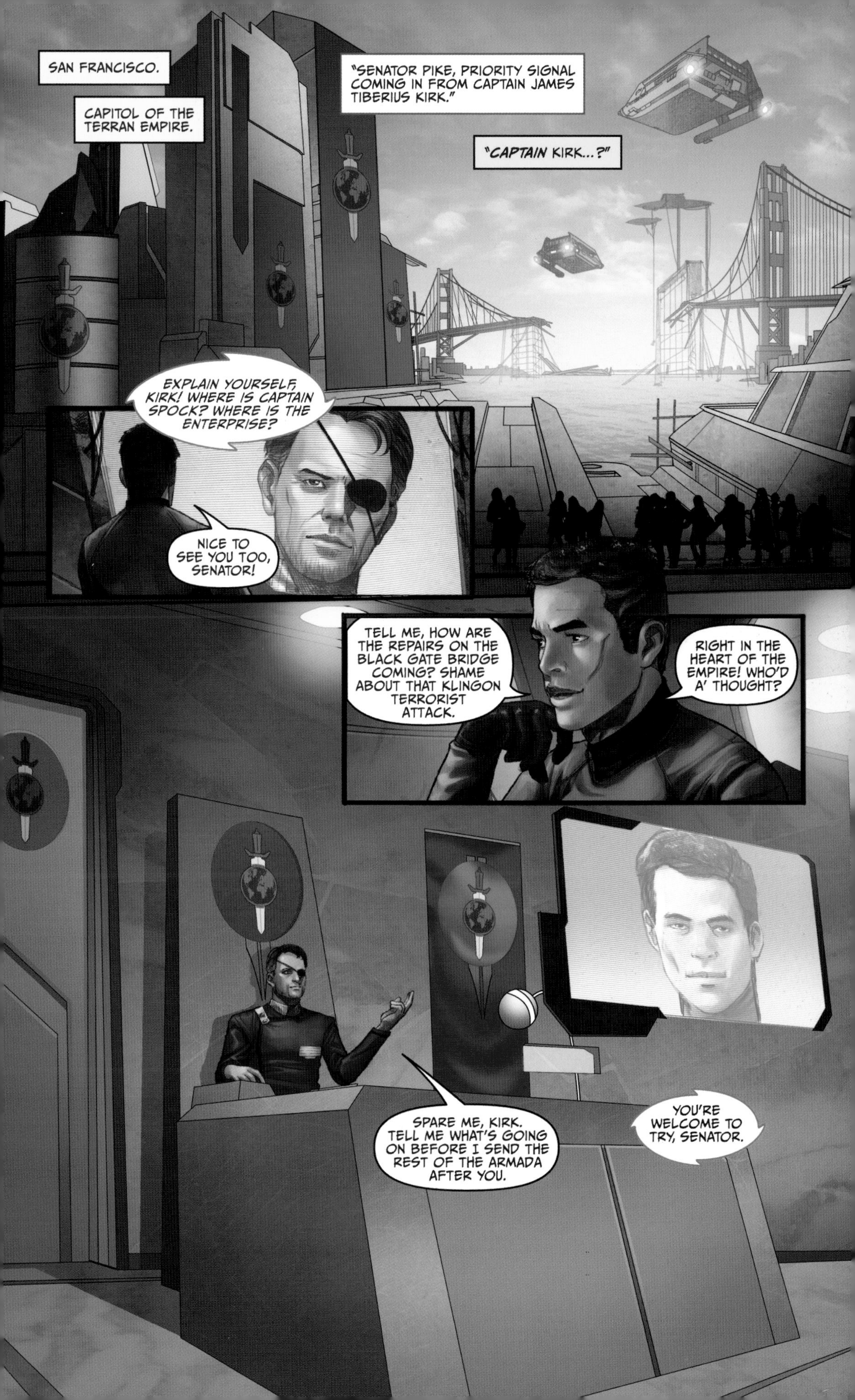
SAN FRANCISCO.
CAPITOL OF THE TERRAN EMPIRE.
"SENATOR PIKE, PRIORITY SIGNAL COMING IN FROM CAPTAIN JAMES TIBERIUS KIRK."
"CAPTAIN KIRK...?"
EXPLAIN YOURSELF, KIRK! WHERE IS CAPTAIN SPOCK? WHERE IS THE ENTERPRISE?
NICE TO SEE YOU TOO, SENATOR!
TELL ME, HOW ARE THE REPAIRS ON THE BLACK GATE BRIDGE COMING? SHAME ABOUT THAT KLINGON TERRORIST ATTACK.
RIGHT IN THE HEART OF THE EMPIRE! WHO'D A' THOUGHT?
SPARE ME, KIRK. TELL ME WHAT'S GOING ON BEFORE I SEND THE REST OF THE ARMADA AFTER YOU.
YOU'RE WELCOME TO TRY, SENATOR.

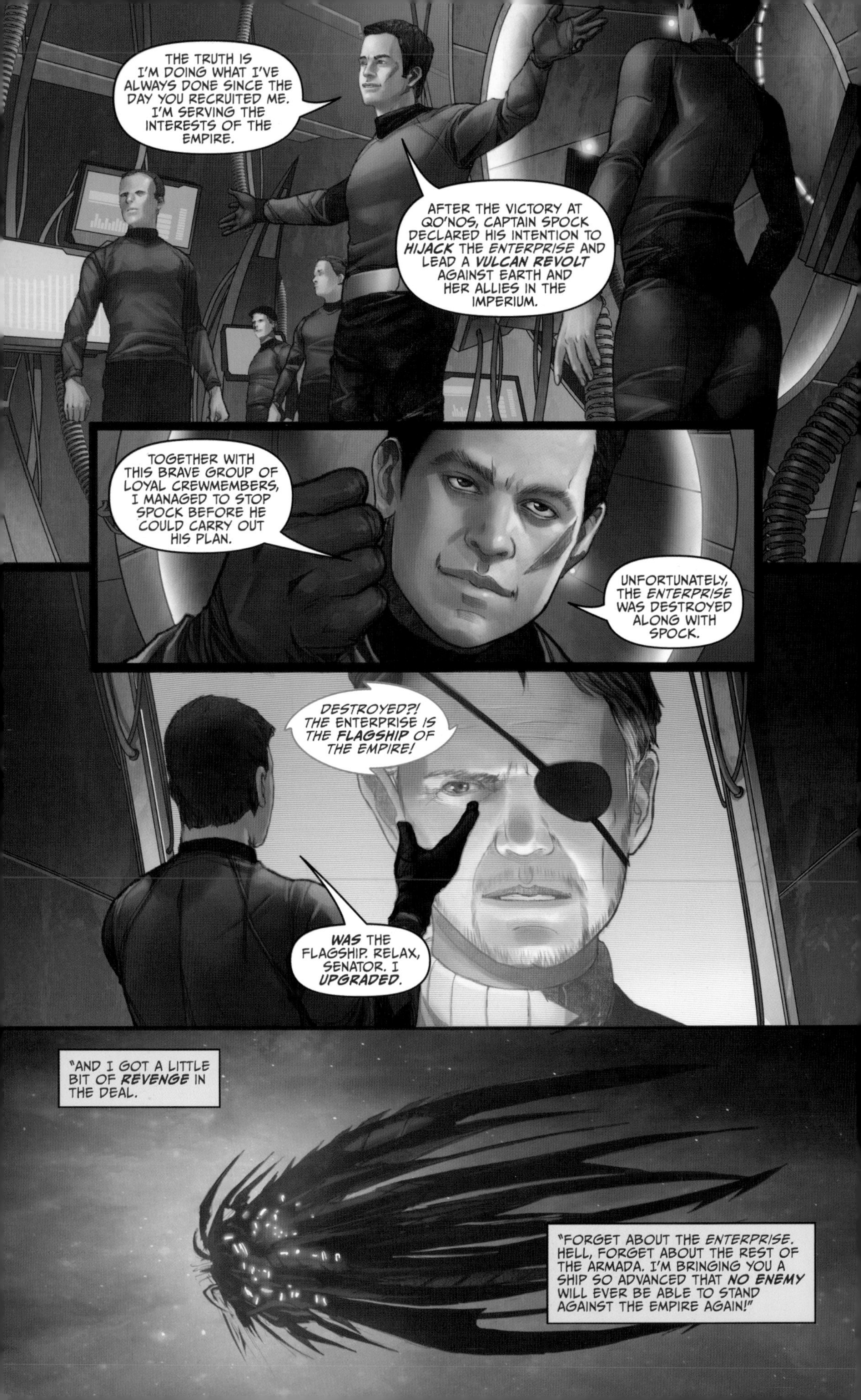
THE TRUTH IS I'M DOING WHAT I'VE ALWAYS DONE SINCE THE DAY YOU RECRUITED ME. I'M SERVING THE INTERESTS OF THE EMPIRE.
AFTER THE VICTORY AT QO'NOS, CAPTAIN SPOCK DECLARED HIS INTENTION TO ***HIJACK*** THE *ENTERPRISE* AND LEAD A ***VULCAN REVOLT*** AGAINST EARTH AND HER ALLIES IN THE IMPERIUM.
TOGETHER WITH THIS BRAVE GROUP OF LOYAL CREWMEMBERS, I MANAGED TO STOP SPOCK BEFORE HE COULD CARRY OUT HIS PLAN.
UNFORTUNATELY, THE *ENTERPRISE* WAS DESTROYED ALONG WITH SPOCK.
*DESTROYED?! THE ENTERPRISE IS THE **FLAGSHIP** OF THE EMPIRE!*
WAS THE FLAGSHIP. RELAX, SENATOR. I ***UPGRADED***.
"AND I GOT A LITTLE BIT OF ***REVENGE*** IN THE DEAL.
"FORGET ABOUT THE *ENTERPRISE*. HELL, FORGET ABOUT THE REST OF THE ARMADA. I'M BRINGING YOU A SHIP SO ADVANCED THAT ***NO ENEMY*** WILL EVER BE ABLE TO STAND AGAINST THE EMPIRE AGAIN!"

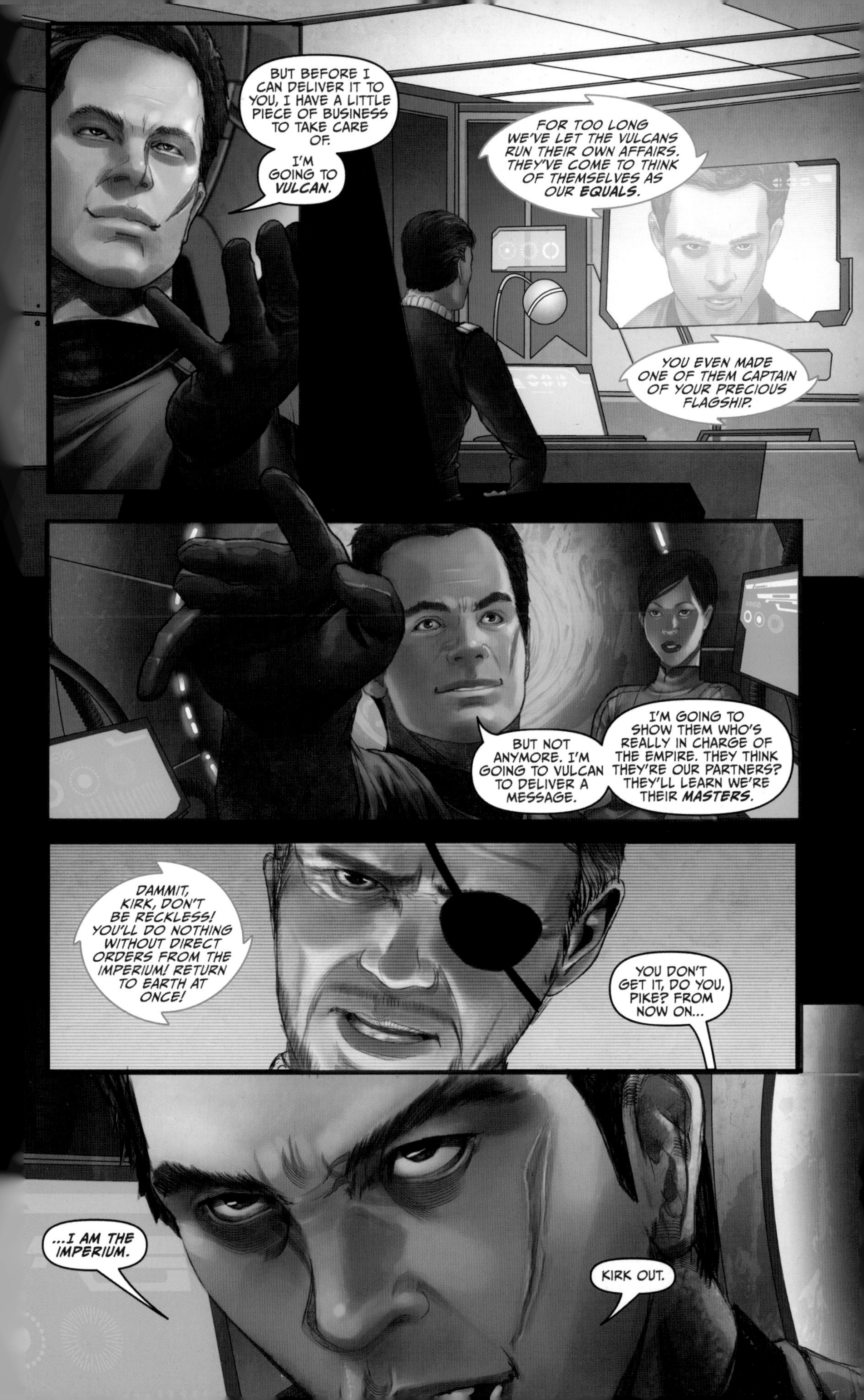
BUT BEFORE I CAN DELIVER IT TO YOU, I HAVE A LITTLE PIECE OF BUSINESS TO TAKE CARE OF.
I'M GOING TO *VULCAN*.
FOR TOO LONG WE'VE LET THE VULCANS RUN THEIR OWN AFFAIRS. THEY'VE COME TO THINK OF THEMSELVES AS OUR **EQUALS**.
YOU EVEN MADE ONE OF THEM CAPTAIN OF YOUR PRECIOUS FLAGSHIP.
BUT NOT ANYMORE. I'M GOING TO VULCAN TO DELIVER A MESSAGE.
I'M GOING TO SHOW THEM WHO'S REALLY IN CHARGE OF THE EMPIRE. THEY THINK THEY'RE OUR PARTNERS? THEY'LL LEARN WE'RE THEIR *MASTERS*.
DAMMIT, KIRK, DON'T BE RECKLESS! YOU'LL DO NOTHING WITHOUT DIRECT ORDERS FROM THE IMPERIUM! RETURN TO EARTH AT ONCE!
YOU DON'T GET IT, DO YOU, PIKE? FROM NOW ON...
...I AM THE IMPERIUM.
KIRK OUT.

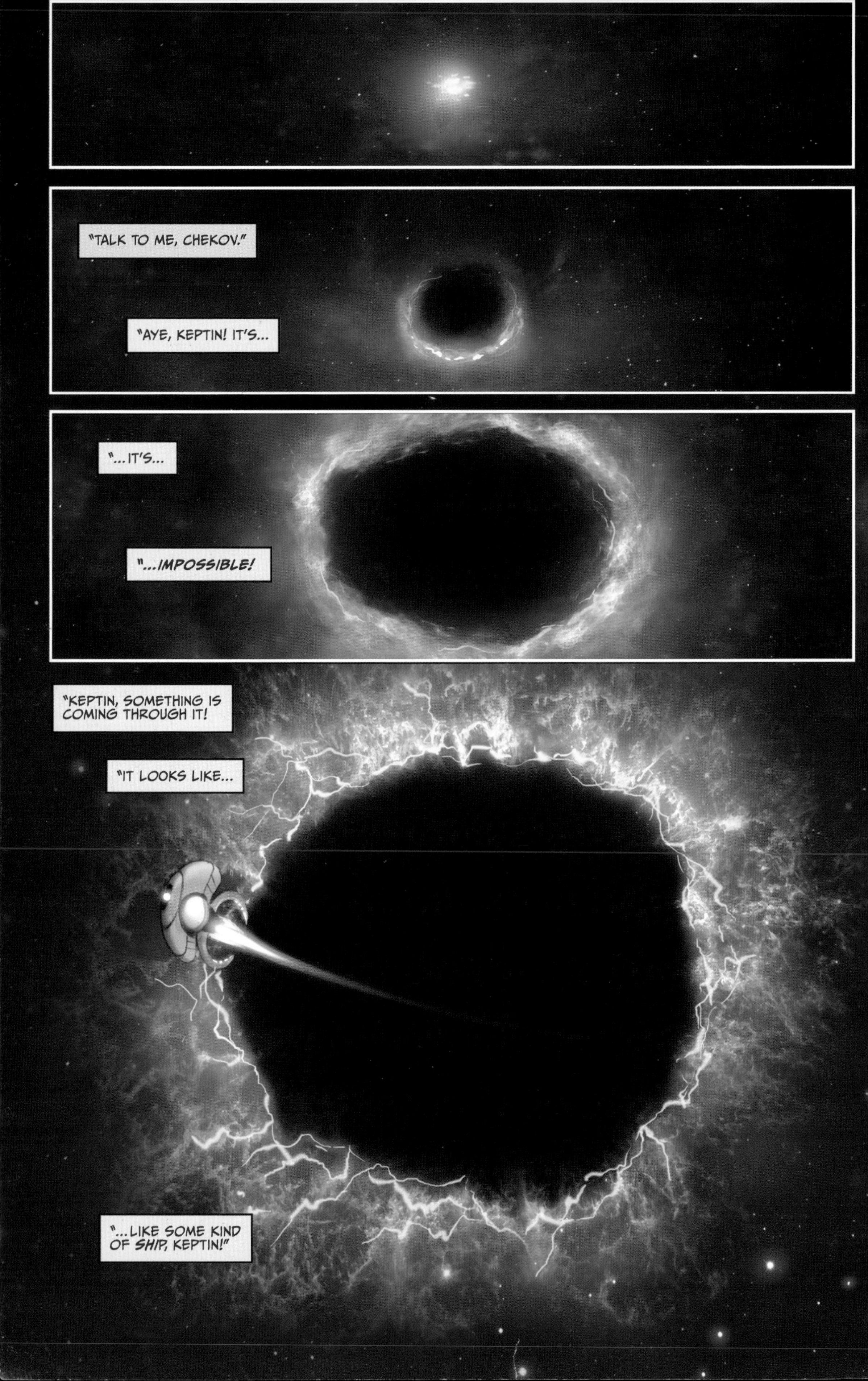
"TALK TO ME, CHEKOV."
"AYE, KEPTIN! IT'S...
"...IT'S...
"...IMPOSSIBLE!
"KEPTIN, SOMETHING IS COMING THROUGH IT!
"IT LOOKS LIKE...
"...LIKE SOME KIND OF SHIP, KEPTIN!"

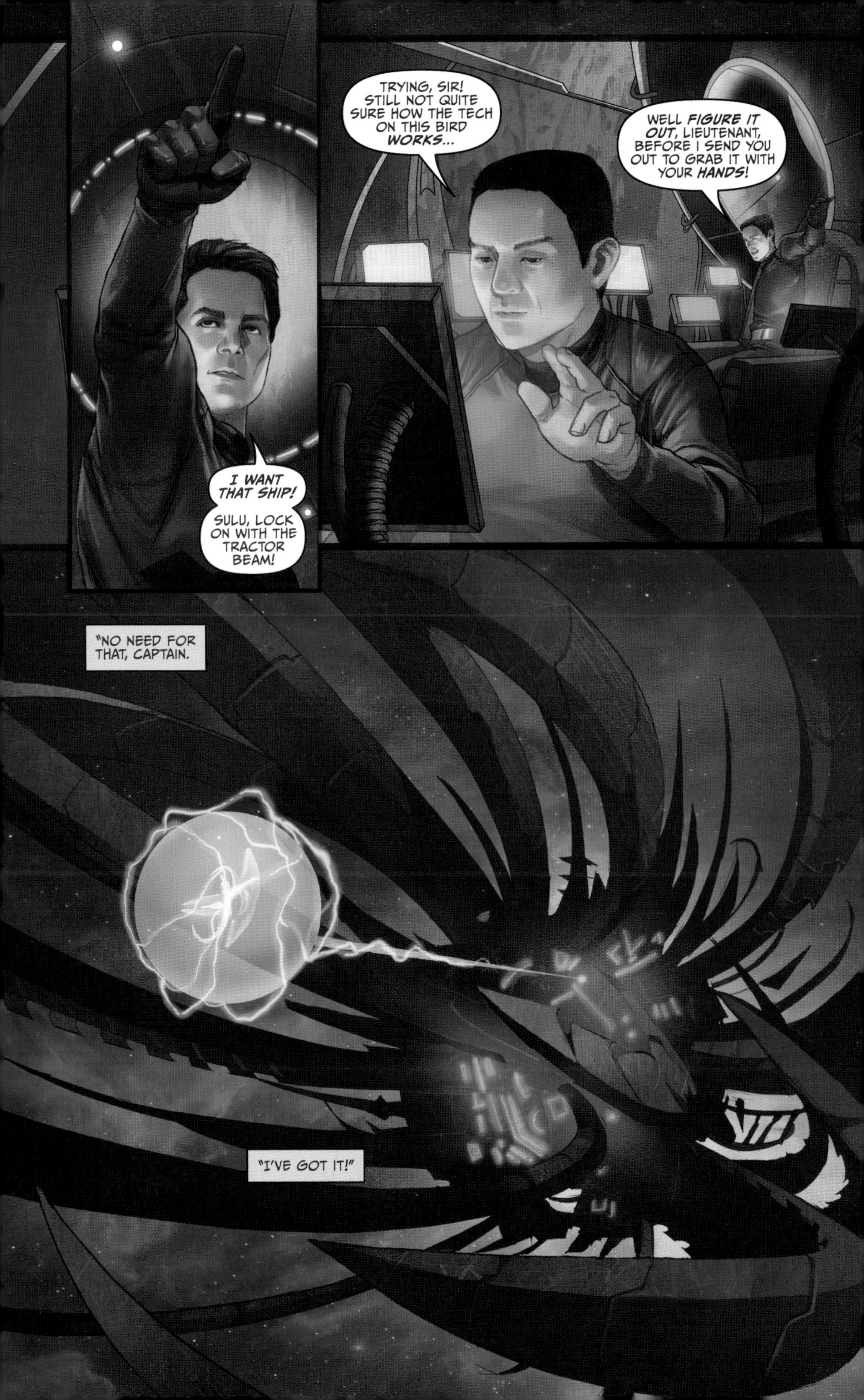
I WANT THAT SHIP!
SULU, LOCK ON WITH THE TRACTOR BEAM!
TRYING, SIR! STILL NOT QUITE SURE HOW THE TECH ON THIS BIRD WORKS...
WELL FIGURE IT OUT, LIEUTENANT, BEFORE I SEND YOU OUT TO GRAB IT WITH YOUR HANDS!
"NO NEED FOR THAT, CAPTAIN.
"I'VE GOT IT!"

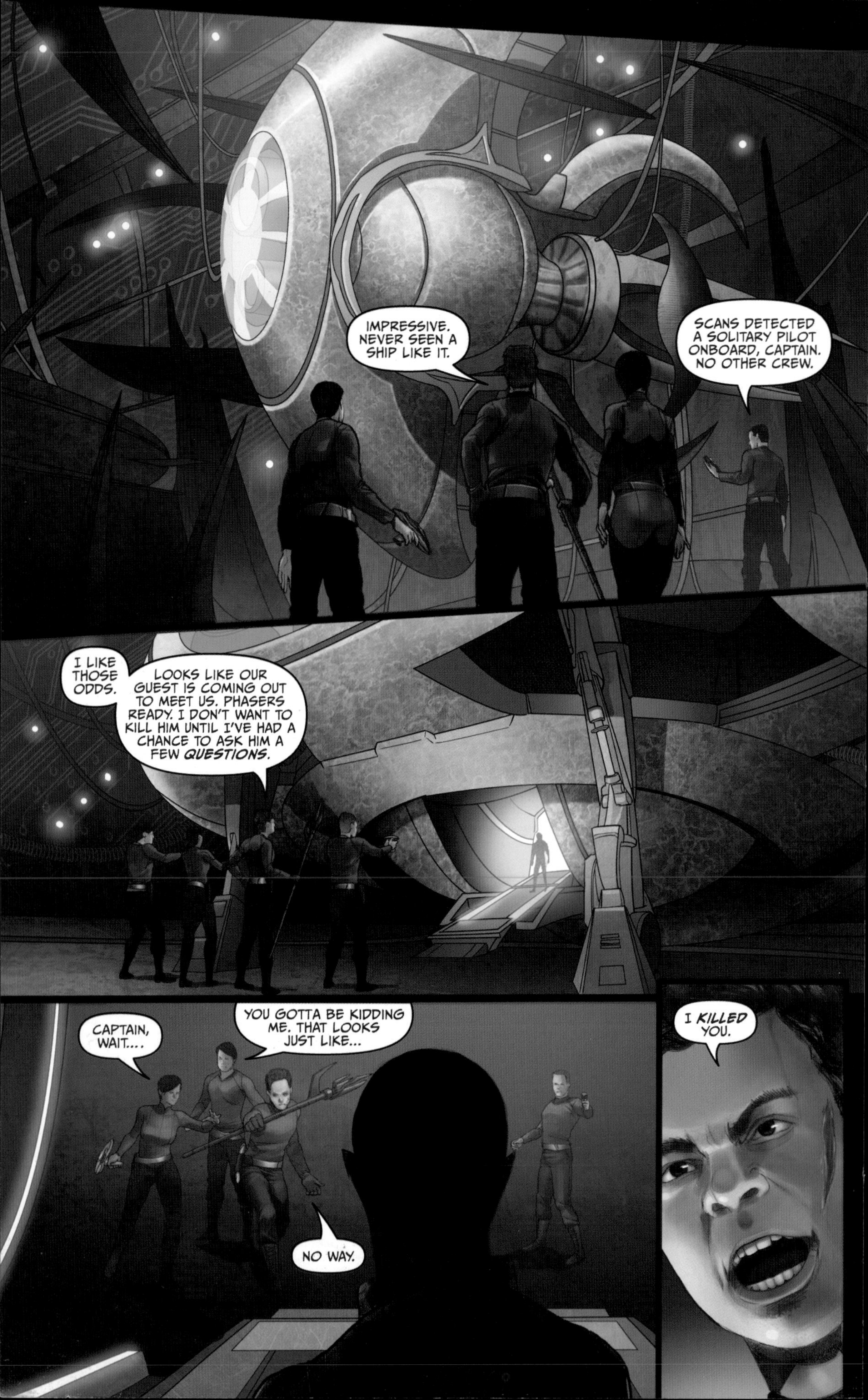
IMPRESSIVE. NEVER SEEN A SHIP LIKE IT.
SCANS DETECTED A SOLITARY PILOT ONBOARD, CAPTAIN. NO OTHER CREW.
I LIKE THOSE ODDS.
LOOKS LIKE OUR GUEST IS COMING OUT TO MEET US. PHASERS READY. I DON'T WANT TO KILL HIM UNTIL I'VE HAD A CHANCE TO ASK HIM A FEW *QUESTIONS*.
CAPTAIN, WAIT....
YOU GOTTA BE KIDDING ME. THAT LOOKS JUST LIKE...
NO WAY.
I *KILLED* YOU.

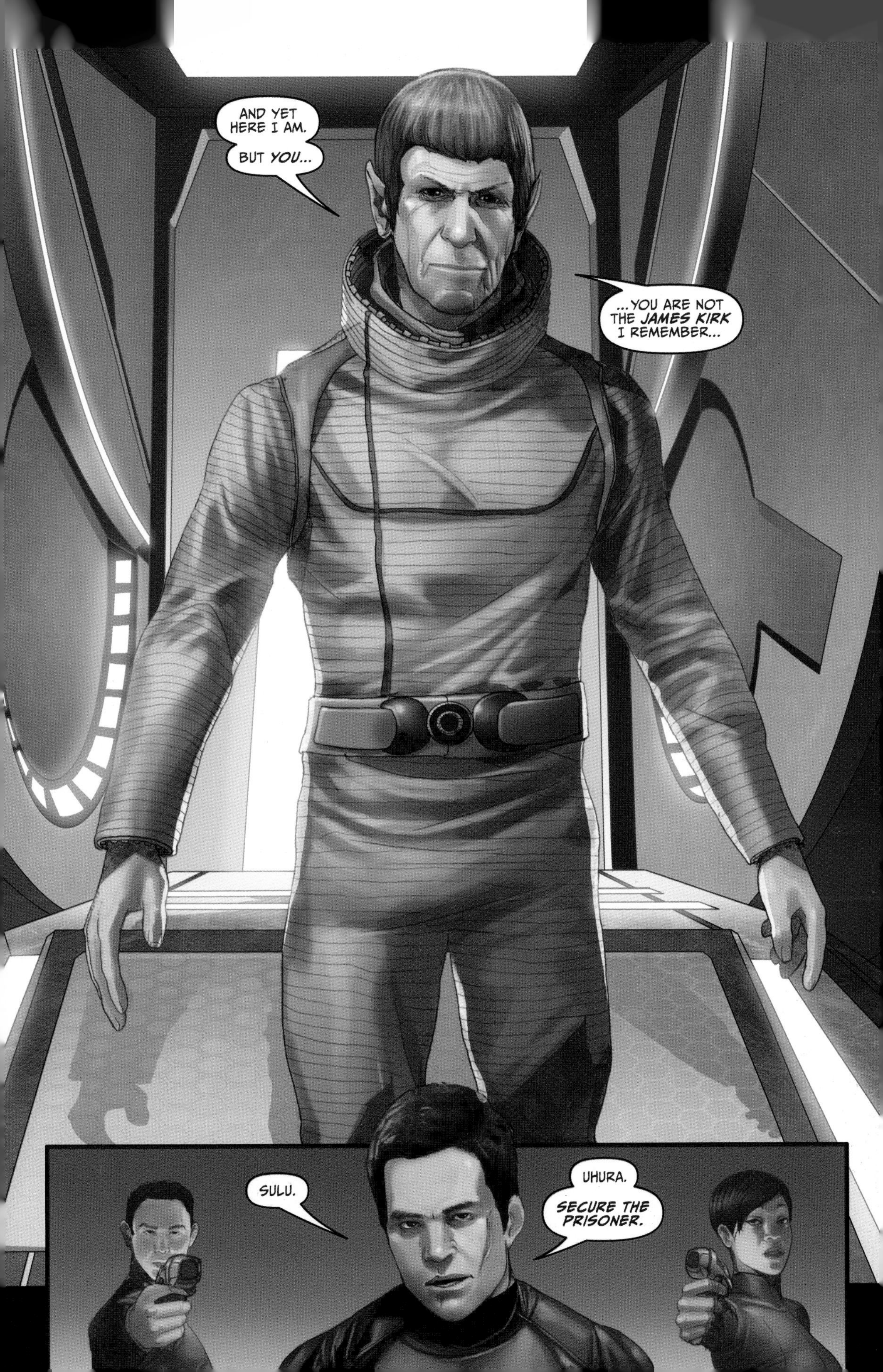
AND YET HERE I AM.
BUT *YOU*...
...YOU ARE NOT THE ***JAMES KIRK*** I REMEMBER...
SULU.
UHURA.
SECURE THE PRISONER.

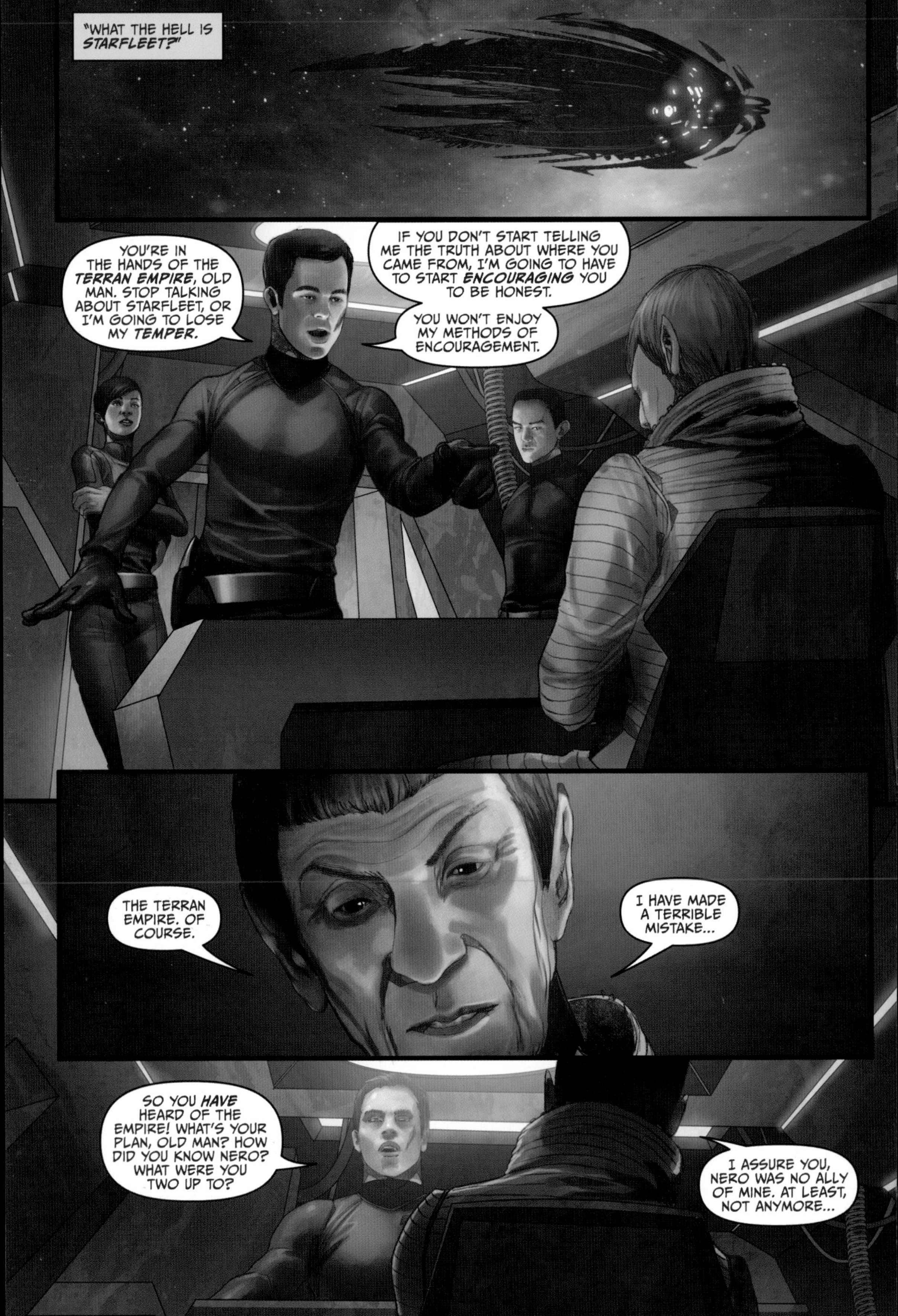
"WHAT THE HELL IS STARFLEET?"
YOU'RE IN THE HANDS OF THE TERRAN EMPIRE, OLD MAN. STOP TALKING ABOUT STARFLEET, OR I'M GOING TO LOSE MY TEMPER.
IF YOU DON'T START TELLING ME THE TRUTH ABOUT WHERE YOU CAME FROM, I'M GOING TO HAVE TO START ENCOURAGING YOU TO BE HONEST.
YOU WON'T ENJOY MY METHODS OF ENCOURAGEMENT.
THE TERRAN EMPIRE. OF COURSE.
I HAVE MADE A TERRIBLE MISTAKE...
SO YOU HAVE HEARD OF THE EMPIRE! WHAT'S YOUR PLAN, OLD MAN? HOW DID YOU KNOW NERO? WHAT WERE YOU TWO UP TO?
I ASSURE YOU, NERO WAS NO ALLY OF MINE. AT LEAST, NOT ANYMORE...

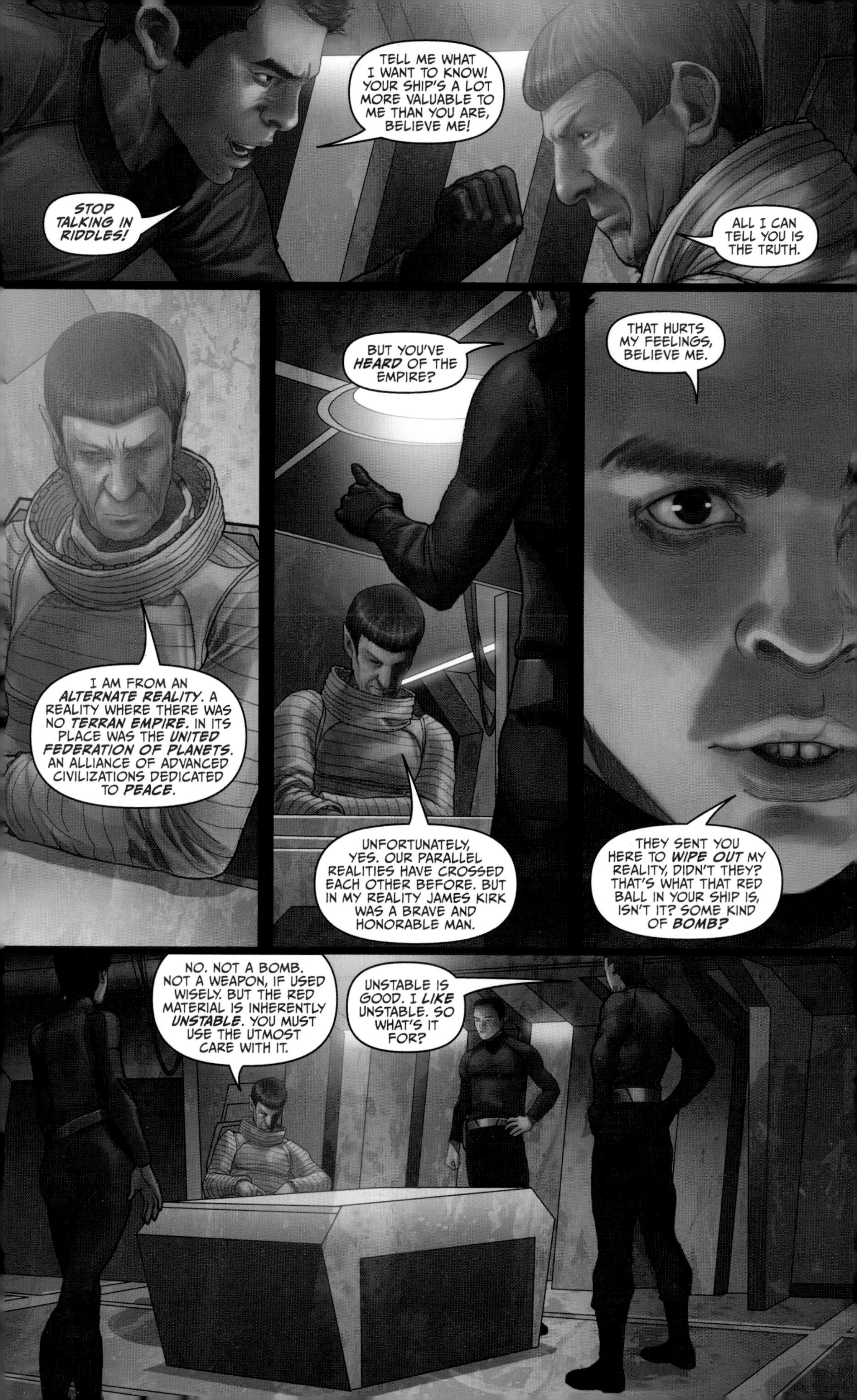
TELL ME WHAT I WANT TO KNOW! YOUR SHIP'S A LOT MORE VALUABLE TO ME THAN YOU ARE, BELIEVE ME!
STOP TALKING IN RIDDLES!
ALL I CAN TELL YOU IS THE TRUTH.
I AM FROM AN ALTERNATE REALITY. A REALITY WHERE THERE WAS NO TERRAN EMPIRE. IN ITS PLACE WAS THE UNITED FEDERATION OF PLANETS. AN ALLIANCE OF ADVANCED CIVILIZATIONS DEDICATED TO PEACE.
BUT YOU'VE HEARD OF THE EMPIRE?
UNFORTUNATELY, YES. OUR PARALLEL REALITIES HAVE CROSSED EACH OTHER BEFORE. BUT IN MY REALITY JAMES KIRK WAS A BRAVE AND HONORABLE MAN.
THAT HURTS MY FEELINGS, BELIEVE ME.
THEY SENT YOU HERE TO WIPE OUT MY REALITY, DIDN'T THEY? THAT'S WHAT THAT RED BALL IN YOUR SHIP IS, ISN'T IT? SOME KIND OF BOMB?
NO. NOT A BOMB. NOT A WEAPON, IF USED WISELY. BUT THE RED MATERIAL IS INHERENTLY UNSTABLE. YOU MUST USE THE UTMOST CARE WITH IT.
UNSTABLE IS GOOD. I LIKE UNSTABLE. SO WHAT'S IT FOR?

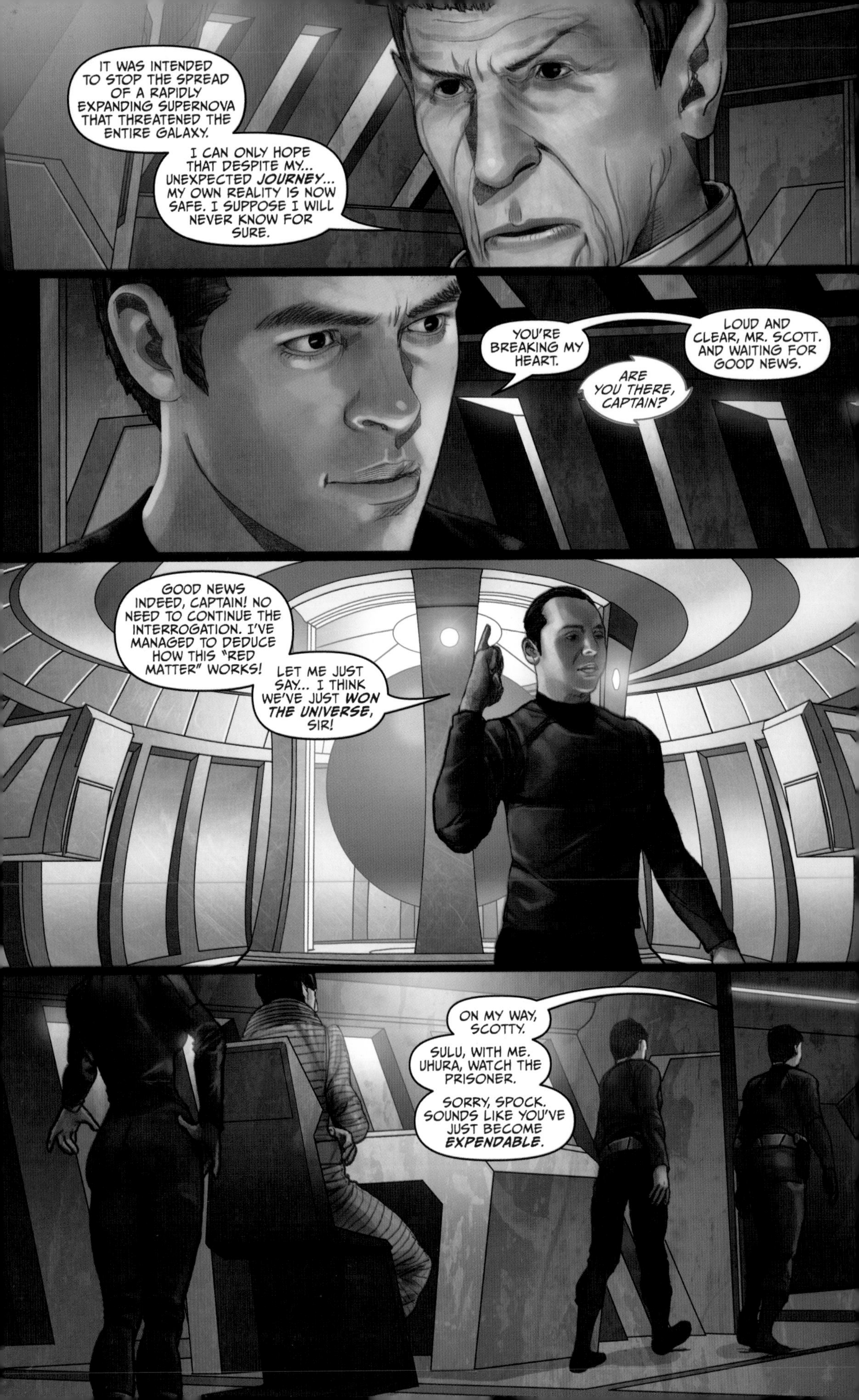
IT WAS INTENDED TO STOP THE SPREAD OF A RAPIDLY EXPANDING SUPERNOVA THAT THREATENED THE ENTIRE GALAXY.
I CAN ONLY HOPE THAT DESPITE MY... UNEXPECTED *JOURNEY*... MY OWN REALITY IS NOW SAFE. I SUPPOSE I WILL NEVER KNOW FOR SURE.
YOU'RE BREAKING MY HEART.
LOUD AND CLEAR, MR. SCOTT. AND WAITING FOR GOOD NEWS.
ARE YOU THERE, CAPTAIN?
GOOD NEWS INDEED, CAPTAIN! NO NEED TO CONTINUE THE INTERROGATION. I'VE MANAGED TO DEDUCE HOW THIS "RED MATTER" WORKS!
LET ME JUST SAY... I THINK WE'VE JUST ***WON THE UNIVERSE***, SIR!
ON MY WAY, SCOTTY.
SULU, WITH ME. UHURA, WATCH THE PRISONER.
SORRY, SPOCK. SOUNDS LIKE YOU'VE JUST BECOME ***EXPENDABLE***.

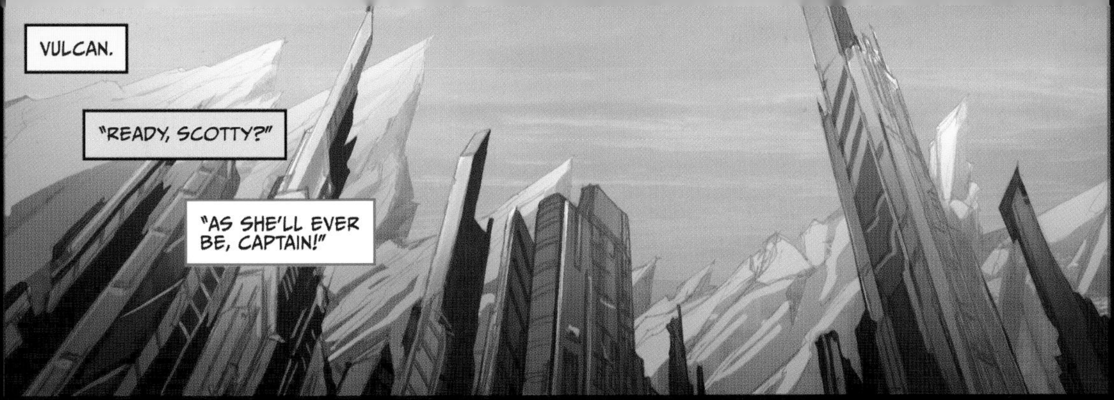
VULCAN.
"READY, SCOTTY?"
"AS SHE'LL EVER BE, CAPTAIN!"

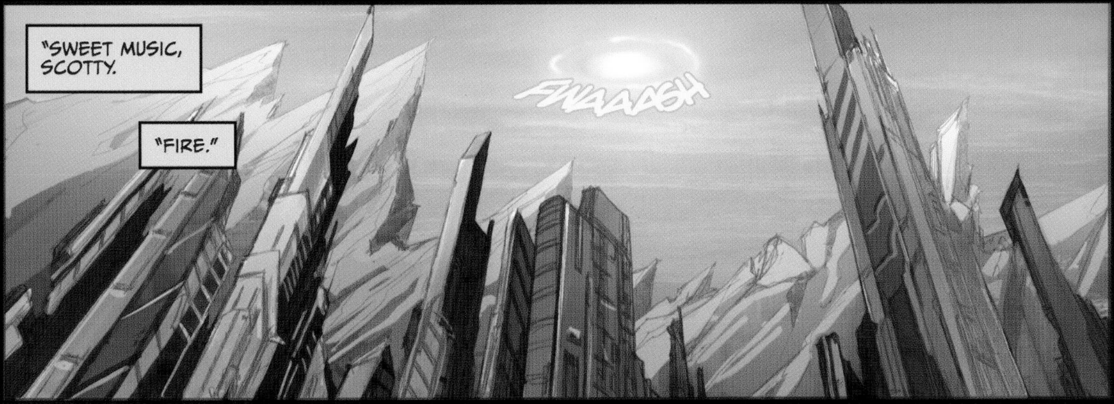
"SWEET MUSIC, SCOTTY.
"FIRE."
FWAAASH

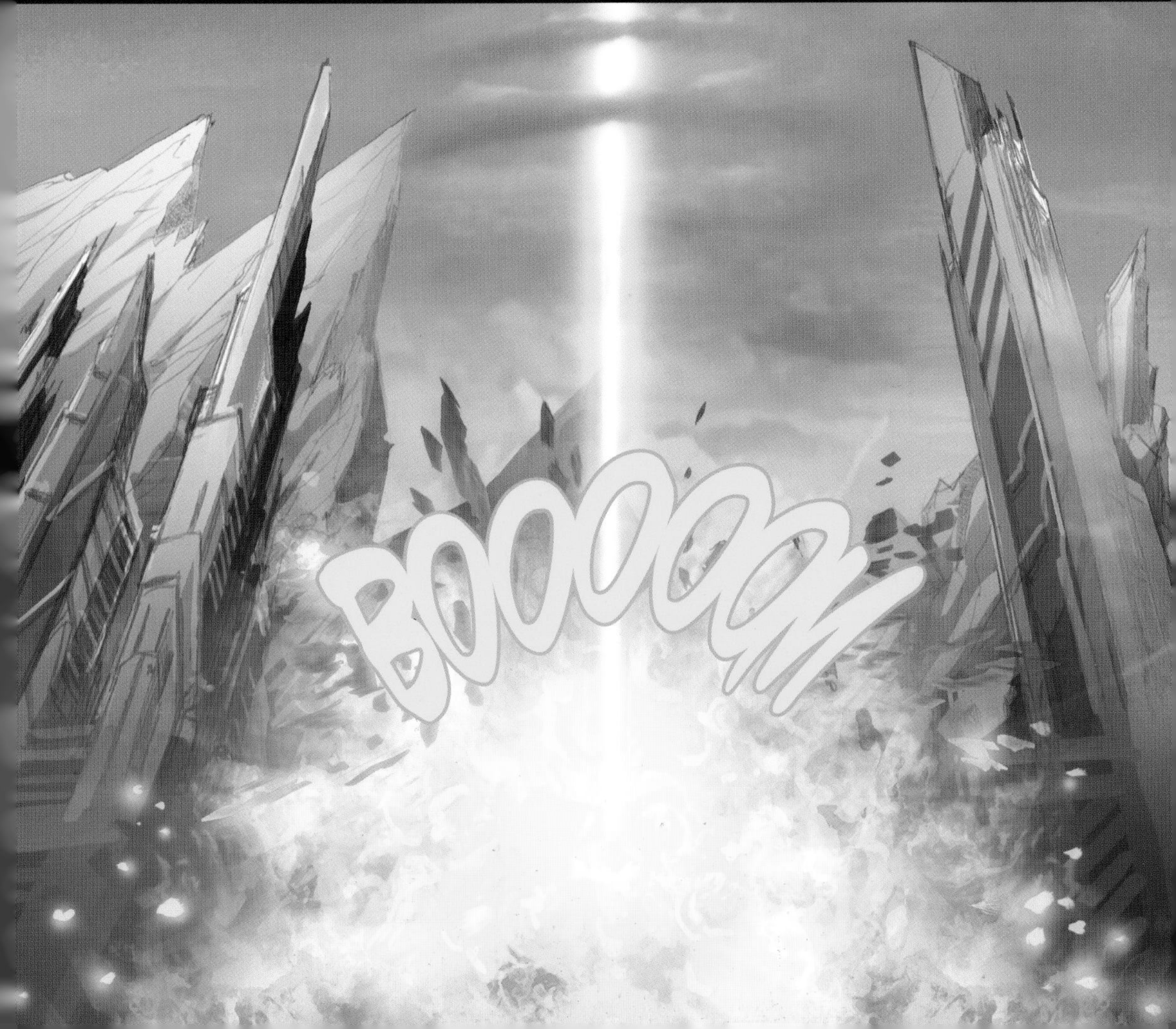
BOOOOOM

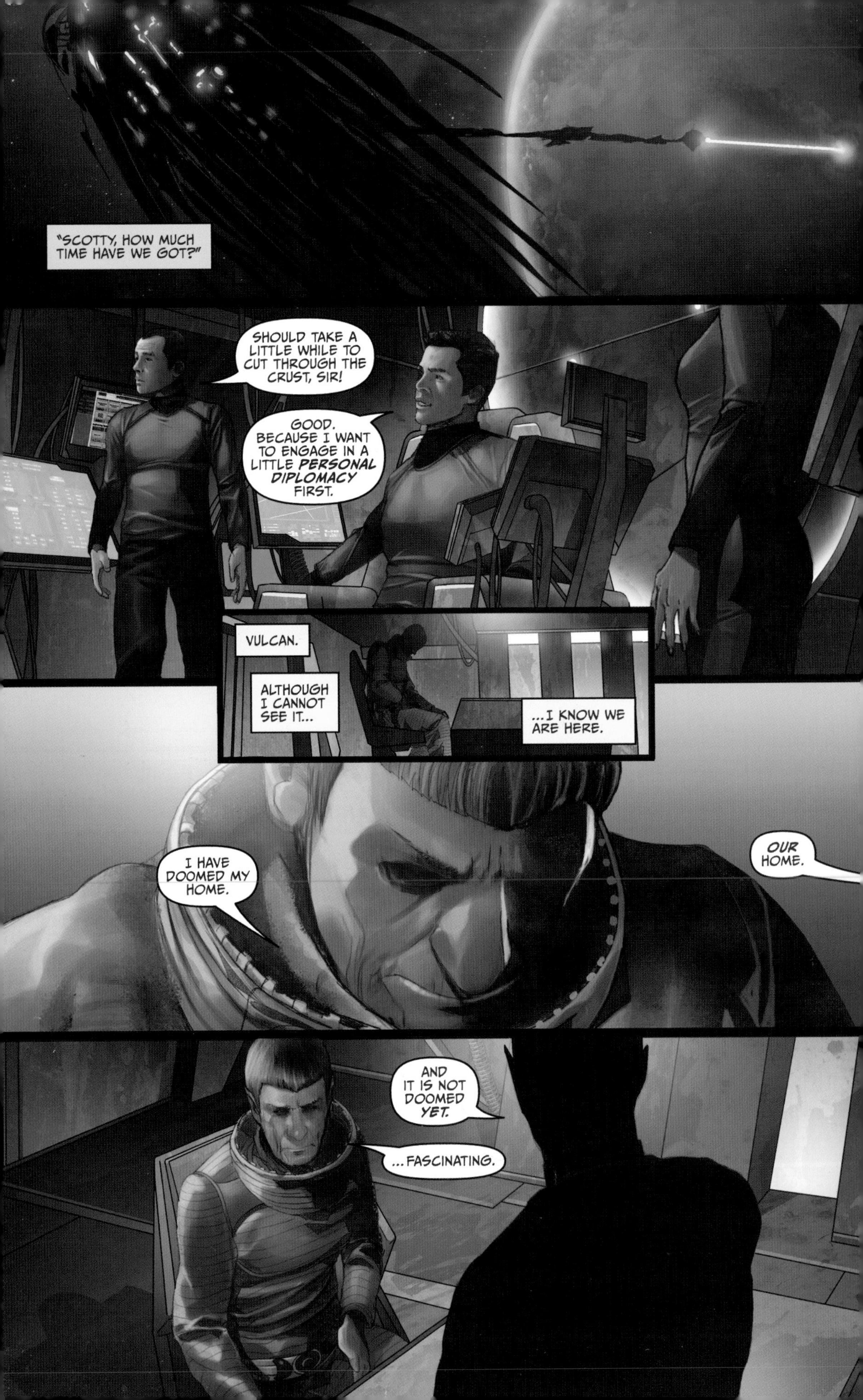
"SCOTTY, HOW MUCH TIME HAVE WE GOT?"
SHOULD TAKE A LITTLE WHILE TO CUT THROUGH THE CRUST, SIR!
GOOD. BECAUSE I WANT TO ENGAGE IN A LITTLE PERSONAL DIPLOMACY FIRST.
VULCAN.
ALTHOUGH I CANNOT SEE IT...
...I KNOW WE ARE HERE.
I HAVE DOOMED MY HOME.
OUR HOME.
AND IT IS NOT DOOMED YET.
...FASCINATING.

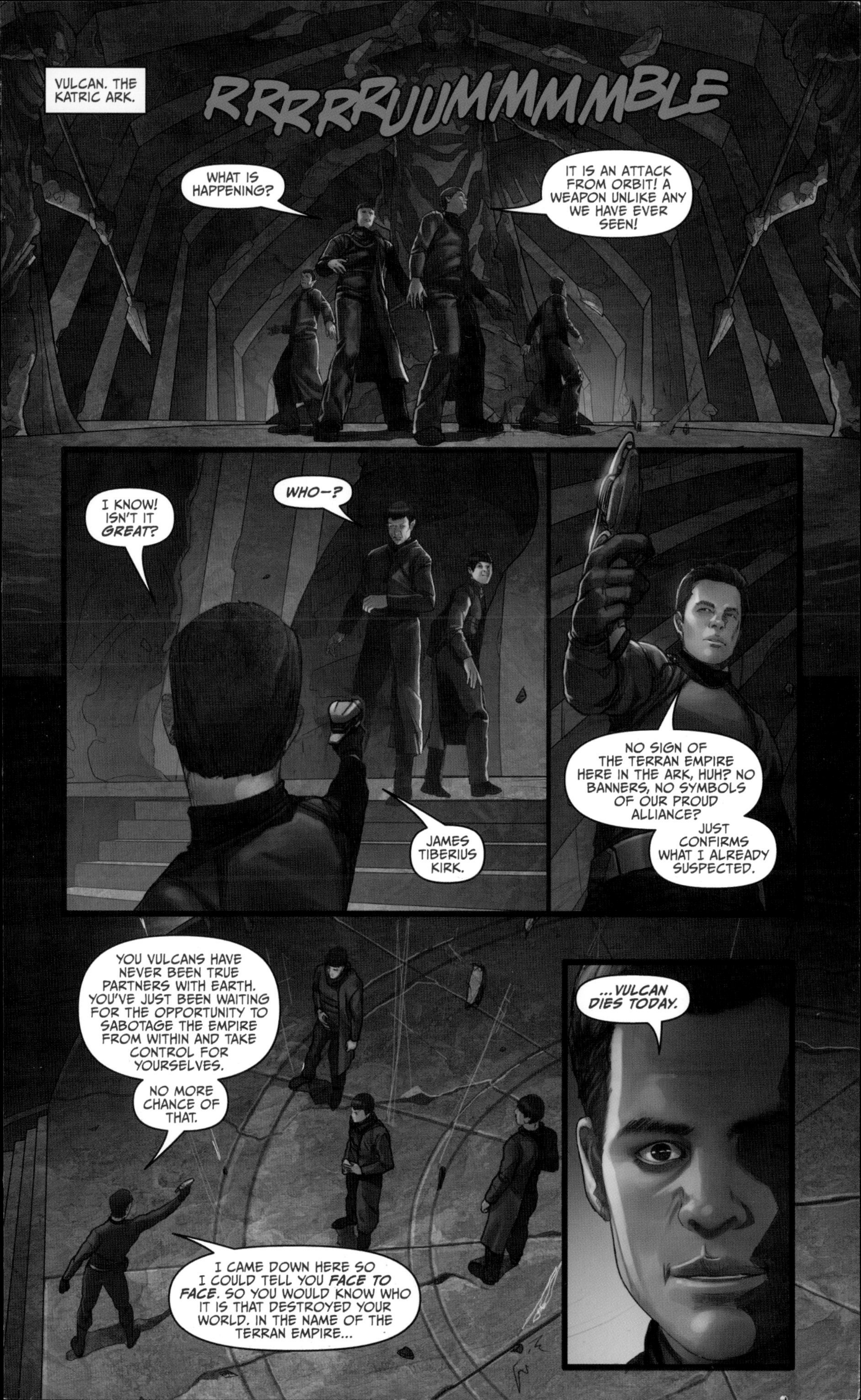

VULCAN. THE KATRIC ARK.
RRRRRUUMMMMMBLE
WHAT IS HAPPENING?
IT IS AN ATTACK FROM ORBIT! A WEAPON UNLIKE ANY WE HAVE EVER SEEN!
WHO–?
I KNOW! ISN'T IT GREAT?
JAMES TIBERIUS KIRK.
NO SIGN OF THE TERRAN EMPIRE HERE IN THE ARK, HUH? NO BANNERS, NO SYMBOLS OF OUR PROUD ALLIANCE?
JUST CONFIRMS WHAT I ALREADY SUSPECTED.
YOU VULCANS HAVE NEVER BEEN TRUE PARTNERS WITH EARTH. YOU'VE JUST BEEN WAITING FOR THE OPPORTUNITY TO SABOTAGE THE EMPIRE FROM WITHIN AND TAKE CONTROL FOR YOURSELVES.
NO MORE CHANCE OF THAT.
I CAME DOWN HERE SO I COULD TELL YOU FACE TO FACE. SO YOU WOULD KNOW WHO IT IS THAT DESTROYED YOUR WORLD. IN THE NAME OF THE TERRAN EMPIRE...
...VULCAN DIES TODAY.

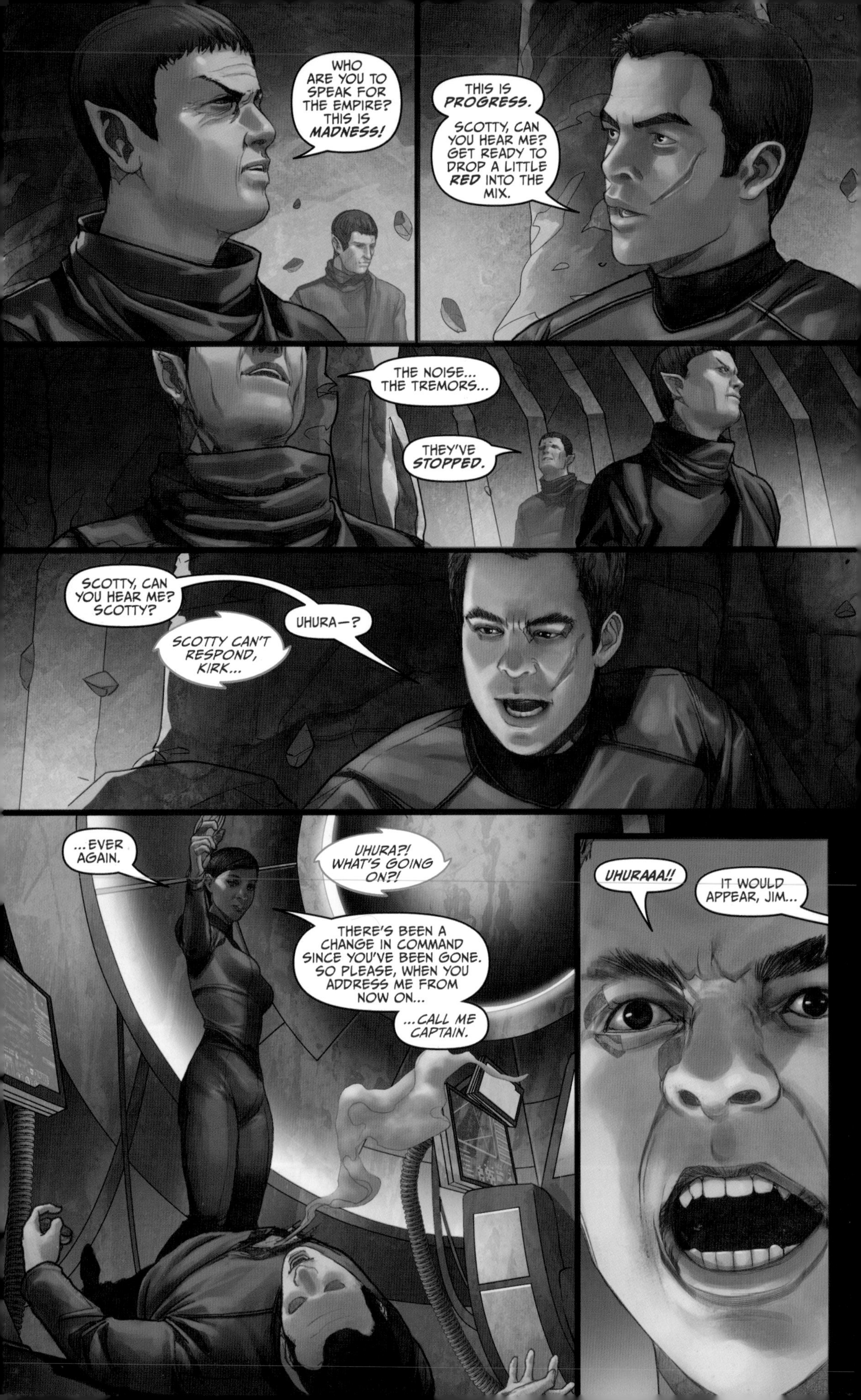
WHO ARE YOU TO SPEAK FOR THE EMPIRE? THIS IS MADNESS!
THIS IS PROGRESS.
SCOTTY, CAN YOU HEAR ME? GET READY TO DROP A LITTLE RED INTO THE MIX.
THE NOISE... THE TREMORS...
THEY'VE STOPPED.
SCOTTY, CAN YOU HEAR ME? SCOTTY?
UHURA—?
SCOTTY CAN'T RESPOND, KIRK...
...EVER AGAIN.
UHURA?! WHAT'S GOING ON?!
THERE'S BEEN A CHANGE IN COMMAND SINCE YOU'VE BEEN GONE. SO PLEASE, WHEN YOU ADDRESS ME FROM NOW ON...
...CALL ME CAPTAIN.
UHURAAA!!
IT WOULD APPEAR, JIM...

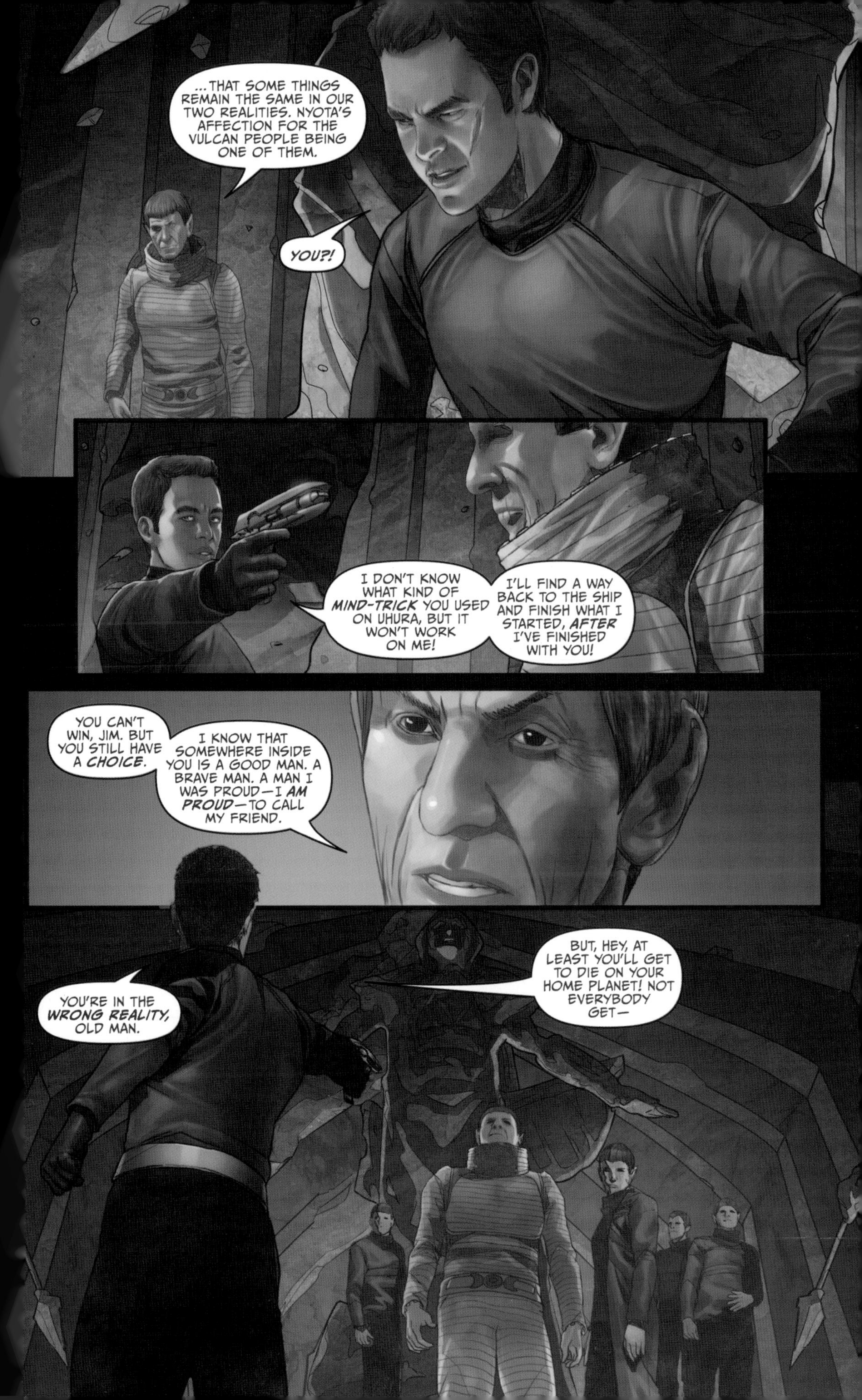
...THAT SOME THINGS REMAIN THE SAME IN OUR TWO REALITIES. NYOTA'S AFFECTION FOR THE VULCAN PEOPLE BEING ONE OF THEM.
YOU?!
I DON'T KNOW WHAT KIND OF MIND-TRICK YOU USED ON UHURA, BUT IT WON'T WORK ON ME!
I'LL FIND A WAY BACK TO THE SHIP AND FINISH WHAT I STARTED, AFTER I'VE FINISHED WITH YOU!
YOU CAN'T WIN, JIM. BUT YOU STILL HAVE A CHOICE.
I KNOW THAT SOMEWHERE INSIDE YOU IS A GOOD MAN. A BRAVE MAN. A MAN I WAS PROUD—I AM PROUD—TO CALL MY FRIEND.
YOU'RE IN THE WRONG REALITY, OLD MAN.
BUT, HEY, AT LEAST YOU'LL GET TO DIE ON YOUR HOME PLANET! NOT EVERYBODY GET—

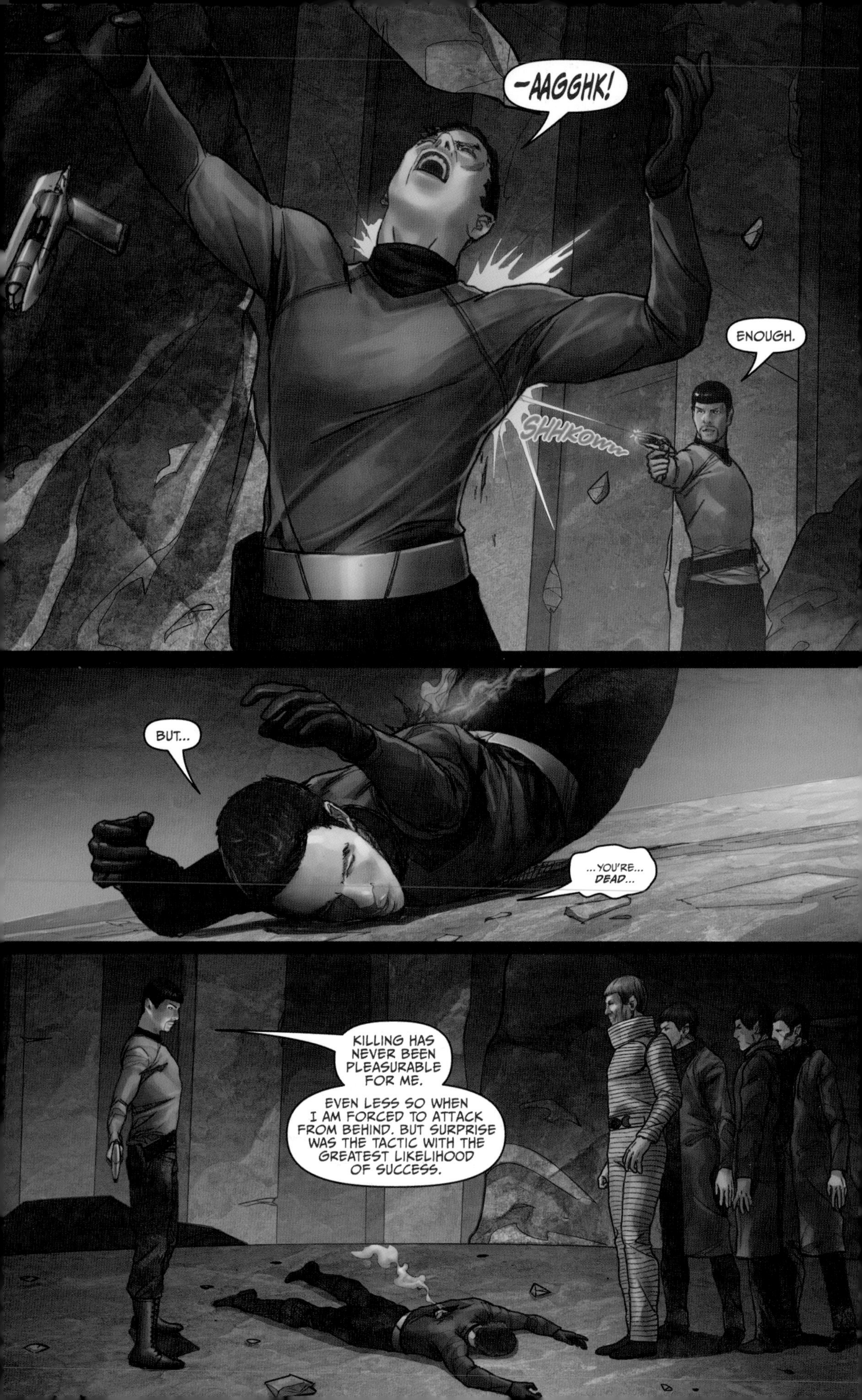
-AAGGHK!
ENOUGH.
SHHKOWW
BUT...
...YOU'RE... DEAD...
KILLING HAS NEVER BEEN PLEASURABLE FOR ME.
EVEN LESS SO WHEN I AM FORCED TO ATTACK FROM BEHIND. BUT SURPRISE WAS THE TACTIC WITH THE GREATEST LIKELIHOOD OF SUCCESS.

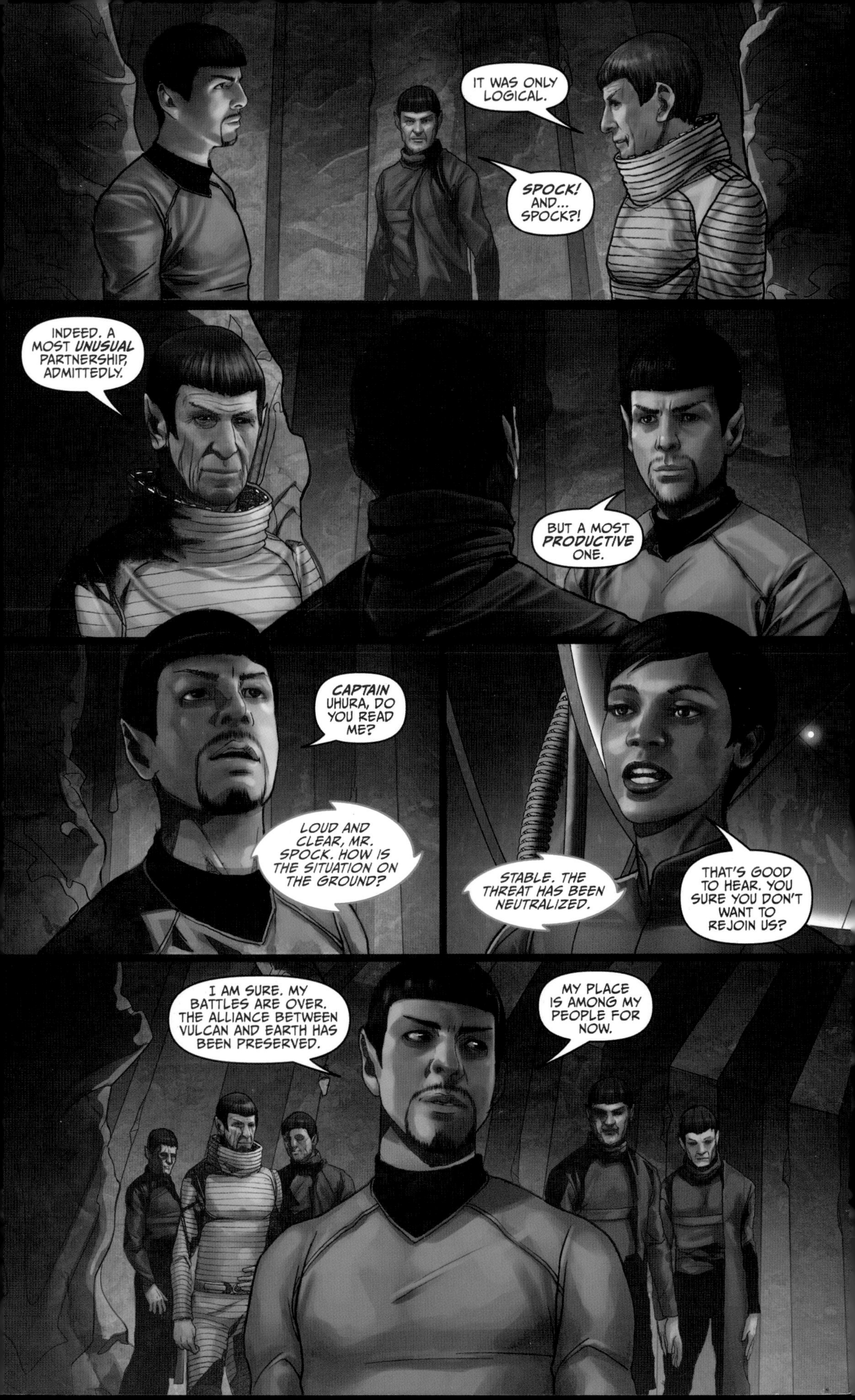
IT WAS ONLY LOGICAL.
SPOCK! AND... SPOCK?!
INDEED. A MOST UNUSUAL PARTNERSHIP, ADMITTEDLY.
BUT A MOST PRODUCTIVE ONE.
CAPTAIN UHURA, DO YOU READ ME?
LOUD AND CLEAR, MR. SPOCK. HOW IS THE SITUATION ON THE GROUND?
STABLE. THE THREAT HAS BEEN NEUTRALIZED.
THAT'S GOOD TO HEAR. YOU SURE YOU DON'T WANT TO REJOIN US?
I AM SURE. MY BATTLES ARE OVER. THE ALLIANCE BETWEEN VULCAN AND EARTH HAS BEEN PRESERVED.
MY PLACE IS AMONG MY PEOPLE FOR NOW.

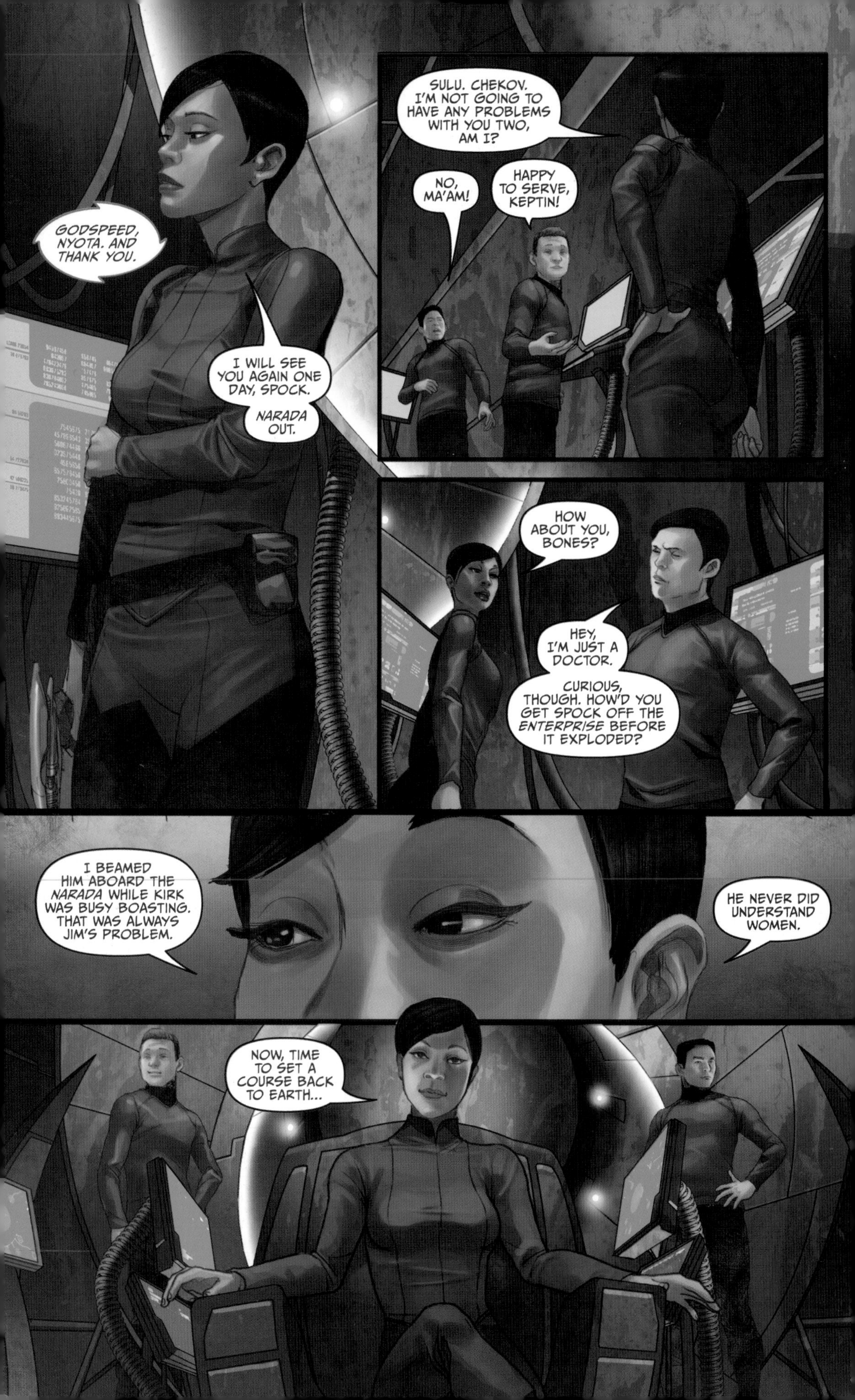
GODSPEED, NYOTA. AND THANK YOU.
I WILL SEE YOU AGAIN ONE DAY, SPOCK.
NARADA OUT.
SULU. CHEKOV. I'M NOT GOING TO HAVE ANY PROBLEMS WITH YOU TWO, AM I?
NO, MA'AM!
HAPPY TO SERVE, KEPTIN!
HOW ABOUT YOU, BONES?
HEY, I'M JUST A DOCTOR.
CURIOUS, THOUGH. HOW'D YOU GET SPOCK OFF THE ENTERPRISE BEFORE IT EXPLODED?
I BEAMED HIM ABOARD THE NARADA WHILE KIRK WAS BUSY BOASTING. THAT WAS ALWAYS JIM'S PROBLEM.
HE NEVER DID UNDERSTAND WOMEN.
NOW, TIME TO SET A COURSE BACK TO EARTH...

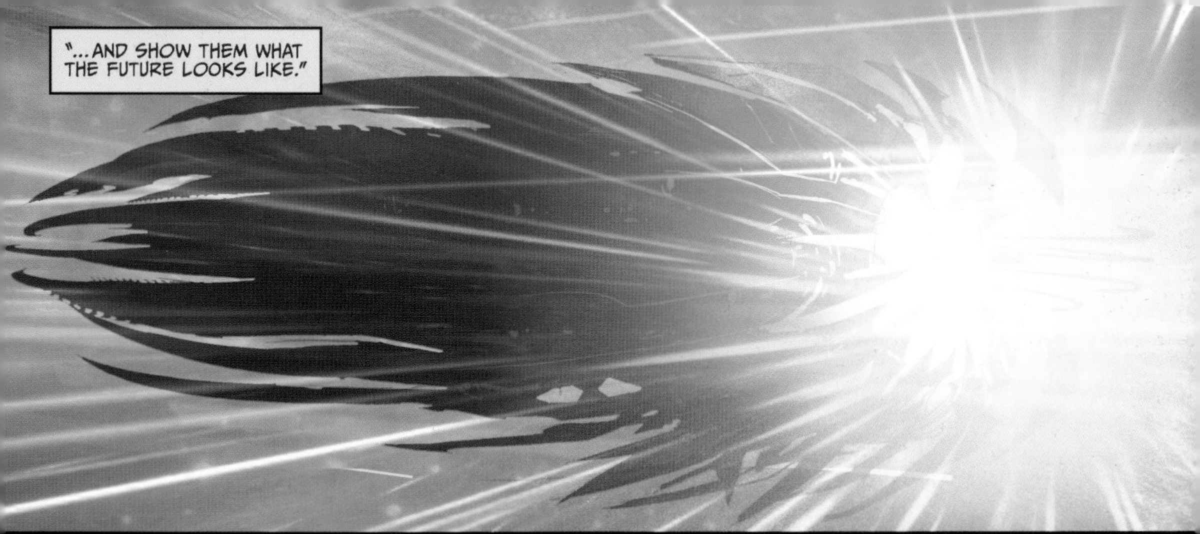
"...AND SHOW THEM WHAT THE FUTURE LOOKS LIKE."

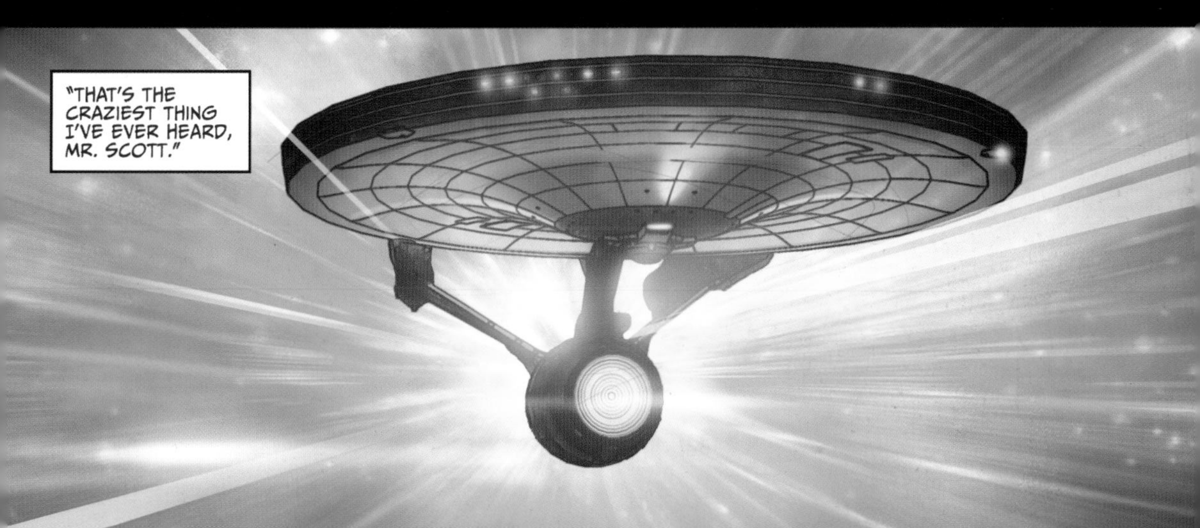
"THAT'S THE CRAZIEST THING I'VE EVER HEARD, MR. SCOTT."

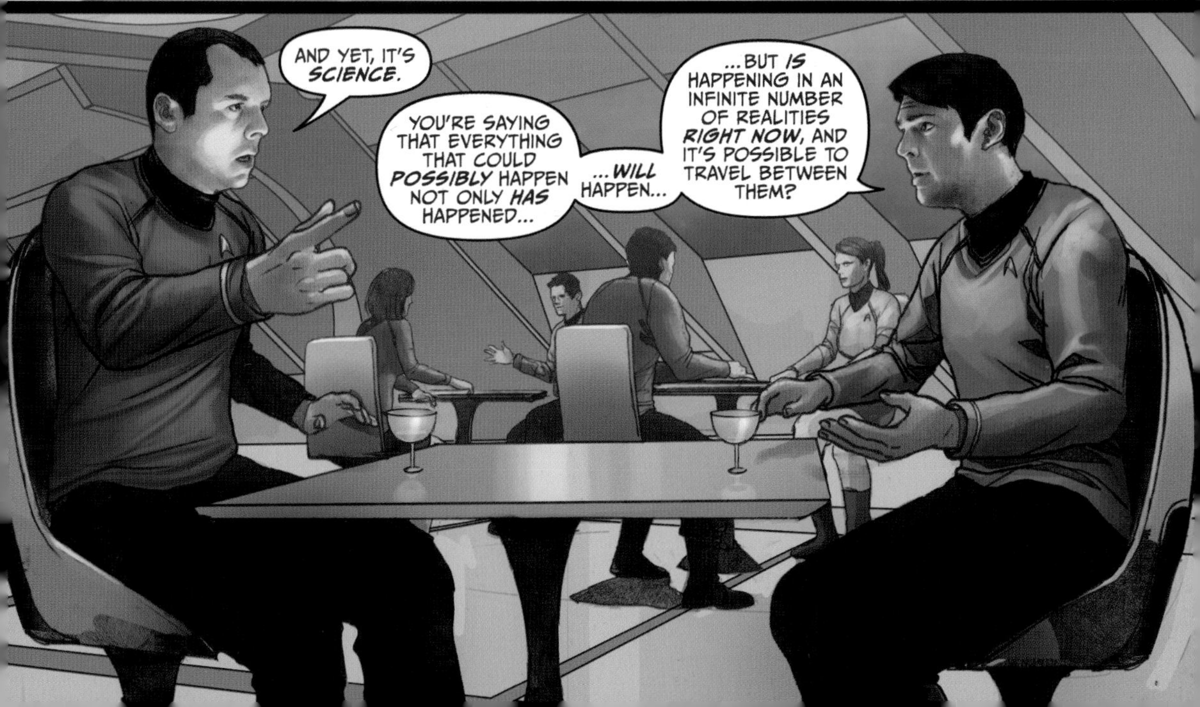
AND YET, IT'S *SCIENCE*.
YOU'RE SAYING THAT EVERYTHING THAT COULD *POSSIBLY* HAPPEN NOT ONLY *HAS* HAPPENED...
...*WILL* HAPPEN...
...BUT *IS* HAPPENING IN AN INFINITE NUMBER OF REALITIES *RIGHT NOW*, AND IT'S POSSIBLE TO TRAVEL BETWEEN THEM?

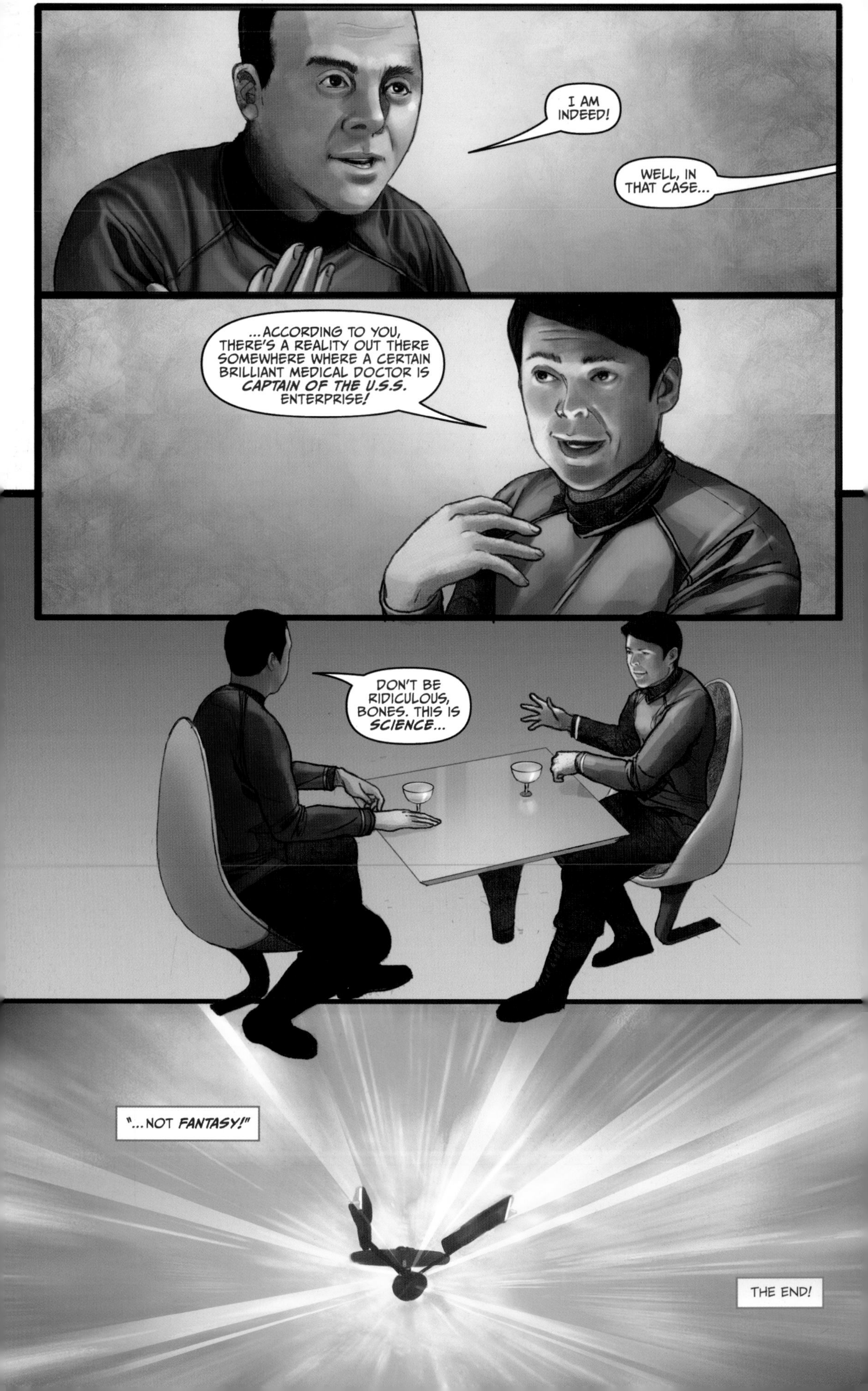
I AM INDEED!
WELL, IN THAT CASE...
...ACCORDING TO YOU, THERE'S A REALITY OUT THERE SOMEWHERE WHERE A CERTAIN BRILLIANT MEDICAL DOCTOR IS CAPTAIN OF THE U.S.S. ENTERPRISE!
DON'T BE RIDICULOUS, BONES. THIS IS SCIENCE...
"...NOT FANTASY!"
THE END!

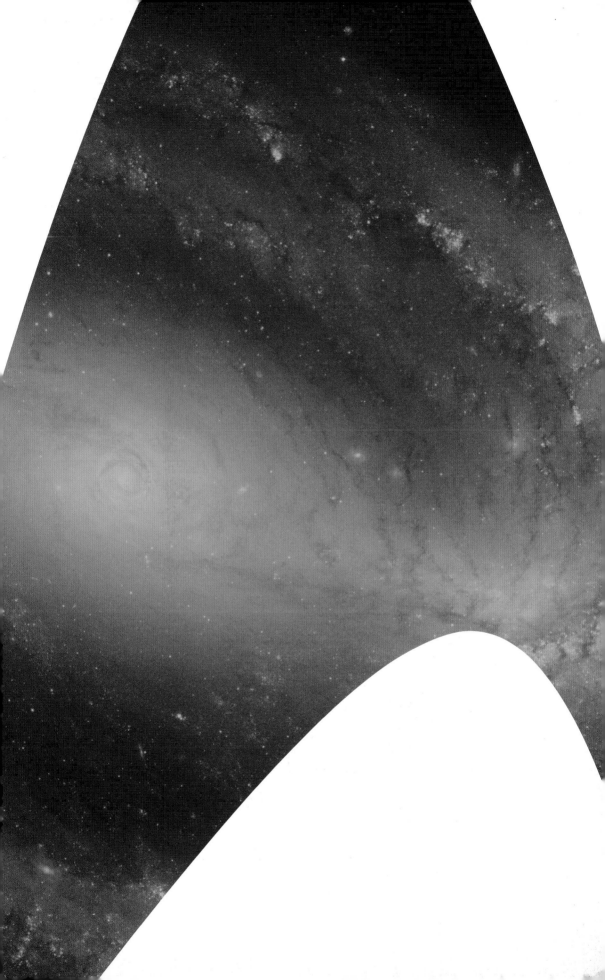

BONES

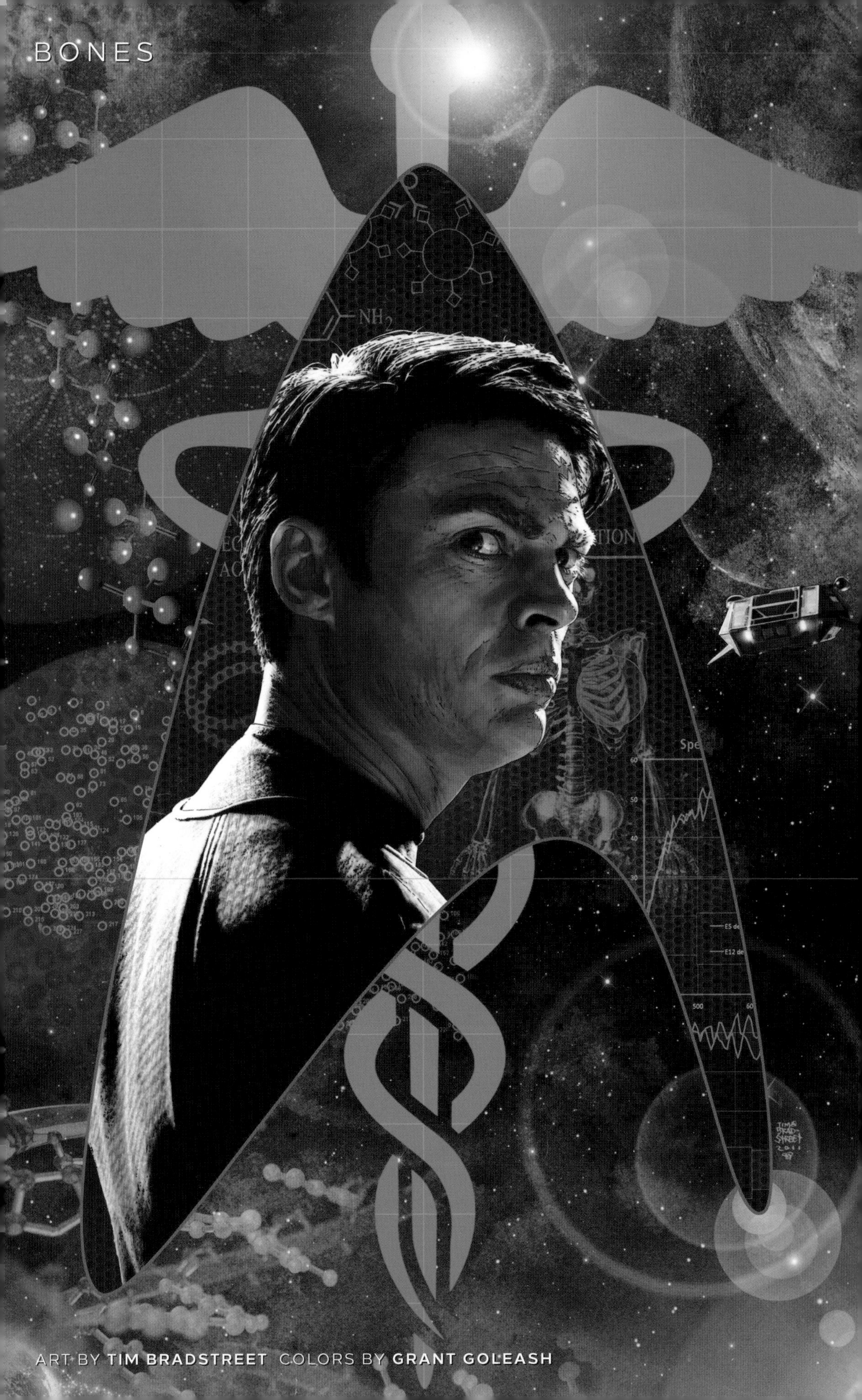

ART BY **TIM BRADSTREET** COLORS BY **GRANT GOLEASH**

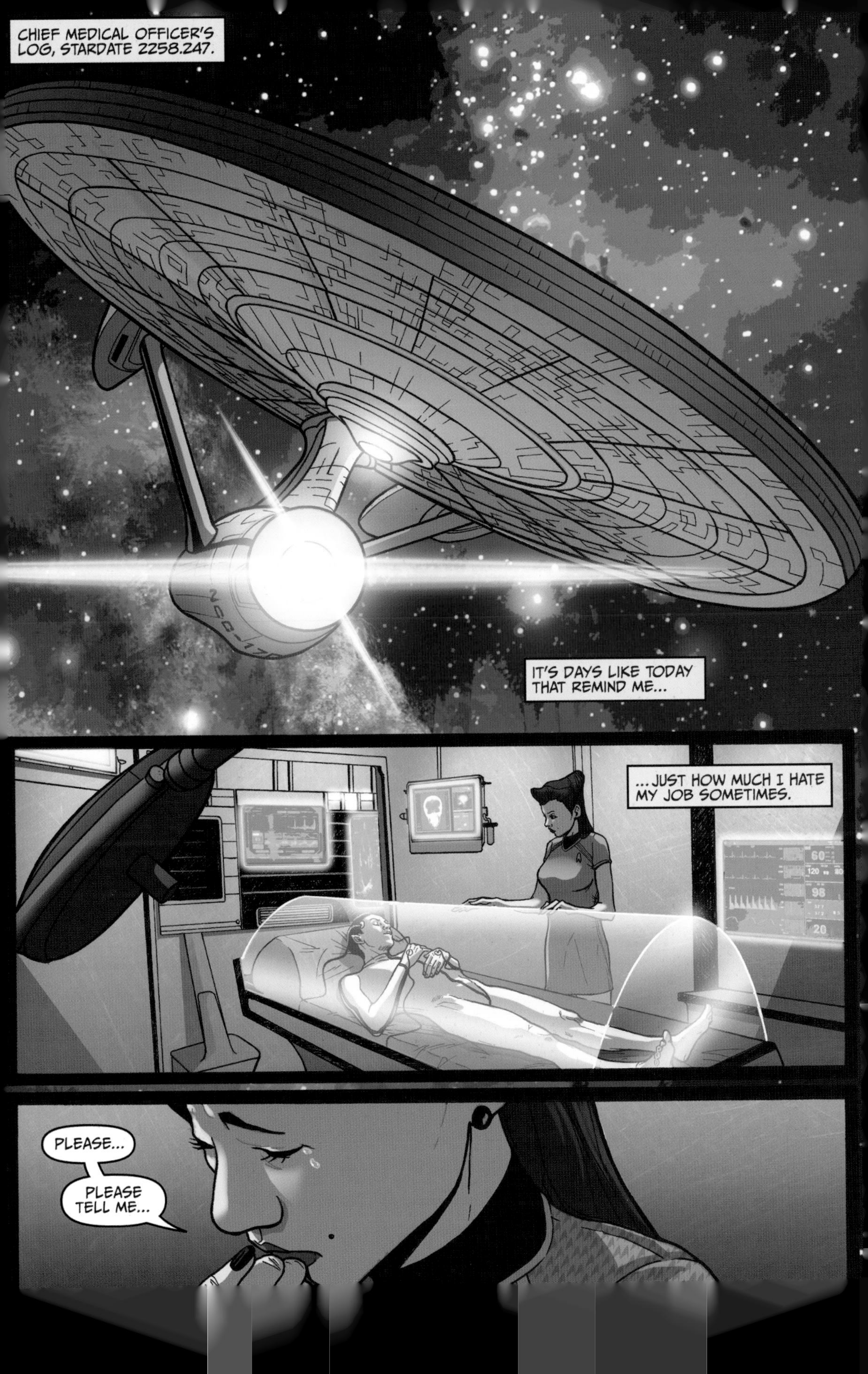
CHIEF MEDICAL OFFICER'S LOG, STARDATE 2258.247.
IT'S DAYS LIKE TODAY THAT REMIND ME...
...JUST HOW MUCH I HATE MY JOB SOMETIMES.
PLEASE...
PLEASE TELL ME...

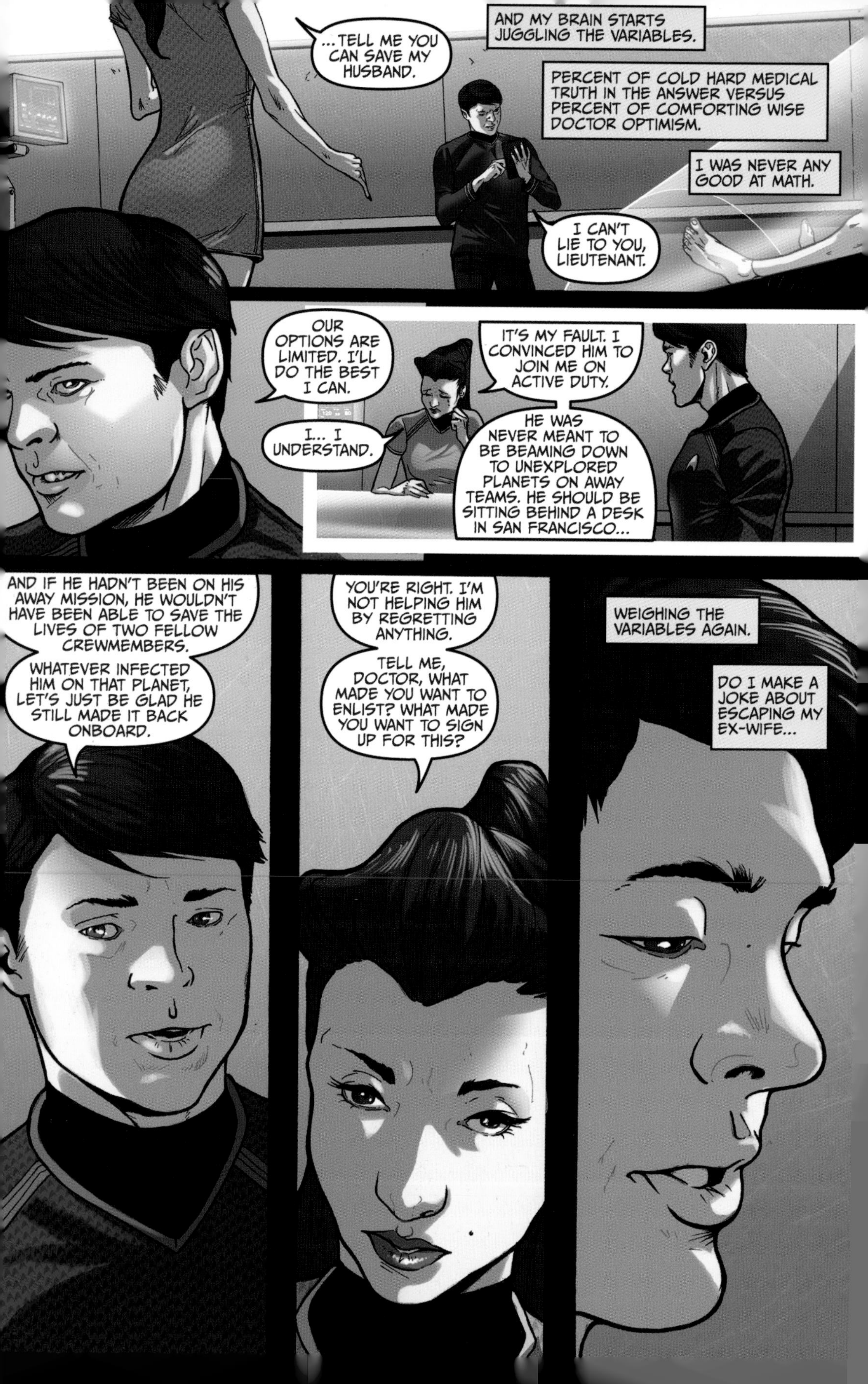
...TELL ME YOU CAN SAVE MY HUSBAND.
AND MY BRAIN STARTS JUGGLING THE VARIABLES.
PERCENT OF COLD HARD MEDICAL TRUTH IN THE ANSWER VERSUS PERCENT OF COMFORTING WISE DOCTOR OPTIMISM.
I WAS NEVER ANY GOOD AT MATH.
I CAN'T LIE TO YOU, LIEUTENANT.
OUR OPTIONS ARE LIMITED. I'LL DO THE BEST I CAN.
I... I UNDERSTAND.
IT'S MY FAULT. I CONVINCED HIM TO JOIN ME ON ACTIVE DUTY.
HE WAS NEVER MEANT TO BE BEAMING DOWN TO UNEXPLORED PLANETS ON AWAY TEAMS. HE SHOULD BE SITTING BEHIND A DESK IN SAN FRANCISCO...
AND IF HE HADN'T BEEN ON HIS AWAY MISSION, HE WOULDN'T HAVE BEEN ABLE TO SAVE THE LIVES OF TWO FELLOW CREWMEMBERS.
WHATEVER INFECTED HIM ON THAT PLANET, LET'S JUST BE GLAD HE STILL MADE IT BACK ONBOARD.
YOU'RE RIGHT. I'M NOT HELPING HIM BY REGRETTING ANYTHING.
TELL ME, DOCTOR, WHAT MADE YOU WANT TO ENLIST? WHAT MADE YOU WANT TO SIGN UP FOR THIS?
WEIGHING THE VARIABLES AGAIN.
DO I MAKE A JOKE ABOUT ESCAPING MY EX-WIFE...

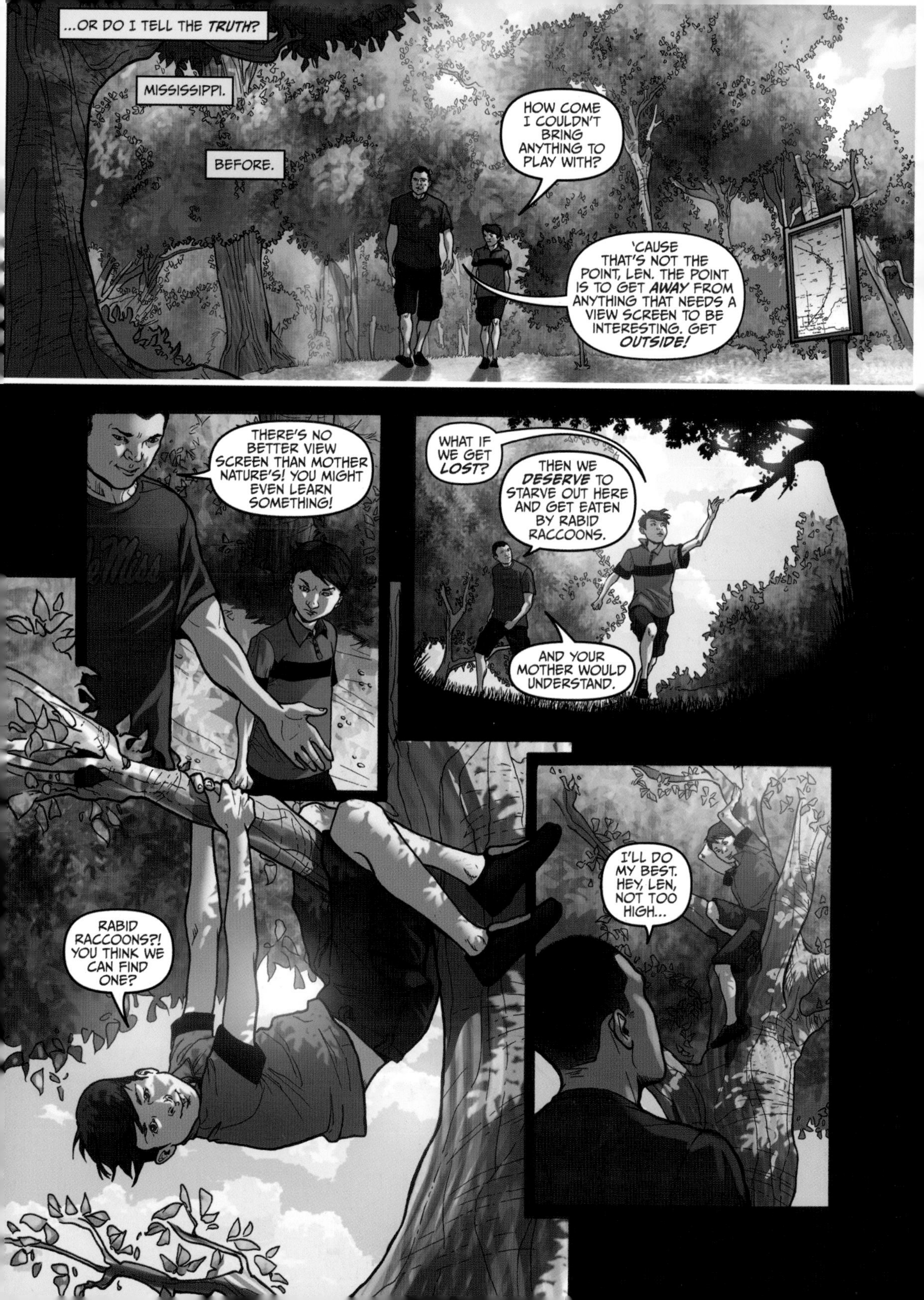
...OR DO I TELL THE *TRUTH*?
MISSISSIPPI.
BEFORE.
HOW COME I COULDN'T BRING ANYTHING TO PLAY WITH?
'CAUSE THAT'S NOT THE POINT, LEN. THE POINT IS TO GET *AWAY* FROM ANYTHING THAT NEEDS A VIEW SCREEN TO BE INTERESTING. GET *OUTSIDE!*
THERE'S NO BETTER VIEW SCREEN THAN MOTHER NATURE'S! YOU MIGHT EVEN LEARN SOMETHING!
WHAT IF WE GET *LOST*?
THEN WE *DESERVE* TO STARVE OUT HERE AND GET EATEN BY RABID RACCOONS.
AND YOUR MOTHER WOULD UNDERSTAND.
RABID RACCOONS?! YOU THINK WE CAN FIND ONE?
I'LL DO MY BEST. HEY, LEN, NOT TOO HIGH...

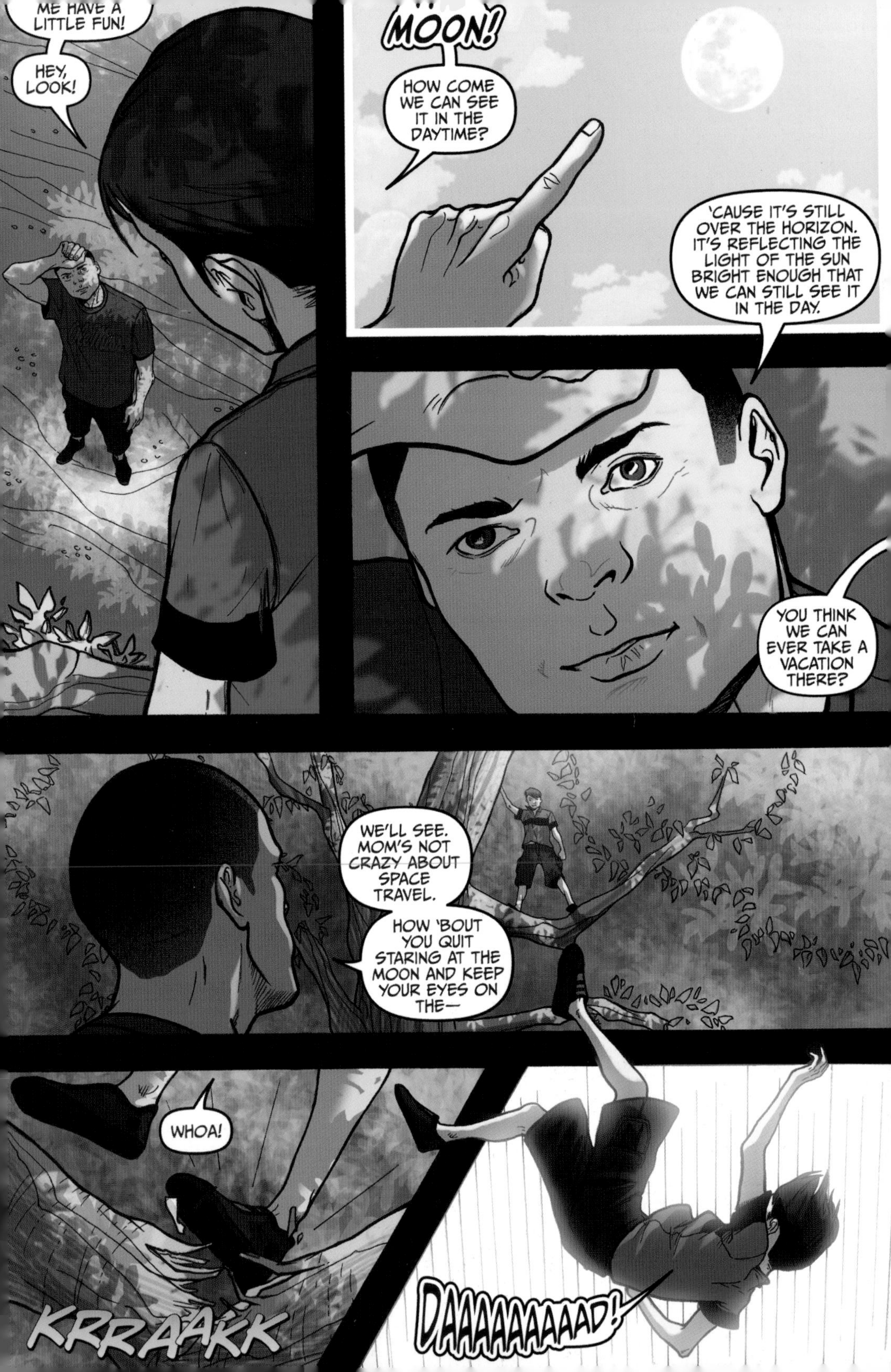
ME HAVE A LITTLE FUN!
HEY, LOOK!
MOON!
HOW COME WE CAN SEE IT IN THE DAYTIME?
'CAUSE IT'S STILL OVER THE HORIZON. IT'S REFLECTING THE LIGHT OF THE SUN BRIGHT ENOUGH THAT WE CAN STILL SEE IT IN THE DAY.
YOU THINK WE CAN EVER TAKE A VACATION THERE?
WE'LL SEE. MOM'S NOT CRAZY ABOUT SPACE TRAVEL.
HOW 'BOUT YOU QUIT STARING AT THE MOON AND KEEP YOUR EYES ON THE—
WHOA!
KRRAAKK
DAAAAAAAAD!

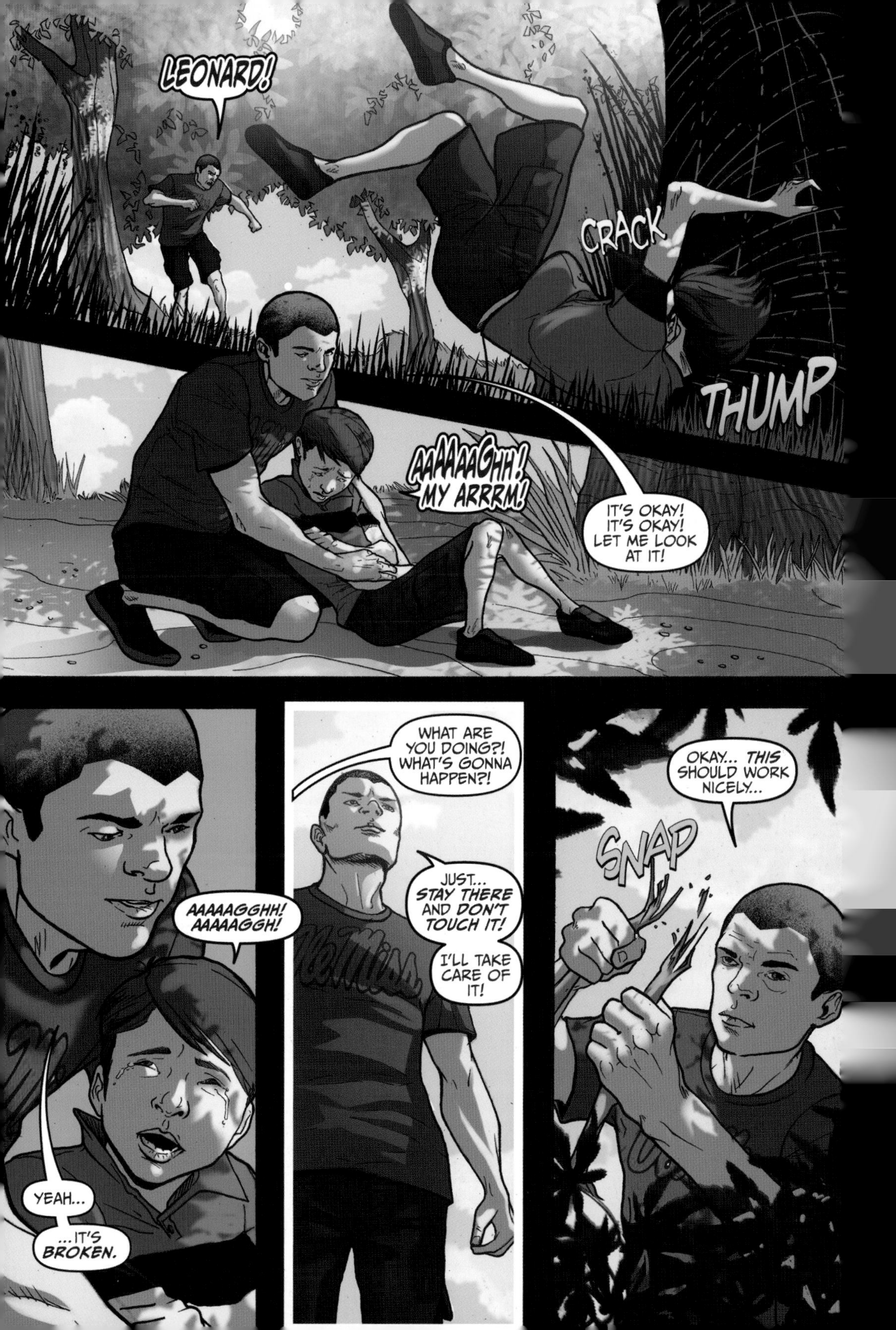
LEONARD!
CRACK
THUMP
AAAAAAGHH! MY ARRRM!
IT'S OKAY! IT'S OKAY! LET ME LOOK AT IT!
AAAAAGGHH! AAAAAGGH!
YEAH...
...IT'S BROKEN.
WHAT ARE YOU DOING?! WHAT'S GONNA HAPPEN?!
JUST... STAY THERE AND DON'T TOUCH IT!
I'LL TAKE CARE OF IT!
OKAY... THIS SHOULD WORK NICELY...
SNAP

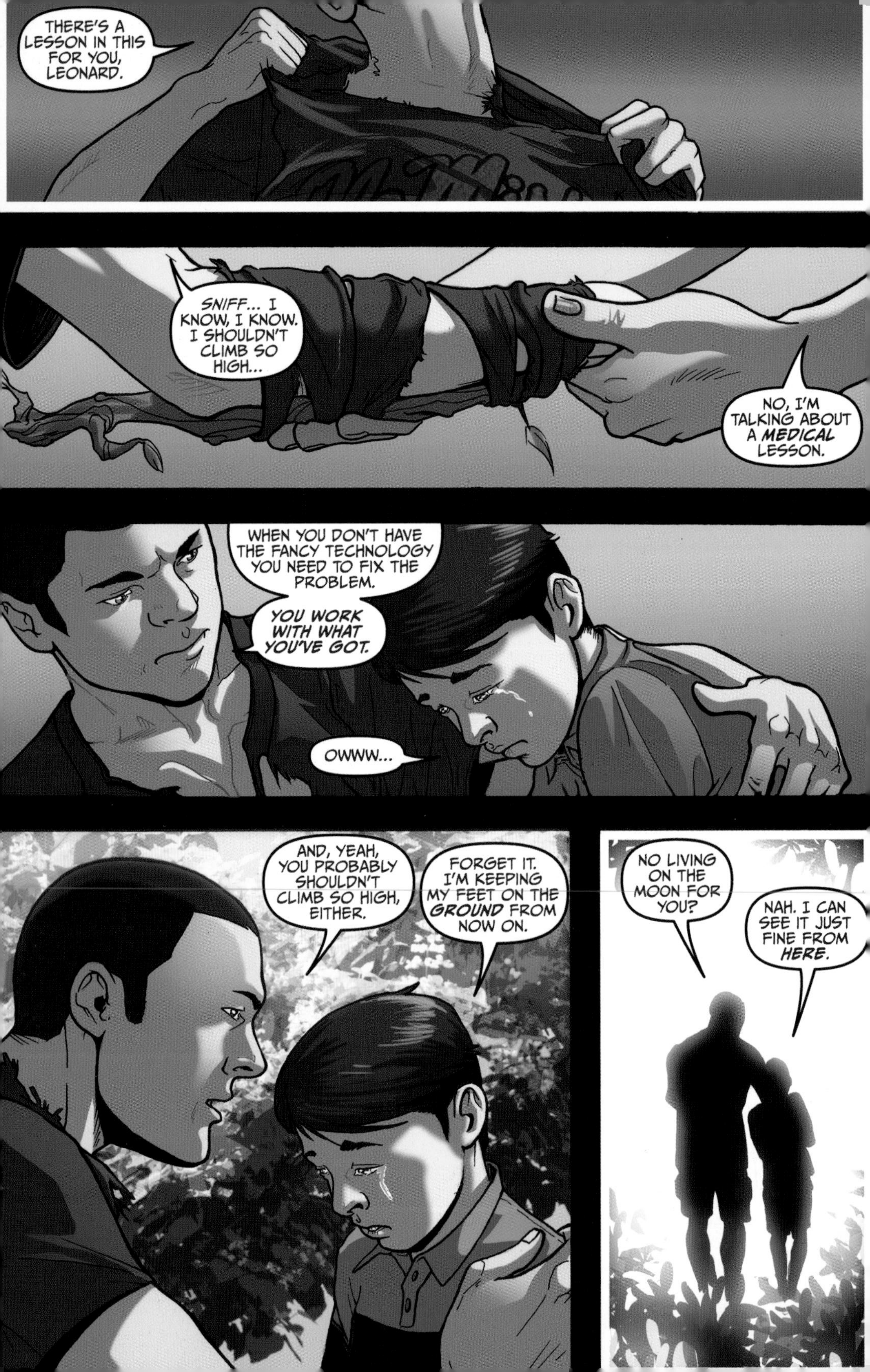
THERE'S A LESSON IN THIS FOR YOU, LEONARD.
SNIFF... I KNOW, I KNOW. I SHOULDN'T CLIMB SO HIGH...
NO, I'M TALKING ABOUT A MEDICAL LESSON.
WHEN YOU DON'T HAVE THE FANCY TECHNOLOGY YOU NEED TO FIX THE PROBLEM.
YOU WORK WITH WHAT YOU'VE GOT.
OWWW...
AND, YEAH, YOU PROBABLY SHOULDN'T CLIMB SO HIGH, EITHER.
FORGET IT. I'M KEEPING MY FEET ON THE GROUND FROM NOW ON.
NO LIVING ON THE MOON FOR YOU?
NAH. I CAN SEE IT JUST FINE FROM HERE.

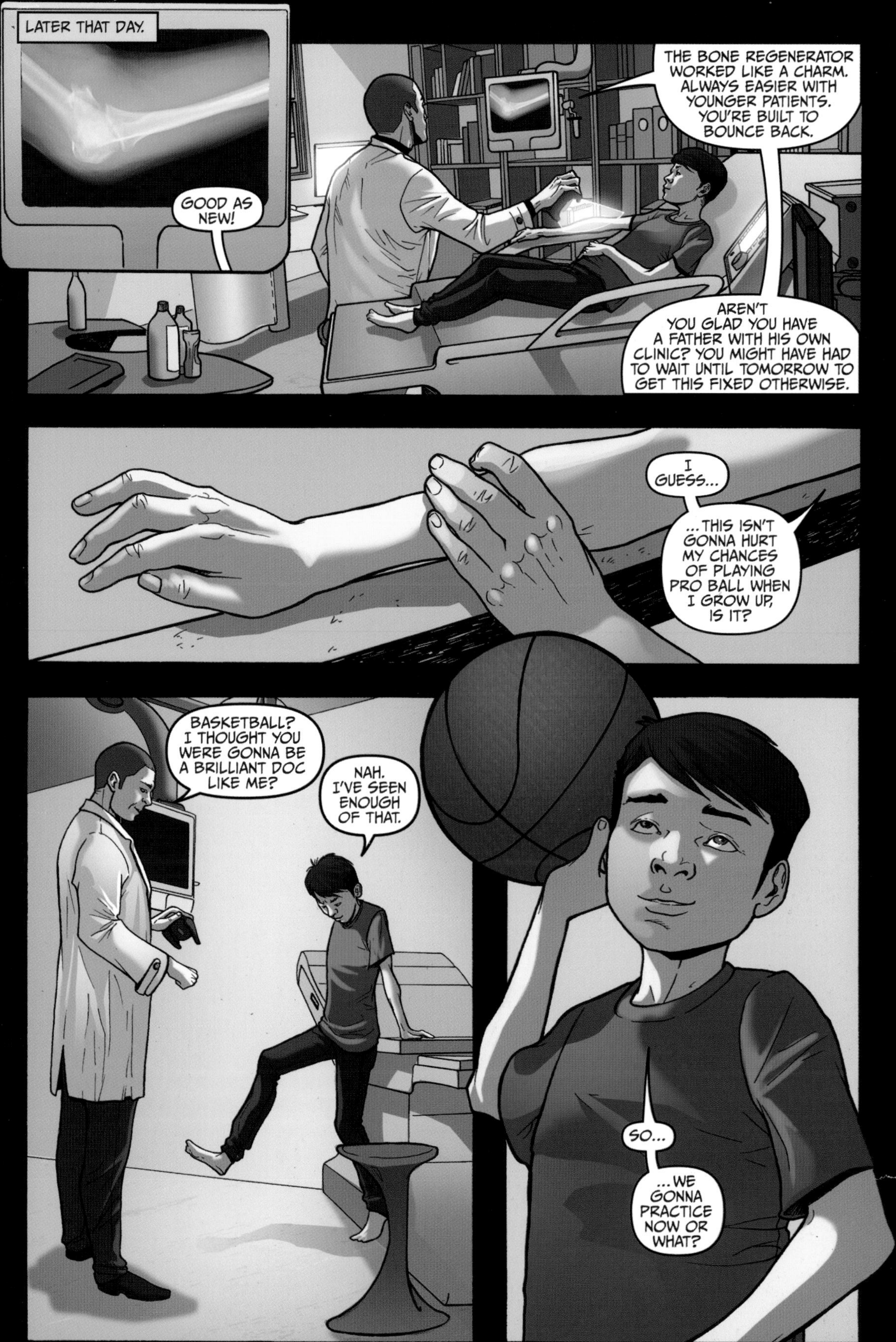
LATER THAT DAY.
THE BONE REGENERATOR WORKED LIKE A CHARM. ALWAYS EASIER WITH YOUNGER PATIENTS. YOU'RE BUILT TO BOUNCE BACK.
GOOD AS NEW!
AREN'T YOU GLAD YOU HAVE A FATHER WITH HIS OWN CLINIC? YOU MIGHT HAVE HAD TO WAIT UNTIL TOMORROW TO GET THIS FIXED OTHERWISE.
I GUESS...
...THIS ISN'T GONNA HURT MY CHANCES OF PLAYING PRO BALL WHEN I GROW UP, IS IT?
BASKETBALL? I THOUGHT YOU WERE GONNA BE A BRILLIANT DOC LIKE ME?
NAH. I'VE SEEN ENOUGH OF THAT.
SO...
...WE GONNA PRACTICE NOW OR WHAT?

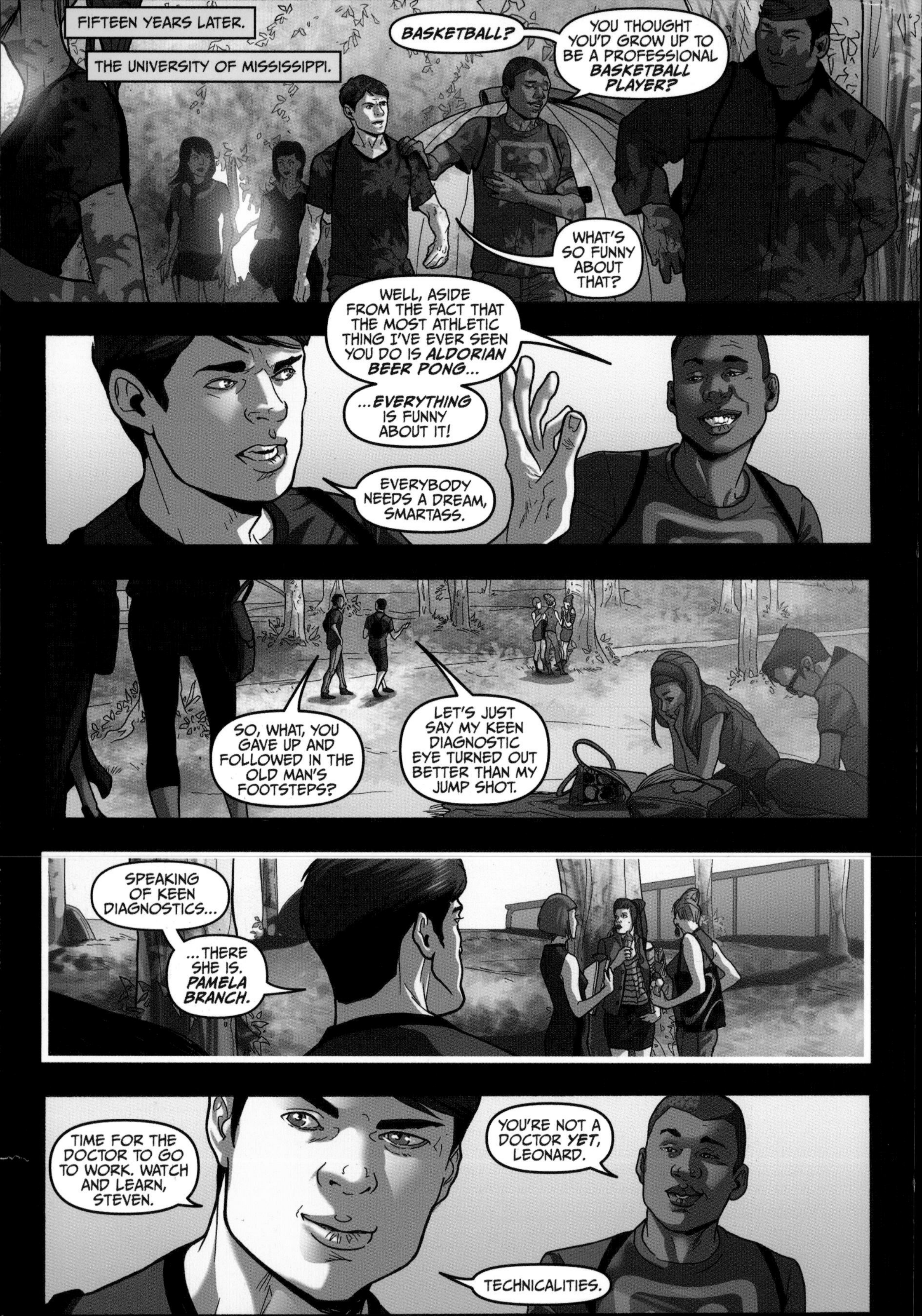
FIFTEEN YEARS LATER.
THE UNIVERSITY OF MISSISSIPPI.
BASKETBALL?
YOU THOUGHT YOU'D GROW UP TO BE A PROFESSIONAL BASKETBALL PLAYER?
WHAT'S SO FUNNY ABOUT THAT?
WELL, ASIDE FROM THE FACT THAT THE MOST ATHLETIC THING I'VE EVER SEEN YOU DO IS ALDORIAN BEER PONG...
...EVERYTHING IS FUNNY ABOUT IT!
EVERYBODY NEEDS A DREAM, SMARTASS.
SO, WHAT, YOU GAVE UP AND FOLLOWED IN THE OLD MAN'S FOOTSTEPS?
LET'S JUST SAY MY KEEN DIAGNOSTIC EYE TURNED OUT BETTER THAN MY JUMP SHOT.
SPEAKING OF KEEN DIAGNOSTICS...
...THERE SHE IS. PAMELA BRANCH.
TIME FOR THE DOCTOR TO GO TO WORK. WATCH AND LEARN, STEVEN.
YOU'RE NOT A DOCTOR YET, LEONARD.
TECHNICALITIES.

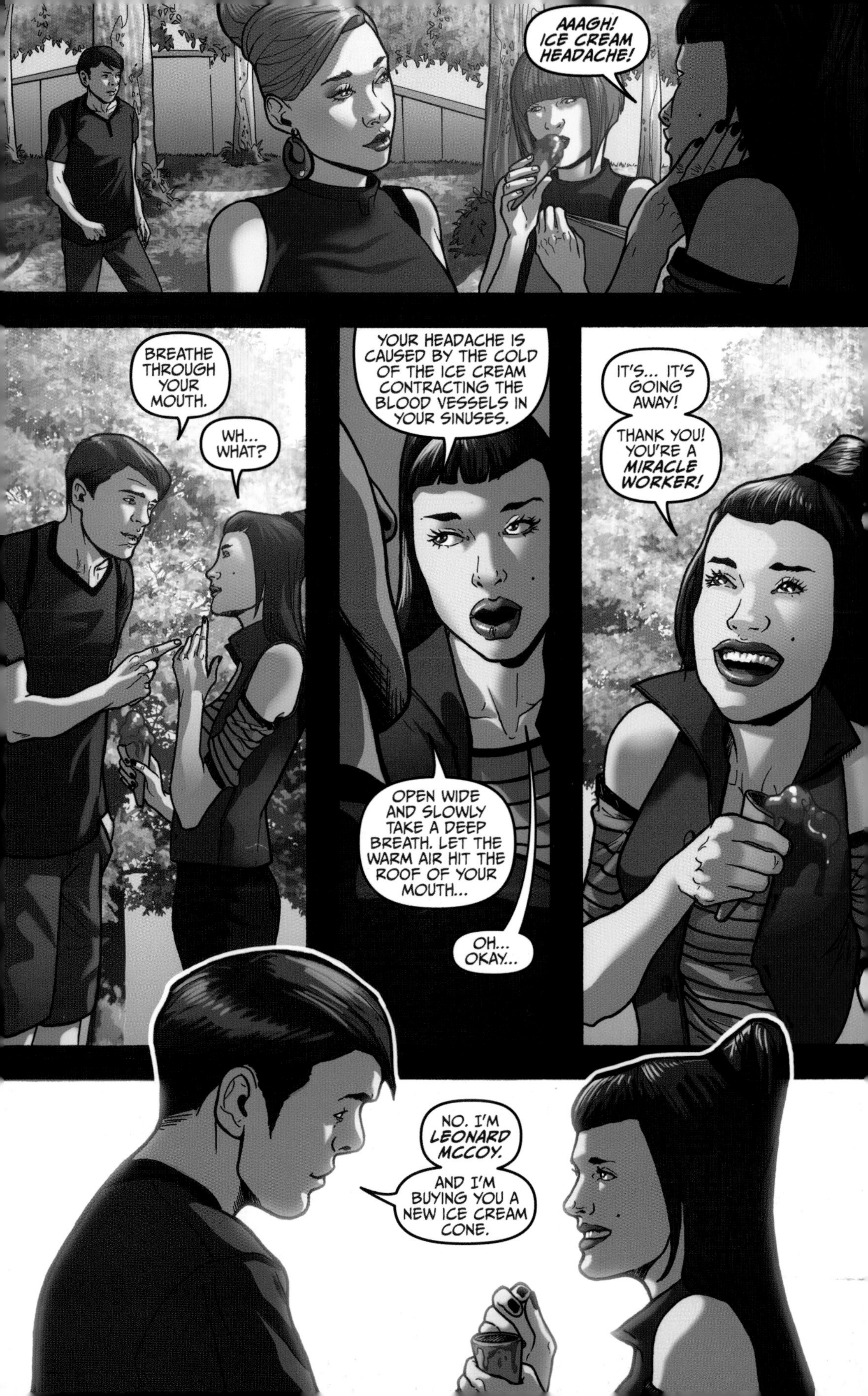
AAAGH! ICE CREAM HEADACHE!
BREATHE THROUGH YOUR MOUTH.
WH... WHAT?
YOUR HEADACHE IS CAUSED BY THE COLD OF THE ICE CREAM CONTRACTING THE BLOOD VESSELS IN YOUR SINUSES.
OPEN WIDE AND SLOWLY TAKE A DEEP BREATH. LET THE WARM AIR HIT THE ROOF OF YOUR MOUTH...
OH... OKAY...
IT'S... IT'S GOING AWAY!
THANK YOU! YOU'RE A MIRACLE WORKER!
NO. I'M LEONARD MCCOY.
AND I'M BUYING YOU A NEW ICE CREAM CONE.

WOW. YOU FINISH FIRST IN YOUR CLASS.

YOU WIN THE MOST PRESTIGIOUS PEDIATRICS JOB IN THE STATE. *AND* YOU GET THE PRETTIEST GIRL IN SCHOOL.

YOU MIGHT HAVE HAD A LOUSY JUMP SHOT, LEN...

...BUT YOU'RE STILL THE CHAMP!

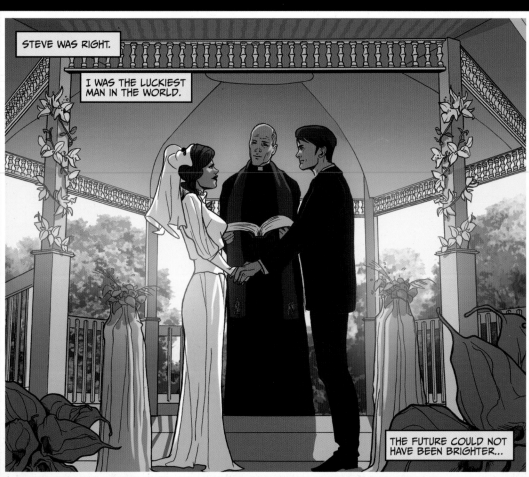

STEVE WAS RIGHT.

I WAS THE LUCKIEST MAN IN THE WORLD.

THE FUTURE COULD NOT HAVE BEEN BRIGHTER...

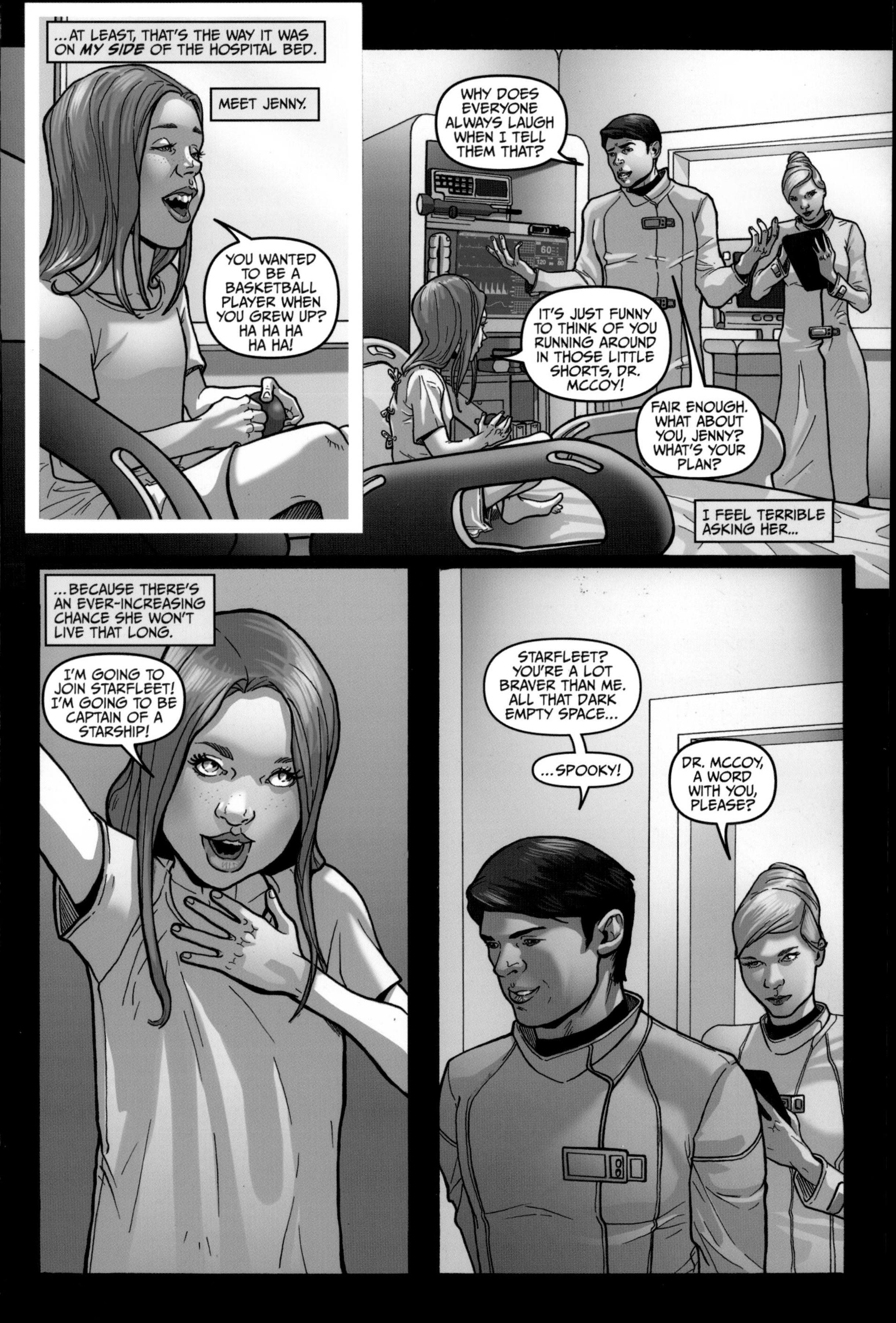
...AT LEAST, THAT'S THE WAY IT WAS ON MY SIDE OF THE HOSPITAL BED.
MEET JENNY.
YOU WANTED TO BE A BASKETBALL PLAYER WHEN YOU GREW UP? HA HA HA HA HA!
WHY DOES EVERYONE ALWAYS LAUGH WHEN I TELL THEM THAT?
IT'S JUST FUNNY TO THINK OF YOU RUNNING AROUND IN THOSE LITTLE SHORTS, DR. MCCOY!
FAIR ENOUGH. WHAT ABOUT YOU, JENNY? WHAT'S YOUR PLAN?
I FEEL TERRIBLE ASKING HER...
...BECAUSE THERE'S AN EVER-INCREASING CHANCE SHE WON'T LIVE THAT LONG.
I'M GOING TO JOIN STARFLEET! I'M GOING TO BE CAPTAIN OF A STARSHIP!
STARFLEET? YOU'RE A LOT BRAVER THAN ME. ALL THAT DARK EMPTY SPACE...
...SPOOKY!
DR. MCCOY, A WORD WITH YOU, PLEASE?

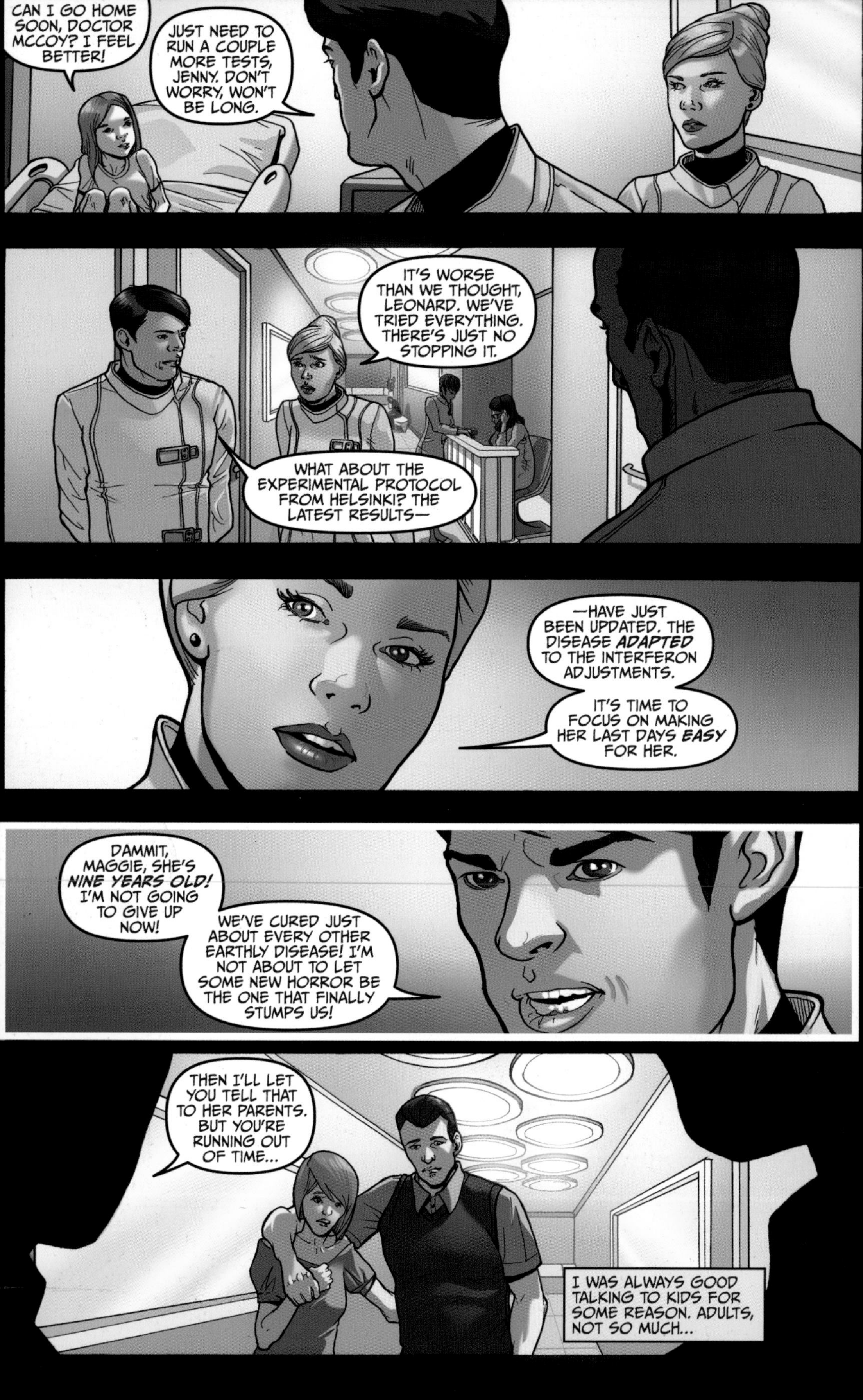
CAN I GO HOME SOON, DOCTOR MCCOY? I FEEL BETTER!
JUST NEED TO RUN A COUPLE MORE TESTS, JENNY. DON'T WORRY, WON'T BE LONG.
IT'S WORSE THAN WE THOUGHT, LEONARD. WE'VE TRIED EVERYTHING. THERE'S JUST NO STOPPING IT.
WHAT ABOUT THE EXPERIMENTAL PROTOCOL FROM HELSINKI? THE LATEST RESULTS—
—HAVE JUST BEEN UPDATED. THE DISEASE *ADAPTED* TO THE INTERFERON ADJUSTMENTS.
IT'S TIME TO FOCUS ON MAKING HER LAST DAYS *EASY* FOR HER.
DAMMIT, MAGGIE, SHE'S *NINE YEARS OLD!* I'M NOT GOING TO GIVE UP NOW!
WE'VE CURED JUST ABOUT EVERY OTHER EARTHLY DISEASE! I'M NOT ABOUT TO LET SOME NEW HORROR BE THE ONE THAT FINALLY STUMPS US!
THEN I'LL LET YOU TELL THAT TO HER PARENTS. BUT YOU'RE RUNNING OUT OF TIME...
I WAS ALWAYS GOOD TALKING TO KIDS FOR SOME REASON. ADULTS, NOT SO MUCH...

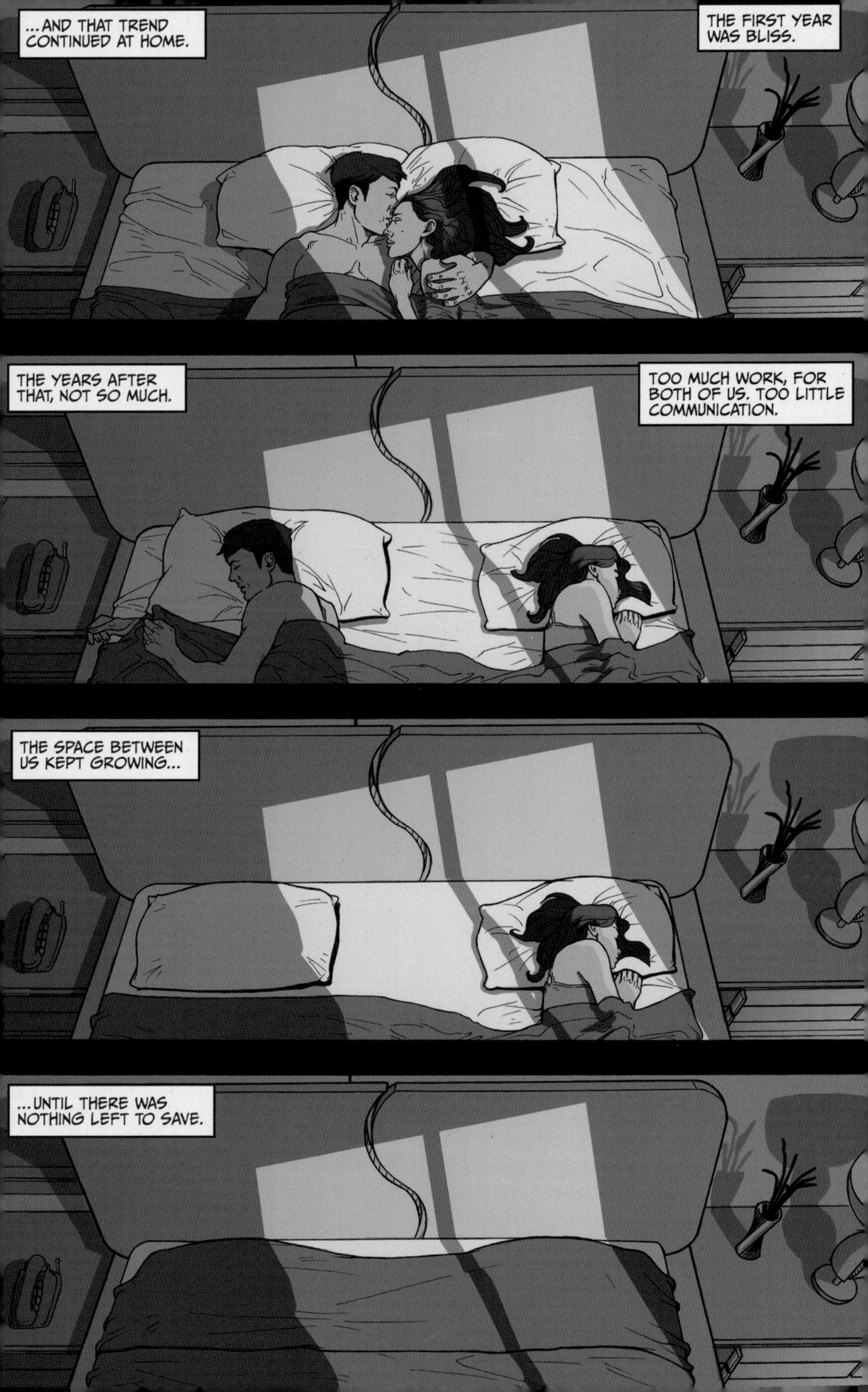
...AND THAT TREND CONTINUED AT HOME.
THE FIRST YEAR WAS BLISS.
THE YEARS AFTER THAT, NOT SO MUCH.
TOO MUCH WORK, FOR BOTH OF US. TOO LITTLE COMMUNICATION.
THE SPACE BETWEEN US KEPT GROWING...
...UNTIL THERE WAS NOTHING LEFT TO SAVE.

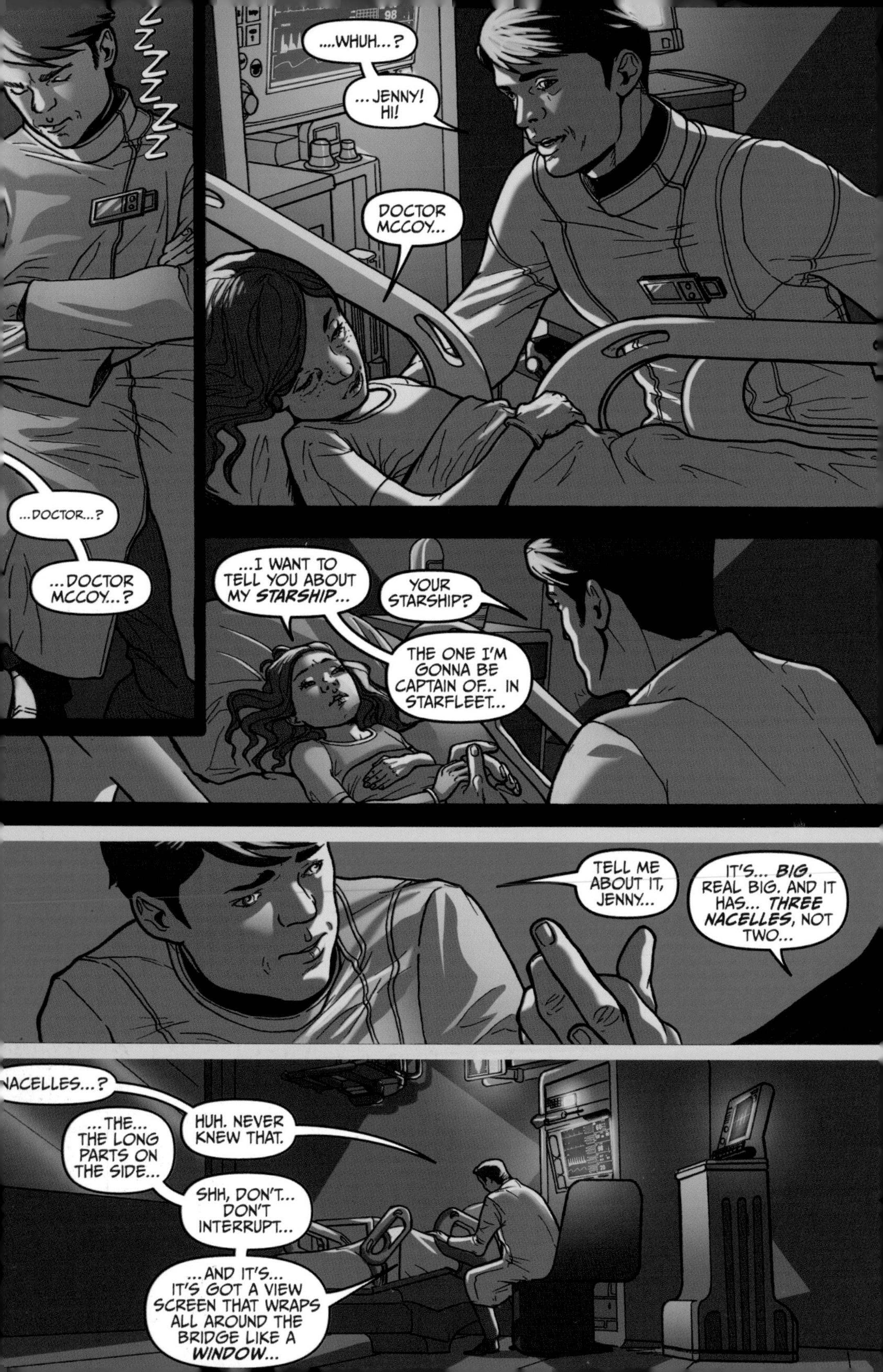
ZZZZZ
....WHUH...?
...JENNY! HI!
DOCTOR MCCOY...
...DOCTOR...?
...DOCTOR MCCOY...?
...I WANT TO TELL YOU ABOUT MY STARSHIP...
YOUR STARSHIP?
THE ONE I'M GONNA BE CAPTAIN OF... IN STARFLEET...
TELL ME ABOUT IT, JENNY...
IT'S... BIG. REAL BIG. AND IT HAS... THREE NACELLES, NOT TWO...
NACELLES...?
...THE... THE LONG PARTS ON THE SIDE...
HUH. NEVER KNEW THAT.
SHH, DON'T... DON'T INTERRUPT...
...AND IT'S... IT'S GOT A VIEW SCREEN THAT WRAPS ALL AROUND THE BRIDGE LIKE A WINDOW...

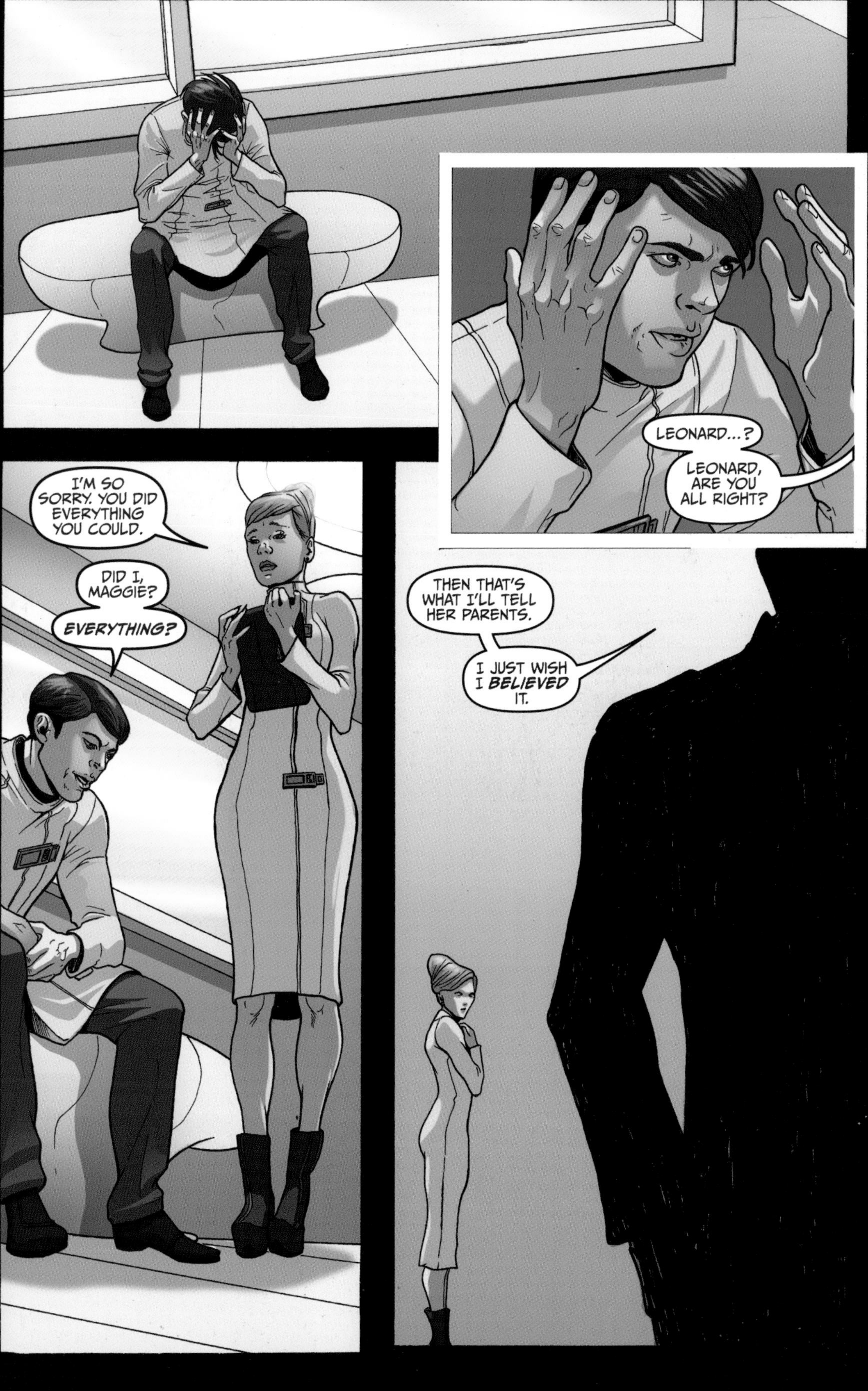
LEONARD...?
LEONARD, ARE YOU ALL RIGHT?
I'M SO SORRY. YOU DID EVERYTHING YOU COULD.
DID I, MAGGIE?
EVERYTHING?
THEN THAT'S WHAT I'LL TELL HER PARENTS.
I JUST WISH I *BELIEVED* IT.

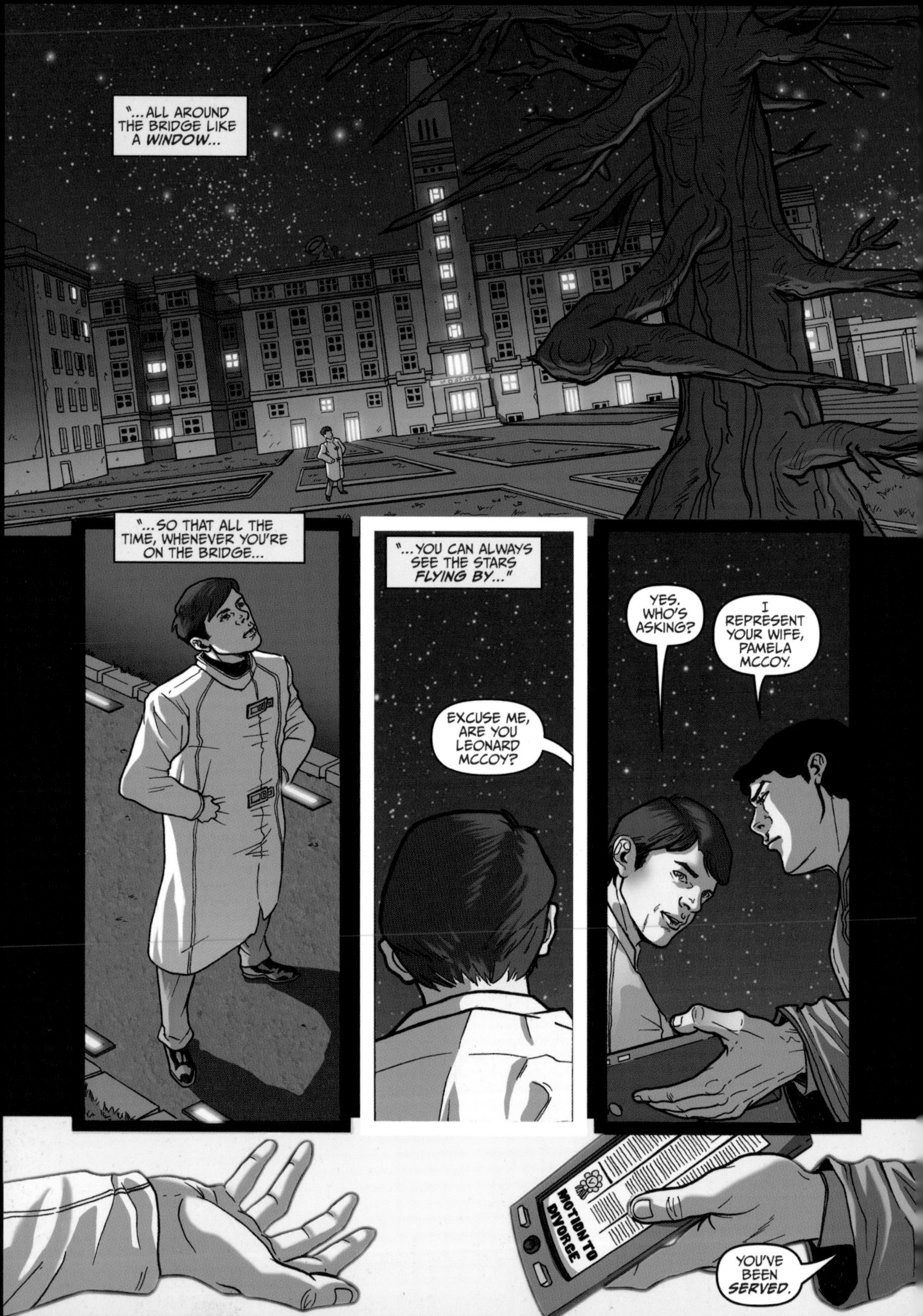
"...ALL AROUND THE BRIDGE LIKE A *WINDOW*...
"...SO THAT ALL THE TIME, WHENEVER YOU'RE ON THE BRIDGE...
"...YOU CAN ALWAYS SEE THE STARS *FLYING BY*..."
EXCUSE ME, ARE YOU LEONARD MCCOY?
YES. WHO'S ASKING?
I REPRESENT YOUR WIFE, PAMELA MCCOY.
MOTION TO DIVORCE
YOU'VE BEEN *SERVED*.

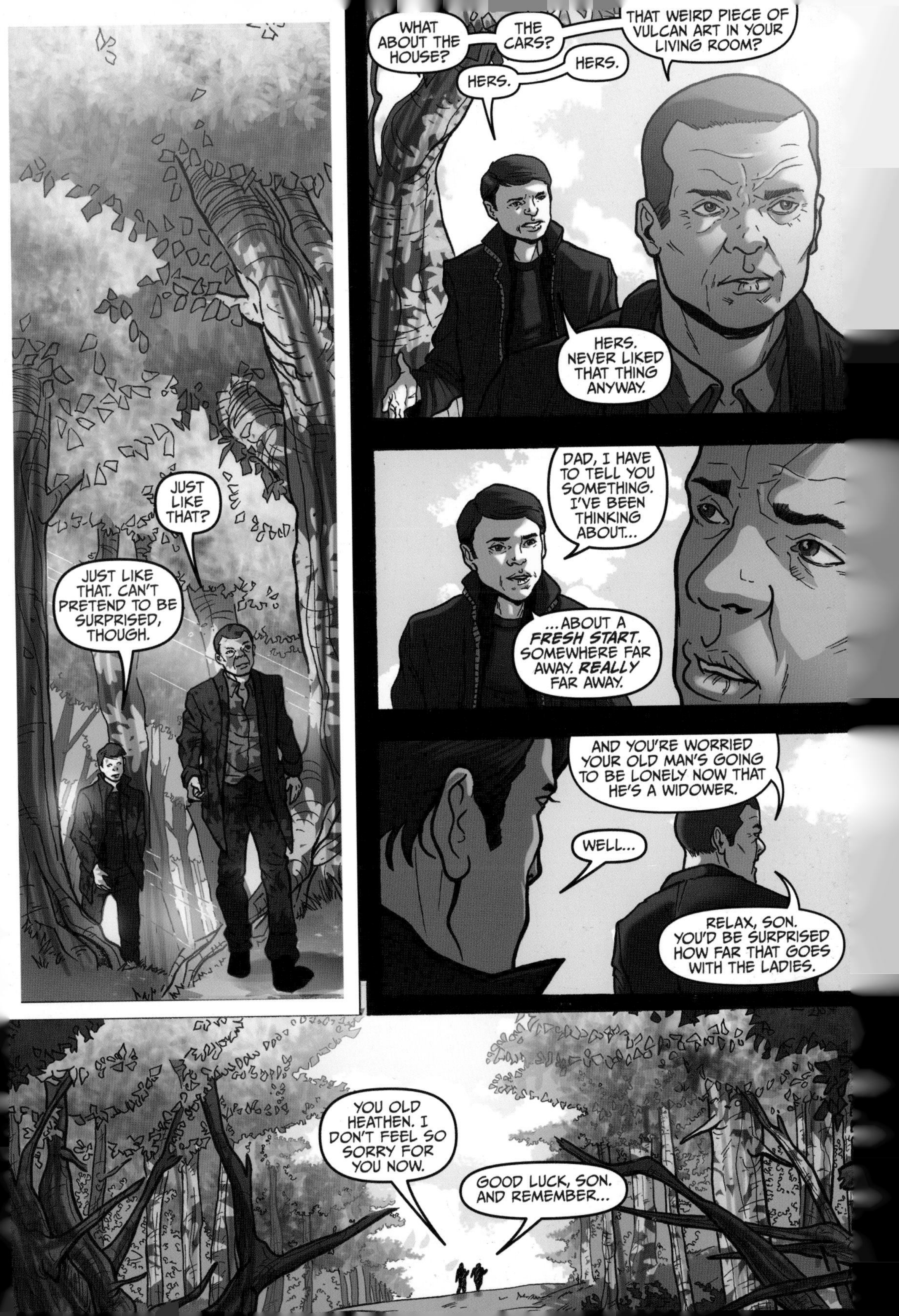

JUST LIKE THAT?
JUST LIKE THAT. CAN'T PRETEND TO BE SURPRISED, THOUGH.
WHAT ABOUT THE HOUSE?
HERS.
THE CARS?
HERS.
THAT WEIRD PIECE OF VULCAN ART IN YOUR LIVING ROOM?
HERS. NEVER LIKED THAT THING ANYWAY.
DAD, I HAVE TO TELL YOU SOMETHING. I'VE BEEN THINKING ABOUT...
...ABOUT A FRESH START. SOMEWHERE FAR AWAY. REALLY FAR AWAY.
AND YOU'RE WORRIED YOUR OLD MAN'S GOING TO BE LONELY NOW THAT HE'S A WIDOWER.
WELL...
RELAX, SON. YOU'D BE SURPRISED HOW FAR THAT GOES WITH THE LADIES.
YOU OLD HEATHEN. I DON'T FEEL SO SORRY FOR YOU NOW.
GOOD LUCK, SON. AND REMEMBER...

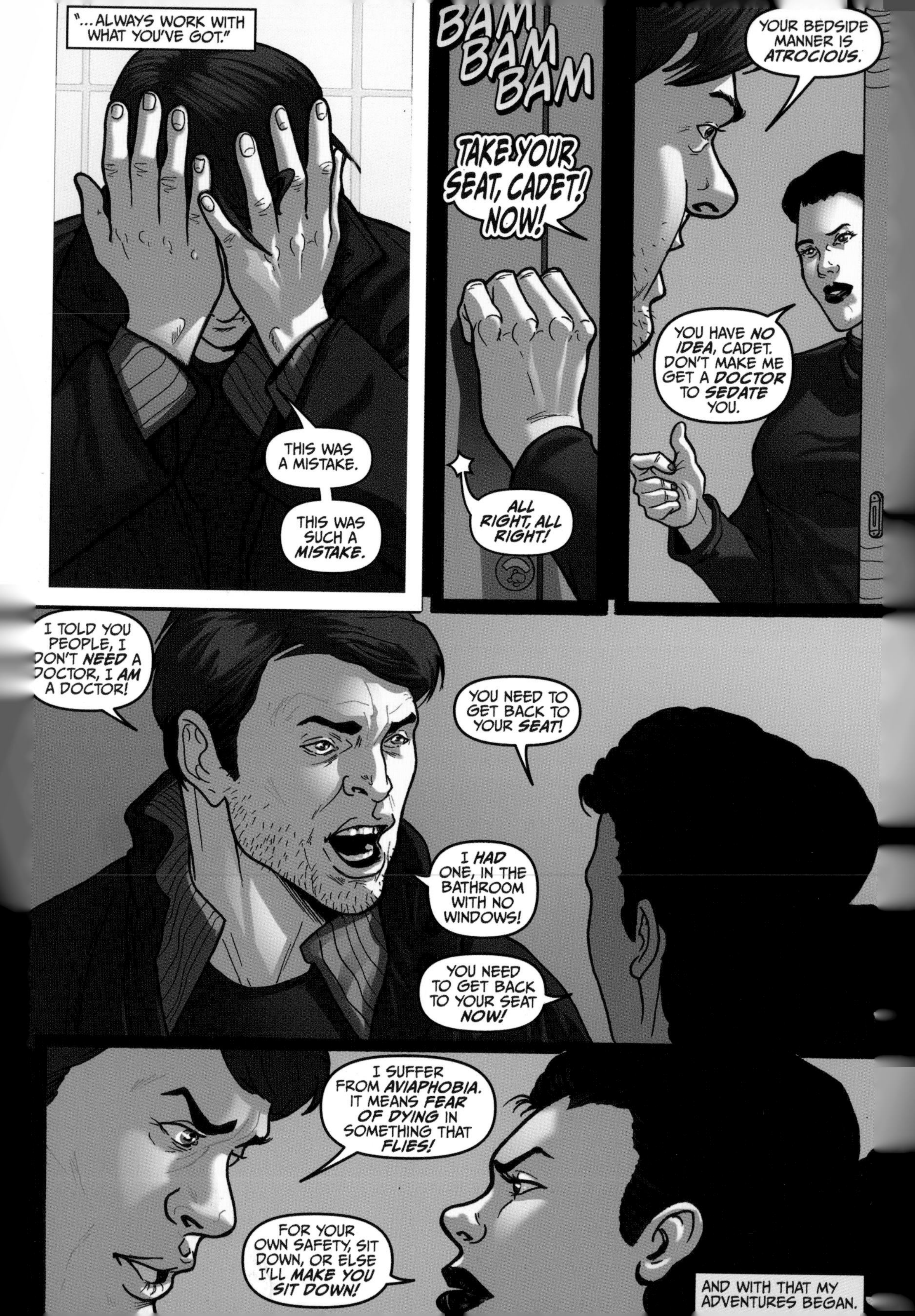
"...ALWAYS WORK WITH WHAT YOU'VE GOT."
THIS WAS A MISTAKE.
THIS WAS SUCH A MISTAKE.
BAM BAM BAM
TAKE YOUR SEAT, CADET! NOW!
ALL RIGHT, ALL RIGHT!
YOUR BEDSIDE MANNER IS ATROCIOUS.
YOU HAVE NO IDEA, CADET. DON'T MAKE ME GET A DOCTOR TO SEDATE YOU.
I TOLD YOU PEOPLE, I DON'T NEED A DOCTOR, I AM A DOCTOR!
YOU NEED TO GET BACK TO YOUR SEAT!
I HAD ONE, IN THE BATHROOM WITH NO WINDOWS!
YOU NEED TO GET BACK TO YOUR SEAT NOW!
I SUFFER FROM AVIAPHOBIA. IT MEANS FEAR OF DYING IN SOMETHING THAT FLIES!
FOR YOUR OWN SAFETY, SIT DOWN, OR ELSE I'LL MAKE YOU SIT DOWN!
AND WITH THAT MY ADVENTURES BEGAN.

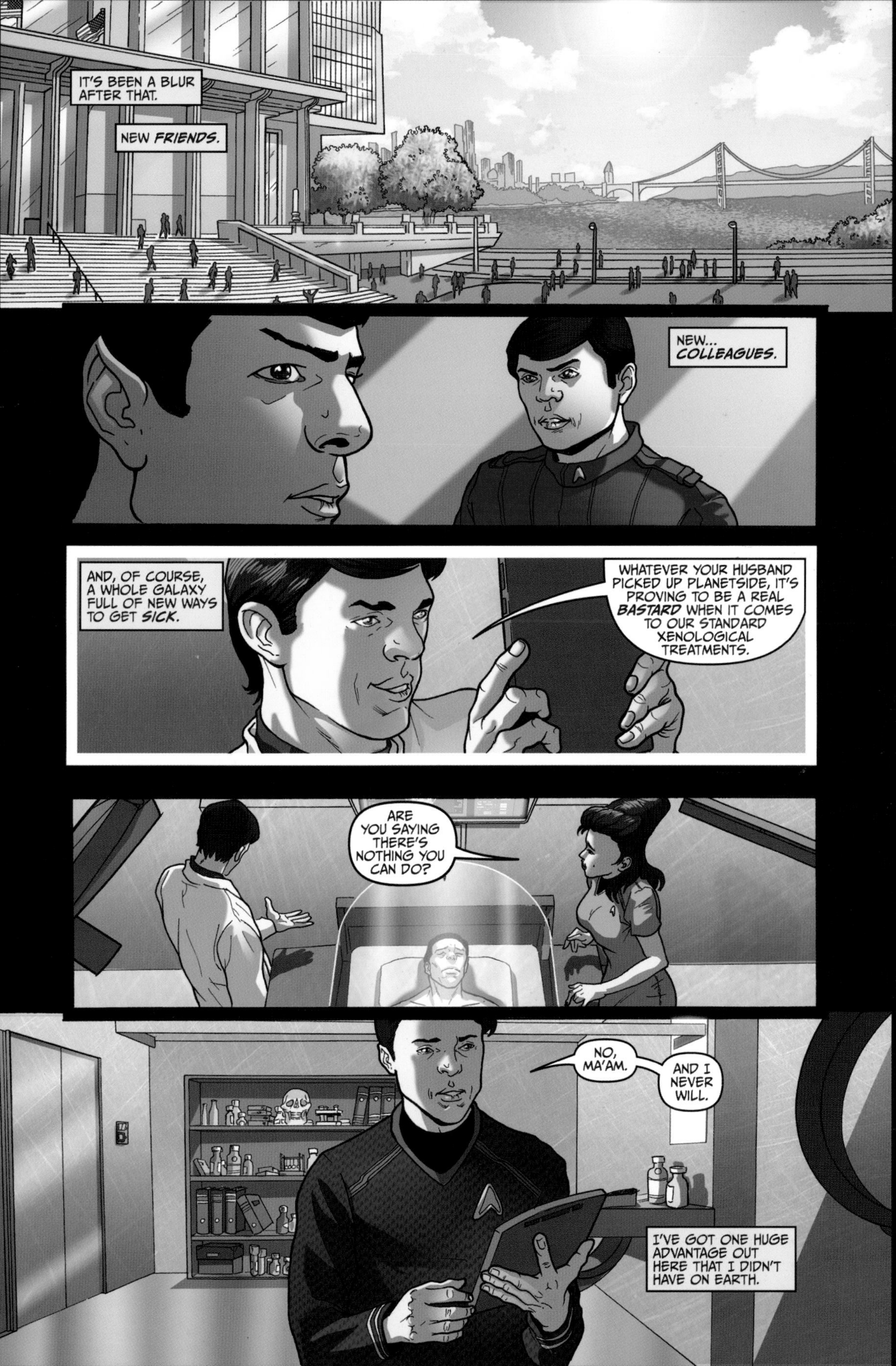
IT'S BEEN A BLUR AFTER THAT.
NEW *FRIENDS*.
NEW... *COLLEAGUES*.
AND, OF COURSE, A WHOLE GALAXY FULL OF NEW WAYS TO GET *SICK*.
WHATEVER YOUR HUSBAND PICKED UP PLANETSIDE, IT'S PROVING TO BE A REAL *BASTARD* WHEN IT COMES TO OUR STANDARD XENOLOGICAL TREATMENTS.
ARE YOU SAYING THERE'S NOTHING YOU CAN DO?
NO, MA'AM.
AND I NEVER WILL.
I'VE GOT ONE HUGE ADVANTAGE OUT HERE THAT I DIDN'T HAVE ON EARTH.

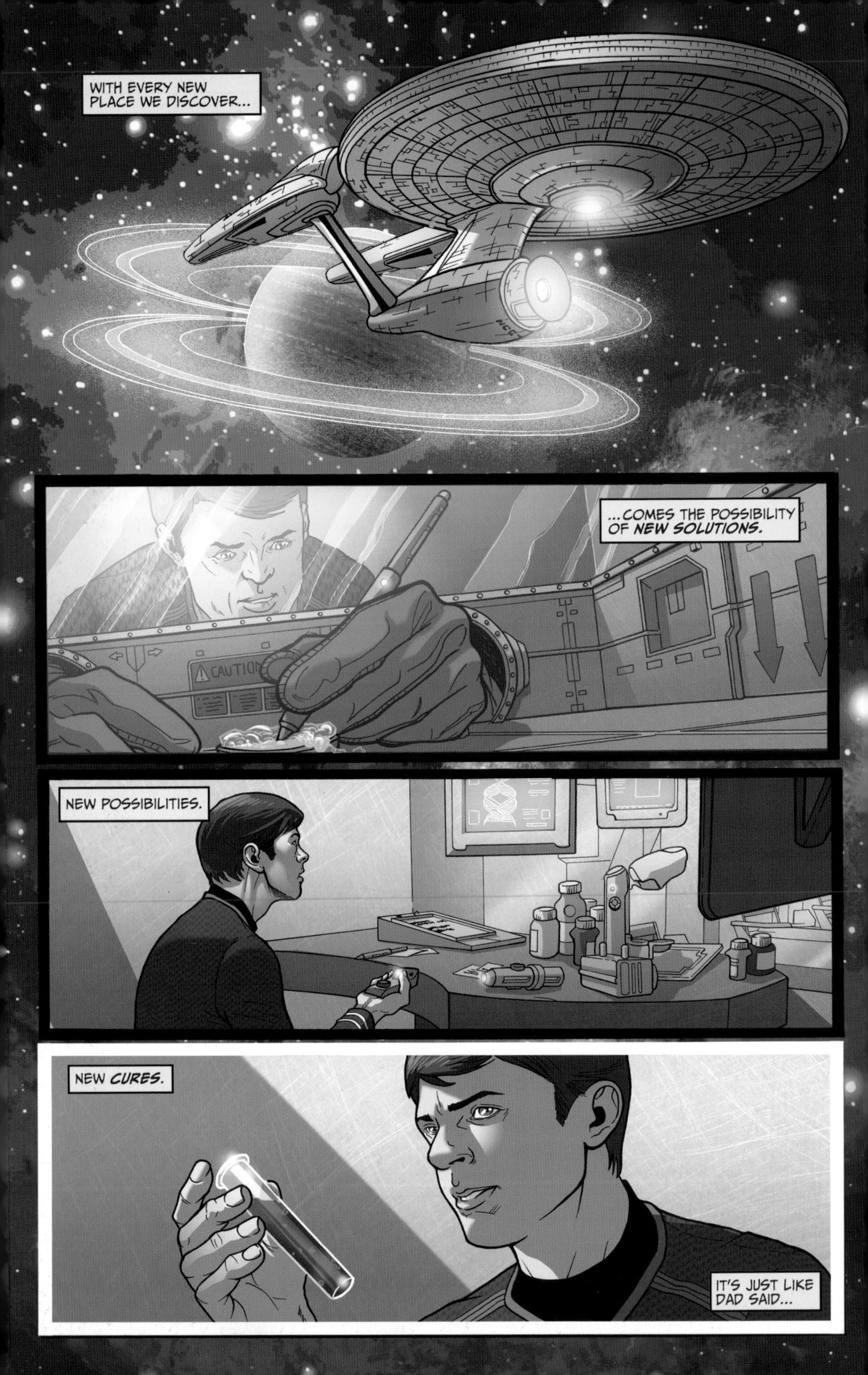
WITH EVERY NEW PLACE WE DISCOVER...
...COMES THE POSSIBILITY OF NEW SOLUTIONS.
CAUTION
NEW POSSIBILITIES.
NEW CURES.
IT'S JUST LIKE DAD SAID...

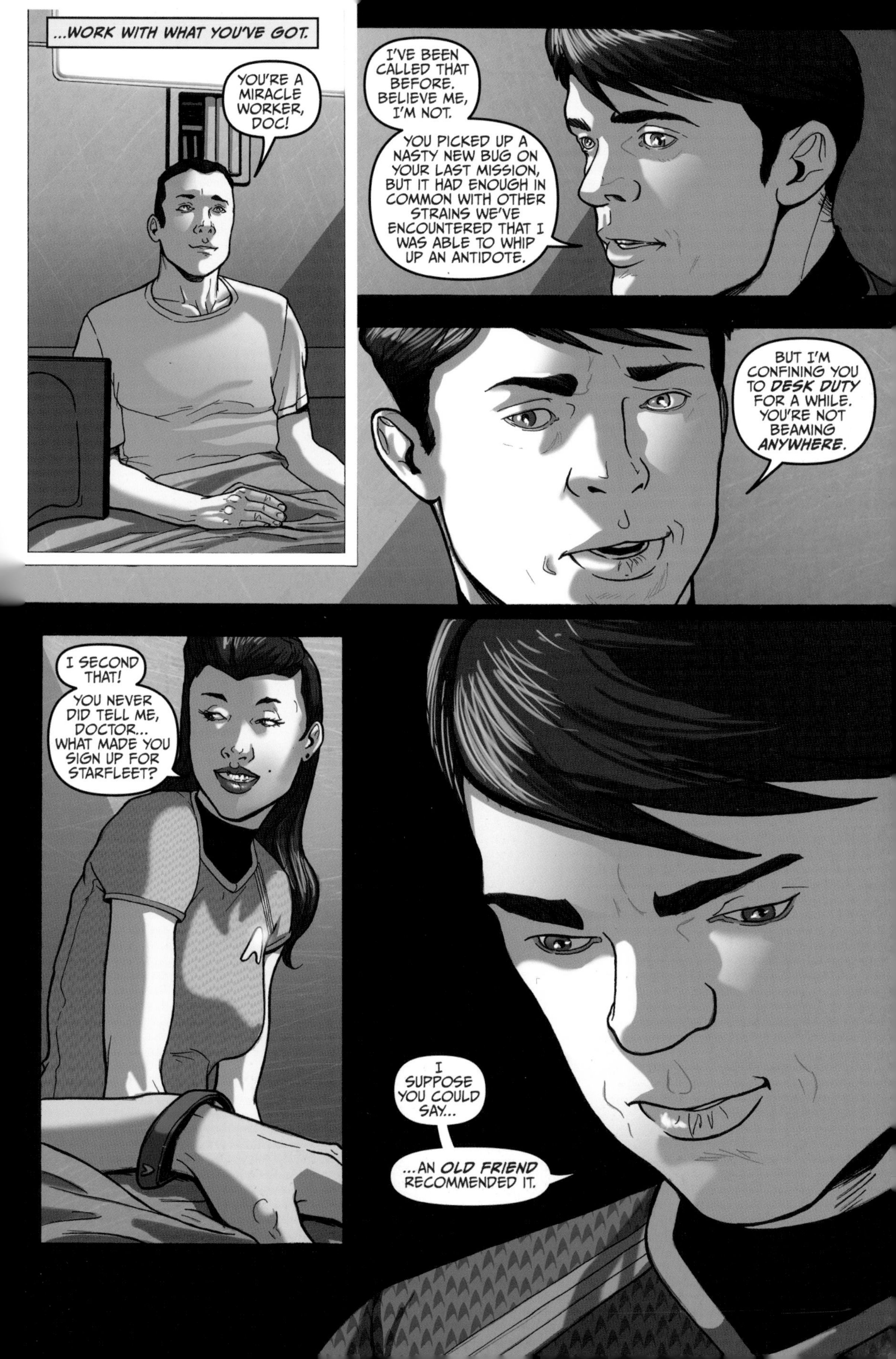
...WORK WITH WHAT YOU'VE GOT.
YOU'RE A MIRACLE WORKER, DOC!
I'VE BEEN CALLED THAT BEFORE. BELIEVE ME, I'M NOT.
YOU PICKED UP A NASTY NEW BUG ON YOUR LAST MISSION, BUT IT HAD ENOUGH IN COMMON WITH OTHER STRAINS WE'VE ENCOUNTERED THAT I WAS ABLE TO WHIP UP AN ANTIDOTE.
BUT I'M CONFINING YOU TO DESK DUTY FOR A WHILE. YOU'RE NOT BEAMING ANYWHERE.
I SECOND THAT!
YOU NEVER DID TELL ME, DOCTOR... WHAT MADE YOU SIGN UP FOR STARFLEET?
I SUPPOSE YOU COULD SAY...
...AN OLD FRIEND RECOMMENDED IT.

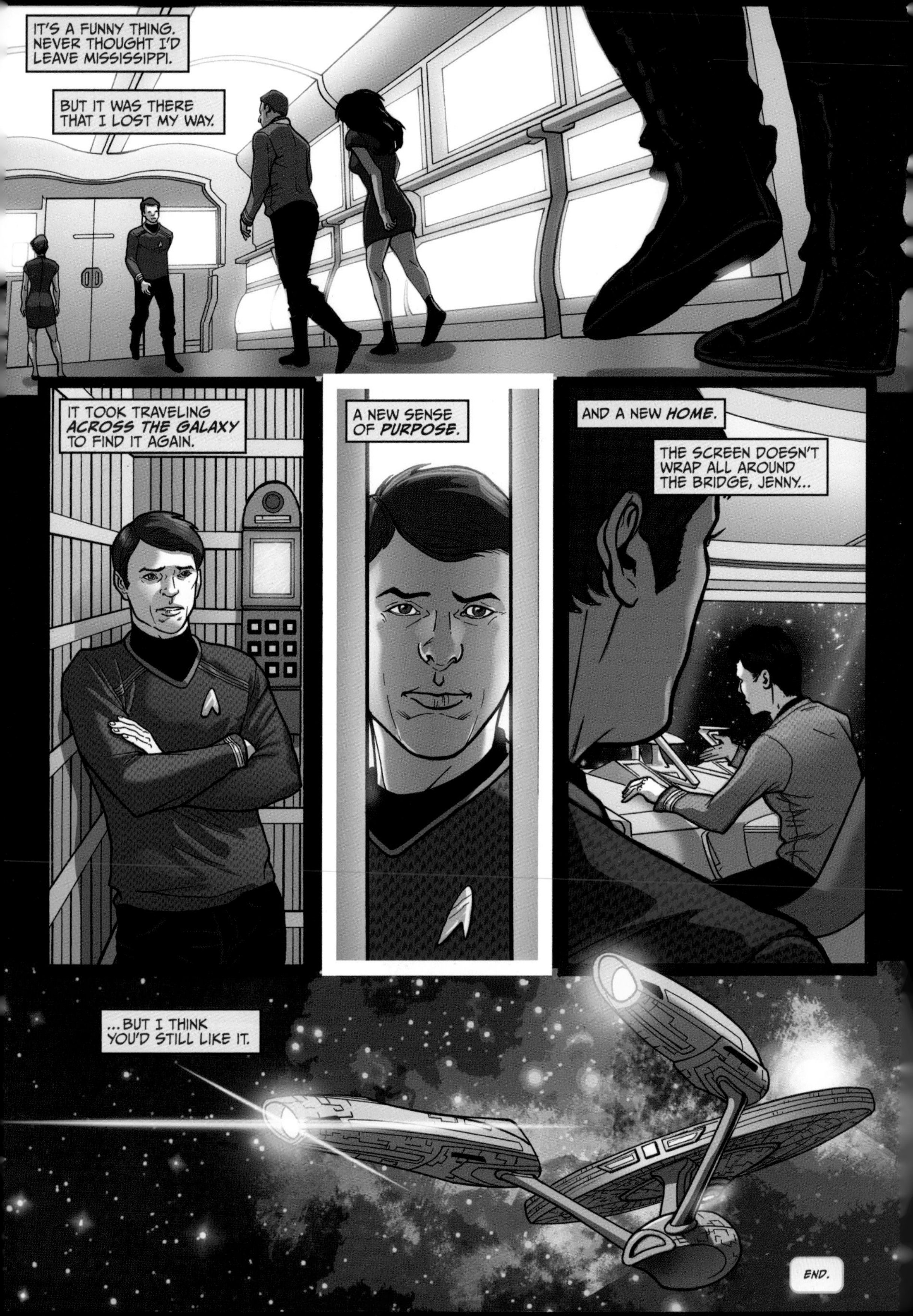
IT'S A FUNNY THING. NEVER THOUGHT I'D LEAVE MISSISSIPPI.
BUT IT WAS THERE THAT I LOST MY WAY.
IT TOOK TRAVELING ACROSS THE GALAXY TO FIND IT AGAIN.
A NEW SENSE OF PURPOSE.
AND A NEW HOME.
THE SCREEN DOESN'T WRAP ALL AROUND THE BRIDGE, JENNY...
...BUT I THINK YOU'D STILL LIKE IT.
END.

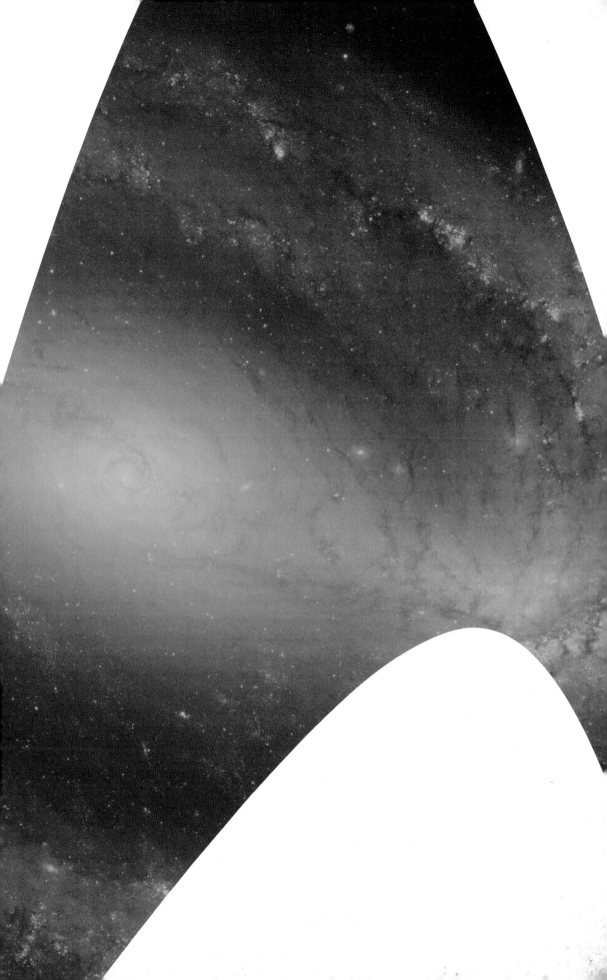

THE VOICE OF A FALLING STAR

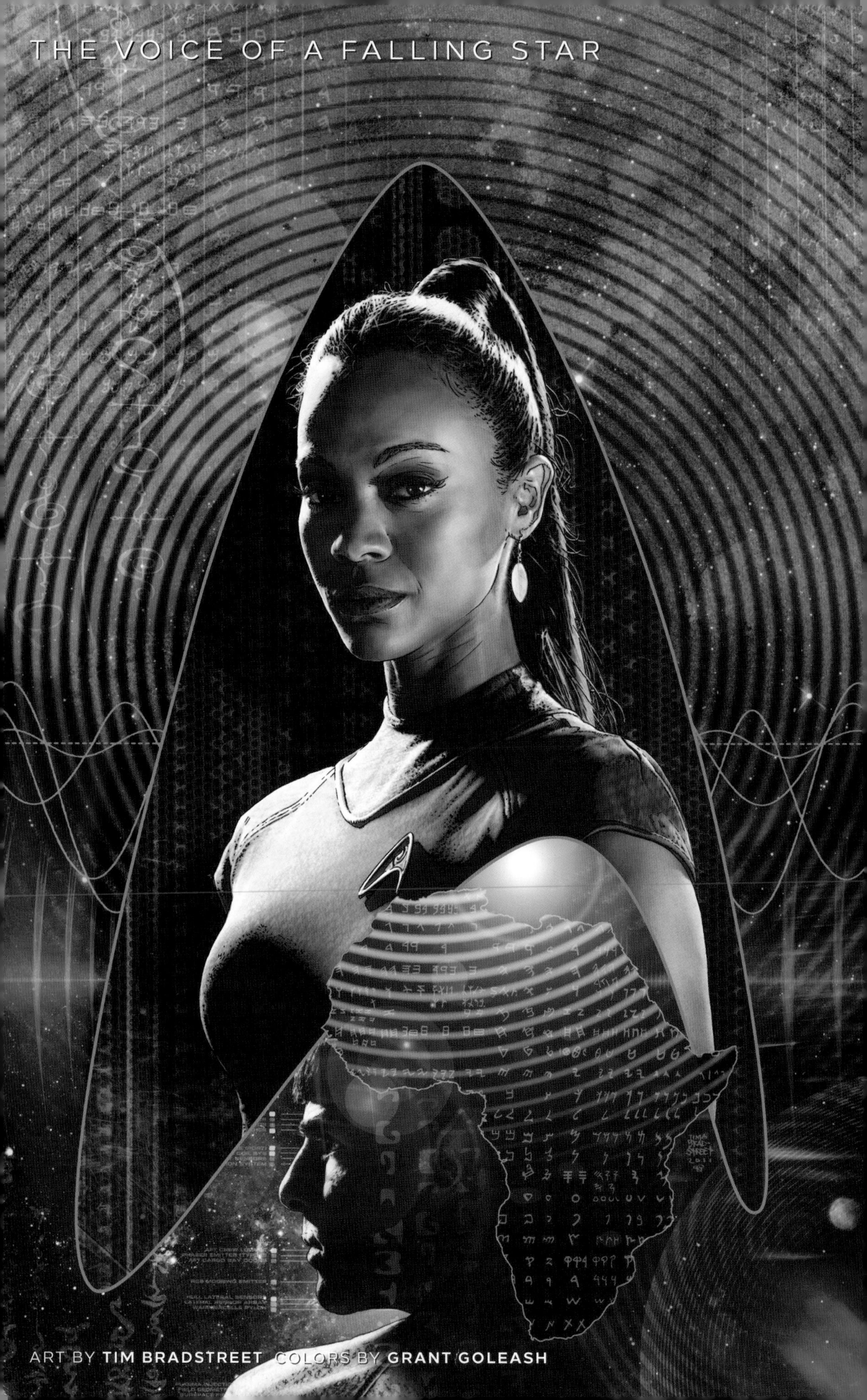

ART BY **TIM BRADSTREET** COLORS BY **GRANT GOLEASH**

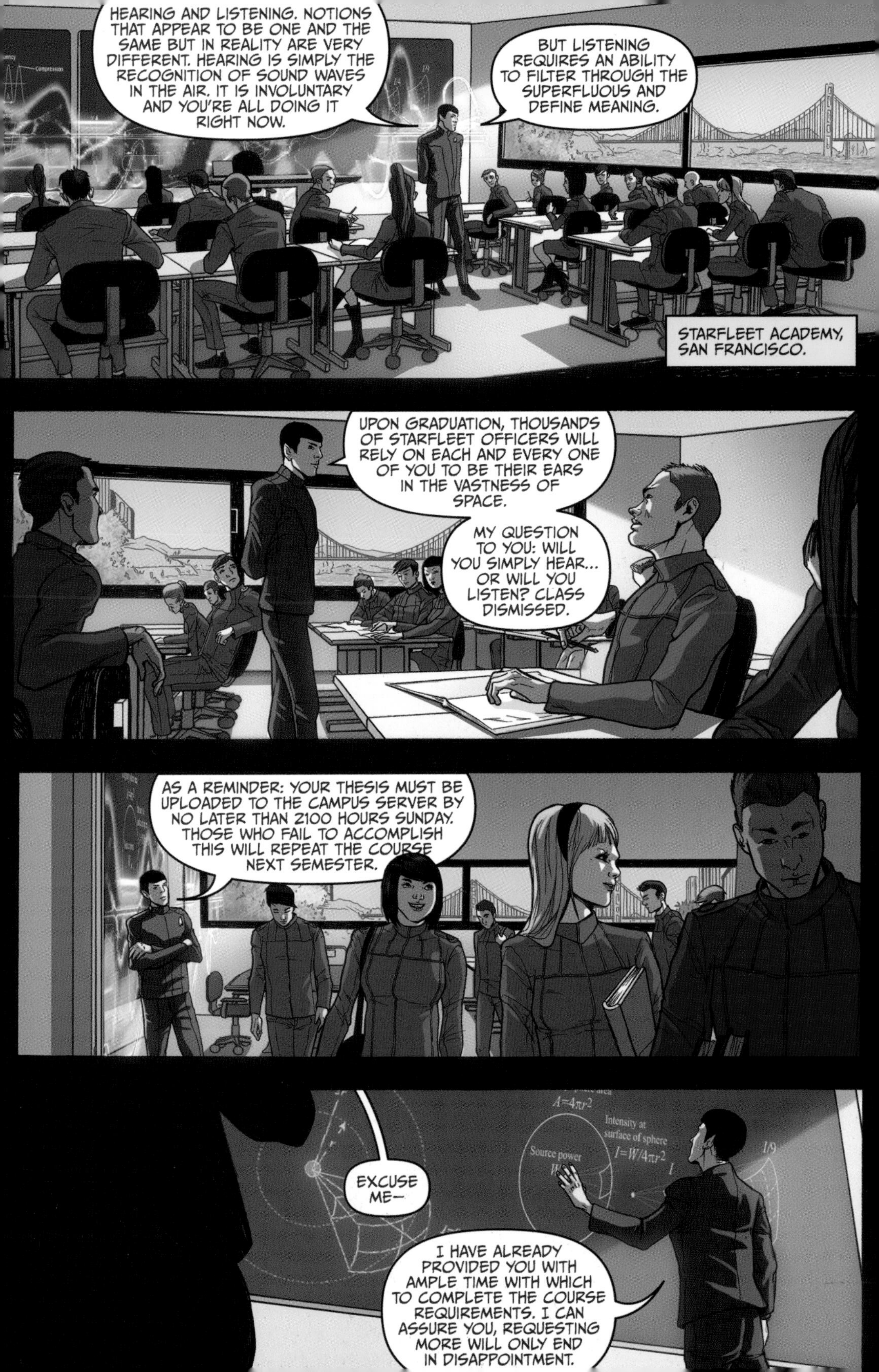
HEARING AND LISTENING. NOTIONS THAT APPEAR TO BE ONE AND THE SAME BUT IN REALITY ARE VERY DIFFERENT. HEARING IS SIMPLY THE RECOGNITION OF SOUND WAVES IN THE AIR. IT IS INVOLUNTARY AND YOU'RE ALL DOING IT RIGHT NOW.
BUT LISTENING REQUIRES AN ABILITY TO FILTER THROUGH THE SUPERFLUOUS AND DEFINE MEANING.
STARFLEET ACADEMY, SAN FRANCISCO.
UPON GRADUATION, THOUSANDS OF STARFLEET OFFICERS WILL RELY ON EACH AND EVERY ONE OF YOU TO BE THEIR EARS IN THE VASTNESS OF SPACE.
MY QUESTION TO YOU: WILL YOU SIMPLY HEAR... OR WILL YOU LISTEN? CLASS DISMISSED.
AS A REMINDER: YOUR THESIS MUST BE UPLOADED TO THE CAMPUS SERVER BY NO LATER THAN 2100 HOURS SUNDAY. THOSE WHO FAIL TO ACCOMPLISH THIS WILL REPEAT THE COURSE NEXT SEMESTER.
$A=4\pi r^2$
Intensity at surface of sphere
$I=W/4\pi r^2$
Source power
EXCUSE ME—
I HAVE ALREADY PROVIDED YOU WITH AMPLE TIME WITH WHICH TO COMPLETE THE COURSE REQUIREMENTS. I CAN ASSURE YOU, REQUESTING MORE WILL ONLY END IN DISAPPOINTMENT.

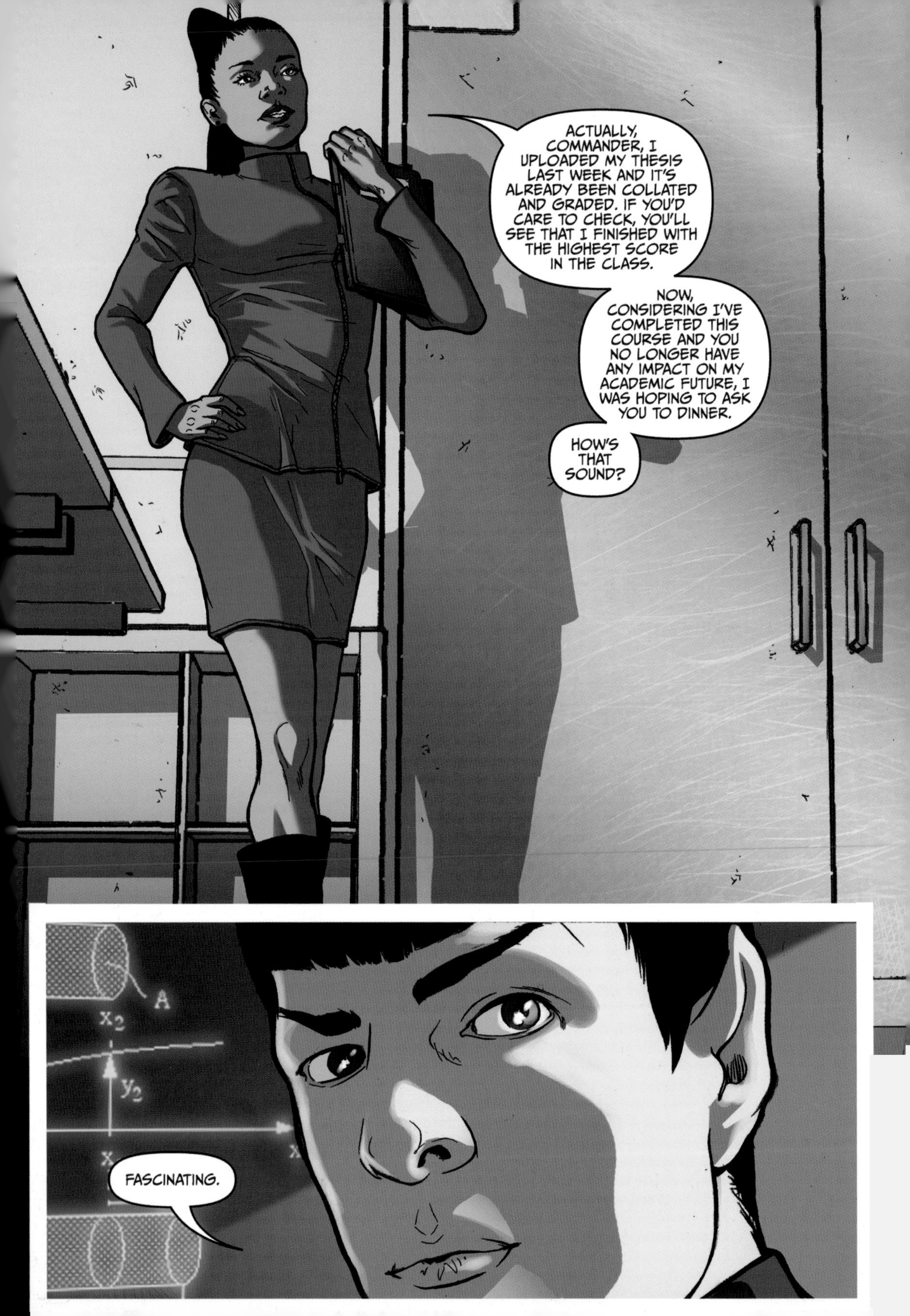
ACTUALLY, COMMANDER, I UPLOADED MY THESIS LAST WEEK AND IT'S ALREADY BEEN COLLATED AND GRADED. IF YOU'D CARE TO CHECK, YOU'LL SEE THAT I FINISHED WITH THE HIGHEST SCORE IN THE CLASS.
NOW, CONSIDERING I'VE COMPLETED THIS COURSE AND YOU NO LONGER HAVE ANY IMPACT ON MY ACADEMIC FUTURE, I WAS HOPING TO ASK YOU TO DINNER.
HOW'S THAT SOUND?
FASCINATING.

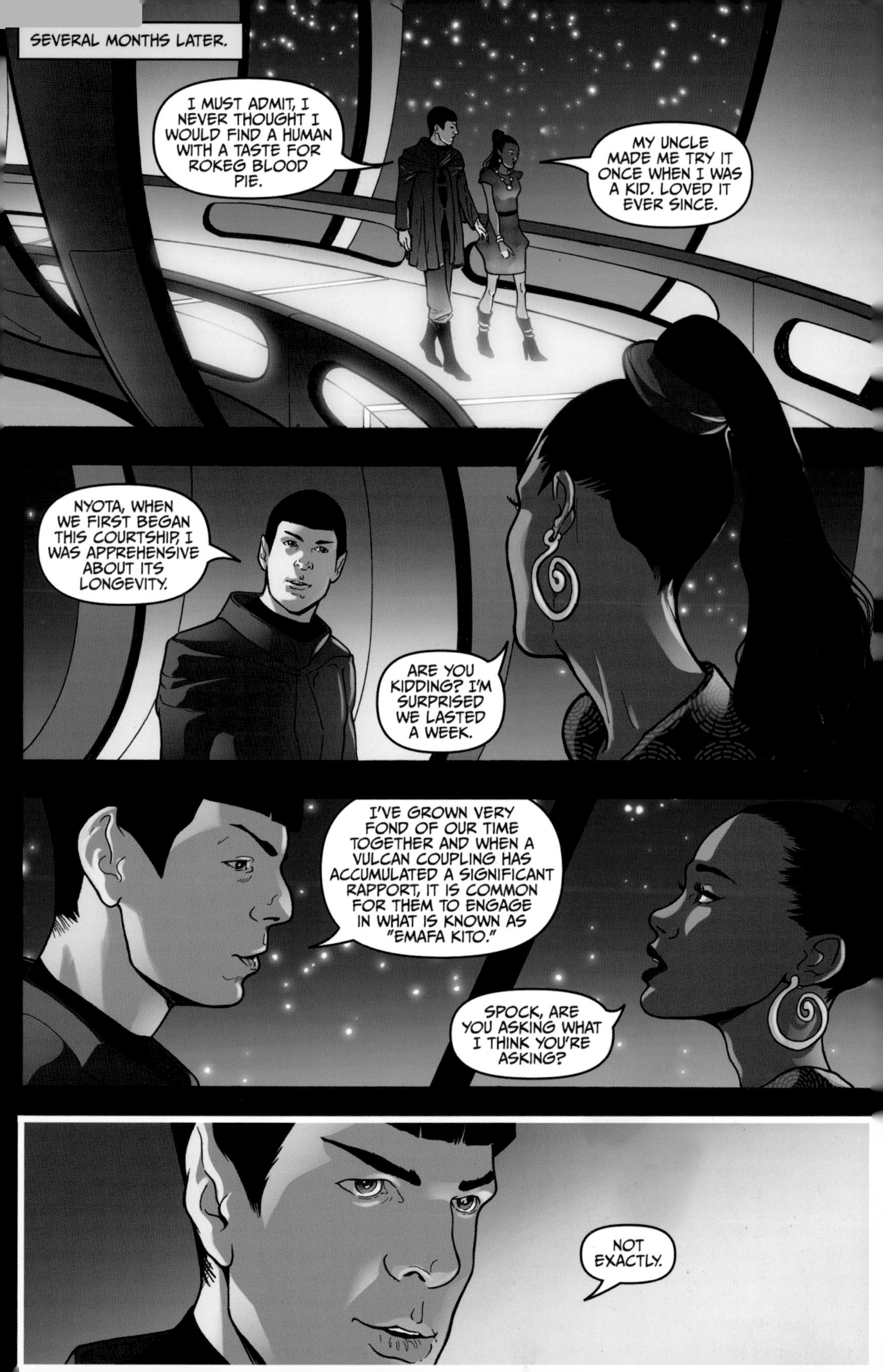
SEVERAL MONTHS LATER.
I MUST ADMIT, I NEVER THOUGHT I WOULD FIND A HUMAN WITH A TASTE FOR ROKEG BLOOD PIE.
MY UNCLE MADE ME TRY IT ONCE WHEN I WAS A KID. LOVED IT EVER SINCE.
NYOTA, WHEN WE FIRST BEGAN THIS COURTSHIP, I WAS APPREHENSIVE ABOUT ITS LONGEVITY.
ARE YOU KIDDING? I'M SURPRISED WE LASTED A WEEK.
I'VE GROWN VERY FOND OF OUR TIME TOGETHER AND WHEN A VULCAN COUPLING HAS ACCUMULATED A SIGNIFICANT RAPPORT, IT IS COMMON FOR THEM TO ENGAGE IN WHAT IS KNOWN AS "EMAFA KITO."
SPOCK, ARE YOU ASKING WHAT I THINK YOU'RE ASKING?
NOT EXACTLY.

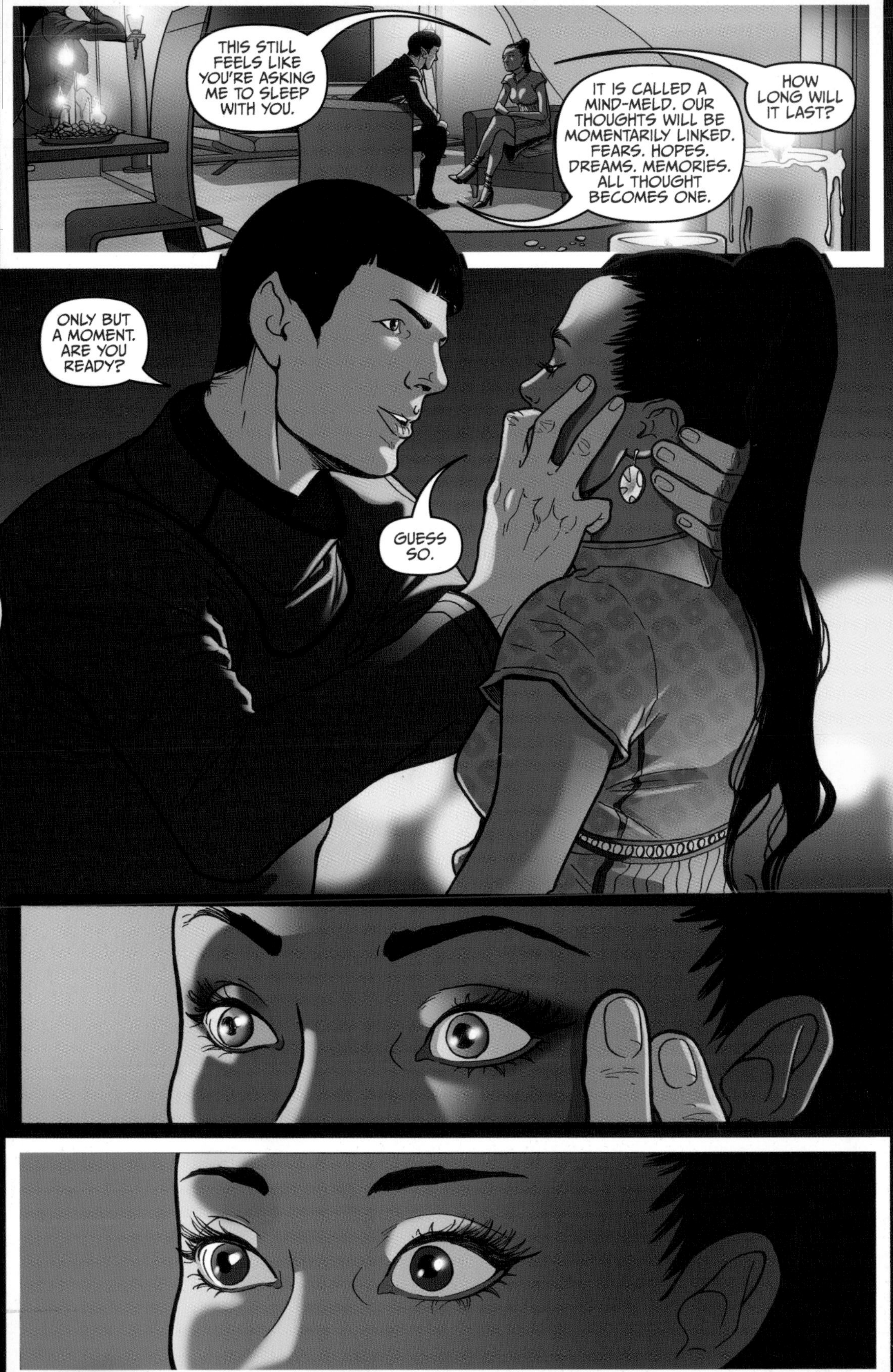
THIS STILL FEELS LIKE YOU'RE ASKING ME TO SLEEP WITH YOU.
IT IS CALLED A MIND-MELD. OUR THOUGHTS WILL BE MOMENTARILY LINKED. FEARS. HOPES. DREAMS. MEMORIES. ALL THOUGHT BECOMES ONE.
HOW LONG WILL IT LAST?
ONLY BUT A MOMENT. ARE YOU READY?
GUESS SO.

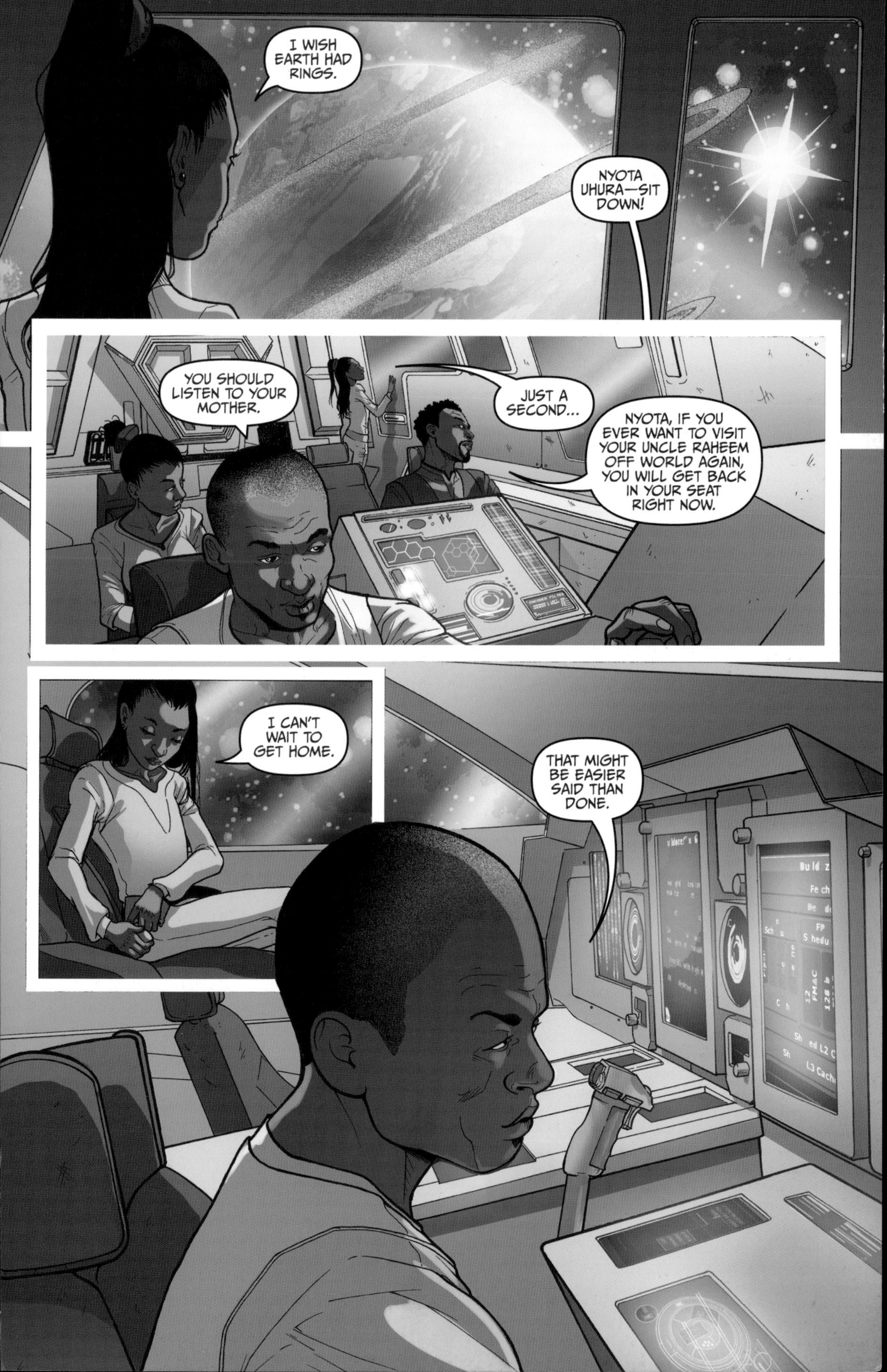
I WISH EARTH HAD RINGS.
NYOTA UHURA—SIT DOWN!
YOU SHOULD LISTEN TO YOUR MOTHER.
JUST A SECOND...
NYOTA, IF YOU EVER WANT TO VISIT YOUR UNCLE RAHEEM OFF WORLD AGAIN, YOU WILL GET BACK IN YOUR SEAT RIGHT NOW.
I CAN'T WAIT TO GET HOME.
THAT MIGHT BE EASIER SAID THAN DONE.

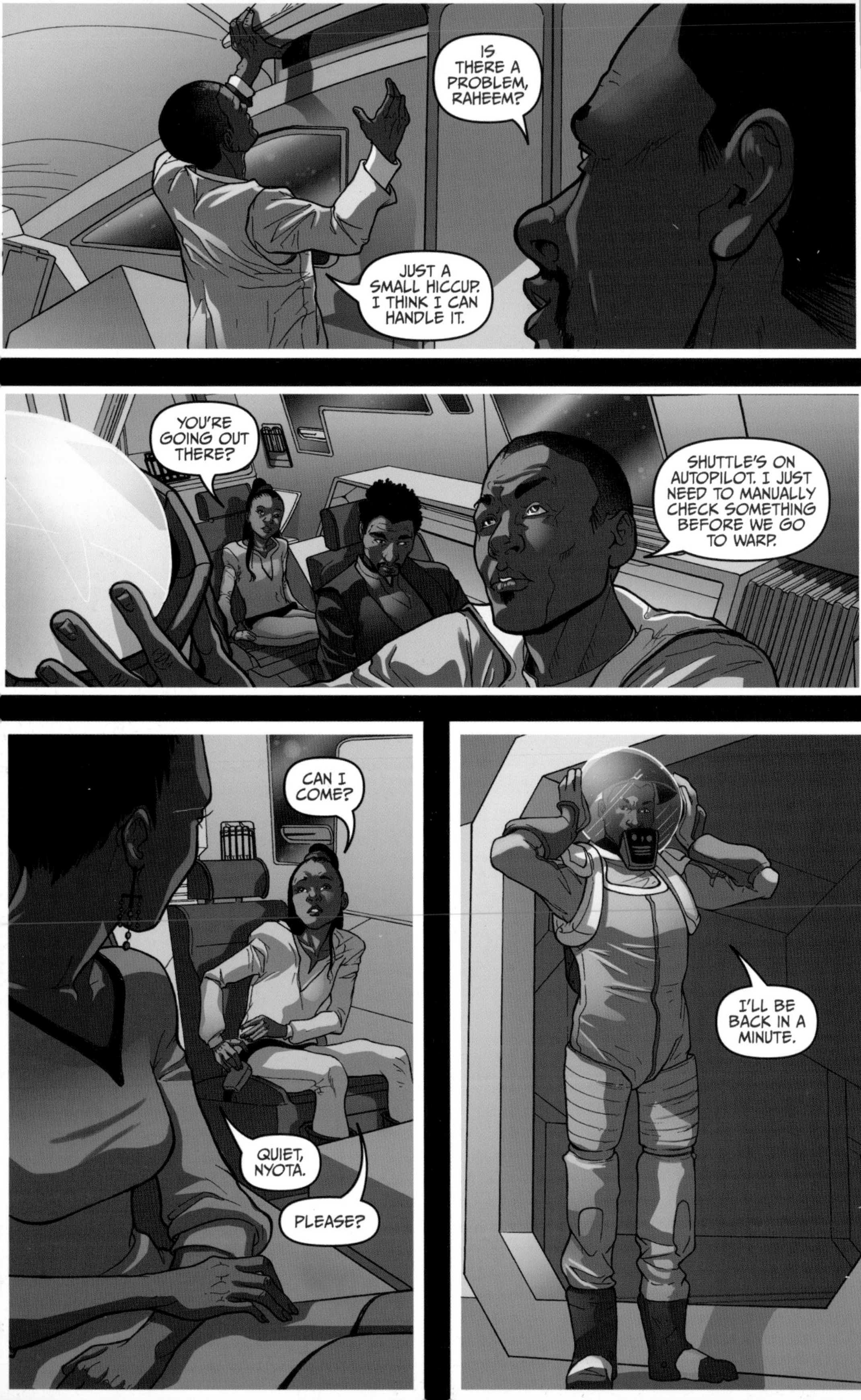
IS THERE A PROBLEM, RAHEEM?
JUST A SMALL HICCUP. I THINK I CAN HANDLE IT.
YOU'RE GOING OUT THERE?
SHUTTLE'S ON AUTOPILOT. I JUST NEED TO MANUALLY CHECK SOMETHING BEFORE WE GO TO WARP.
CAN I COME?
QUIET, NYOTA.
PLEASE?
I'LL BE BACK IN A MINUTE.

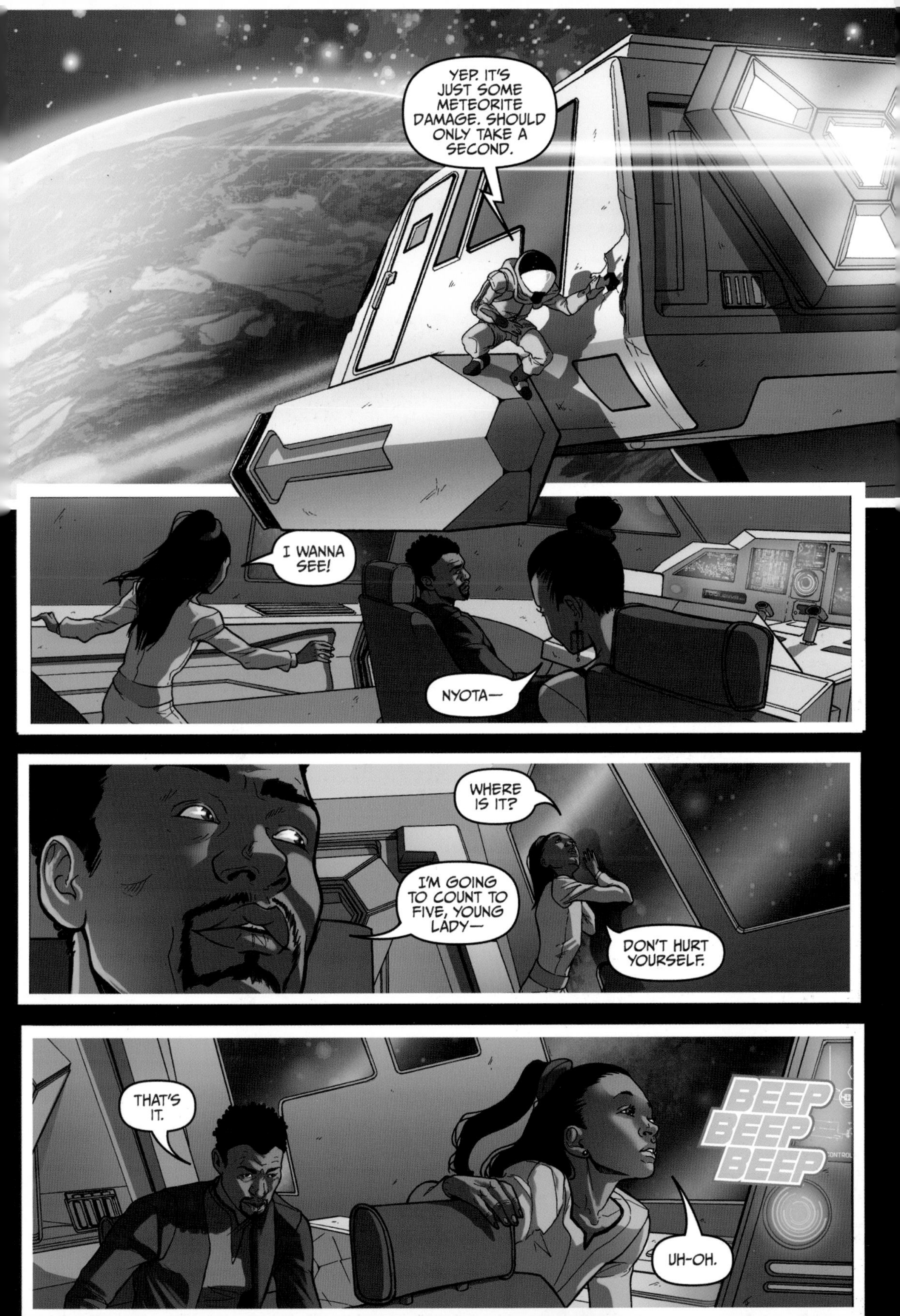
YEP. IT'S JUST SOME METEORITE DAMAGE. SHOULD ONLY TAKE A SECOND.
I WANNA SEE!
NYOTA—
WHERE IS IT?
I'M GOING TO COUNT TO FIVE, YOUNG LADY—
DON'T HURT YOURSELF.
THAT'S IT.
BEEP BEEP BEEP
UH-OH.

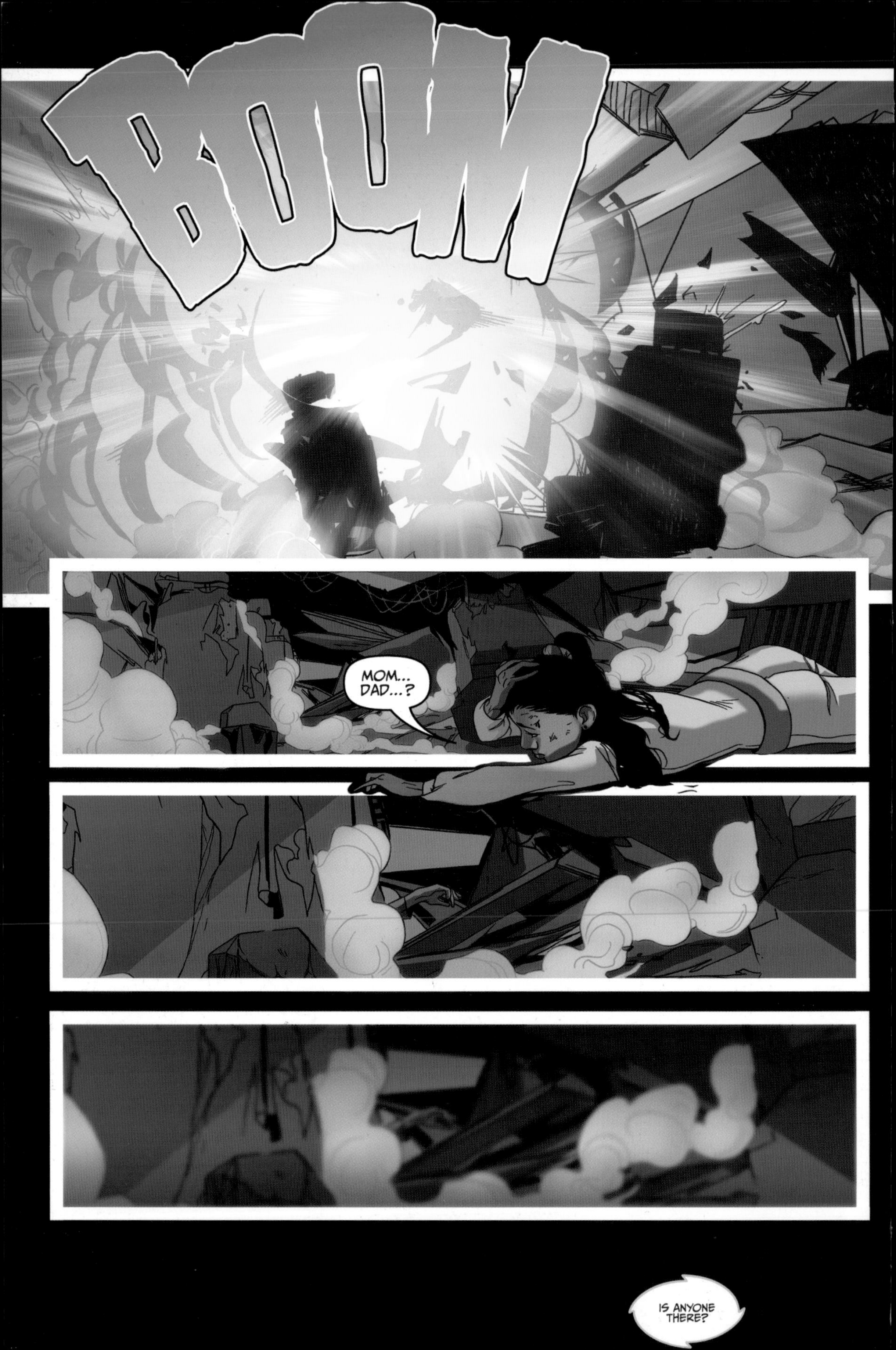
BOOM
MOM... DAD...?
IS ANYONE THERE?

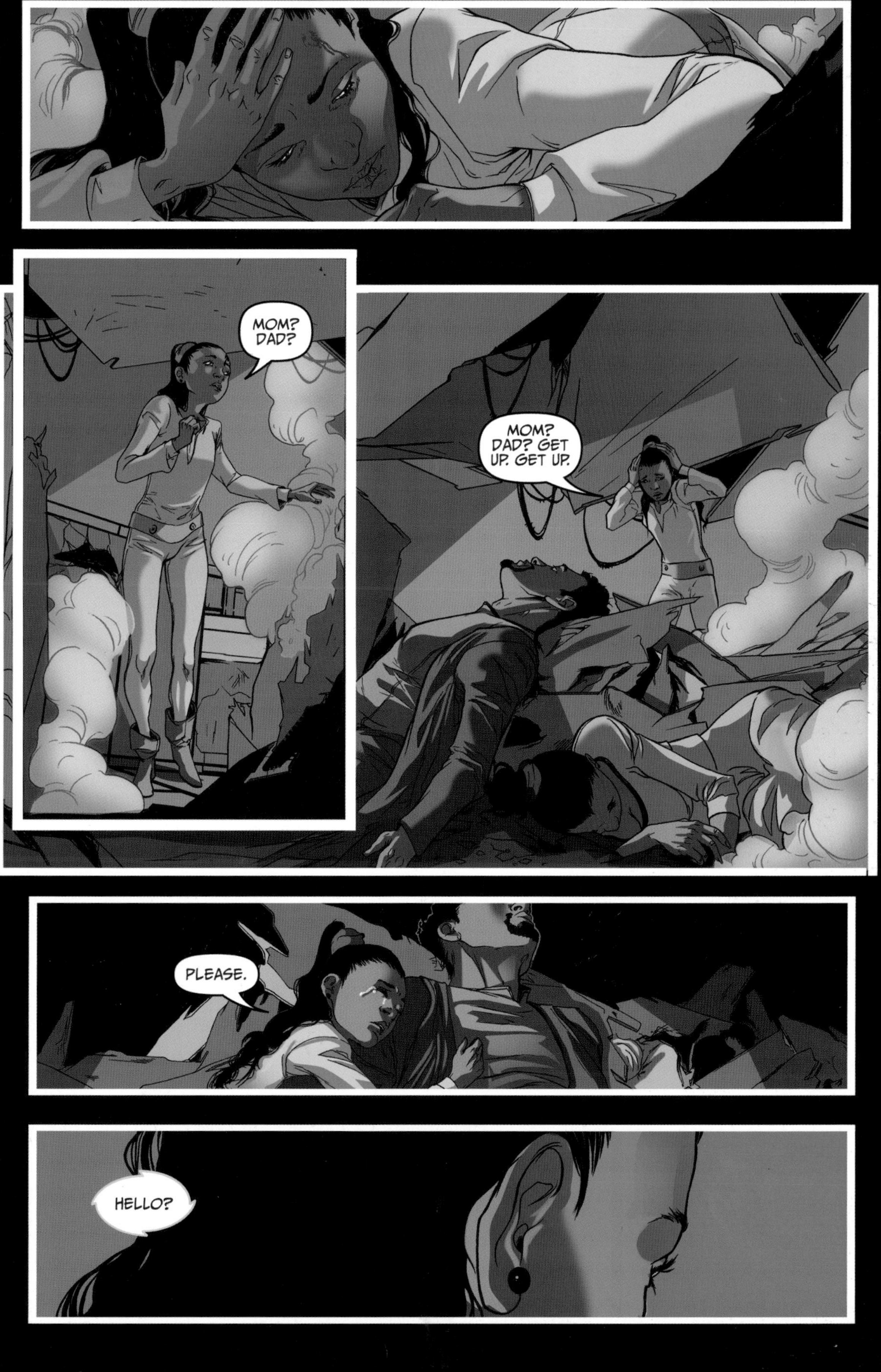
MOM? DAD?
MOM? DAD? GET UP. GET UP.
PLEASE.
HELLO?

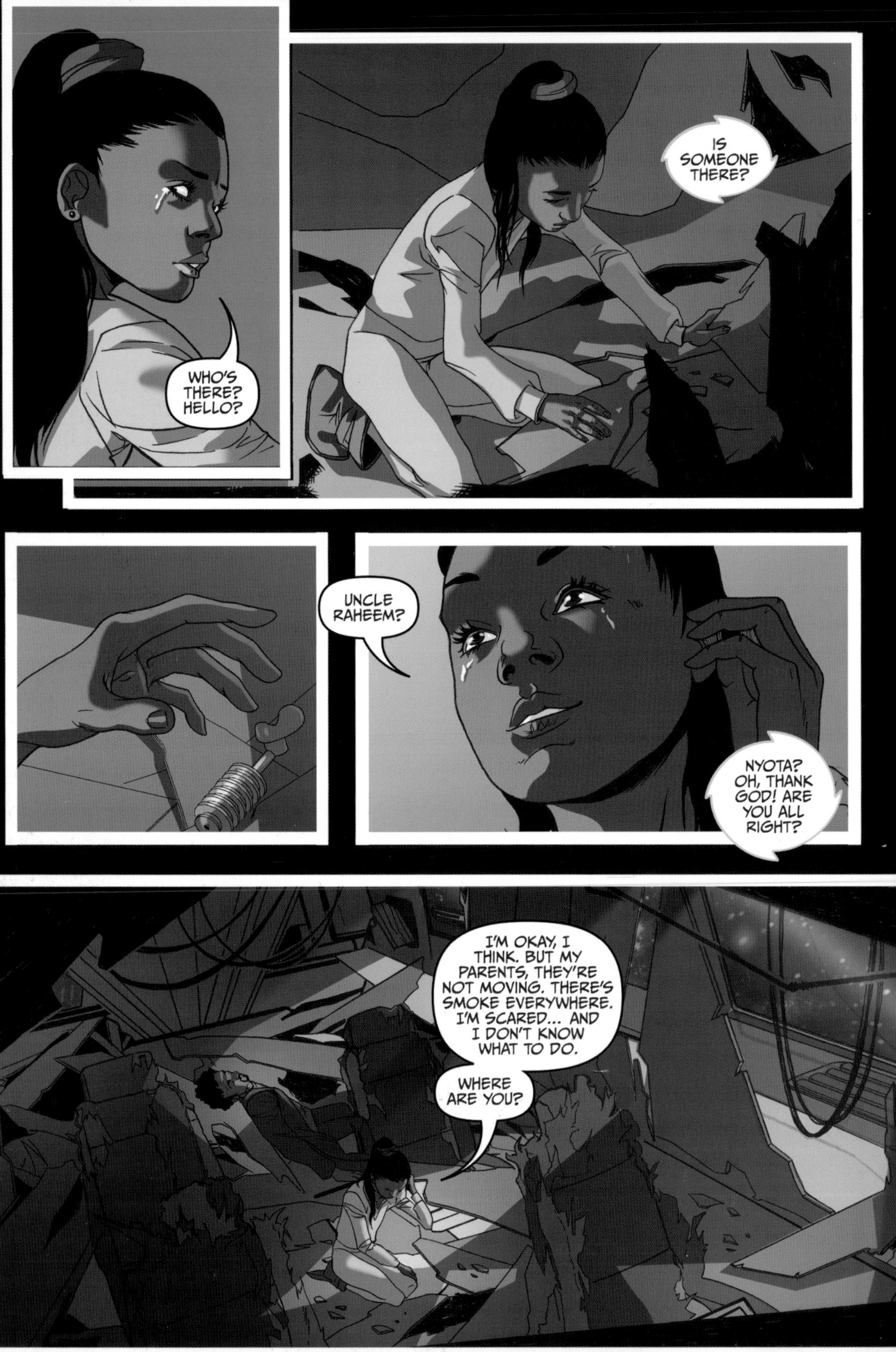
WHO'S THERE? HELLO?
IS SOMEONE THERE?
UNCLE RAHEEM?
NYOTA? OH, THANK GOD! ARE YOU ALL RIGHT?
I'M OKAY, I THINK. BUT MY PARENTS, THEY'RE NOT MOVING. THERE'S SMOKE EVERYWHERE. I'M SCARED... AND I DON'T KNOW WHAT TO DO.
WHERE ARE YOU?

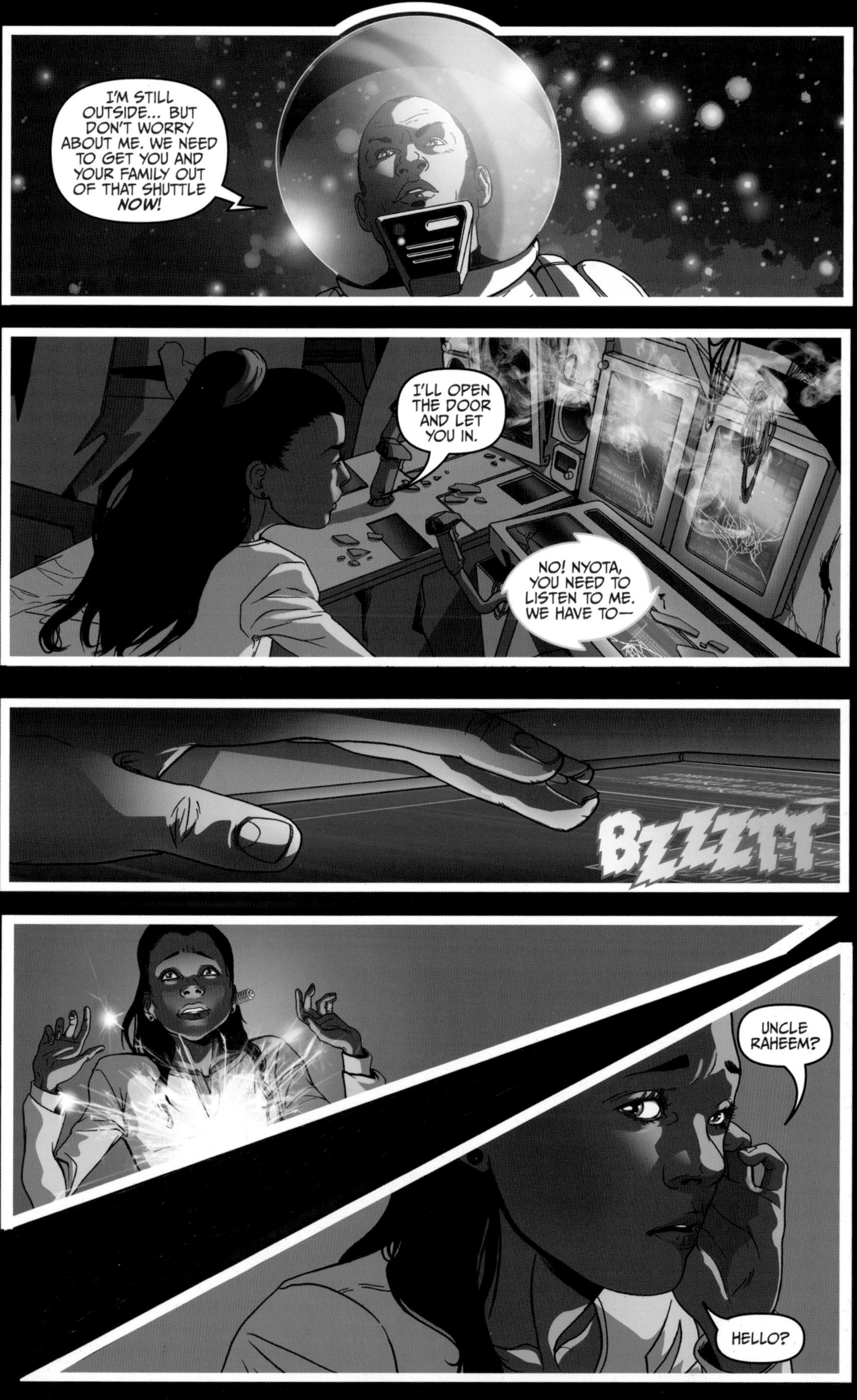
I'M STILL OUTSIDE... BUT DON'T WORRY ABOUT ME. WE NEED TO GET YOU AND YOUR FAMILY OUT OF THAT SHUTTLE NOW!
I'LL OPEN THE DOOR AND LET YOU IN.
NO! NYOTA, YOU NEED TO LISTEN TO ME. WE HAVE TO—
BZZZTT
UNCLE RAHEEM?
HELLO?

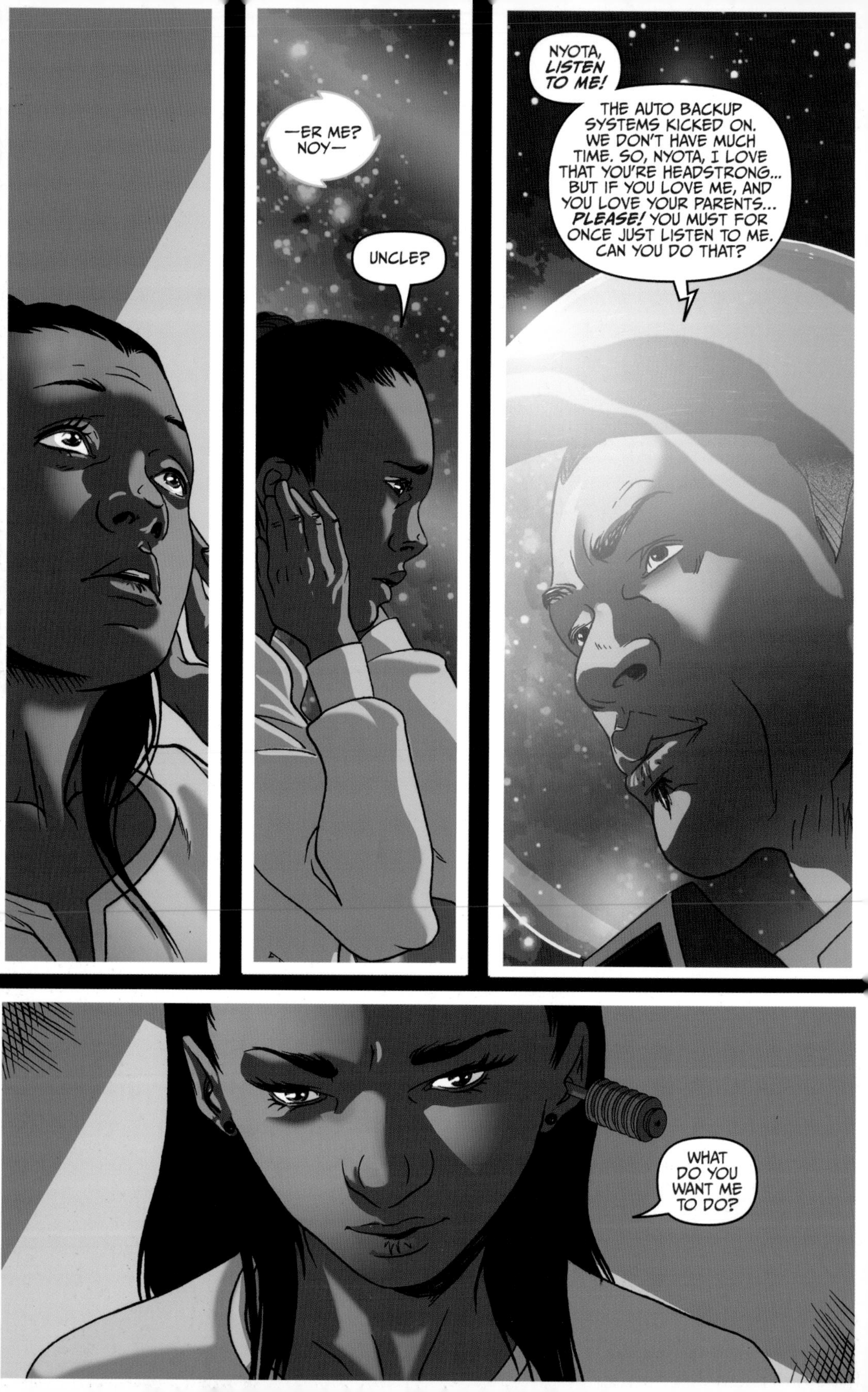
—ER ME? NOY—
UNCLE?
NYOTA, LISTEN TO ME!
THE AUTO BACKUP SYSTEMS KICKED ON. WE DON'T HAVE MUCH TIME. SO, NYOTA, I LOVE THAT YOU'RE HEADSTRONG... BUT IF YOU LOVE ME, AND YOU LOVE YOUR PARENTS... PLEASE! YOU MUST FOR ONCE JUST LISTEN TO ME. CAN YOU DO THAT?
WHAT DO YOU WANT ME TO DO?

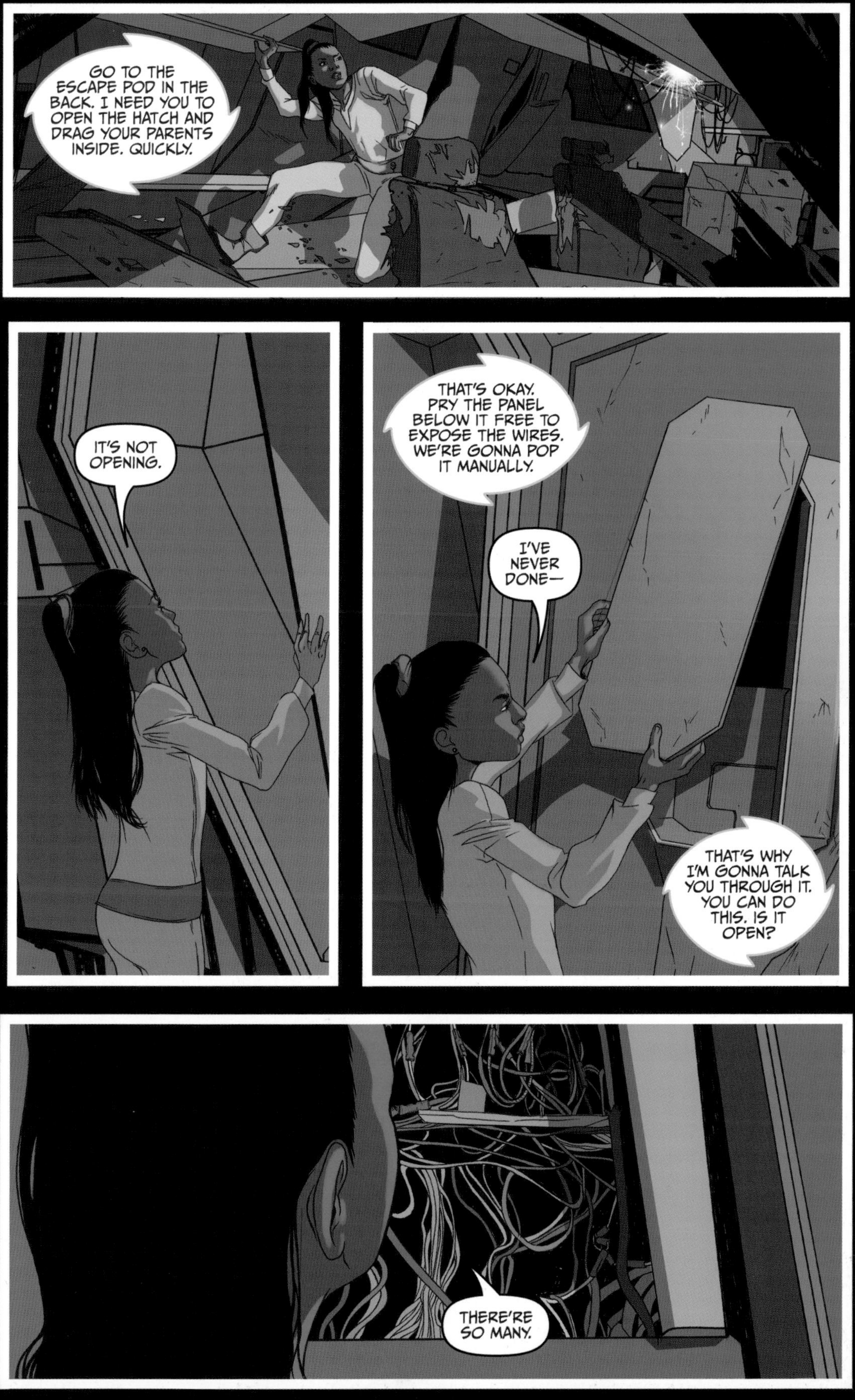
GO TO THE ESCAPE POD IN THE BACK. I NEED YOU TO OPEN THE HATCH AND DRAG YOUR PARENTS INSIDE. QUICKLY.
IT'S NOT OPENING.
THAT'S OKAY. PRY THE PANEL BELOW IT FREE TO EXPOSE THE WIRES. WE'RE GONNA POP IT MANUALLY.
I'VE NEVER DONE—
THAT'S WHY I'M GONNA TALK YOU THROUGH IT. YOU CAN DO THIS. IS IT OPEN?
THERE'RE SO MANY.

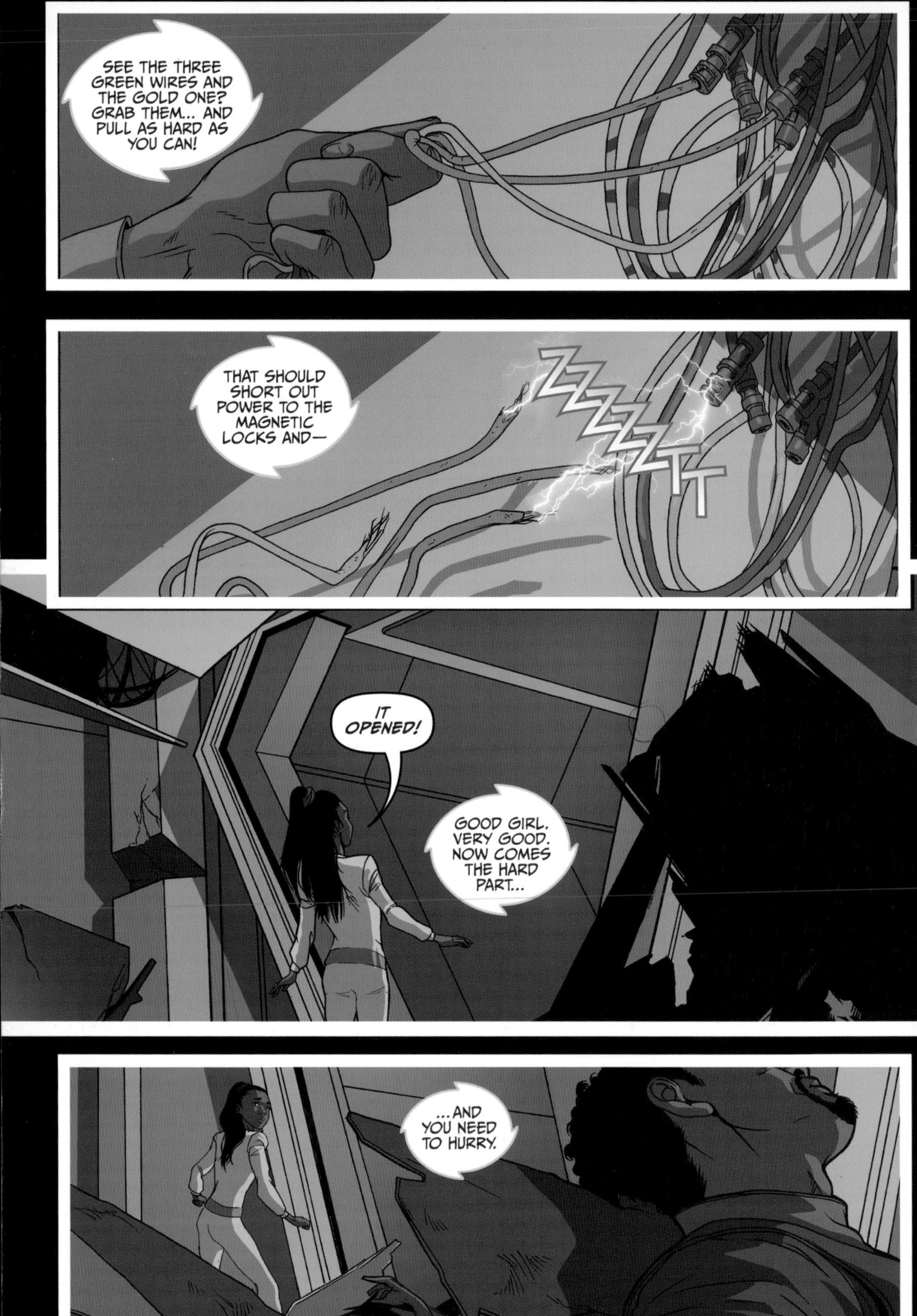
SEE THE THREE GREEN WIRES AND THE GOLD ONE? GRAB THEM... AND PULL AS HARD AS YOU CAN!
THAT SHOULD SHORT OUT POWER TO THE MAGNETIC LOCKS AND—
ZZZZZTT
IT OPENED!
GOOD GIRL. VERY GOOD. NOW COMES THE HARD PART...
...AND YOU NEED TO HURRY.

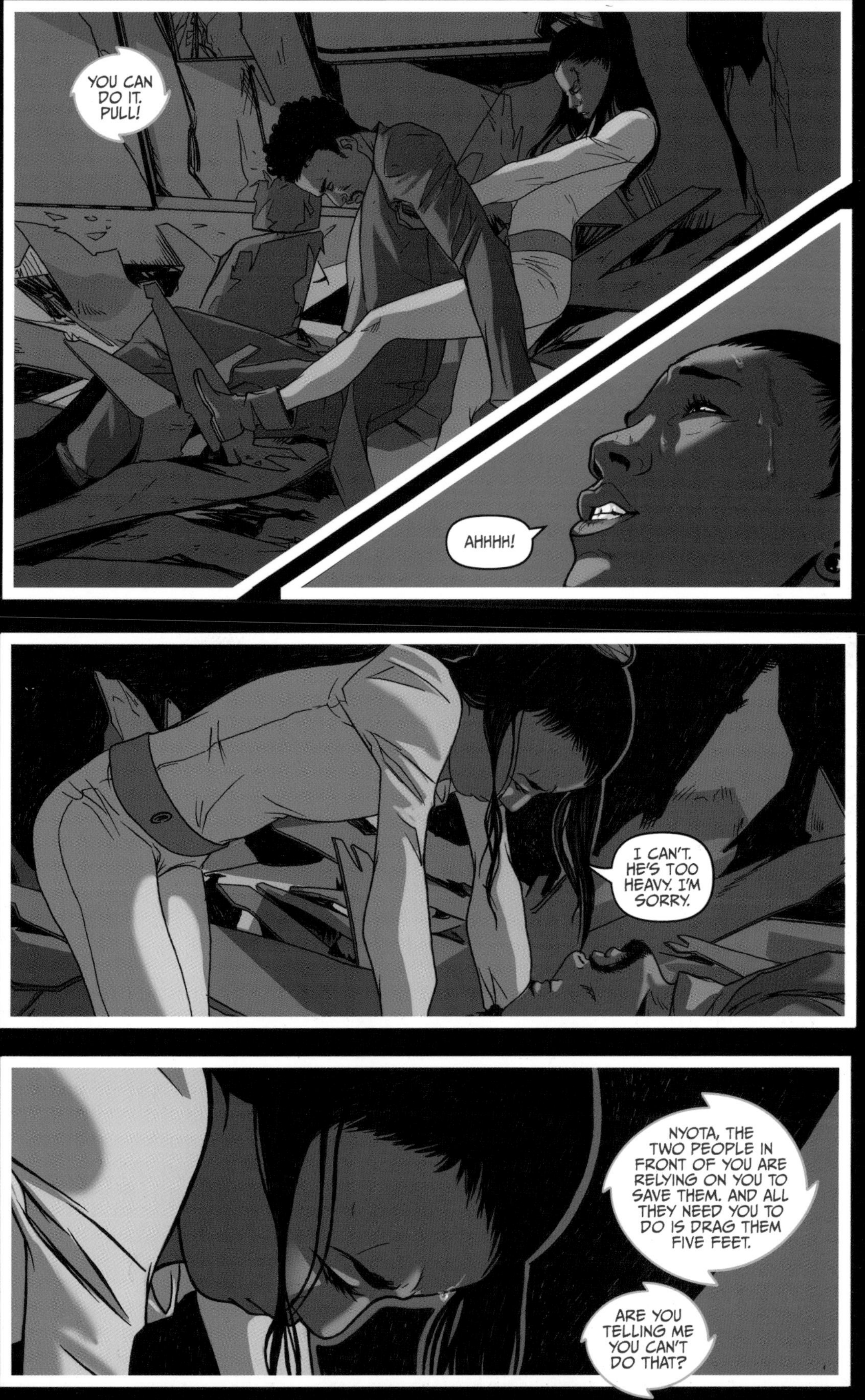
YOU CAN DO IT. PULL!
AHHHH!
I CAN'T. HE'S TOO HEAVY. I'M SORRY.
NYOTA, THE TWO PEOPLE IN FRONT OF YOU ARE RELYING ON YOU TO SAVE THEM. AND ALL THEY NEED YOU TO DO IS DRAG THEM FIVE FEET.
ARE YOU TELLING ME YOU CAN'T DO THAT?

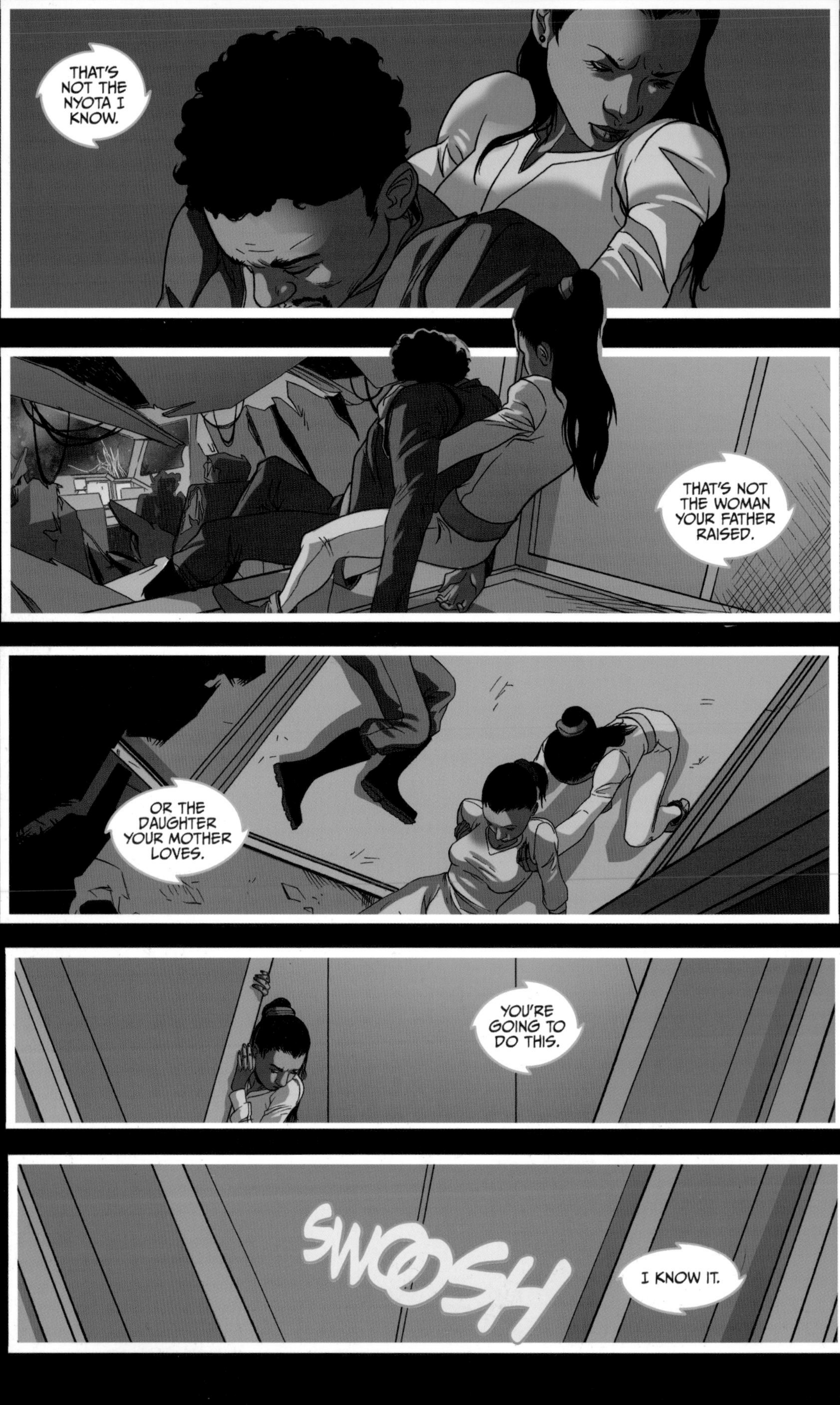
THAT'S NOT THE NYOTA I KNOW.
THAT'S NOT THE WOMAN YOUR FATHER RAISED.
OR THE DAUGHTER YOUR MOTHER LOVES.
YOU'RE GOING TO DO THIS.
SWOOSH
I KNOW IT.

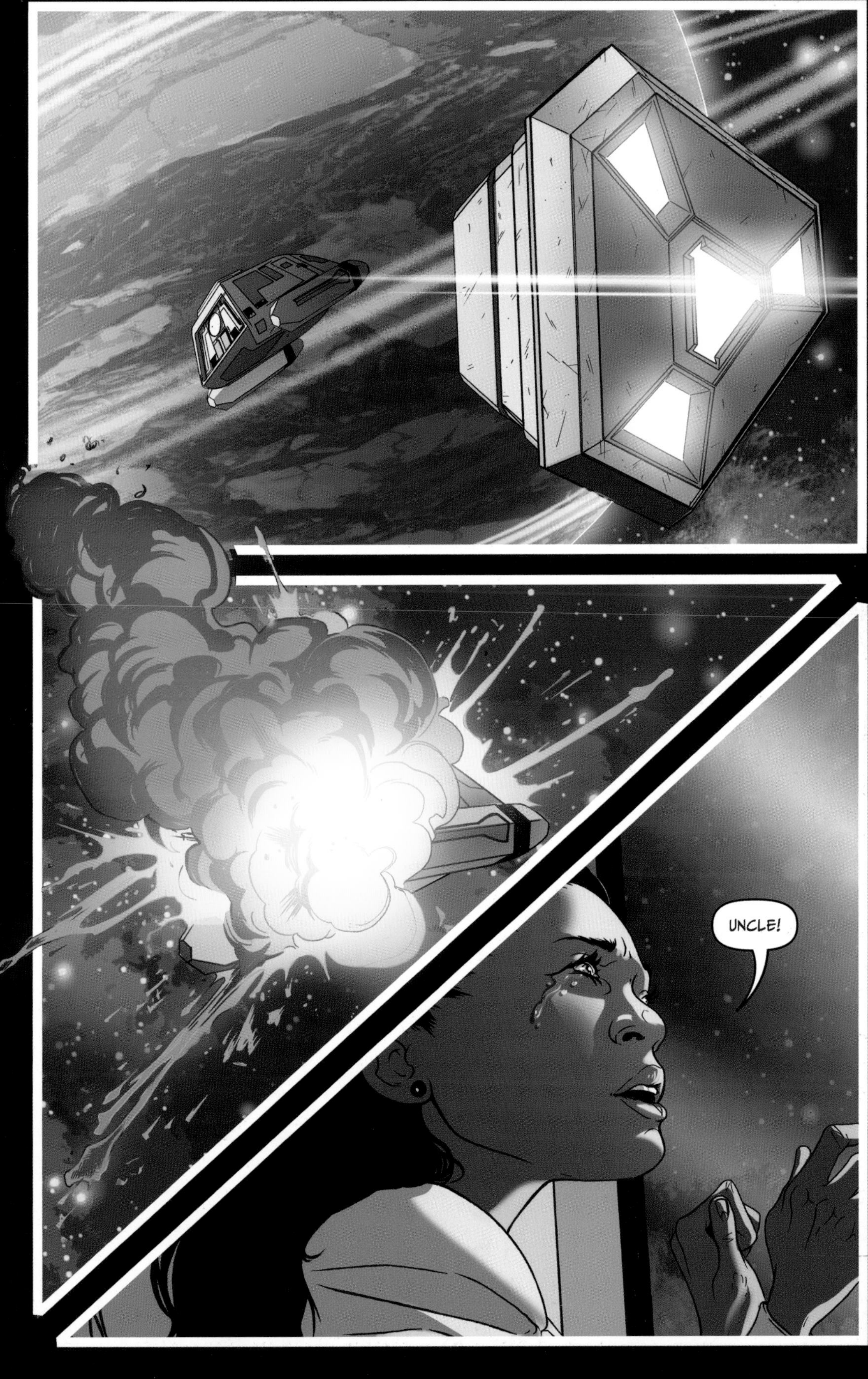
UNCLE!

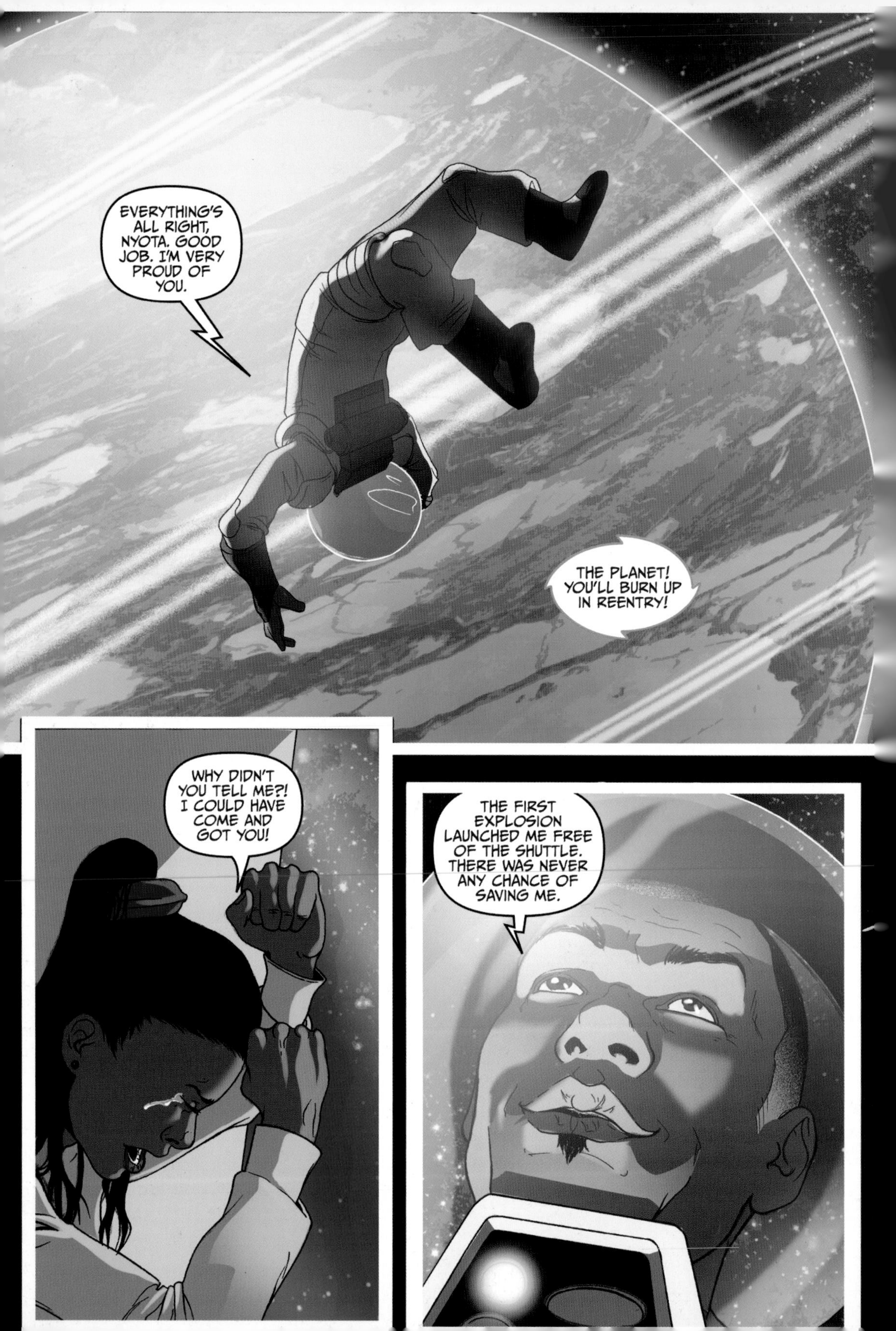
EVERYTHING'S ALL RIGHT, NYOTA. GOOD JOB. I'M VERY PROUD OF YOU.
THE PLANET! YOU'LL BURN UP IN REENTRY!
WHY DIDN'T YOU TELL ME?! I COULD HAVE COME AND GOT YOU!
THE FIRST EXPLOSION LAUNCHED ME FREE OF THE SHUTTLE. THERE WAS NEVER ANY CHANCE OF SAVING ME.

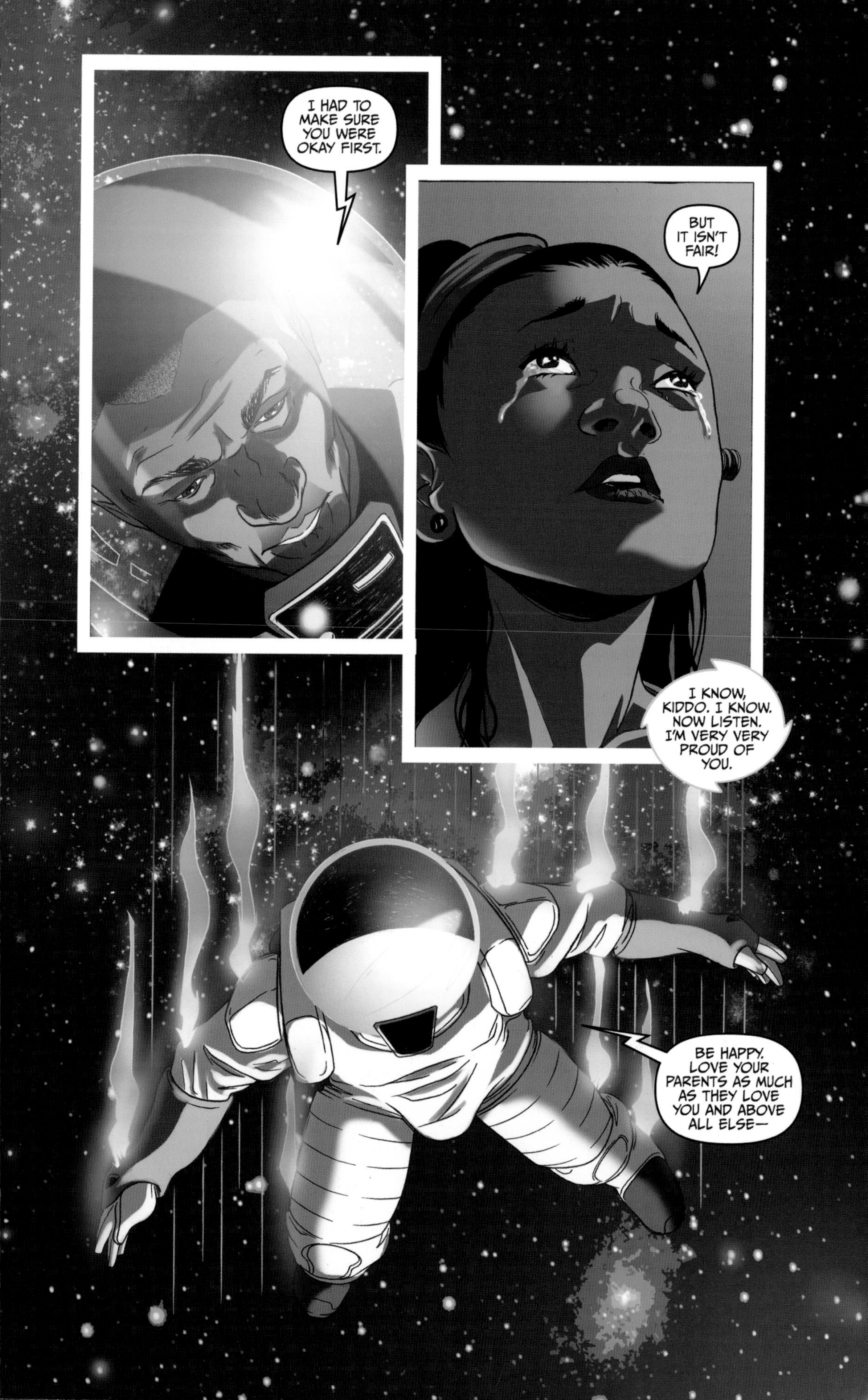

I HAD TO MAKE SURE YOU WERE OKAY FIRST.
BUT IT ISN'T FAIR!
I KNOW, KIDDO. I KNOW. NOW LISTEN. I'M VERY VERY PROUD OF YOU.
BE HAPPY. LOVE YOUR PARENTS AS MUCH AS THEY LOVE YOU AND ABOVE ALL ELSE—

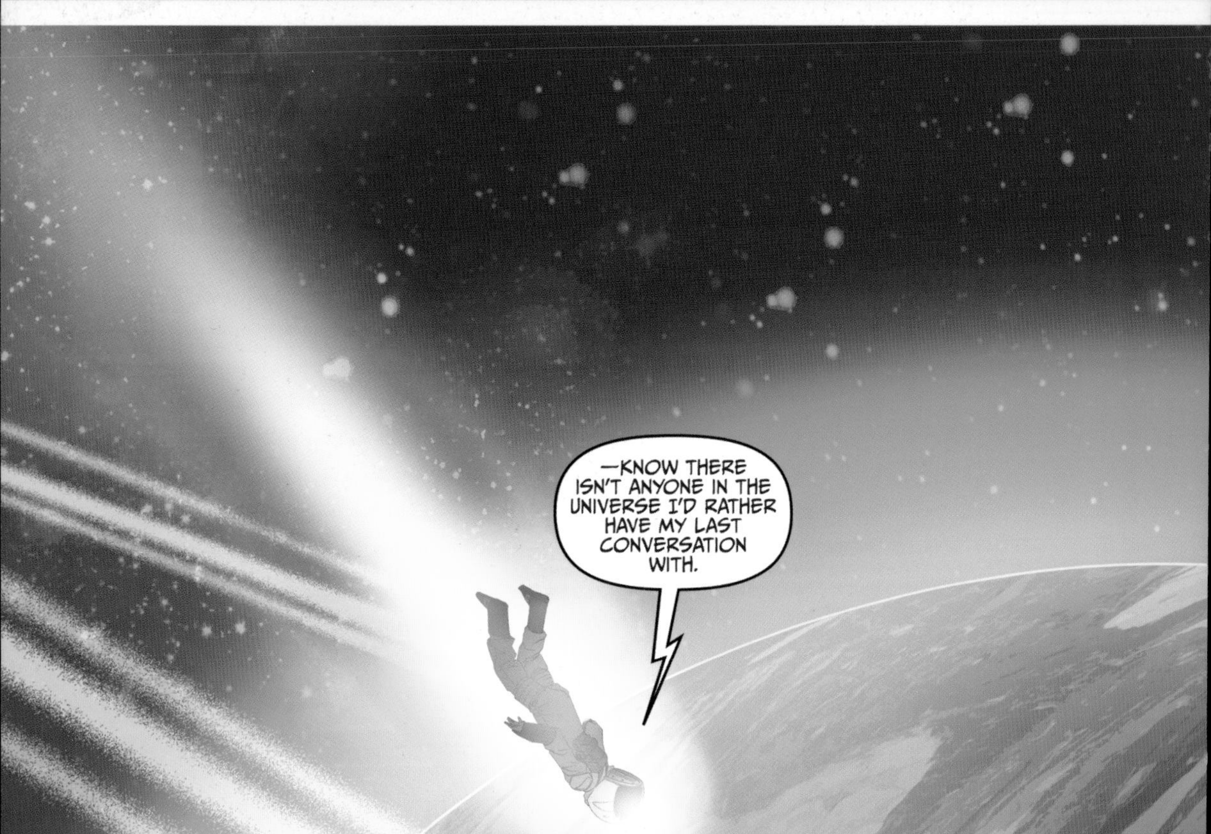
—KNOW THERE ISN'T ANYONE IN THE UNIVERSE I'D RATHER HAVE MY LAST CONVERSATION WITH.

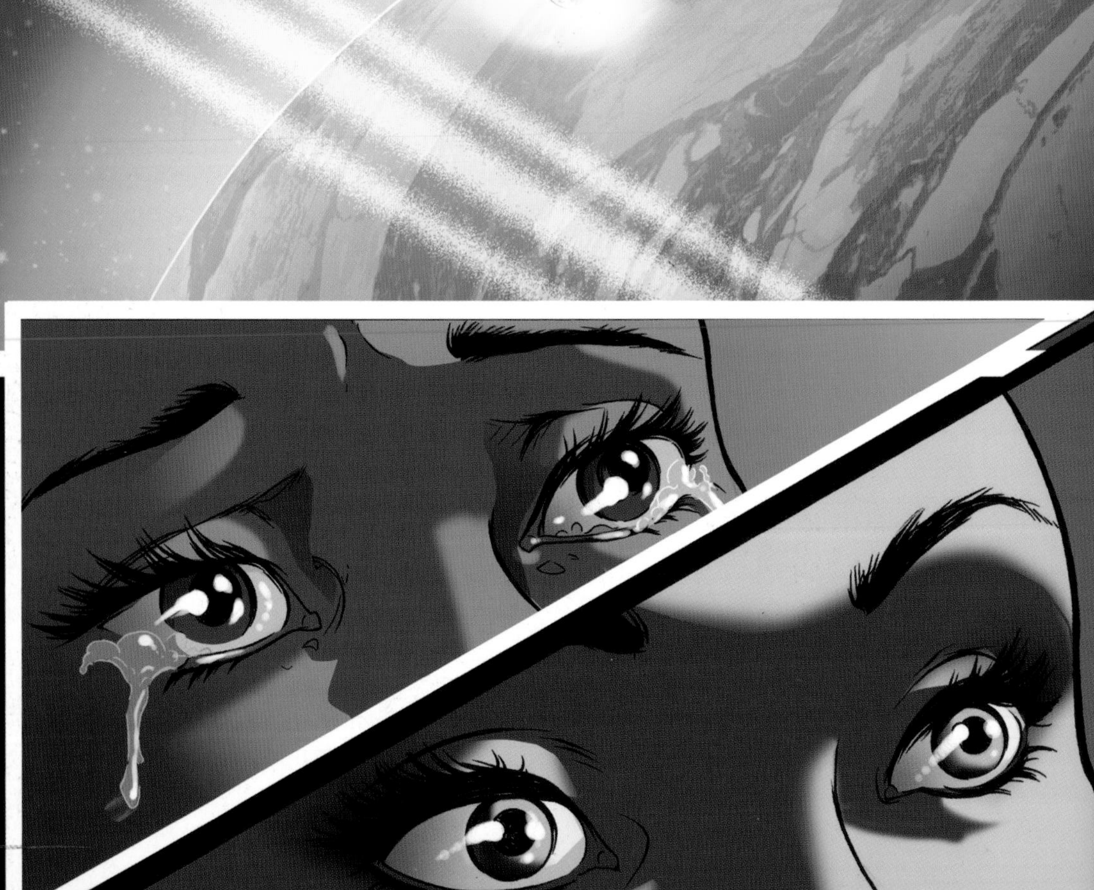

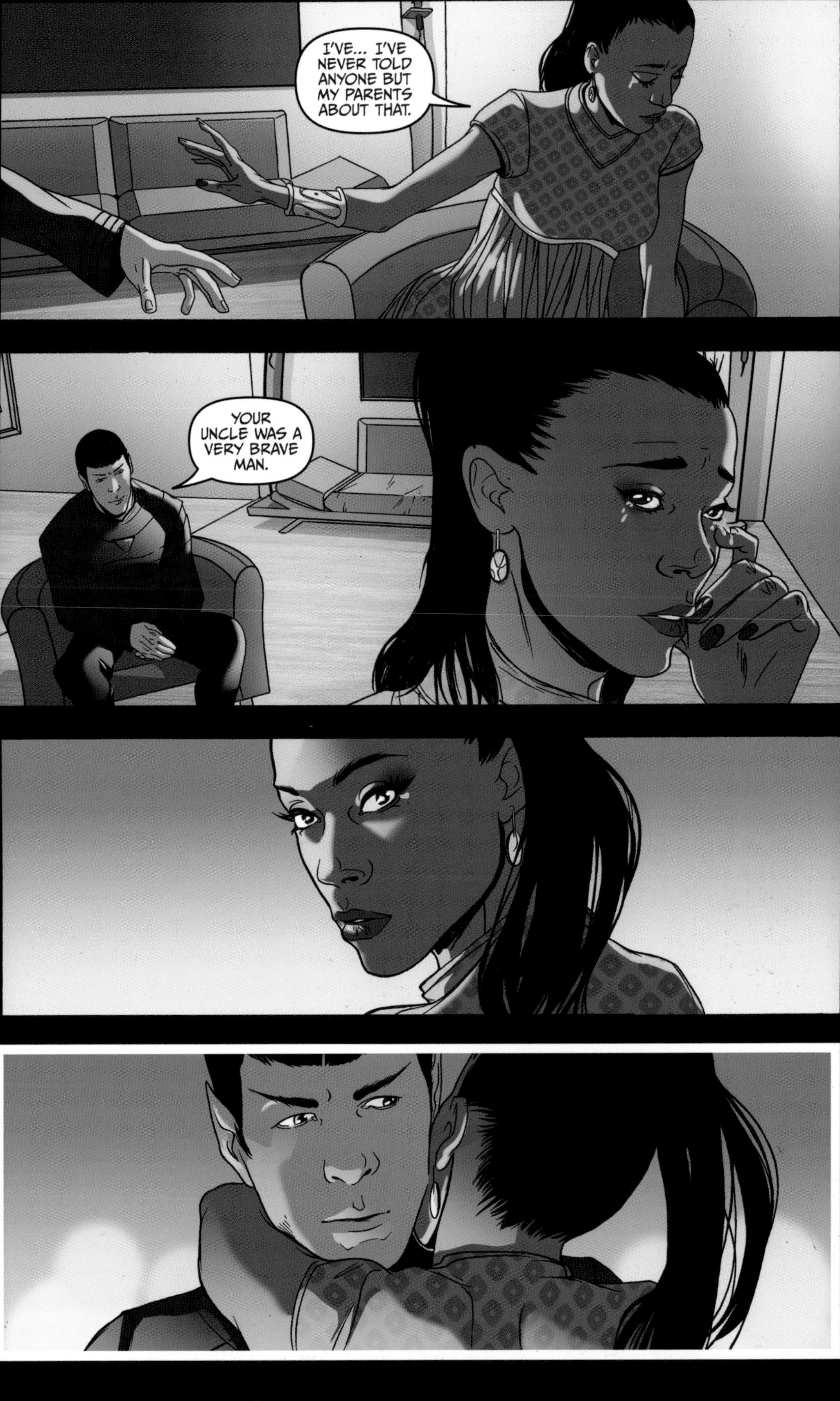
I'VE... I'VE NEVER TOLD ANYONE BUT MY PARENTS ABOUT THAT.
YOUR UNCLE WAS A VERY BRAVE MAN.

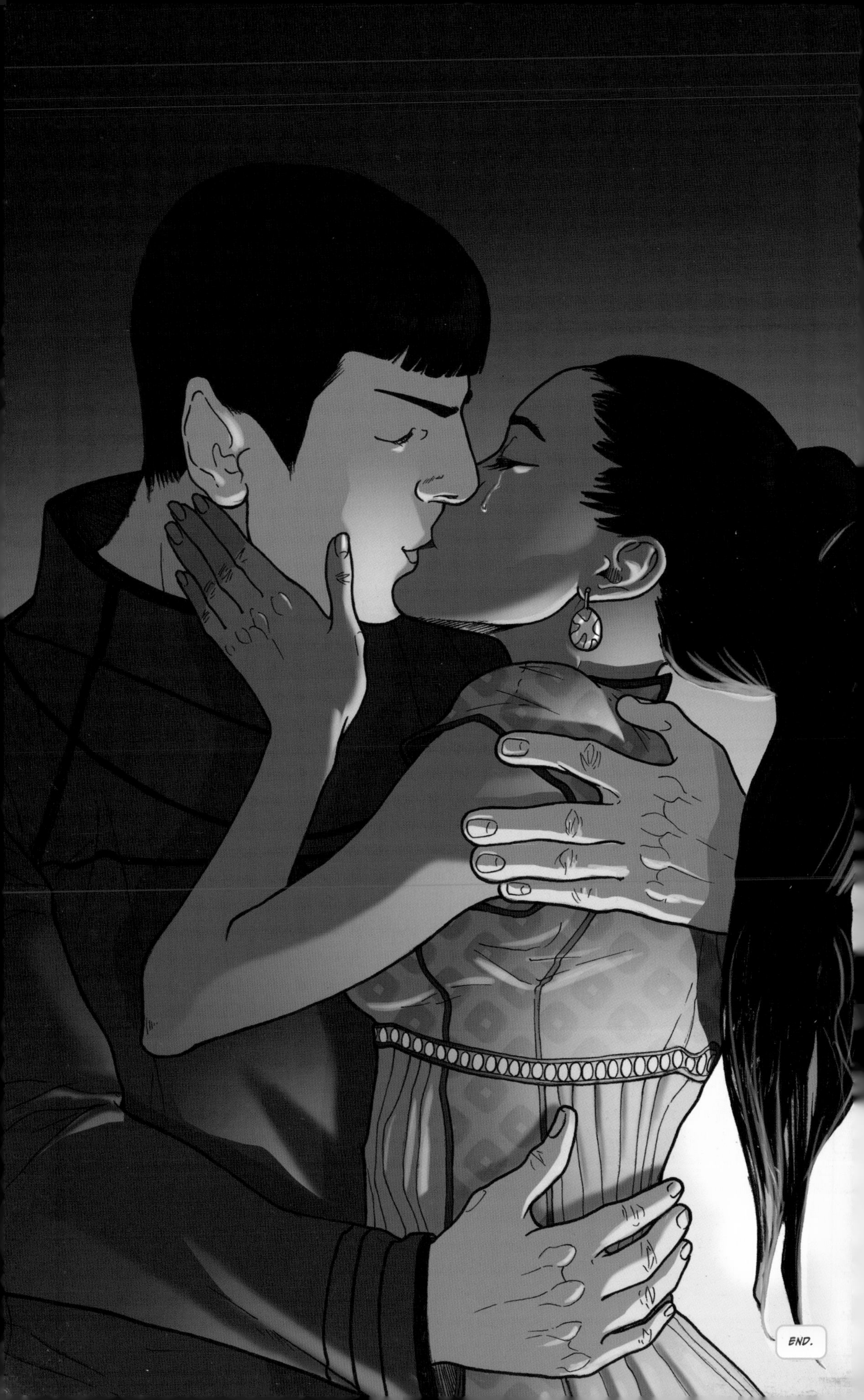
END.

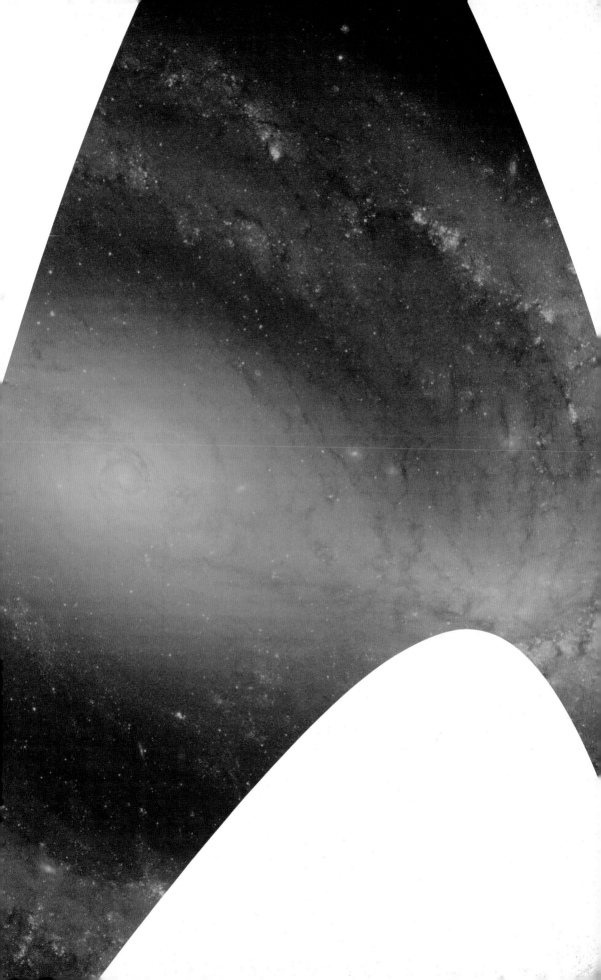

SCOTTY

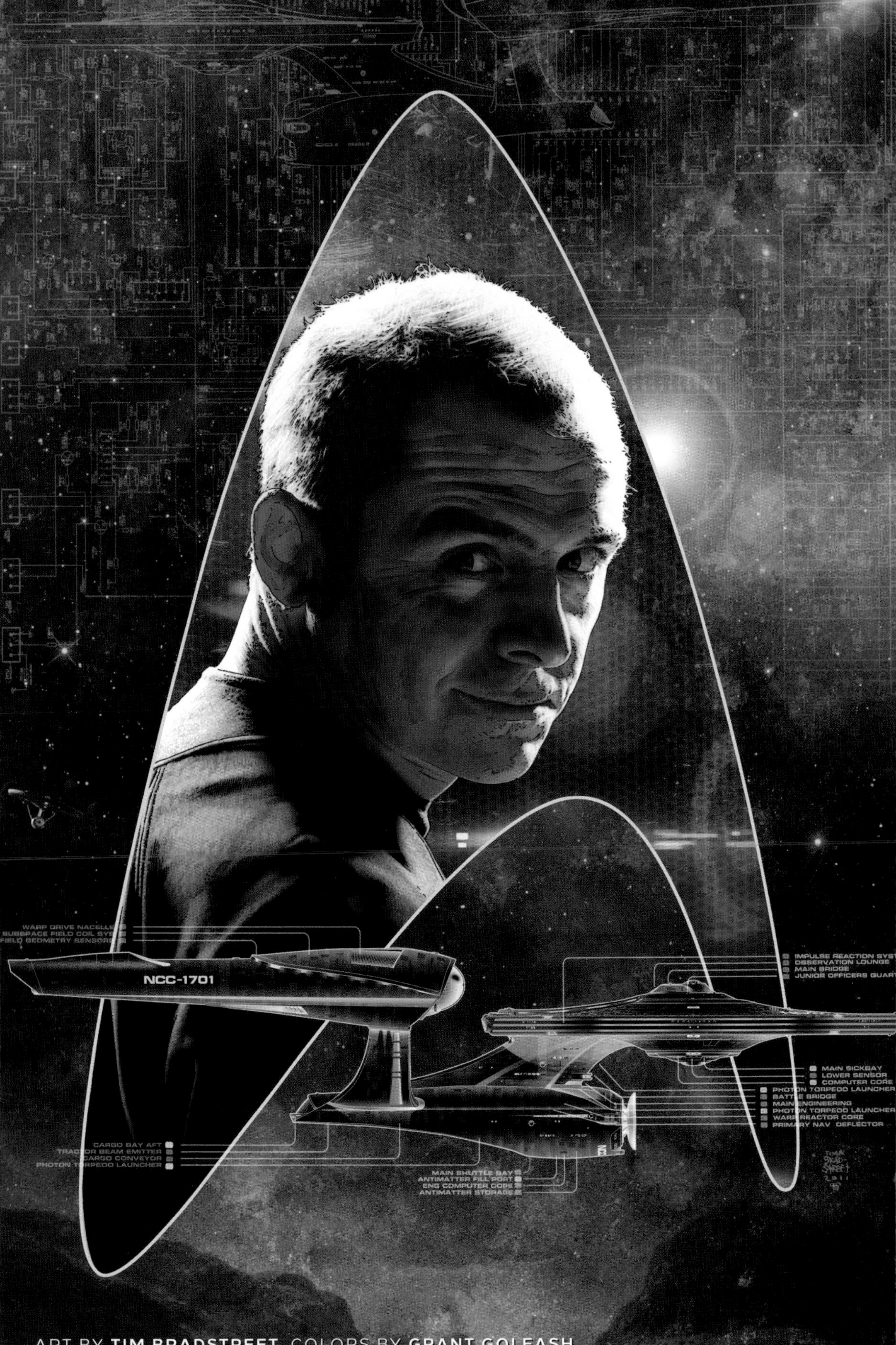
WARP DRIVE NACELLE
SUBSPACE FIELD COIL SYS
FIELD GEOMETRY SENSORS
NCC-1701
IMPULSE REACTION SYST
OBSERVATION LOUNGE
MAIN BRIDGE
JUNIOR OFFICERS QUART
MAIN SICKBAY
LOWER SENSOR
COMPUTER CORE
PHOTON TORPEDO LAUNCHER
BATTLE BRIDGE
MAIN ENGINEERING
PHOTON TORPEDO LAUNCHER
WARP REACTOR CORE
PRIMARY NAV DEFLECTOR
CARGO BAY AFT
TRACTOR BEAM EMITTER
CARGO CONVEYOR
PHOTON TORPEDO LAUNCHER
MAIN SHUTTLE BAY
ANTIMATTER FILL PORT
ENG COMPUTER CORE
ANTIMATTER STORAGE

ART BY **TIM BRADSTREET** COLORS BY **GRANT GOLEASH**

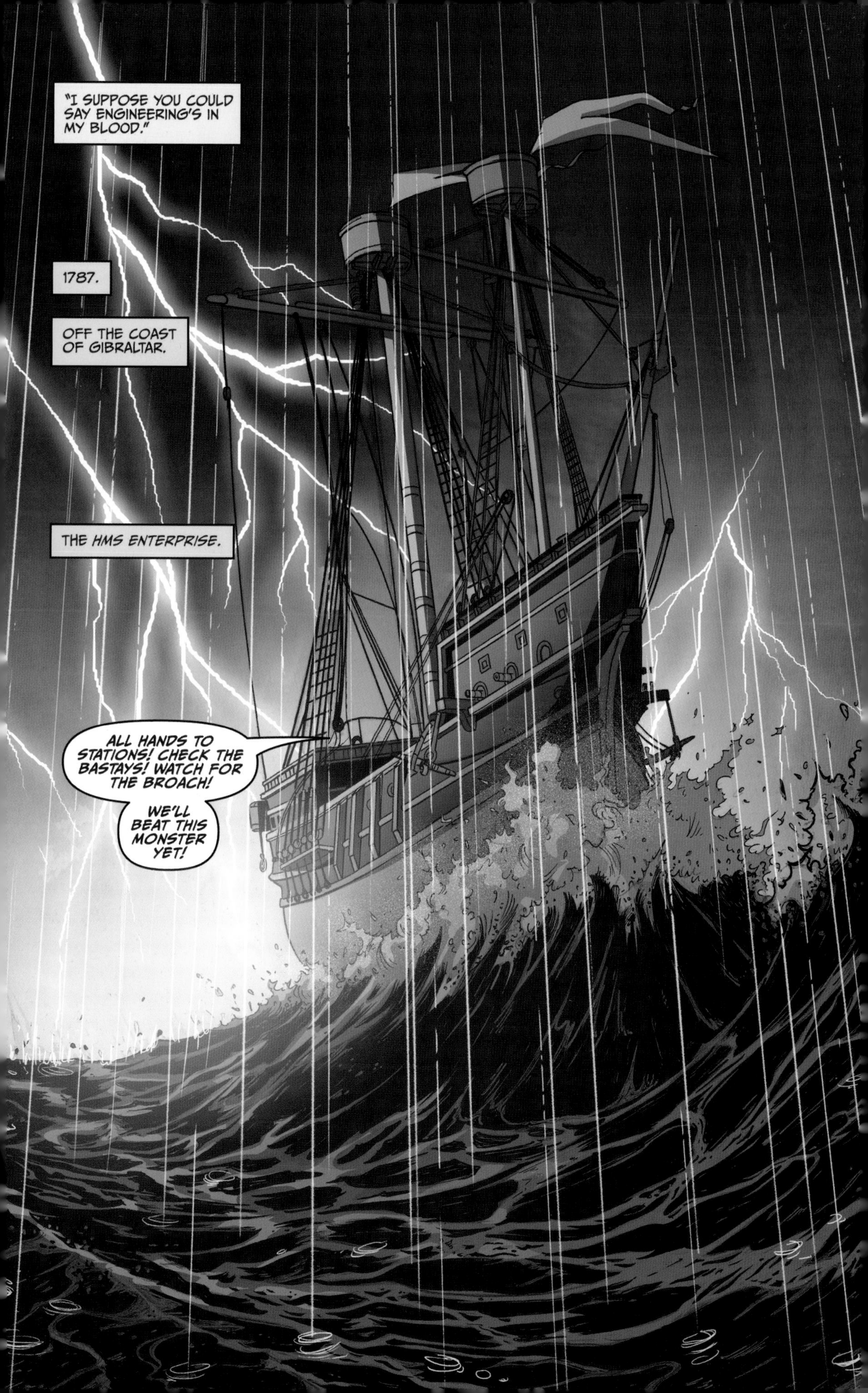
"I SUPPOSE YOU COULD SAY ENGINEERING'S IN MY BLOOD."
1787.
OFF THE COAST OF GIBRALTAR.
THE *HMS ENTERPRISE*.
ALL HANDS TO STATIONS! CHECK THE BASTAYS! WATCH FOR THE BROACH!
WE'LL BEAT THIS MONSTER YET!

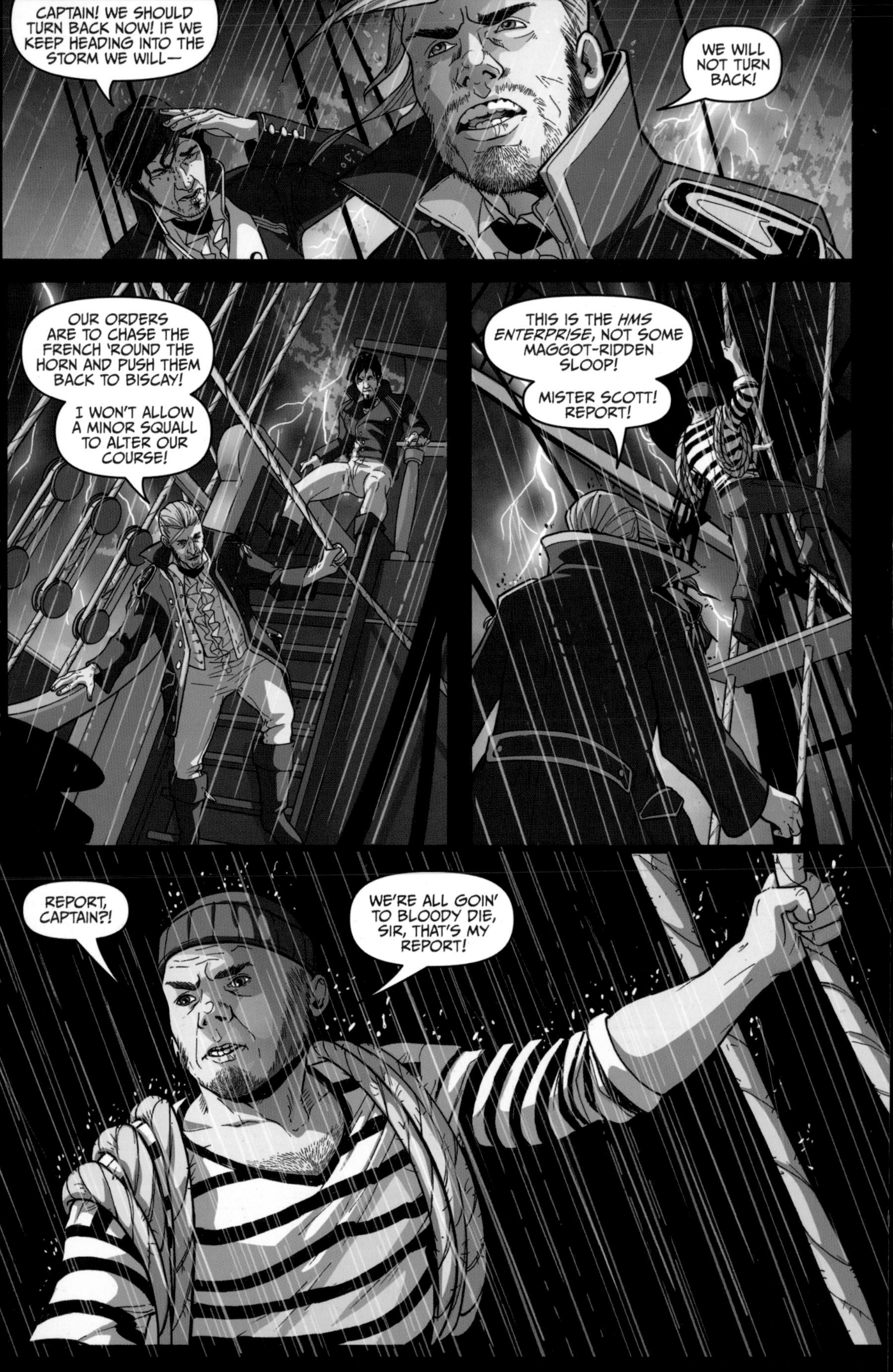
CAPTAIN! WE SHOULD TURN BACK NOW! IF WE KEEP HEADING INTO THE STORM WE WILL—
WE WILL NOT TURN BACK!
OUR ORDERS ARE TO CHASE THE FRENCH 'ROUND THE HORN AND PUSH THEM BACK TO BISCAY!
I WON'T ALLOW A MINOR SQUALL TO ALTER OUR COURSE!
THIS IS THE *HMS ENTERPRISE*, NOT SOME MAGGOT-RIDDEN SLOOP!
MISTER SCOTT! REPORT!
REPORT, CAPTAIN?!
WE'RE ALL GOIN' TO BLOODY DIE, SIR, THAT'S MY REPORT!

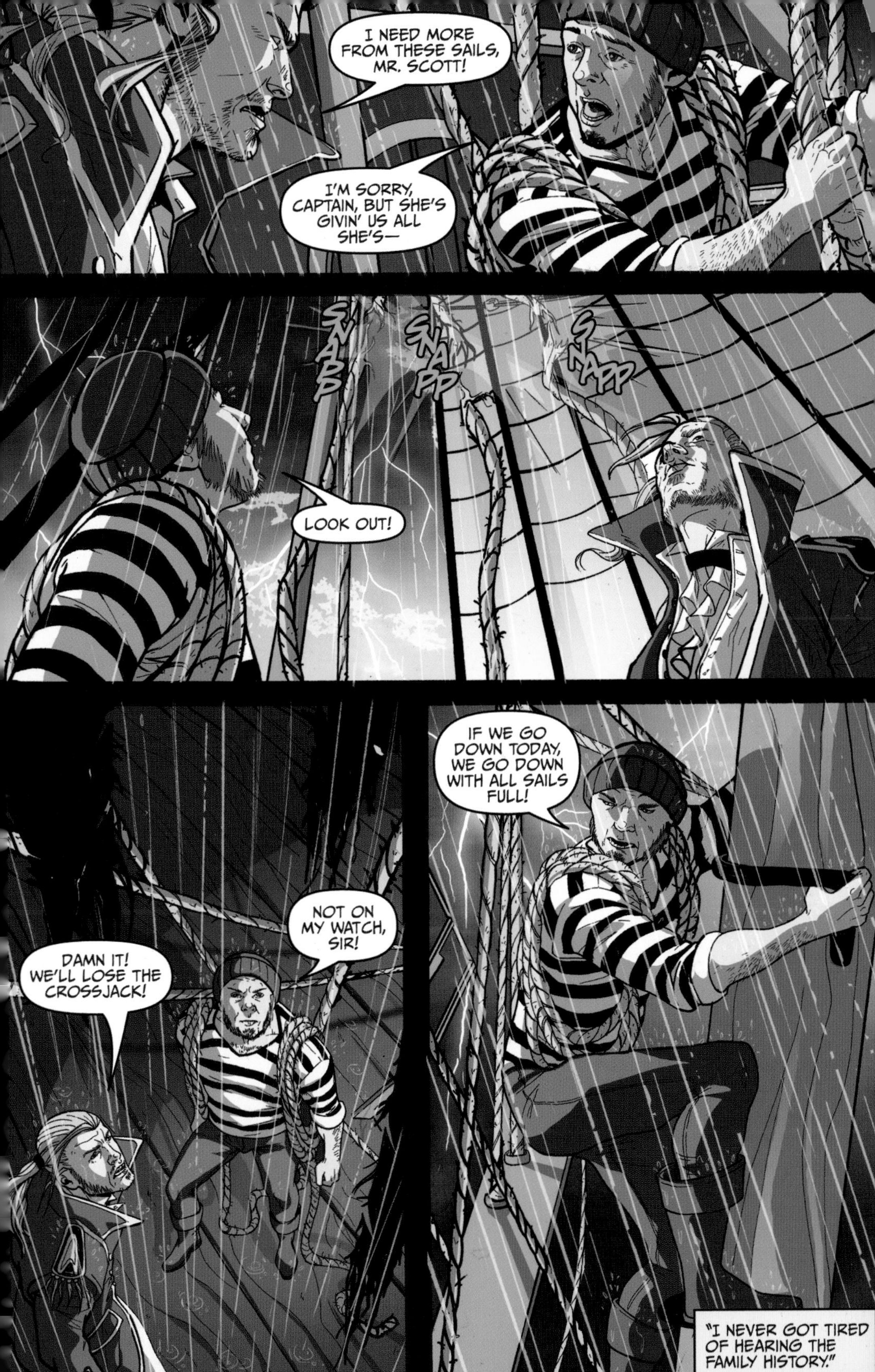
I NEED MORE FROM THESE SAILS, MR. SCOTT!
I'M SORRY, CAPTAIN, BUT SHE'S GIVIN' US ALL SHE'S—
SNAPP
SNAPP
SNAPP
LOOK OUT!
DAMN IT! WE'LL LOSE THE CROSSJACK!
NOT ON MY WATCH, SIR!
IF WE GO DOWN TODAY, WE GO DOWN WITH ALL SAILS FULL!
"I NEVER GOT TIRED OF HEARING THE FAMILY HISTORY."

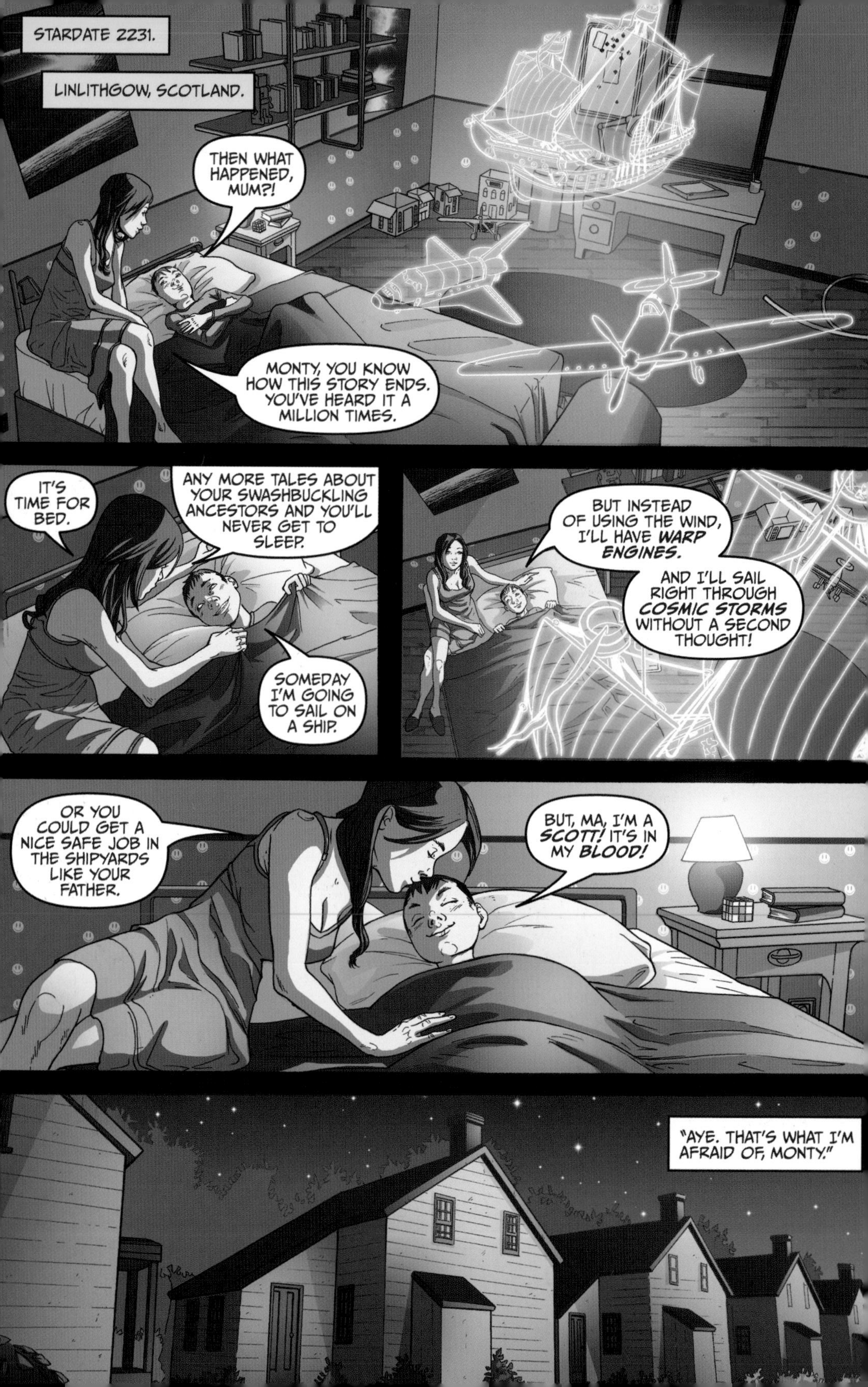
STARDATE 2231.
LINLITHGOW, SCOTLAND.
THEN WHAT HAPPENED, MUM?!
MONTY, YOU KNOW HOW THIS STORY ENDS. YOU'VE HEARD IT A MILLION TIMES.
IT'S TIME FOR BED.
ANY MORE TALES ABOUT YOUR SWASHBUCKLING ANCESTORS AND YOU'LL NEVER GET TO SLEEP.
SOMEDAY I'M GOING TO SAIL ON A SHIP.
BUT INSTEAD OF USING THE WIND, I'LL HAVE WARP ENGINES.
AND I'LL SAIL RIGHT THROUGH COSMIC STORMS WITHOUT A SECOND THOUGHT!
OR YOU COULD GET A NICE SAFE JOB IN THE SHIPYARDS LIKE YOUR FATHER.
BUT, MA, I'M A SCOTT! IT'S IN MY BLOOD!
"AYE. THAT'S WHAT I'M AFRAID OF, MONTY."

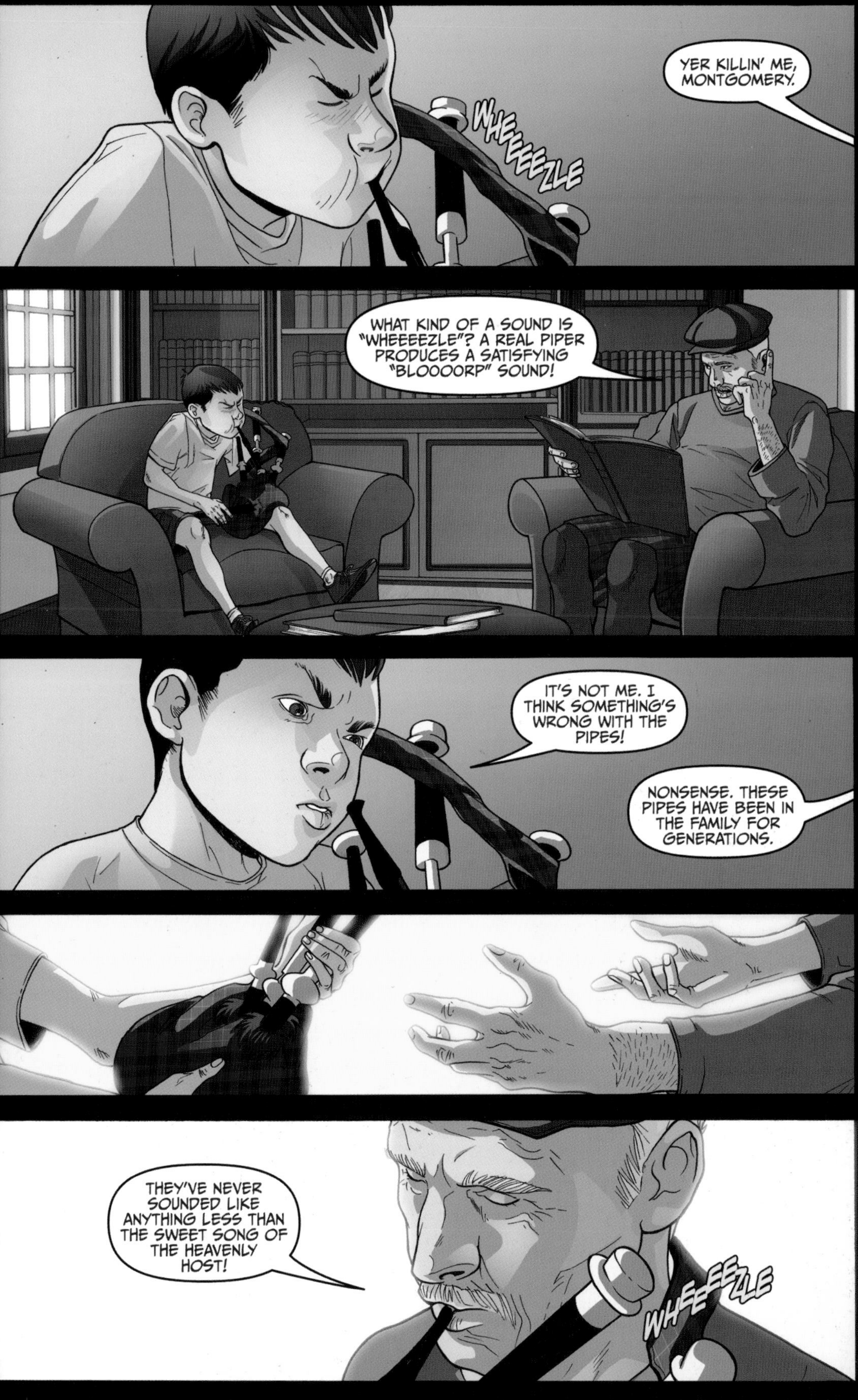
YER KILLIN' ME, MONTGOMERY.
WHEEEEZLE
WHAT KIND OF A SOUND IS "WHEEEEZLE"? A REAL PIPER PRODUCES A SATISFYING "BLOOOORP" SOUND!
IT'S NOT ME. I THINK SOMETHING'S WRONG WITH THE PIPES!
NONSENSE. THESE PIPES HAVE BEEN IN THE FAMILY FOR GENERATIONS.
THEY'VE NEVER SOUNDED LIKE ANYTHING LESS THAN THE SWEET SONG OF THE HEAVENLY HOST!
WHEEEEZLE

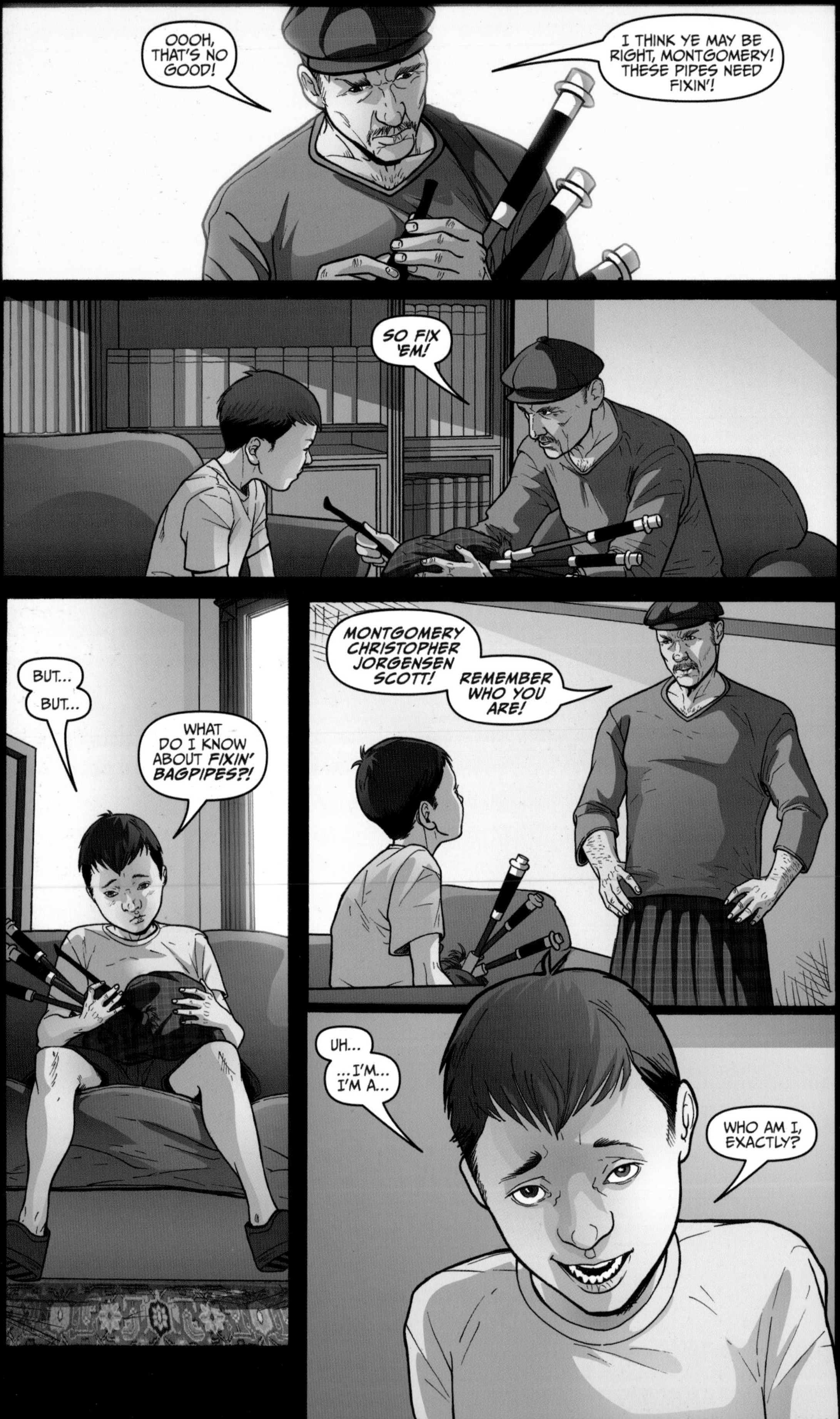

OOOH, THAT'S NO GOOD!
I THINK YE MAY BE RIGHT, MONTGOMERY! THESE PIPES NEED FIXIN'!
SO FIX 'EM!
BUT...
BUT...
WHAT DO I KNOW ABOUT FIXIN' BAGPIPES?!
MONTGOMERY CHRISTOPHER JORGENSEN SCOTT!
REMEMBER WHO YOU ARE!
UH...
...I'M... I'M A...
WHO AM I, EXACTLY?

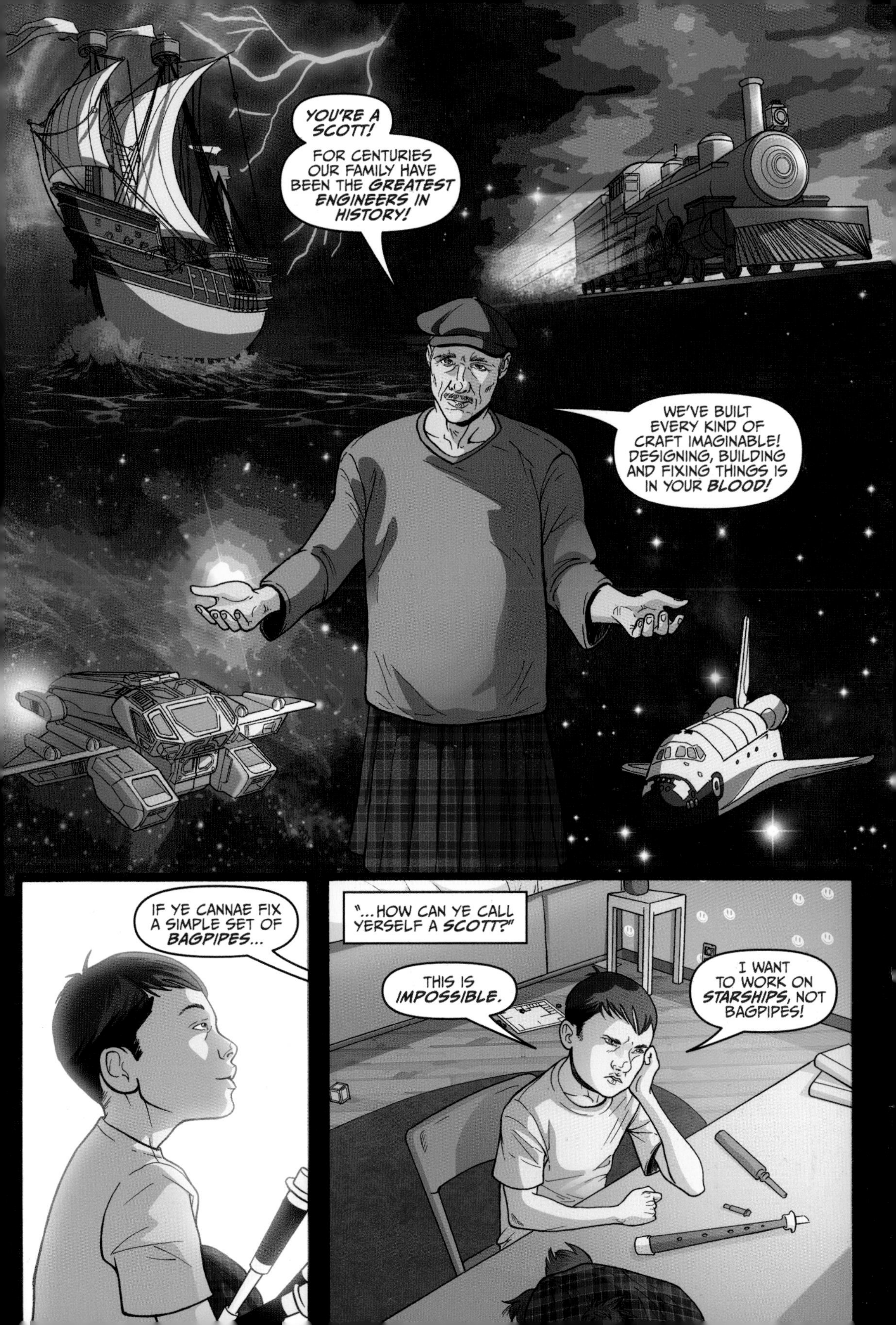
YOU'RE A SCOTT!
FOR CENTURIES OUR FAMILY HAVE BEEN THE GREATEST ENGINEERS IN HISTORY!
WE'VE BUILT EVERY KIND OF CRAFT IMAGINABLE! DESIGNING, BUILDING AND FIXING THINGS IS IN YOUR BLOOD!
IF YE CANNAE FIX A SIMPLE SET OF BAGPIPES...
"...HOW CAN YE CALL YERSELF A SCOTT?"
THIS IS IMPOSSIBLE.
I WANT TO WORK ON STARSHIPS, NOT BAGPIPES!

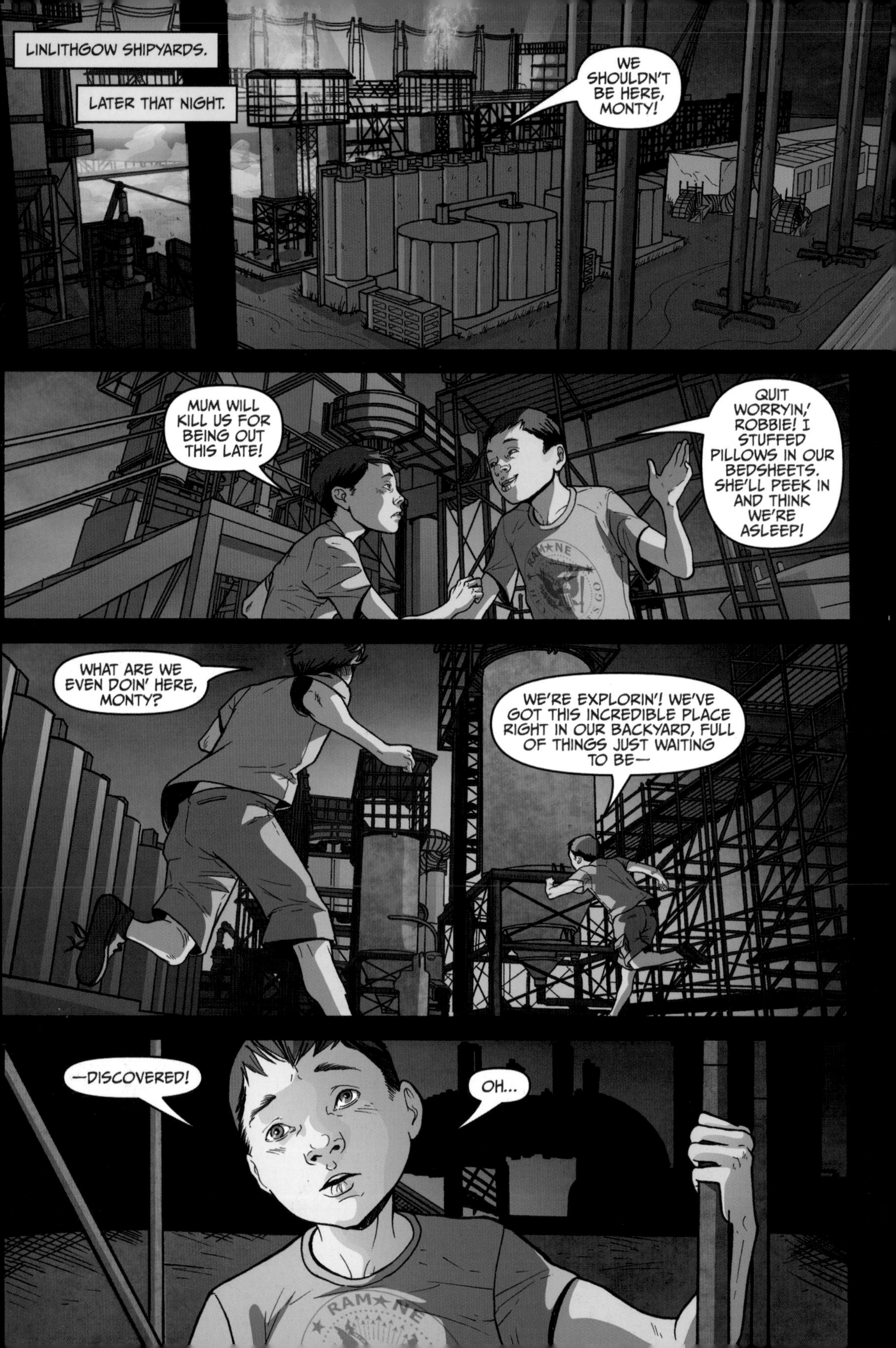
LINLITHGOW SHIPYARDS.
LATER THAT NIGHT.
WE SHOULDN'T BE HERE, MONTY!
MUM WILL KILL US FOR BEING OUT THIS LATE!
QUIT WORRYIN,' ROBBIE! I STUFFED PILLOWS IN OUR BEDSHEETS. SHE'LL PEEK IN AND THINK WE'RE ASLEEP!
WHAT ARE WE EVEN DOIN' HERE, MONTY?
WE'RE EXPLORIN'! WE'VE GOT THIS INCREDIBLE PLACE RIGHT IN OUR BACKYARD, FULL OF THINGS JUST WAITING TO BE—
—DISCOVERED!
OH...

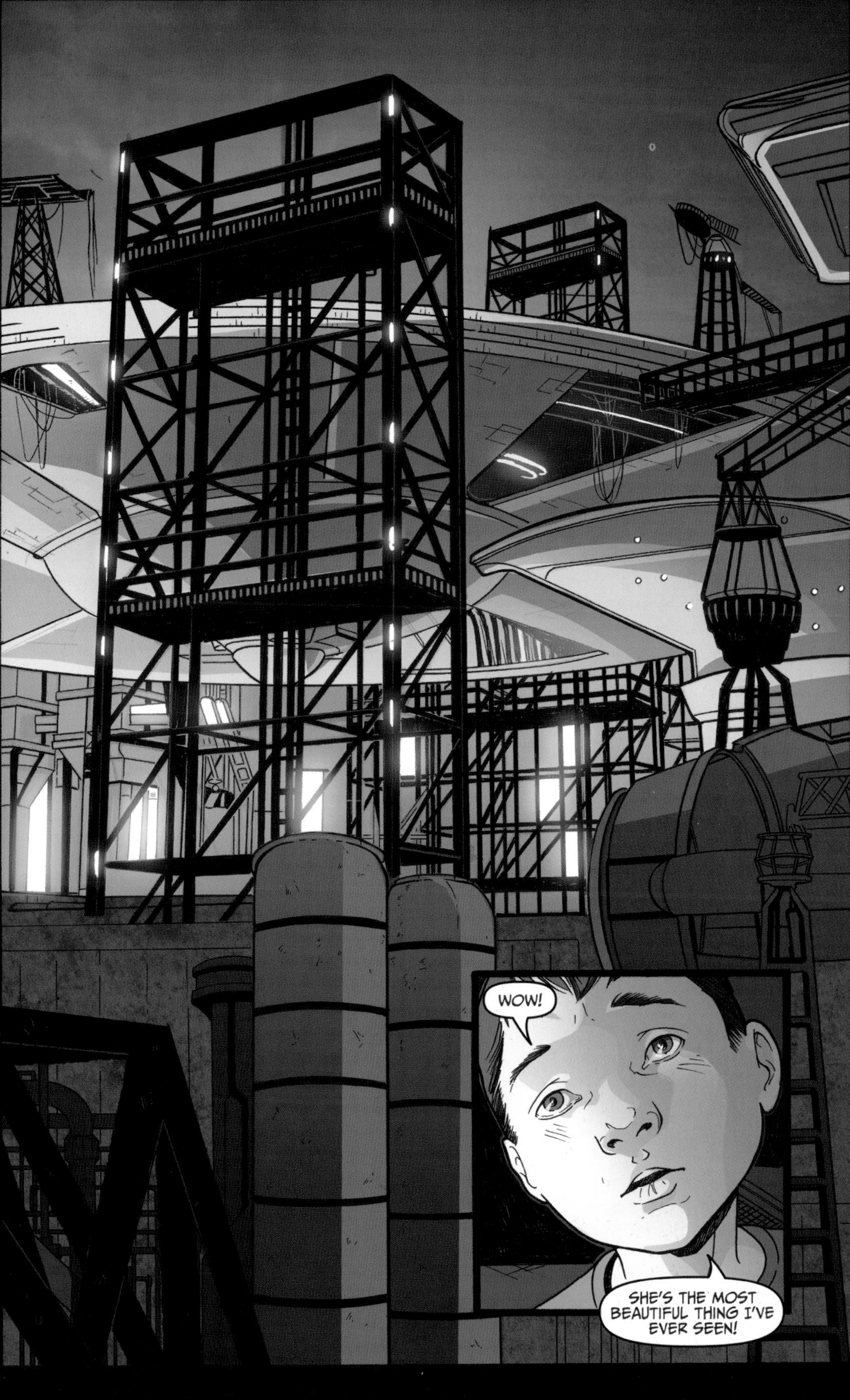
WOW!
SHE'S THE MOST BEAUTIFUL THING I'VE EVER SEEN!

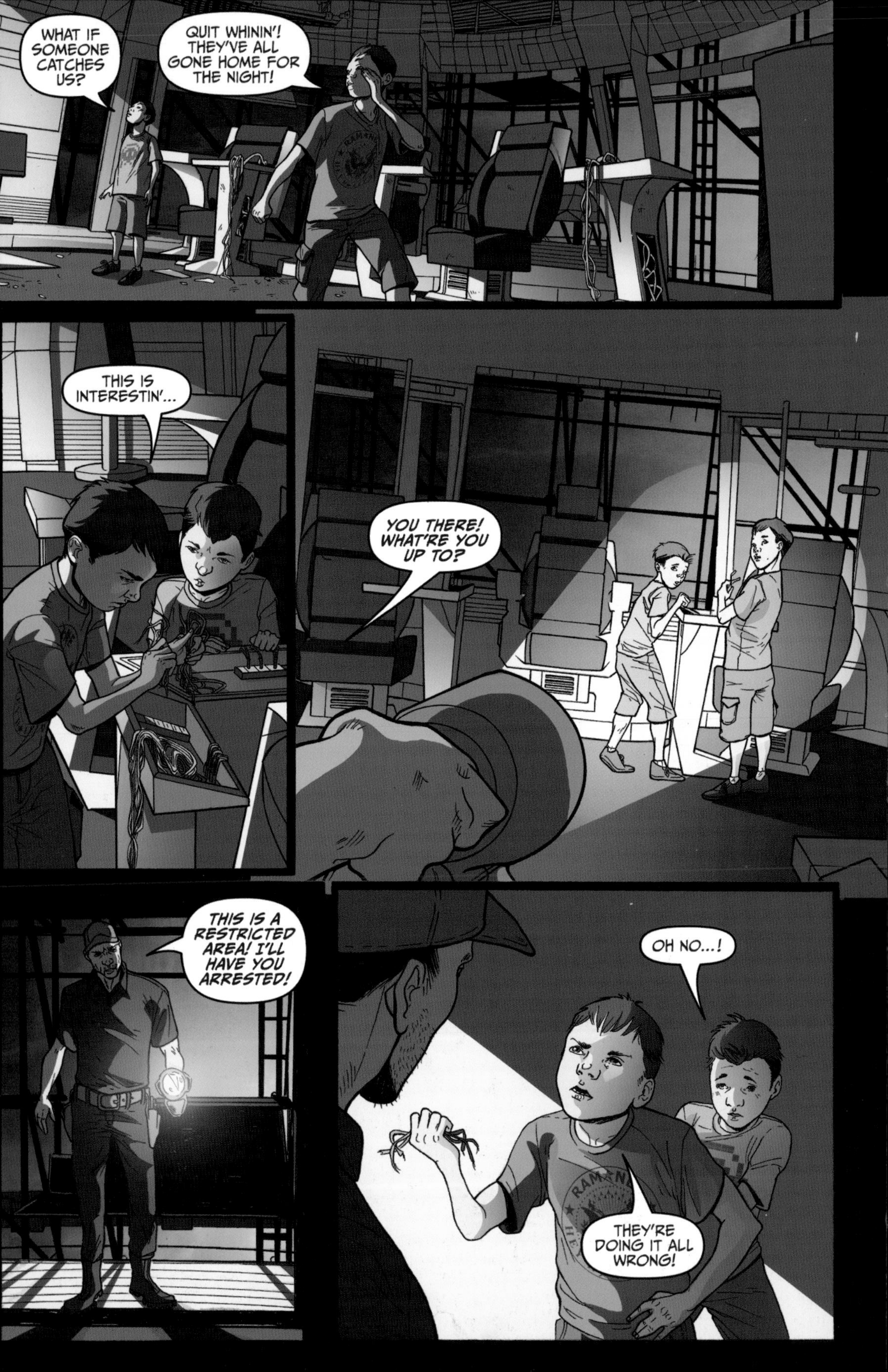
WHAT IF SOMEONE CATCHES US?
QUIT WHININ'! THEY'VE ALL GONE HOME FOR THE NIGHT!
THIS IS INTERESTIN'...
YOU THERE! WHAT'RE YOU UP TO?
THIS IS A RESTRICTED AREA! I'LL HAVE YOU ARRESTED!
OH NO...!
THEY'RE DOING IT ALL WRONG!

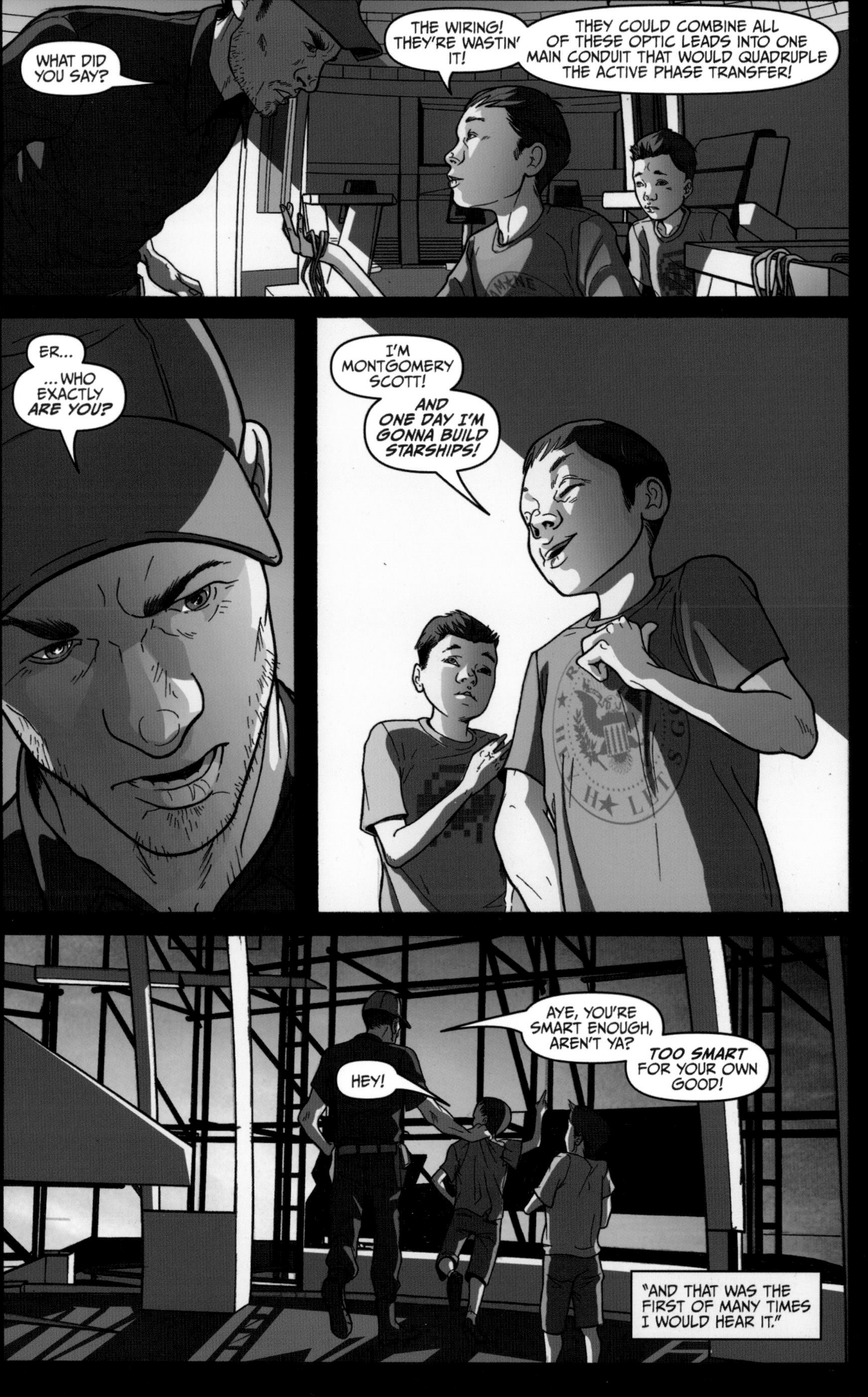

WHAT DID YOU SAY?
THE WIRING! THEY'RE WASTIN' IT!
THEY COULD COMBINE ALL OF THESE OPTIC LEADS INTO ONE MAIN CONDUIT THAT WOULD QUADRUPLE THE ACTIVE PHASE TRANSFER!
ER...
...WHO EXACTLY ARE YOU?
I'M MONTGOMERY SCOTT!
AND ONE DAY I'M GONNA BUILD STARSHIPS!
AYE, YOU'RE SMART ENOUGH, AREN'T YA?
TOO SMART FOR YOUR OWN GOOD!
HEY!
"AND THAT WAS THE FIRST OF MANY TIMES I WOULD HEAR IT."

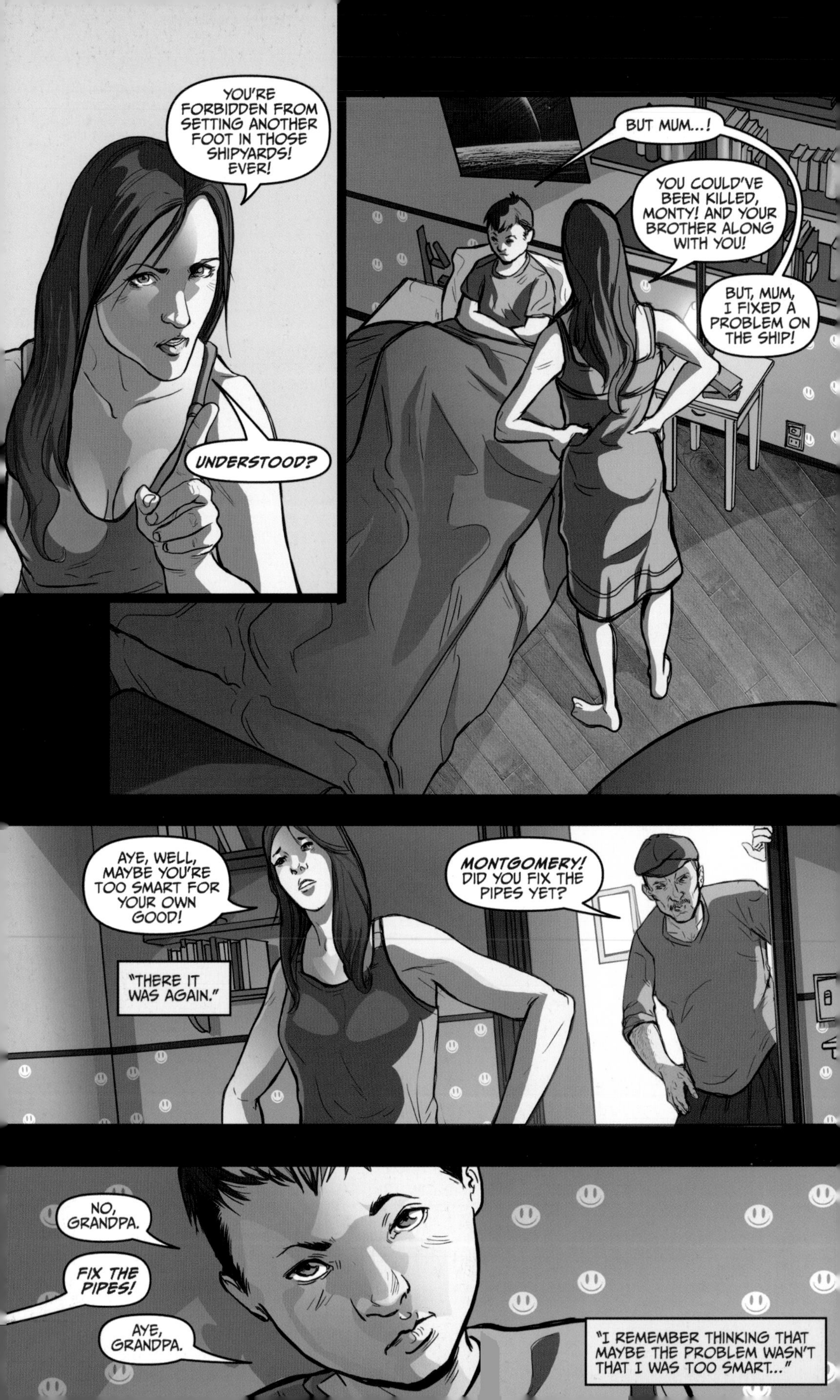
YOU'RE FORBIDDEN FROM SETTING ANOTHER FOOT IN THOSE SHIPYARDS! EVER!
UNDERSTOOD?
BUT MUM...!
YOU COULD'VE BEEN KILLED, MONTY! AND YOUR BROTHER ALONG WITH YOU!
BUT, MUM, I FIXED A PROBLEM ON THE SHIP!
AYE, WELL, MAYBE YOU'RE TOO SMART FOR YOUR OWN GOOD!
"THERE IT WAS AGAIN."
MONTGOMERY! DID YOU FIX THE PIPES YET?
NO, GRANDPA.
FIX THE PIPES!
AYE, GRANDPA.
"I REMEMBER THINKING THAT MAYBE THE PROBLEM WASN'T THAT I WAS TOO SMART..."

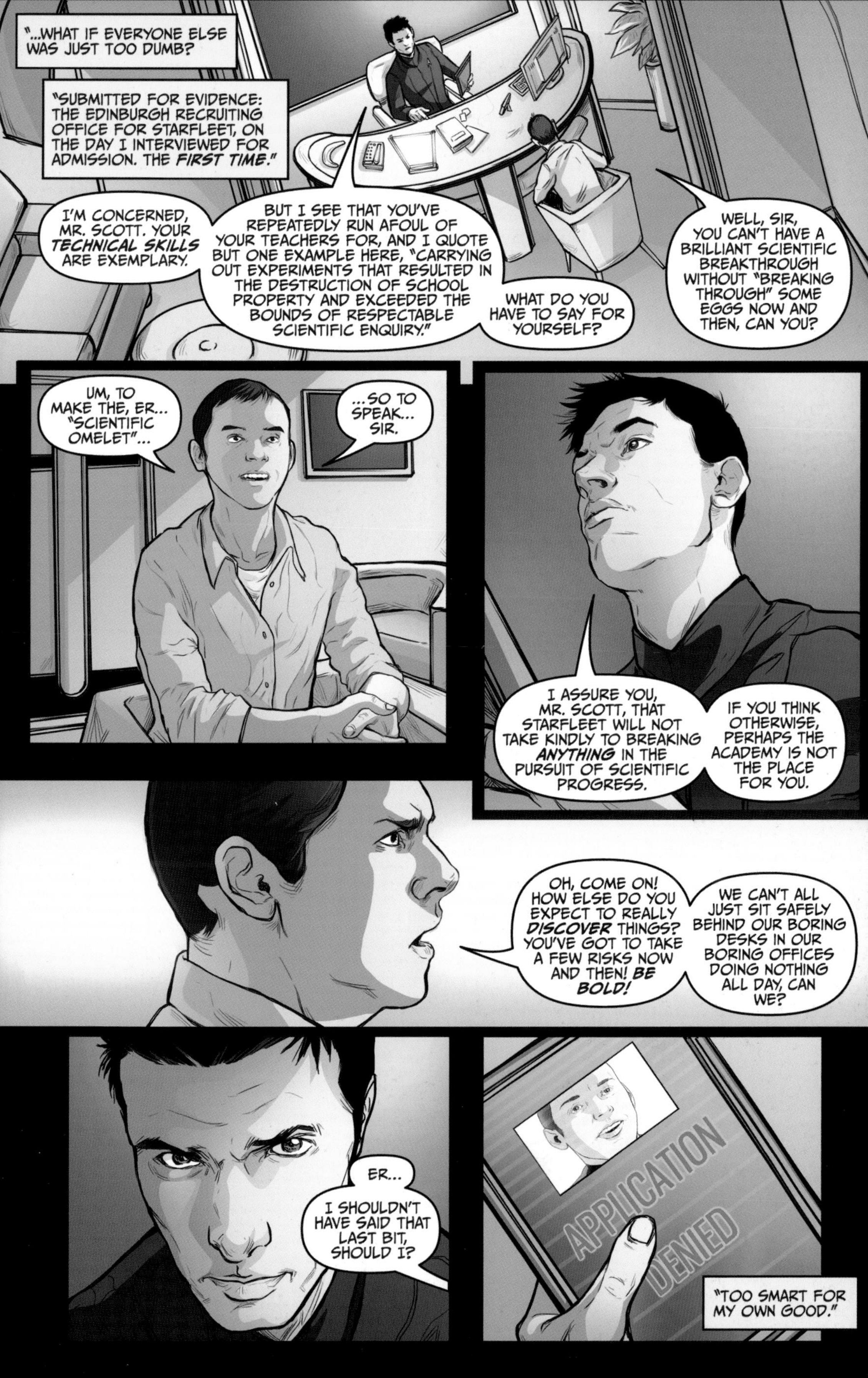
"...WHAT IF EVERYONE ELSE WAS JUST TOO DUMB?
"SUBMITTED FOR EVIDENCE: THE EDINBURGH RECRUITING OFFICE FOR STARFLEET, ON THE DAY I INTERVIEWED FOR ADMISSION. THE *FIRST TIME*."
I'M CONCERNED, MR. SCOTT. YOUR ***TECHNICAL SKILLS*** ARE EXEMPLARY.
BUT I SEE THAT YOU'VE REPEATEDLY RUN AFOUL OF YOUR TEACHERS FOR, AND I QUOTE BUT ONE EXAMPLE HERE, "CARRYING OUT EXPERIMENTS THAT RESULTED IN THE DESTRUCTION OF SCHOOL PROPERTY AND EXCEEDED THE BOUNDS OF RESPECTABLE SCIENTIFIC ENQUIRY."
WHAT DO YOU HAVE TO SAY FOR YOURSELF?
WELL, SIR, YOU CAN'T HAVE A BRILLIANT SCIENTIFIC BREAKTHROUGH WITHOUT "BREAKING THROUGH" SOME EGGS NOW AND THEN, CAN YOU?
UM, TO MAKE THE, ER... "SCIENTIFIC OMELET"...
...SO TO SPEAK... SIR.
I ASSURE YOU, MR. SCOTT, THAT STARFLEET WILL NOT TAKE KINDLY TO BREAKING ***ANYTHING*** IN THE PURSUIT OF SCIENTIFIC PROGRESS.
IF YOU THINK OTHERWISE, PERHAPS THE ACADEMY IS NOT THE PLACE FOR YOU.
OH, COME ON! HOW ELSE DO YOU EXPECT TO REALLY ***DISCOVER*** THINGS? YOU'VE GOT TO TAKE A FEW RISKS NOW AND THEN! ***BE BOLD!***
WE CAN'T ALL JUST SIT SAFELY BEHIND OUR BORING DESKS IN OUR BORING OFFICES DOING NOTHING ALL DAY, CAN WE?
ER...
I SHOULDN'T HAVE SAID THAT LAST BIT, SHOULD I?
APPLICATION DENIED
"TOO SMART FOR MY OWN GOOD."

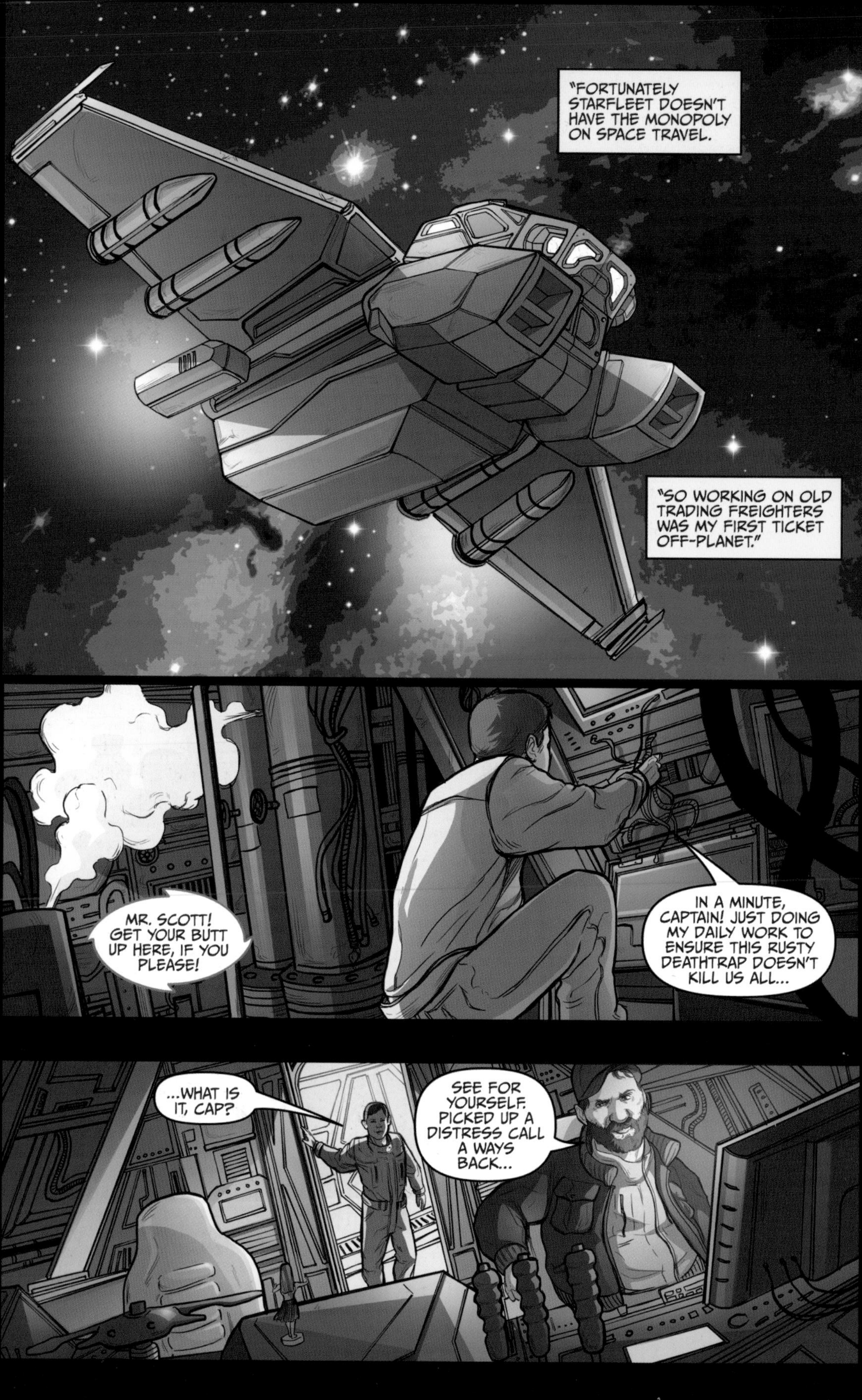
"FORTUNATELY STARFLEET DOESN'T HAVE THE MONOPOLY ON SPACE TRAVEL.
"SO WORKING ON OLD TRADING FREIGHTERS WAS MY FIRST TICKET OFF-PLANET."
MR. SCOTT! GET YOUR BUTT UP HERE, IF YOU PLEASE!
IN A MINUTE, CAPTAIN! JUST DOING MY DAILY WORK TO ENSURE THIS RUSTY DEATHTRAP DOESN'T KILL US ALL...
...WHAT IS IT, CAP?
SEE FOR YOURSELF. PICKED UP A DISTRESS CALL A WAYS BACK...

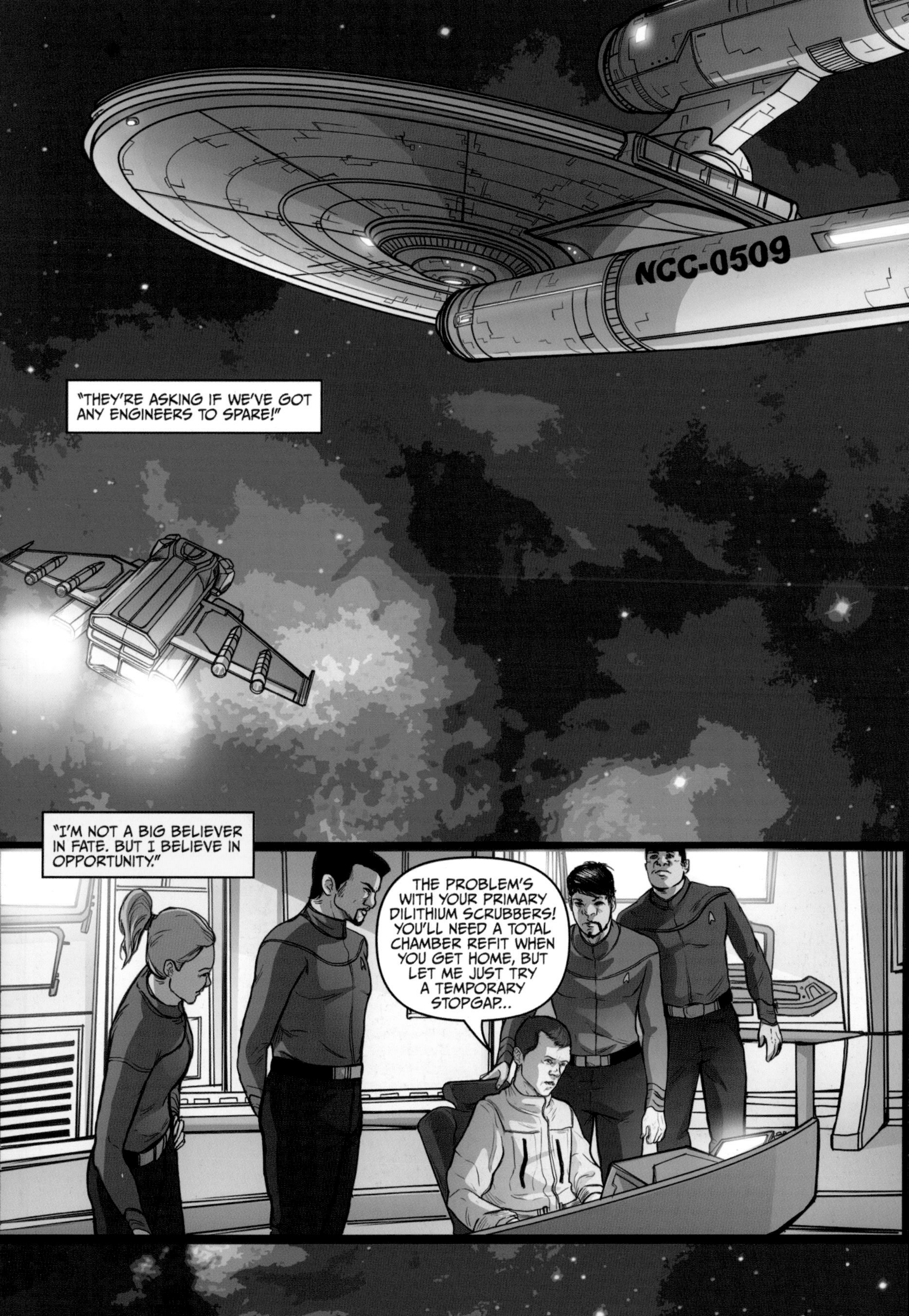
NCC-0509
"THEY'RE ASKING IF WE'VE GOT ANY ENGINEERS TO SPARE!"
"I'M NOT A BIG BELIEVER IN FATE. BUT I BELIEVE IN OPPORTUNITY."
THE PROBLEM'S WITH YOUR PRIMARY DILITHIUM SCRUBBERS! YOU'LL NEED A TOTAL CHAMBER REFIT WHEN YOU GET HOME, BUT LET ME JUST TRY A TEMPORARY STOPGAP...

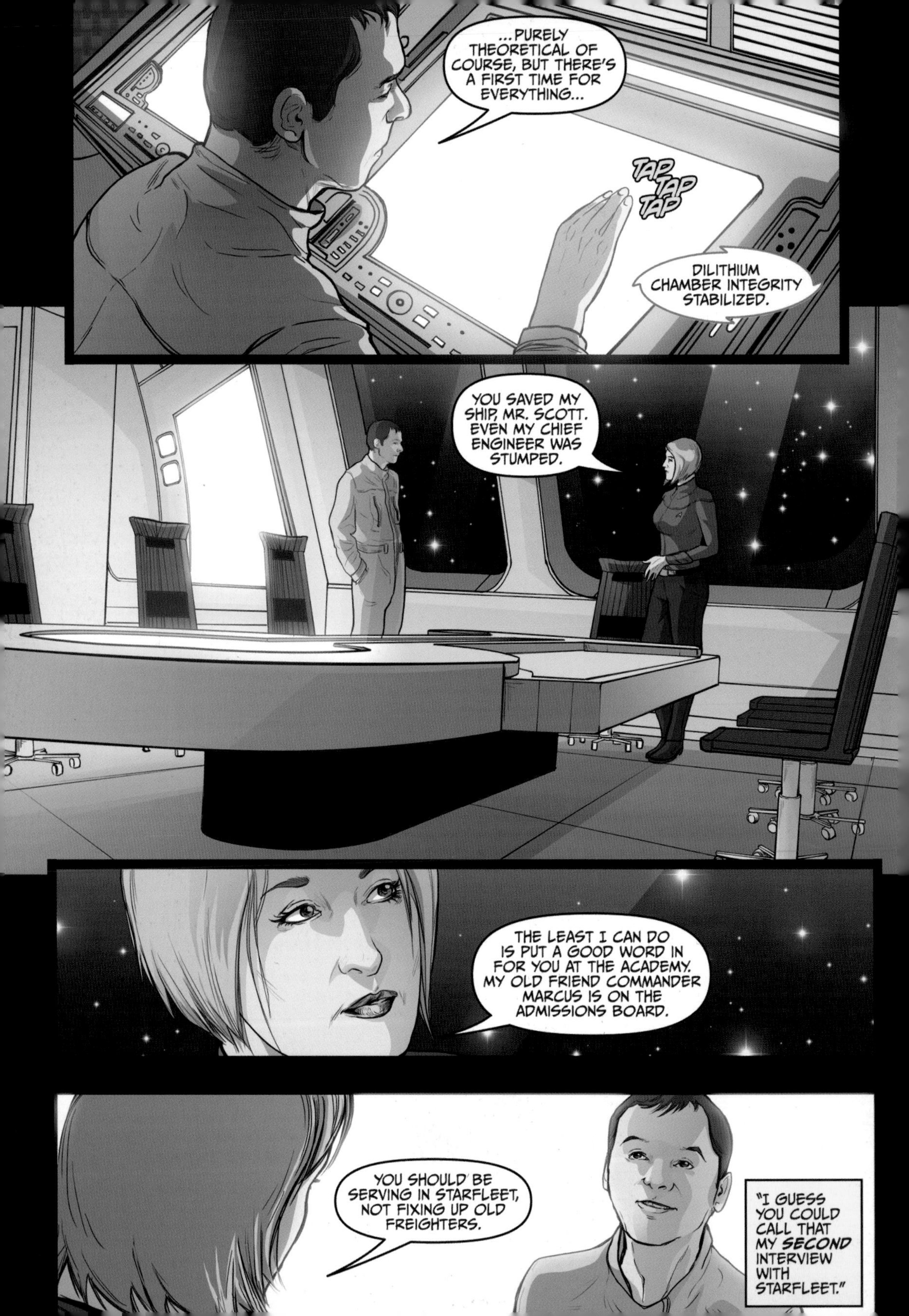
...PURELY THEORETICAL OF COURSE, BUT THERE'S A FIRST TIME FOR EVERYTHING...
TAP TAP TAP
DILITHIUM CHAMBER INTEGRITY STABILIZED.
YOU SAVED MY SHIP, MR. SCOTT. EVEN MY CHIEF ENGINEER WAS STUMPED.
THE LEAST I CAN DO IS PUT A GOOD WORD IN FOR YOU AT THE ACADEMY. MY OLD FRIEND COMMANDER MARCUS IS ON THE ADMISSIONS BOARD.
YOU SHOULD BE SERVING IN STARFLEET, NOT FIXING UP OLD FREIGHTERS.
"I GUESS YOU COULD CALL THAT MY *SECOND* INTERVIEW WITH STARFLEET."

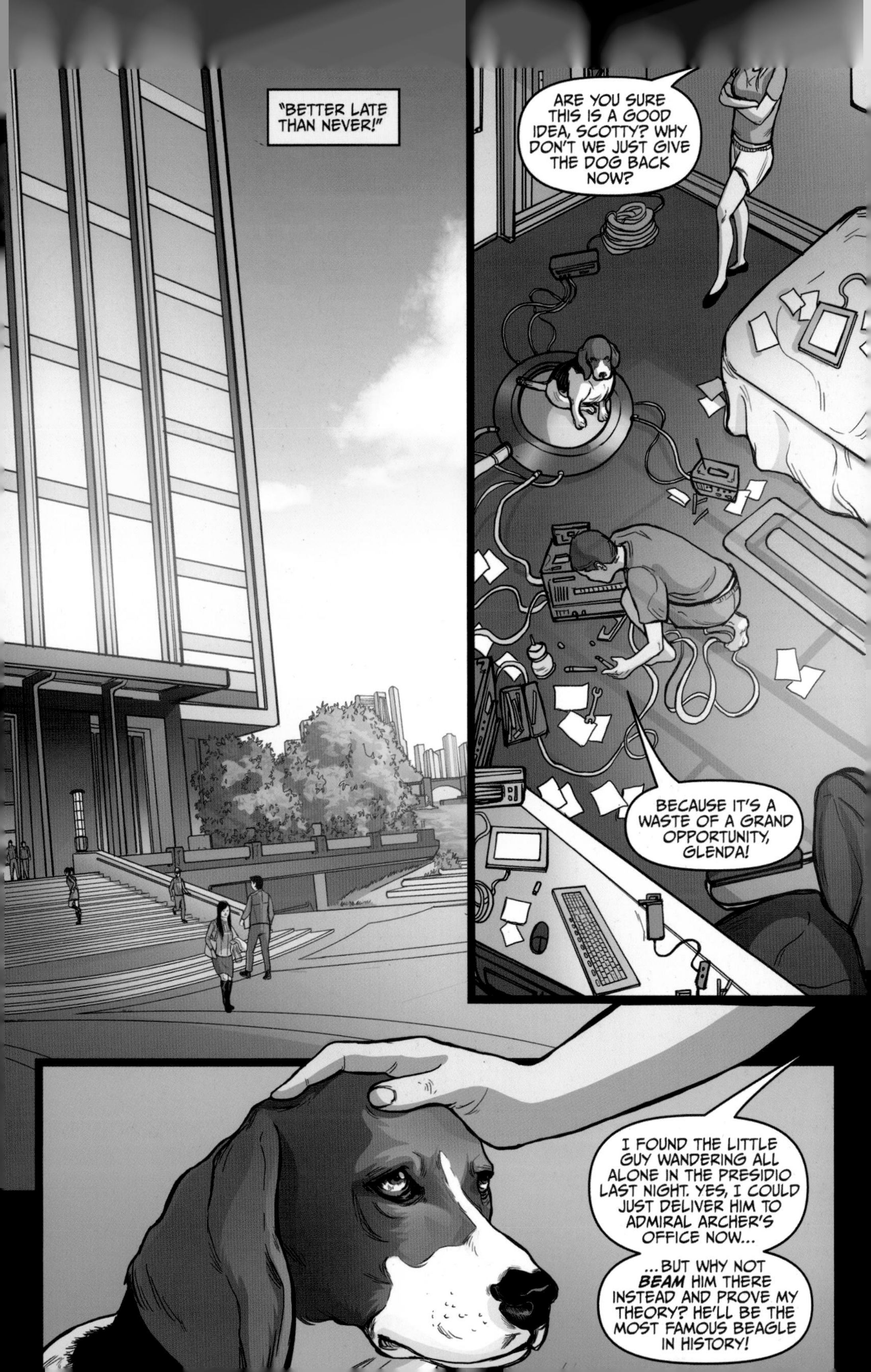
"BETTER LATE THAN NEVER!"
ARE YOU SURE THIS IS A GOOD IDEA, SCOTTY? WHY DON'T WE JUST GIVE THE DOG BACK NOW?
BECAUSE IT'S A WASTE OF A GRAND OPPORTUNITY, GLENDA!
I FOUND THE LITTLE GUY WANDERING ALL ALONE IN THE PRESIDIO LAST NIGHT. YES, I COULD JUST DELIVER HIM TO ADMIRAL ARCHER'S OFFICE NOW...
...BUT WHY NOT BEAM HIM THERE INSTEAD AND PROVE MY THEORY? HE'LL BE THE MOST FAMOUS BEAGLE IN HISTORY!

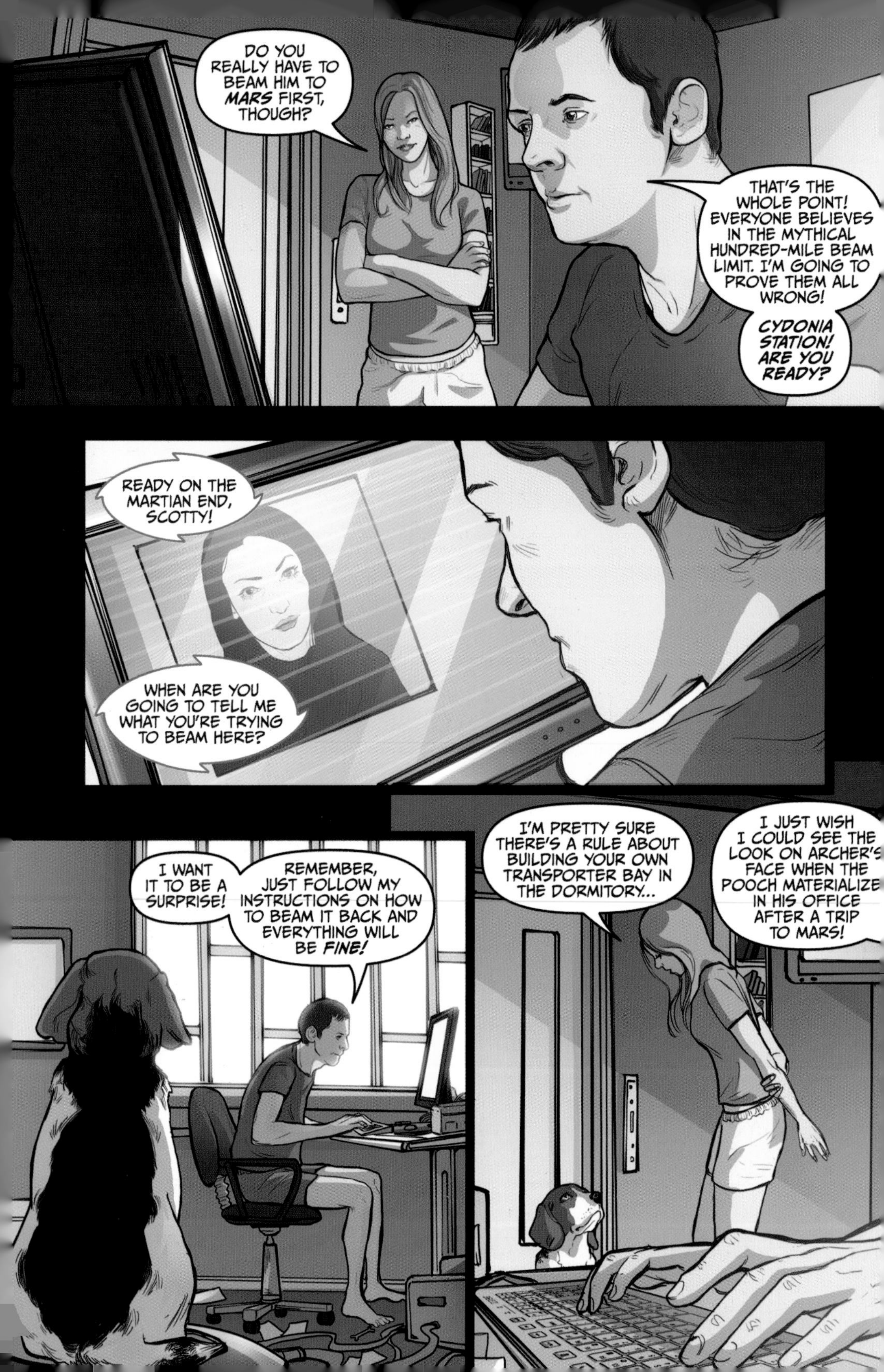
DO YOU REALLY HAVE TO BEAM HIM TO *MARS* FIRST, THOUGH?
THAT'S THE WHOLE POINT! EVERYONE BELIEVES IN THE MYTHICAL HUNDRED-MILE BEAM LIMIT. I'M GOING TO PROVE THEM ALL WRONG!
CYDONIA STATION! ARE YOU READY?
READY ON THE MARTIAN END, SCOTTY!
WHEN ARE YOU GOING TO TELL ME WHAT YOU'RE TRYING TO BEAM HERE?
I WANT IT TO BE A SURPRISE!
REMEMBER, JUST FOLLOW MY INSTRUCTIONS ON HOW TO BEAM IT BACK AND EVERYTHING WILL BE *FINE!*
I'M PRETTY SURE THERE'S A RULE ABOUT BUILDING YOUR OWN TRANSPORTER BAY IN THE DORMITORY...
I JUST WISH I COULD SEE THE LOOK ON ARCHER'S FACE WHEN THE POOCH MATERIALIZE IN HIS OFFICE AFTER A TRIP TO MARS!

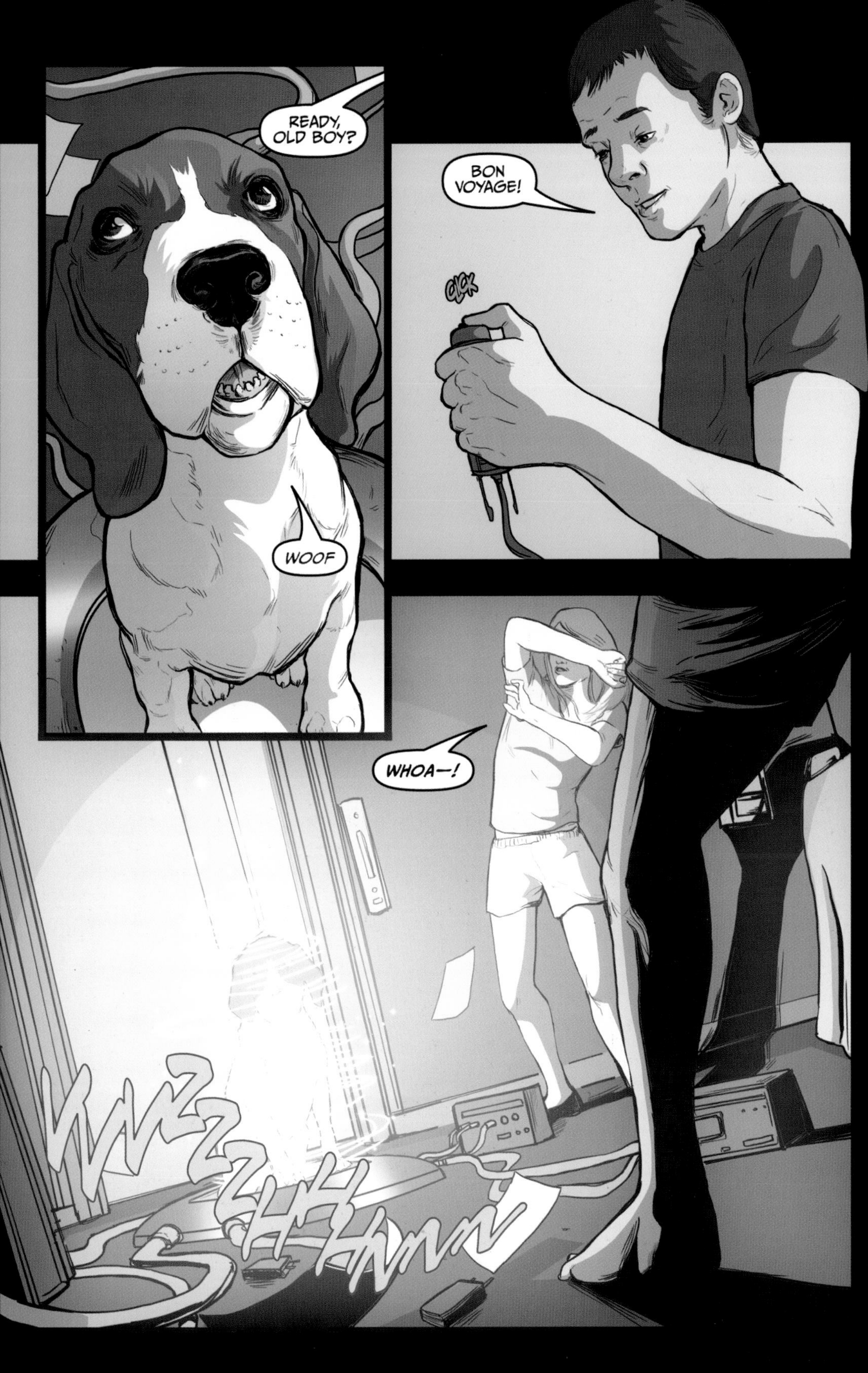

READY, OLD BOY?
WOOF
BON VOYAGE!
CLICK
WHOA—!
VVVZZZZHHHMMM

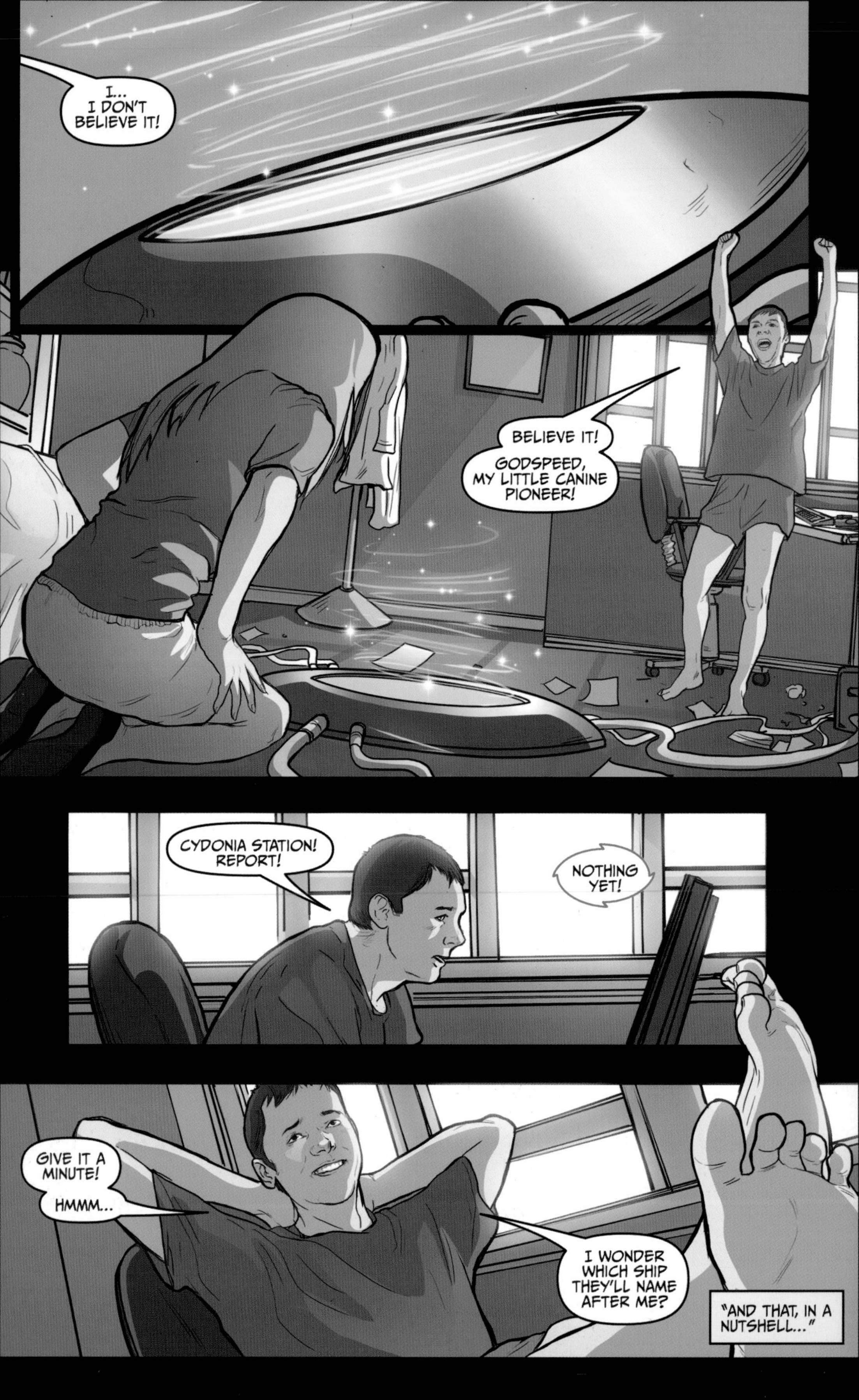
I...
I DON'T BELIEVE IT!
BELIEVE IT!
GODSPEED, MY LITTLE CANINE PIONEER!
CYDONIA STATION! REPORT!
NOTHING YET!
GIVE IT A MINUTE!
HMMM...
I WONDER WHICH SHIP THEY'LL NAME AFTER ME?
"AND THAT, IN A NUTSHELL..."

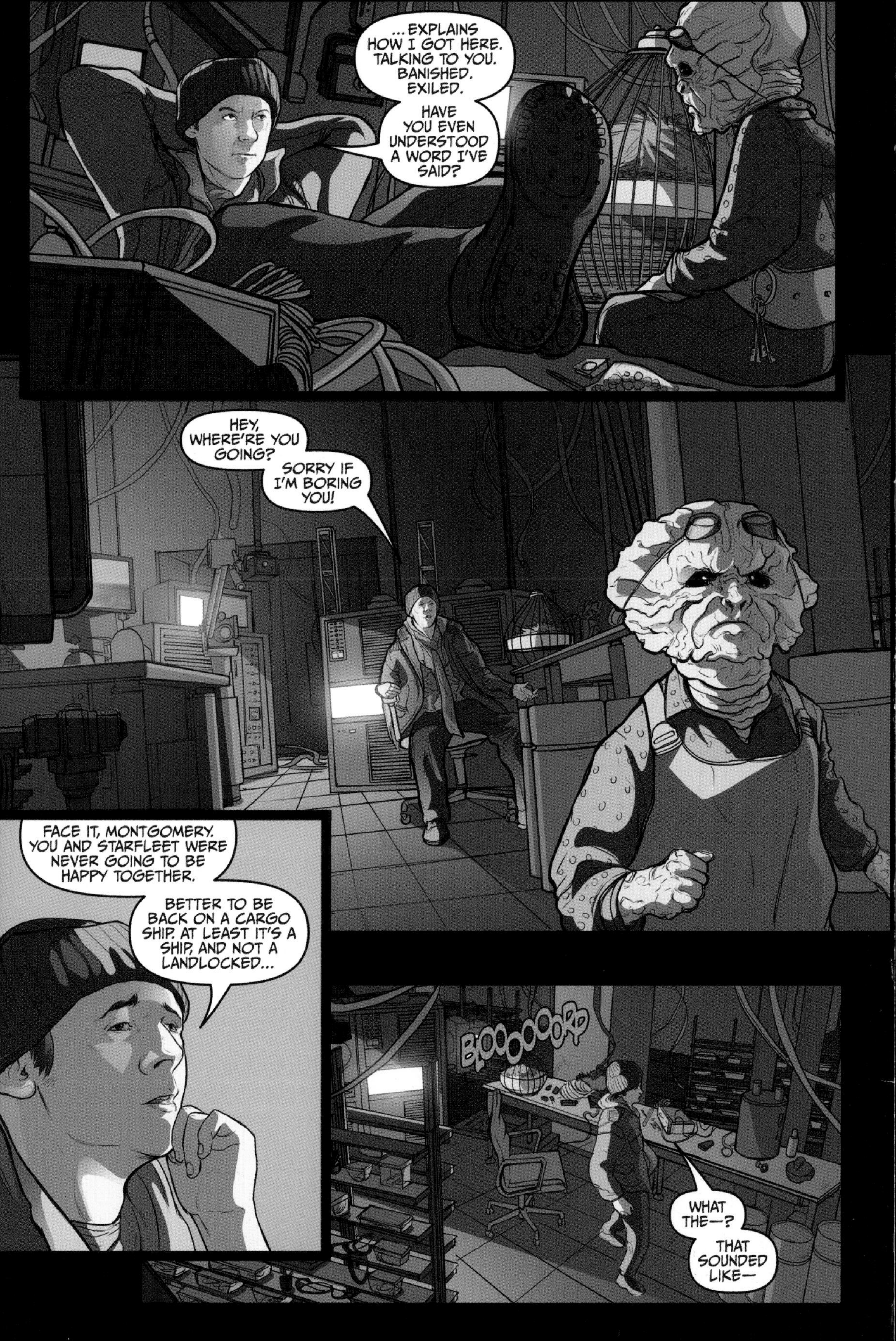
...EXPLAINS HOW I GOT HERE. TALKING TO YOU. BANISHED. EXILED.
HAVE YOU EVEN UNDERSTOOD A WORD I'VE SAID?
HEY, WHERE'RE YOU GOING?
SORRY IF I'M BORING YOU!
FACE IT, MONTGOMERY. YOU AND STARFLEET WERE NEVER GOING TO BE HAPPY TOGETHER.
BETTER TO BE BACK ON A CARGO SHIP. AT LEAST IT'S A SHIP, AND NOT A LANDLOCKED...
BLOOOOOORP
WHAT THE—?
THAT SOUNDED LIKE—

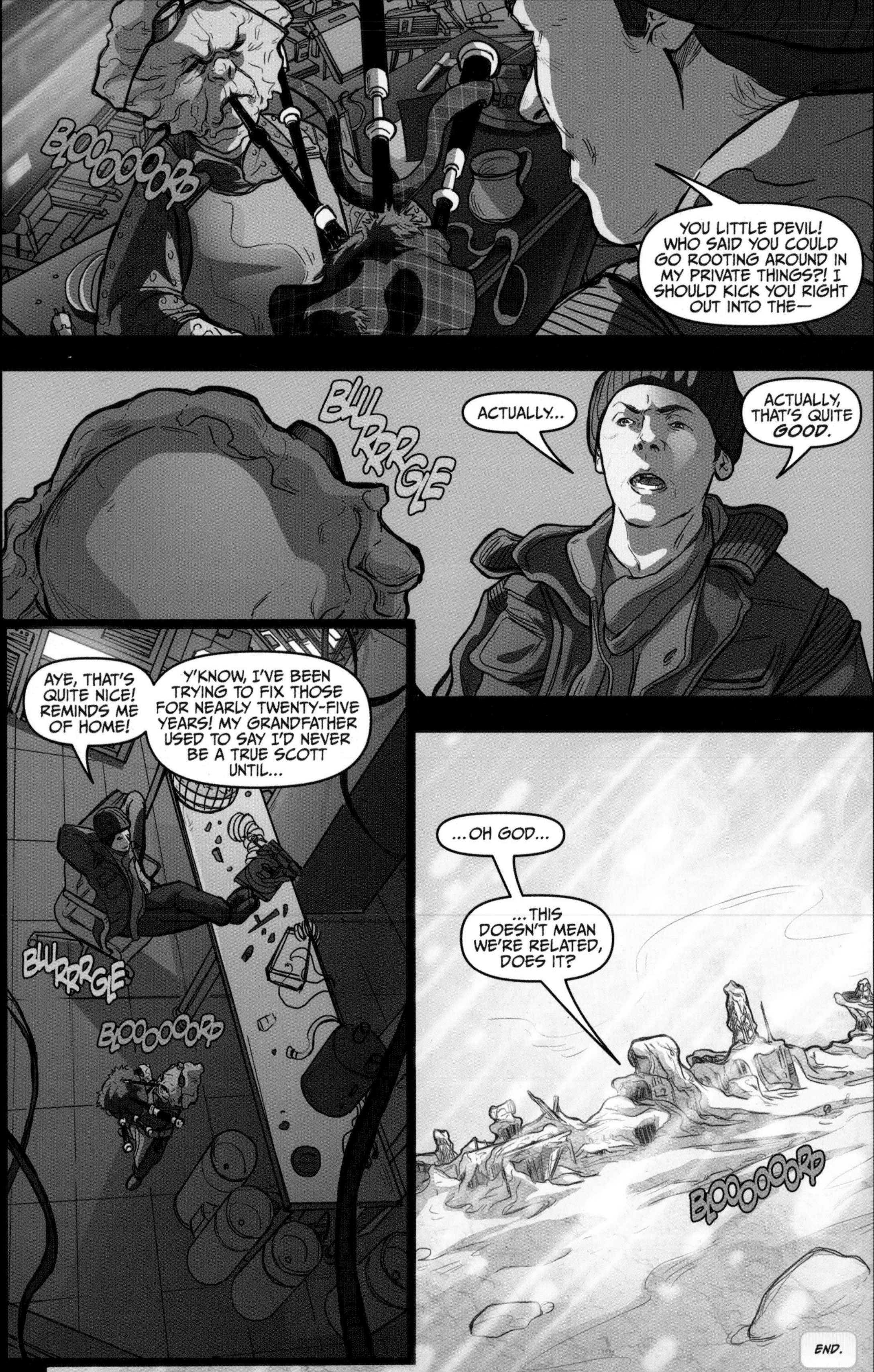
BLOOOOOORD
YOU LITTLE DEVIL! WHO SAID YOU COULD GO ROOTING AROUND IN MY PRIVATE THINGS?! I SHOULD KICK YOU RIGHT OUT INTO THE—
BLURRRGLE
ACTUALLY...
ACTUALLY, THAT'S QUITE GOOD.
AYE, THAT'S QUITE NICE! REMINDS ME OF HOME!
Y'KNOW, I'VE BEEN TRYING TO FIX THOSE FOR NEARLY TWENTY-FIVE YEARS! MY GRANDFATHER USED TO SAY I'D NEVER BE A TRUE SCOTT UNTIL...
BLURRRGLE
BLOOOOOORD
...OH GOD...
...THIS DOESN'T MEAN WE'RE RELATED, DOES IT?
BLOOOOOORD
END.

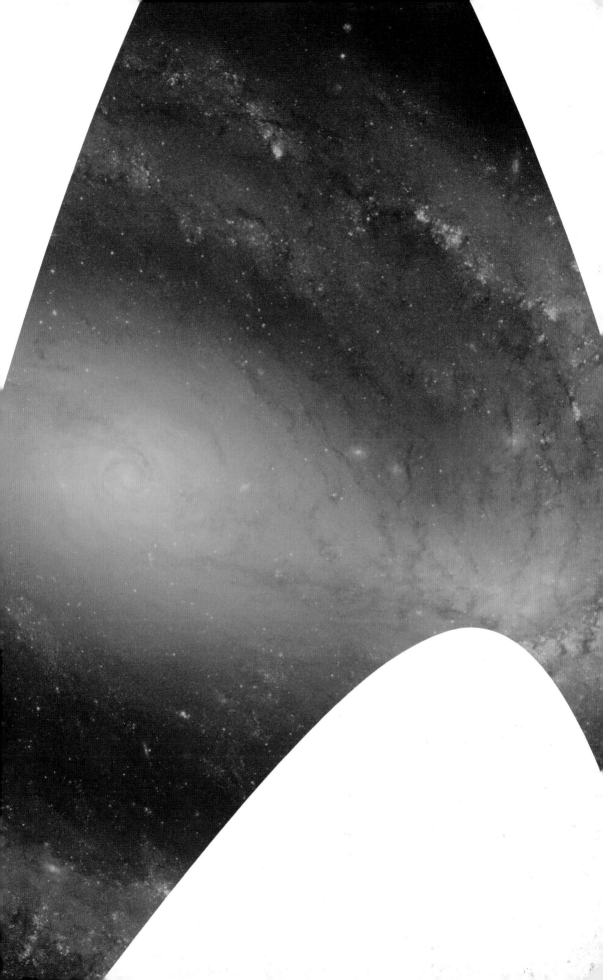

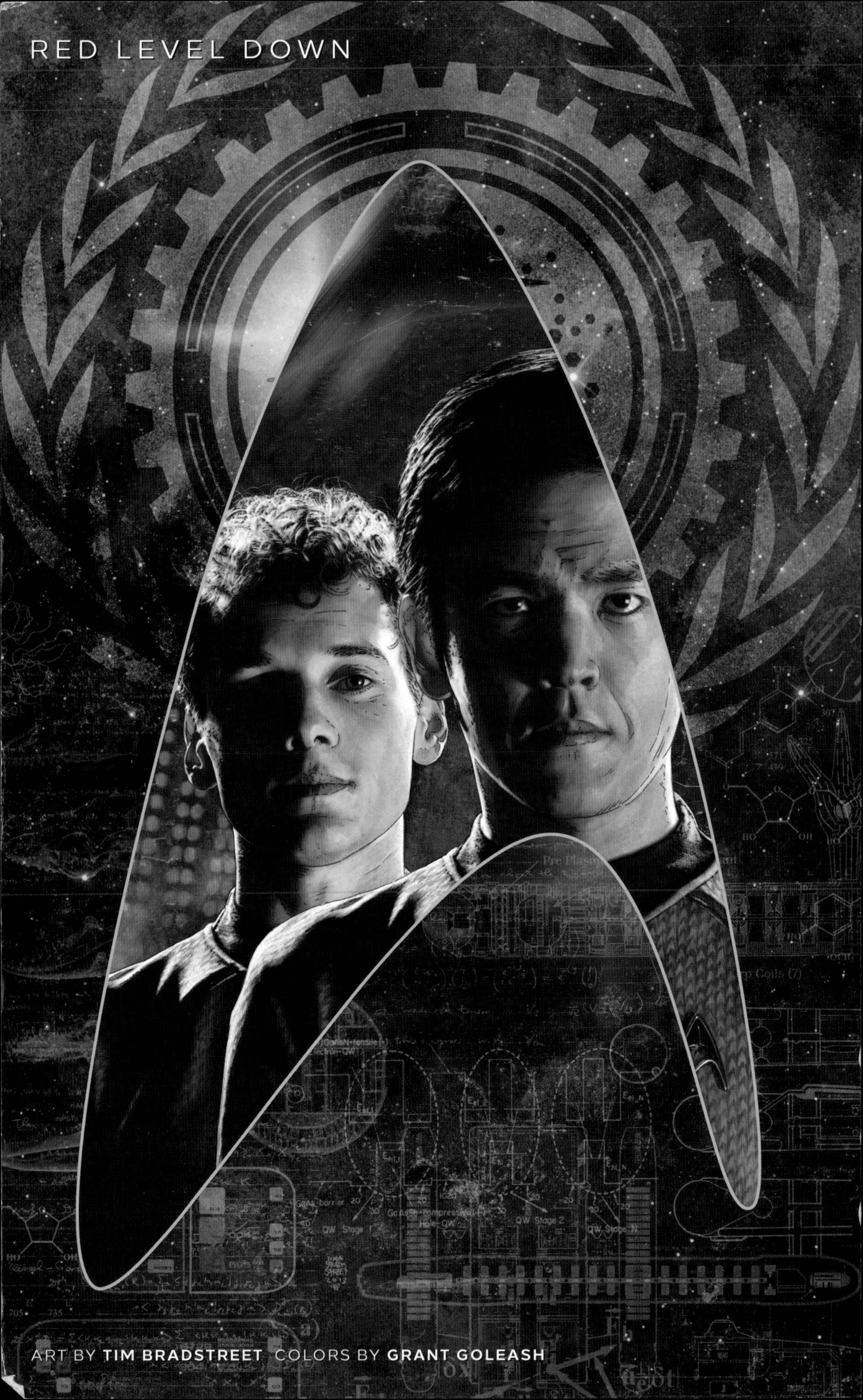
RED LEVEL DOWN
ART BY **TIM BRADSTREET** COLORS BY **GRANT GOLEASH**

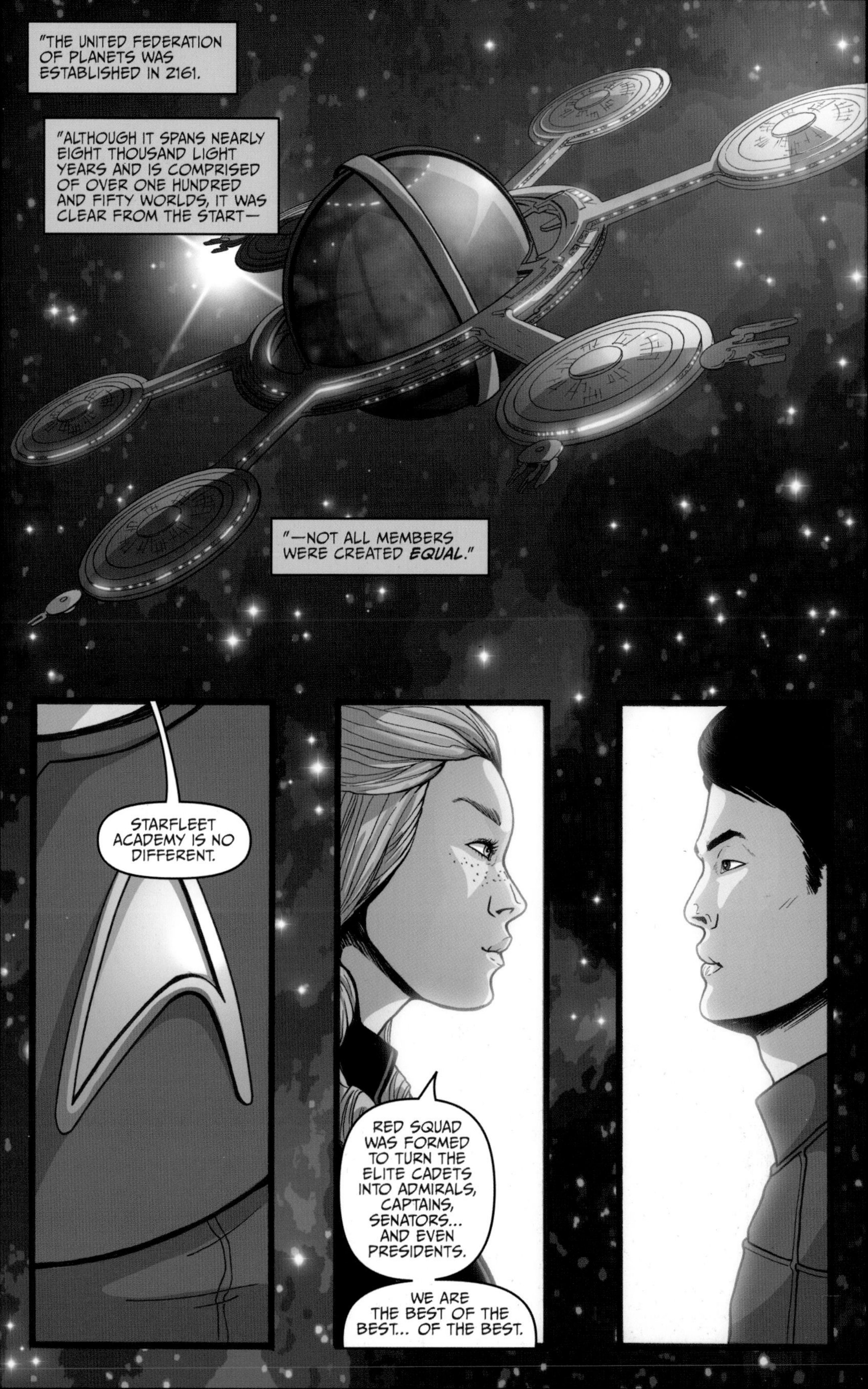
"THE UNITED FEDERATION OF PLANETS WAS ESTABLISHED IN 2161.
"ALTHOUGH IT SPANS NEARLY EIGHT THOUSAND LIGHT YEARS AND IS COMPRISED OF OVER ONE HUNDRED AND FIFTY WORLDS, IT WAS CLEAR FROM THE START—
"—NOT ALL MEMBERS WERE CREATED *EQUAL*."
STARFLEET ACADEMY IS NO DIFFERENT.
RED SQUAD WAS FORMED TO TURN THE ELITE CADETS INTO ADMIRALS, CAPTAINS, SENATORS... AND EVEN PRESIDENTS.
WE ARE THE BEST OF THE BEST... OF THE BEST.

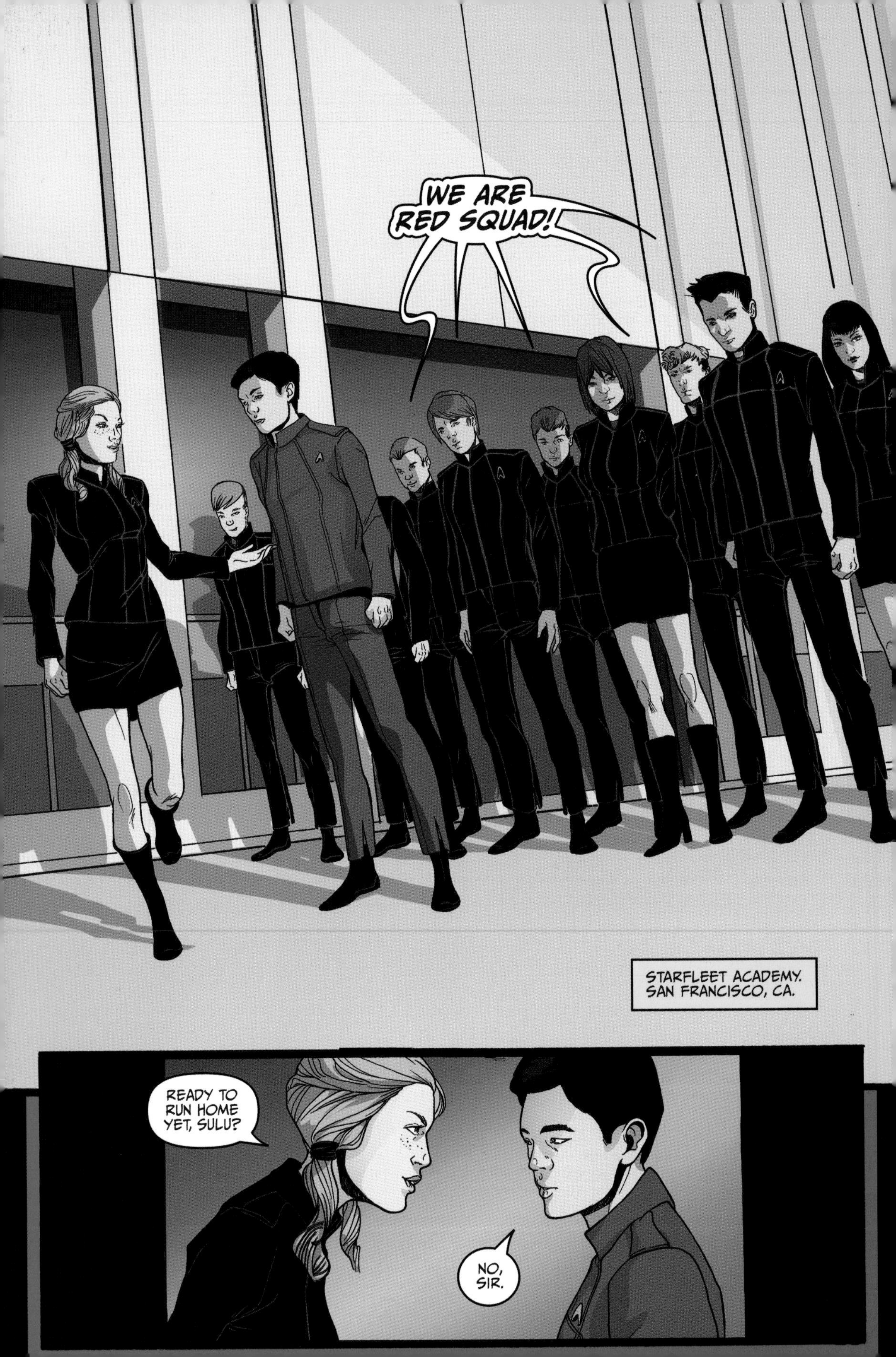
WE ARE RED SQUAD!
STARFLEET ACADEMY. SAN FRANCISCO, CA.
READY TO RUN HOME YET, SULU?
NO, SIR.

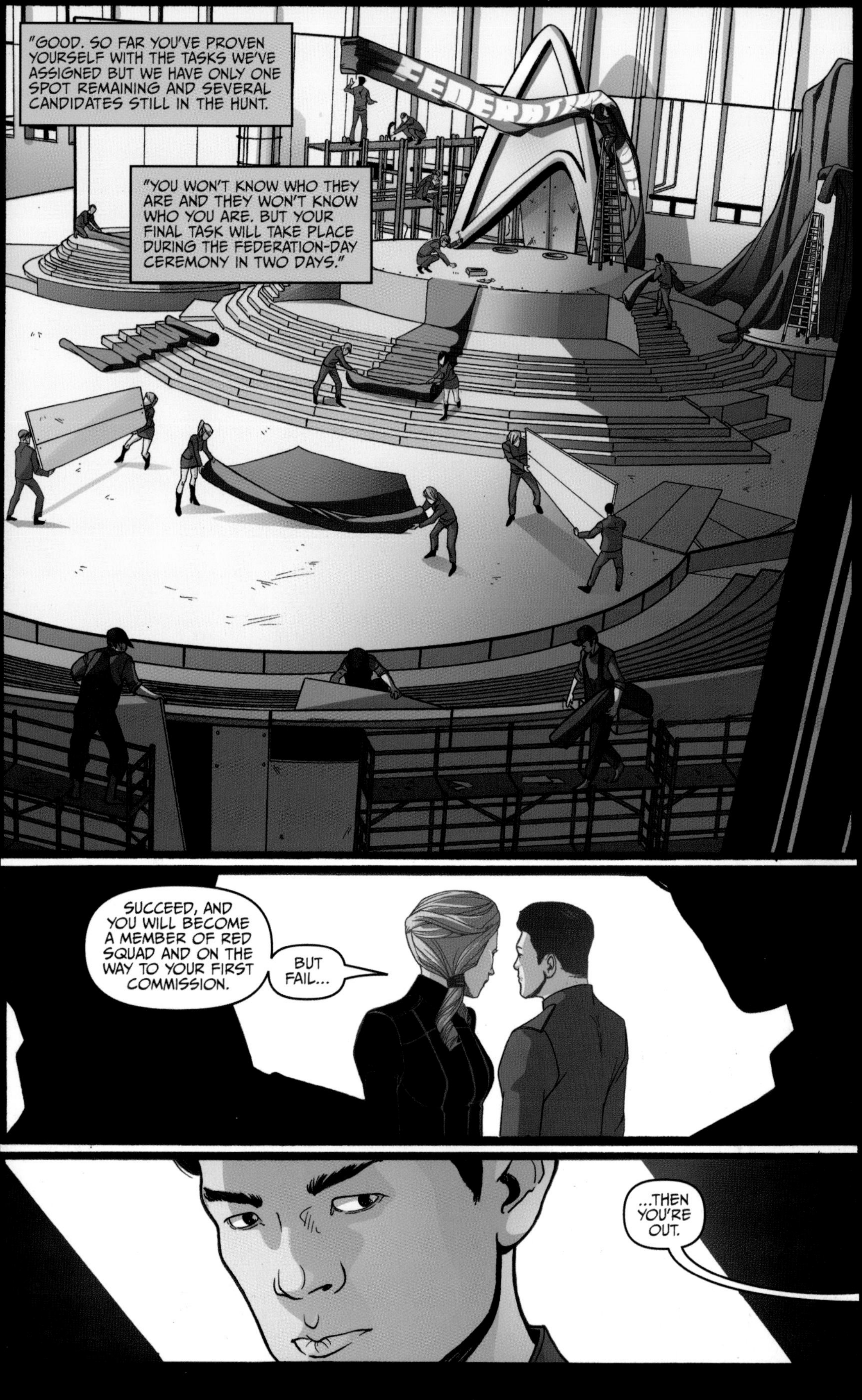
"GOOD. SO FAR YOU'VE PROVEN YOURSELF WITH THE TASKS WE'VE ASSIGNED BUT WE HAVE ONLY ONE SPOT REMAINING AND SEVERAL CANDIDATES STILL IN THE HUNT.
"YOU WON'T KNOW WHO THEY ARE AND THEY WON'T KNOW WHO YOU ARE. BUT YOUR FINAL TASK WILL TAKE PLACE DURING THE FEDERATION-DAY CEREMONY IN TWO DAYS."
SUCCEED, AND YOU WILL BECOME A MEMBER OF RED SQUAD AND ON THE WAY TO YOUR FIRST COMMISSION.
BUT FAIL...
...THEN YOU'RE OUT.

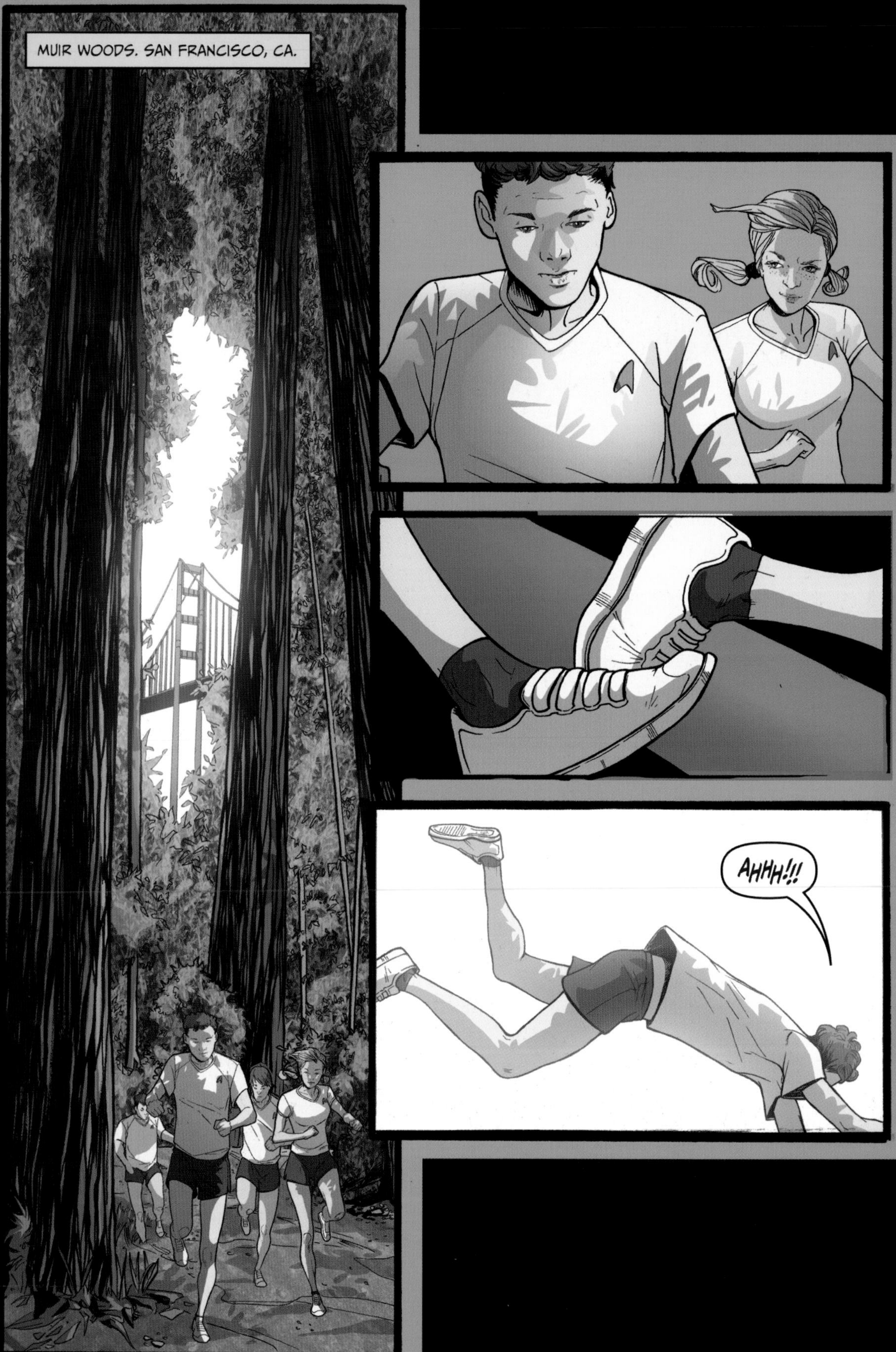
MUIR WOODS. SAN FRANCISCO, CA.
AHHH!!!

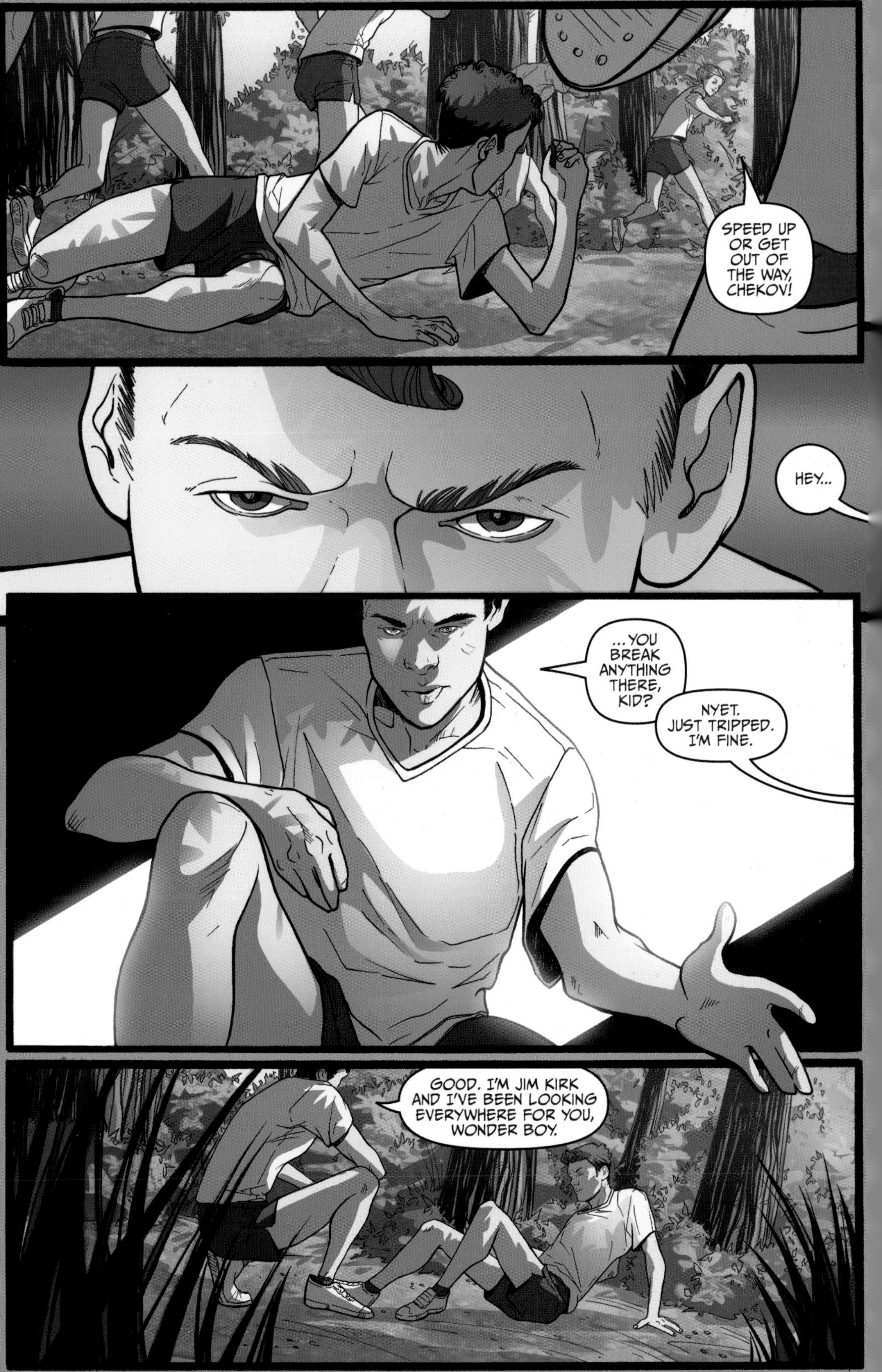
SPEED UP OR GET OUT OF THE WAY, CHEKOV!
HEY...
...YOU BREAK ANYTHING THERE, KID?
NYET. JUST TRIPPED. I'M FINE.
GOOD. I'M JIM KIRK AND I'VE BEEN LOOKING EVERYWHERE FOR YOU, WONDER BOY.

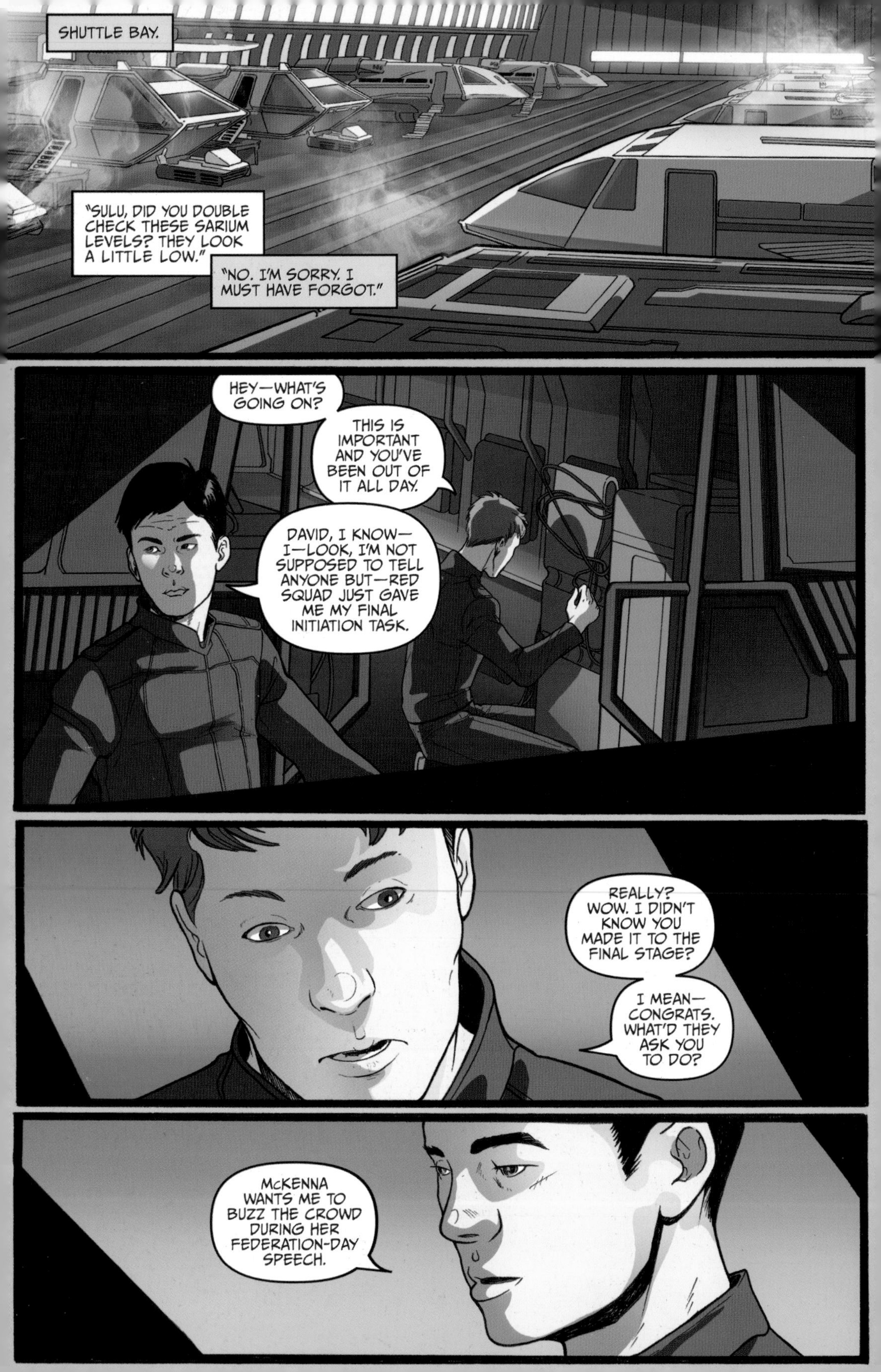
SHUTTLE BAY.
"SULU, DID YOU DOUBLE CHECK THESE SARIUM LEVELS? THEY LOOK A LITTLE LOW."
"NO. I'M SORRY. I MUST HAVE FORGOT."
HEY—WHAT'S GOING ON?
THIS IS IMPORTANT AND YOU'VE BEEN OUT OF IT ALL DAY.
DAVID, I KNOW—I—LOOK, I'M NOT SUPPOSED TO TELL ANYONE BUT—RED SQUAD JUST GAVE ME MY FINAL INITIATION TASK.
REALLY? WOW. I DIDN'T KNOW YOU MADE IT TO THE FINAL STAGE?
I MEAN—CONGRATS. WHAT'D THEY ASK YOU TO DO?
McKENNA WANTS ME TO BUZZ THE CROWD DURING HER FEDERATION-DAY SPEECH.

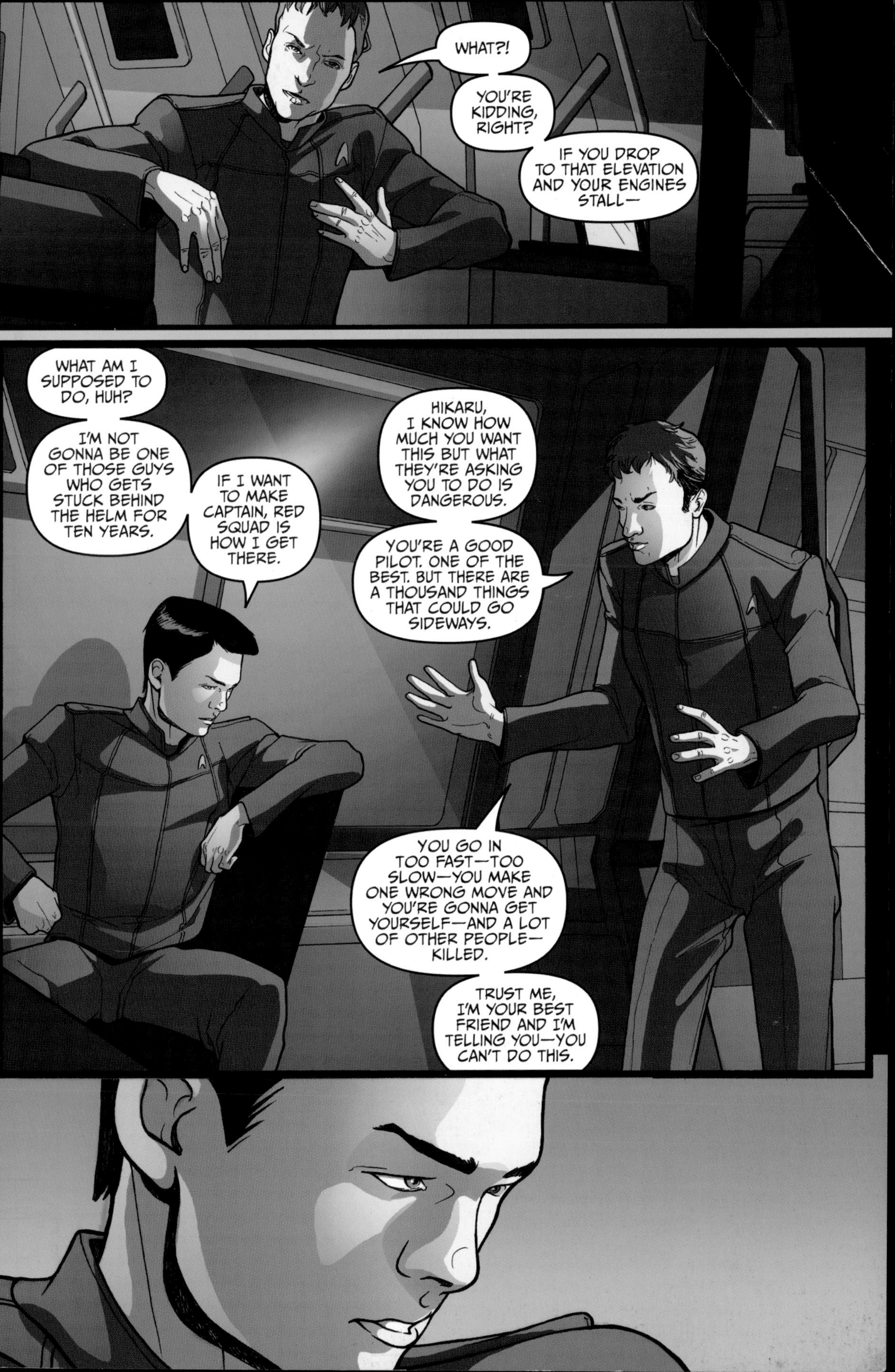
WHAT?!
YOU'RE KIDDING, RIGHT?
IF YOU DROP TO THAT ELEVATION AND YOUR ENGINES STALL—
WHAT AM I SUPPOSED TO DO, HUH?
I'M NOT GONNA BE ONE OF THOSE GUYS WHO GETS STUCK BEHIND THE HELM FOR TEN YEARS.
IF I WANT TO MAKE CAPTAIN, RED SQUAD IS HOW I GET THERE.
HIKARU, I KNOW HOW MUCH YOU WANT THIS BUT WHAT THEY'RE ASKING YOU TO DO IS DANGEROUS.
YOU'RE A GOOD PILOT. ONE OF THE BEST. BUT THERE ARE A THOUSAND THINGS THAT COULD GO SIDEWAYS.
YOU GO IN TOO FAST—TOO SLOW—YOU MAKE ONE WRONG MOVE AND YOU'RE GONNA GET YOURSELF—AND A LOT OF OTHER PEOPLE—KILLED.
TRUST ME, I'M YOUR BEST FRIEND AND I'M TELLING YOU—YOU CAN'T DO THIS.

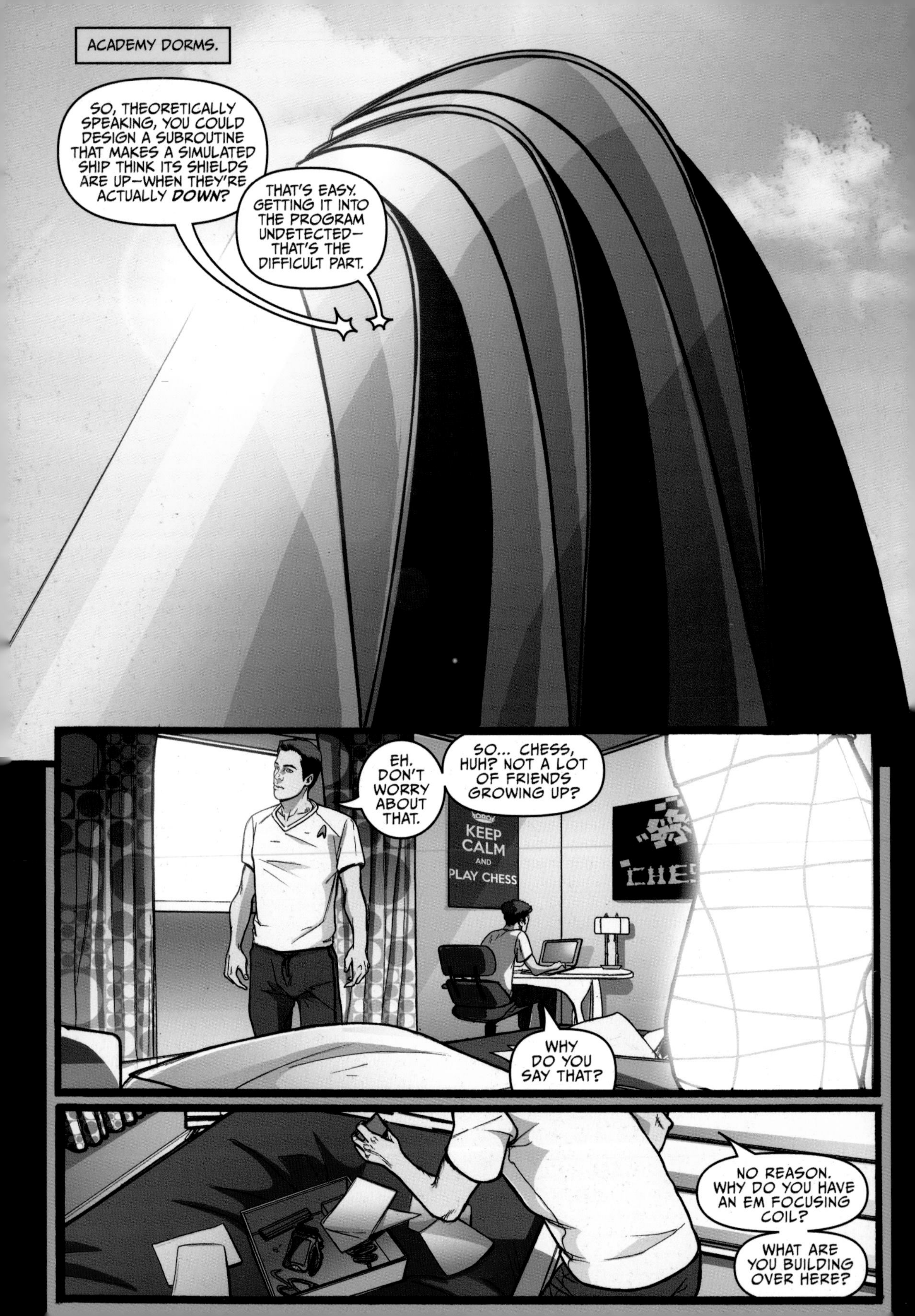
ACADEMY DORMS.
SO, THEORETICALLY SPEAKING, YOU COULD DESIGN A SUBROUTINE THAT MAKES A SIMULATED SHIP THINK ITS SHIELDS ARE UP—WHEN THEY'RE ACTUALLY **DOWN**?
THAT'S EASY. GETTING IT INTO THE PROGRAM UNDETECTED—THAT'S THE DIFFICULT PART.
SO... CHESS, HUH? NOT A LOT OF FRIENDS GROWING UP?
EH. DON'T WORRY ABOUT THAT.
KEEP CALM AND PLAY CHESS
WHY DO YOU SAY THAT?
NO REASON. WHY DO YOU HAVE AN EM FOCUSING COIL?
WHAT ARE YOU BUILDING OVER HERE?

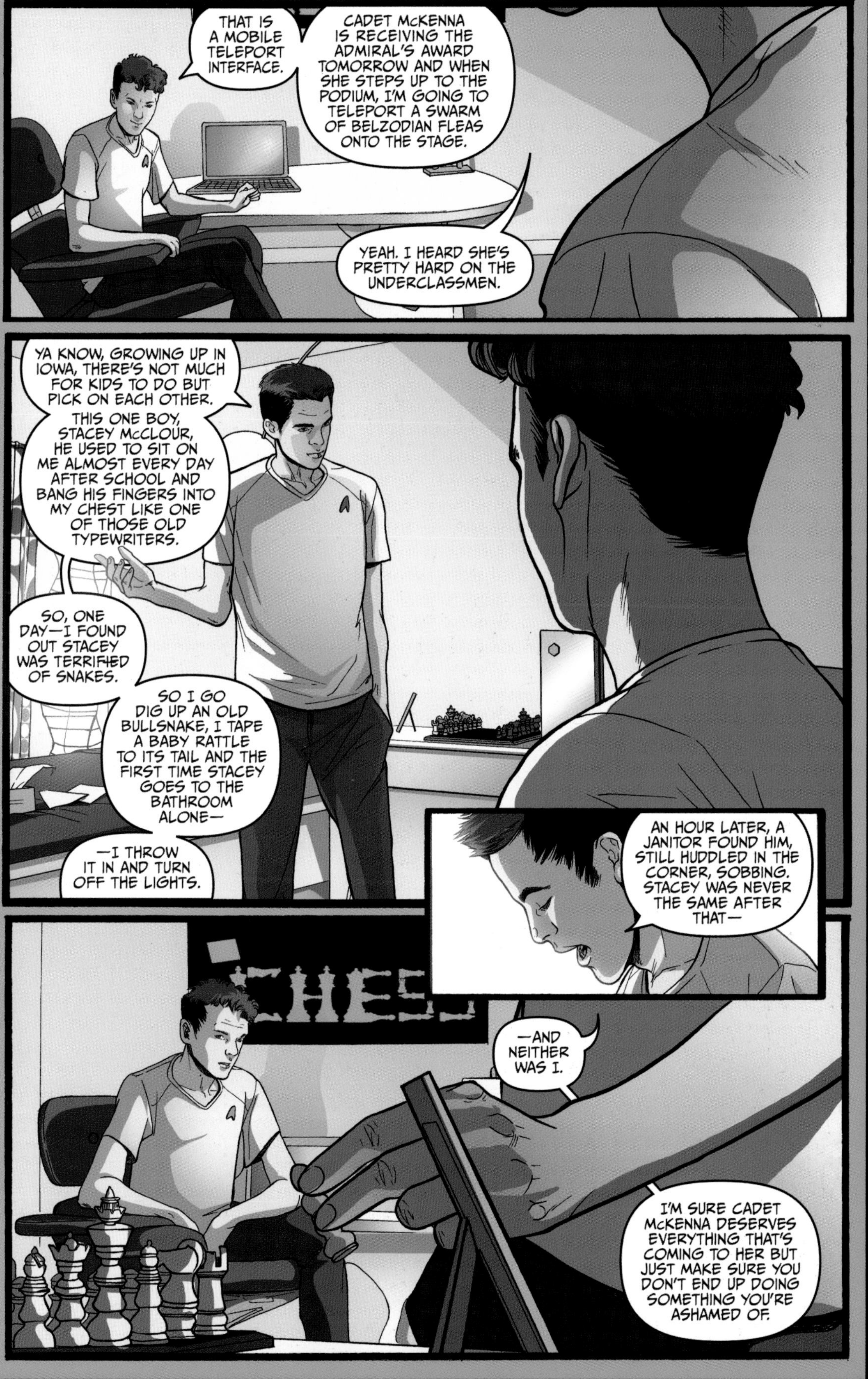
THAT IS A MOBILE TELEPORT INTERFACE.
CADET McKENNA IS RECEIVING THE ADMIRAL'S AWARD TOMORROW AND WHEN SHE STEPS UP TO THE PODIUM, I'M GOING TO TELEPORT A SWARM OF BELZODIAN FLEAS ONTO THE STAGE.
YEAH. I HEARD SHE'S PRETTY HARD ON THE UNDERCLASSMEN.
YA KNOW, GROWING UP IN IOWA, THERE'S NOT MUCH FOR KIDS TO DO BUT PICK ON EACH OTHER.
THIS ONE BOY, STACEY McCLOUR, HE USED TO SIT ON ME ALMOST EVERY DAY AFTER SCHOOL AND BANG HIS FINGERS INTO MY CHEST LIKE ONE OF THOSE OLD TYPEWRITERS.
SO, ONE DAY—I FOUND OUT STACEY WAS TERRIFIED OF SNAKES.
SO I GO DIG UP AN OLD BULLSNAKE, I TAPE A BABY RATTLE TO ITS TAIL AND THE FIRST TIME STACEY GOES TO THE BATHROOM ALONE—
—I THROW IT IN AND TURN OFF THE LIGHTS.
AN HOUR LATER, A JANITOR FOUND HIM, STILL HUDDLED IN THE CORNER, SOBBING. STACEY WAS NEVER THE SAME AFTER THAT—
—AND NEITHER WAS I.
I'M SURE CADET McKENNA DESERVES EVERYTHING THAT'S COMING TO HER BUT JUST MAKE SURE YOU DON'T END UP DOING SOMETHING YOU'RE ASHAMED OF.

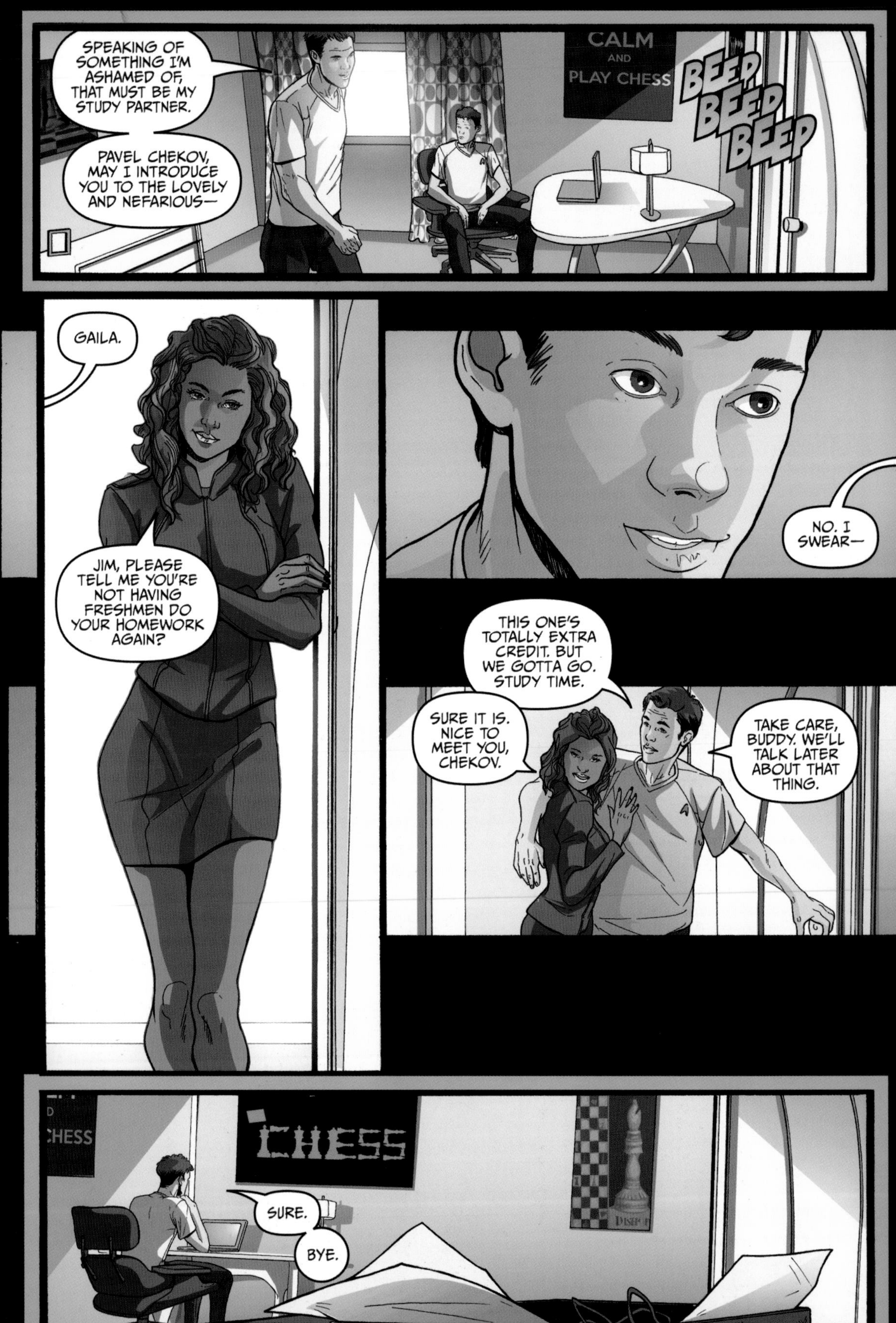
SPEAKING OF SOMETHING I'M ASHAMED OF, THAT MUST BE MY STUDY PARTNER.
PAVEL CHEKOV, MAY I INTRODUCE YOU TO THE LOVELY AND NEFARIOUS—
CALM AND PLAY CHESS
BEEP BEEP BEEP
GAILA.
JIM, PLEASE TELL ME YOU'RE NOT HAVING FRESHMEN DO YOUR HOMEWORK AGAIN?
NO. I SWEAR—
THIS ONE'S TOTALLY EXTRA CREDIT. BUT WE GOTTA GO. STUDY TIME.
SURE IT IS. NICE TO MEET YOU, CHEKOV.
TAKE CARE, BUDDY. WE'LL TALK LATER ABOUT THAT THING.
CHESS
SURE.
BYE.

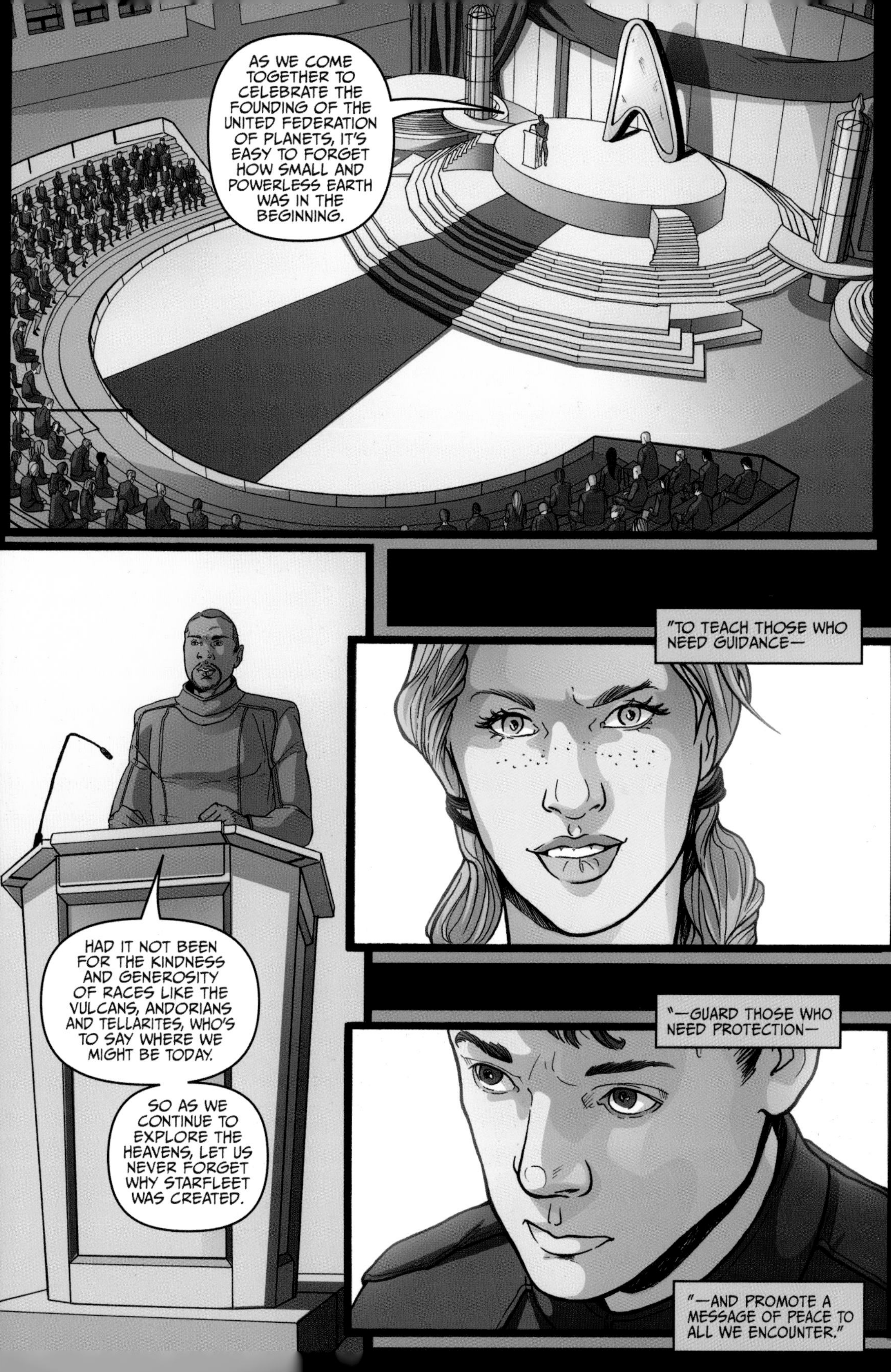
AS WE COME TOGETHER TO CELEBRATE THE FOUNDING OF THE UNITED FEDERATION OF PLANETS, IT'S EASY TO FORGET HOW SMALL AND POWERLESS EARTH WAS IN THE BEGINNING.
"TO TEACH THOSE WHO NEED GUIDANCE—
HAD IT NOT BEEN FOR THE KINDNESS AND GENEROSITY OF RACES LIKE THE VULCANS, ANDORIANS AND TELLARITES, WHO'S TO SAY WHERE WE MIGHT BE TODAY.
SO AS WE CONTINUE TO EXPLORE THE HEAVENS, LET US NEVER FORGET WHY STARFLEET WAS CREATED.
"—GUARD THOSE WHO NEED PROTECTION—
"—AND PROMOTE A MESSAGE OF PEACE TO ALL WE ENCOUNTER."

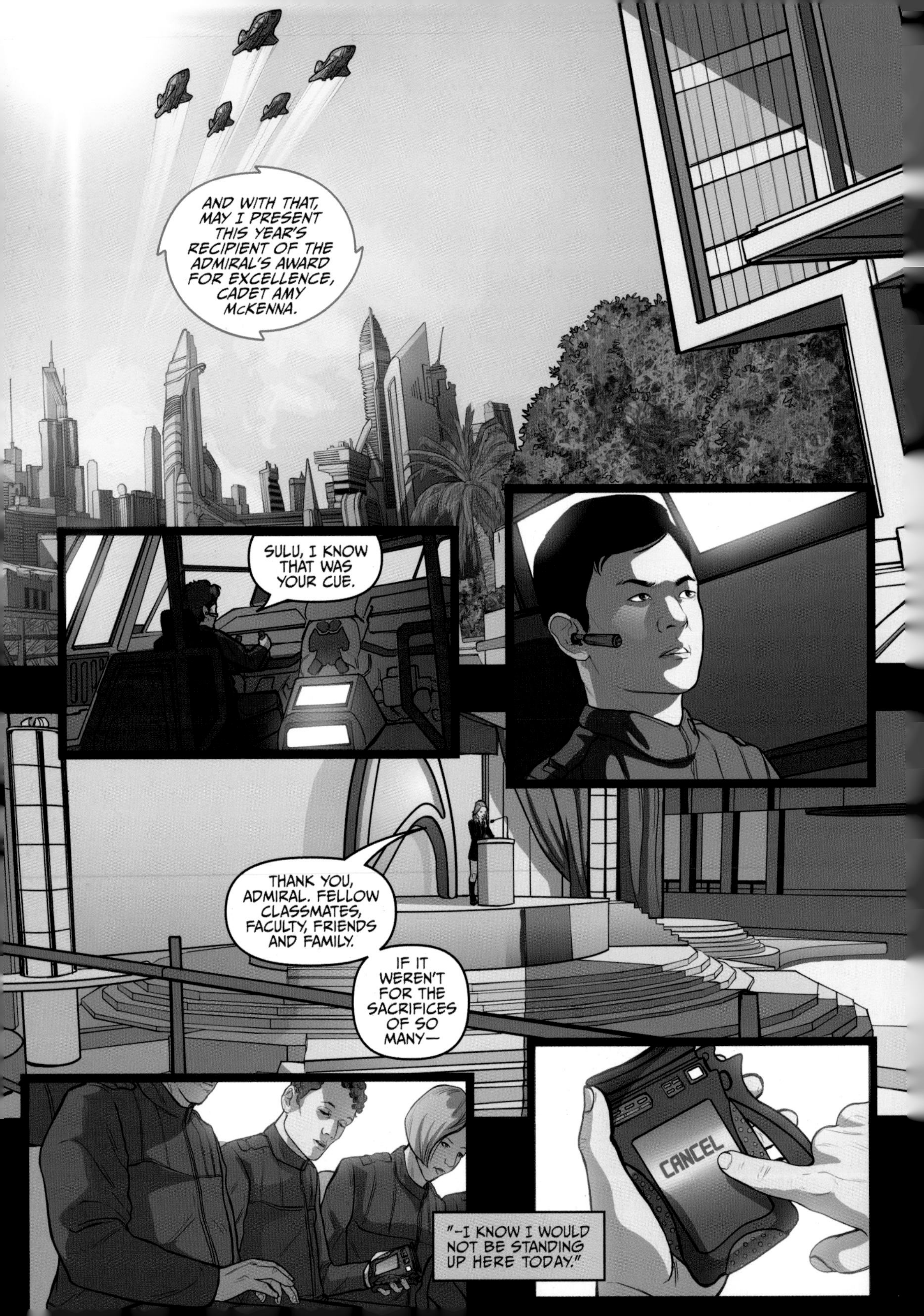
AND WITH THAT, MAY I PRESENT THIS YEAR'S RECIPIENT OF THE ADMIRAL'S AWARD FOR EXCELLENCE, CADET AMY McKENNA.
SULU, I KNOW THAT WAS YOUR CUE.
THANK YOU, ADMIRAL. FELLOW CLASSMATES, FACULTY, FRIENDS AND FAMILY.
IF IT WEREN'T FOR THE SACRIFICES OF SO MANY—
CANCEL
"—I KNOW I WOULD NOT BE STANDING UP HERE TODAY."

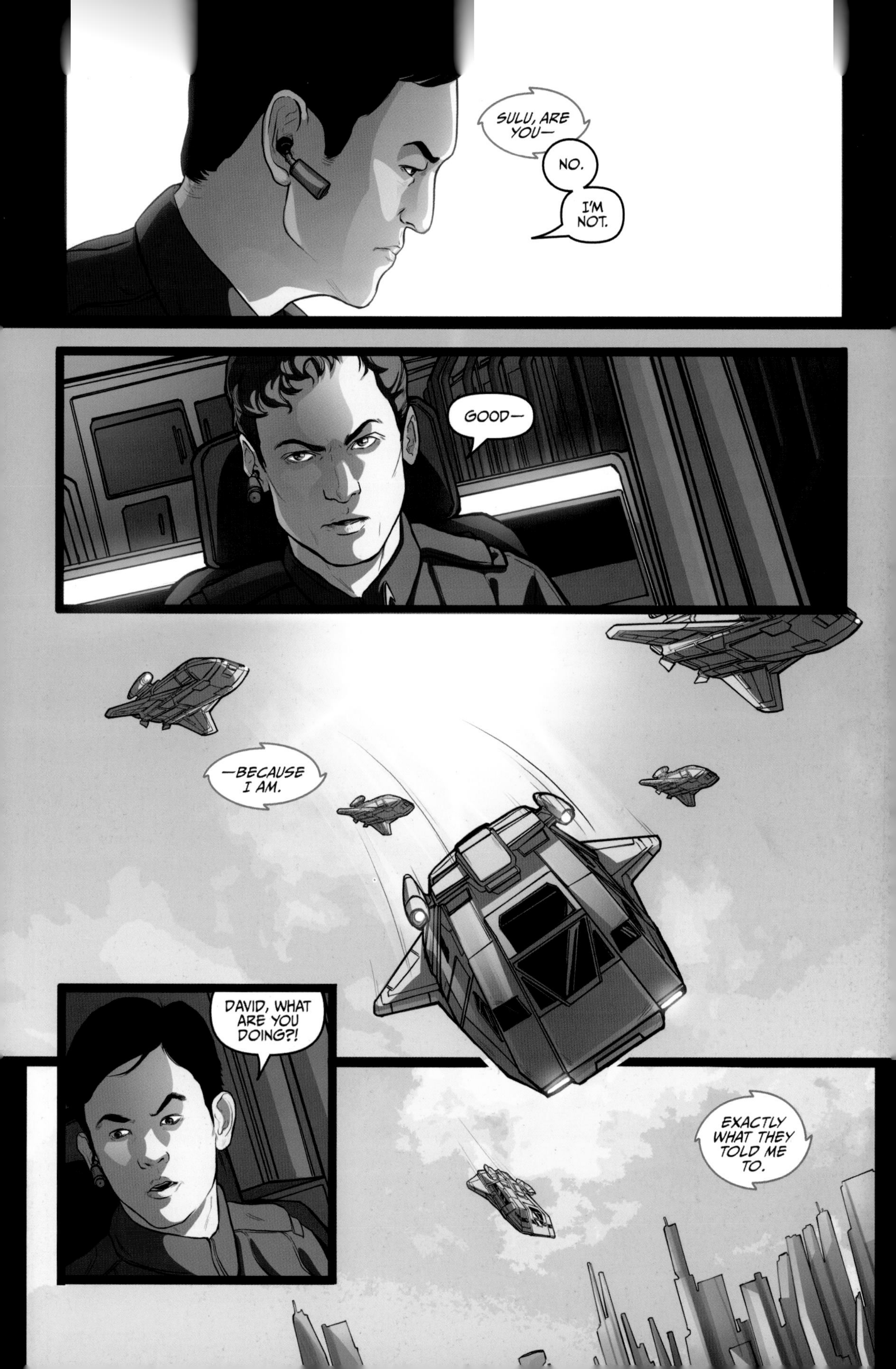
SULU, ARE YOU—
NO.
I'M NOT.
GOOD—
—BECAUSE I AM.
DAVID, WHAT ARE YOU DOING?!
EXACTLY WHAT THEY TOLD ME TO.

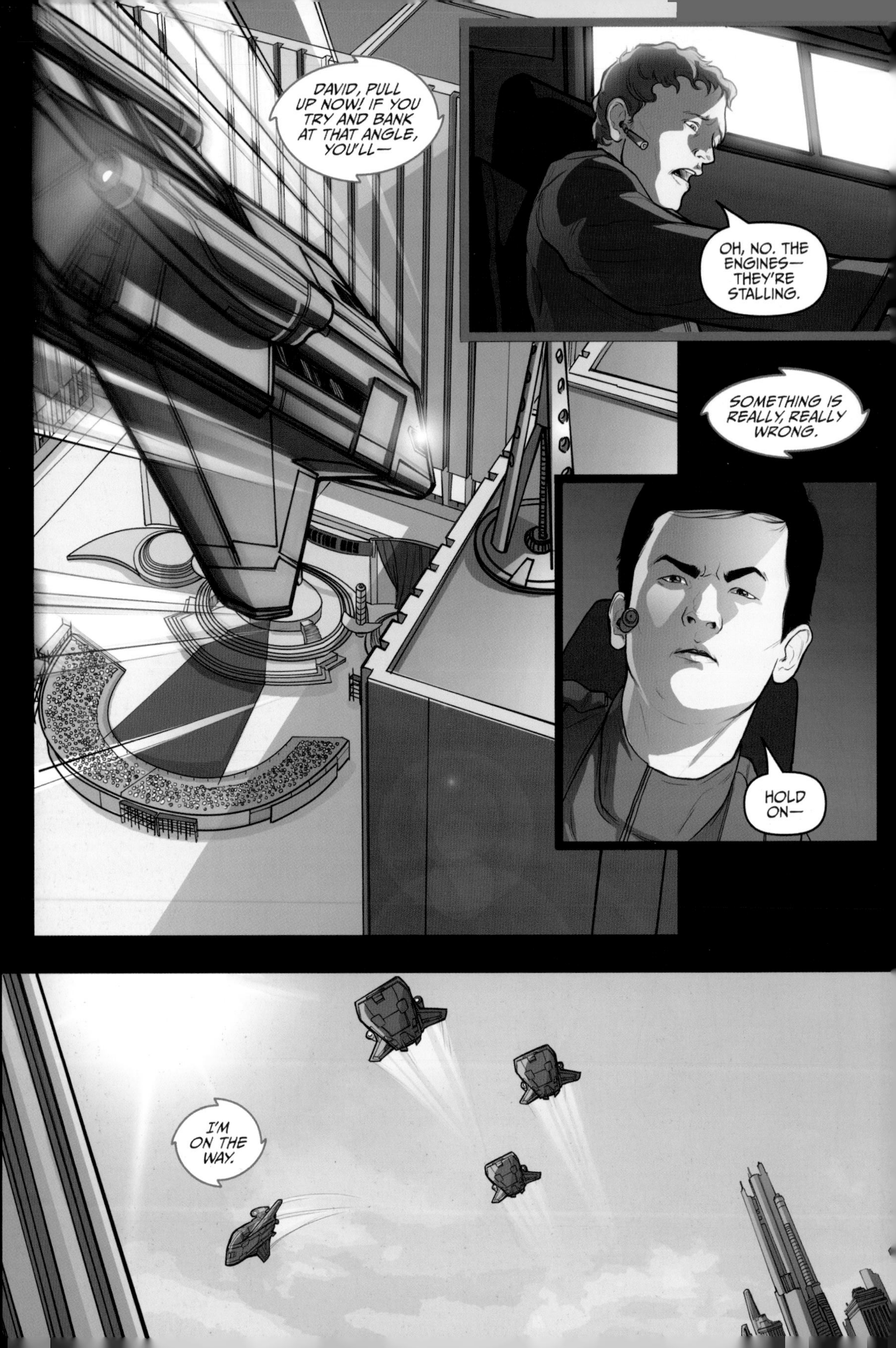
DAVID, PULL UP NOW! IF YOU TRY AND BANK AT THAT ANGLE, YOU'LL—
OH, NO. THE ENGINES— THEY'RE STALLING.
SOMETHING IS REALLY, REALLY WRONG.
HOLD ON—
I'M ON THE WAY.

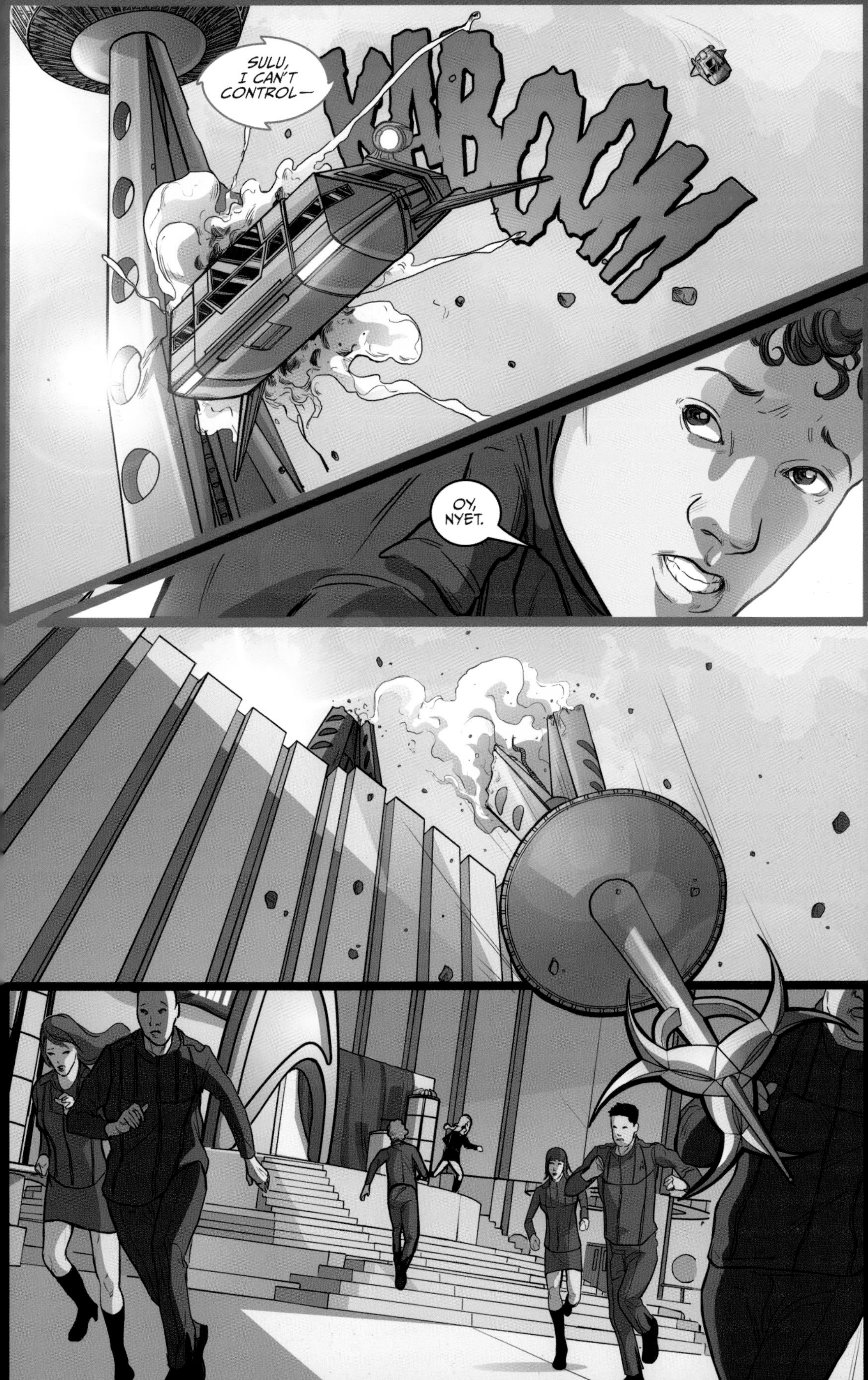
SULU, I CAN'T CONTROL—
KABOOM
OY, NYET.

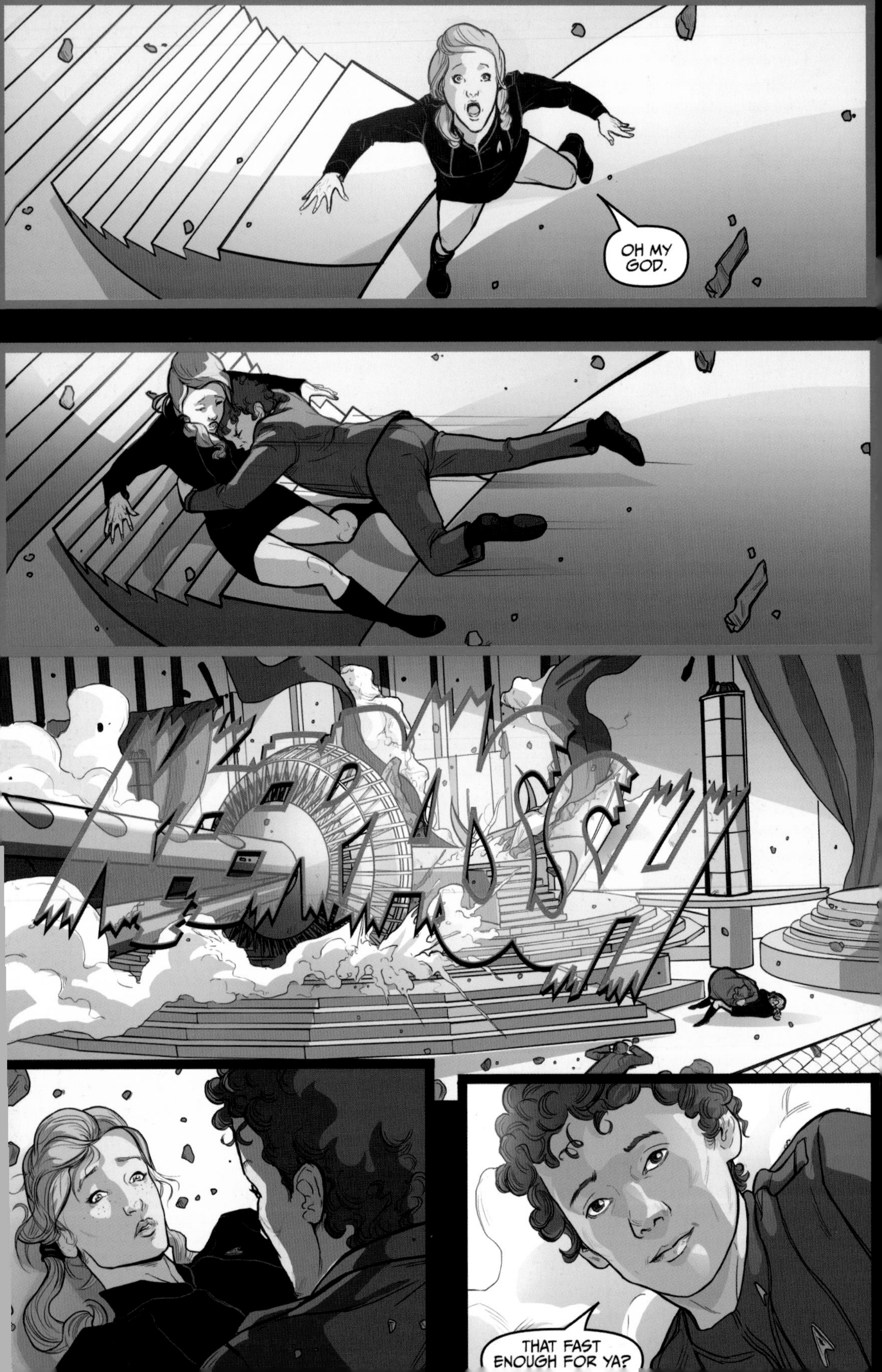
OH MY GOD.
THAT FAST ENOUGH FOR YA?

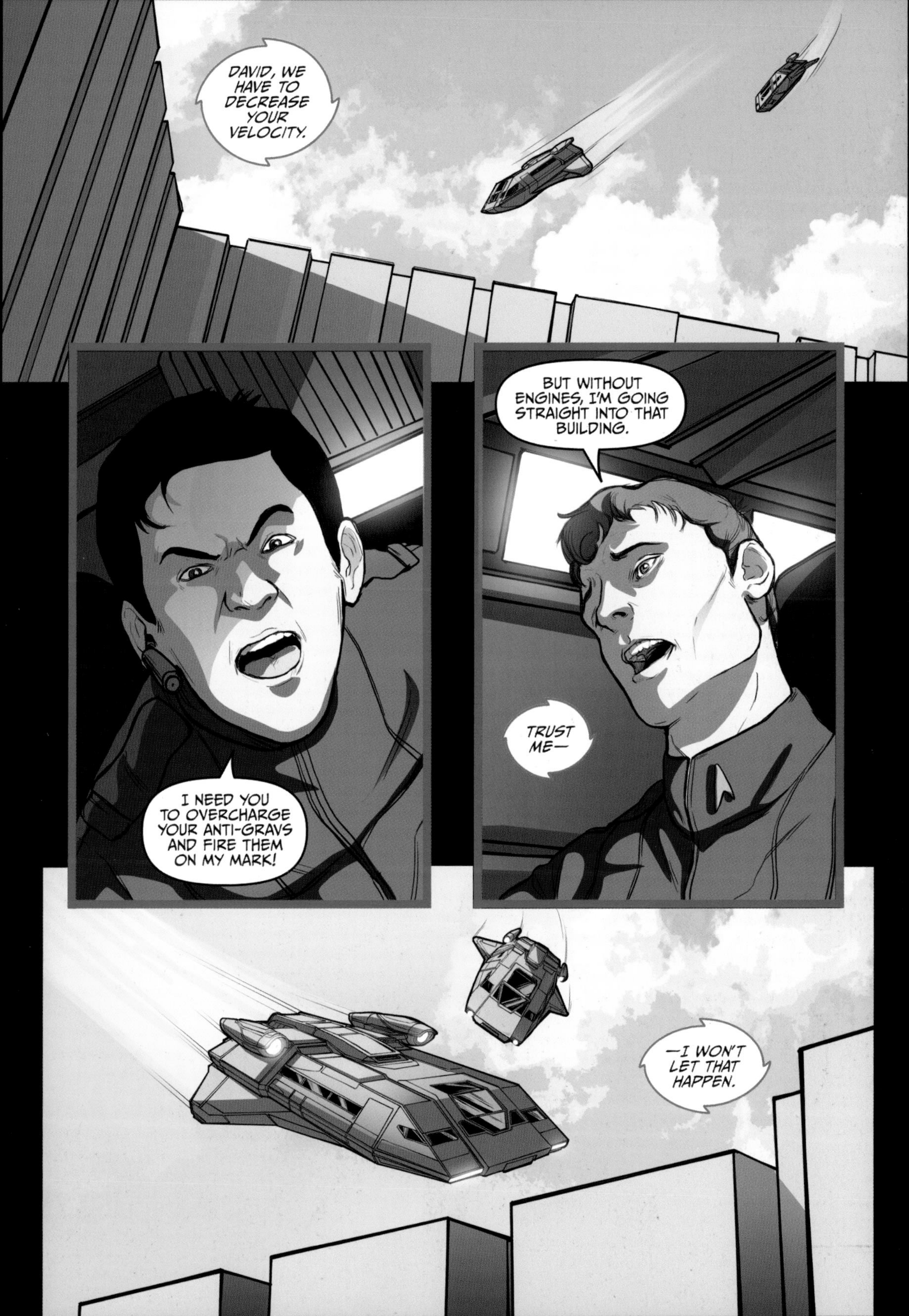
DAVID, WE HAVE TO DECREASE YOUR VELOCITY.
I NEED YOU TO OVERCHARGE YOUR ANTI-GRAVS AND FIRE THEM ON MY MARK!
BUT WITHOUT ENGINES, I'M GOING STRAIGHT INTO THAT BUILDING.
TRUST ME—
—I WON'T LET THAT HAPPEN.

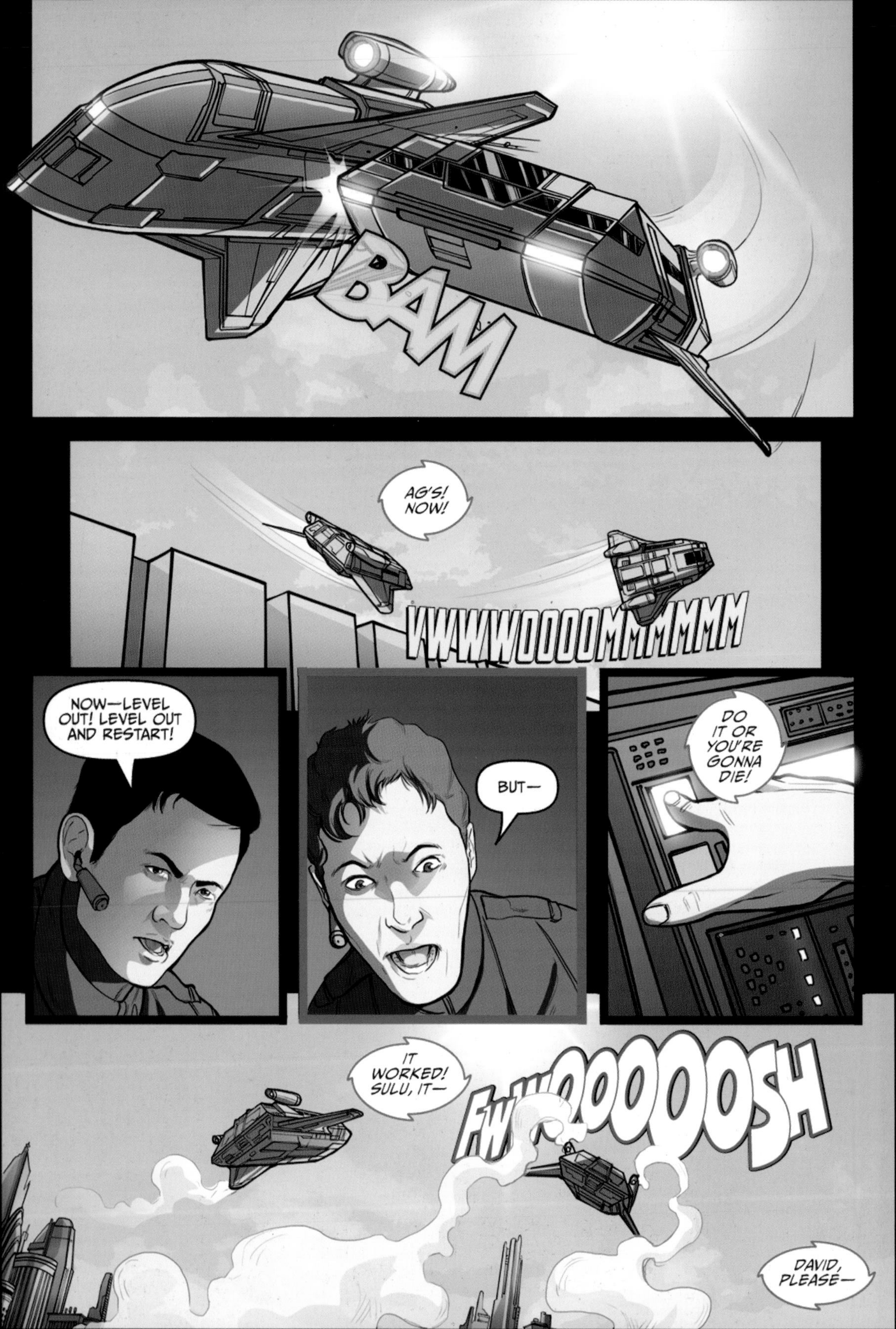
BAM
AG'S! NOW!
VWWWOOOOMMMMMMM
NOW—LEVEL OUT! LEVEL OUT AND RESTART!
BUT—
DO IT OR YOU'RE GONNA DIE!
IT WORKED! SULU, IT—
FWOOOOOOSH
DAVID, PLEASE—

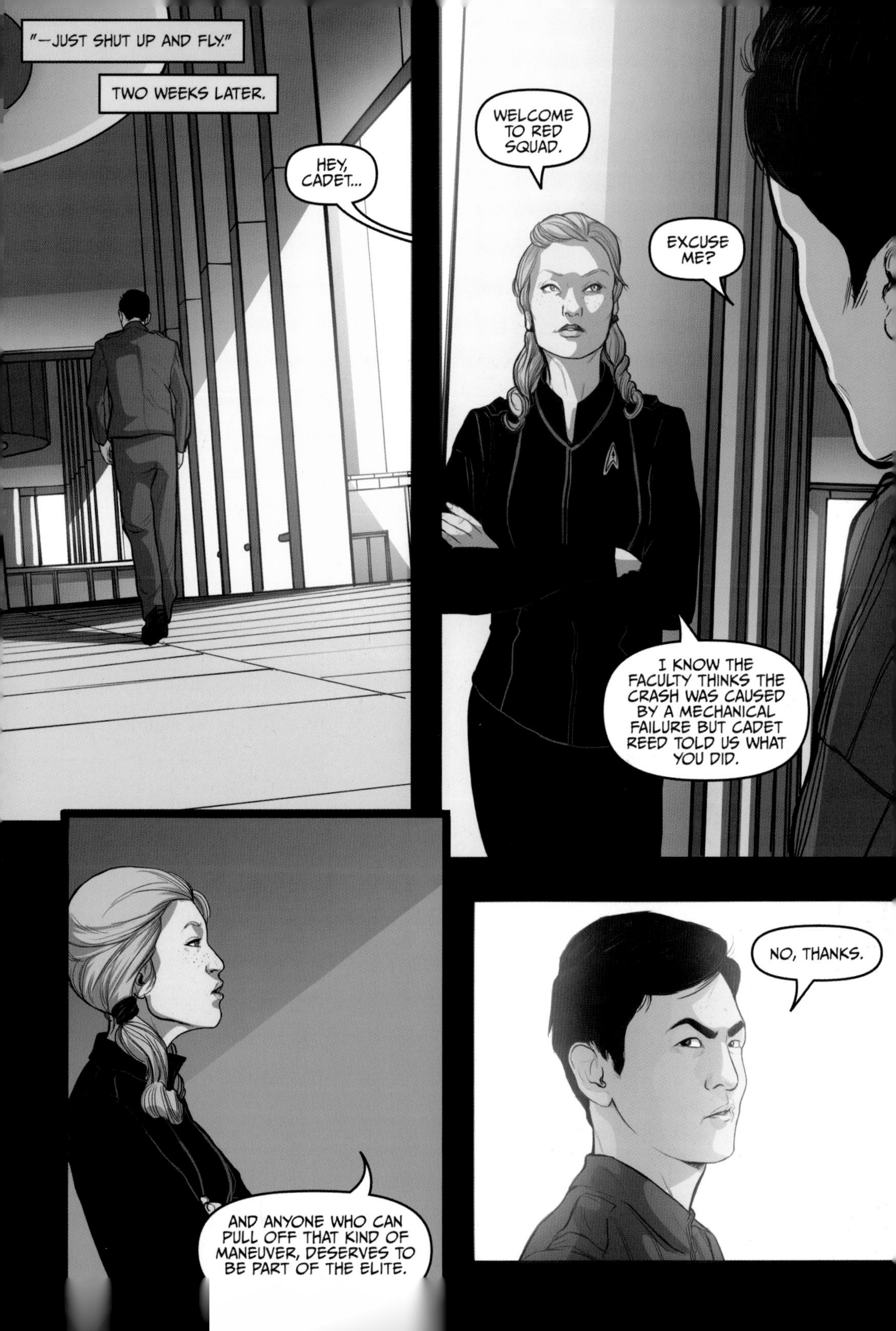
"—JUST SHUT UP AND FLY."
TWO WEEKS LATER.
HEY, CADET...
WELCOME TO RED SQUAD.
EXCUSE ME?
I KNOW THE FACULTY THINKS THE CRASH WAS CAUSED BY A MECHANICAL FAILURE BUT CADET REED TOLD US WHAT YOU DID.
AND ANYONE WHO CAN PULL OFF THAT KIND OF MANEUVER, DESERVES TO BE PART OF THE ELITE.
NO, THANKS.

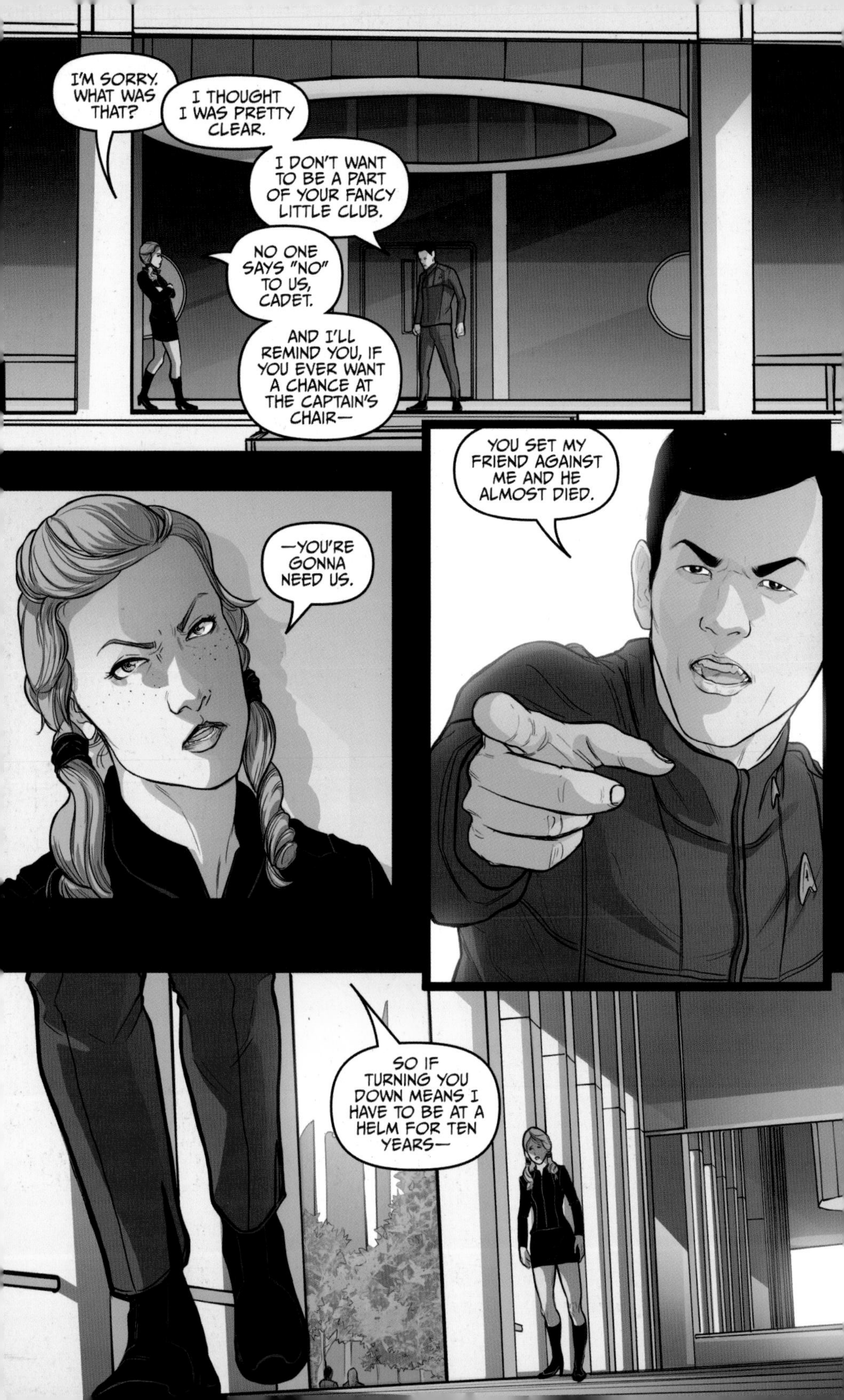
I'M SORRY. WHAT WAS THAT?
I THOUGHT I WAS PRETTY CLEAR.
I DON'T WANT TO BE A PART OF YOUR FANCY LITTLE CLUB.
NO ONE SAYS "NO" TO US, CADET.
AND I'LL REMIND YOU, IF YOU EVER WANT A CHANCE AT THE CAPTAIN'S CHAIR—
—YOU'RE GONNA NEED US.
YOU SET MY FRIEND AGAINST ME AND HE ALMOST DIED.
SO IF TURNING YOU DOWN MEANS I HAVE TO BE AT A HELM FOR TEN YEARS—

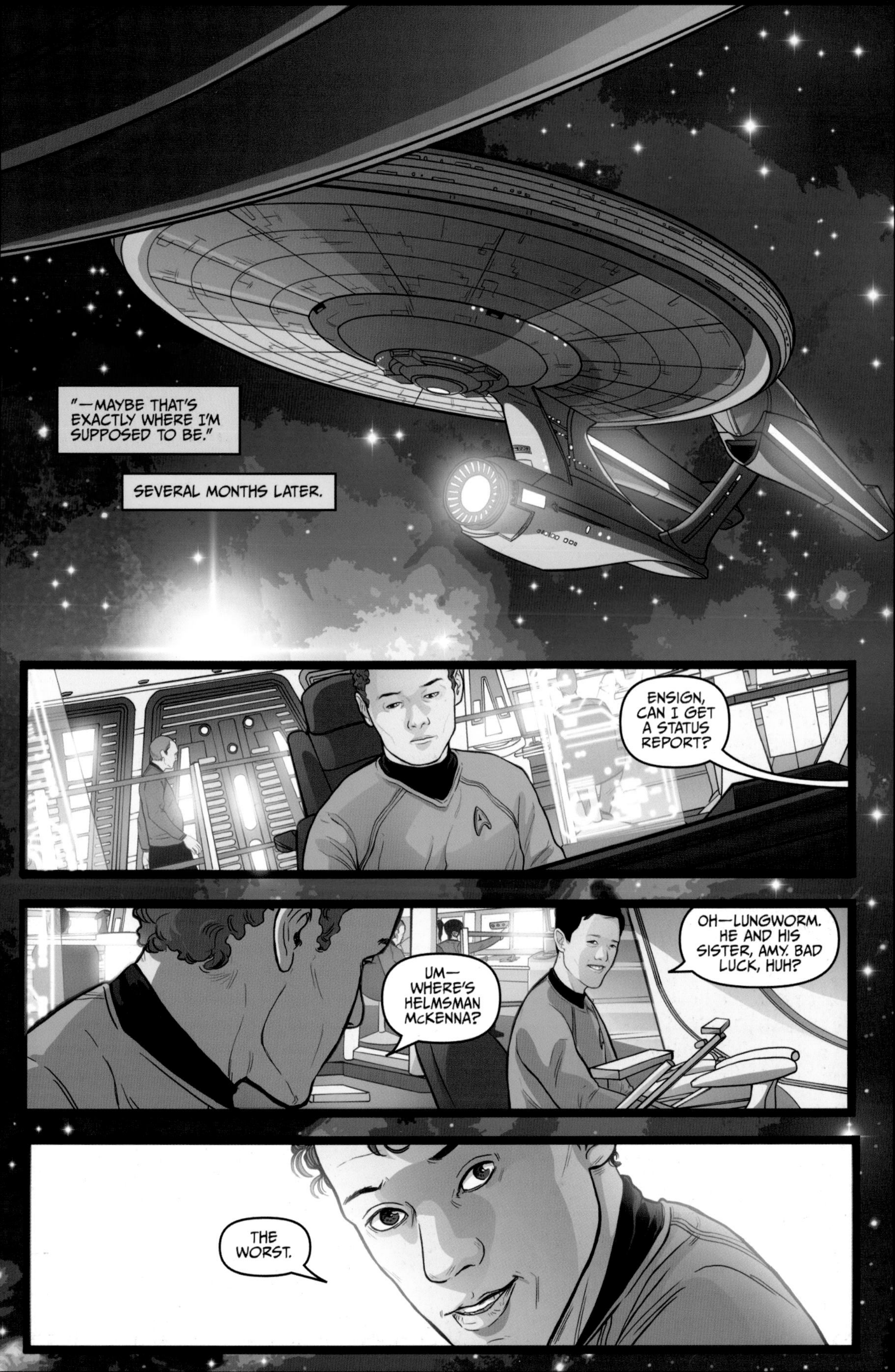
"—MAYBE THAT'S EXACTLY WHERE I'M SUPPOSED TO BE."
SEVERAL MONTHS LATER.
ENSIGN, CAN I GET A STATUS REPORT?
UM—WHERE'S HELMSMAN McKENNA?
OH—LUNGWORM. HE AND HIS SISTER, AMY. BAD LUCK, HUH?
THE WORST.

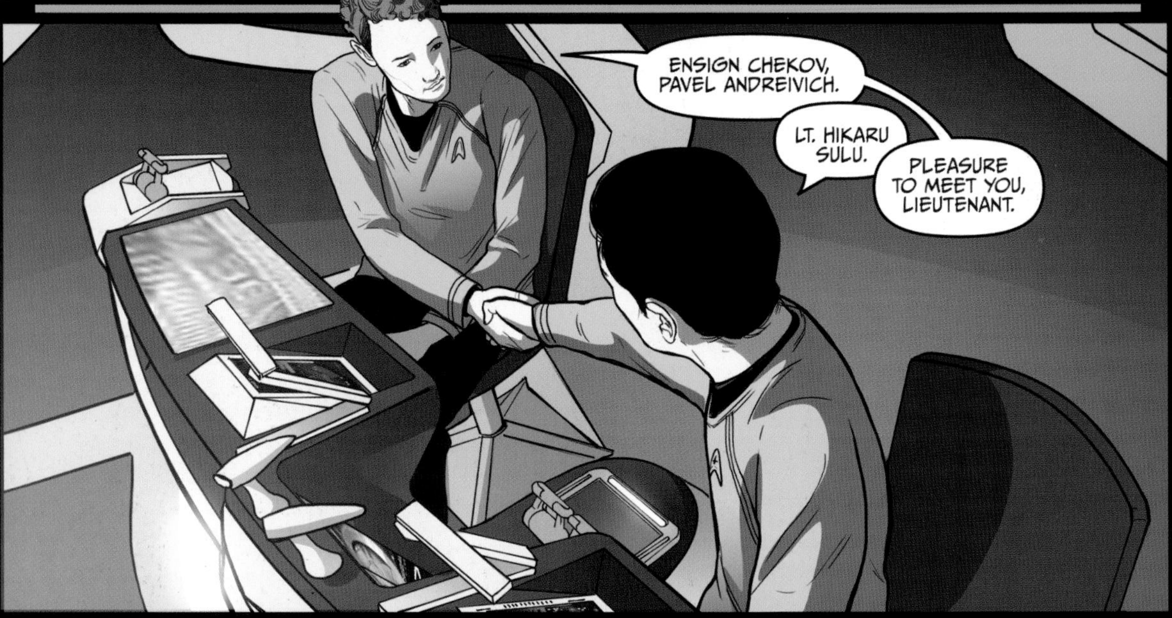
ENSIGN CHEKOV, PAVEL ANDREIVICH.
LT. HIKARU SULU.
PLEASURE TO MEET YOU, LIEUTENANT.

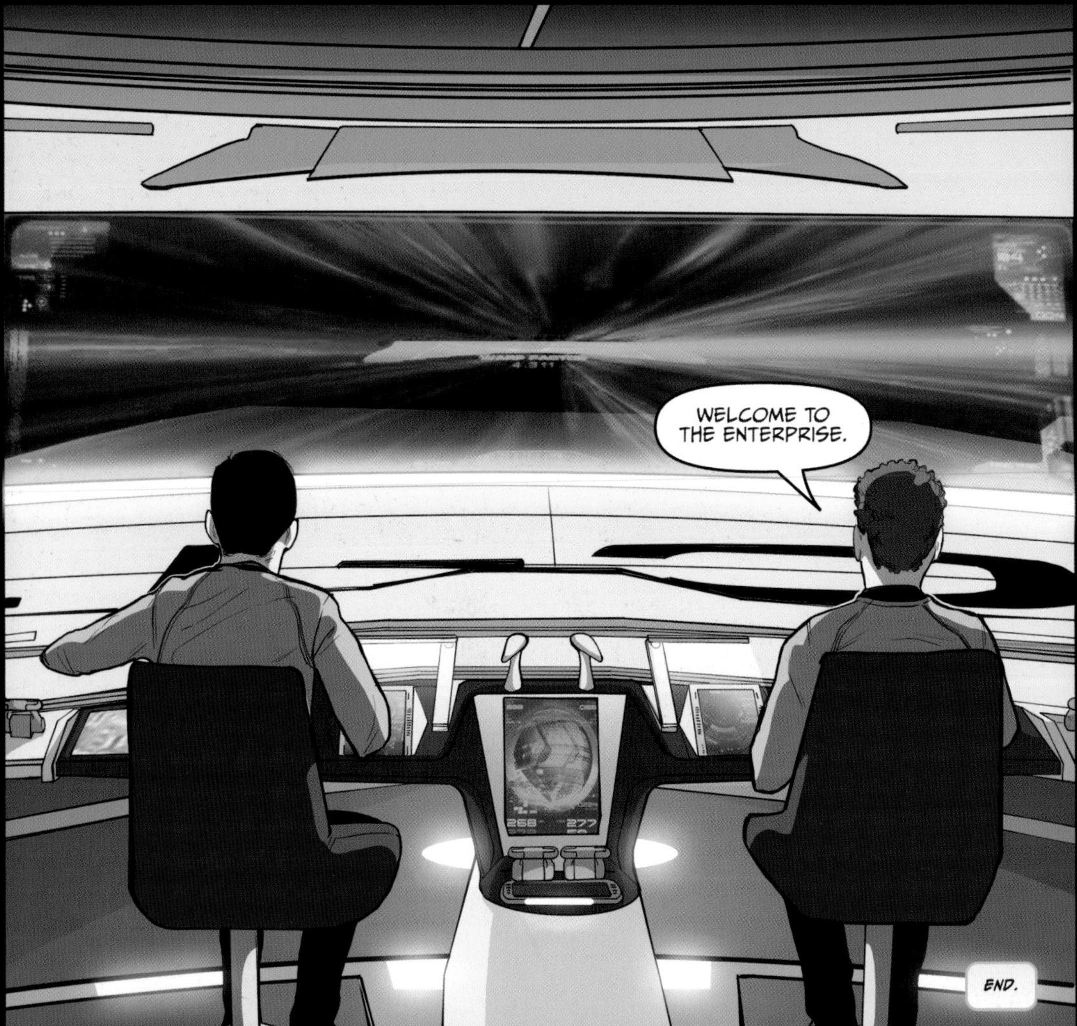
WELCOME TO THE ENTERPRISE.
END.

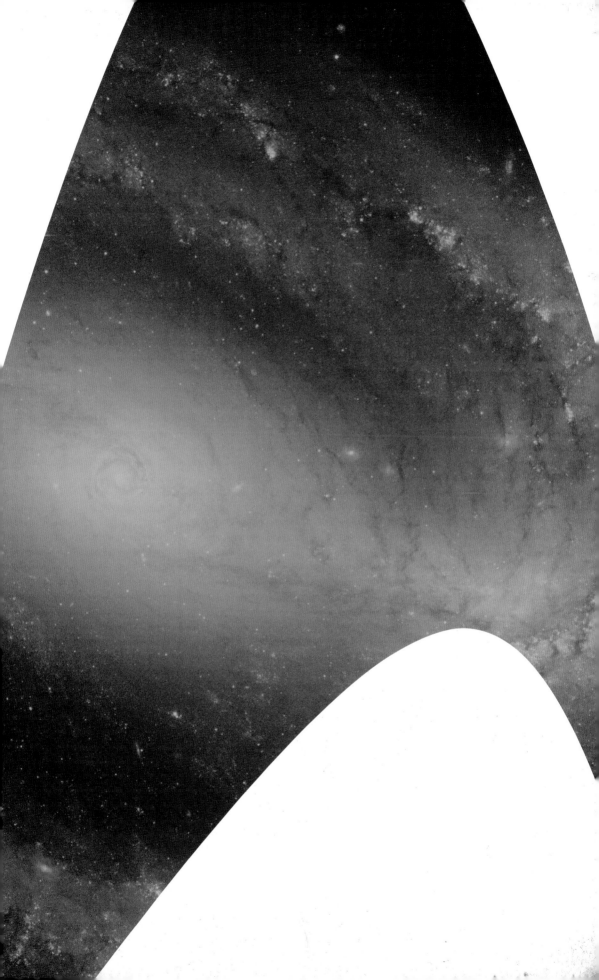

AFTER DARKNESS

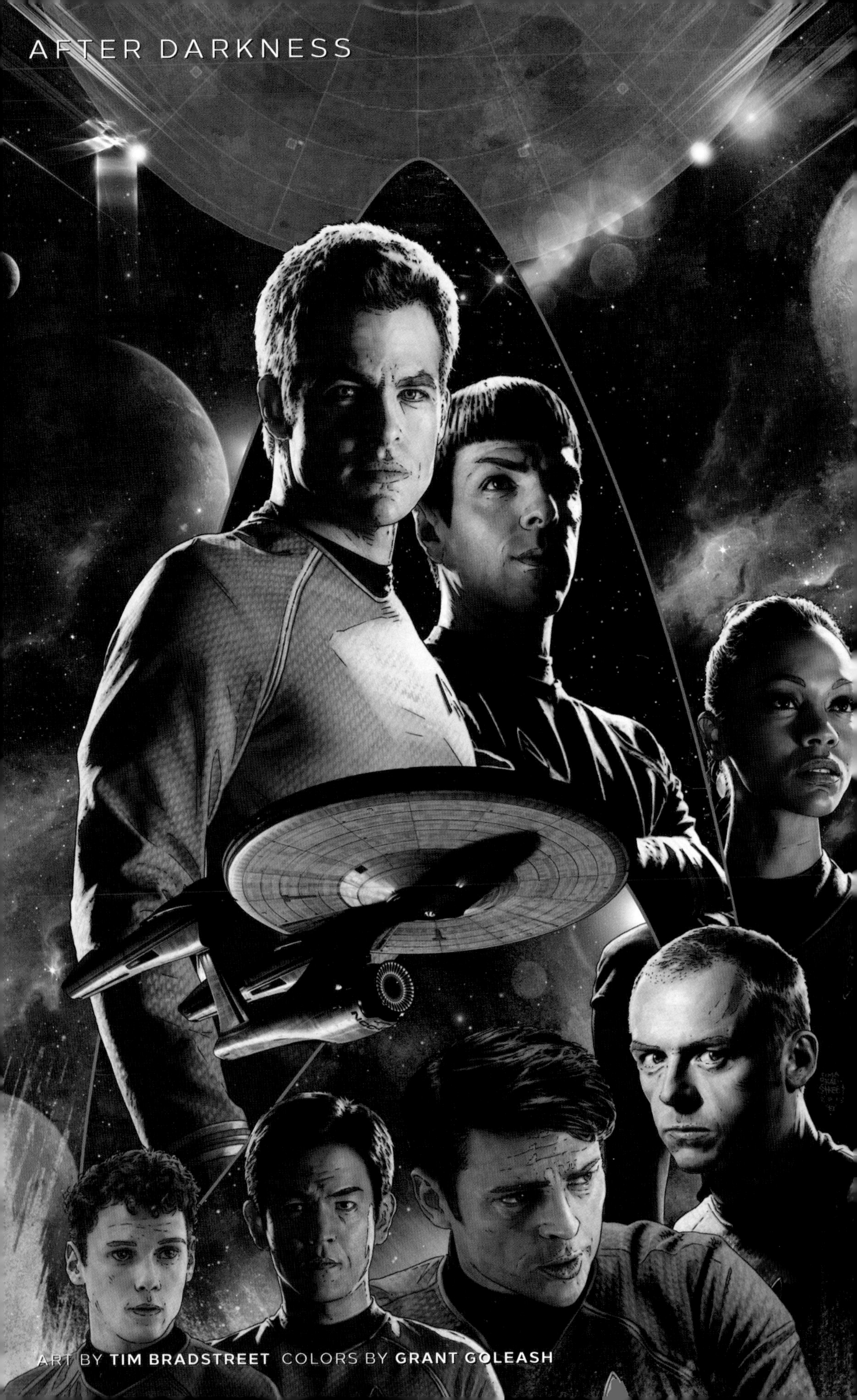

ART BY **TIM BRADSTREET** COLORS BY **GRANT GOLEASH**

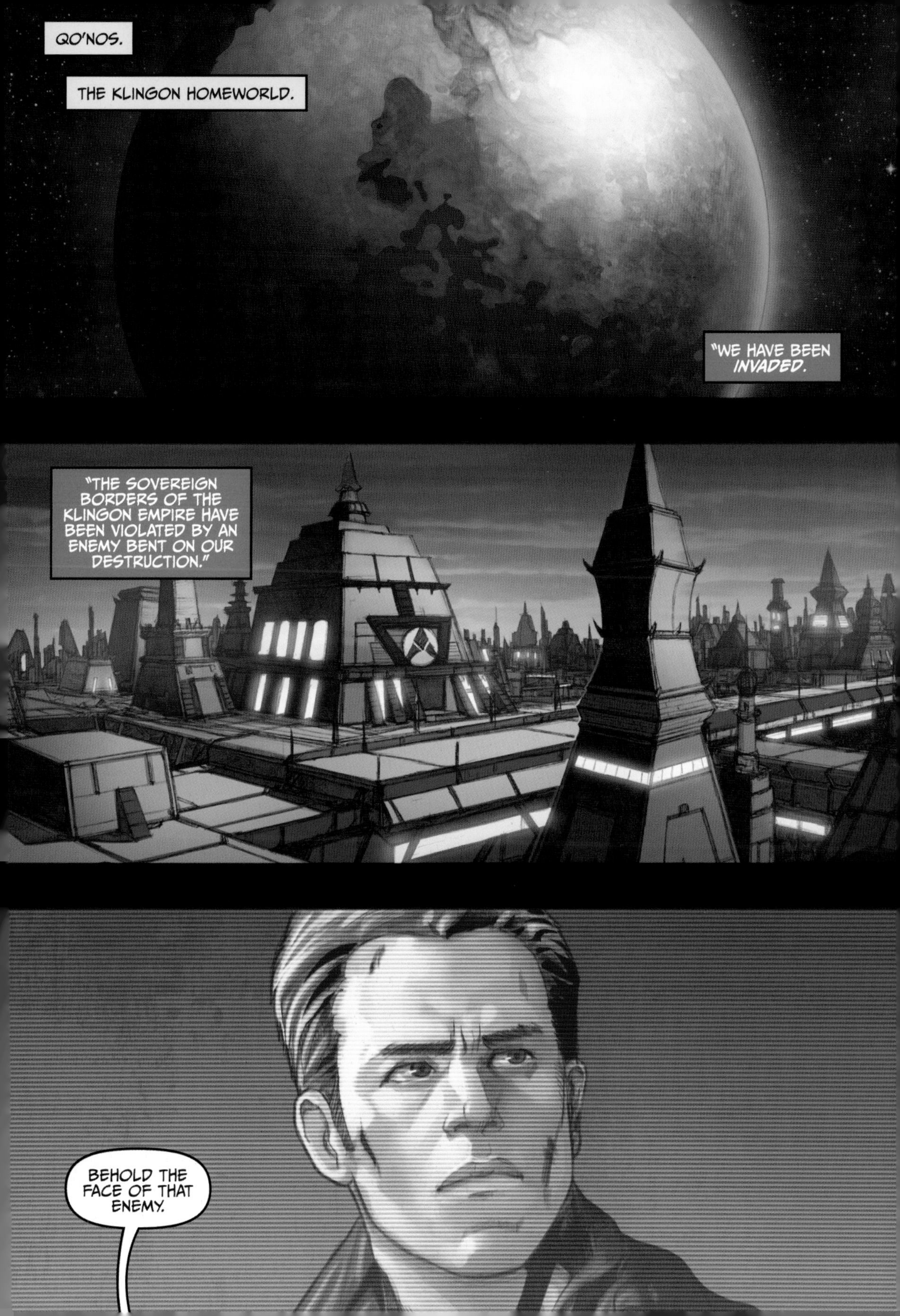
QO'NOS.
THE KLINGON HOMEWORLD.
"WE HAVE BEEN INVADED.
"THE SOVEREIGN BORDERS OF THE KLINGON EMPIRE HAVE BEEN VIOLATED BY AN ENEMY BENT ON OUR DESTRUCTION."
BEHOLD THE FACE OF THAT ENEMY.

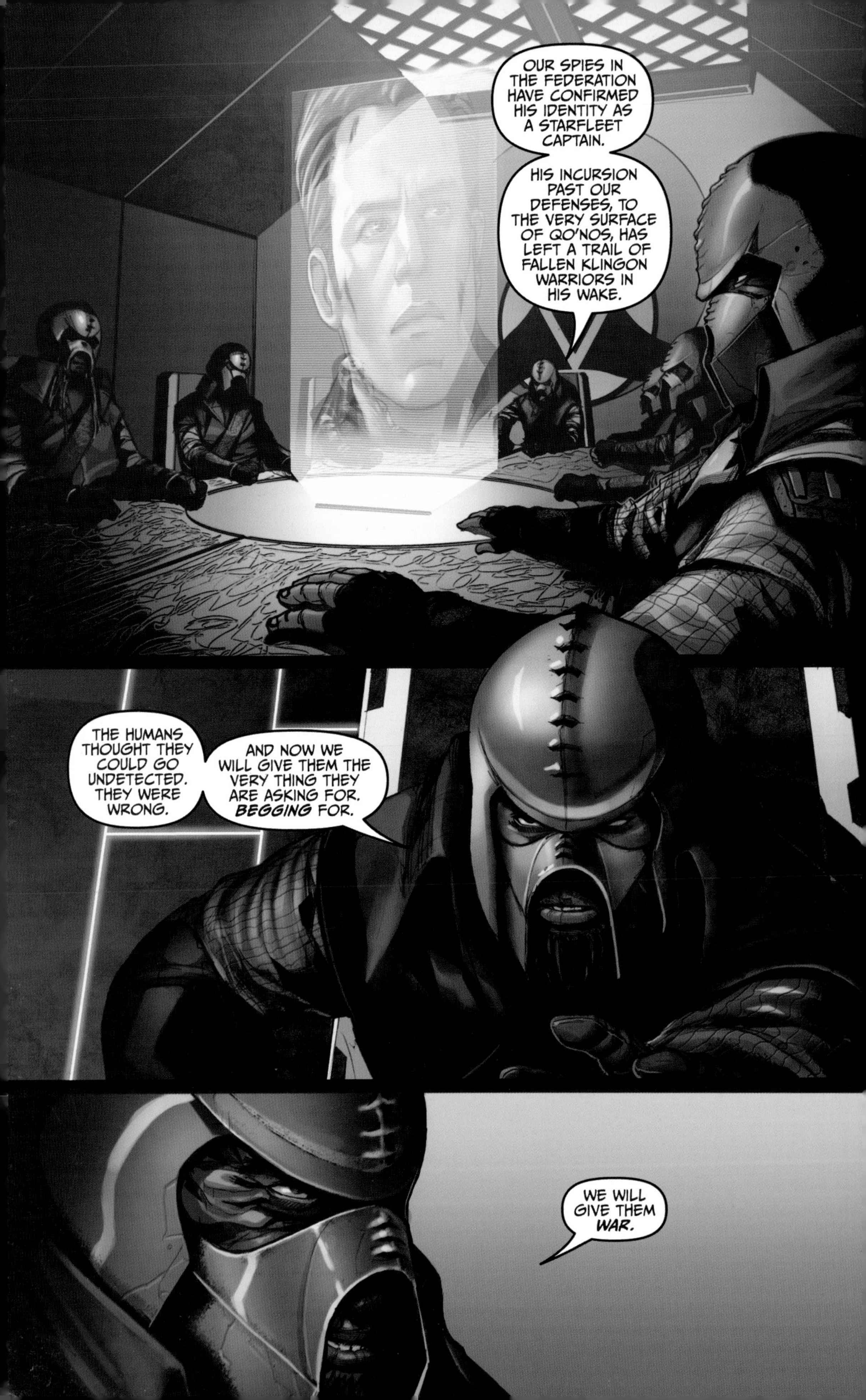
OUR SPIES IN THE FEDERATION HAVE CONFIRMED HIS IDENTITY AS A STARFLEET CAPTAIN.
HIS INCURSION PAST OUR DEFENSES, TO THE VERY SURFACE OF QO'NOS, HAS LEFT A TRAIL OF FALLEN KLINGON WARRIORS IN HIS WAKE.
THE HUMANS THOUGHT THEY COULD GO UNDETECTED. THEY WERE WRONG.
AND NOW WE WILL GIVE THEM THE VERY THING THEY ARE ASKING FOR. *BEGGING* FOR.
WE WILL GIVE THEM *WAR.*

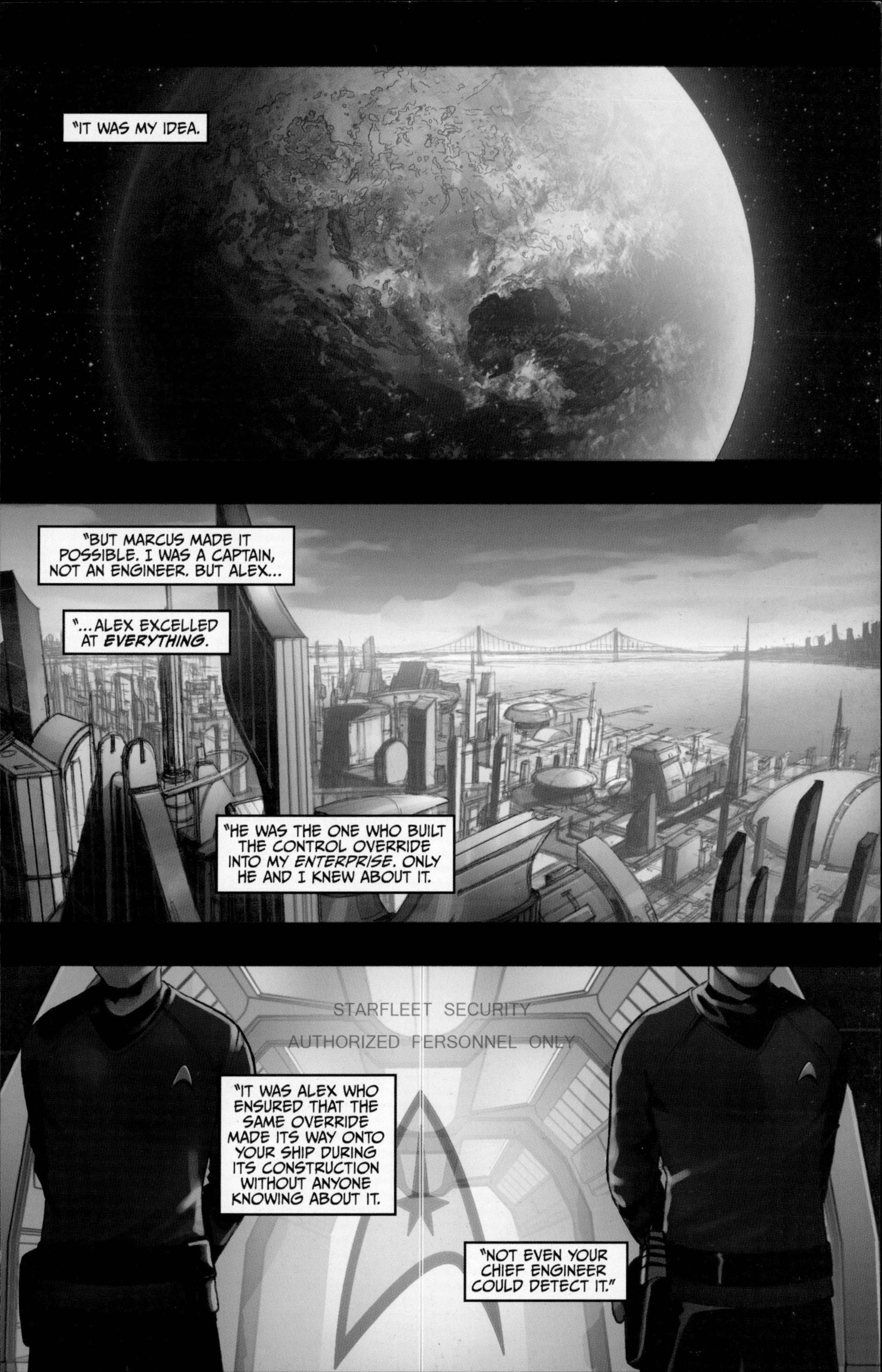
"IT WAS MY IDEA.
"BUT MARCUS MADE IT POSSIBLE. I WAS A CAPTAIN, NOT AN ENGINEER. BUT ALEX...
"...ALEX EXCELLED AT *EVERYTHING*.
"HE WAS THE ONE WHO BUILT THE CONTROL OVERRIDE INTO MY *ENTERPRISE*. ONLY HE AND I KNEW ABOUT IT.
STARFLEET SECURITY
AUTHORIZED PERSONNEL ONLY
"IT WAS ALEX WHO ENSURED THAT THE SAME OVERRIDE MADE ITS WAY ONTO YOUR SHIP DURING ITS CONSTRUCTION WITHOUT ANYONE KNOWING ABOUT IT.
"NOT EVEN YOUR CHIEF ENGINEER COULD DETECT IT."

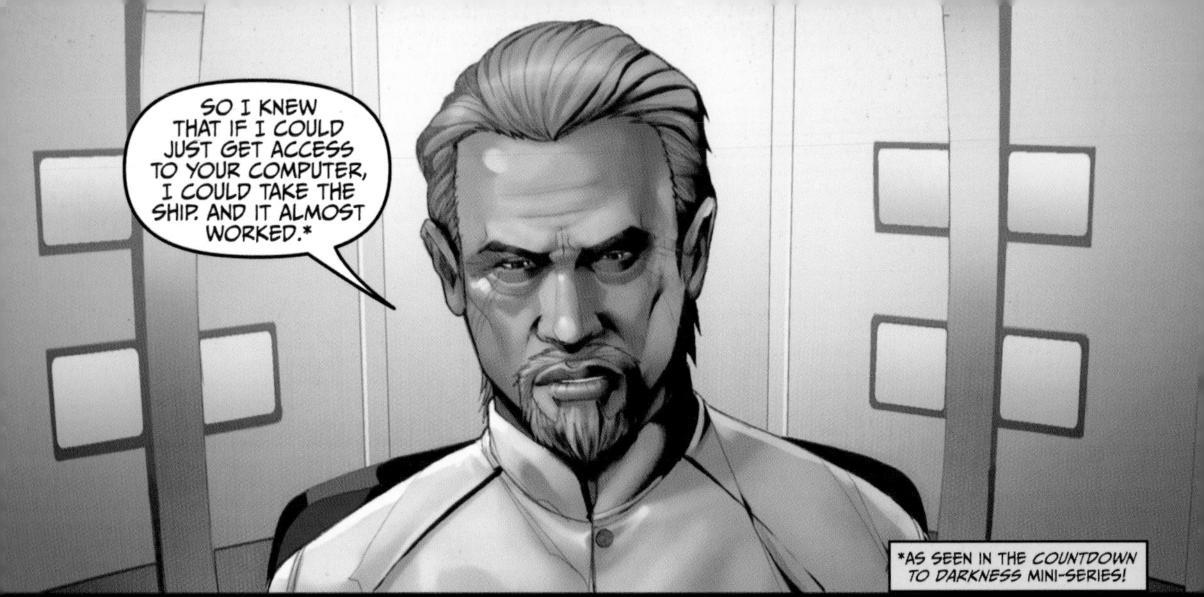
SO I KNEW THAT IF I COULD JUST GET ACCESS TO YOUR COMPUTER, I COULD TAKE THE SHIP. AND IT ALMOST WORKED.*
*AS SEEN IN THE *COUNTDOWN TO DARKNESS* MINI-SERIES!

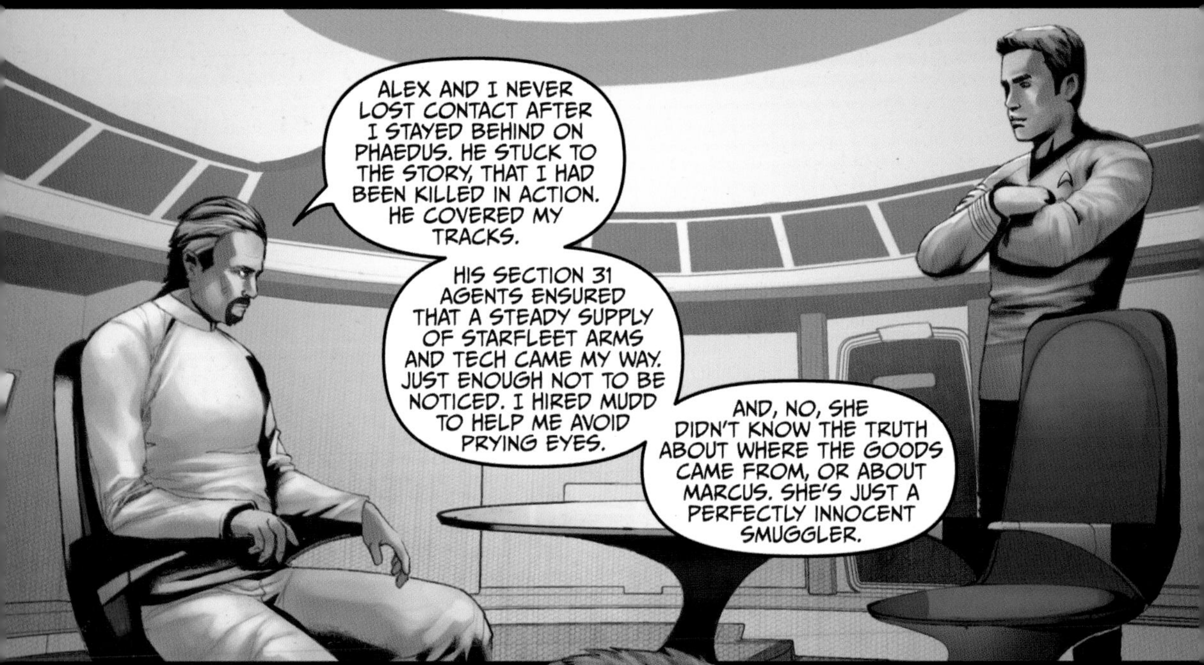
ALEX AND I NEVER LOST CONTACT AFTER I STAYED BEHIND ON PHAEDUS. HE STUCK TO THE STORY, THAT I HAD BEEN KILLED IN ACTION. HE COVERED MY TRACKS.
HIS SECTION 31 AGENTS ENSURED THAT A STEADY SUPPLY OF STARFLEET ARMS AND TECH CAME MY WAY. JUST ENOUGH NOT TO BE NOTICED. I HIRED MUDD TO HELP ME AVOID PRYING EYES.
AND, NO, SHE DIDN'T KNOW THE TRUTH ABOUT WHERE THE GOODS CAME FROM, OR ABOUT MARCUS. SHE'S JUST A PERFECTLY INNOCENT SMUGGLER.

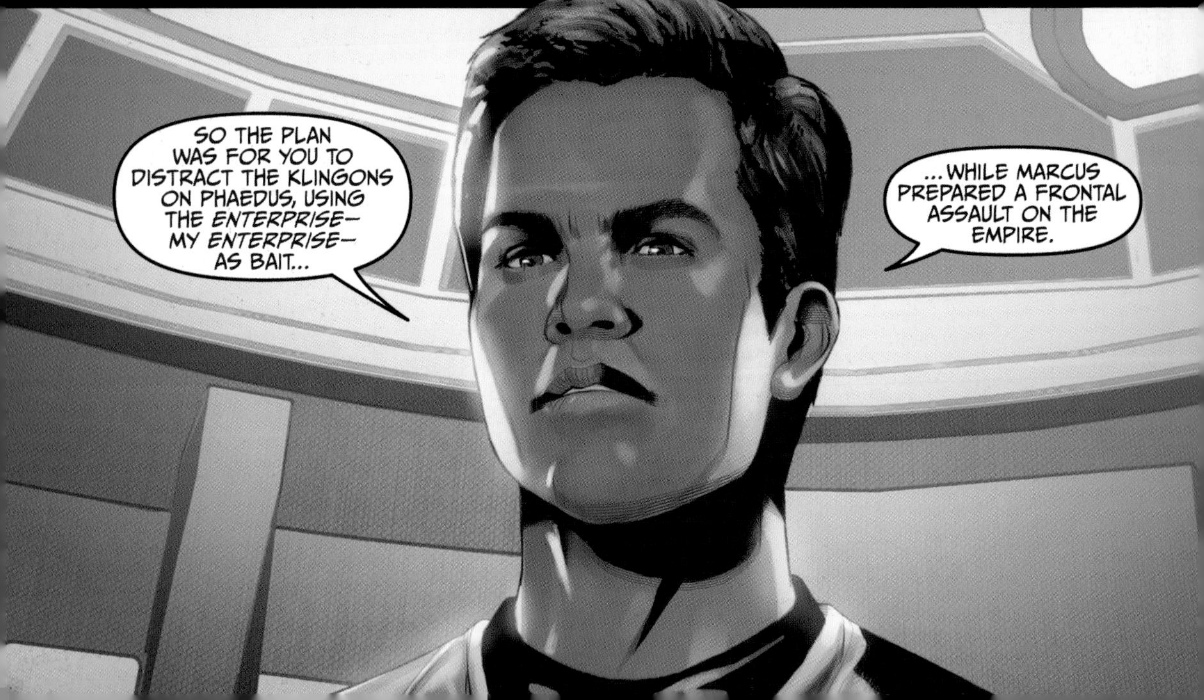
SO THE PLAN WAS FOR YOU TO DISTRACT THE KLINGONS ON PHAEDUS, USING THE *ENTERPRISE*— MY *ENTERPRISE*— AS BAIT...
...WHILE MARCUS PREPARED A FRONTAL ASSAULT ON THE EMPIRE.

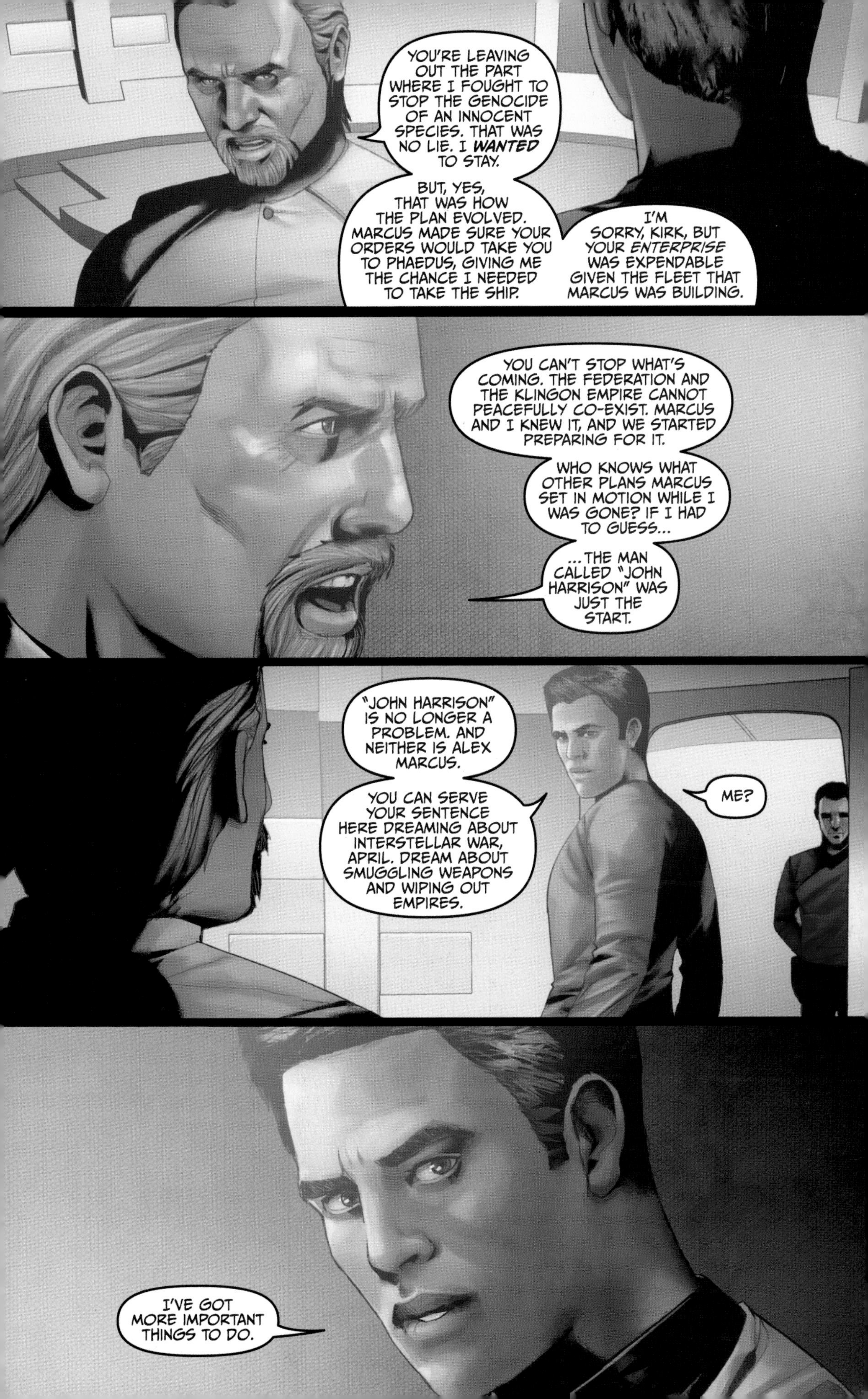
YOU'RE LEAVING OUT THE PART WHERE I FOUGHT TO STOP THE GENOCIDE OF AN INNOCENT SPECIES. THAT WAS NO LIE. I *WANTED* TO STAY.
BUT, YES, THAT WAS HOW THE PLAN EVOLVED. MARCUS MADE SURE YOUR ORDERS WOULD TAKE YOU TO PHAEDUS, GIVING ME THE CHANCE I NEEDED TO TAKE THE SHIP.
I'M SORRY, KIRK, BUT YOUR *ENTERPRISE* WAS EXPENDABLE GIVEN THE FLEET THAT MARCUS WAS BUILDING.
YOU CAN'T STOP WHAT'S COMING. THE FEDERATION AND THE KLINGON EMPIRE CANNOT PEACEFULLY CO-EXIST. MARCUS AND I KNEW IT, AND WE STARTED PREPARING FOR IT.
WHO KNOWS WHAT OTHER PLANS MARCUS SET IN MOTION WHILE I WAS GONE? IF I HAD TO GUESS...
...THE MAN CALLED "JOHN HARRISON" WAS JUST THE START.
"JOHN HARRISON" IS NO LONGER A PROBLEM. AND NEITHER IS ALEX MARCUS.
YOU CAN SERVE YOUR SENTENCE HERE DREAMING ABOUT INTERSTELLAR WAR, APRIL. DREAM ABOUT SMUGGLING WEAPONS AND WIPING OUT EMPIRES.
ME?
I'VE GOT MORE IMPORTANT THINGS TO DO.

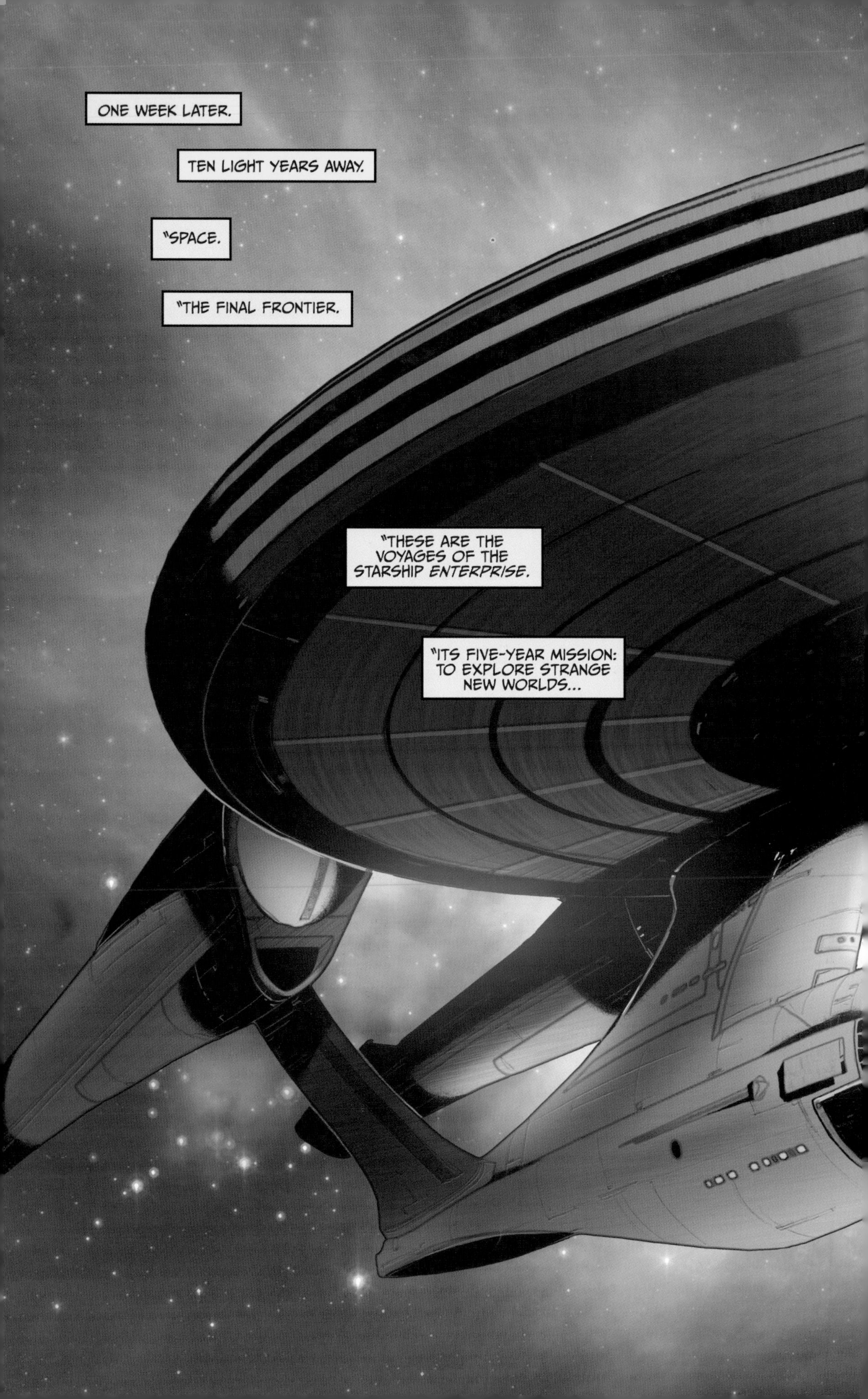
ONE WEEK LATER.
TEN LIGHT YEARS AWAY.
"SPACE.
"THE FINAL FRONTIER.
"THESE ARE THE VOYAGES OF THE STARSHIP *ENTERPRISE*.
"ITS FIVE-YEAR MISSION: TO EXPLORE STRANGE NEW WORLDS...

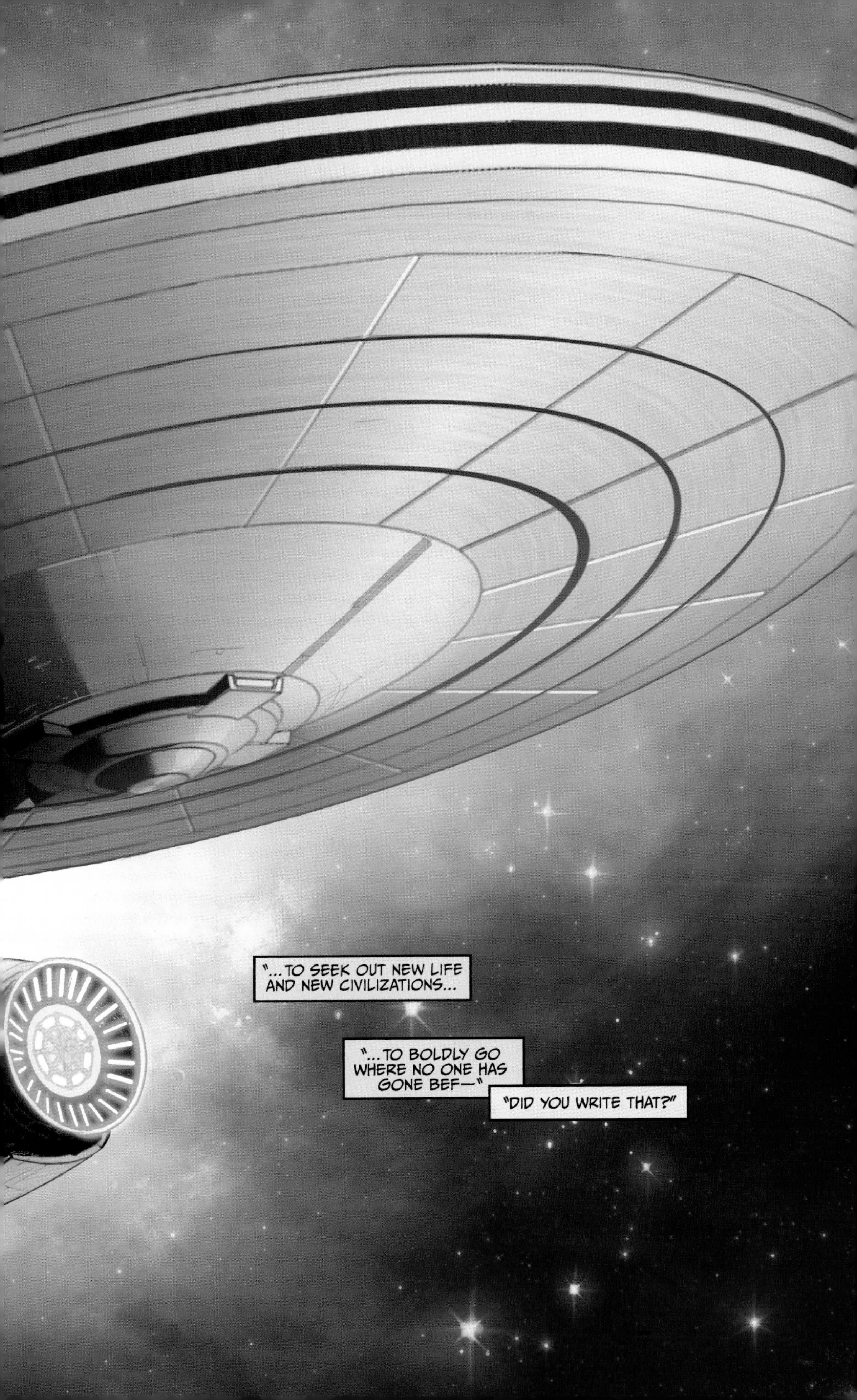
"...TO SEEK OUT NEW LIFE AND NEW CIVILIZATIONS...
"...TO BOLDLY GO WHERE NO ONE HAS GONE BEF—"
"DID YOU WRITE THAT?"

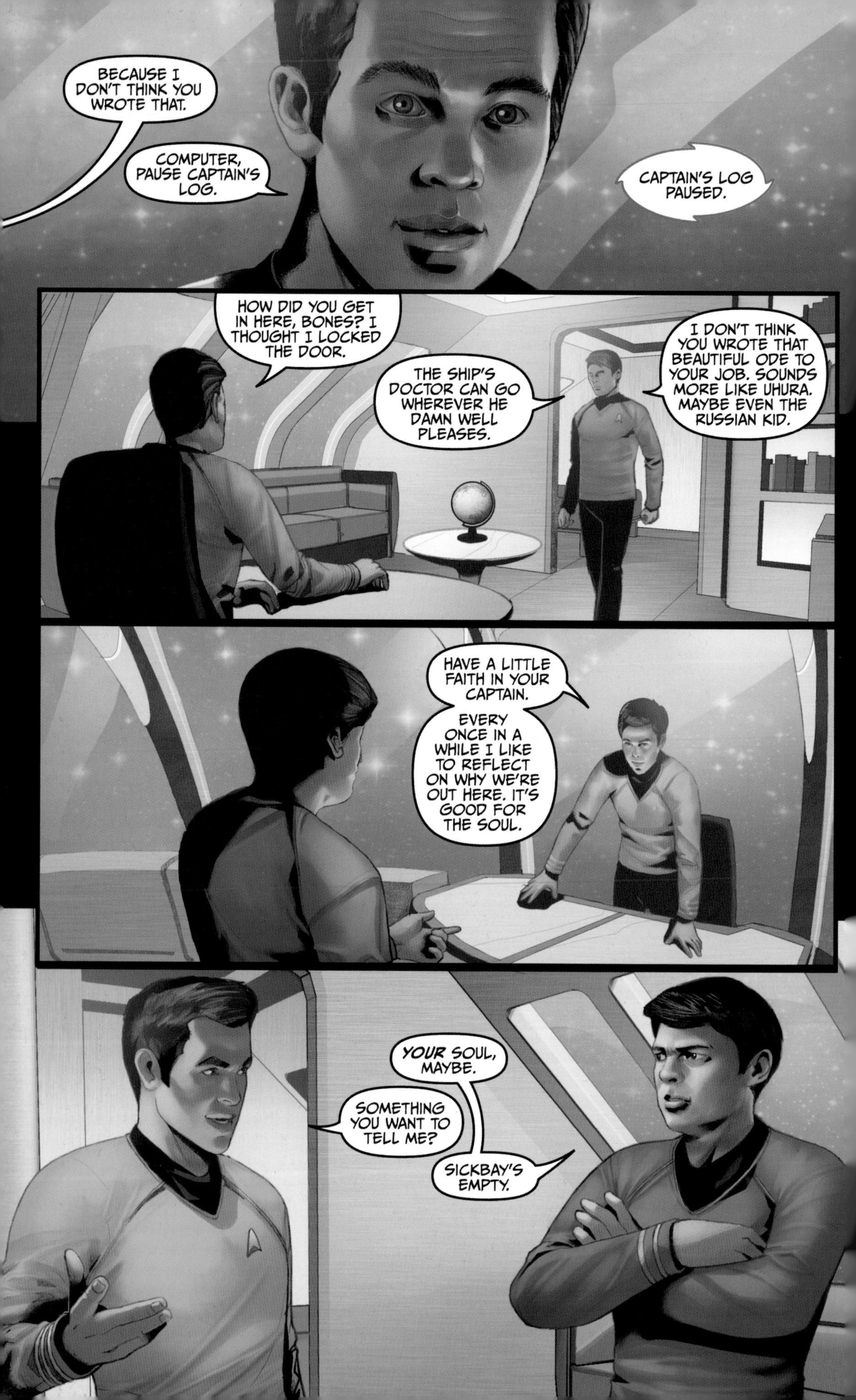
BECAUSE I DON'T THINK YOU WROTE THAT.
COMPUTER, PAUSE CAPTAIN'S LOG.
CAPTAIN'S LOG PAUSED.
HOW DID YOU GET IN HERE, BONES? I THOUGHT I LOCKED THE DOOR.
THE SHIP'S DOCTOR CAN GO WHEREVER HE DAMN WELL PLEASES.
I DON'T THINK YOU WROTE THAT BEAUTIFUL ODE TO YOUR JOB. SOUNDS MORE LIKE UHURA. MAYBE EVEN THE RUSSIAN KID.
HAVE A LITTLE FAITH IN YOUR CAPTAIN.
EVERY ONCE IN A WHILE I LIKE TO REFLECT ON WHY WE'RE OUT HERE. IT'S GOOD FOR THE SOUL.
YOUR SOUL, MAYBE.
SOMETHING YOU WANT TO TELL ME?
SICKBAY'S EMPTY.

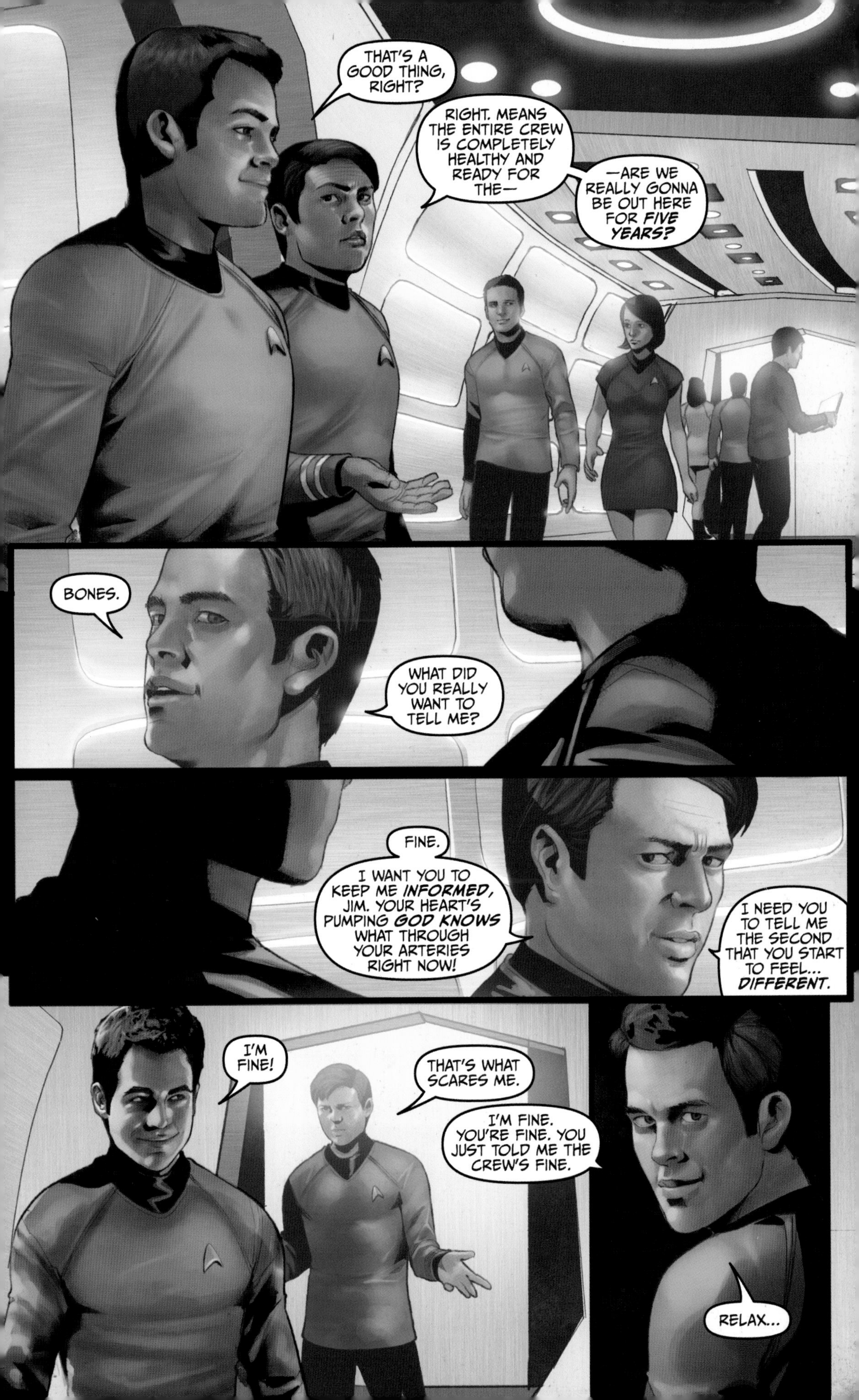
THAT'S A GOOD THING, RIGHT?
RIGHT. MEANS THE ENTIRE CREW IS COMPLETELY HEALTHY AND READY FOR THE—
—ARE WE REALLY GONNA BE OUT HERE FOR *FIVE YEARS?*
BONES.
WHAT DID YOU REALLY WANT TO TELL ME?
FINE.
I WANT YOU TO KEEP ME *INFORMED*, JIM. YOUR HEART'S PUMPING ***GOD KNOWS*** WHAT THROUGH YOUR ARTERIES RIGHT NOW!
I NEED YOU TO TELL ME THE SECOND THAT YOU START TO FEEL... *DIFFERENT*.
I'M FINE!
THAT'S WHAT SCARES ME.
I'M FINE. YOU'RE FINE. YOU JUST TOLD ME THE CREW'S FINE.
RELAX...

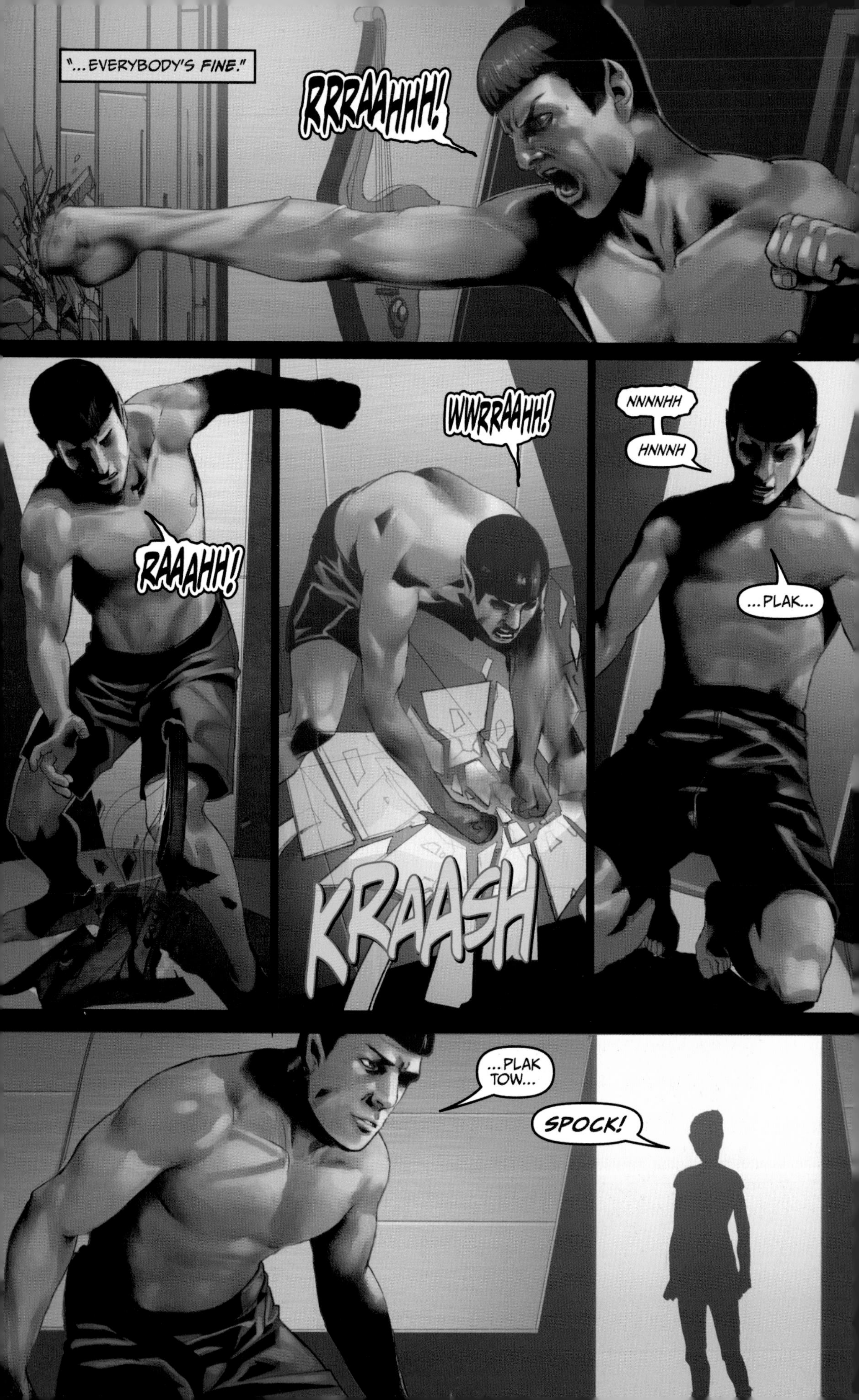
"...EVERYBODY'S FINE."
RRRAAHHH!
RAAAHH!
WWRRAAHH!
KRAASH
NNNNHH
HNNNH
...PLAK...
...PLAK TOW...
SPOCK!

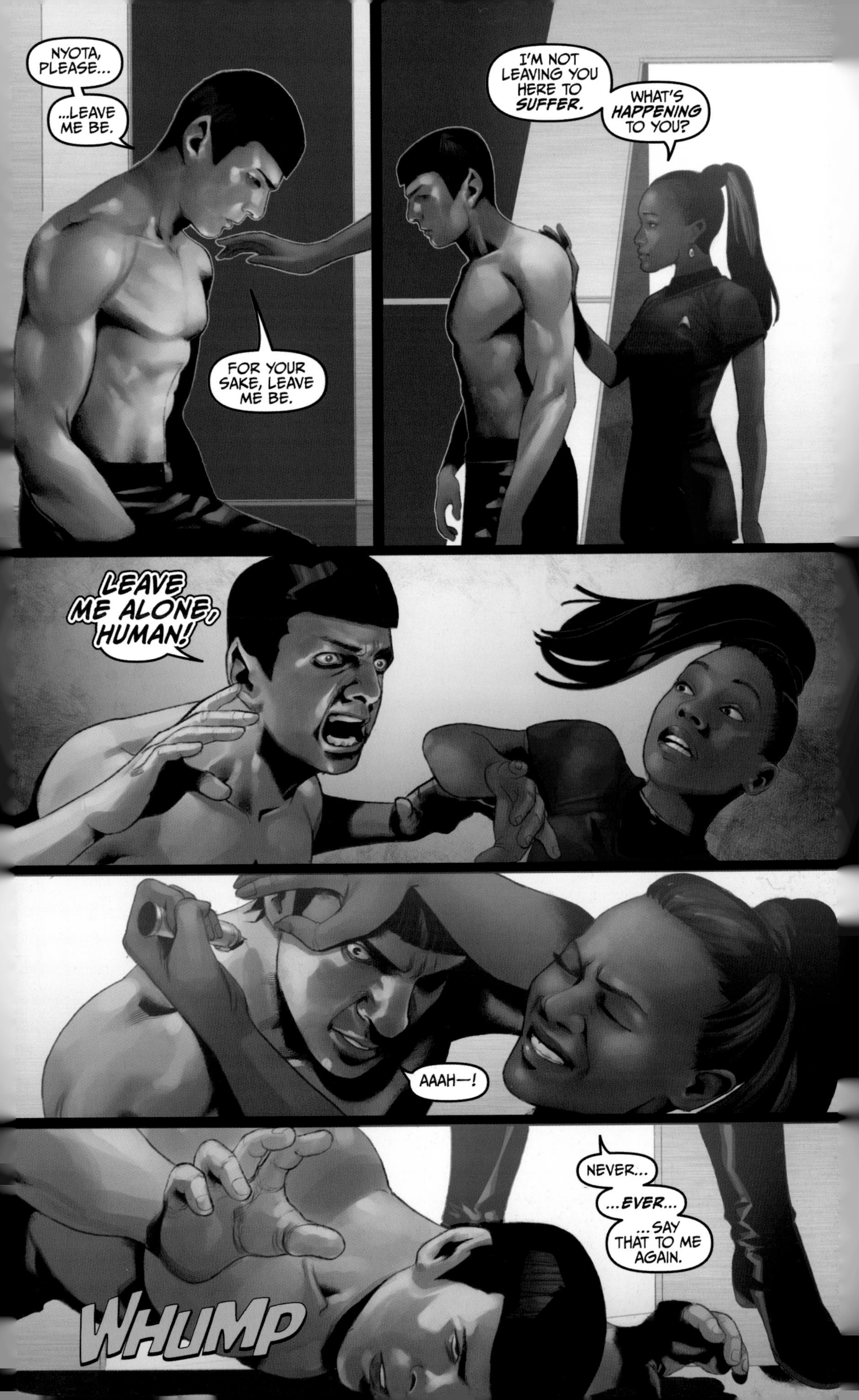
NYOTA, PLEASE...
...LEAVE ME BE.
FOR YOUR SAKE, LEAVE ME BE.
I'M NOT LEAVING YOU HERE TO *SUFFER*.
WHAT'S *HAPPENING* TO YOU?
LEAVE ME ALONE, HUMAN!
AAAH—!
NEVER...
...*EVER*...
...SAY THAT TO ME AGAIN.
WHUMP

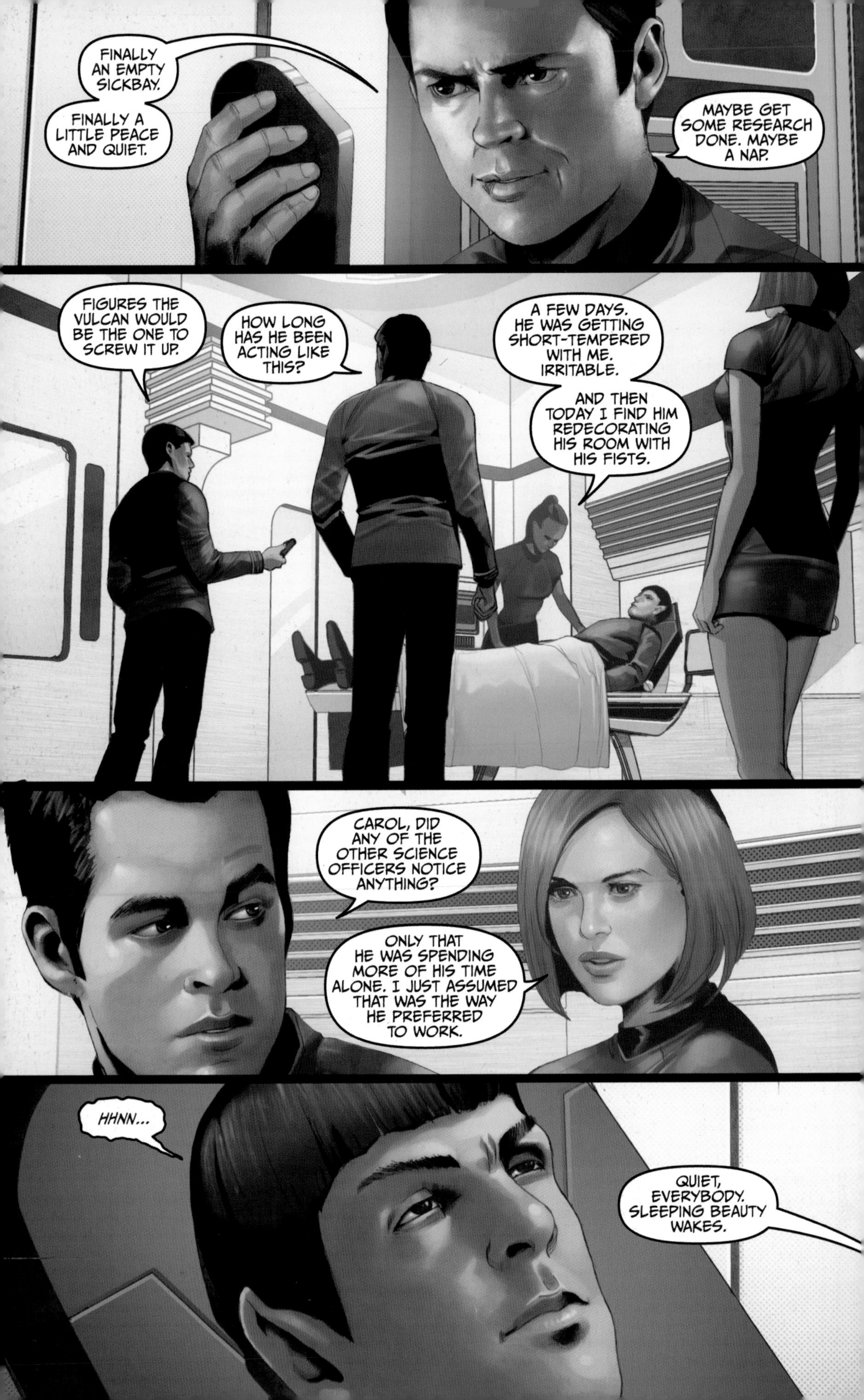
FINALLY AN EMPTY SICKBAY.
FINALLY A LITTLE PEACE AND QUIET.
MAYBE GET SOME RESEARCH DONE. MAYBE A NAP.
FIGURES THE VULCAN WOULD BE THE ONE TO SCREW IT UP.
HOW LONG HAS HE BEEN ACTING LIKE THIS?
A FEW DAYS. HE WAS GETTING SHORT-TEMPERED WITH ME. IRRITABLE.
AND THEN TODAY I FIND HIM REDECORATING HIS ROOM WITH HIS FISTS.
CAROL, DID ANY OF THE OTHER SCIENCE OFFICERS NOTICE ANYTHING?
ONLY THAT HE WAS SPENDING MORE OF HIS TIME ALONE. I JUST ASSUMED THAT WAS THE WAY HE PREFERRED TO WORK.
HHNN...
QUIET, EVERYBODY. SLEEPING BEAUTY WAKES.

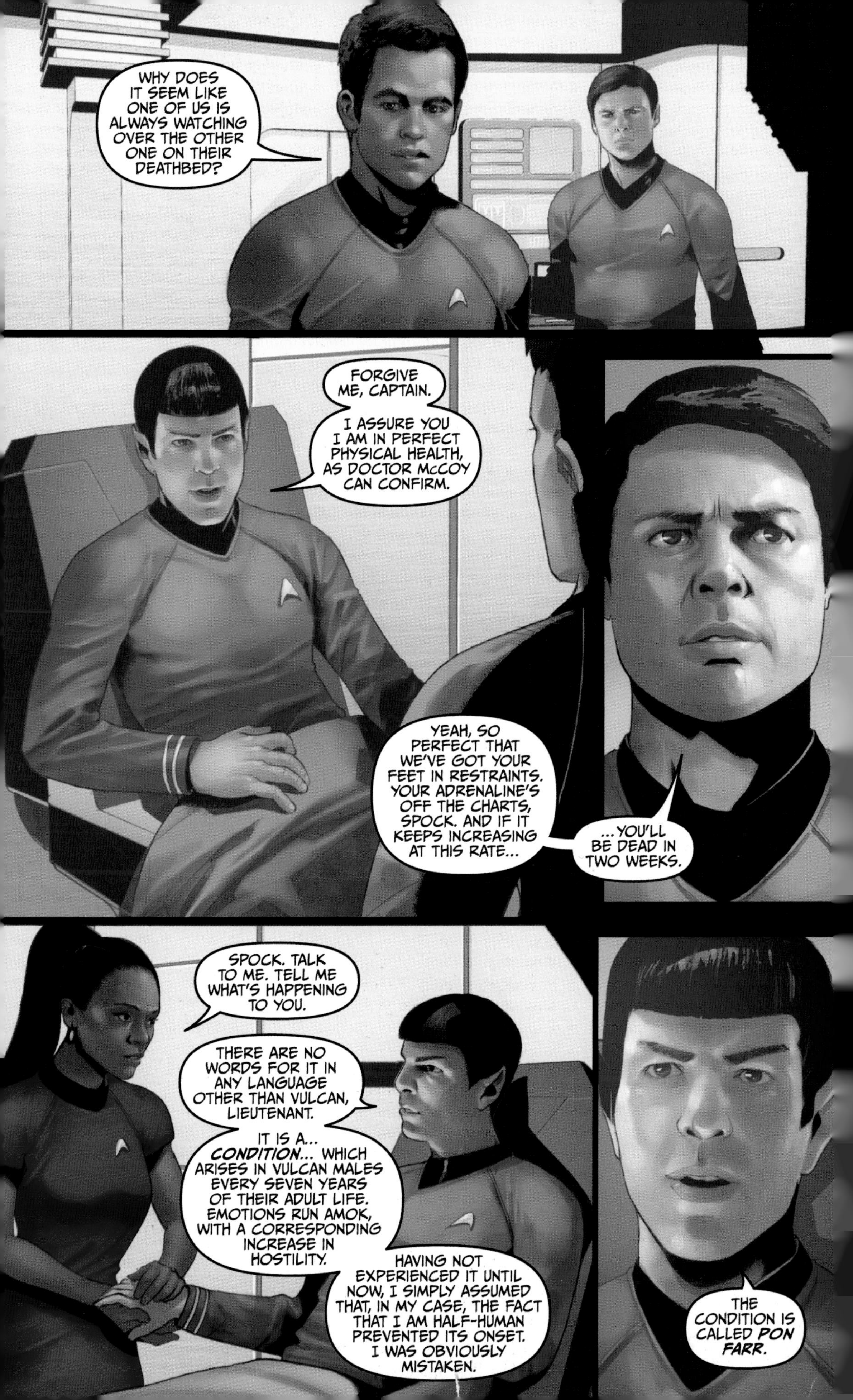
WHY DOES IT SEEM LIKE ONE OF US IS ALWAYS WATCHING OVER THE OTHER ONE ON THEIR DEATHBED?
FORGIVE ME, CAPTAIN.
I ASSURE YOU I AM IN PERFECT PHYSICAL HEALTH, AS DOCTOR McCOY CAN CONFIRM.
YEAH, SO PERFECT THAT WE'VE GOT YOUR FEET IN RESTRAINTS. YOUR ADRENALINE'S OFF THE CHARTS, SPOCK. AND IF IT KEEPS INCREASING AT THIS RATE...
...YOU'LL BE DEAD IN TWO WEEKS.
SPOCK. TALK TO ME. TELL ME WHAT'S HAPPENING TO YOU.
THERE ARE NO WORDS FOR IT IN ANY LANGUAGE OTHER THAN VULCAN, LIEUTENANT.
IT IS A... *CONDITION*... WHICH ARISES IN VULCAN MALES EVERY SEVEN YEARS OF THEIR ADULT LIFE. EMOTIONS RUN AMOK, WITH A CORRESPONDING INCREASE IN HOSTILITY.
HAVING NOT EXPERIENCED IT UNTIL NOW, I SIMPLY ASSUMED THAT, IN MY CASE, THE FACT THAT I AM HALF-HUMAN PREVENTED ITS ONSET. I WAS OBVIOUSLY MISTAKEN.
THE CONDITION IS CALLED *PON FARR*.

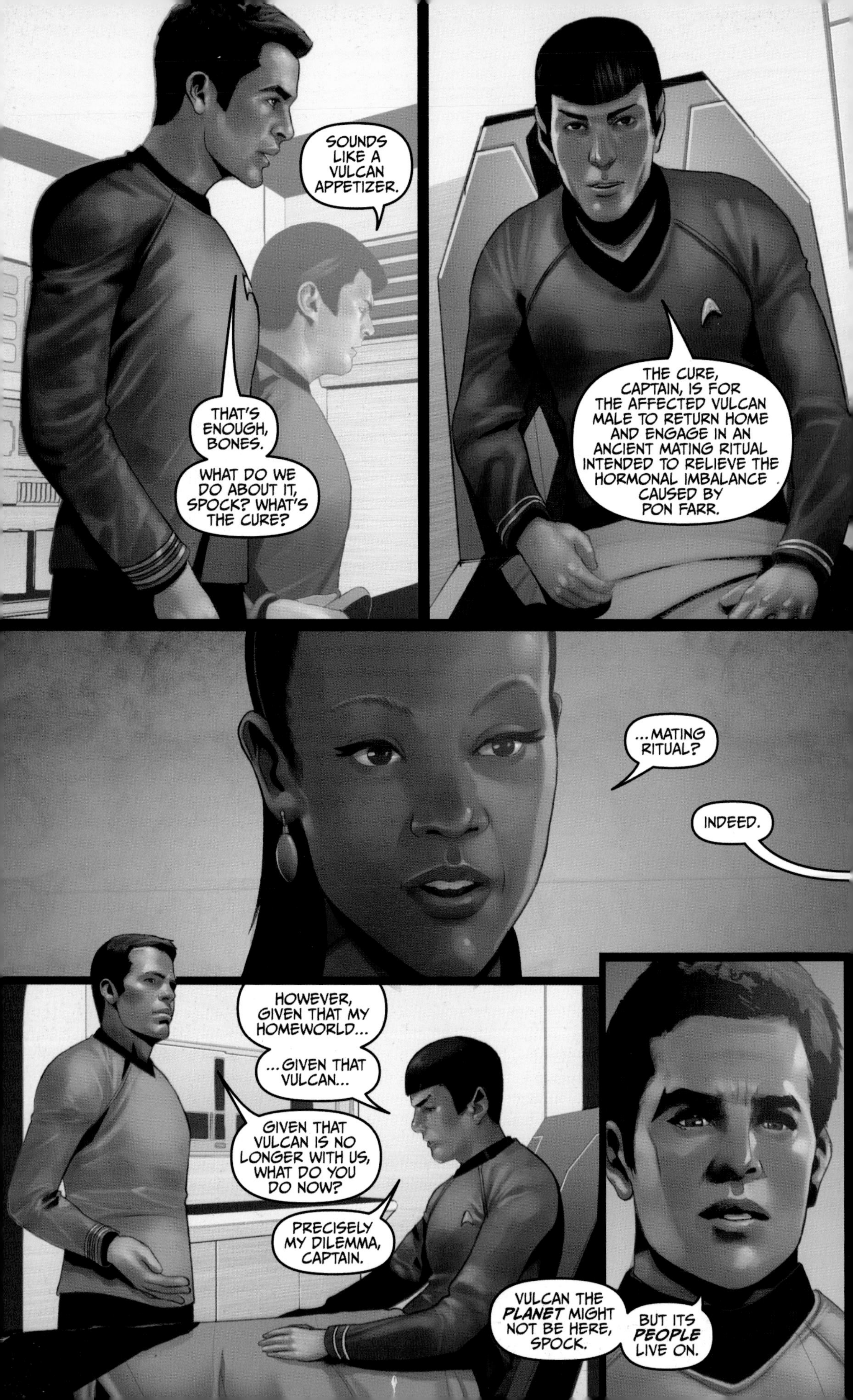
SOUNDS LIKE A VULCAN APPETIZER.
THAT'S ENOUGH, BONES.
WHAT DO WE DO ABOUT IT, SPOCK? WHAT'S THE CURE?
THE CURE, CAPTAIN, IS FOR THE AFFECTED VULCAN MALE TO RETURN HOME AND ENGAGE IN AN ANCIENT MATING RITUAL INTENDED TO RELIEVE THE HORMONAL IMBALANCE CAUSED BY PON FARR.
...MATING RITUAL?
INDEED.
HOWEVER, GIVEN THAT MY HOMEWORLD...
...GIVEN THAT VULCAN...
GIVEN THAT VULCAN IS NO LONGER WITH US, WHAT DO YOU DO NOW?
PRECISELY MY DILEMMA, CAPTAIN.
VULCAN THE *PLANET* MIGHT NOT BE HERE, SPOCK.
BUT ITS *PEOPLE* LIVE ON.

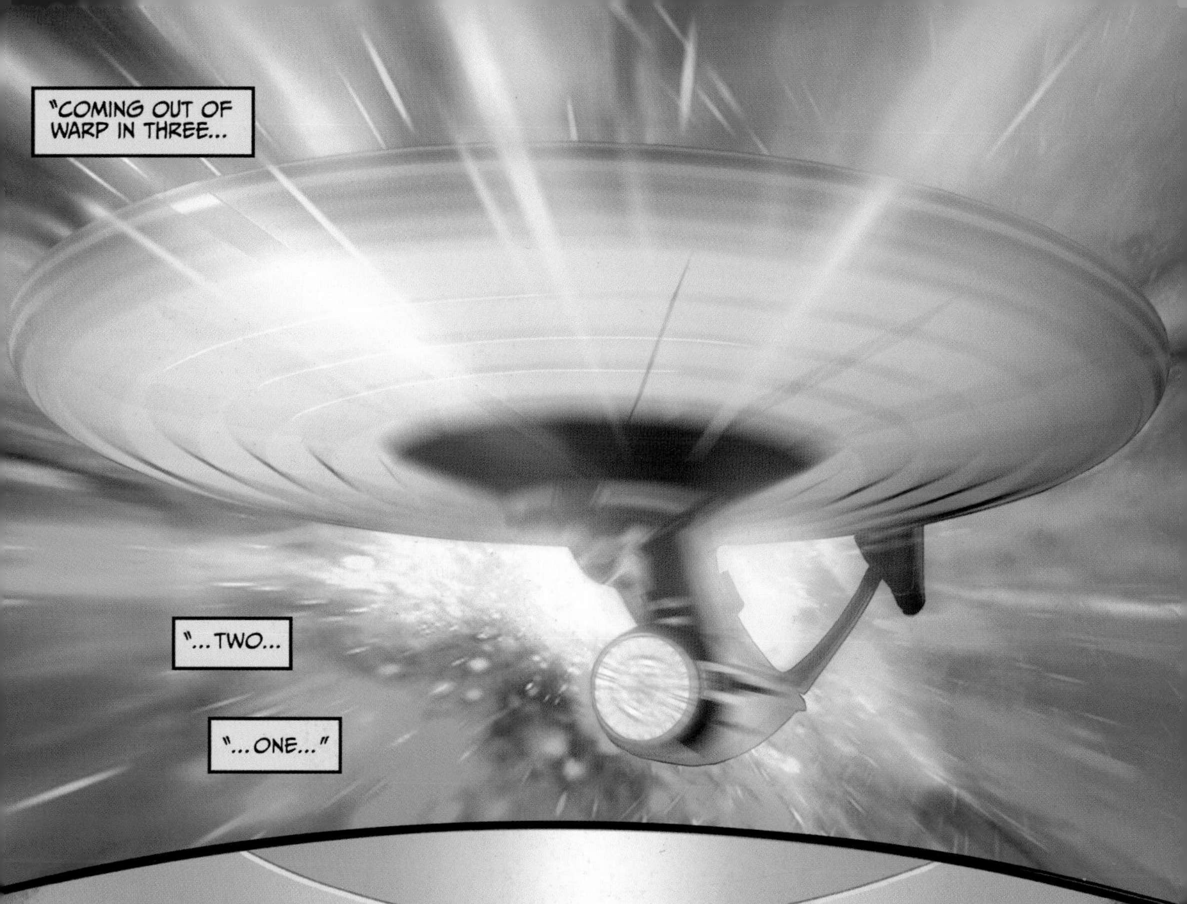
"COMING OUT OF WARP IN THREE...
"...TWO...
"...ONE..."

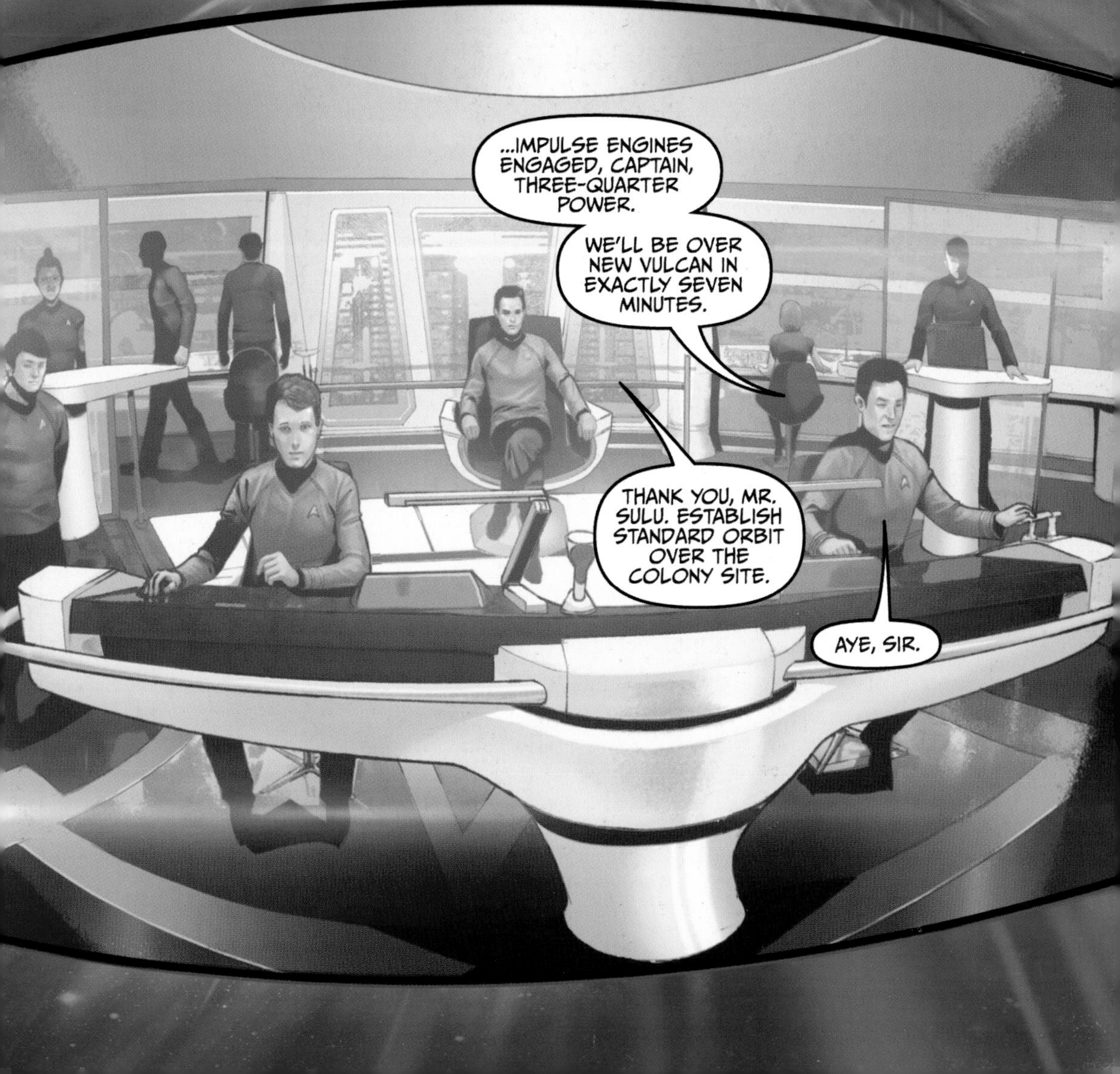
...IMPULSE ENGINES ENGAGED, CAPTAIN, THREE-QUARTER POWER.
WE'LL BE OVER NEW VULCAN IN EXACTLY SEVEN MINUTES.
THANK YOU, MR. SULU. ESTABLISH STANDARD ORBIT OVER THE COLONY SITE.
AYE, SIR.

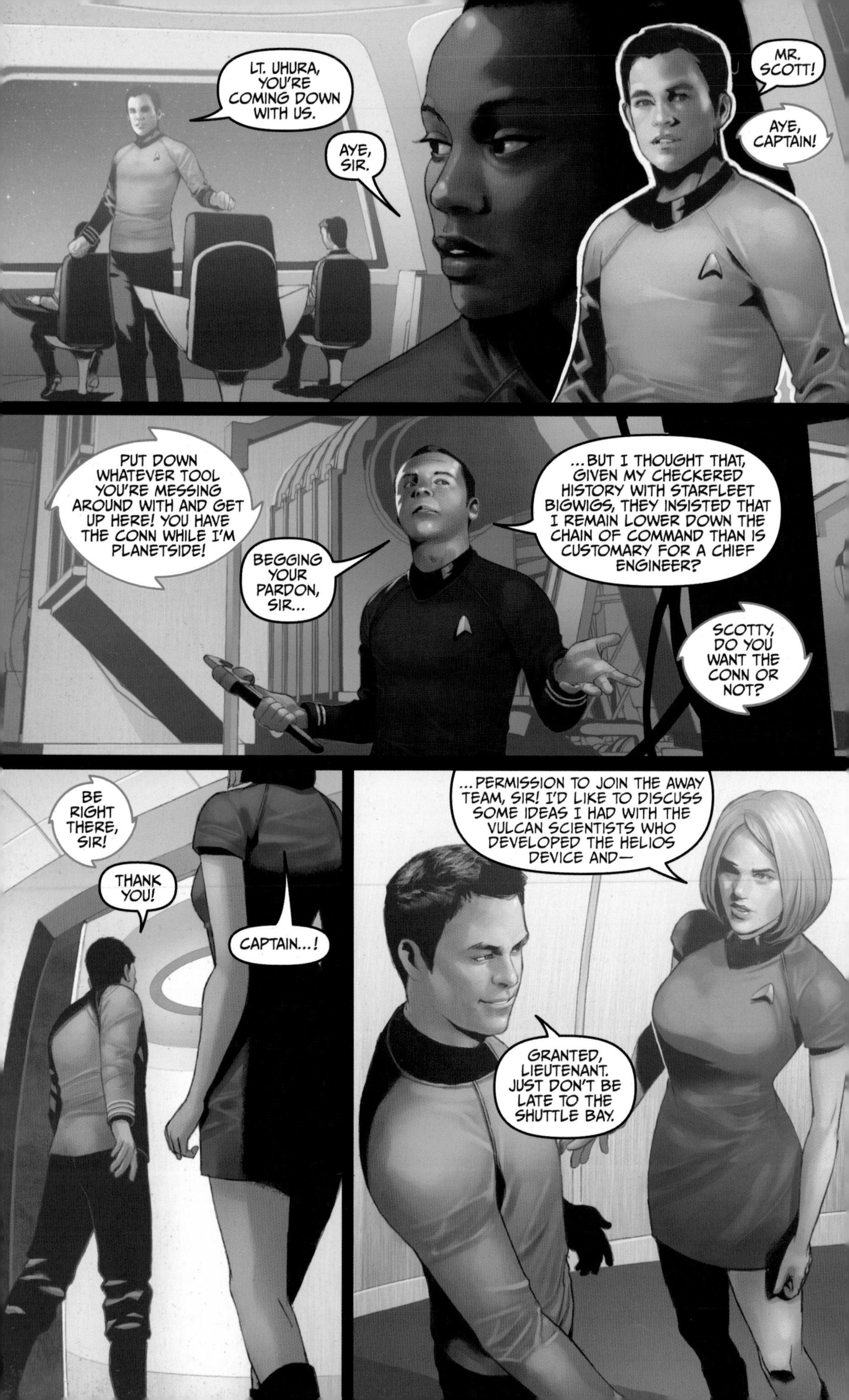
LT. UHURA, YOU'RE COMING DOWN WITH US.
AYE, SIR.
MR. SCOTT!
AYE, CAPTAIN!
PUT DOWN WHATEVER TOOL YOU'RE MESSING AROUND WITH AND GET UP HERE! YOU HAVE THE CONN WHILE I'M PLANETSIDE!
BEGGING YOUR PARDON, SIR...
...BUT I THOUGHT THAT, GIVEN MY CHECKERED HISTORY WITH STARFLEET BIGWIGS, THEY INSISTED THAT I REMAIN LOWER DOWN THE CHAIN OF COMMAND THAN IS CUSTOMARY FOR A CHIEF ENGINEER?
SCOTTY, DO YOU WANT THE CONN OR NOT?
BE RIGHT THERE, SIR!
THANK YOU!
CAPTAIN...!
...PERMISSION TO JOIN THE AWAY TEAM, SIR! I'D LIKE TO DISCUSS SOME IDEAS I HAD WITH THE VULCAN SCIENTISTS WHO DEVELOPED THE HELIOS DEVICE AND—
GRANTED, LIEUTENANT. JUST DON'T BE LATE TO THE SHUTTLE BAY.

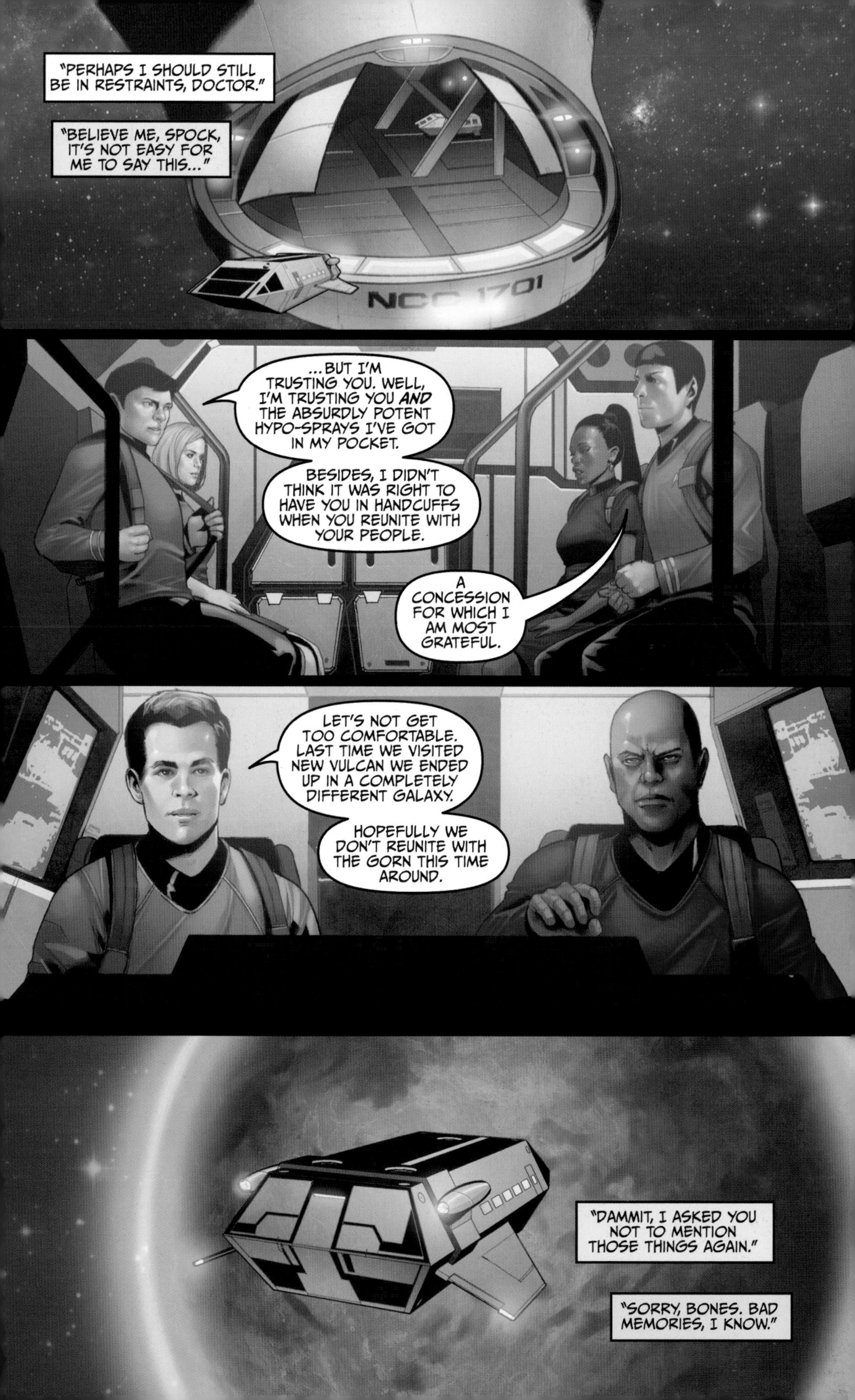
"PERHAPS I SHOULD STILL BE IN RESTRAINTS, DOCTOR."
"BELIEVE ME, SPOCK, IT'S NOT EASY FOR ME TO SAY THIS..."
NCC-1701
...BUT I'M TRUSTING YOU. WELL, I'M TRUSTING YOU *AND* THE ABSURDLY POTENT HYPO-SPRAYS I'VE GOT IN MY POCKET.
BESIDES, I DIDN'T THINK IT WAS RIGHT TO HAVE YOU IN HANDCUFFS WHEN YOU REUNITE WITH YOUR PEOPLE.
A CONCESSION FOR WHICH I AM MOST GRATEFUL.
LET'S NOT GET TOO COMFORTABLE. LAST TIME WE VISITED NEW VULCAN WE ENDED UP IN A COMPLETELY DIFFERENT GALAXY.
HOPEFULLY WE DON'T REUNITE WITH THE GORN THIS TIME AROUND.
"DAMMIT, I ASKED YOU NOT TO MENTION THOSE THINGS AGAIN."
"SORRY, BONES. BAD MEMORIES, I KNOW."

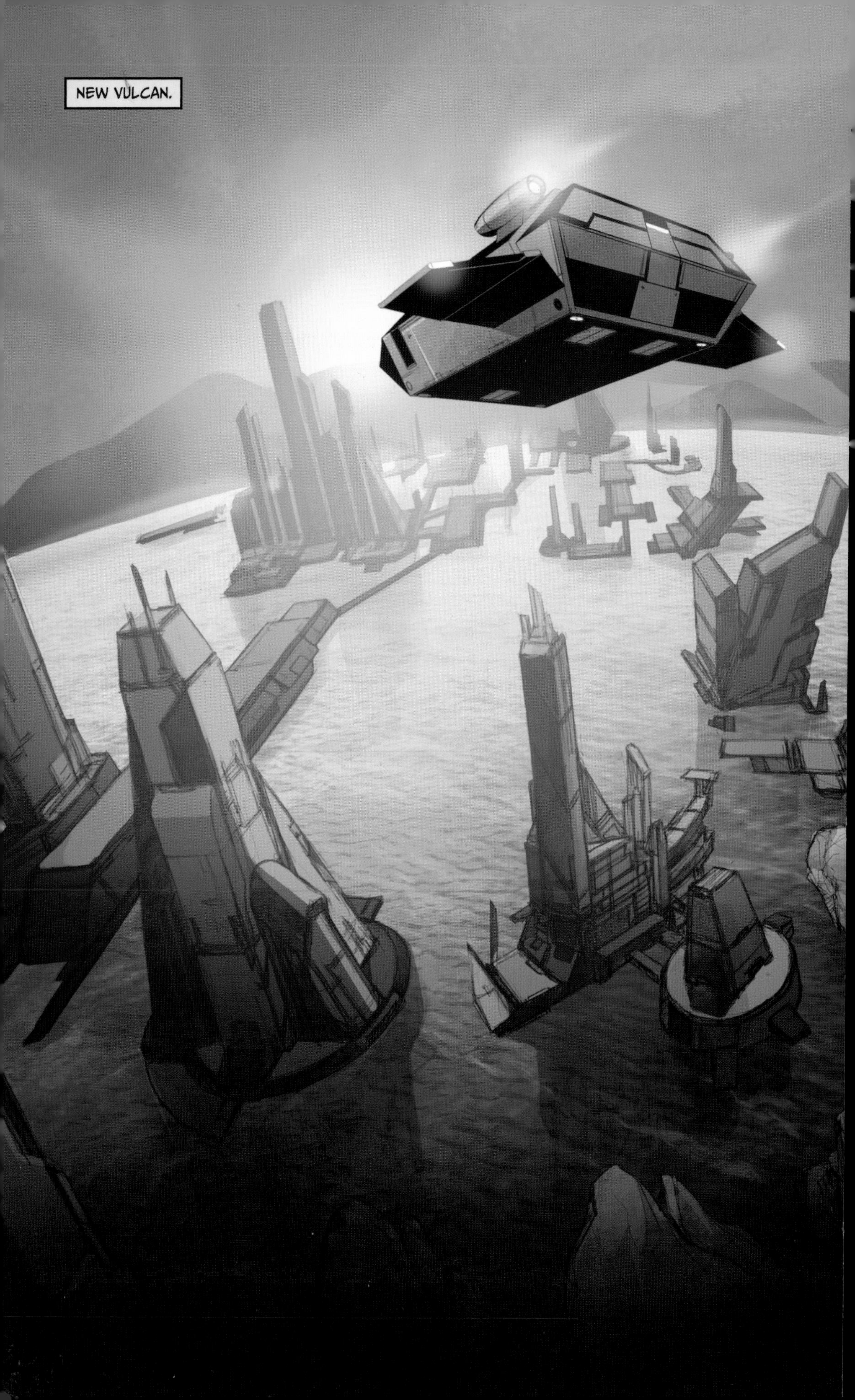
NEW VULCAN.

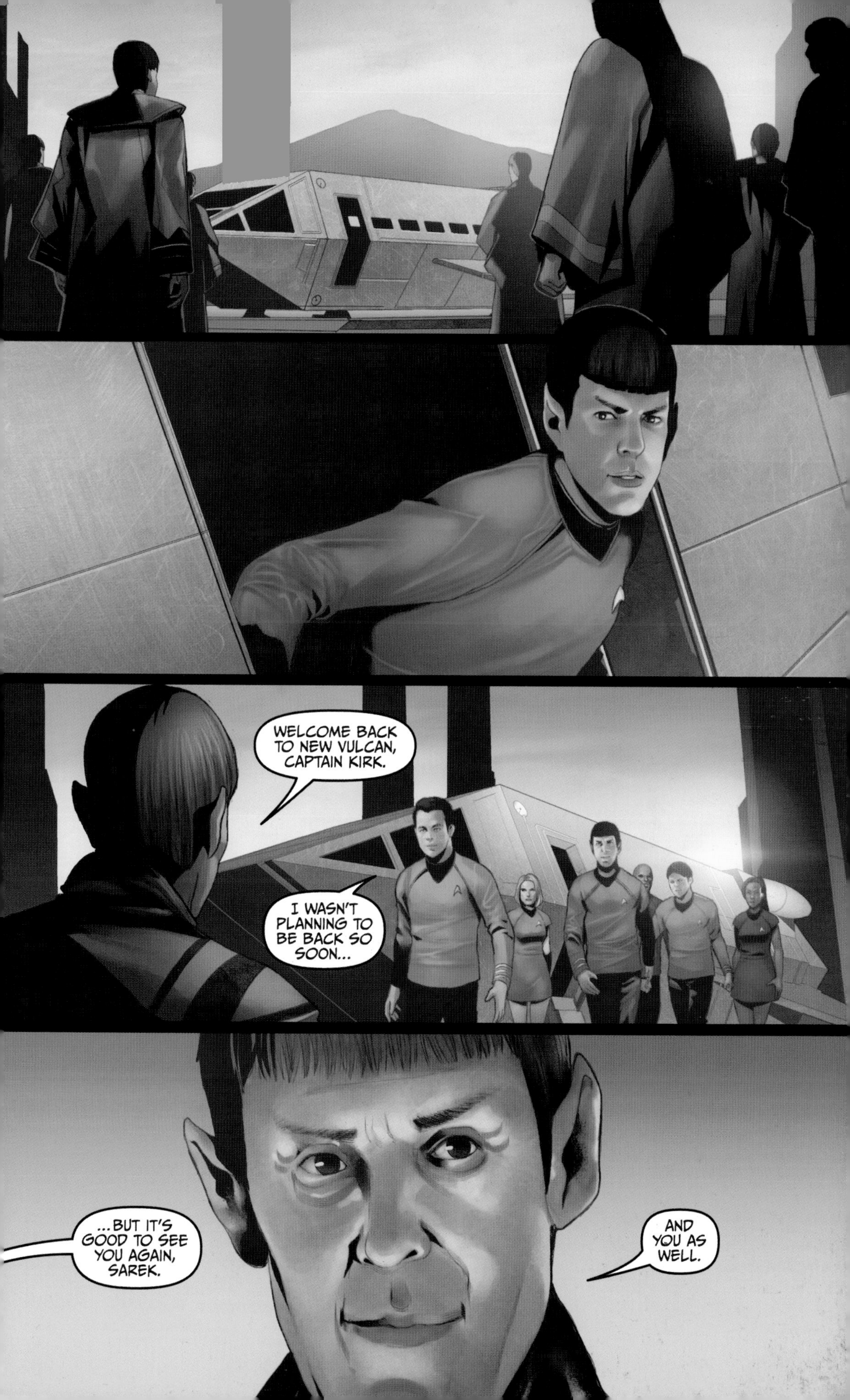
WELCOME BACK TO NEW VULCAN, CAPTAIN KIRK.
I WASN'T PLANNING TO BE BACK SO SOON...
...BUT IT'S GOOD TO SEE YOU AGAIN, SAREK.
AND YOU AS WELL.

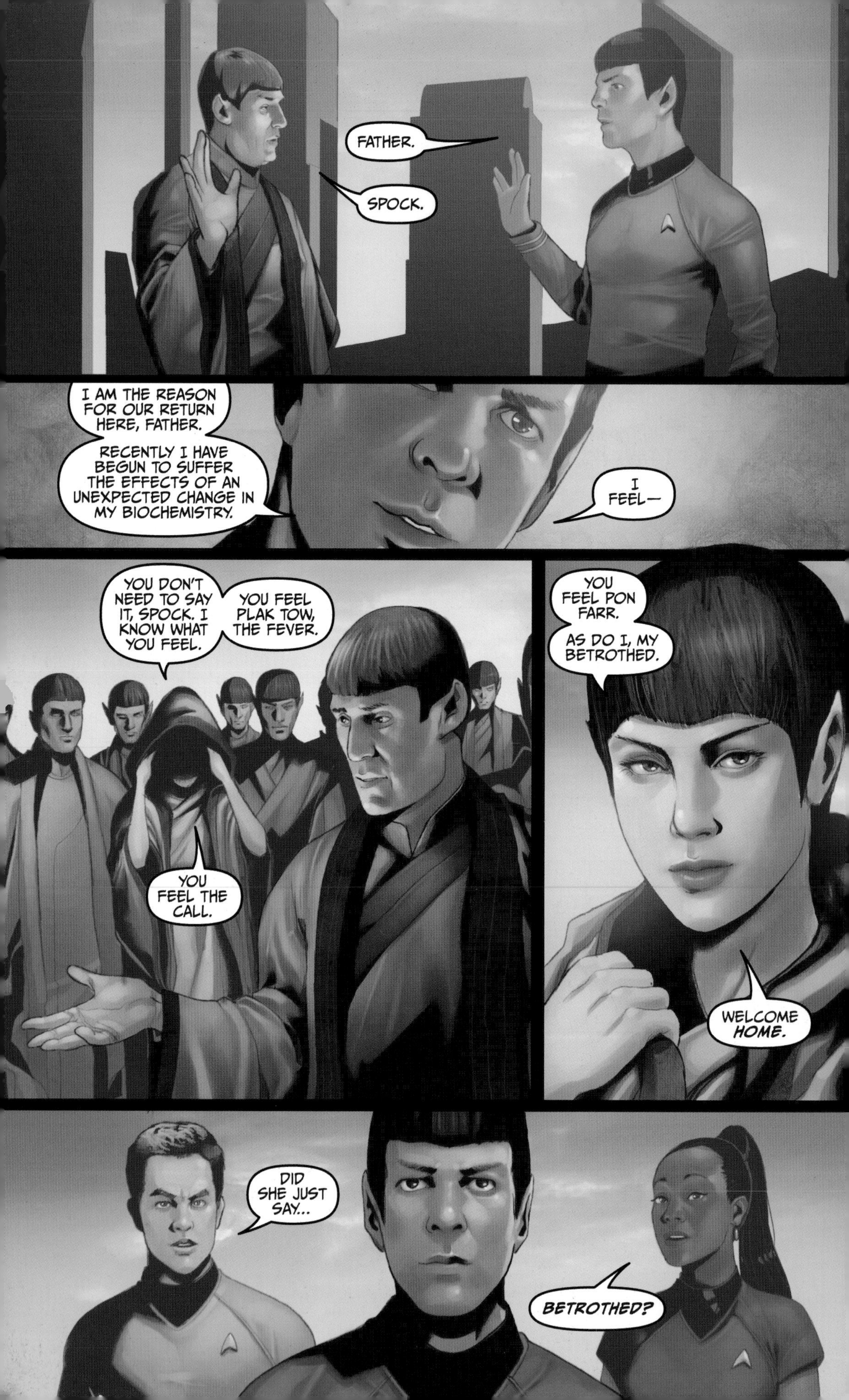
FATHER.
SPOCK.
I AM THE REASON FOR OUR RETURN HERE, FATHER.
RECENTLY I HAVE BEGUN TO SUFFER THE EFFECTS OF AN UNEXPECTED CHANGE IN MY BIOCHEMISTRY.
I FEEL—
YOU DON'T NEED TO SAY IT, SPOCK. I KNOW WHAT YOU FEEL.
YOU FEEL PLAK TOW, THE FEVER.
YOU FEEL THE CALL.
YOU FEEL PON FARR.
AS DO I, MY BETROTHED.
WELCOME *HOME.*
DID SHE JUST SAY...
BETROTHED?

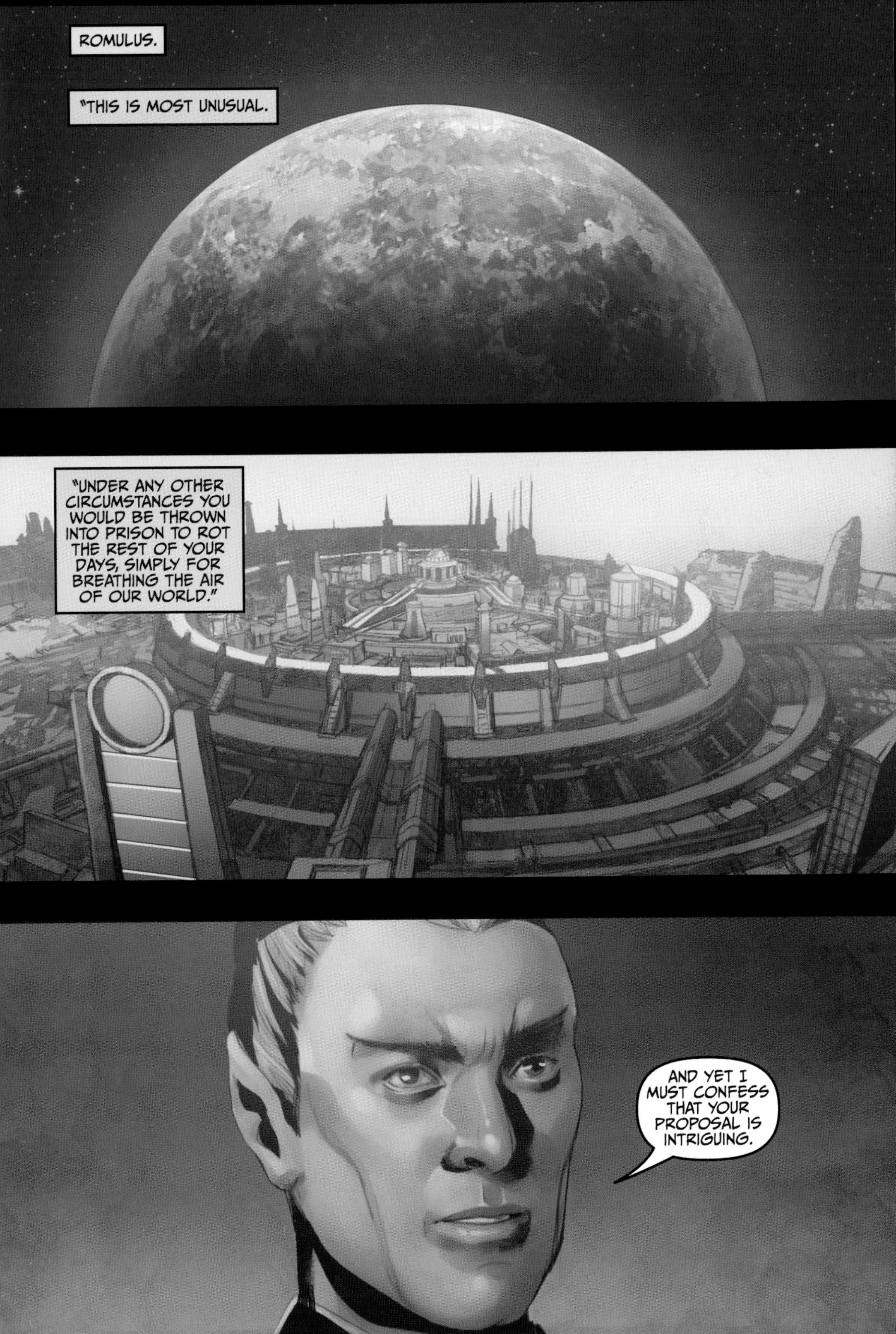
ROMULUS.
"THIS IS MOST UNUSUAL.
"UNDER ANY OTHER CIRCUMSTANCES YOU WOULD BE THROWN INTO PRISON TO ROT THE REST OF YOUR DAYS, SIMPLY FOR BREATHING THE AIR OF OUR WORLD."
AND YET I MUST CONFESS THAT YOUR PROPOSAL IS INTRIGUING.

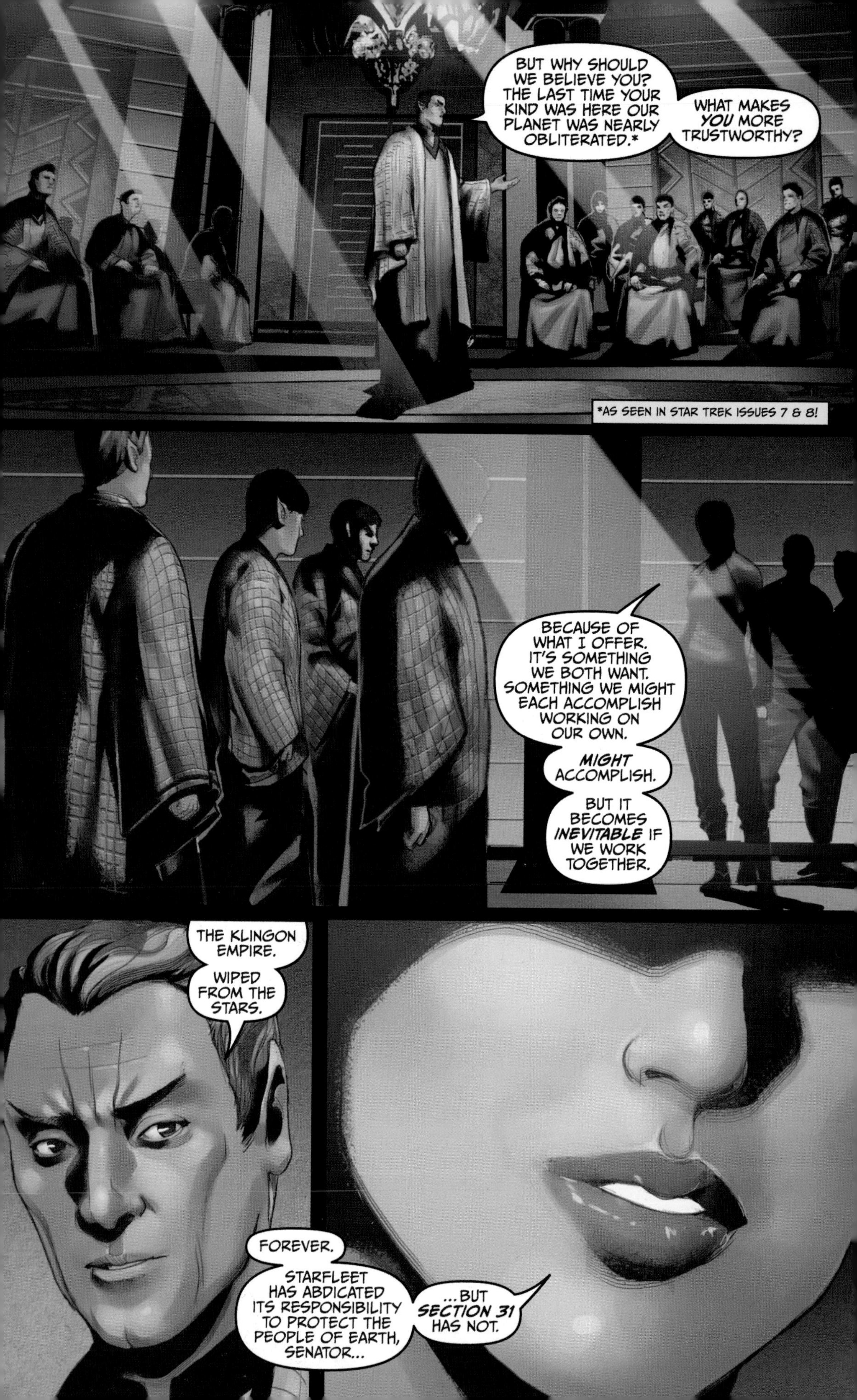

BUT WHY SHOULD WE BELIEVE YOU? THE LAST TIME YOUR KIND WAS HERE OUR PLANET WAS NEARLY OBLITERATED.*
WHAT MAKES *YOU* MORE TRUSTWORTHY?
*AS SEEN IN STAR TREK ISSUES 7 & 8!
BECAUSE OF WHAT I OFFER. IT'S SOMETHING WE BOTH WANT. SOMETHING WE MIGHT EACH ACCOMPLISH WORKING ON OUR OWN.
MIGHT ACCOMPLISH.
BUT IT BECOMES *INEVITABLE* IF WE WORK TOGETHER.
THE KLINGON EMPIRE.
WIPED FROM THE STARS.
FOREVER.
STARFLEET HAS ABDICATED ITS RESPONSIBILITY TO PROTECT THE PEOPLE OF EARTH, SENATOR...
...BUT *SECTION 31* HAS NOT.

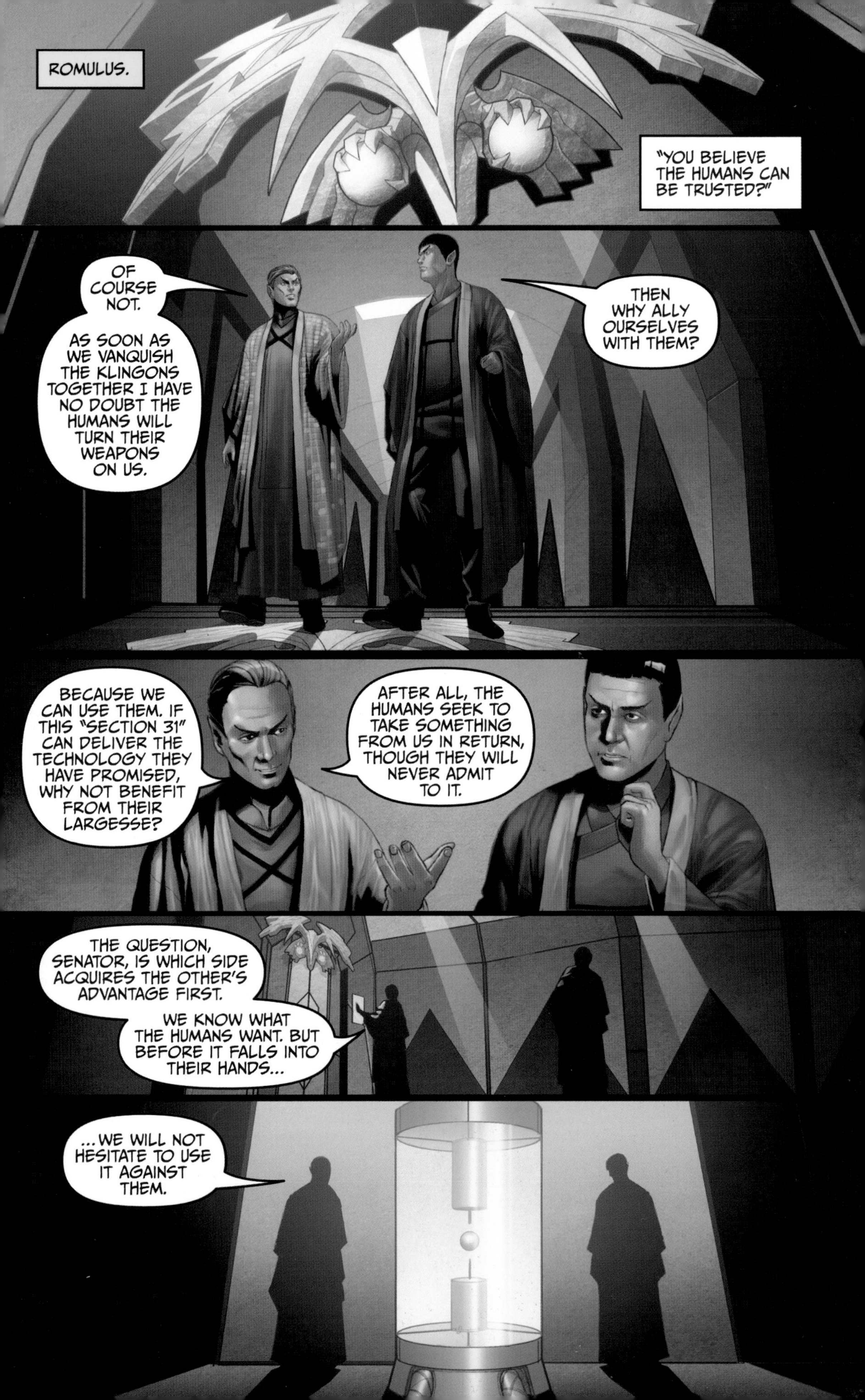
ROMULUS.
"YOU BELIEVE THE HUMANS CAN BE TRUSTED?"
OF COURSE NOT.
AS SOON AS WE VANQUISH THE KLINGONS TOGETHER I HAVE NO DOUBT THE HUMANS WILL TURN THEIR WEAPONS ON US.
THEN WHY ALLY OURSELVES WITH THEM?
BECAUSE WE CAN USE THEM. IF THIS "SECTION 31" CAN DELIVER THE TECHNOLOGY THEY HAVE PROMISED, WHY NOT BENEFIT FROM THEIR LARGESSE?
AFTER ALL, THE HUMANS SEEK TO TAKE SOMETHING FROM US IN RETURN, THOUGH THEY WILL NEVER ADMIT TO IT.
THE QUESTION, SENATOR, IS WHICH SIDE ACQUIRES THE OTHER'S ADVANTAGE FIRST.
WE KNOW WHAT THE HUMANS WANT. BUT BEFORE IT FALLS INTO THEIR HANDS...
...WE WILL NOT HESITATE TO USE IT AGAINST THEM.

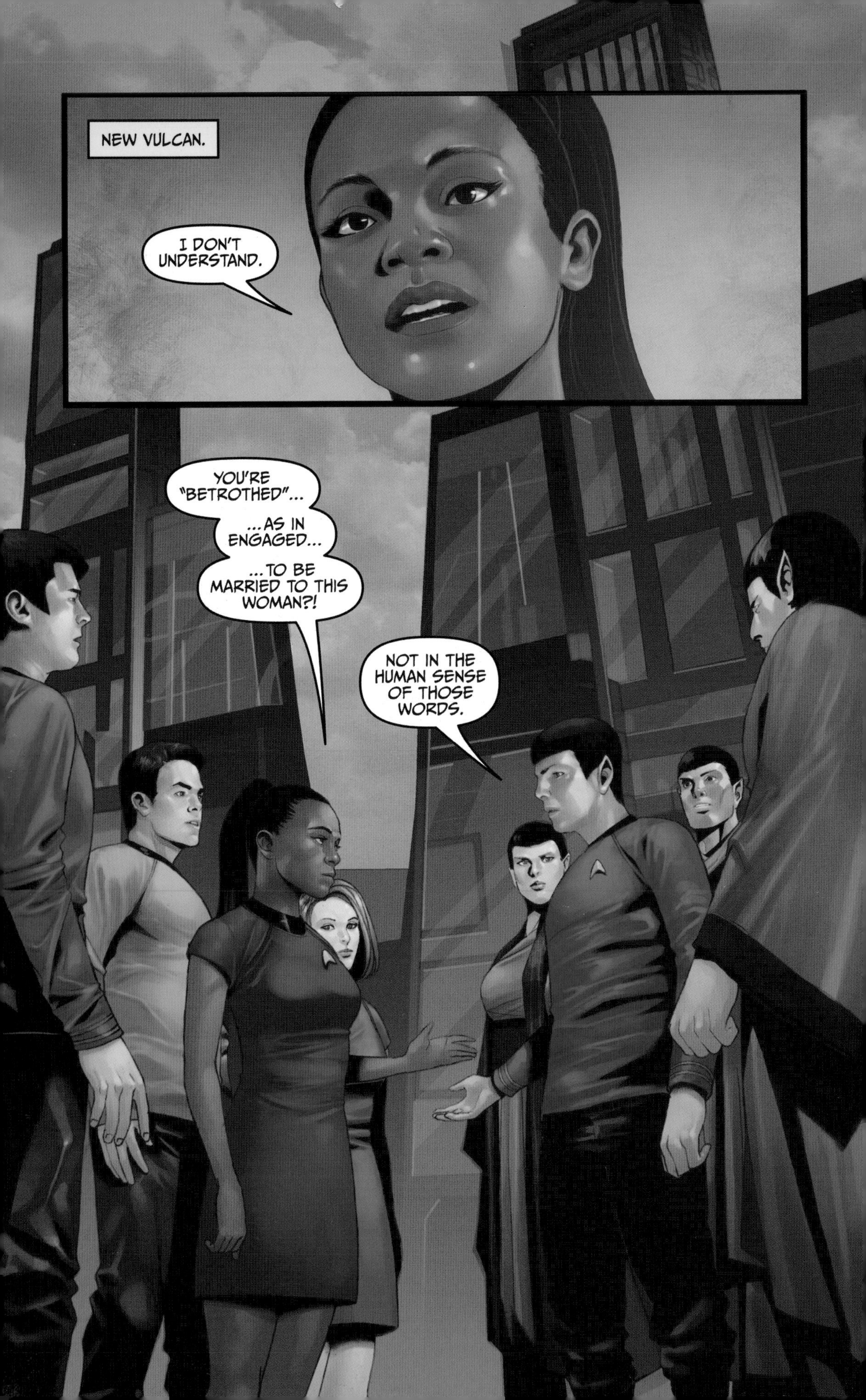
NEW VULCAN.
I DON'T UNDERSTAND.
YOU'RE "BETROTHED"...
...AS IN ENGAGED...
...TO BE MARRIED TO THIS WOMAN?!
NOT IN THE HUMAN SENSE OF THOSE WORDS.

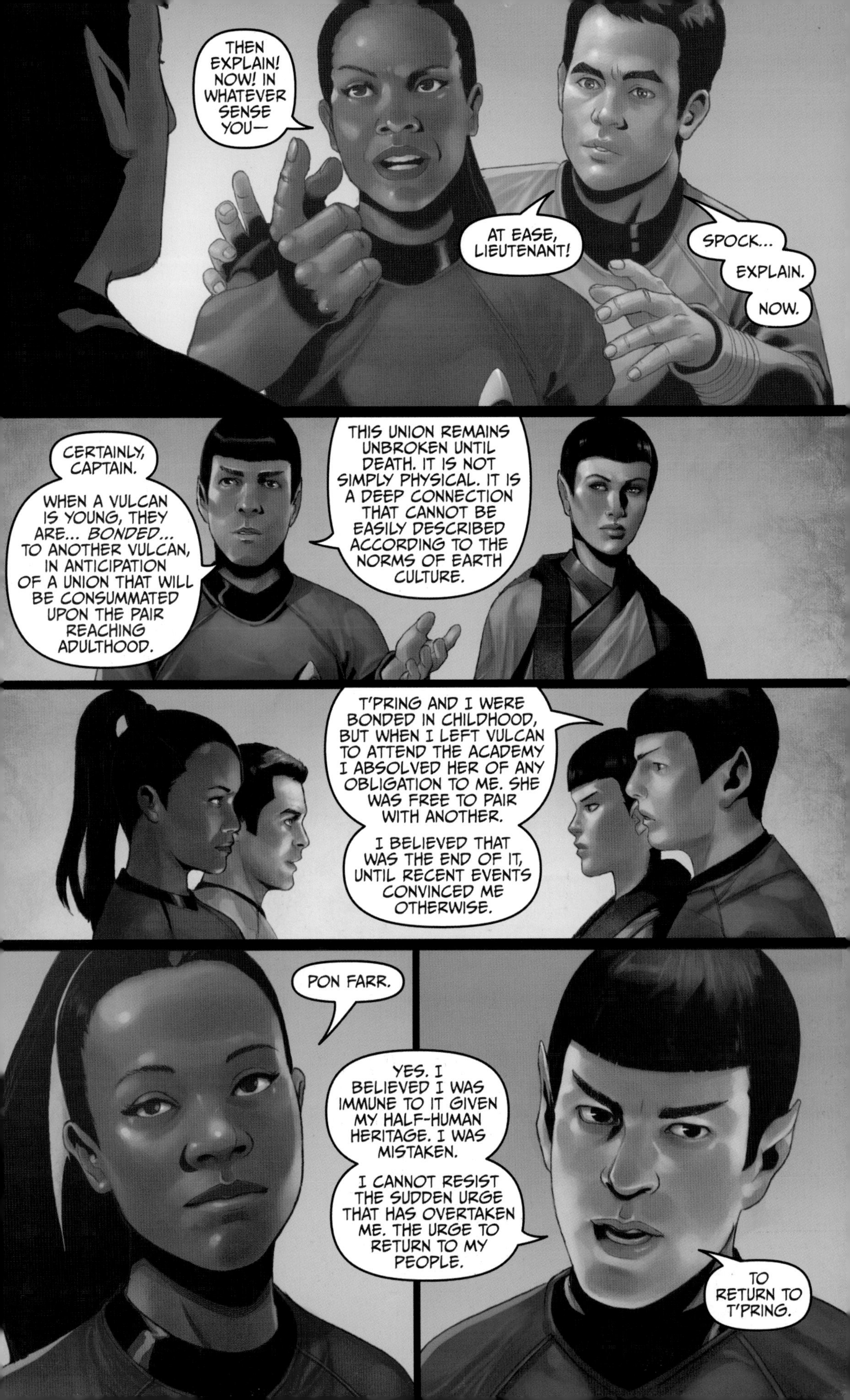
THEN EXPLAIN! NOW! IN WHATEVER SENSE YOU—
AT EASE, LIEUTENANT!
SPOCK...
EXPLAIN.
NOW.
CERTAINLY, CAPTAIN.
WHEN A VULCAN IS YOUNG, THEY ARE... *BONDED*... TO ANOTHER VULCAN, IN ANTICIPATION OF A UNION THAT WILL BE CONSUMMATED UPON THE PAIR REACHING ADULTHOOD.
THIS UNION REMAINS UNBROKEN UNTIL DEATH. IT IS NOT SIMPLY PHYSICAL. IT IS A DEEP CONNECTION THAT CANNOT BE EASILY DESCRIBED ACCORDING TO THE NORMS OF EARTH CULTURE.
T'PRING AND I WERE BONDED IN CHILDHOOD, BUT WHEN I LEFT VULCAN TO ATTEND THE ACADEMY I ABSOLVED HER OF ANY OBLIGATION TO ME. SHE WAS FREE TO PAIR WITH ANOTHER.
I BELIEVED THAT WAS THE END OF IT, UNTIL RECENT EVENTS CONVINCED ME OTHERWISE.
PON FARR.
YES. I BELIEVED I WAS IMMUNE TO IT GIVEN MY HALF-HUMAN HERITAGE. I WAS MISTAKEN.
I CANNOT RESIST THE SUDDEN URGE THAT HAS OVERTAKEN ME. THE URGE TO RETURN TO MY PEOPLE.
TO RETURN TO T'PRING.

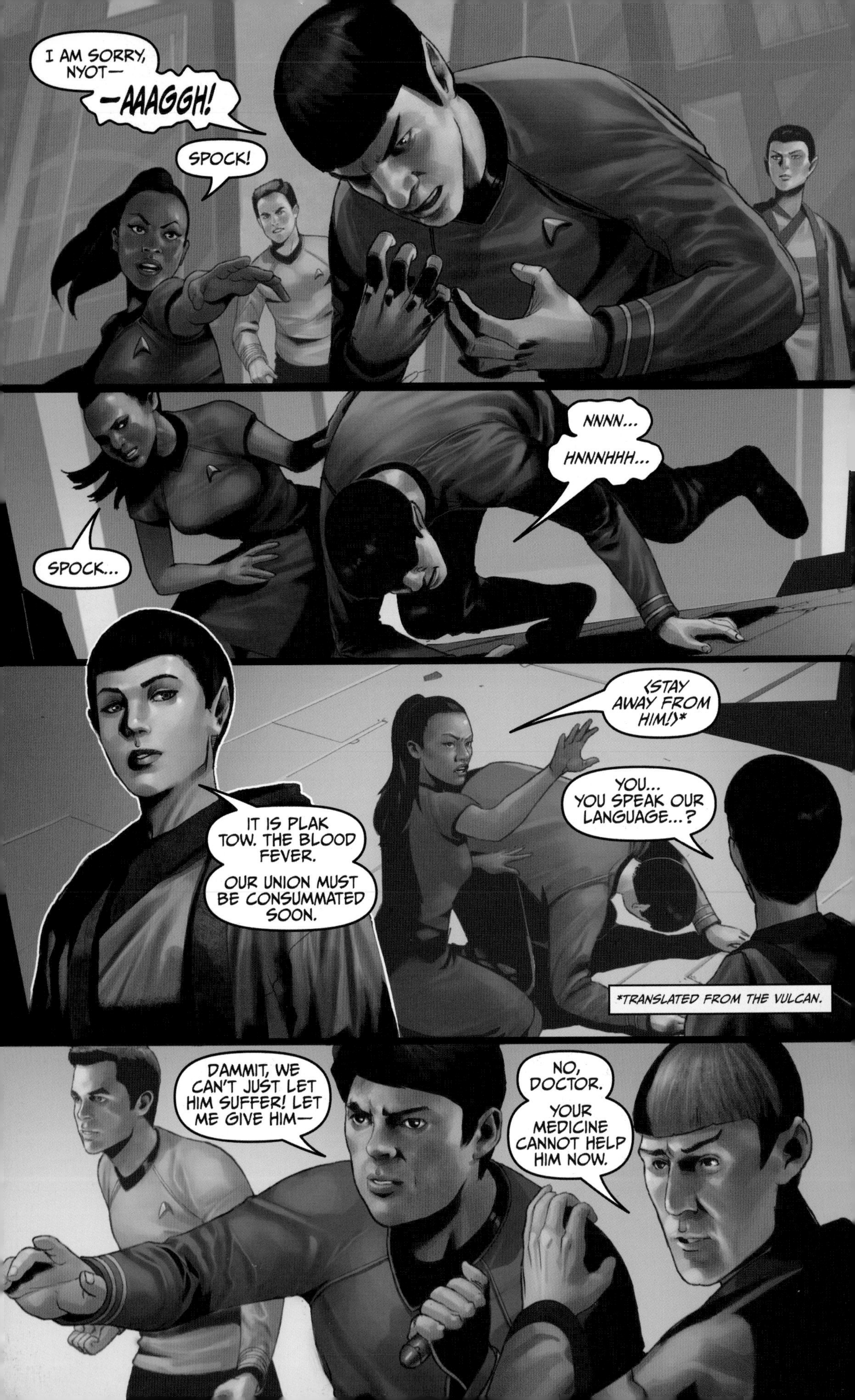
I AM SORRY, NYOT—
—AAAGGH!
SPOCK!
NNNN...
HNNNHHH...
SPOCK...
⟨STAY AWAY FROM HIM!⟩*
IT IS PLAK TOW. THE BLOOD FEVER.
OUR UNION MUST BE CONSUMMATED SOON.
YOU... YOU SPEAK OUR LANGUAGE...?
*TRANSLATED FROM THE VULCAN.
DAMMIT, WE CAN'T JUST LET HIM SUFFER! LET ME GIVE HIM—
NO, DOCTOR.
YOUR MEDICINE CANNOT HELP HIM NOW.

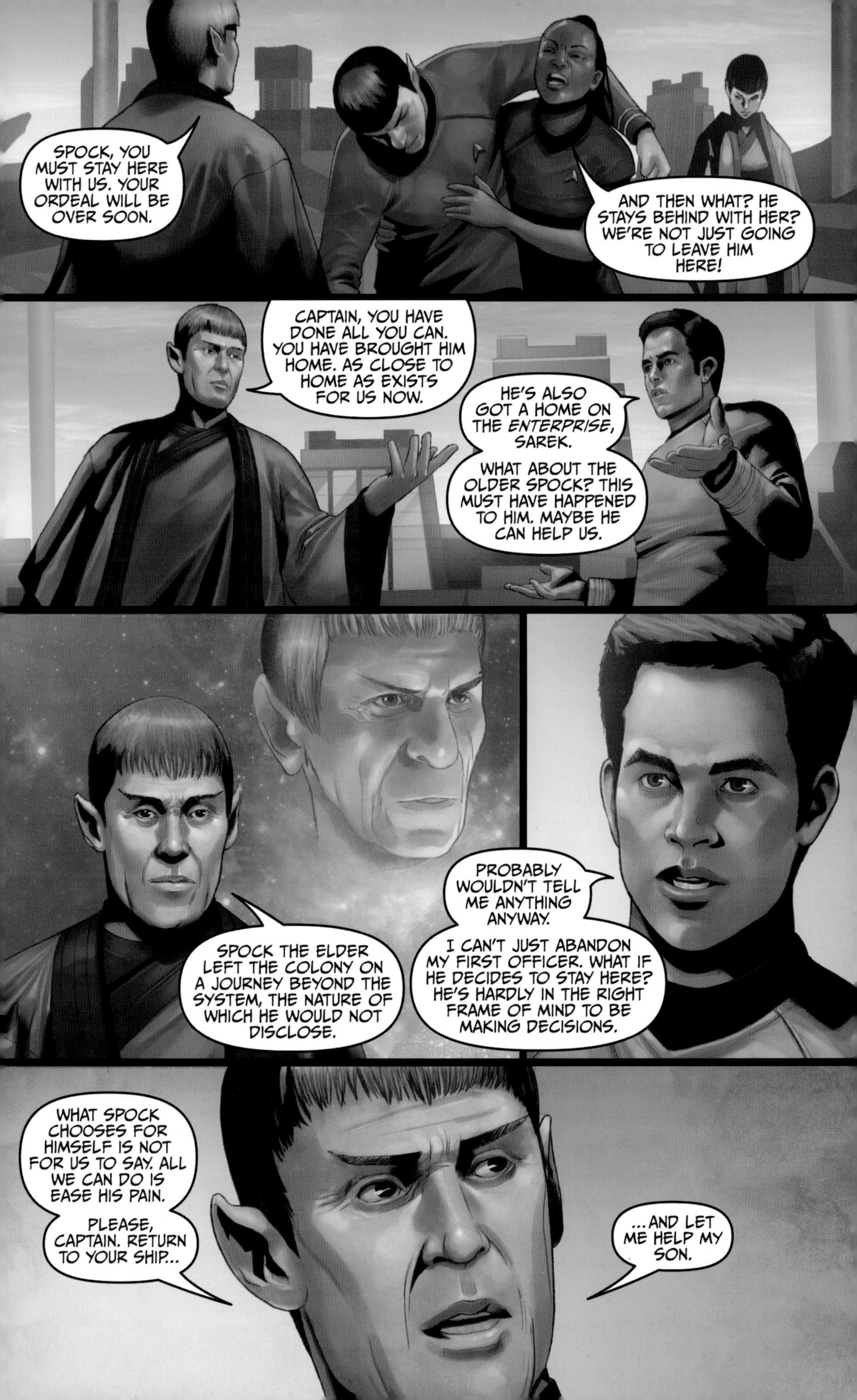
SPOCK, YOU MUST STAY HERE WITH US. YOUR ORDEAL WILL BE OVER SOON.
AND THEN WHAT? HE STAYS BEHIND WITH HER? WE'RE NOT JUST GOING TO LEAVE HIM HERE!
CAPTAIN, YOU HAVE DONE ALL YOU CAN. YOU HAVE BROUGHT HIM HOME. AS CLOSE TO HOME AS EXISTS FOR US NOW.
HE'S ALSO GOT A HOME ON THE *ENTERPRISE*, SAREK.
WHAT ABOUT THE OLDER SPOCK? THIS MUST HAVE HAPPENED TO HIM. MAYBE HE CAN HELP US.
SPOCK THE ELDER LEFT THE COLONY ON A JOURNEY BEYOND THE SYSTEM, THE NATURE OF WHICH HE WOULD NOT DISCLOSE.
PROBABLY WOULDN'T TELL ME ANYTHING ANYWAY.
I CAN'T JUST ABANDON MY FIRST OFFICER. WHAT IF HE DECIDES TO STAY HERE? HE'S HARDLY IN THE RIGHT FRAME OF MIND TO BE MAKING DECISIONS.
WHAT SPOCK CHOOSES FOR HIMSELF IS NOT FOR US TO SAY. ALL WE CAN DO IS EASE HIS PAIN.
PLEASE, CAPTAIN. RETURN TO YOUR SHIP...
...AND LET ME HELP MY SON.

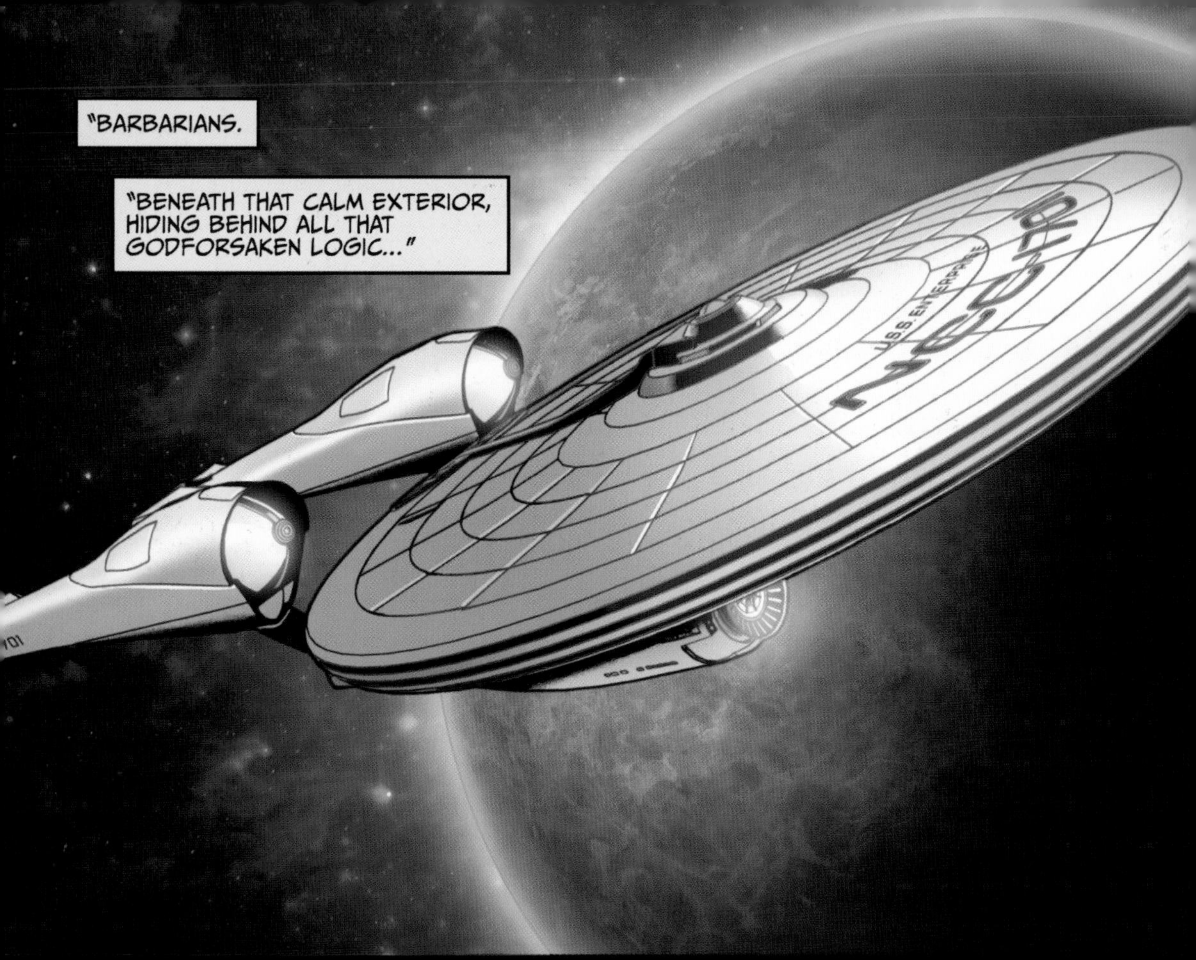
"BARBARIANS.
"BENEATH THAT CALM EXTERIOR, HIDING BEHIND ALL THAT GODFORSAKEN LOGIC..."

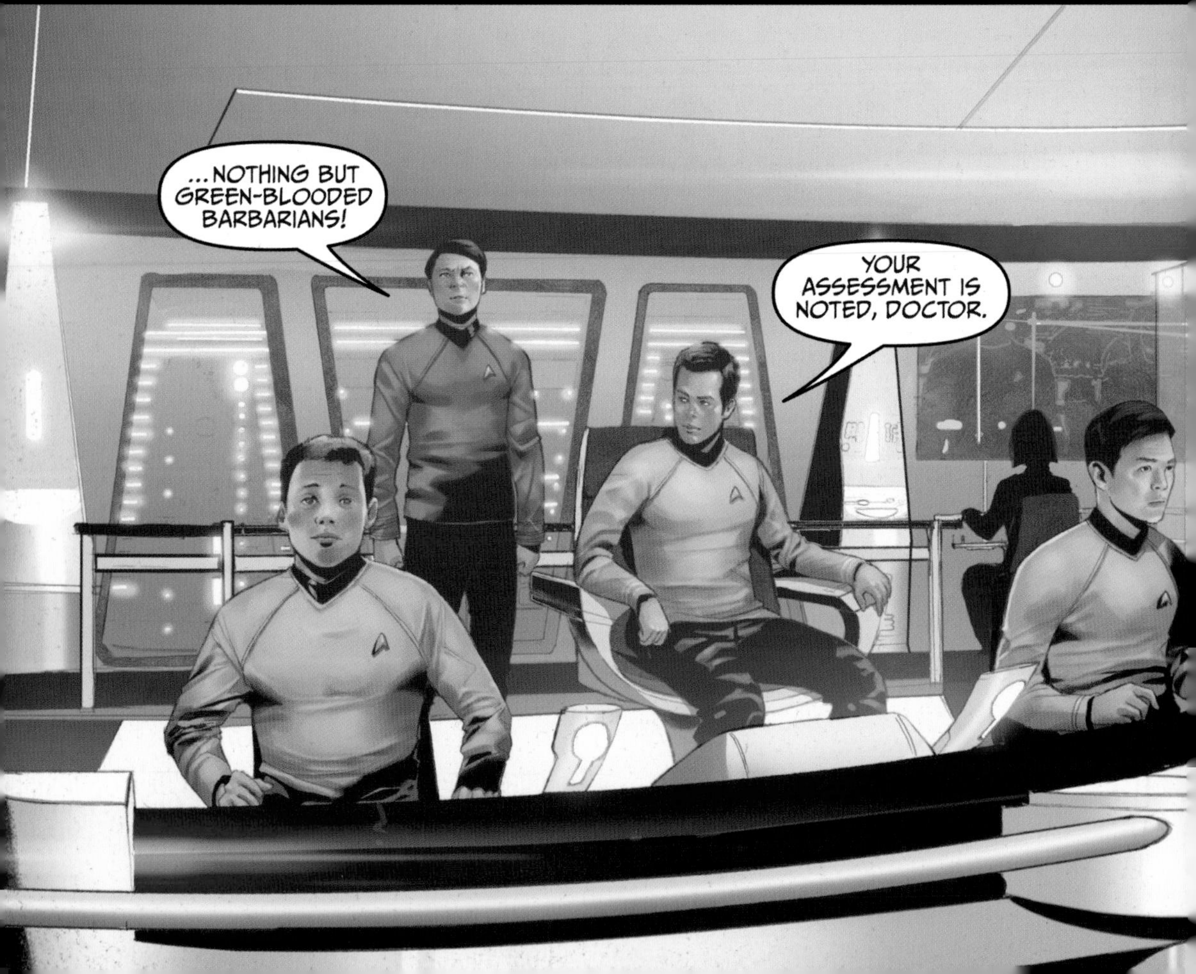
...NOTHING BUT GREEN-BLOODED BARBARIANS!
YOUR ASSESSMENT IS NOTED, DOCTOR.

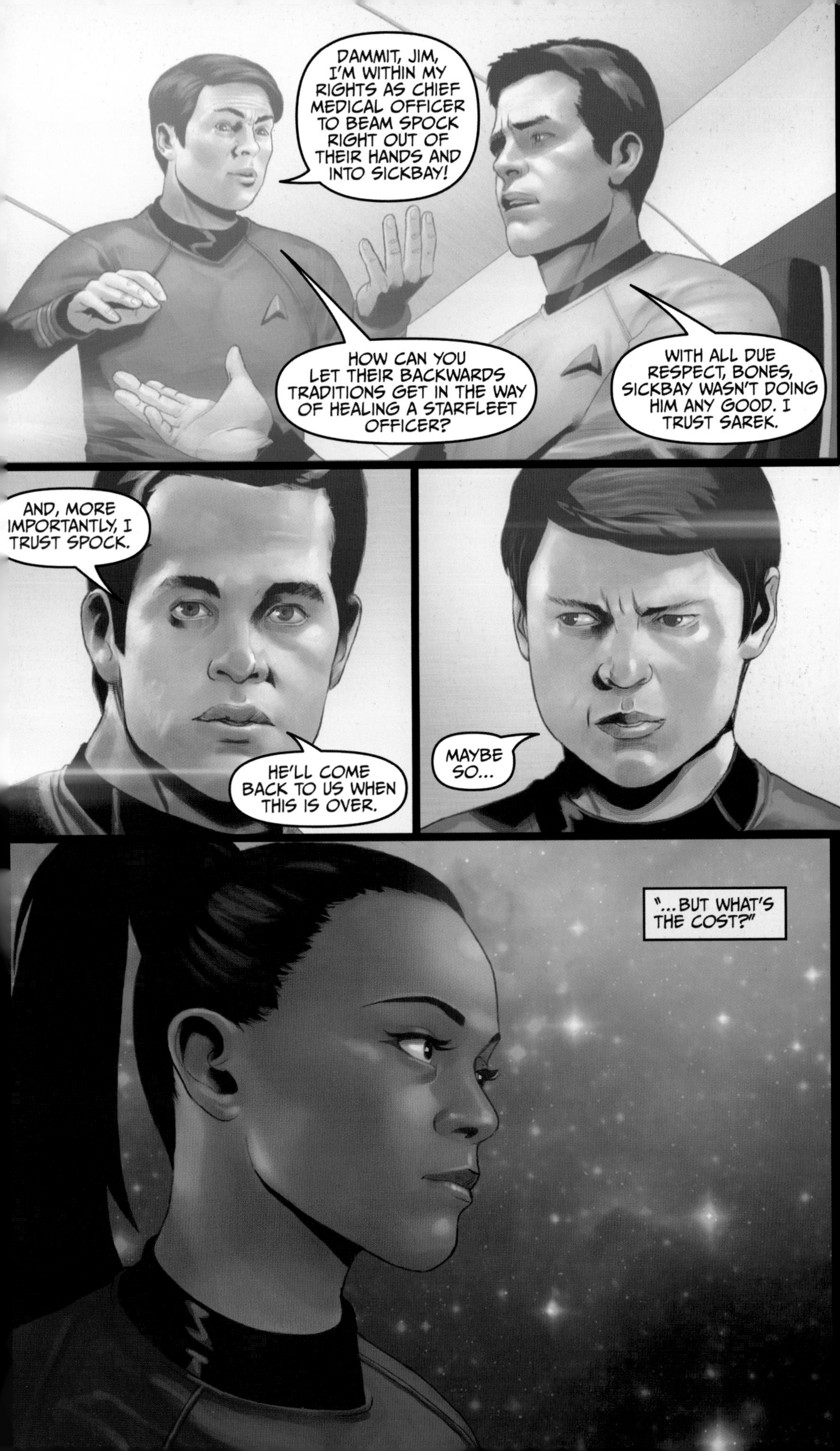
DAMMIT, JIM, I'M WITHIN MY RIGHTS AS CHIEF MEDICAL OFFICER TO BEAM SPOCK RIGHT OUT OF THEIR HANDS AND INTO SICKBAY!
HOW CAN YOU LET THEIR BACKWARDS TRADITIONS GET IN THE WAY OF HEALING A STARFLEET OFFICER?
WITH ALL DUE RESPECT, BONES, SICKBAY WASN'T DOING HIM ANY GOOD. I TRUST SAREK.
AND, MORE IMPORTANTLY, I TRUST SPOCK.
HE'LL COME BACK TO US WHEN THIS IS OVER.
MAYBE SO...
"...BUT WHAT'S THE COST?"

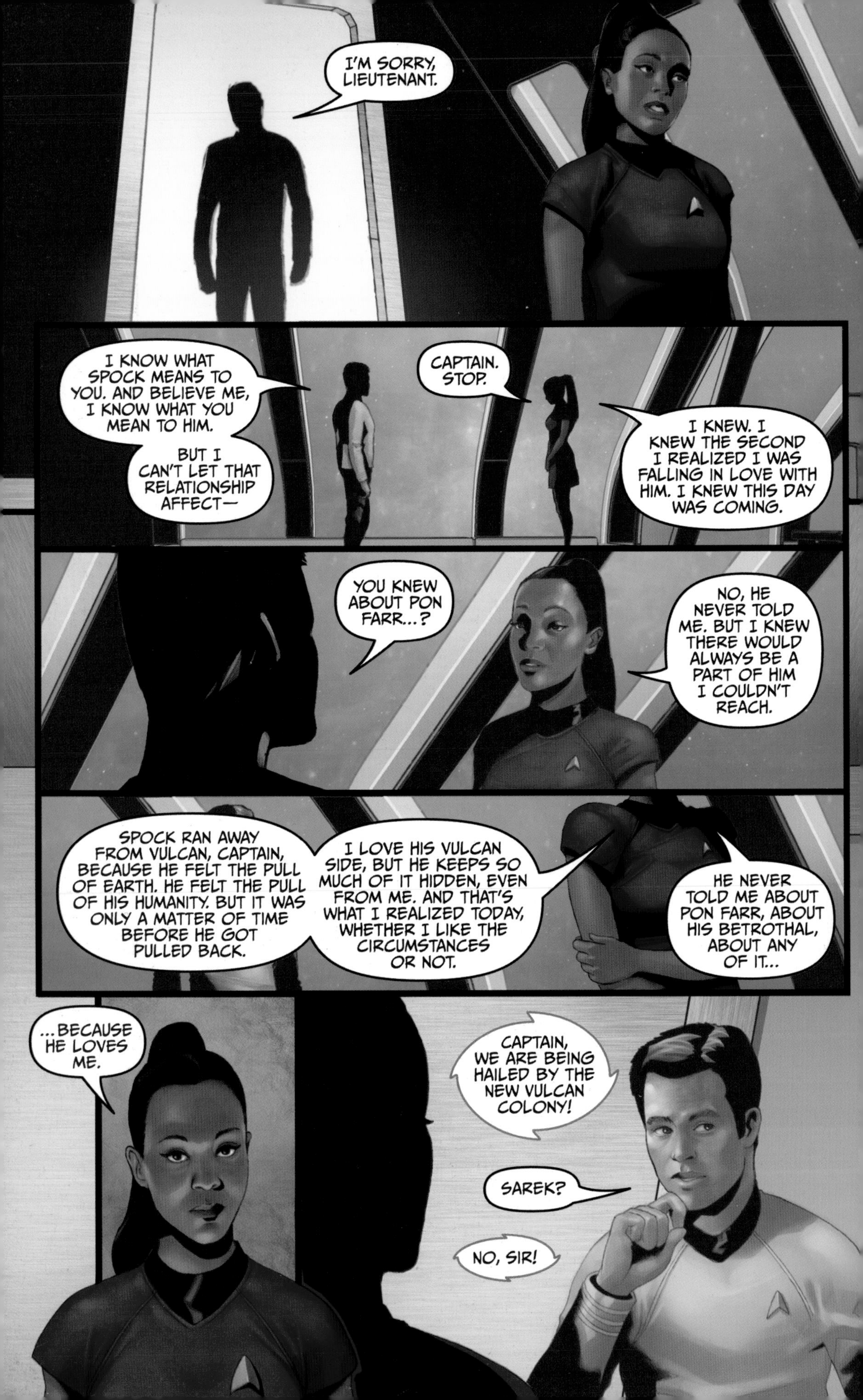
I'M SORRY, LIEUTENANT.
I KNOW WHAT SPOCK MEANS TO YOU. AND BELIEVE ME, I KNOW WHAT YOU MEAN TO HIM.
BUT I CAN'T LET THAT RELATIONSHIP AFFECT—
CAPTAIN. STOP.
I KNEW. I KNEW THE SECOND I REALIZED I WAS FALLING IN LOVE WITH HIM. I KNEW THIS DAY WAS COMING.
YOU KNEW ABOUT PON FARR...?
NO, HE NEVER TOLD ME. BUT I KNEW THERE WOULD ALWAYS BE A PART OF HIM I COULDN'T REACH.
SPOCK RAN AWAY FROM VULCAN, CAPTAIN, BECAUSE HE FELT THE PULL OF EARTH. HE FELT THE PULL OF HIS HUMANITY. BUT IT WAS ONLY A MATTER OF TIME BEFORE HE GOT PULLED BACK.
I LOVE HIS VULCAN SIDE, BUT HE KEEPS SO MUCH OF IT HIDDEN, EVEN FROM ME. AND THAT'S WHAT I REALIZED TODAY, WHETHER I LIKE THE CIRCUMSTANCES OR NOT.
HE NEVER TOLD ME ABOUT PON FARR, ABOUT HIS BETROTHAL, ABOUT ANY OF IT...
...BECAUSE HE LOVES ME.
CAPTAIN, WE ARE BEING HAILED BY THE NEW VULCAN COLONY!
SAREK?
NO, SIR!

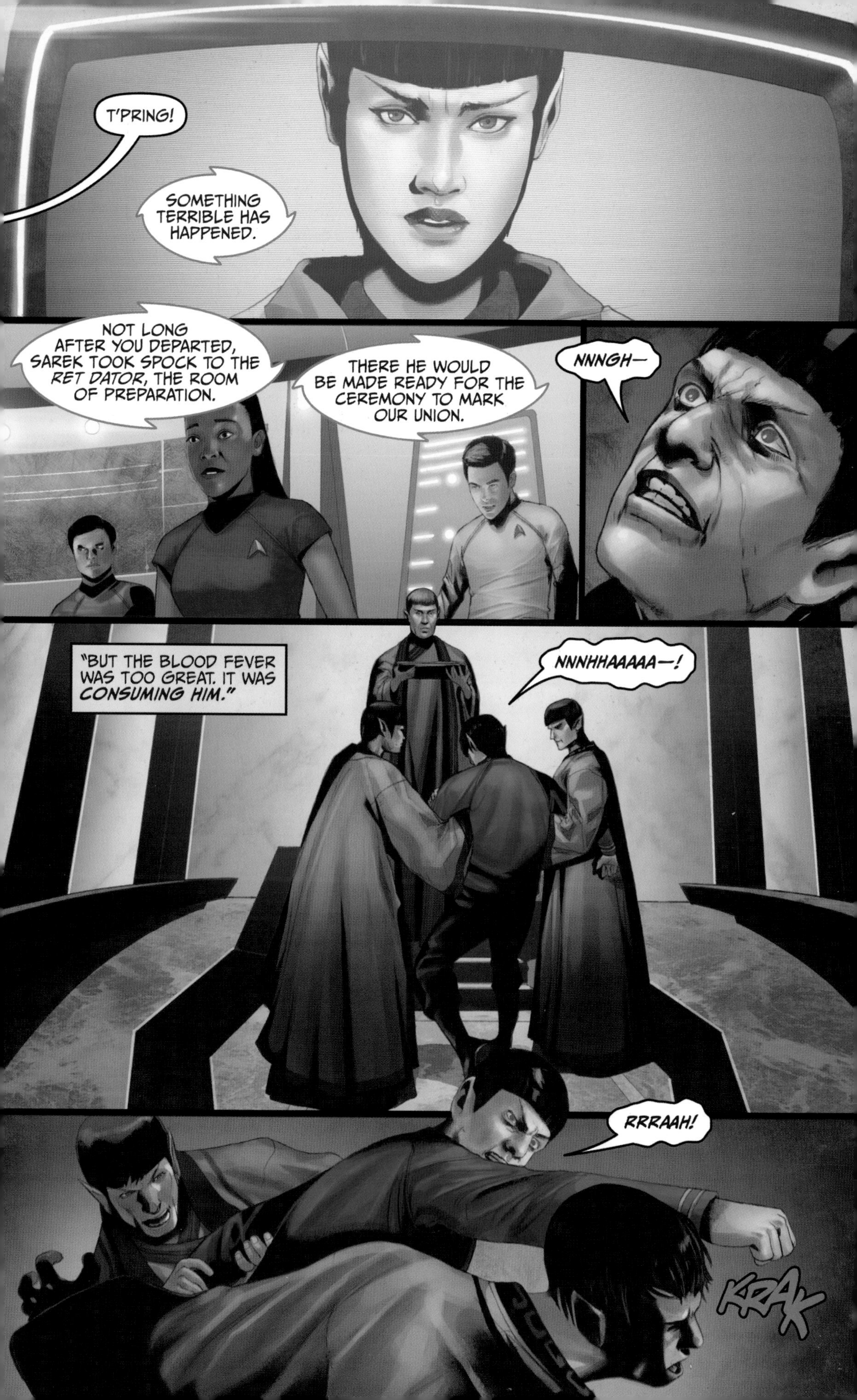
T'PRING!
SOMETHING TERRIBLE HAS HAPPENED.
NOT LONG AFTER YOU DEPARTED, SAREK TOOK SPOCK TO THE RET DATOR, THE ROOM OF PREPARATION.
THERE HE WOULD BE MADE READY FOR THE CEREMONY TO MARK OUR UNION.
NNNGH—
"BUT THE BLOOD FEVER WAS TOO GREAT. IT WAS CONSUMING HIM."
NNNHHAAAAA—!
RRRAAH!
KRAK

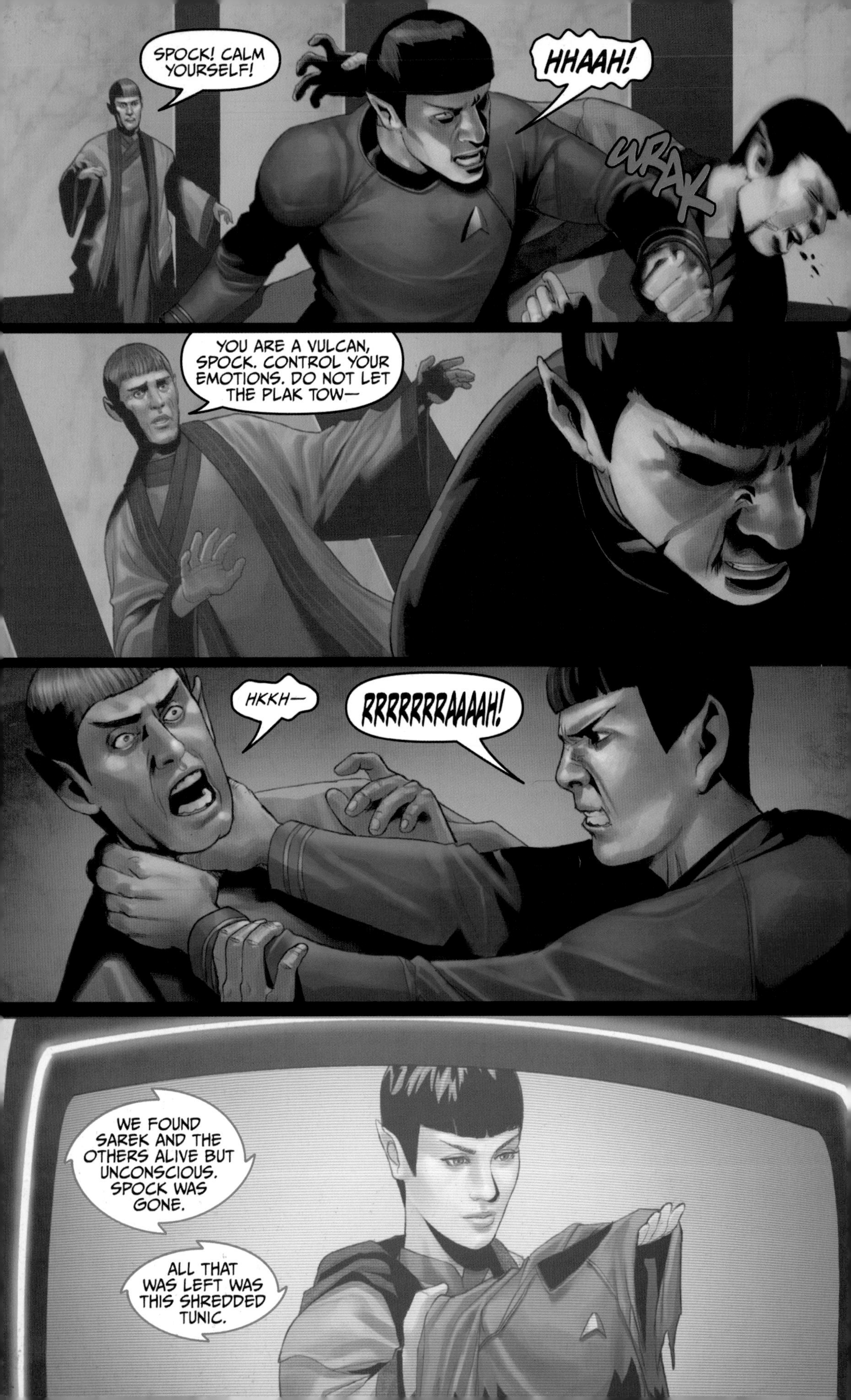
SPOCK! CALM YOURSELF!
HHAAH!
WRAK
YOU ARE A VULCAN, SPOCK. CONTROL YOUR EMOTIONS. DO NOT LET THE PLAK TOW—
HKKH—
RRRRRRRAAAAH!
WE FOUND SAREK AND THE OTHERS ALIVE BUT UNCONSCIOUS. SPOCK WAS GONE.
ALL THAT WAS LEFT WAS THIS SHREDDED TUNIC.

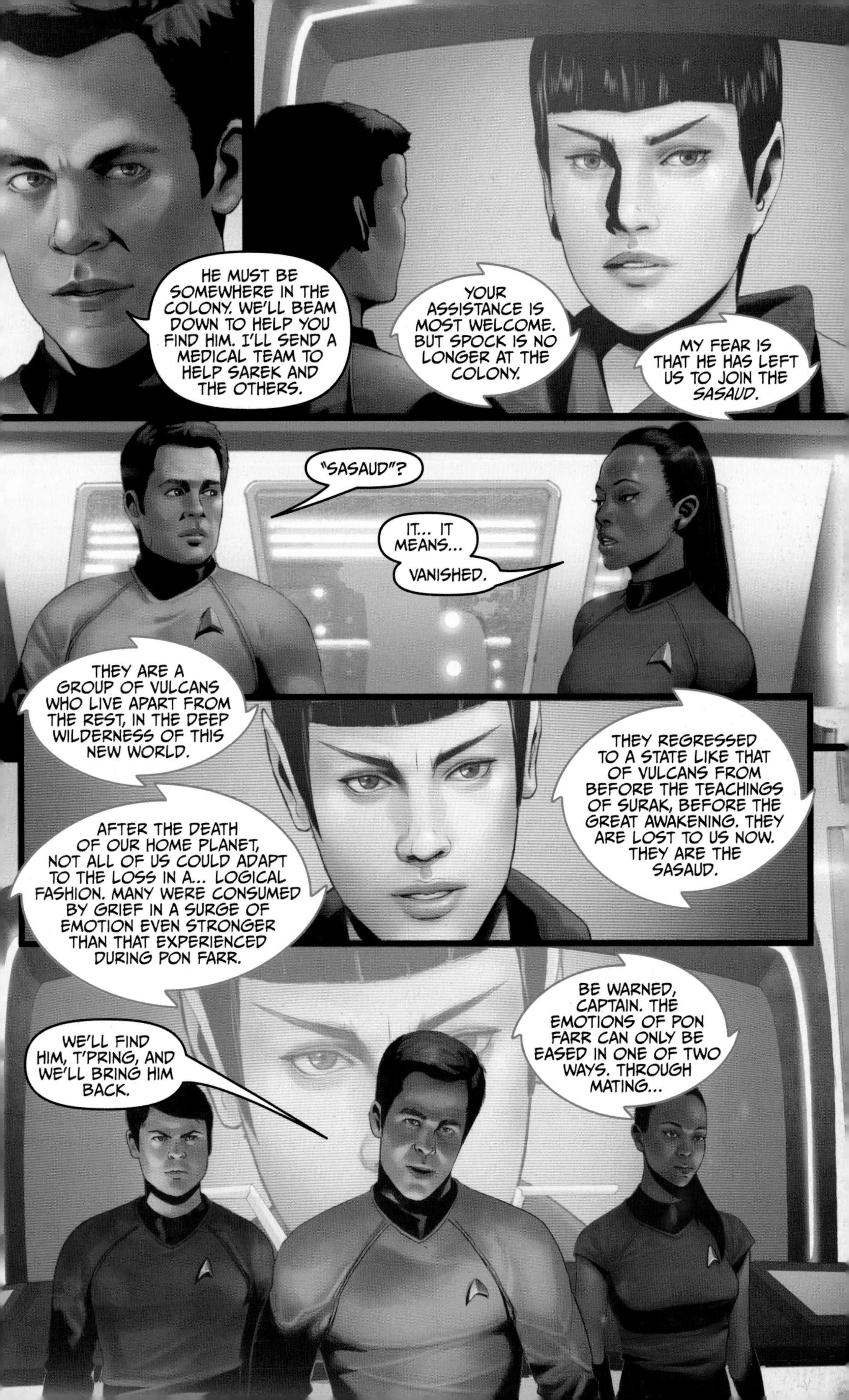
HE MUST BE SOMEWHERE IN THE COLONY. WE'LL BEAM DOWN TO HELP YOU FIND HIM. I'LL SEND A MEDICAL TEAM TO HELP SAREK AND THE OTHERS.
YOUR ASSISTANCE IS MOST WELCOME. BUT SPOCK IS NO LONGER AT THE COLONY.
MY FEAR IS THAT HE HAS LEFT US TO JOIN THE SASAUD.
"SASAUD"?
IT... IT MEANS...
VANISHED.
THEY ARE A GROUP OF VULCANS WHO LIVE APART FROM THE REST, IN THE DEEP WILDERNESS OF THIS NEW WORLD.
AFTER THE DEATH OF OUR HOME PLANET, NOT ALL OF US COULD ADAPT TO THE LOSS IN A... LOGICAL FASHION. MANY WERE CONSUMED BY GRIEF IN A SURGE OF EMOTION EVEN STRONGER THAN THAT EXPERIENCED DURING PON FARR.
THEY REGRESSED TO A STATE LIKE THAT OF VULCANS FROM BEFORE THE TEACHINGS OF SURAK, BEFORE THE GREAT AWAKENING. THEY ARE LOST TO US NOW. THEY ARE THE SASAUD.
WE'LL FIND HIM, T'PRING, AND WE'LL BRING HIM BACK.
BE WARNED, CAPTAIN. THE EMOTIONS OF PON FARR CAN ONLY BE EASED IN ONE OF TWO WAYS. THROUGH MATING...

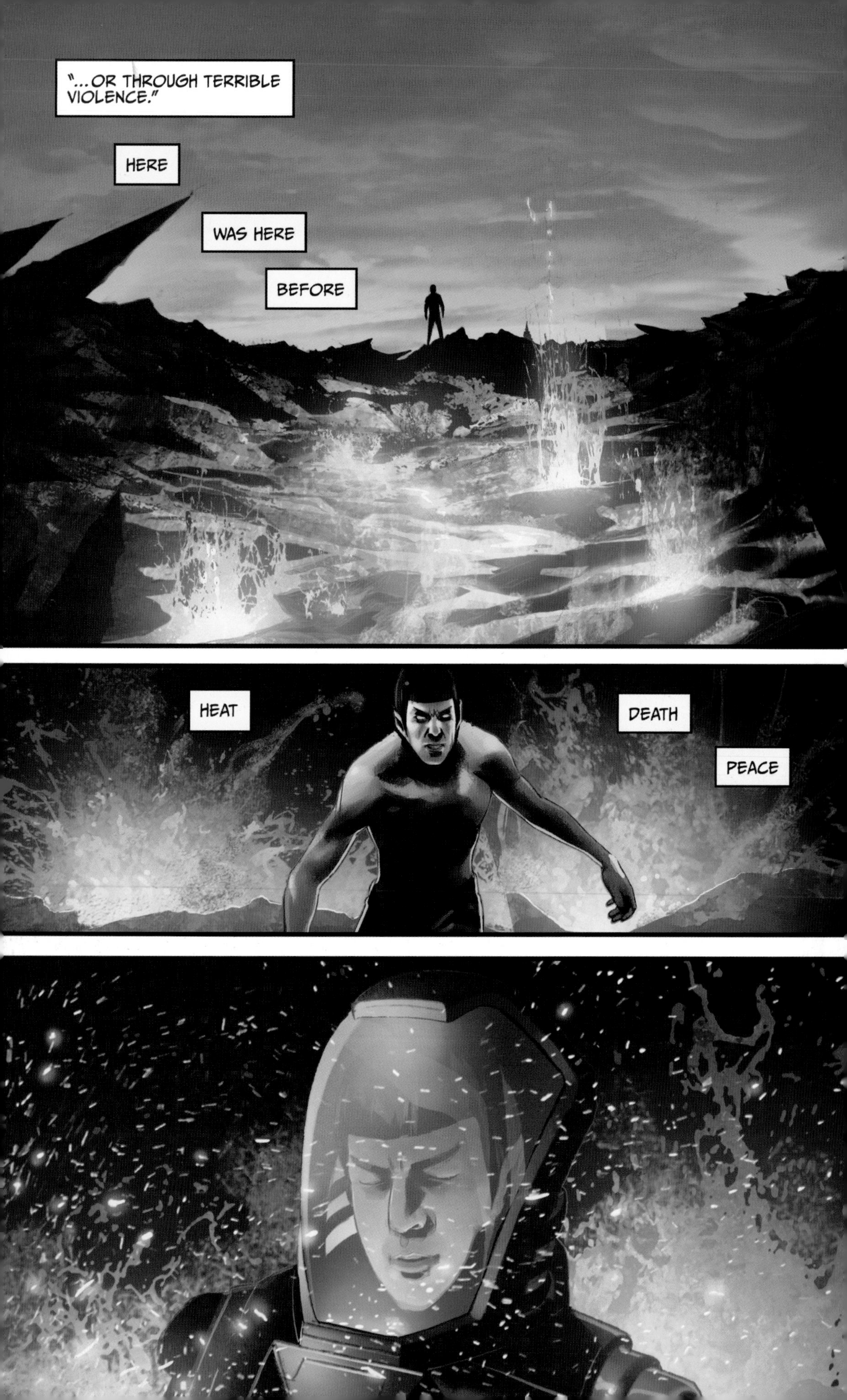
"...OR THROUGH TERRIBLE VIOLENCE."
HERE
WAS HERE
BEFORE
HEAT
DEATH
PEACE

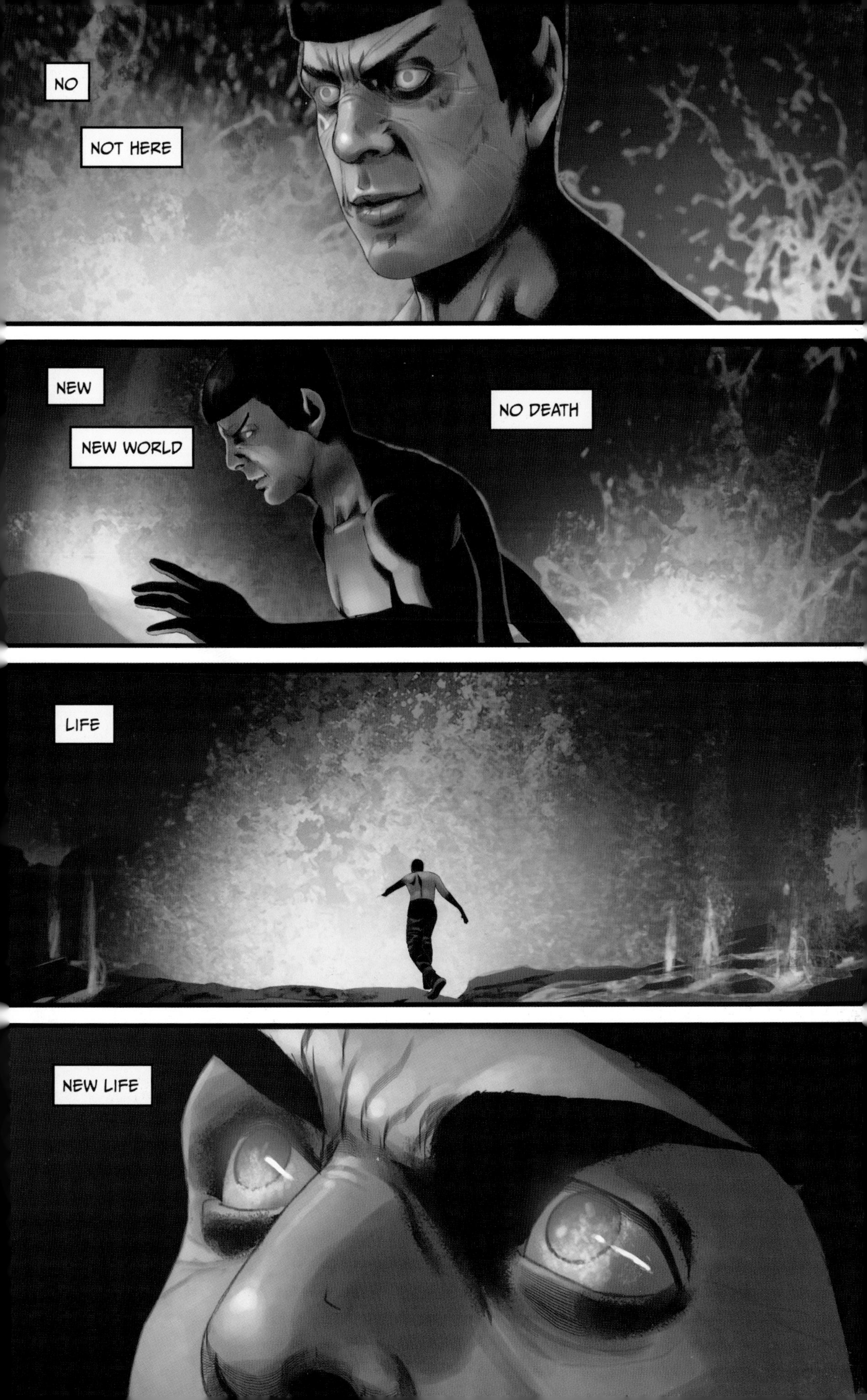
NO
NOT HERE
NEW
NEW WORLD
NO DEATH
LIFE
NEW LIFE

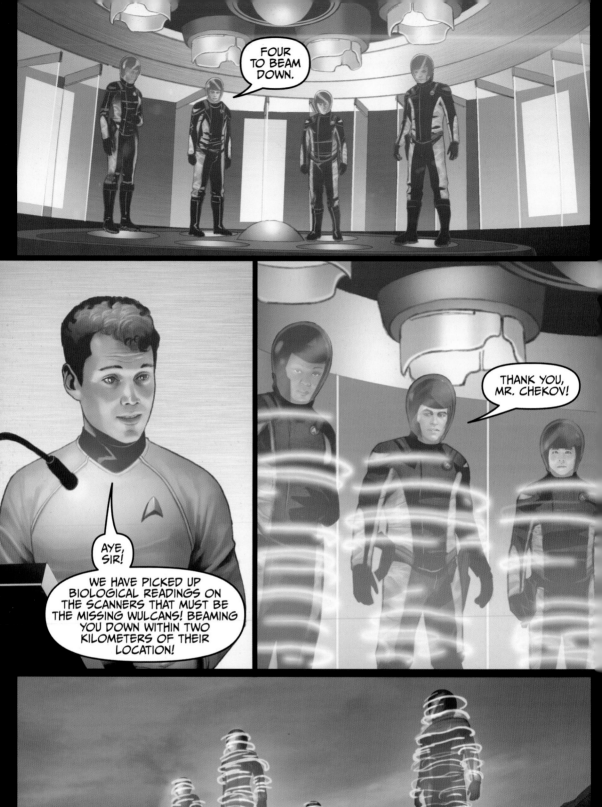

FOUR TO BEAM DOWN.

THANK YOU, MR. CHEKOV!

AYE, SIR!

WE HAVE PICKED UP BIOLOGICAL READINGS ON THE SCANNERS THAT MUST BE THE MISSING WULCANS! BEAMING YOU DOWN WITHIN TWO KILOMETERS OF THEIR LOCATION!

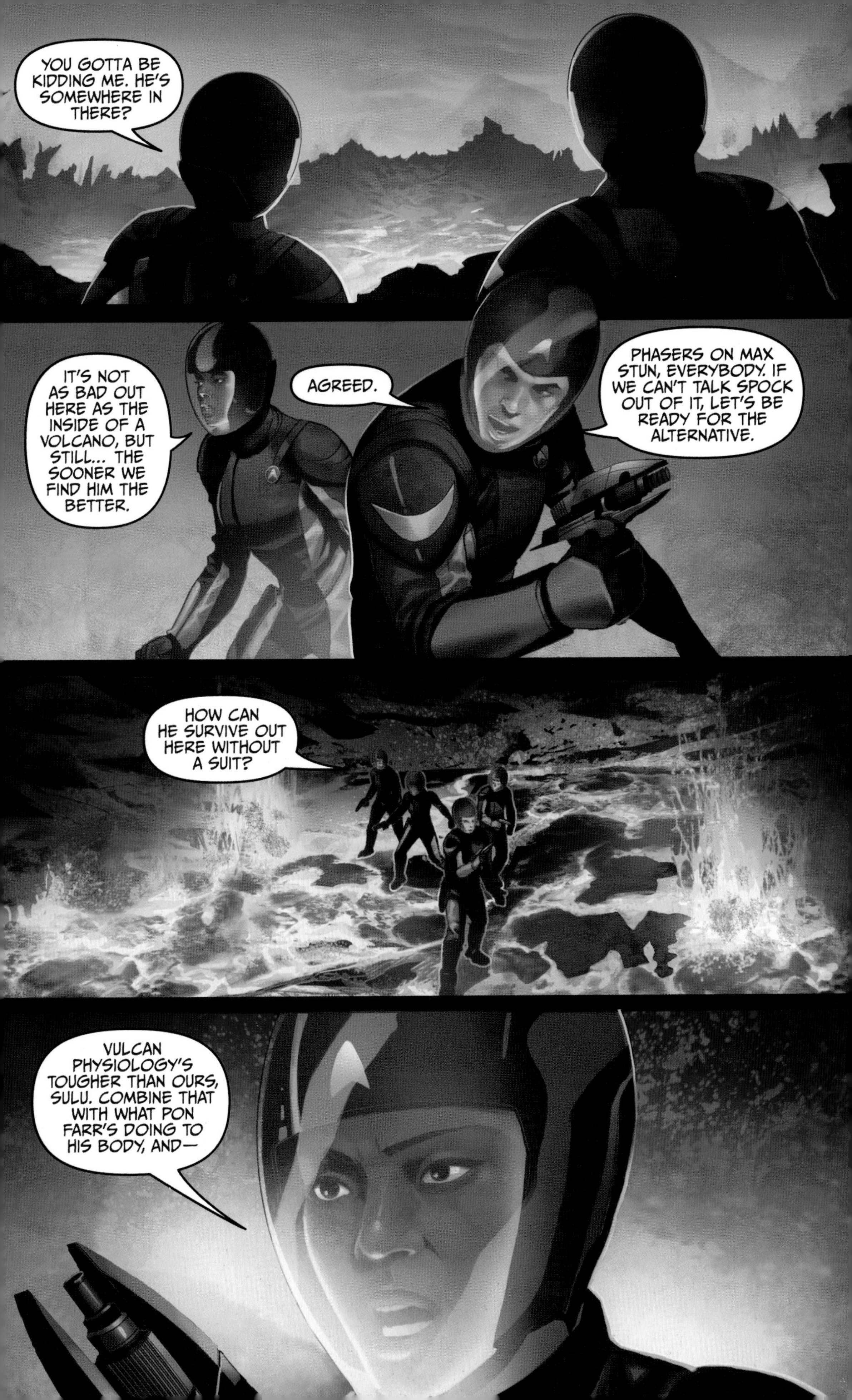
YOU GOTTA BE KIDDING ME. HE'S SOMEWHERE IN THERE?
IT'S NOT AS BAD OUT HERE AS THE INSIDE OF A VOLCANO, BUT STILL... THE SOONER WE FIND HIM THE BETTER.
AGREED.
PHASERS ON MAX STUN, EVERYBODY. IF WE CAN'T TALK SPOCK OUT OF IT, LET'S BE READY FOR THE ALTERNATIVE.
HOW CAN HE SURVIVE OUT HERE WITHOUT A SUIT?
VULCAN PHYSIOLOGY'S TOUGHER THAN OURS, SULU. COMBINE THAT WITH WHAT PON FARR'S DOING TO HIS BODY, AND—

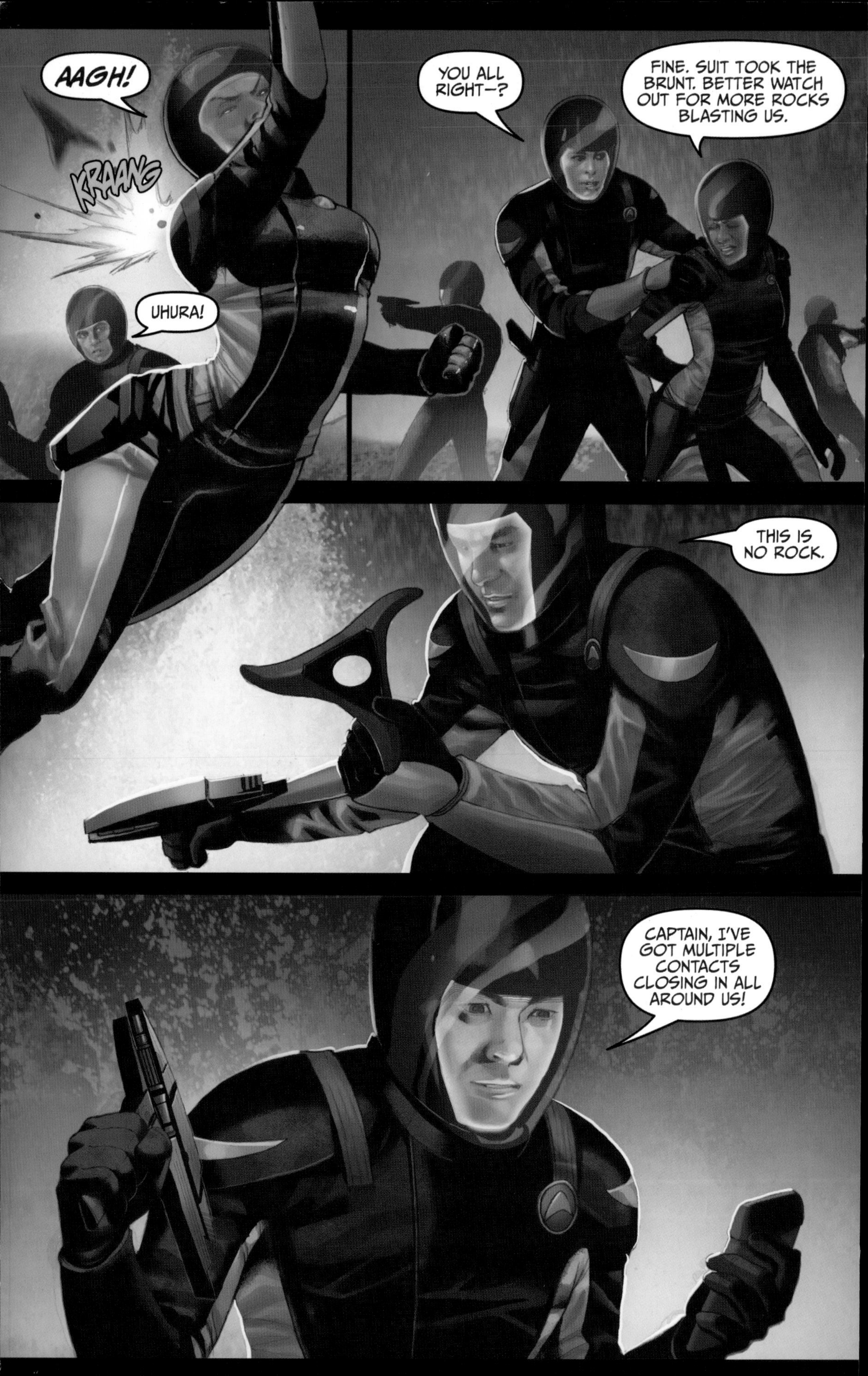
AAGH!
KRAANG
UHURA!
YOU ALL RIGHT—?
FINE. SUIT TOOK THE BRUNT. BETTER WATCH OUT FOR MORE ROCKS BLASTING US.
THIS IS NO ROCK.
CAPTAIN, I'VE GOT MULTIPLE CONTACTS CLOSING IN ALL AROUND US!

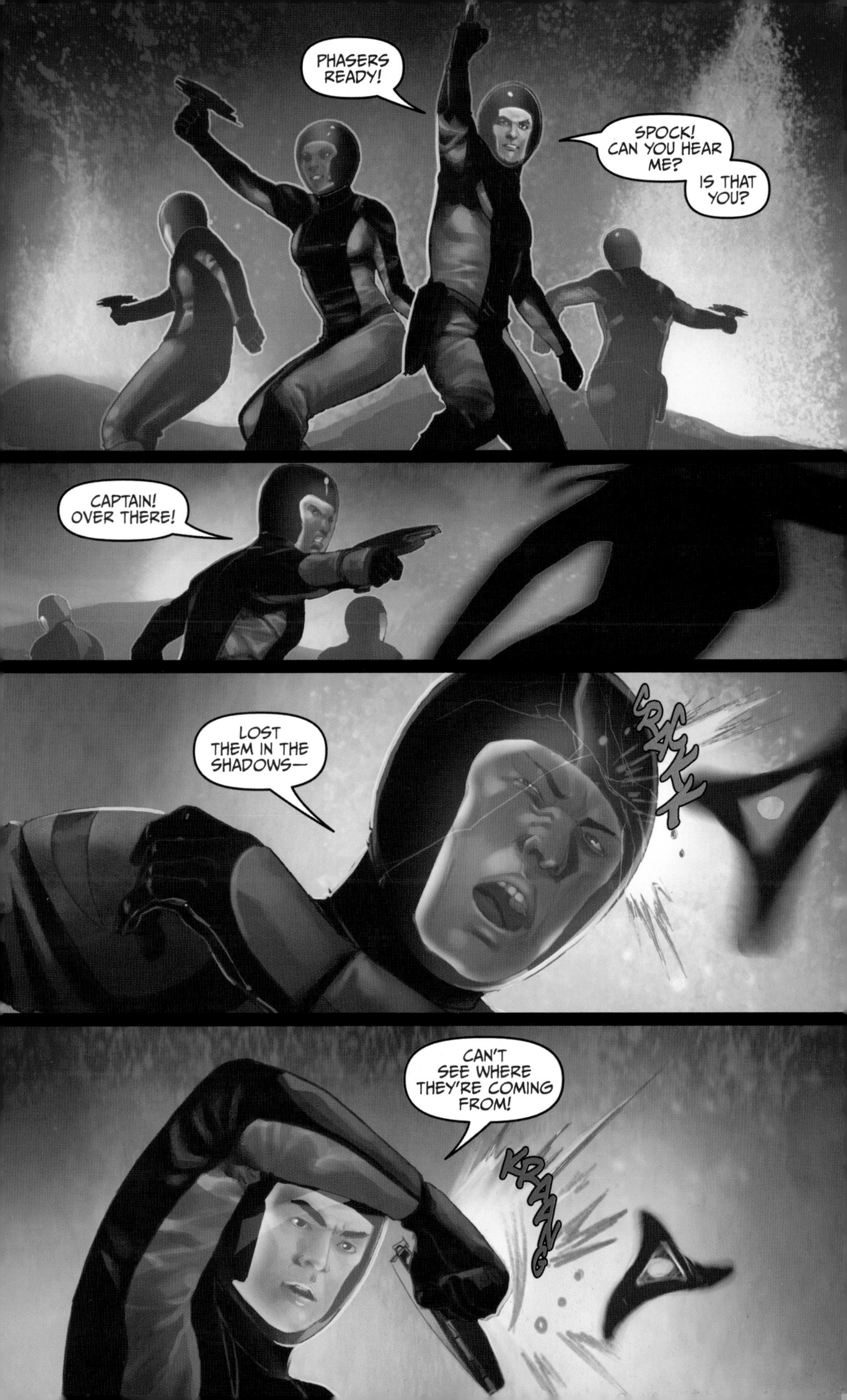
PHASERS READY!
SPOCK! CAN YOU HEAR ME?
IS THAT YOU?
CAPTAIN! OVER THERE!
LOST THEM IN THE SHADOWS—
CRAKK
CAN'T SEE WHERE THEY'RE COMING FROM!
KRAANG

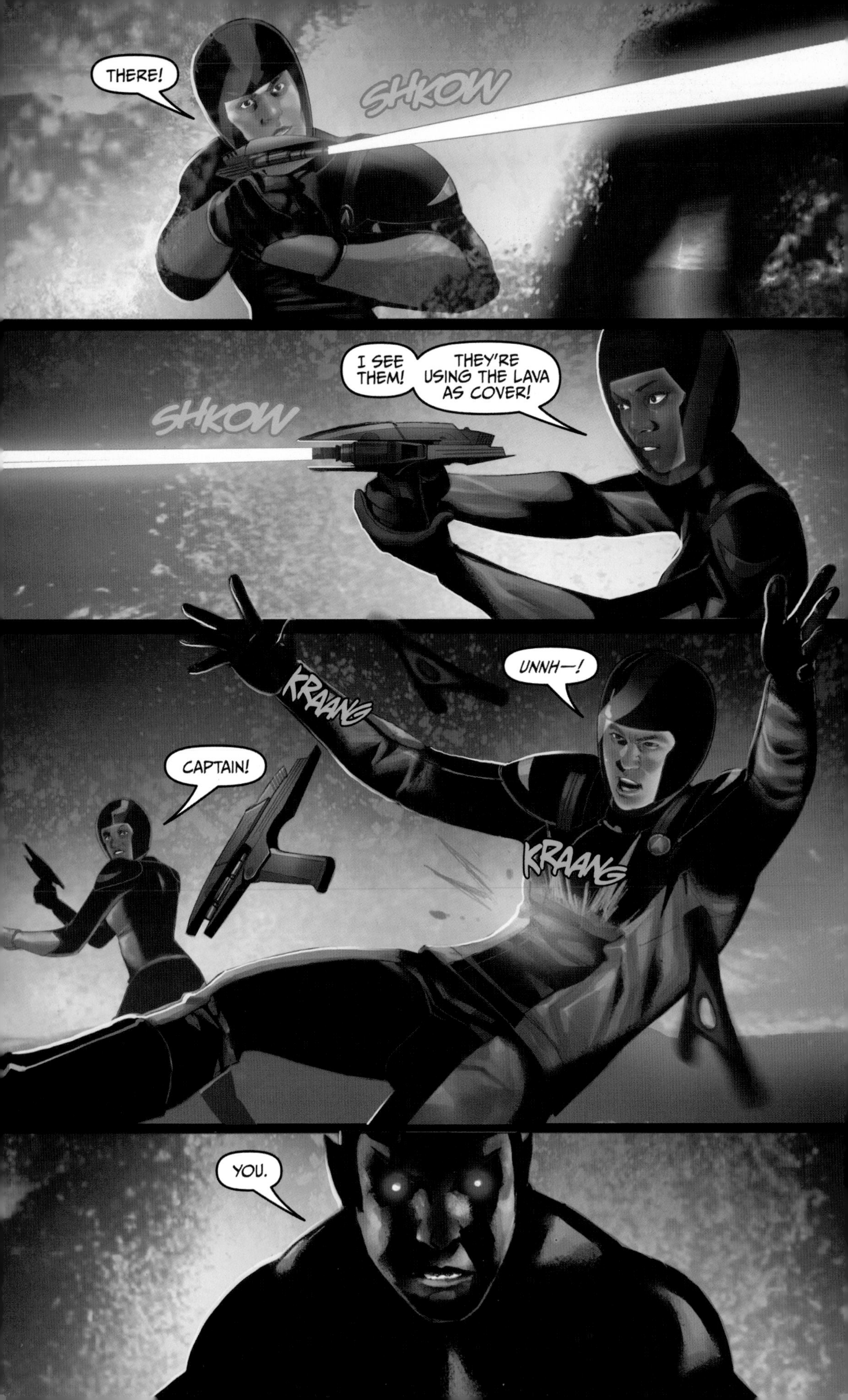
THERE!
SHKOW
I SEE THEM!
THEY'RE USING THE LAVA AS COVER!
SHKOW
UNNH—!
KRAANG
CAPTAIN!
KRAANG
YOU.

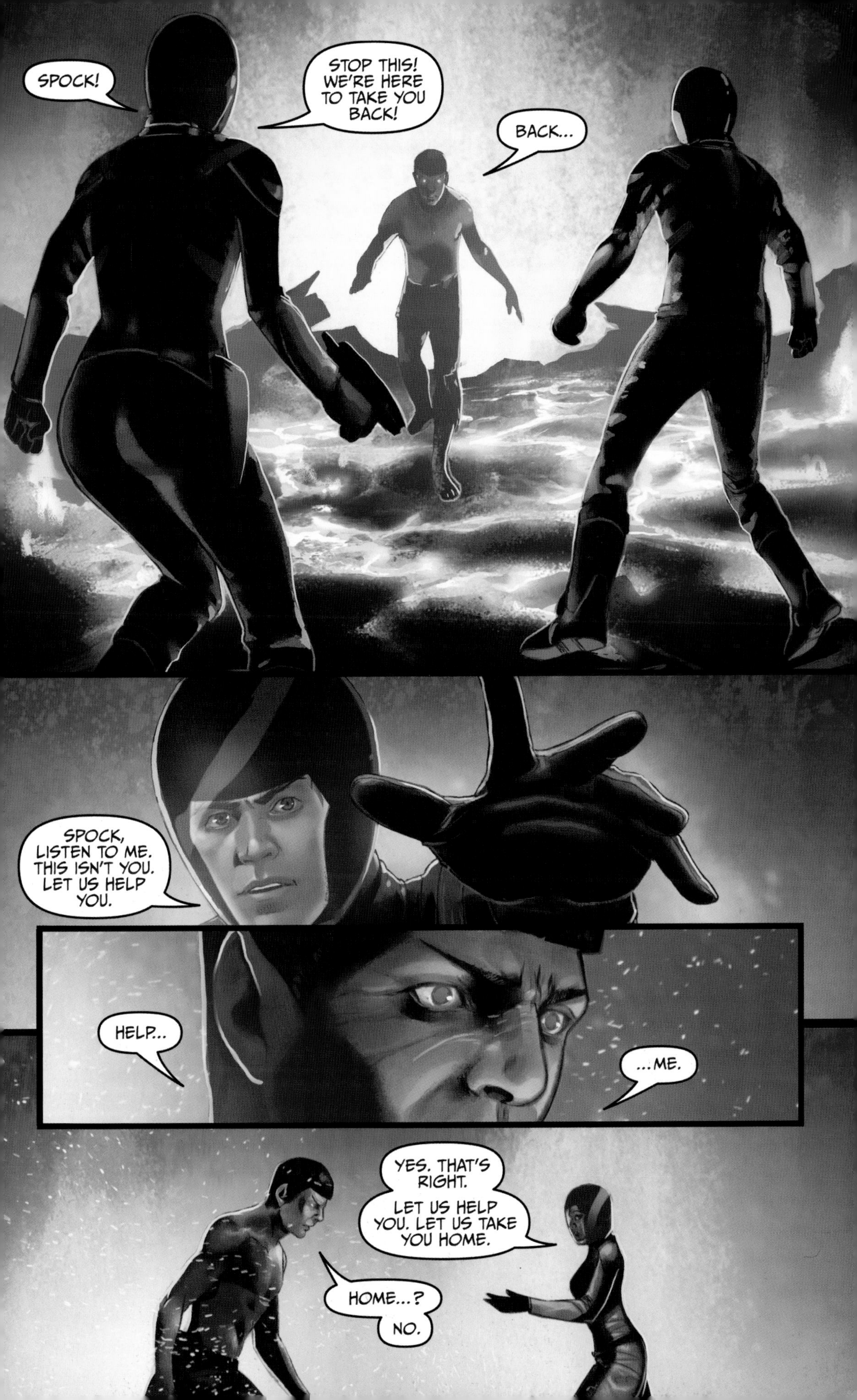
SPOCK!
STOP THIS! WE'RE HERE TO TAKE YOU BACK!
BACK...
SPOCK, LISTEN TO ME. THIS ISN'T YOU. LET US HELP YOU.
HELP...
...ME.
YES. THAT'S RIGHT.
LET US HELP YOU. LET US TAKE YOU HOME.
HOME...?
NO.

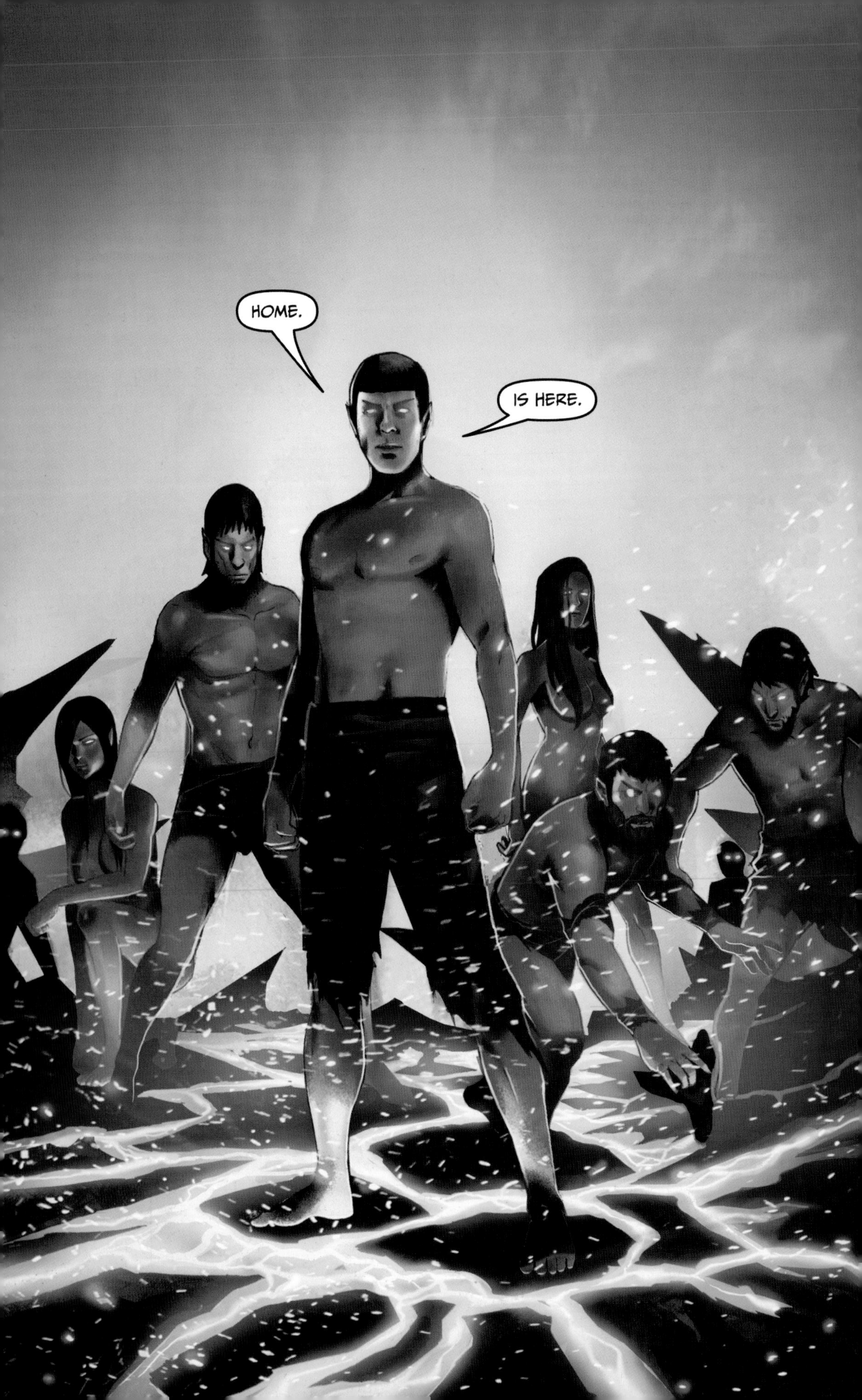
HOME.
IS HERE.

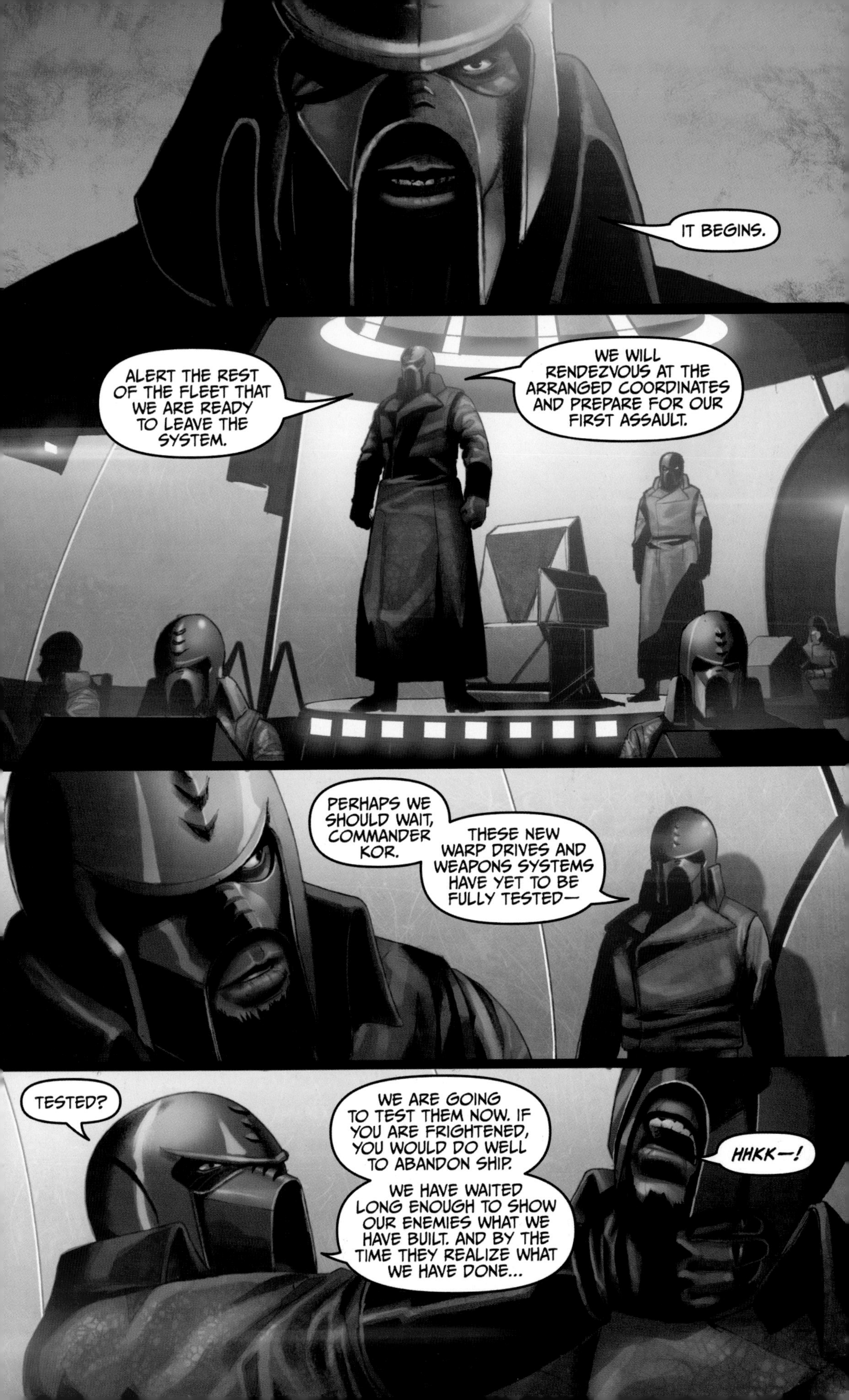
IT BEGINS.
ALERT THE REST OF THE FLEET THAT WE ARE READY TO LEAVE THE SYSTEM.
WE WILL RENDEZVOUS AT THE ARRANGED COORDINATES AND PREPARE FOR OUR FIRST ASSAULT.
PERHAPS WE SHOULD WAIT, COMMANDER KOR.
THESE NEW WARP DRIVES AND WEAPONS SYSTEMS HAVE YET TO BE FULLY TESTED—
TESTED?
WE ARE GOING TO TEST THEM NOW. IF YOU ARE FRIGHTENED, YOU WOULD DO WELL TO ABANDON SHIP.
WE HAVE WAITED LONG ENOUGH TO SHOW OUR ENEMIES WHAT WE HAVE BUILT. AND BY THE TIME THEY REALIZE WHAT WE HAVE DONE...
HHKK—!

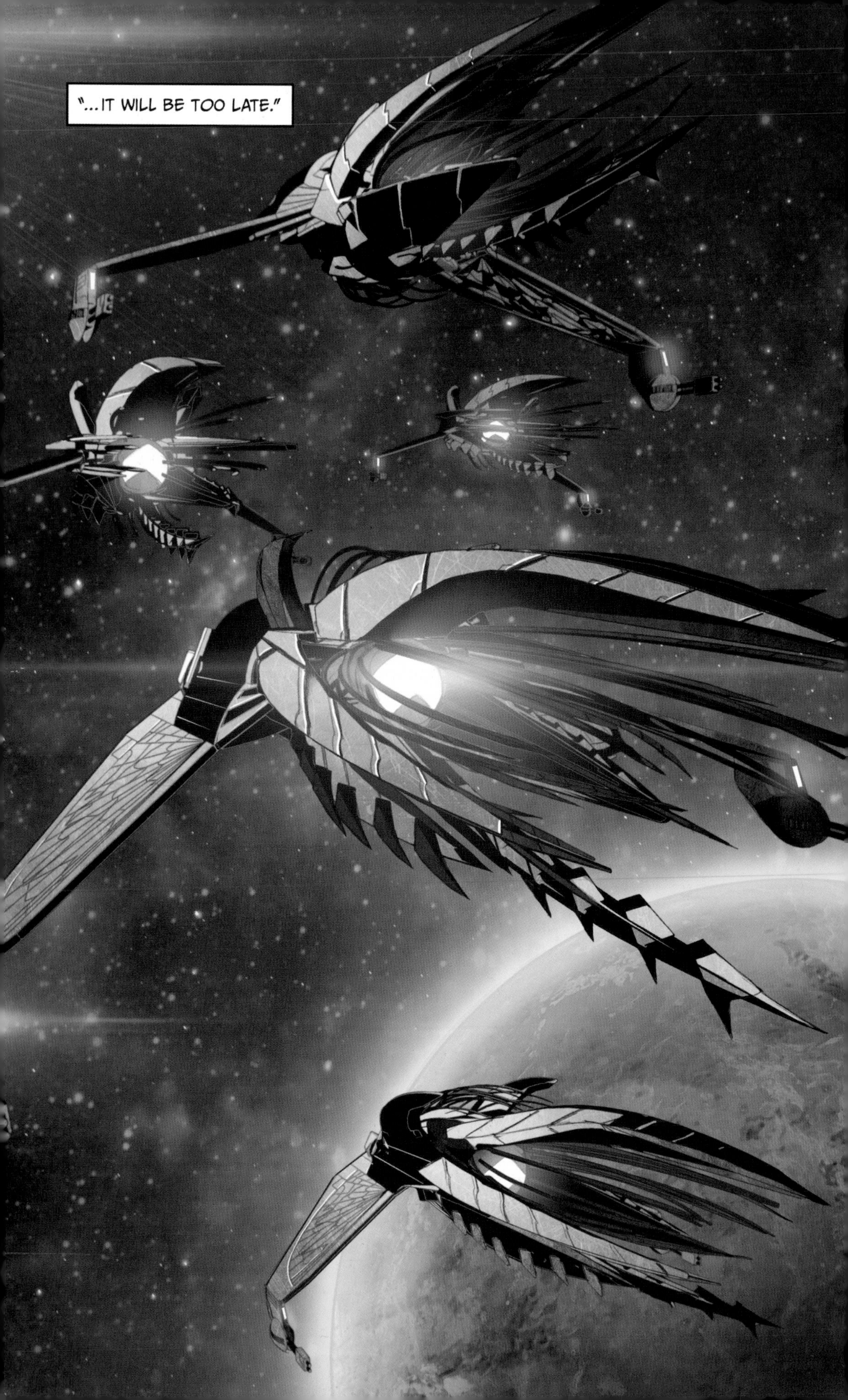
"...IT WILL BE TOO LATE."

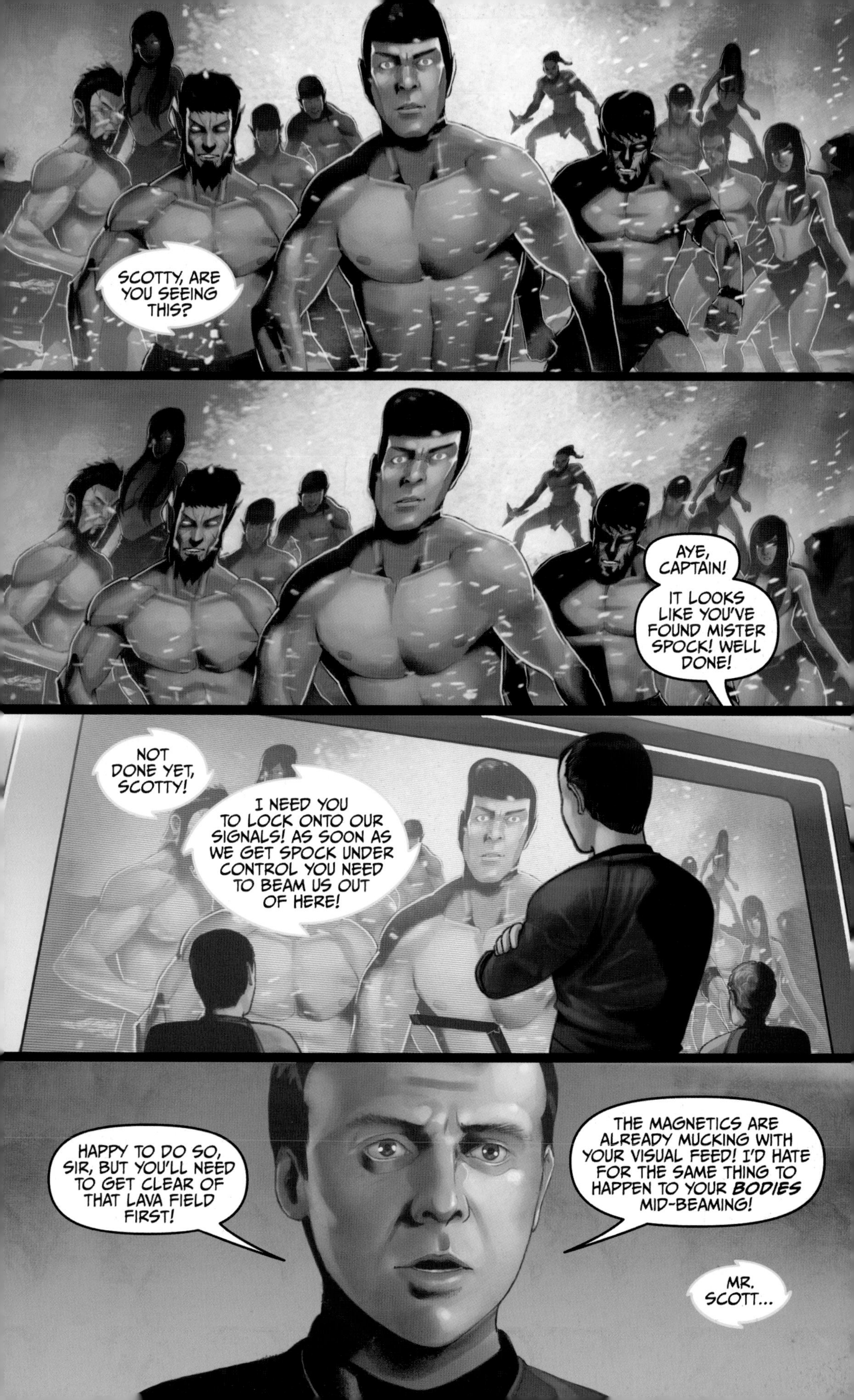
SCOTTY, ARE YOU SEEING THIS?
AYE, CAPTAIN!
IT LOOKS LIKE YOU'VE FOUND MISTER SPOCK! WELL DONE!
NOT DONE YET, SCOTTY!
I NEED YOU TO LOCK ONTO OUR SIGNALS! AS SOON AS WE GET SPOCK UNDER CONTROL YOU NEED TO BEAM US OUT OF HERE!
HAPPY TO DO SO, SIR, BUT YOU'LL NEED TO GET CLEAR OF THAT LAVA FIELD FIRST!
THE MAGNETICS ARE ALREADY MUCKING WITH YOUR VISUAL FEED! I'D HATE FOR THE SAME THING TO HAPPEN TO YOUR *BODIES* MID-BEAMING!
MR. SCOTT...

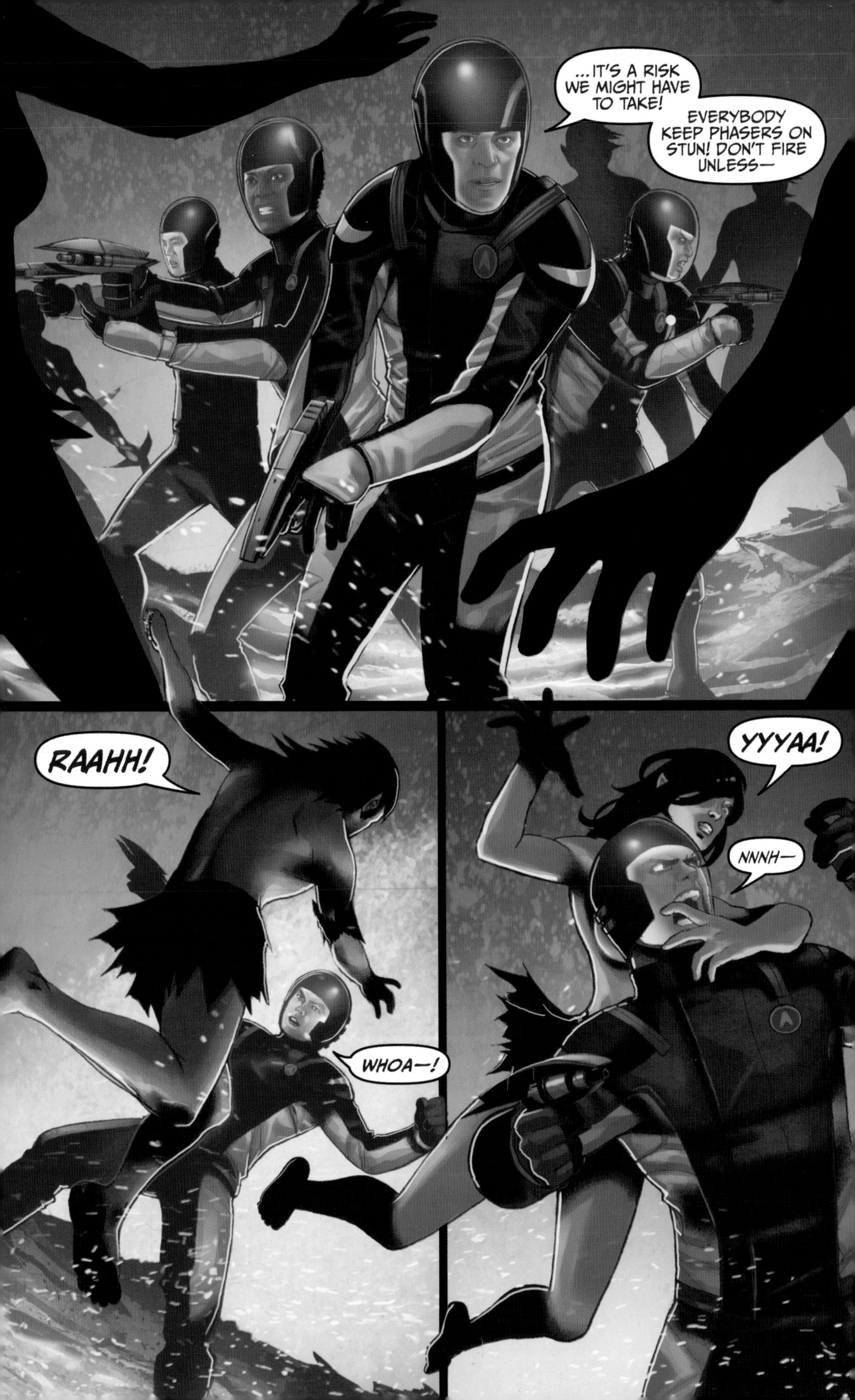

...IT'S A RISK WE MIGHT HAVE TO TAKE!
EVERYBODY KEEP PHASERS ON STUN! DON'T FIRE UNLESS—
RAAHH!
WHOA—!
YYYAA!
NNNH—

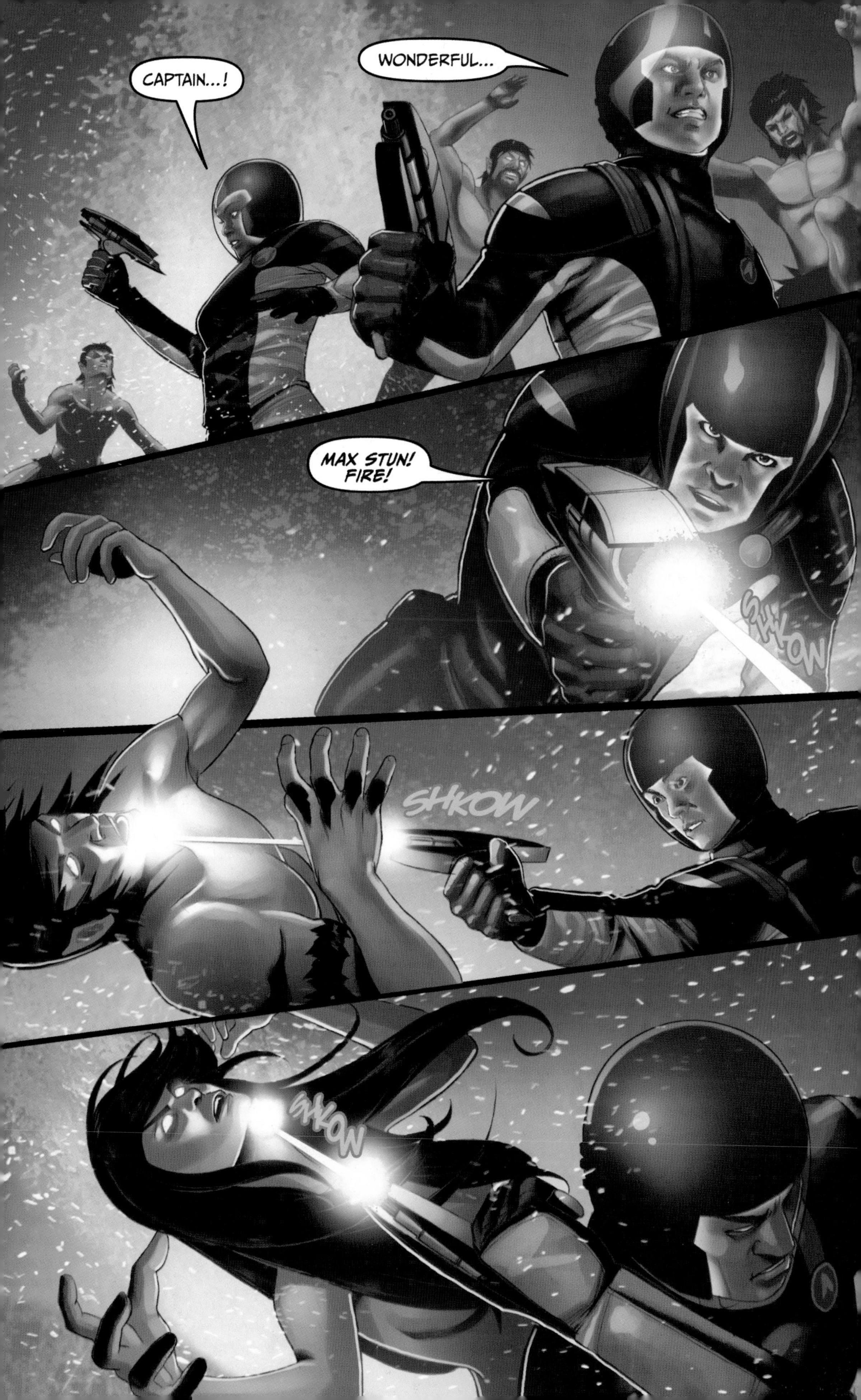
CAPTAIN...!
WONDERFUL...
MAX STUN! FIRE!
SHKOW
SHKOW
SHKOW

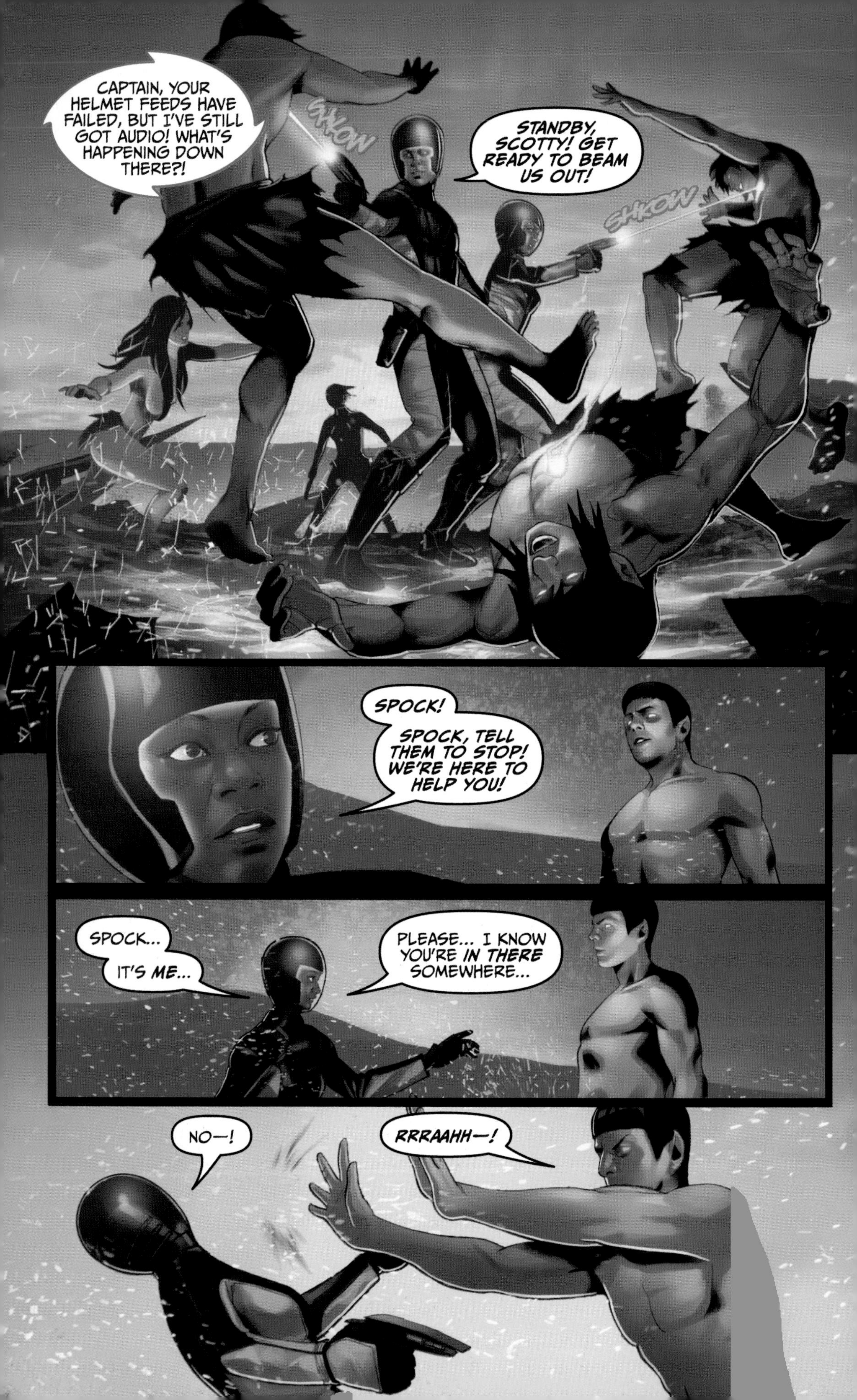
CAPTAIN, YOUR HELMET FEEDS HAVE FAILED, BUT I'VE STILL GOT AUDIO! WHAT'S HAPPENING DOWN THERE?!
SHKOW
STANDBY, SCOTTY! GET READY TO BEAM US OUT!
SHKOW
SPOCK!
SPOCK, TELL THEM TO STOP! WE'RE HERE TO HELP YOU!
SPOCK...
IT'S ME...
PLEASE... I KNOW YOU'RE IN THERE SOMEWHERE...
NO—!
RRRAAHH—!

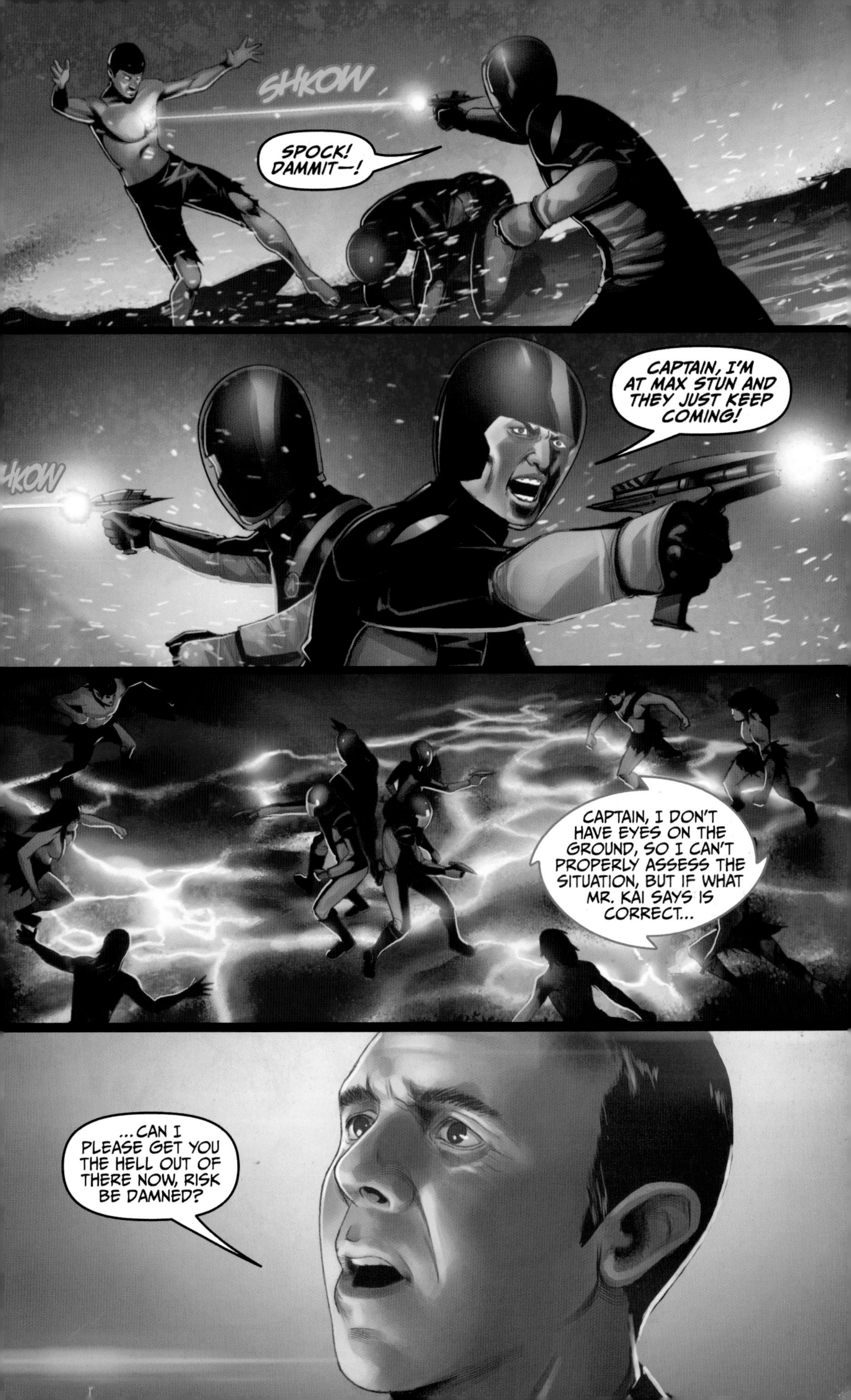
SHKOW
SPOCK! DAMMIT—!
CAPTAIN, I'M AT MAX STUN AND THEY JUST KEEP COMING!
SHKOW
CAPTAIN, I DON'T HAVE EYES ON THE GROUND, SO I CAN'T PROPERLY ASSESS THE SITUATION, BUT IF WHAT MR. KAI SAYS IS CORRECT...
...CAN I PLEASE GET YOU THE HELL OUT OF THERE NOW, RISK BE DAMNED?

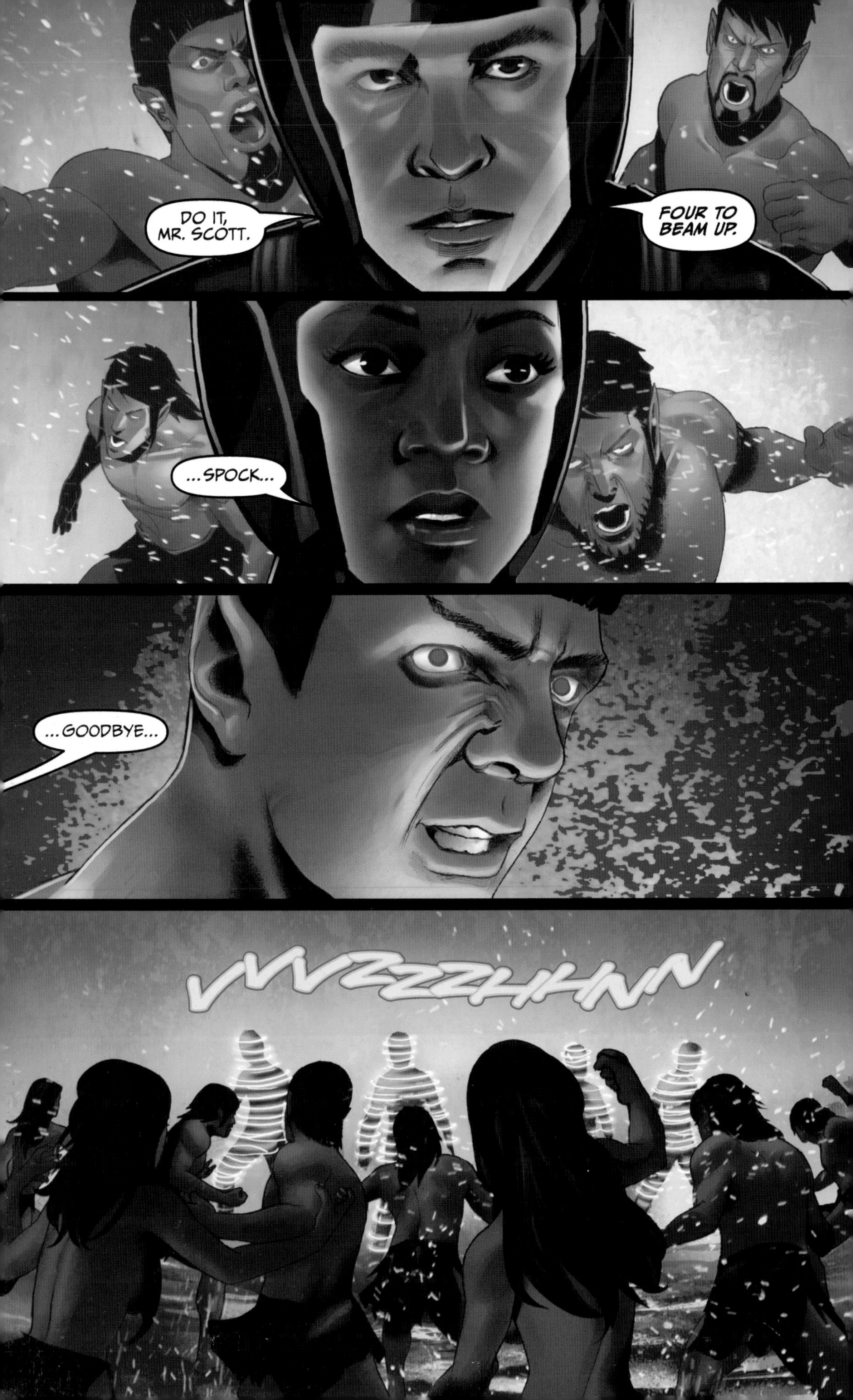
DO IT, MR. SCOTT.
FOUR TO BEAM UP.
...SPOCK...
...GOODBYE...
VVVZZZHHNN

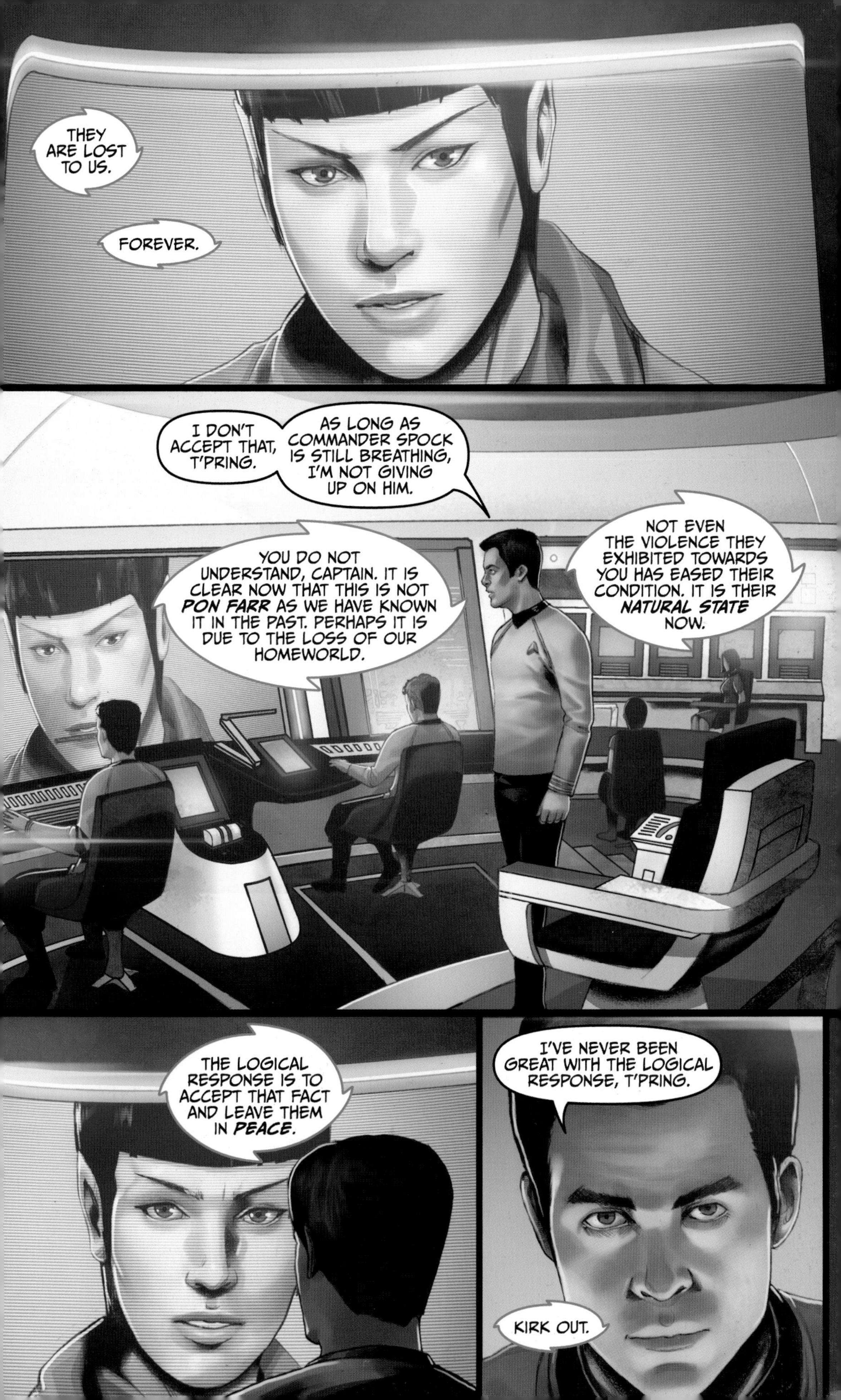
THEY ARE LOST TO US.
FOREVER.
I DON'T ACCEPT THAT, T'PRING.
AS LONG AS COMMANDER SPOCK IS STILL BREATHING, I'M NOT GIVING UP ON HIM.
YOU DO NOT UNDERSTAND, CAPTAIN. IT IS CLEAR NOW THAT THIS IS NOT PON FARR AS WE HAVE KNOWN IT IN THE PAST. PERHAPS IT IS DUE TO THE LOSS OF OUR HOMEWORLD.
NOT EVEN THE VIOLENCE THEY EXHIBITED TOWARDS YOU HAS EASED THEIR CONDITION. IT IS THEIR NATURAL STATE NOW.
THE LOGICAL RESPONSE IS TO ACCEPT THAT FACT AND LEAVE THEM IN PEACE.
I'VE NEVER BEEN GREAT WITH THE LOGICAL RESPONSE, T'PRING.
KIRK OUT.

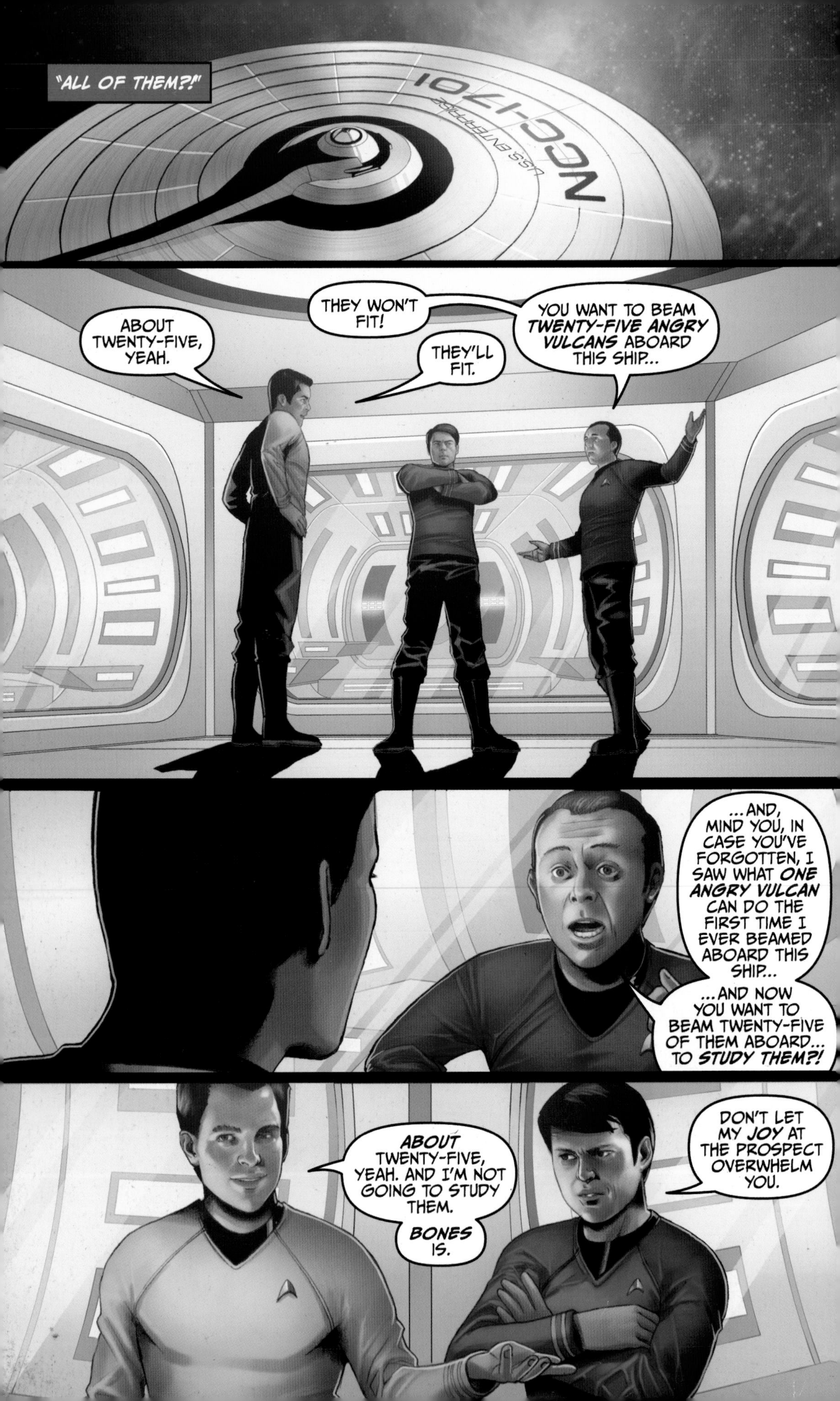
"ALL OF THEM?!"
NCC-1701
U.S.S. ENTERPRISE
ABOUT TWENTY-FIVE, YEAH.
THEY WON'T FIT!
THEY'LL FIT.
YOU WANT TO BEAM TWENTY-FIVE ANGRY VULCANS ABOARD THIS SHIP...
...AND, MIND YOU, IN CASE YOU'VE FORGOTTEN, I SAW WHAT ONE ANGRY VULCAN CAN DO THE FIRST TIME I EVER BEAMED ABOARD THIS SHIP...
...AND NOW YOU WANT TO BEAM TWENTY-FIVE OF THEM ABOARD... TO STUDY THEM?!
ABOUT TWENTY-FIVE, YEAH. AND I'M NOT GOING TO STUDY THEM.
BONES IS.
DON'T LET MY JOY AT THE PROSPECT OVERWHELM YOU.

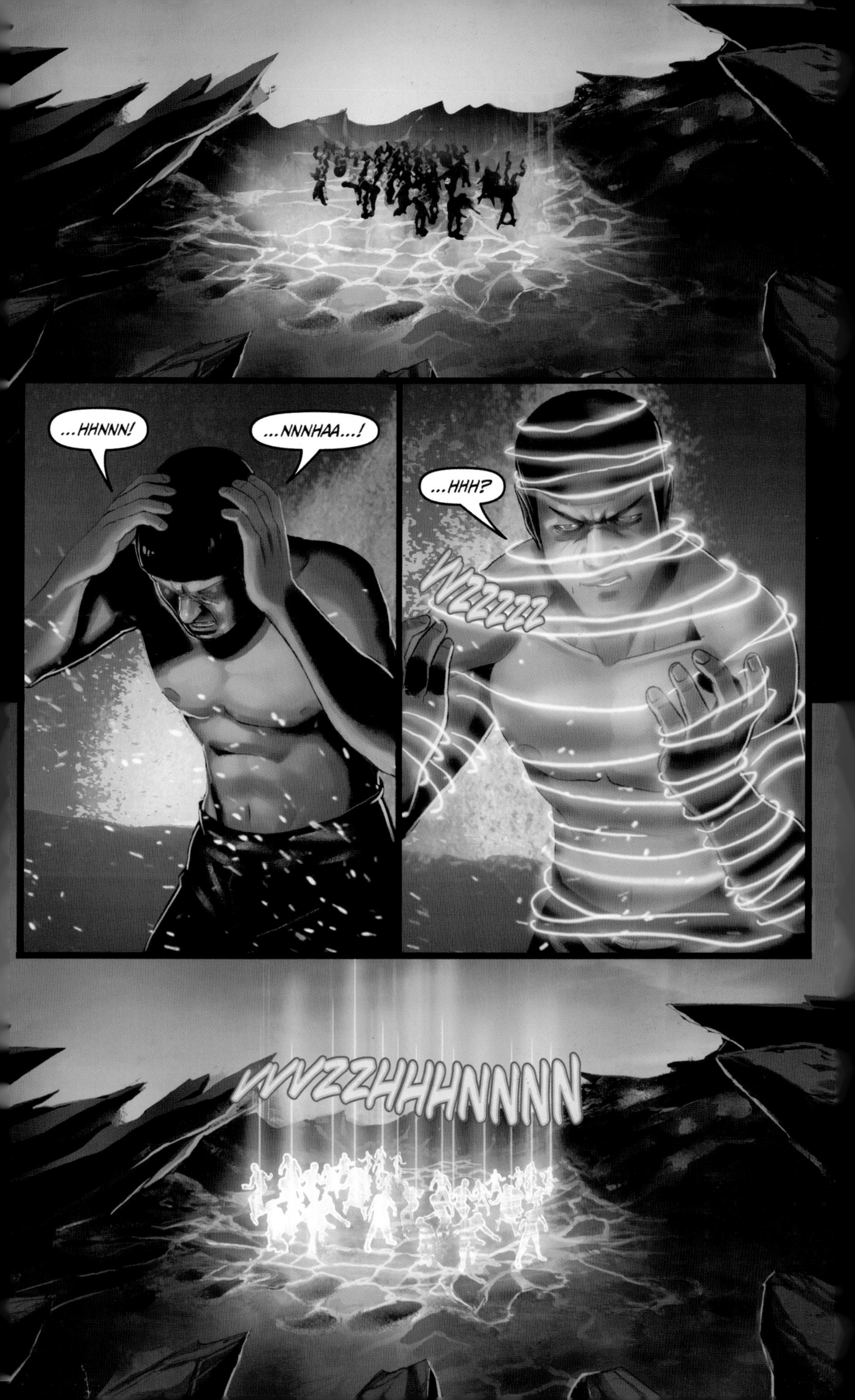
...HHNNN!
...NNNHAA...!
...HHH?
WZZZZZ
VVVZZHHHNNNNN

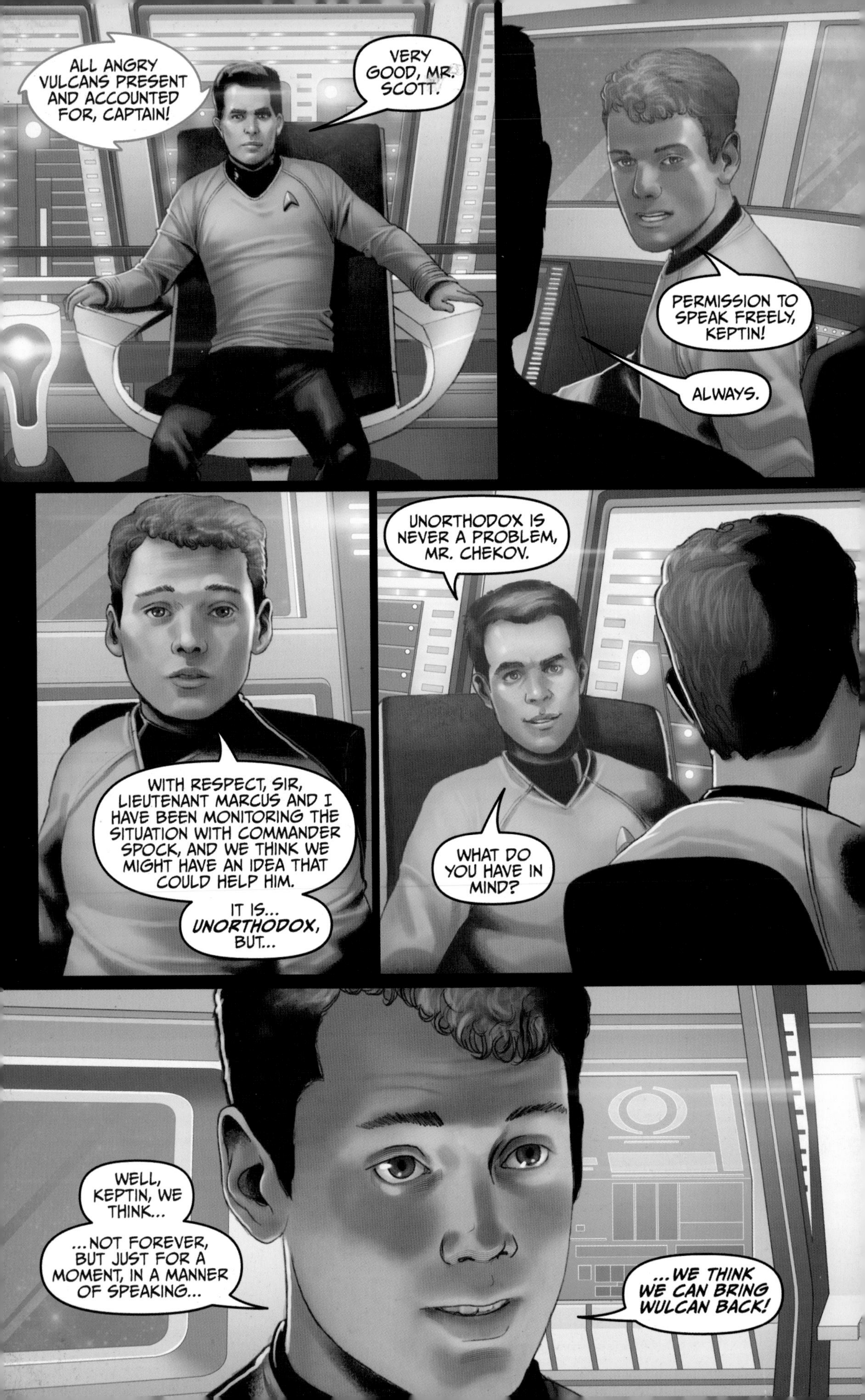

ALL ANGRY VULCANS PRESENT AND ACCOUNTED FOR, CAPTAIN!
VERY GOOD, MR. SCOTT.
PERMISSION TO SPEAK FREELY, KEPTIN!
ALWAYS.
WITH RESPECT, SIR, LIEUTENANT MARCUS AND I HAVE BEEN MONITORING THE SITUATION WITH COMMANDER SPOCK, AND WE THINK WE MIGHT HAVE AN IDEA THAT COULD HELP HIM.
IT IS... *UNORTHODOX*, BUT...
UNORTHODOX IS NEVER A PROBLEM, MR. CHEKOV.
WHAT DO YOU HAVE IN MIND?
WELL, KEPTIN, WE THINK...
...NOT FOREVER, BUT JUST FOR A MOMENT, IN A MANNER OF SPEAKING...
...WE THINK WE CAN BRING WULCAN BACK!

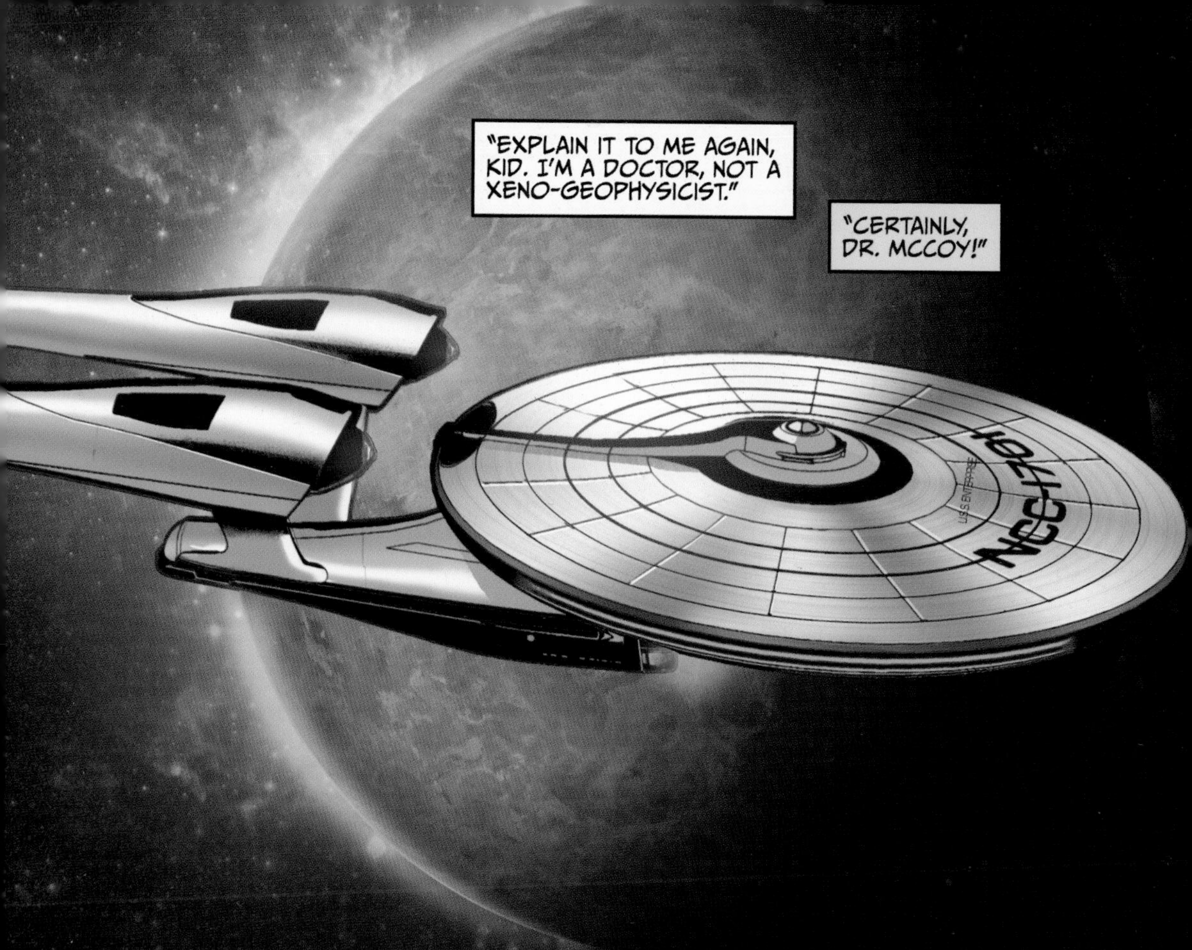
"EXPLAIN IT TO ME AGAIN, KID. I'M A DOCTOR, NOT A XENO-GEOPHYSICIST."
"CERTAINLY, DR. MCCOY!"
NCC-1701

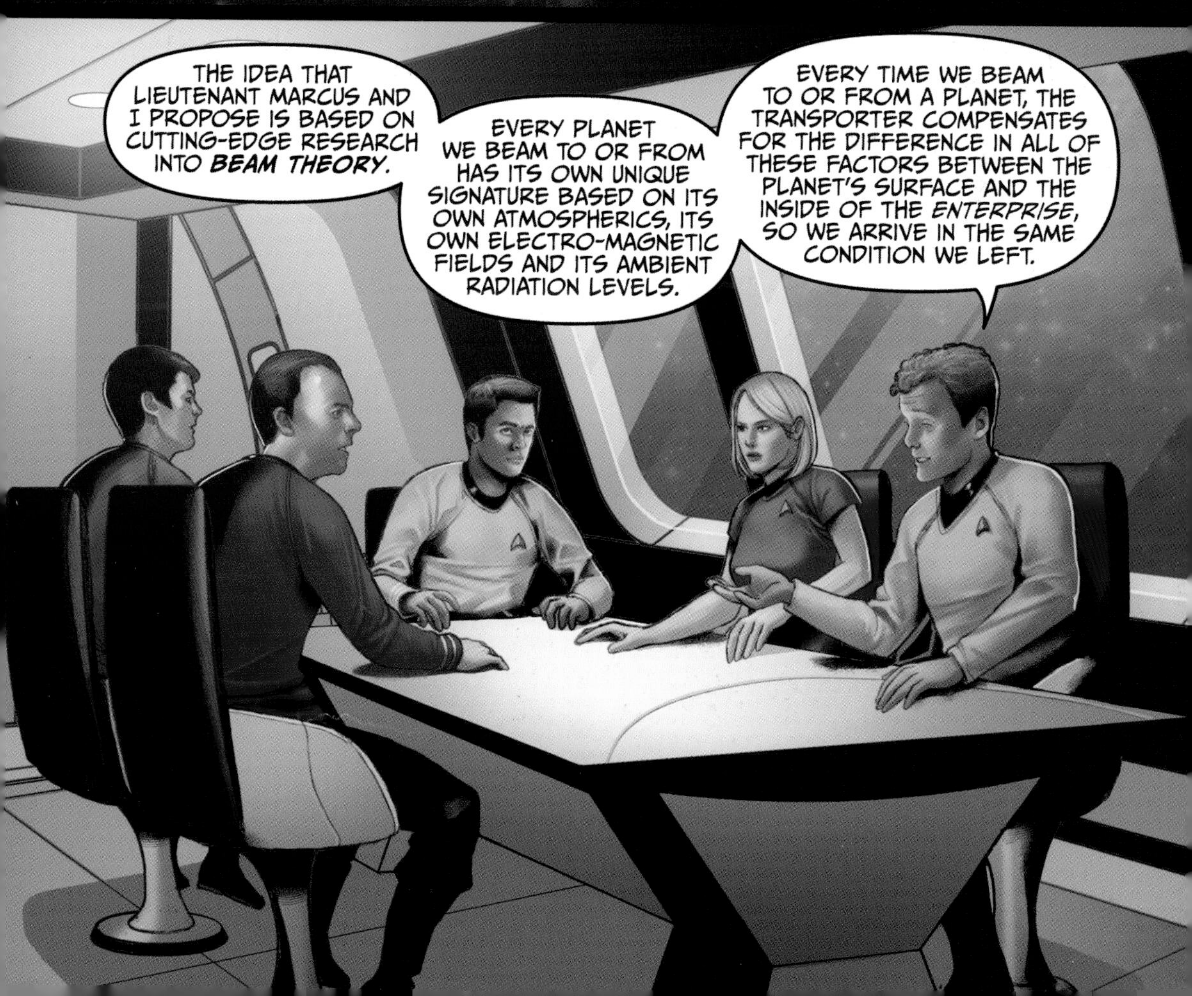
THE IDEA THAT LIEUTENANT MARCUS AND I PROPOSE IS BASED ON CUTTING-EDGE RESEARCH INTO ***BEAM THEORY***.
EVERY PLANET WE BEAM TO OR FROM HAS ITS OWN UNIQUE SIGNATURE BASED ON ITS OWN ATMOSPHERICS, ITS OWN ELECTRO-MAGNETIC FIELDS AND ITS AMBIENT RADIATION LEVELS.
EVERY TIME WE BEAM TO OR FROM A PLANET, THE TRANSPORTER COMPENSATES FOR THE DIFFERENCE IN ALL OF THESE FACTORS BETWEEN THE PLANET'S SURFACE AND THE INSIDE OF THE *ENTERPRISE*, SO WE ARRIVE IN THE SAME CONDITION WE LEFT.

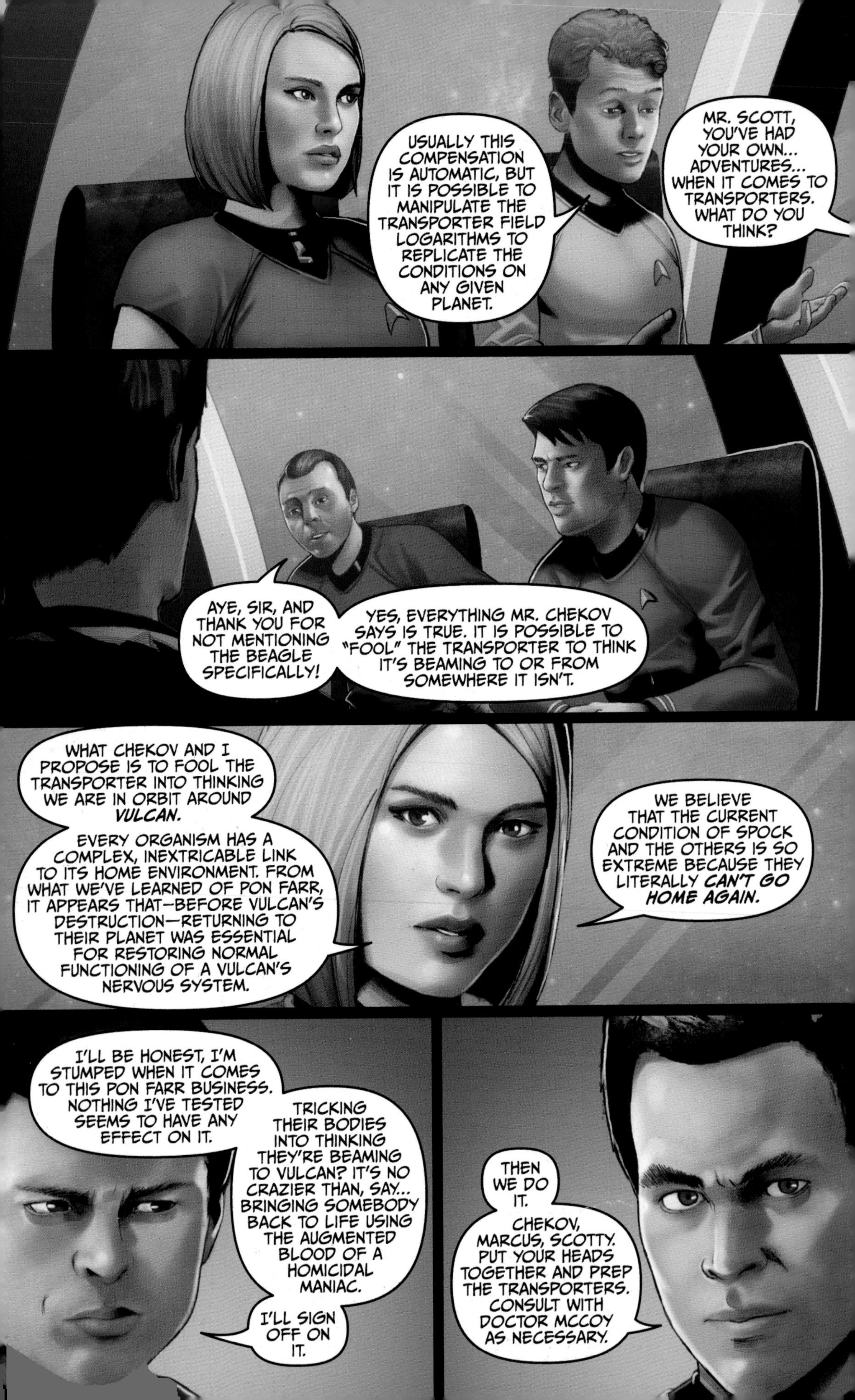
USUALLY THIS COMPENSATION IS AUTOMATIC, BUT IT IS POSSIBLE TO MANIPULATE THE TRANSPORTER FIELD LOGARITHMS TO REPLICATE THE CONDITIONS ON ANY GIVEN PLANET.
MR. SCOTT, YOU'VE HAD YOUR OWN... ADVENTURES... WHEN IT COMES TO TRANSPORTERS. WHAT DO YOU THINK?
AYE, SIR, AND THANK YOU FOR NOT MENTIONING THE BEAGLE SPECIFICALLY!
YES, EVERYTHING MR. CHEKOV SAYS IS TRUE. IT IS POSSIBLE TO "FOOL" THE TRANSPORTER TO THINK IT'S BEAMING TO OR FROM SOMEWHERE IT ISN'T.
WHAT CHEKOV AND I PROPOSE IS TO FOOL THE TRANSPORTER INTO THINKING WE ARE IN ORBIT AROUND ***VULCAN.***
EVERY ORGANISM HAS A COMPLEX, INEXTRICABLE LINK TO ITS HOME ENVIRONMENT. FROM WHAT WE'VE LEARNED OF PON FARR, IT APPEARS THAT—BEFORE VULCAN'S DESTRUCTION—RETURNING TO THEIR PLANET WAS ESSENTIAL FOR RESTORING NORMAL FUNCTIONING OF A VULCAN'S NERVOUS SYSTEM.
WE BELIEVE THAT THE CURRENT CONDITION OF SPOCK AND THE OTHERS IS SO EXTREME BECAUSE THEY LITERALLY ***CAN'T GO HOME AGAIN.***
I'LL BE HONEST, I'M STUMPED WHEN IT COMES TO THIS PON FARR BUSINESS. NOTHING I'VE TESTED SEEMS TO HAVE ANY EFFECT ON IT.
TRICKING THEIR BODIES INTO THINKING THEY'RE BEAMING TO VULCAN? IT'S NO CRAZIER THAN, SAY... BRINGING SOMEBODY BACK TO LIFE USING THE AUGMENTED BLOOD OF A HOMICIDAL MANIAC.
I'LL SIGN OFF ON IT.
THEN WE DO IT.
CHEKOV, MARCUS, SCOTTY. PUT YOUR HEADS TOGETHER AND PREP THE TRANSPORTERS. CONSULT WITH DOCTOR MCCOY AS NECESSARY.

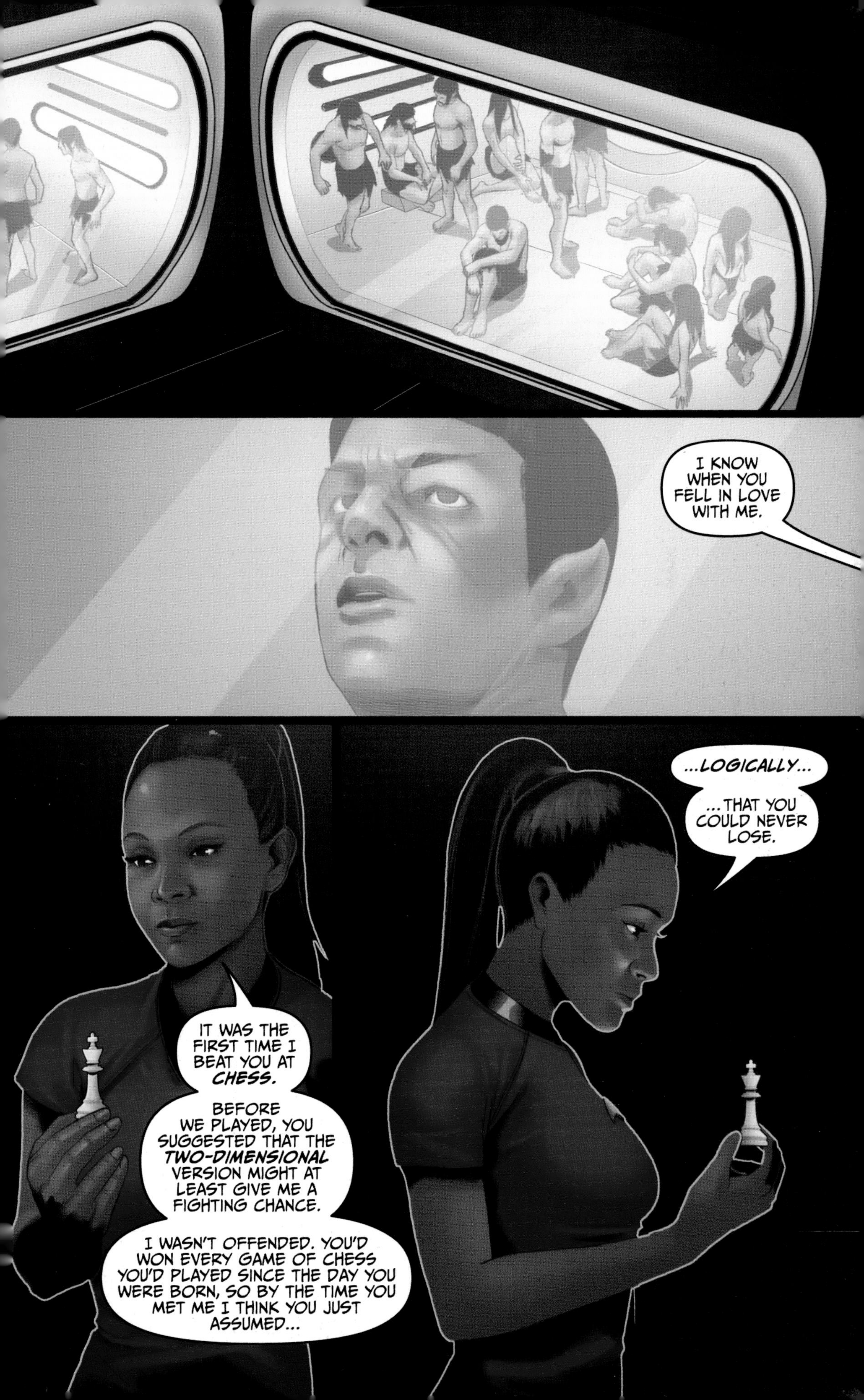
I KNOW WHEN YOU FELL IN LOVE WITH ME.
IT WAS THE FIRST TIME I BEAT YOU AT *CHESS.*
BEFORE WE PLAYED, YOU SUGGESTED THAT THE *TWO-DIMENSIONAL* VERSION MIGHT AT LEAST GIVE ME A FIGHTING CHANCE.
I WASN'T OFFENDED. YOU'D WON EVERY GAME OF CHESS YOU'D PLAYED SINCE THE DAY YOU WERE BORN, SO BY THE TIME YOU MET ME I THINK YOU JUST ASSUMED...
...*LOGICALLY*...
...THAT YOU COULD NEVER LOSE.

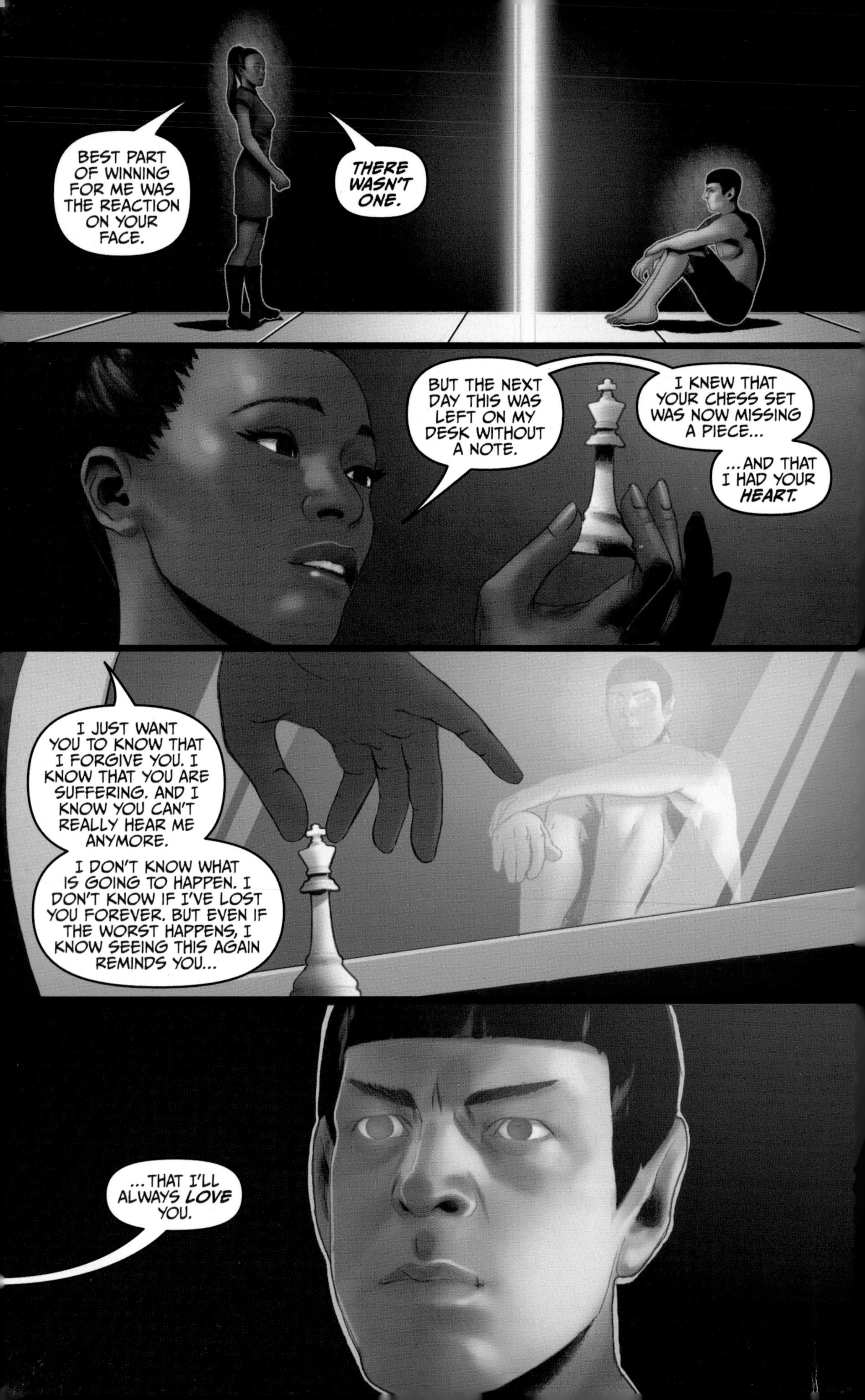
BEST PART OF WINNING FOR ME WAS THE REACTION ON YOUR FACE.
THERE WASN'T ONE.
BUT THE NEXT DAY THIS WAS LEFT ON MY DESK WITHOUT A NOTE.
I KNEW THAT YOUR CHESS SET WAS NOW MISSING A PIECE...
...AND THAT I HAD YOUR HEART.
I JUST WANT YOU TO KNOW THAT I FORGIVE YOU. I KNOW THAT YOU ARE SUFFERING. AND I KNOW YOU CAN'T REALLY HEAR ME ANYMORE.
I DON'T KNOW WHAT IS GOING TO HAPPEN. I DON'T KNOW IF I'VE LOST YOU FOREVER. BUT EVEN IF THE WORST HAPPENS, I KNOW SEEING THIS AGAIN REMINDS YOU...
...THAT I'LL ALWAYS LOVE YOU.

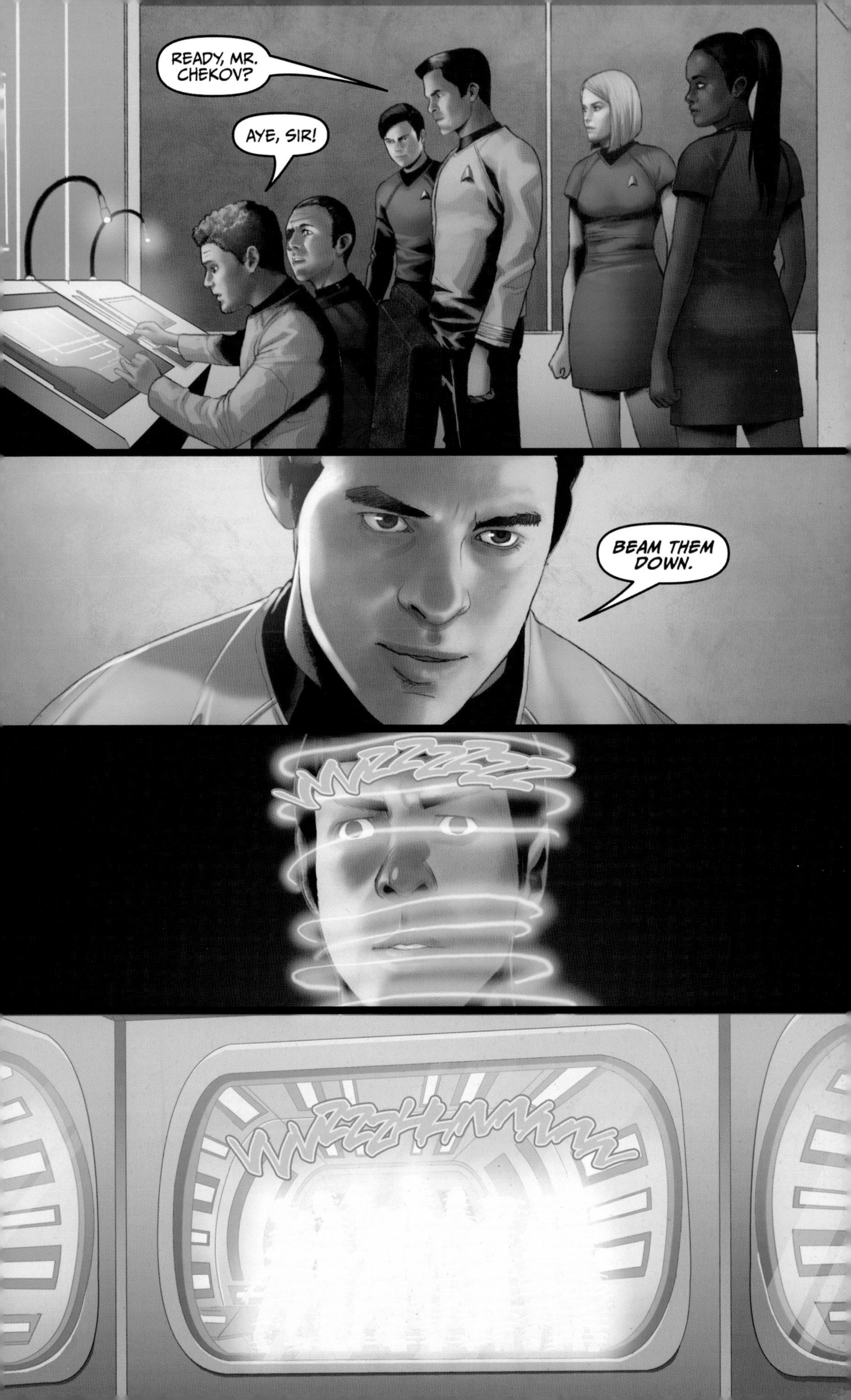
READY, MR. CHEKOV?
AYE, SIR!
BEAM THEM DOWN.
WWZZZZZZ
WWZZZHWWWWW

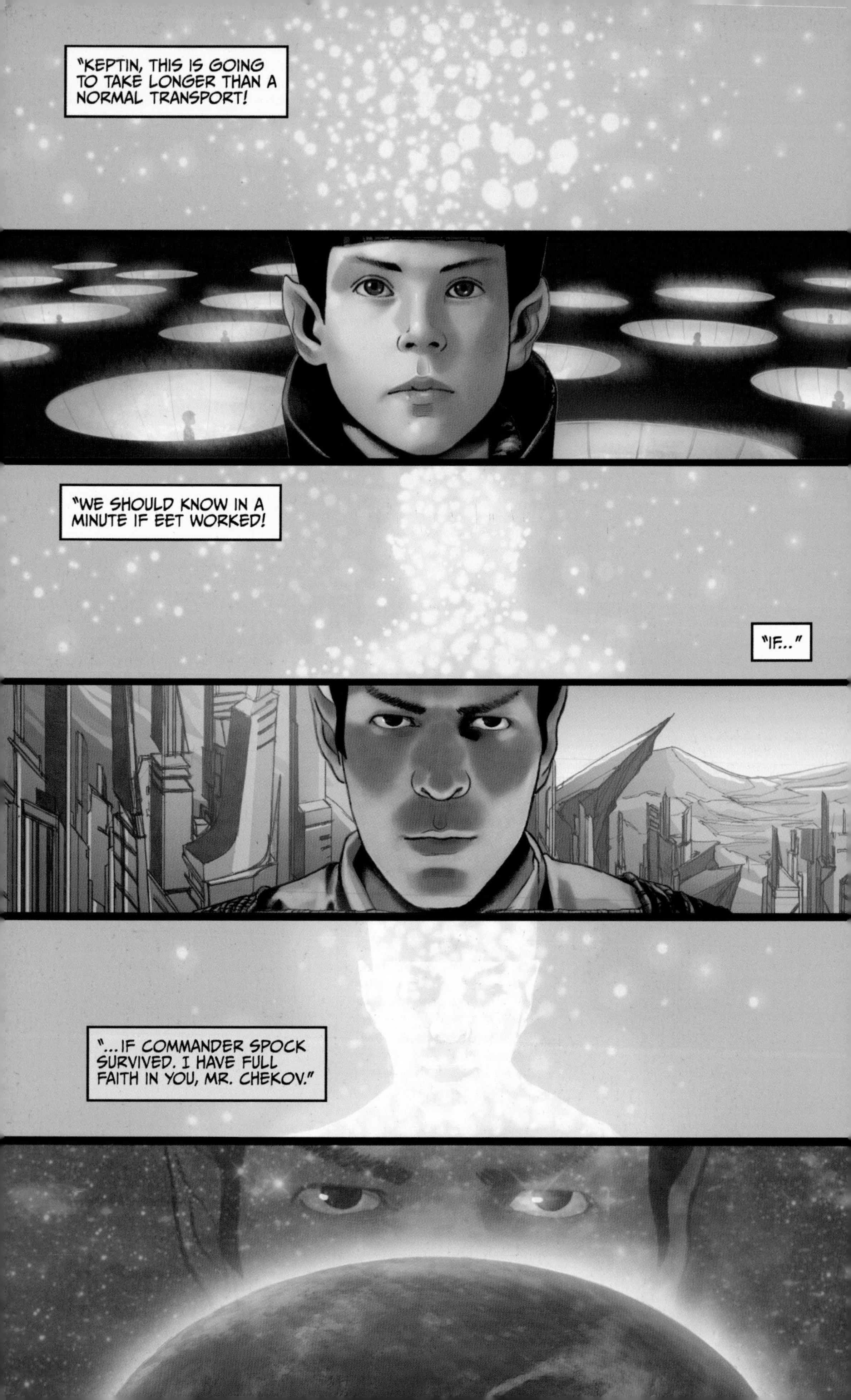
"KEPTIN, THIS IS GOING TO TAKE LONGER THAN A NORMAL TRANSPORT!
"WE SHOULD KNOW IN A MINUTE IF EET WORKED!
"IF..."
"...IF COMMANDER SPOCK SURVIVED. I HAVE FULL FAITH IN YOU, MR. CHEKOV."

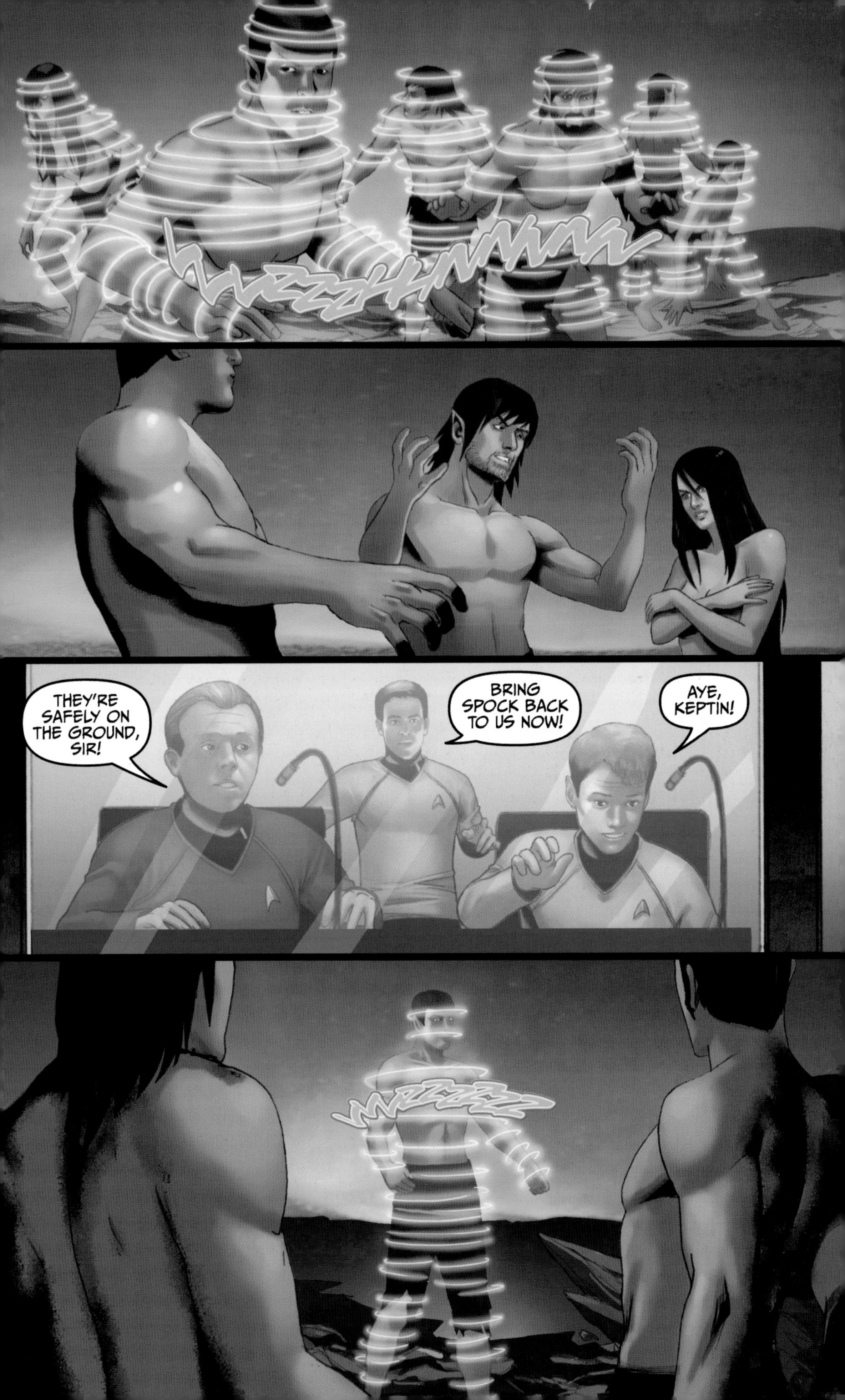
THEY'RE SAFELY ON THE GROUND, SIR!
BRING SPOCK BACK TO US NOW!
AYE, KEPTIN!

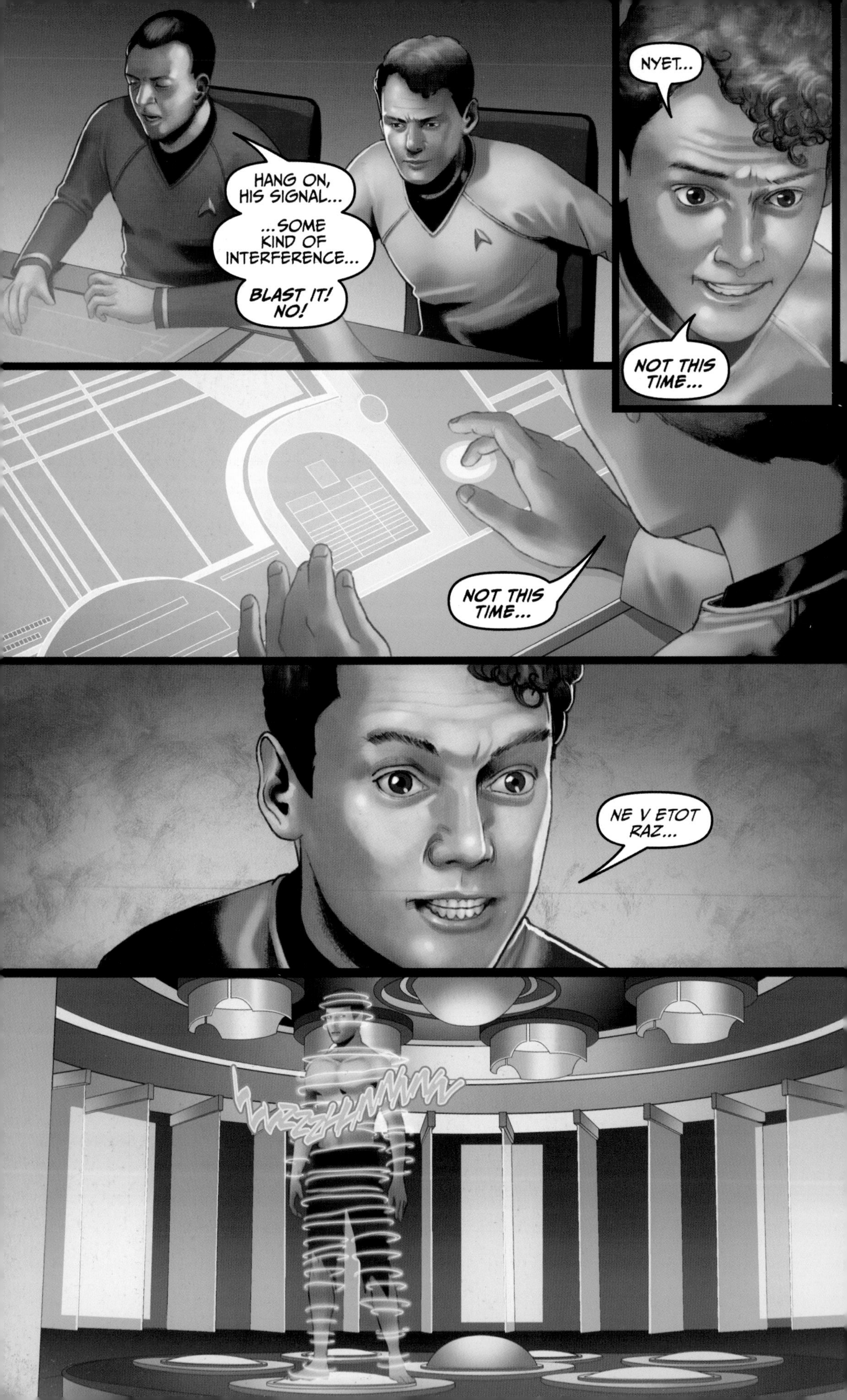

HANG ON, HIS SIGNAL...
...SOME KIND OF INTERFERENCE...
BLAST IT! NO!
NYET...
NOT THIS TIME...
NOT THIS TIME...
NE V ETOT RAZ...
VWEEEHHMMMMM

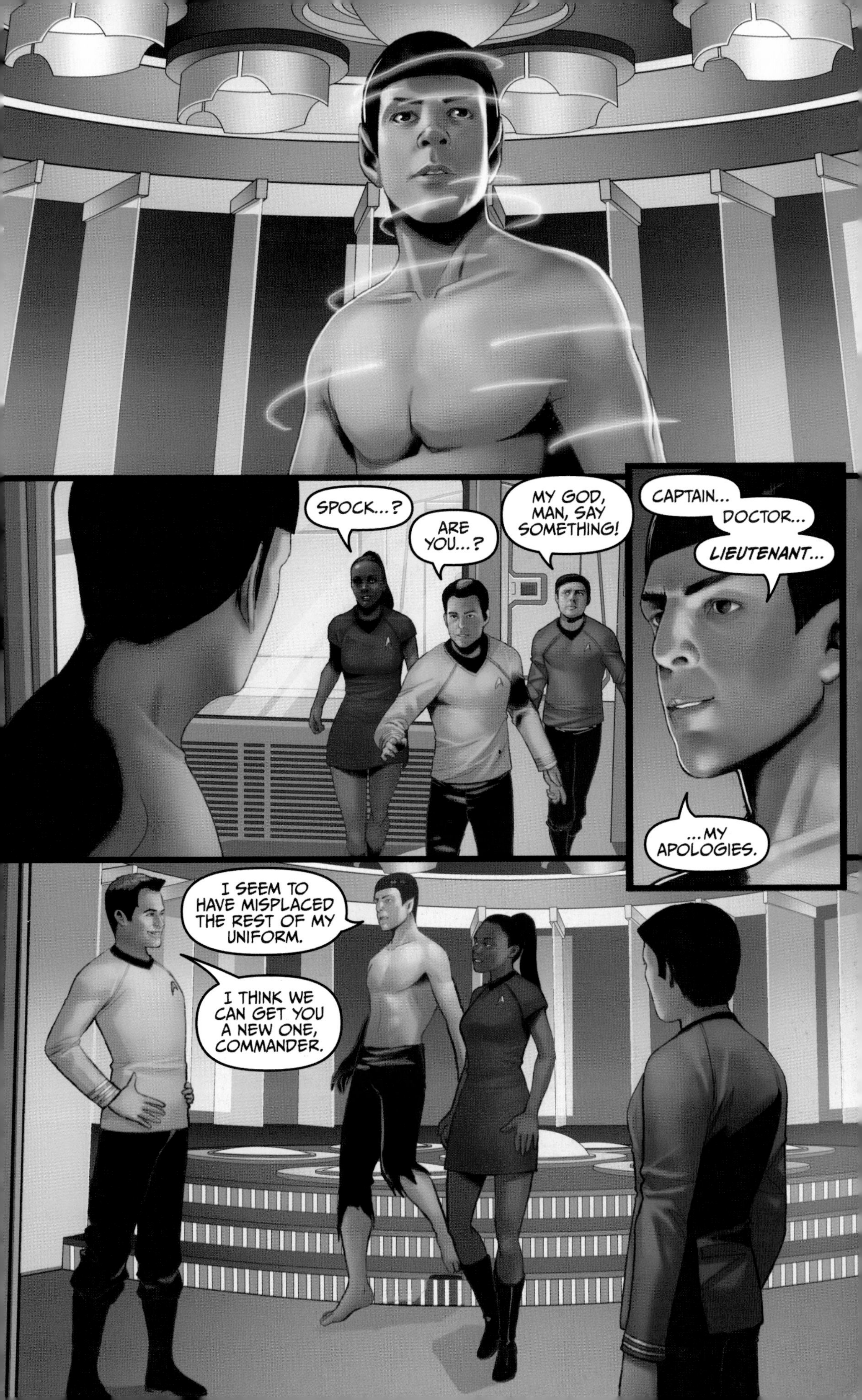
SPOCK...?
ARE YOU...?
MY GOD, MAN, SAY SOMETHING!
CAPTAIN...
DOCTOR...
LIEUTENANT...
...MY APOLOGIES.
I SEEM TO HAVE MISPLACED THE REST OF MY UNIFORM.
I THINK WE CAN GET YOU A NEW ONE, COMMANDER.

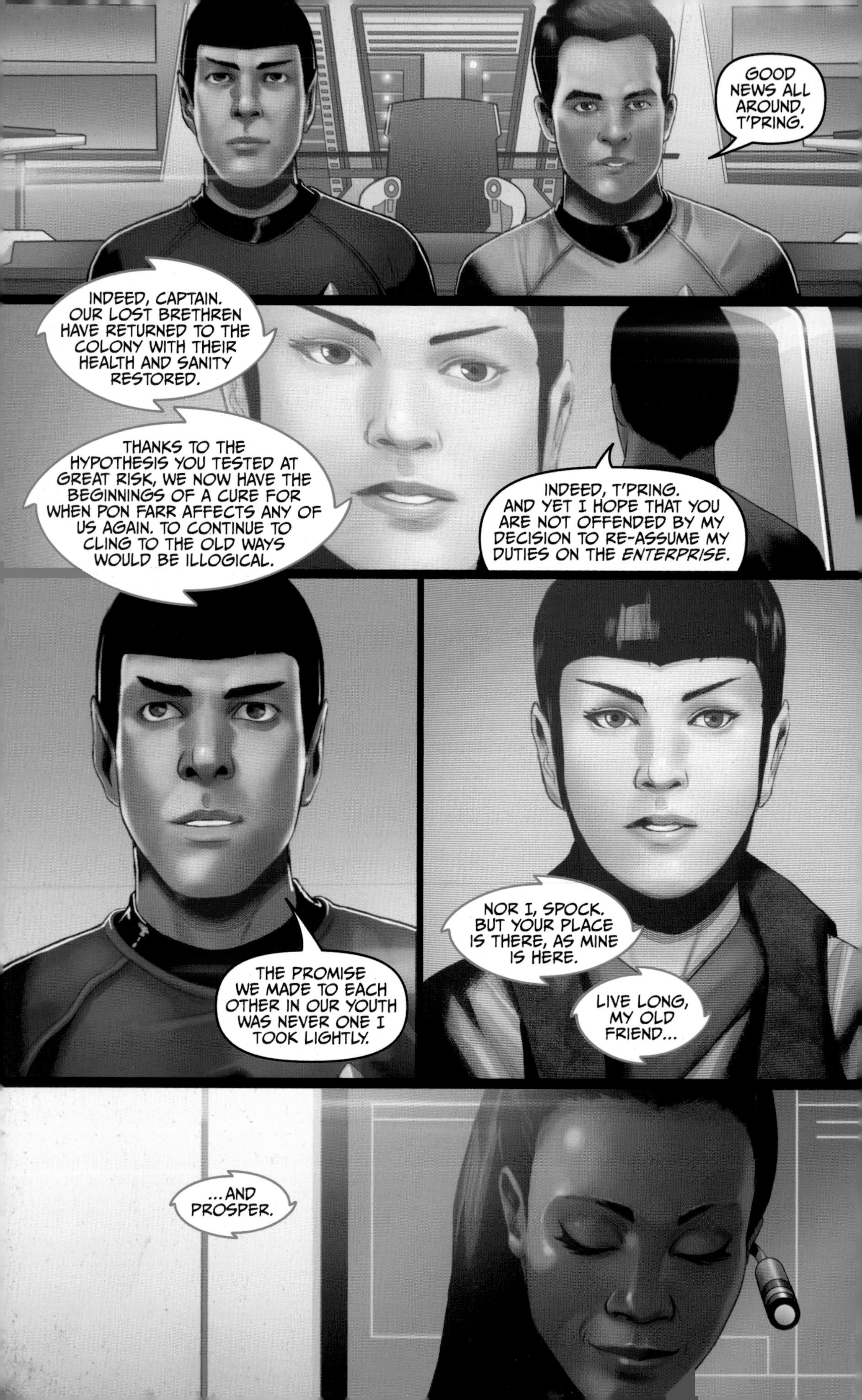
GOOD NEWS ALL AROUND, T'PRING.
INDEED, CAPTAIN. OUR LOST BRETHREN HAVE RETURNED TO THE COLONY WITH THEIR HEALTH AND SANITY RESTORED.
THANKS TO THE HYPOTHESIS YOU TESTED AT GREAT RISK, WE NOW HAVE THE BEGINNINGS OF A CURE FOR WHEN PON FARR AFFECTS ANY OF US AGAIN. TO CONTINUE TO CLING TO THE OLD WAYS WOULD BE ILLOGICAL.
INDEED, T'PRING. AND YET I HOPE THAT YOU ARE NOT OFFENDED BY MY DECISION TO RE-ASSUME MY DUTIES ON THE *ENTERPRISE*.
THE PROMISE WE MADE TO EACH OTHER IN OUR YOUTH WAS NEVER ONE I TOOK LIGHTLY.
NOR I, SPOCK. BUT YOUR PLACE IS THERE, AS MINE IS HERE.
LIVE LONG, MY OLD FRIEND...
...AND PROSPER.

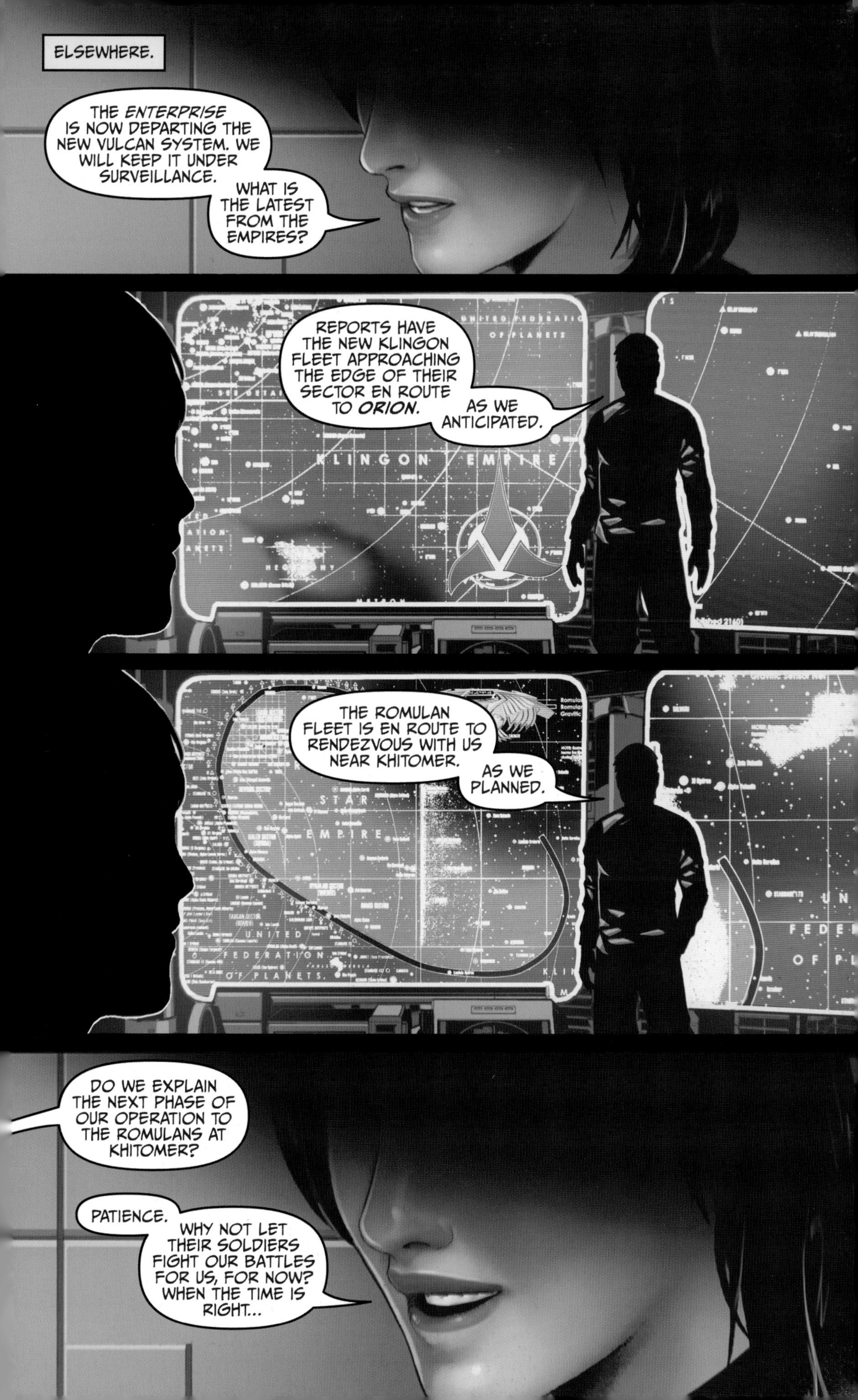
ELSEWHERE.
THE ENTERPRISE IS NOW DEPARTING THE NEW VULCAN SYSTEM. WE WILL KEEP IT UNDER SURVEILLANCE.
WHAT IS THE LATEST FROM THE EMPIRES?
REPORTS HAVE THE NEW KLINGON FLEET APPROACHING THE EDGE OF THEIR SECTOR EN ROUTE TO ORION.
AS WE ANTICIPATED.
KLINGON EMPIRE
THE ROMULAN FLEET IS EN ROUTE TO RENDEZVOUS WITH US NEAR KHITOMER.
AS WE PLANNED.
STAR EMPIRE
UNITED FEDERATION OF PLANETS
DO WE EXPLAIN THE NEXT PHASE OF OUR OPERATION TO THE ROMULANS AT KHITOMER?
PATIENCE.
WHY NOT LET THEIR SOLDIERS FIGHT OUR BATTLES FOR US, FOR NOW? WHEN THE TIME IS RIGHT...

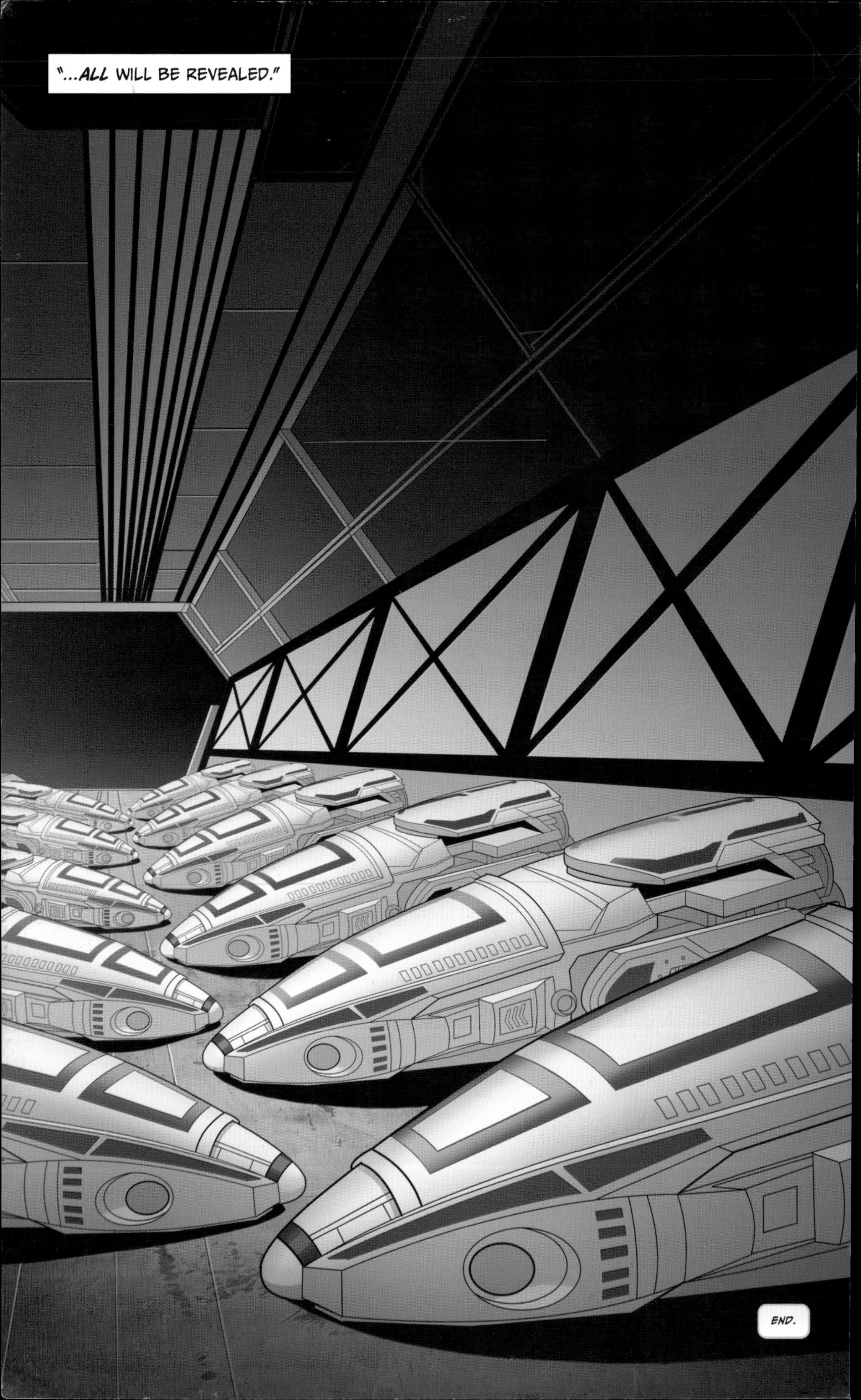
"...ALL WILL BE REVEALED."
END.

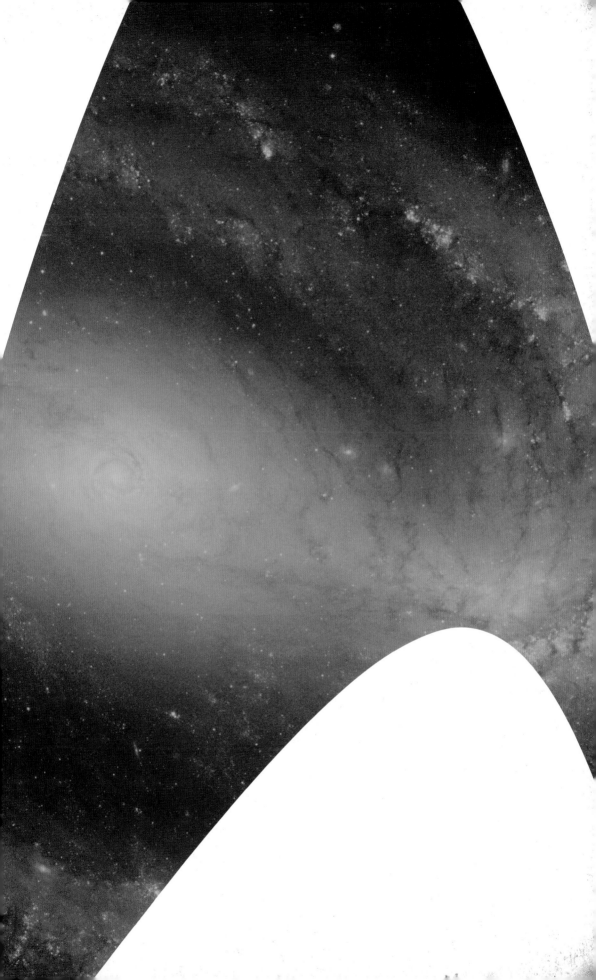

PREDATORY

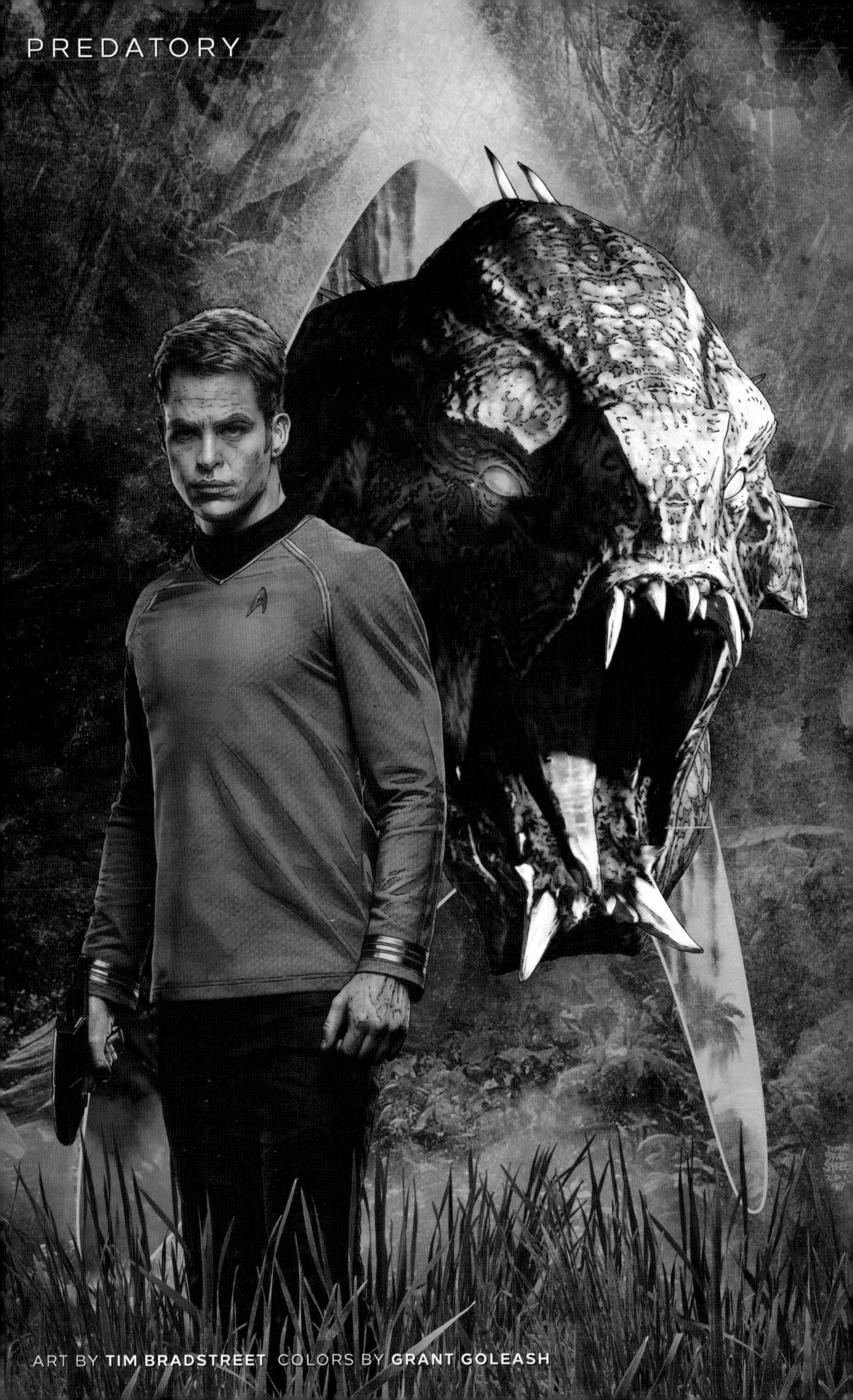

ART BY **TIM BRADSTREET** COLORS BY **GRANT GOLEASH**

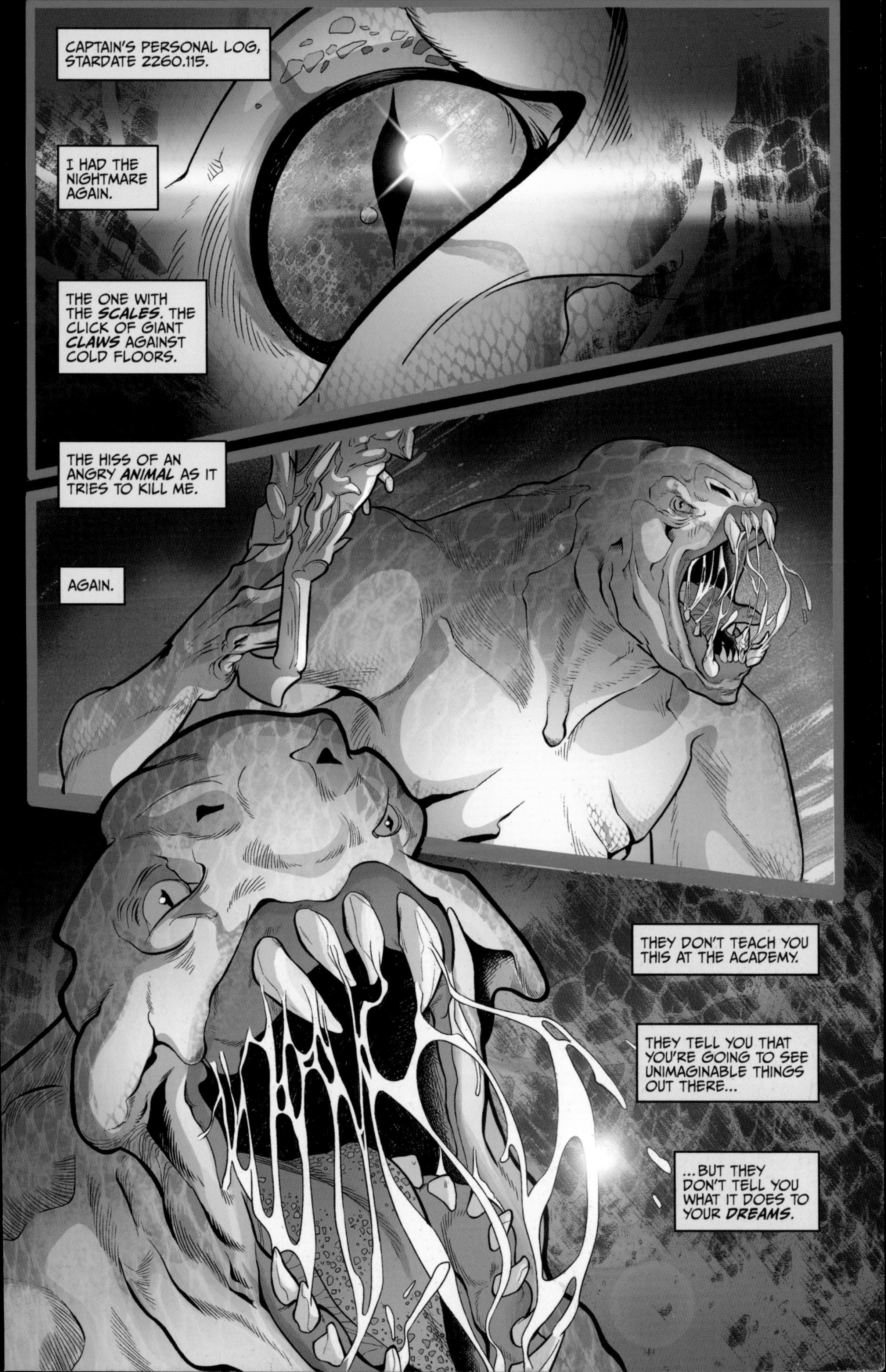
CAPTAIN'S PERSONAL LOG, STARDATE 2260.115.
I HAD THE NIGHTMARE AGAIN.
THE ONE WITH THE *SCALES*. THE CLICK OF GIANT *CLAWS* AGAINST COLD FLOORS.
THE HISS OF AN ANGRY *ANIMAL* AS IT TRIES TO KILL ME.
AGAIN.
THEY DON'T TEACH YOU THIS AT THE ACADEMY.
THEY TELL YOU THAT YOU'RE GOING TO SEE UNIMAGINABLE THINGS OUT THERE...
...BUT THEY DON'T TELL YOU WHAT IT DOES TO YOUR *DREAMS*.

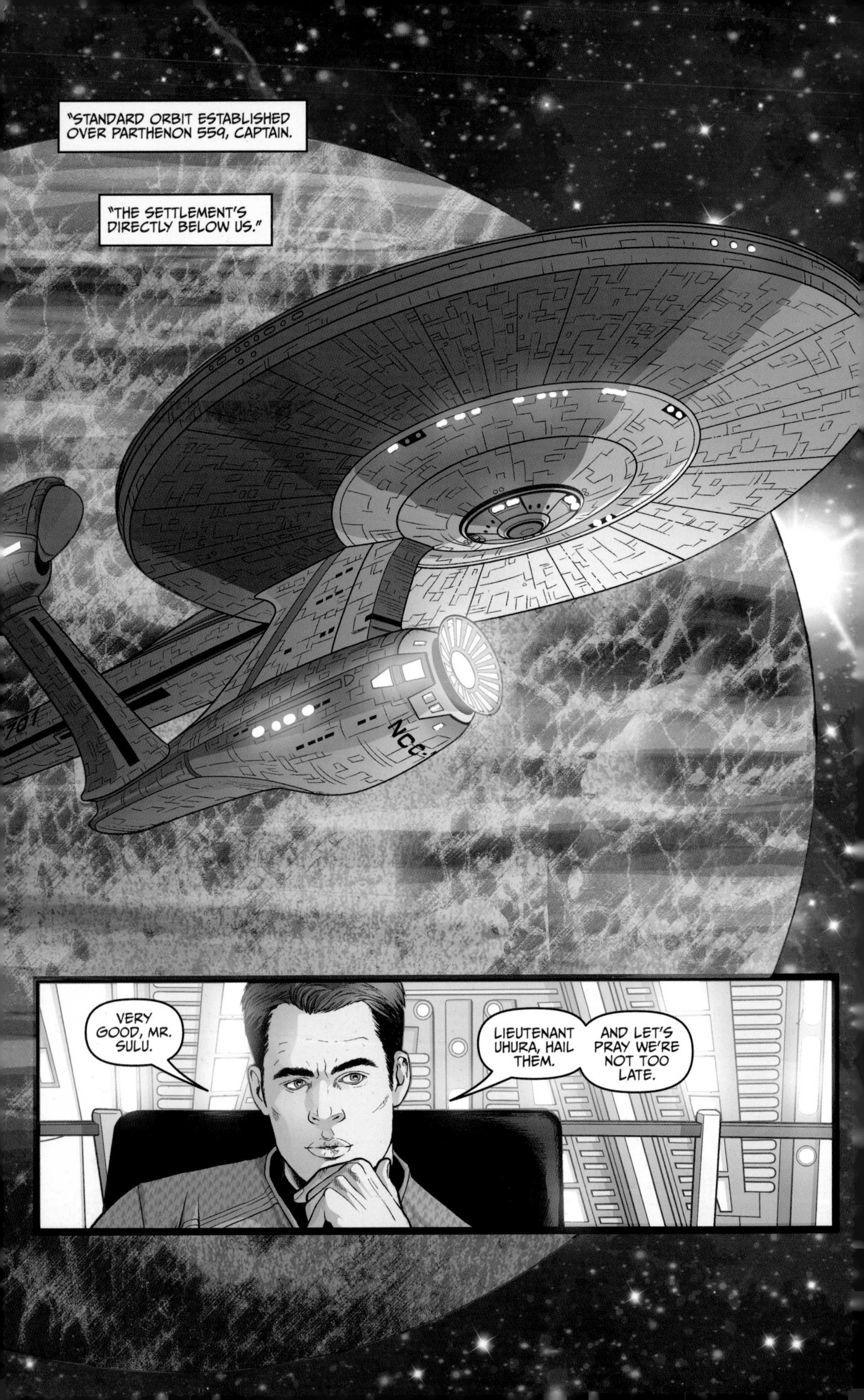
"STANDARD ORBIT ESTABLISHED OVER PARTHENON 559, CAPTAIN.
"THE SETTLEMENT'S DIRECTLY BELOW US."
NCC-
VERY GOOD, MR. SULU.
LIEUTENANT UHURA, HAIL THEM.
AND LET'S PRAY WE'RE NOT TOO LATE.

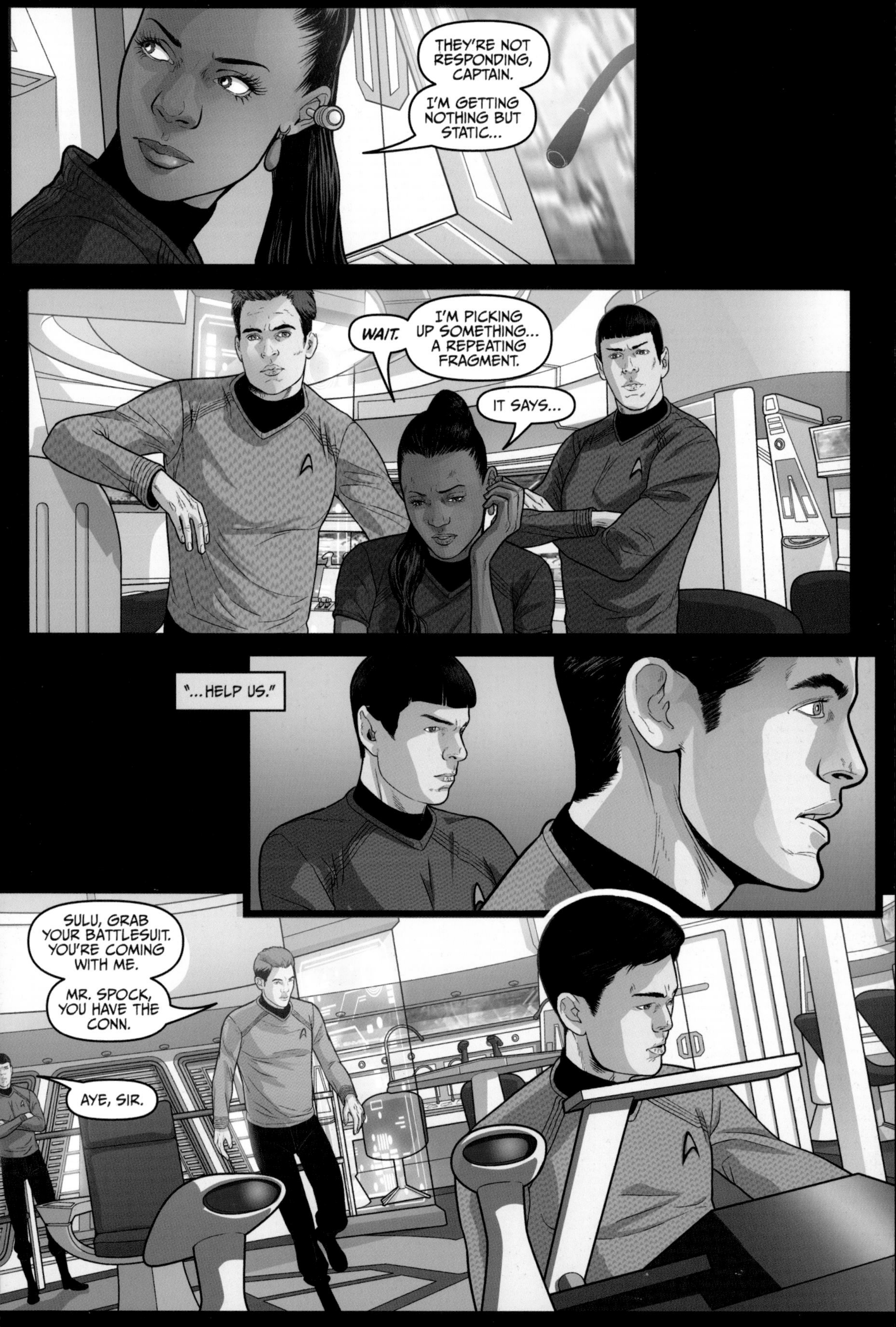
THEY'RE NOT RESPONDING, CAPTAIN.
I'M GETTING NOTHING BUT STATIC...
WAIT.
I'M PICKING UP SOMETHING... A REPEATING FRAGMENT.
IT SAYS...
"...HELP US."
SULU, GRAB YOUR BATTLESUIT. YOU'RE COMING WITH ME.
MR. SPOCK, YOU HAVE THE CONN.
AYE, SIR.

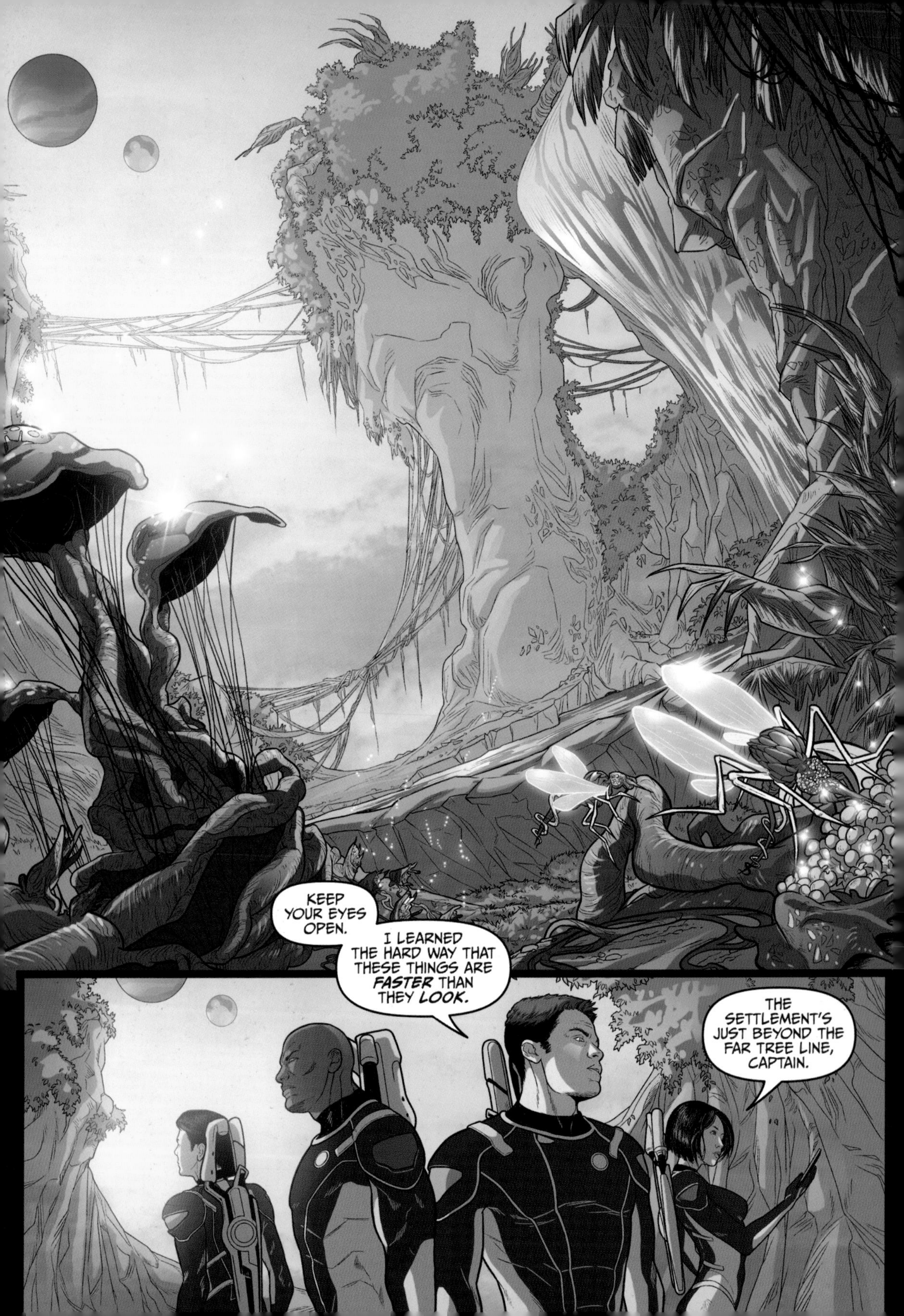
KEEP YOUR EYES OPEN.
I LEARNED THE HARD WAY THAT THESE THINGS ARE *FASTER* THAN THEY *LOOK.*
THE SETTLEMENT'S JUST BEYOND THE FAR TREE LINE, CAPTAIN.

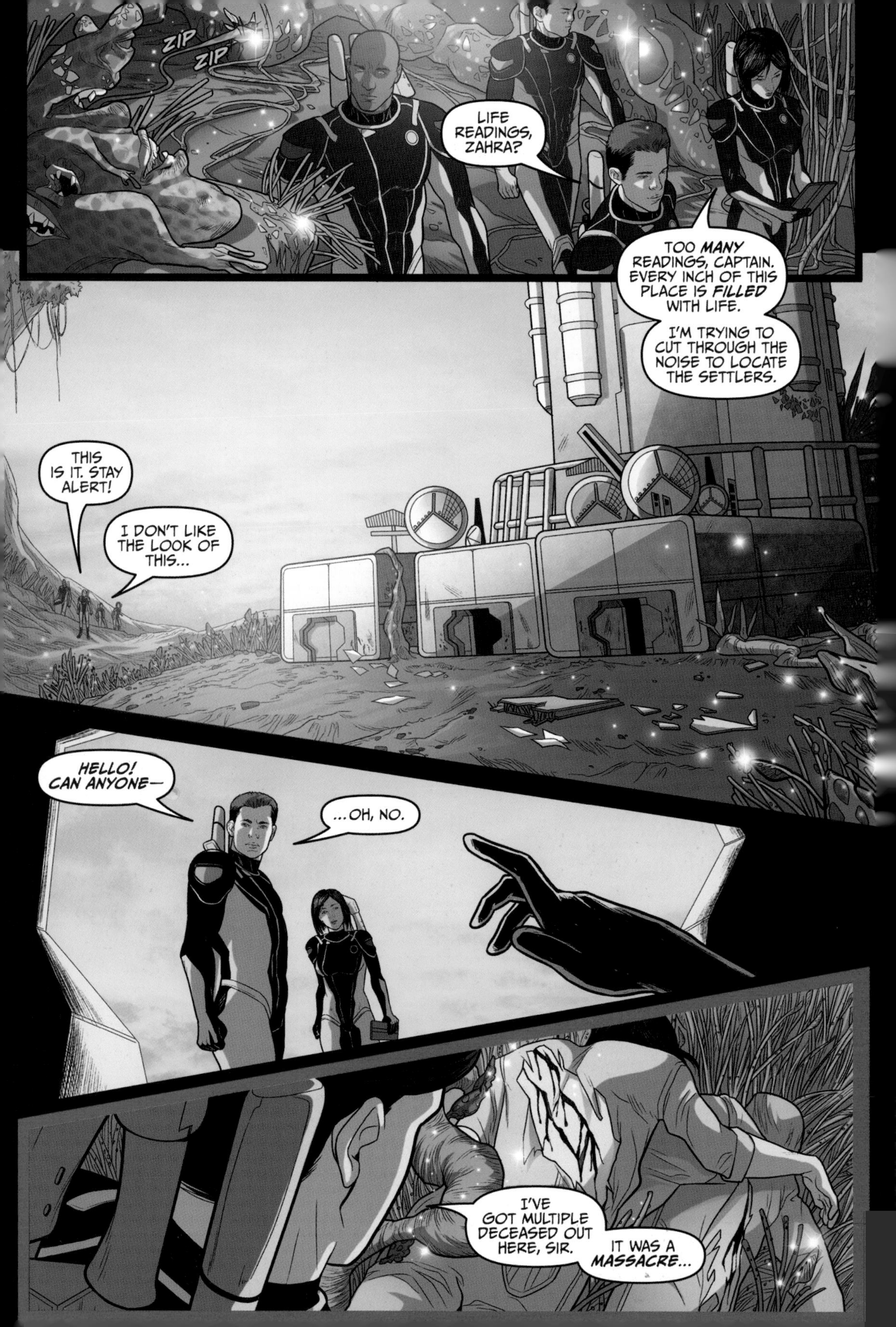
ZIP
ZIP
LIFE READINGS, ZAHRA?
TOO MANY READINGS, CAPTAIN. EVERY INCH OF THIS PLACE IS FILLED WITH LIFE.
I'M TRYING TO CUT THROUGH THE NOISE TO LOCATE THE SETTLERS.
THIS IS IT. STAY ALERT!
I DON'T LIKE THE LOOK OF THIS...
HELLO! CAN ANYONE—
...OH, NO.
I'VE GOT MULTIPLE DECEASED OUT HERE, SIR.
IT WAS A MASSACRE...

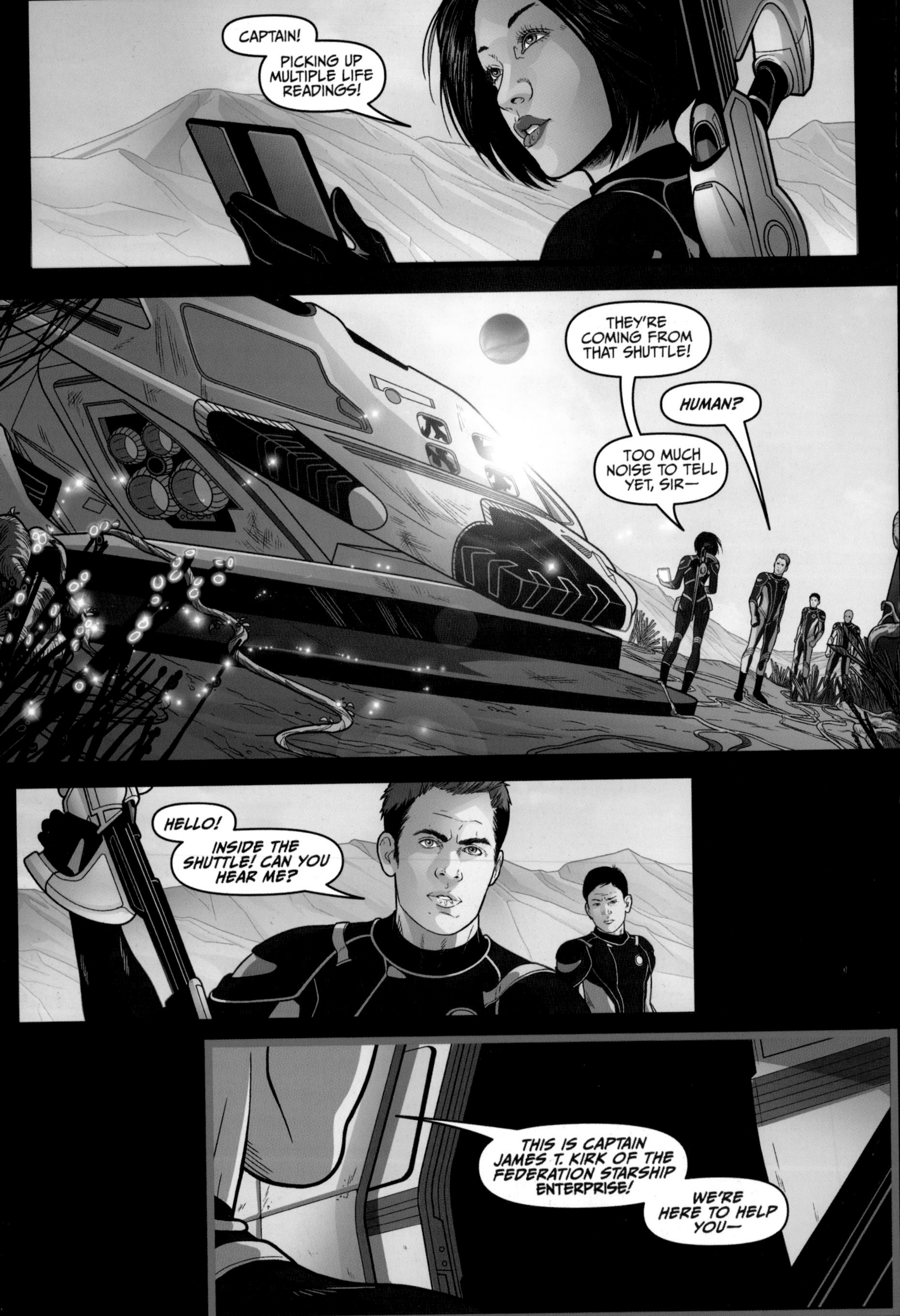
CAPTAIN!
PICKING UP MULTIPLE LIFE READINGS!
THEY'RE COMING FROM THAT SHUTTLE!
HUMAN?
TOO MUCH NOISE TO TELL YET, SIR—
HELLO!
INSIDE THE SHUTTLE! CAN YOU HEAR ME?
THIS IS CAPTAIN JAMES T. KIRK OF THE FEDERATION STARSHIP ENTERPRISE!
WE'RE HERE TO HELP YOU—

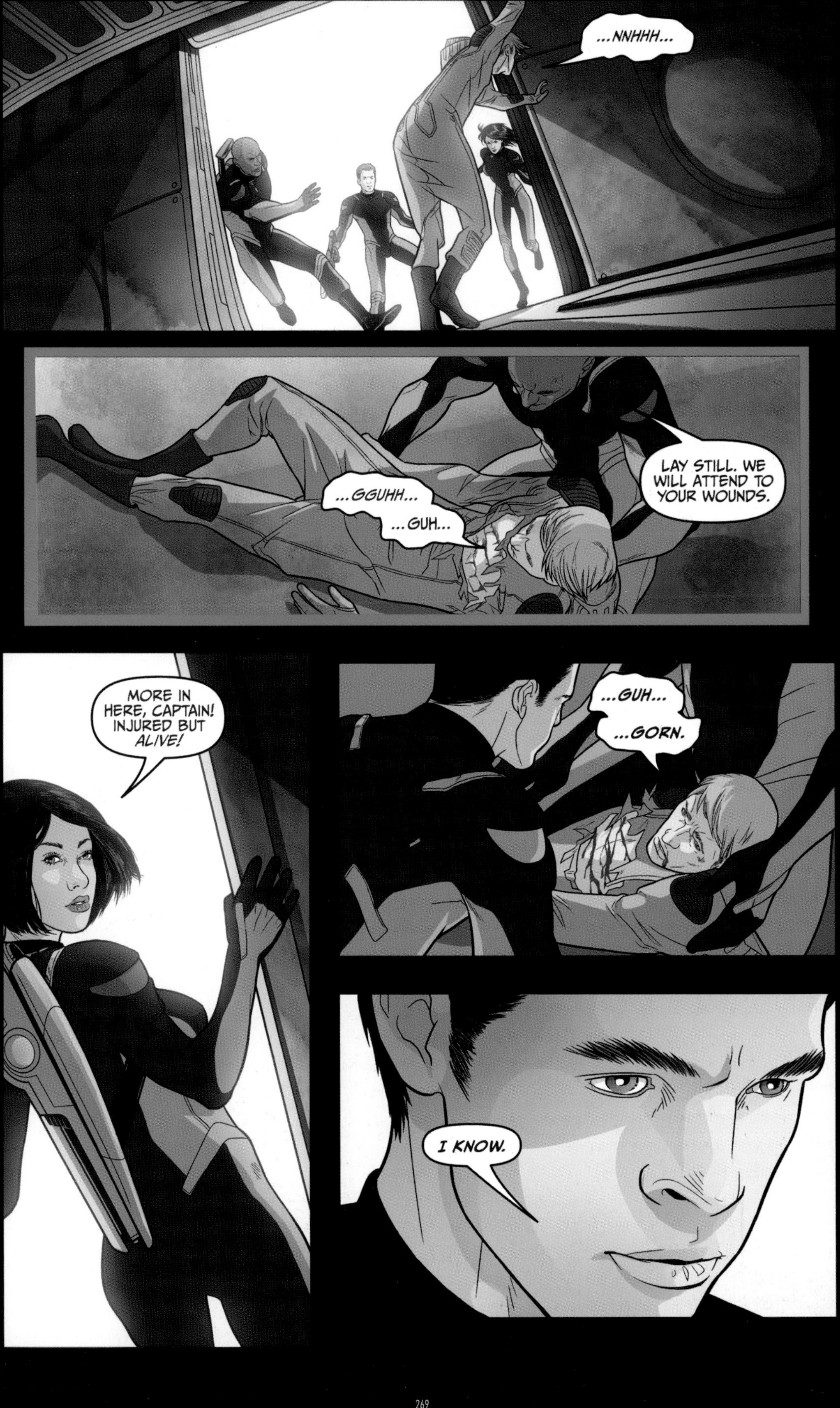
...NNHHH...
LAY STILL. WE WILL ATTEND TO YOUR WOUNDS.
...GGUHH...
...GUH...
MORE IN HERE, CAPTAIN! INJURED BUT ALIVE!
...GUH...
...GORN.
I KNOW.

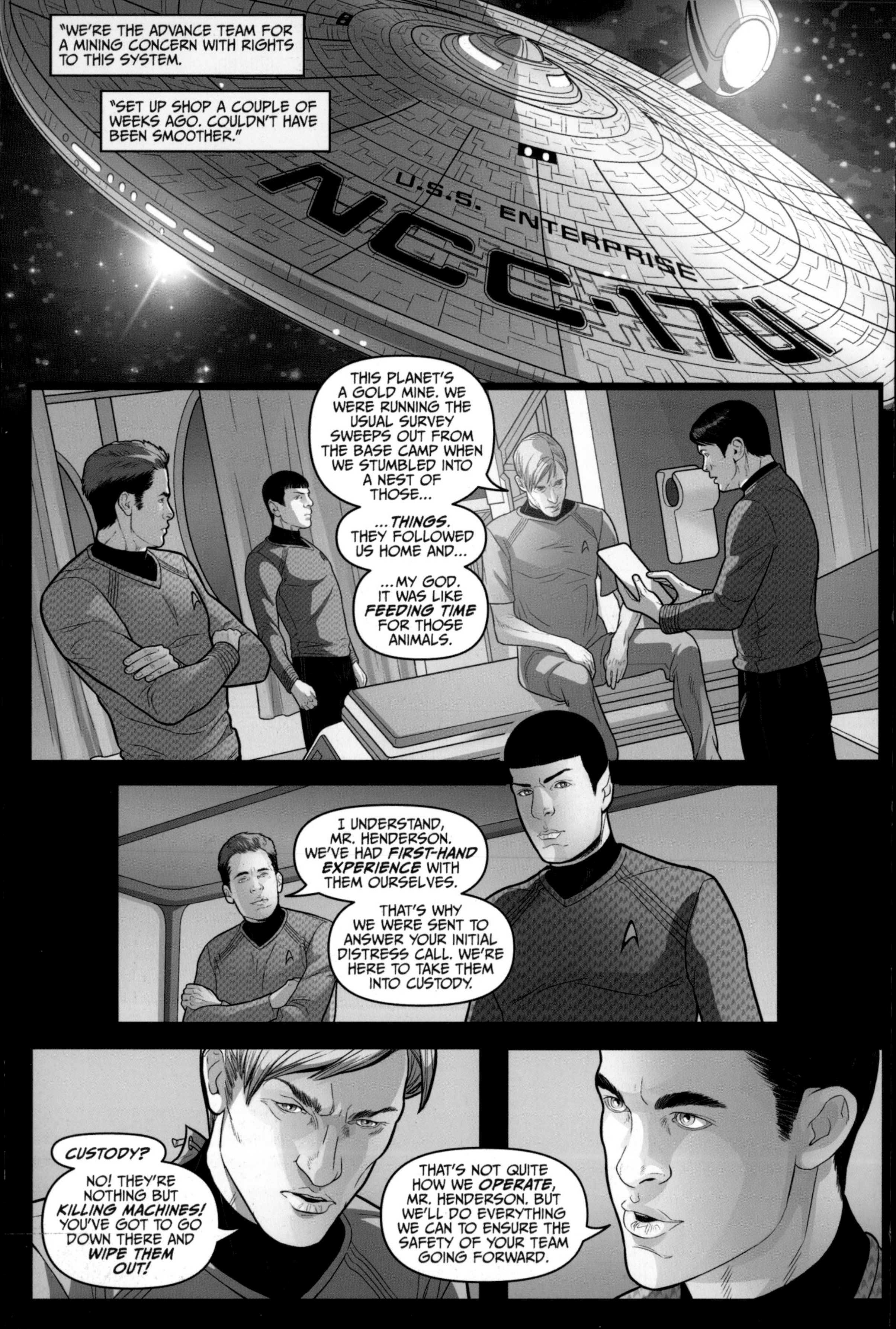
"WE'RE THE ADVANCE TEAM FOR A MINING CONCERN WITH RIGHTS TO THIS SYSTEM.
"SET UP SHOP A COUPLE OF WEEKS AGO. COULDN'T HAVE BEEN SMOOTHER."
U.S.S. ENTERPRISE
NCC-1701
THIS PLANET'S A GOLD MINE. WE WERE RUNNING THE USUAL SURVEY SWEEPS OUT FROM THE BASE CAMP WHEN WE STUMBLED INTO A NEST OF THOSE...
...THINGS. THEY FOLLOWED US HOME AND...
...MY GOD. IT WAS LIKE FEEDING TIME FOR THOSE ANIMALS.
I UNDERSTAND, MR. HENDERSON. WE'VE HAD FIRST-HAND EXPERIENCE WITH THEM OURSELVES.
THAT'S WHY WE WERE SENT TO ANSWER YOUR INITIAL DISTRESS CALL. WE'RE HERE TO TAKE THEM INTO CUSTODY.
CUSTODY?
NO! THEY'RE NOTHING BUT KILLING MACHINES! YOU'VE GOT TO GO DOWN THERE AND WIPE THEM OUT!
THAT'S NOT QUITE HOW WE OPERATE, MR. HENDERSON. BUT WE'LL DO EVERYTHING WE CAN TO ENSURE THE SAFETY OF YOUR TEAM GOING FORWARD.

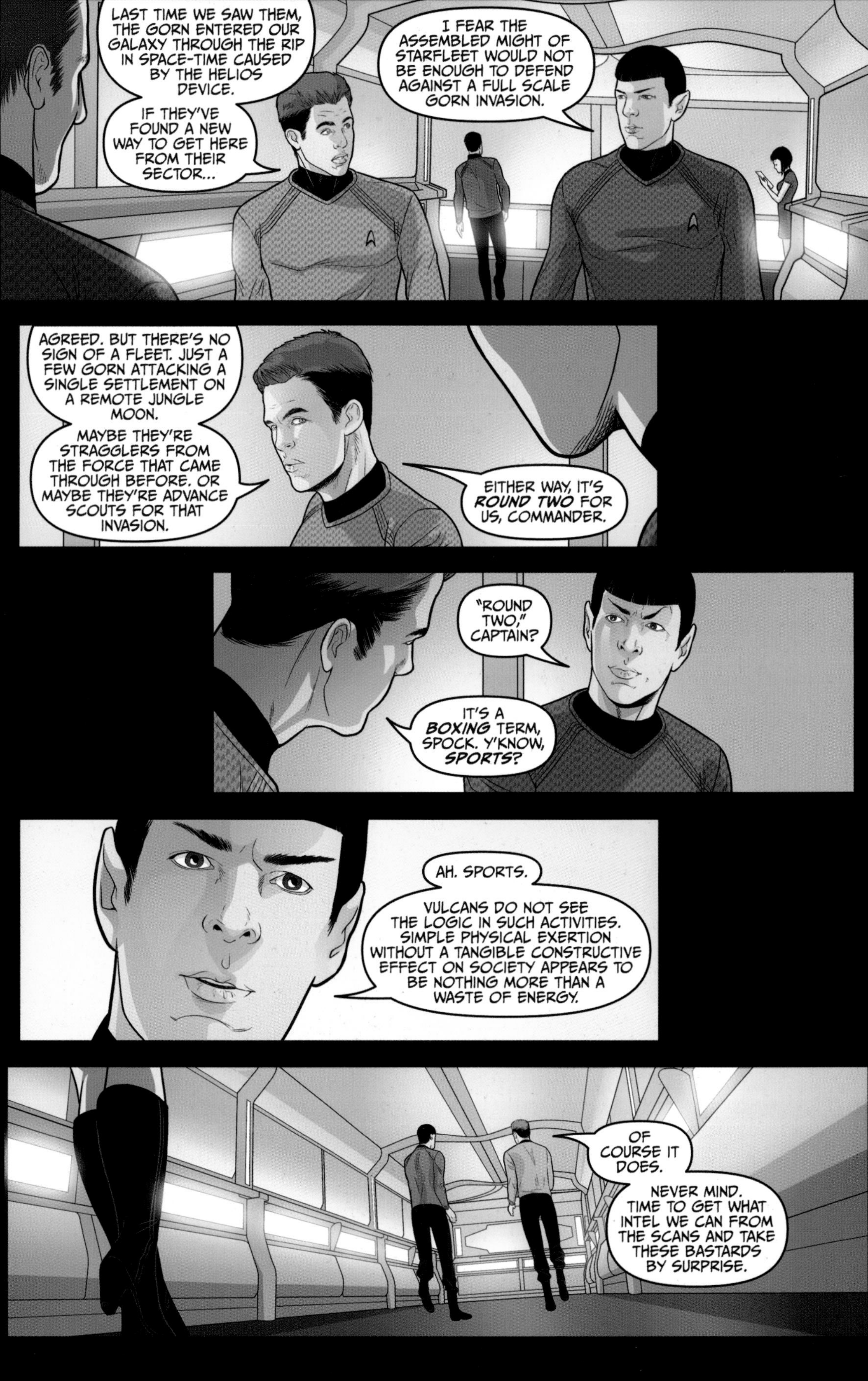
LAST TIME WE SAW THEM, THE GORN ENTERED OUR GALAXY THROUGH THE RIP IN SPACE-TIME CAUSED BY THE HELIOS DEVICE.
IF THEY'VE FOUND A NEW WAY TO GET HERE FROM THEIR SECTOR...
I FEAR THE ASSEMBLED MIGHT OF STARFLEET WOULD NOT BE ENOUGH TO DEFEND AGAINST A FULL SCALE GORN INVASION.
AGREED. BUT THERE'S NO SIGN OF A FLEET. JUST A FEW GORN ATTACKING A SINGLE SETTLEMENT ON A REMOTE JUNGLE MOON.
MAYBE THEY'RE STRAGGLERS FROM THE FORCE THAT CAME THROUGH BEFORE. OR MAYBE THEY'RE ADVANCE SCOUTS FOR THAT INVASION.
EITHER WAY, IT'S *ROUND TWO* FOR US, COMMANDER.
"ROUND TWO," CAPTAIN?
IT'S A *BOXING* TERM, SPOCK. Y'KNOW, *SPORTS?*
AH. SPORTS.
VULCANS DO NOT SEE THE LOGIC IN SUCH ACTIVITIES. SIMPLE PHYSICAL EXERTION WITHOUT A TANGIBLE CONSTRUCTIVE EFFECT ON SOCIETY APPEARS TO BE NOTHING MORE THAN A WASTE OF ENERGY.
OF COURSE IT DOES.
NEVER MIND. TIME TO GET WHAT INTEL WE CAN FROM THE SCANS AND TAKE THESE BASTARDS BY SURPRISE.

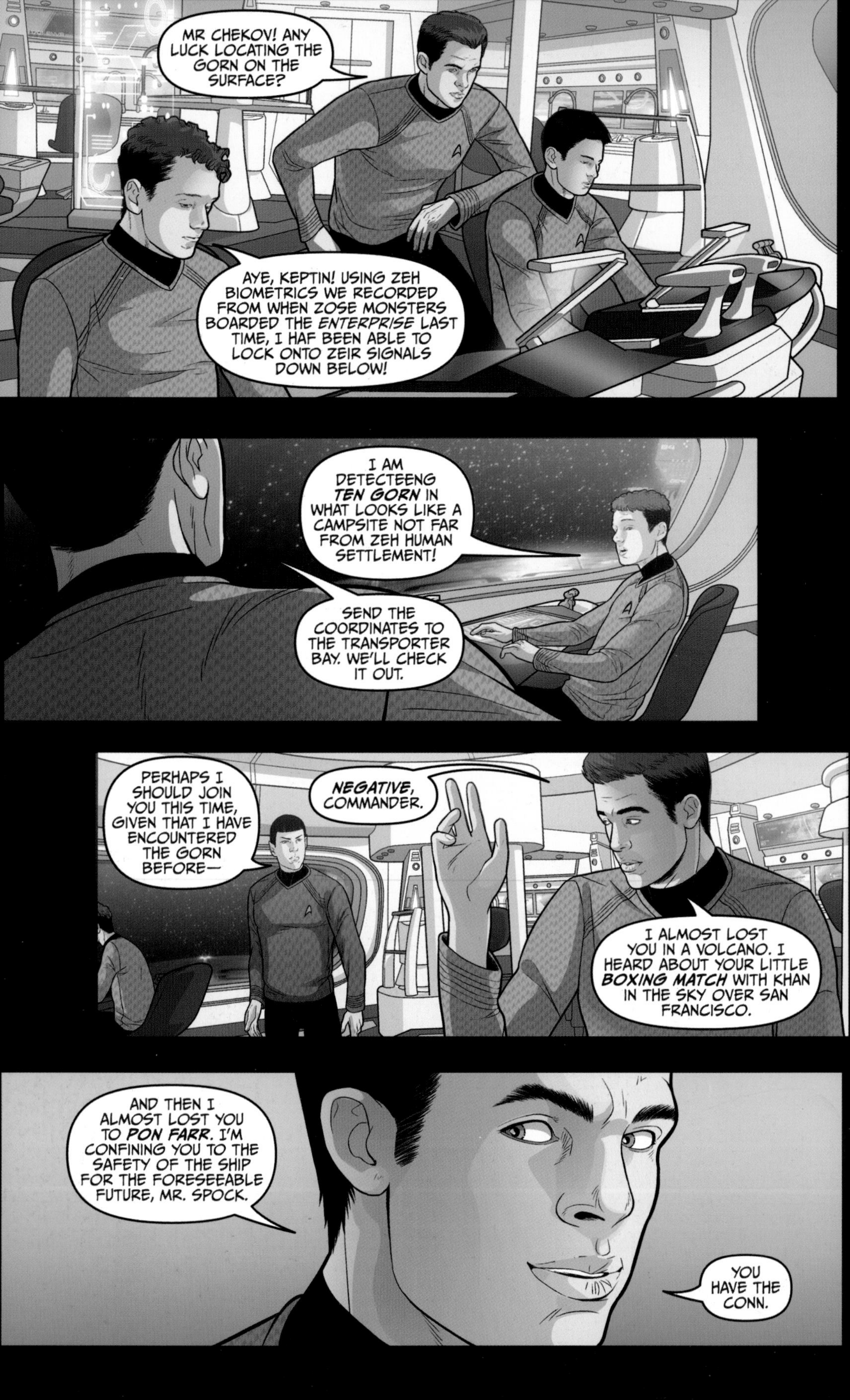

MR CHEKOV! ANY LUCK LOCATING THE GORN ON THE SURFACE?
AYE, KEPTIN! USING ZEH BIOMETRICS WE RECORDED FROM WHEN ZOSE MONSTERS BOARDED THE *ENTERPRISE* LAST TIME, I HAF BEEN ABLE TO LOCK ONTO ZEIR SIGNALS DOWN BELOW!
I AM DETECTEENG ***TEN GORN*** IN WHAT LOOKS LIKE A CAMPSITE NOT FAR FROM ZEH HUMAN SETTLEMENT!
SEND THE COORDINATES TO THE TRANSPORTER BAY. WE'LL CHECK IT OUT.
PERHAPS I SHOULD JOIN YOU THIS TIME, GIVEN THAT I HAVE ENCOUNTERED THE GORN BEFORE—
NEGATIVE, COMMANDER.
I ALMOST LOST YOU IN A VOLCANO. I HEARD ABOUT YOUR LITTLE ***BOXING MATCH*** WITH KHAN IN THE SKY OVER SAN FRANCISCO.
AND THEN I ALMOST LOST YOU TO ***PON FARR***. I'M CONFINING YOU TO THE SAFETY OF THE SHIP FOR THE FORESEEABLE FUTURE, MR. SPOCK.
YOU HAVE THE CONN.

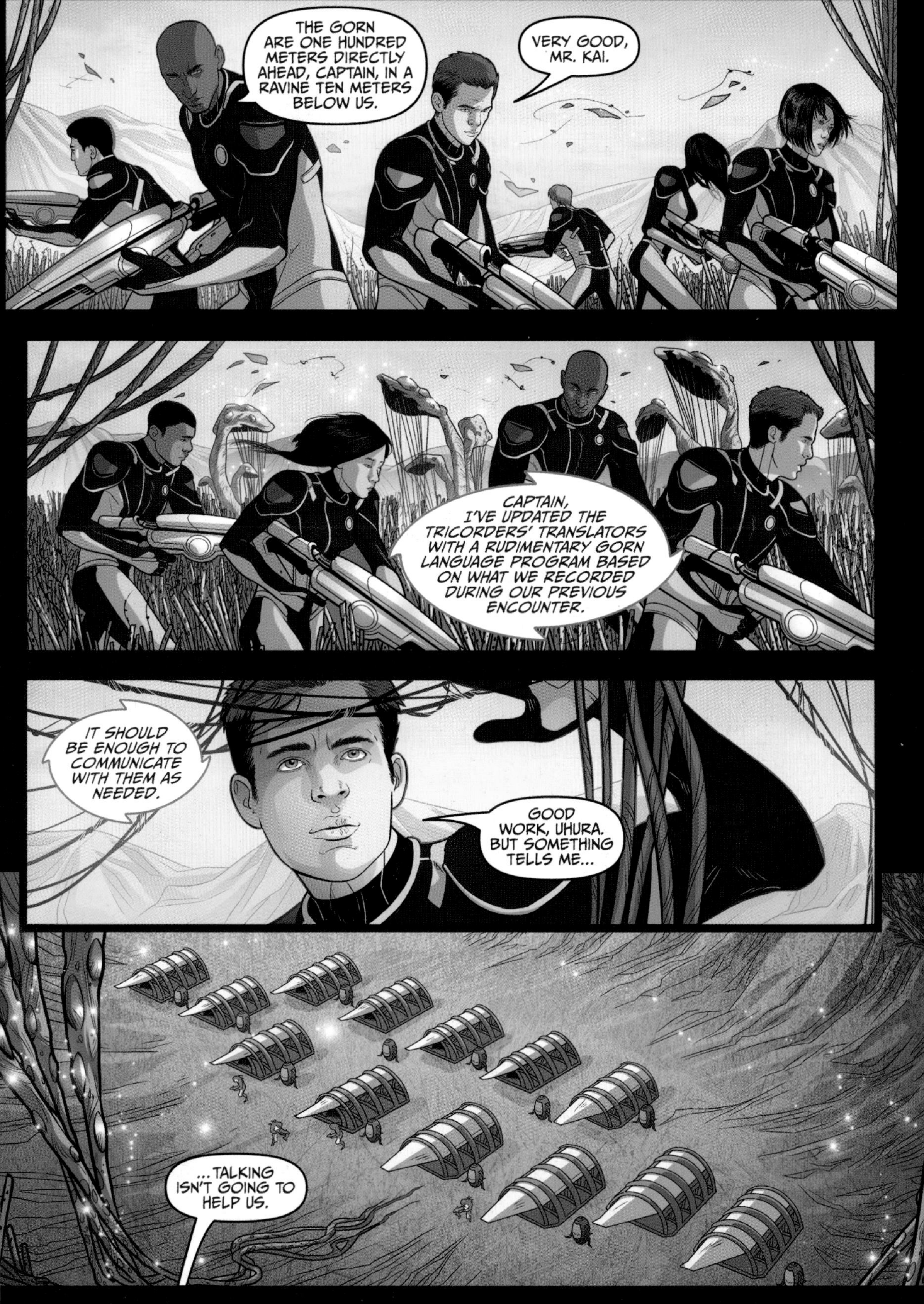
THE GORN ARE ONE HUNDRED METERS DIRECTLY AHEAD, CAPTAIN, IN A RAVINE TEN METERS BELOW US.
VERY GOOD, MR. KAI.
CAPTAIN, I'VE UPDATED THE TRICORDERS' TRANSLATORS WITH A RUDIMENTARY GORN LANGUAGE PROGRAM BASED ON WHAT WE RECORDED DURING OUR PREVIOUS ENCOUNTER.
IT SHOULD BE ENOUGH TO COMMUNICATE WITH THEM AS NEEDED.
GOOD WORK, UHURA. BUT SOMETHING TELLS ME...
...TALKING ISN'T GOING TO HELP US.

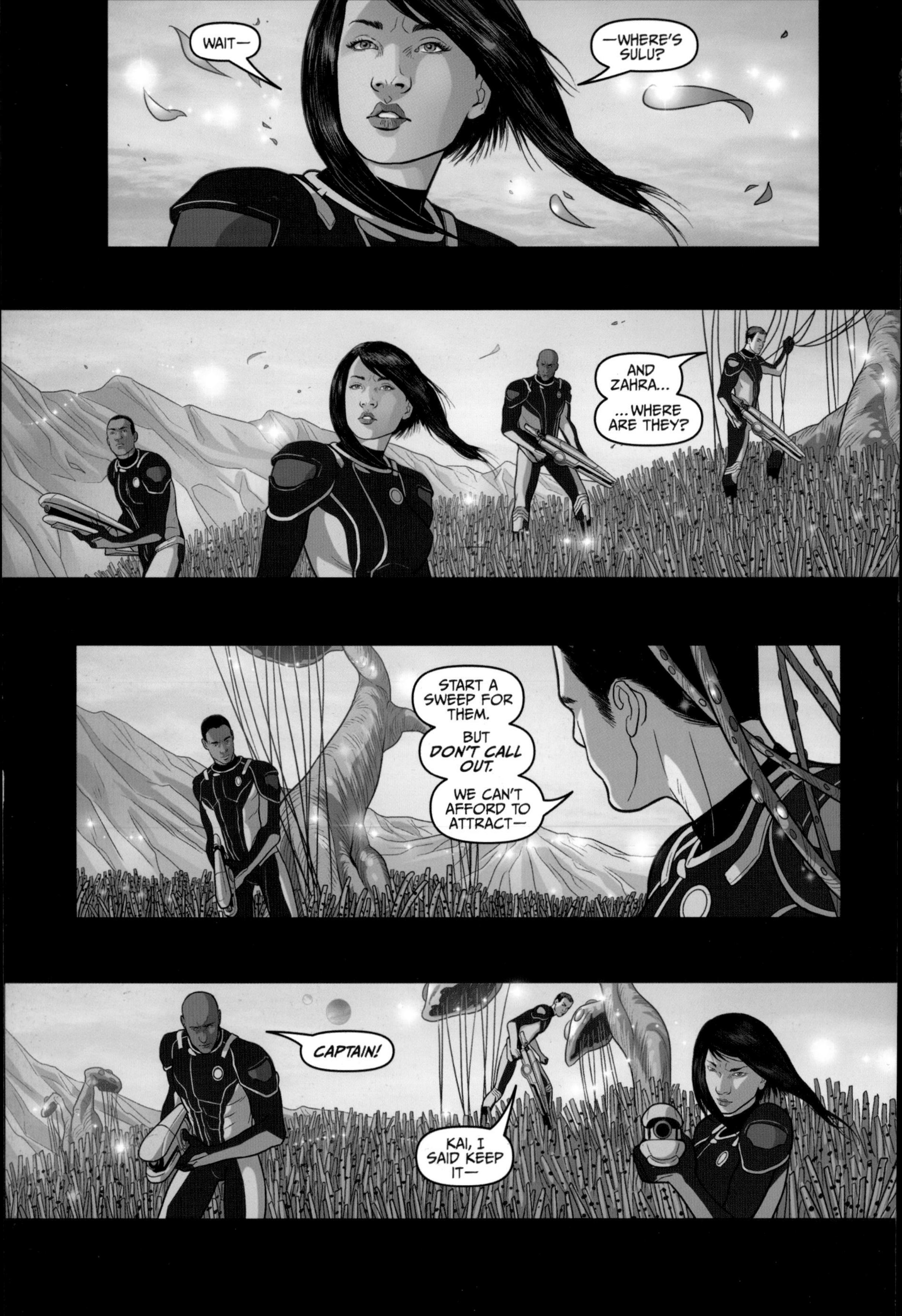
WAIT—
—WHERE'S SULU?
AND ZAHRA...
...WHERE ARE THEY?
START A SWEEP FOR THEM.
BUT *DON'T CALL OUT.*
WE CAN'T AFFORD TO ATTRACT—
CAPTAIN!
KAI, I SAID KEEP IT—

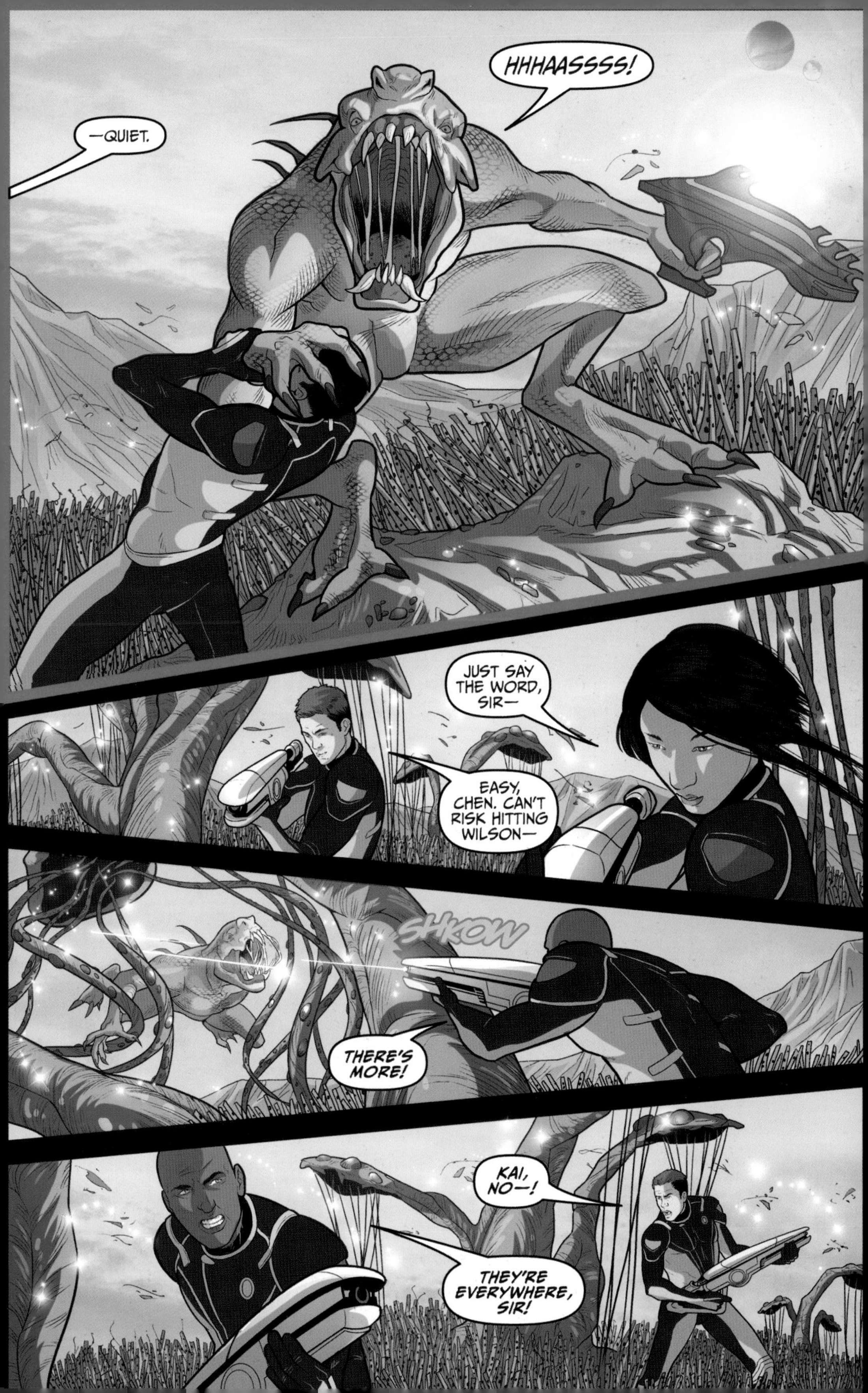
HHHAASSSS!
—QUIET.
JUST SAY THE WORD, SIR—
EASY, CHEN. CAN'T RISK HITTING WILSON—
SHKOW
THERE'S MORE!
KAI, NO—!
THEY'RE EVERYWHERE, SIR!

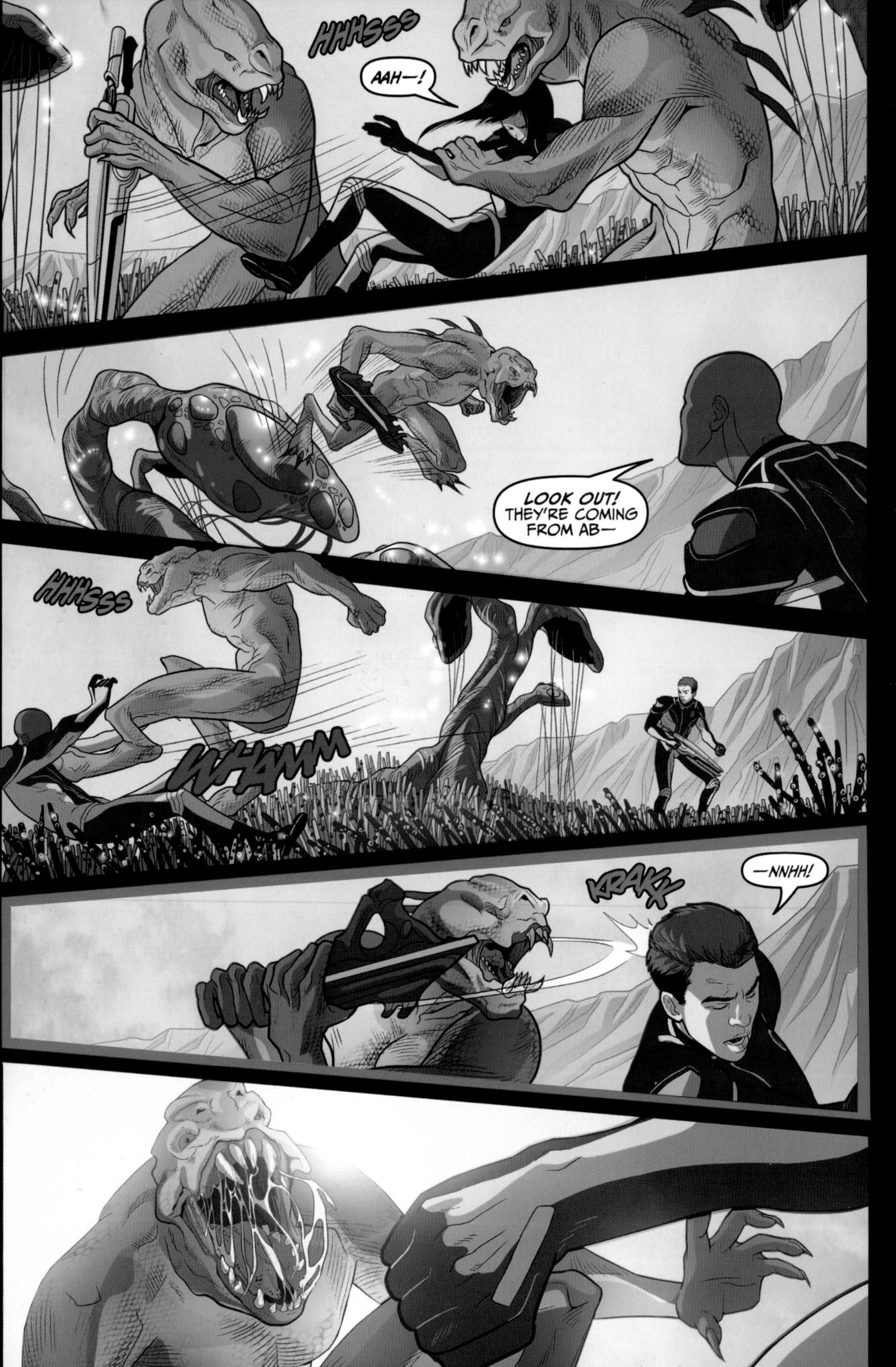
HHHSSS
AAH—!
LOOK OUT! THEY'RE COMING FROM AB—
HHHSSS
WHAMM
KRAKK
—NNHH!

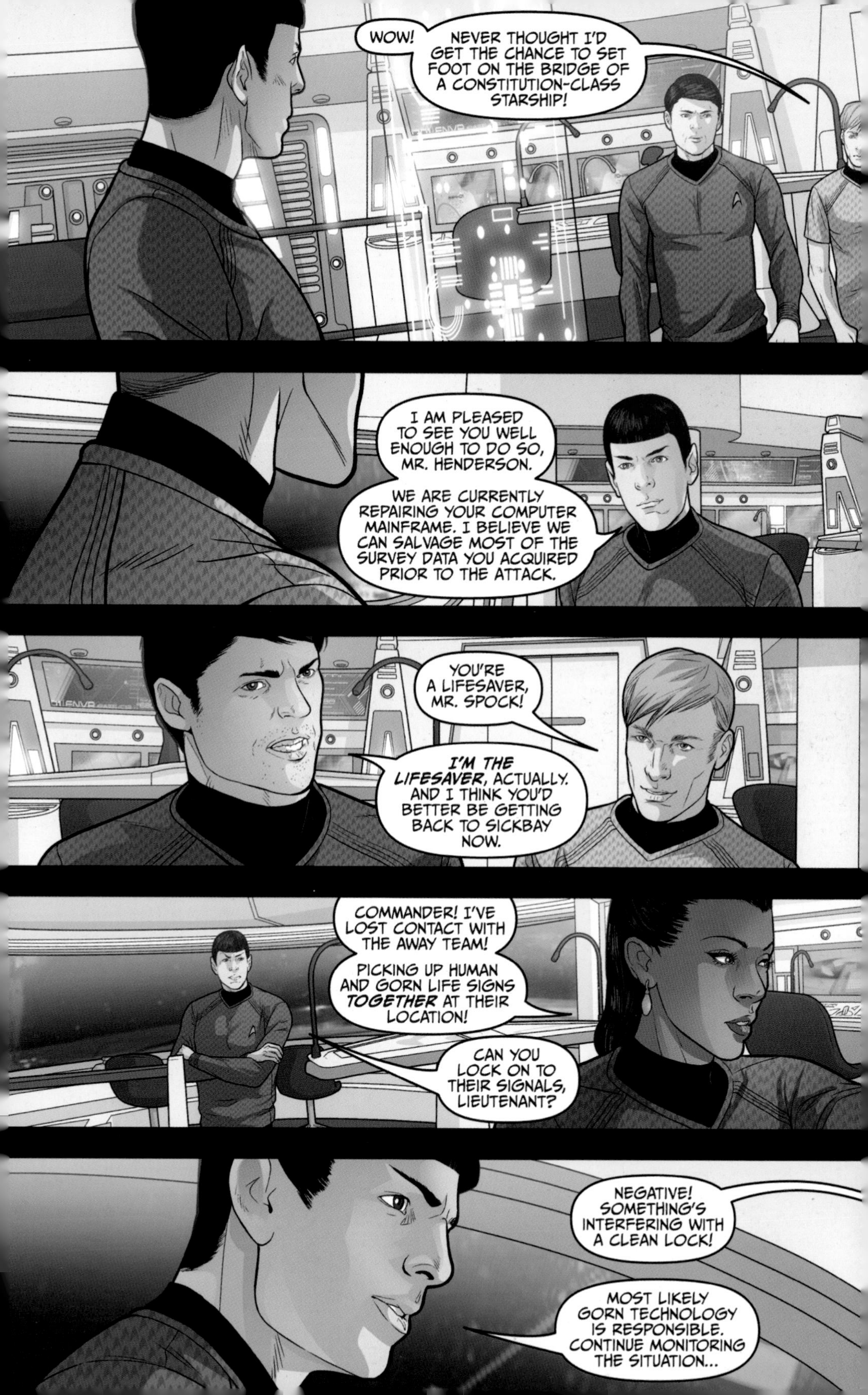
WOW!
NEVER THOUGHT I'D GET THE CHANCE TO SET FOOT ON THE BRIDGE OF A CONSTITUTION-CLASS STARSHIP!
I AM PLEASED TO SEE YOU WELL ENOUGH TO DO SO, MR. HENDERSON.
WE ARE CURRENTLY REPAIRING YOUR COMPUTER MAINFRAME. I BELIEVE WE CAN SALVAGE MOST OF THE SURVEY DATA YOU ACQUIRED PRIOR TO THE ATTACK.
YOU'RE A LIFESAVER, MR. SPOCK!
I'M THE LIFESAVER, ACTUALLY. AND I THINK YOU'D BETTER BE GETTING BACK TO SICKBAY NOW.
COMMANDER! I'VE LOST CONTACT WITH THE AWAY TEAM!
PICKING UP HUMAN AND GORN LIFE SIGNS *TOGETHER* AT THEIR LOCATION!
CAN YOU LOCK ON TO THEIR SIGNALS, LIEUTENANT?
NEGATIVE! SOMETHING'S INTERFERING WITH A CLEAN LOCK!
MOST LIKELY GORN TECHNOLOGY IS RESPONSIBLE. CONTINUE MONITORING THE SITUATION...

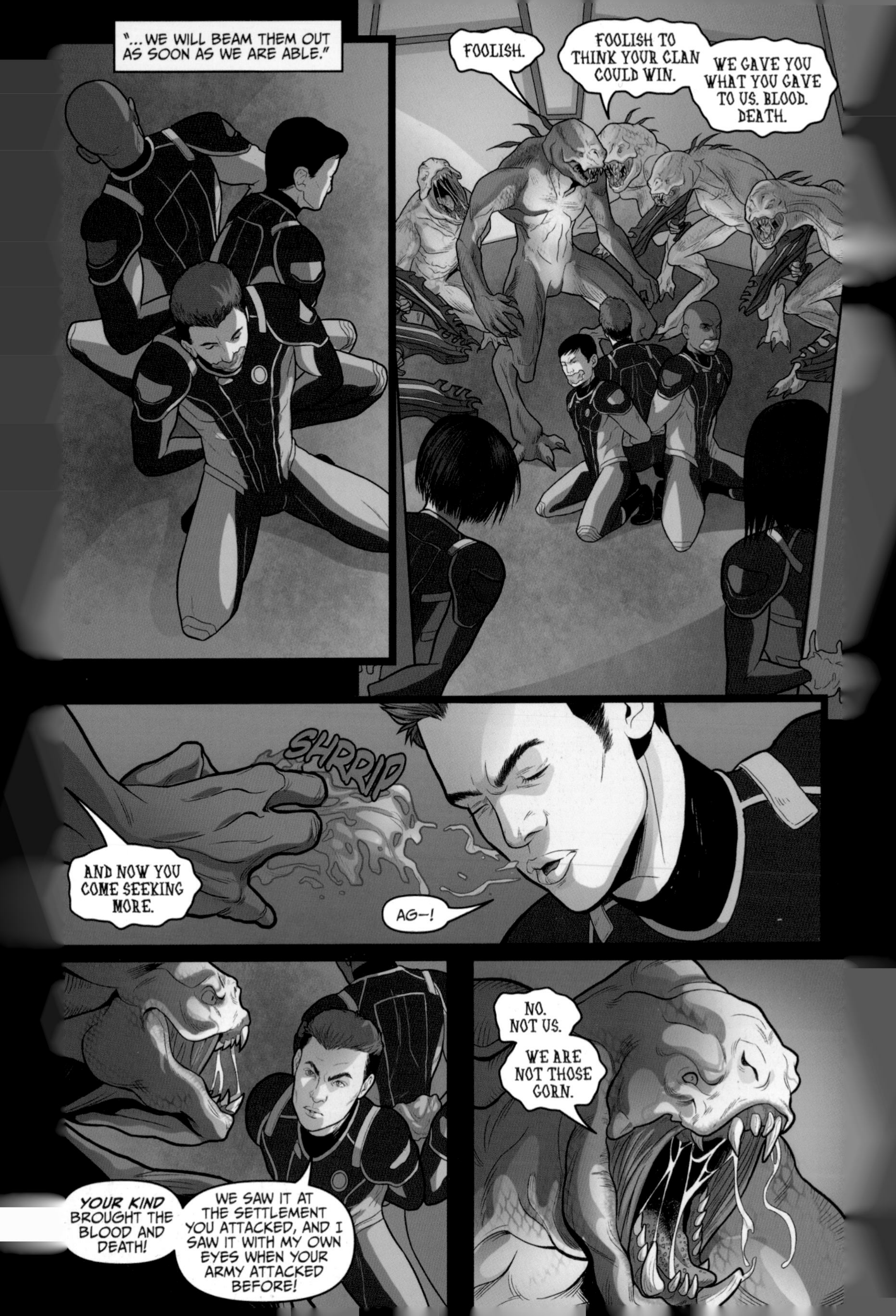
"...WE WILL BEAM THEM OUT AS SOON AS WE ARE ABLE."
FOOLISH.
FOOLISH TO THINK YOUR CLAN COULD WIN.
WE GAVE YOU WHAT YOU GAVE TO US. BLOOD. DEATH.
SHRRIP
AND NOW YOU COME SEEKING MORE.
AG—!
YOUR KIND BROUGHT THE BLOOD AND DEATH!
WE SAW IT AT THE SETTLEMENT YOU ATTACKED, AND I SAW IT WITH MY OWN EYES WHEN YOUR ARMY ATTACKED BEFORE!
NO. NOT US.
WE ARE NOT THOSE GORN.

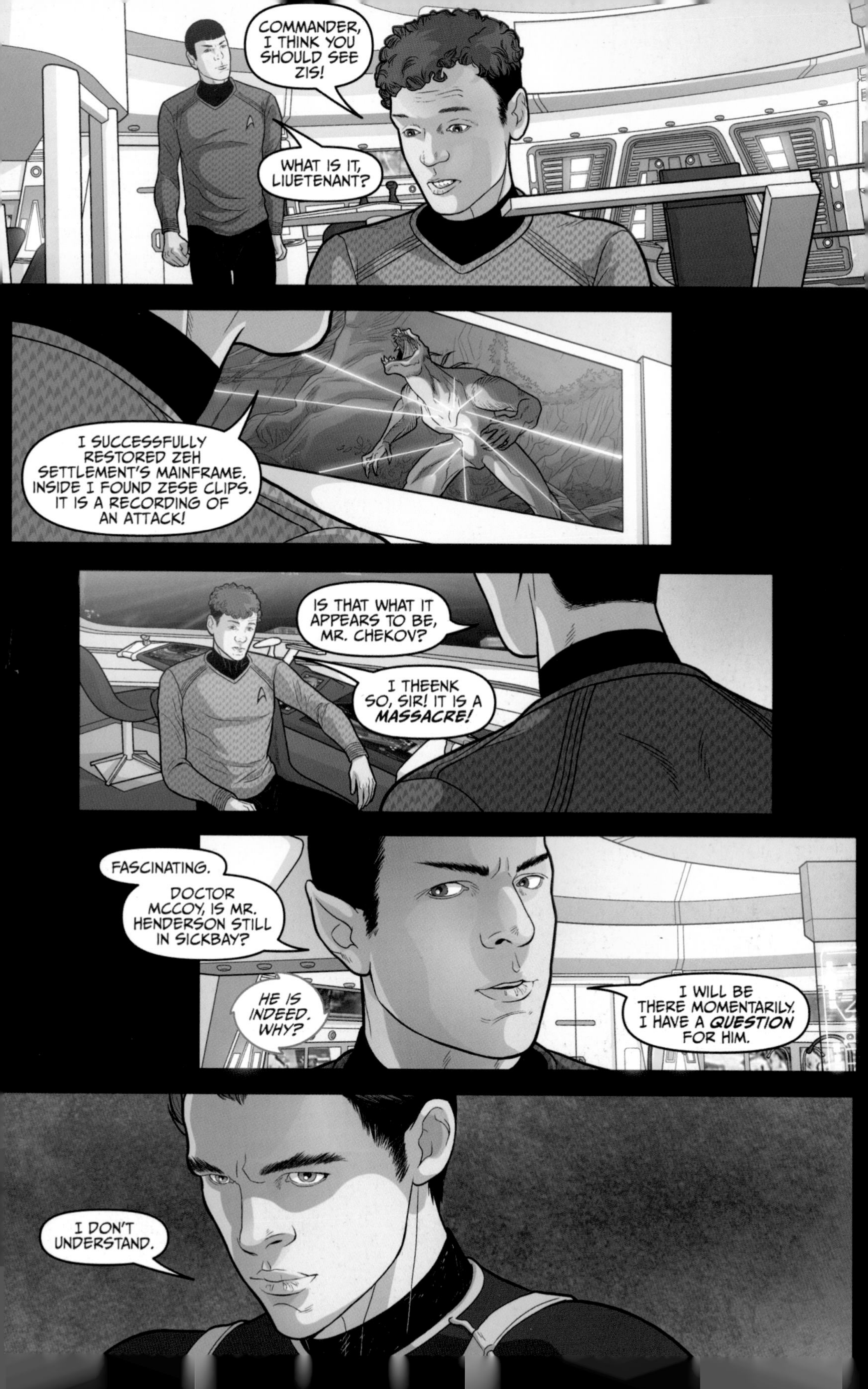
COMMANDER, I THINK YOU SHOULD SEE ZIS!
WHAT IS IT, LIUETENANT?
I SUCCESSFULLY RESTORED ZEH SETTLEMENT'S MAINFRAME. INSIDE I FOUND ZESE CLIPS. IT IS A RECORDING OF AN ATTACK!
IS THAT WHAT IT APPEARS TO BE, MR. CHEKOV?
I THEENK SO, SIR! IT IS A *MASSACRE!*
FASCINATING.
DOCTOR MCCOY, IS MR. HENDERSON STILL IN SICKBAY?
HE IS INDEED. WHY?
I WILL BE THERE MOMENTARILY. I HAVE A *QUESTION* FOR HIM.
I DON'T UNDERSTAND.

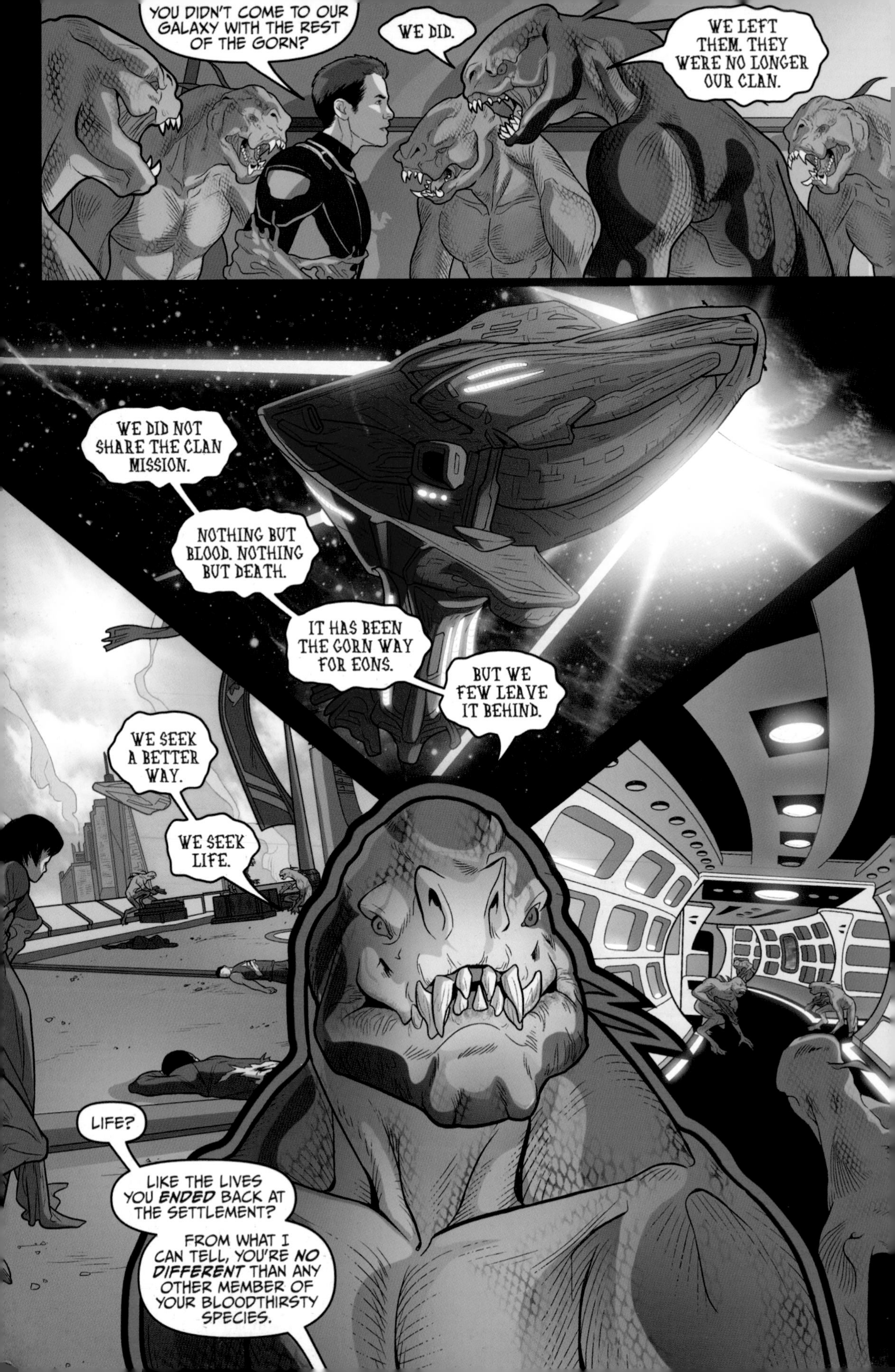
YOU DIDN'T COME TO OUR GALAXY WITH THE REST OF THE GORN?
WE DID.
WE LEFT THEM. THEY WERE NO LONGER OUR CLAN.
WE DID NOT SHARE THE CLAN MISSION.
NOTHING BUT BLOOD. NOTHING BUT DEATH.
IT HAS BEEN THE GORN WAY FOR EONS.
BUT WE FEW LEAVE IT BEHIND.
WE SEEK A BETTER WAY.
WE SEEK LIFE.
LIFE?
LIKE THE LIVES YOU ENDED BACK AT THE SETTLEMENT?
FROM WHAT I CAN TELL, YOU'RE NO DIFFERENT THAN ANY OTHER MEMBER OF YOUR BLOODTHIRSTY SPECIES.

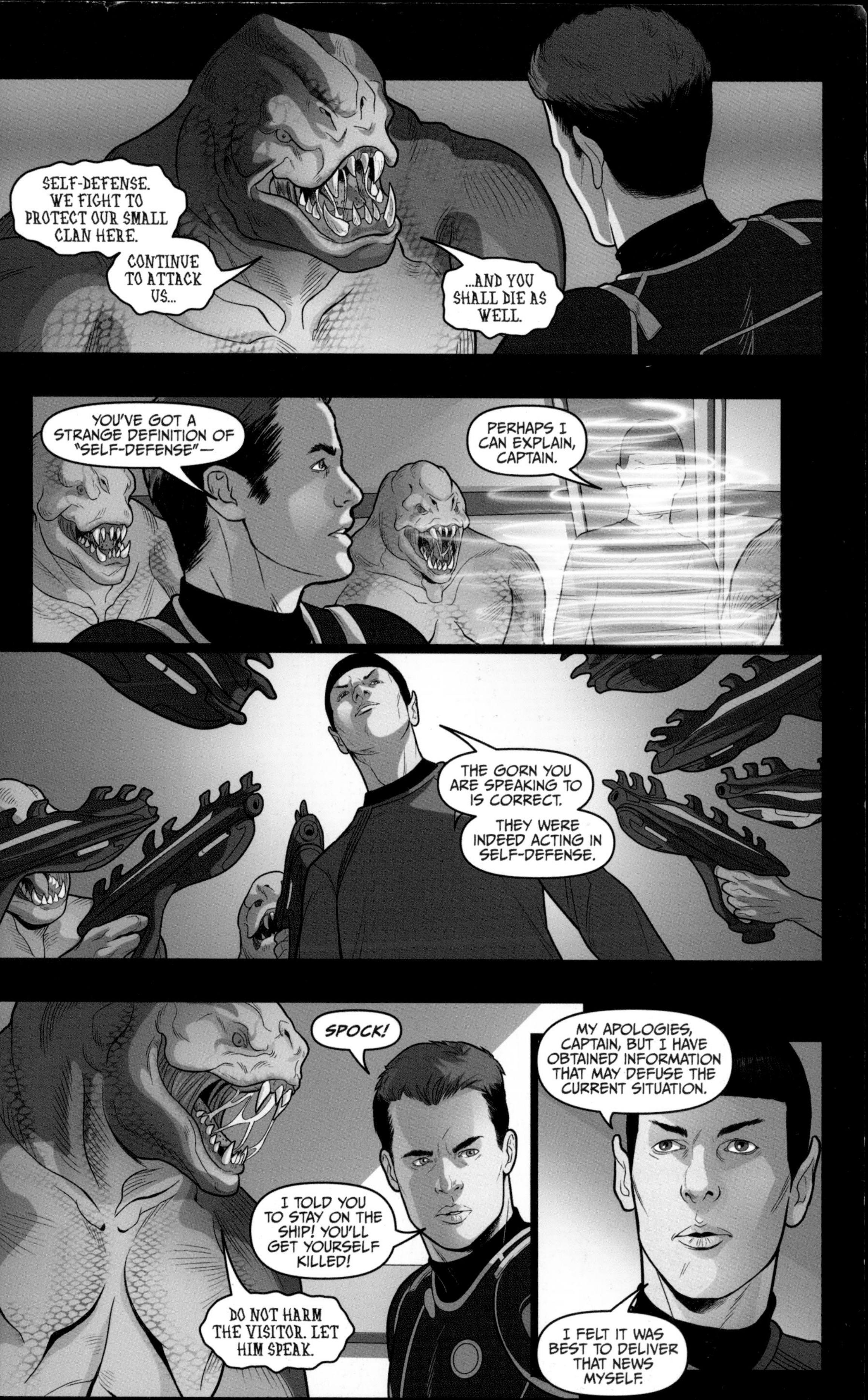
SELF-DEFENSE. WE FIGHT TO PROTECT OUR SMALL CLAN HERE.
CONTINUE TO ATTACK US...
...AND YOU SHALL DIE AS WELL.
YOU'VE GOT A STRANGE DEFINITION OF "SELF-DEFENSE"—
PERHAPS I CAN EXPLAIN, CAPTAIN.
THE GORN YOU ARE SPEAKING TO IS CORRECT.
THEY WERE INDEED ACTING IN SELF-DEFENSE.
SPOCK!
I TOLD YOU TO STAY ON THE SHIP! YOU'LL GET YOURSELF KILLED!
DO NOT HARM THE VISITOR. LET HIM SPEAK.
MY APOLOGIES, CAPTAIN, BUT I HAVE OBTAINED INFORMATION THAT MAY DEFUSE THE CURRENT SITUATION.
I FELT IT WAS BEST TO DELIVER THAT NEWS MYSELF.

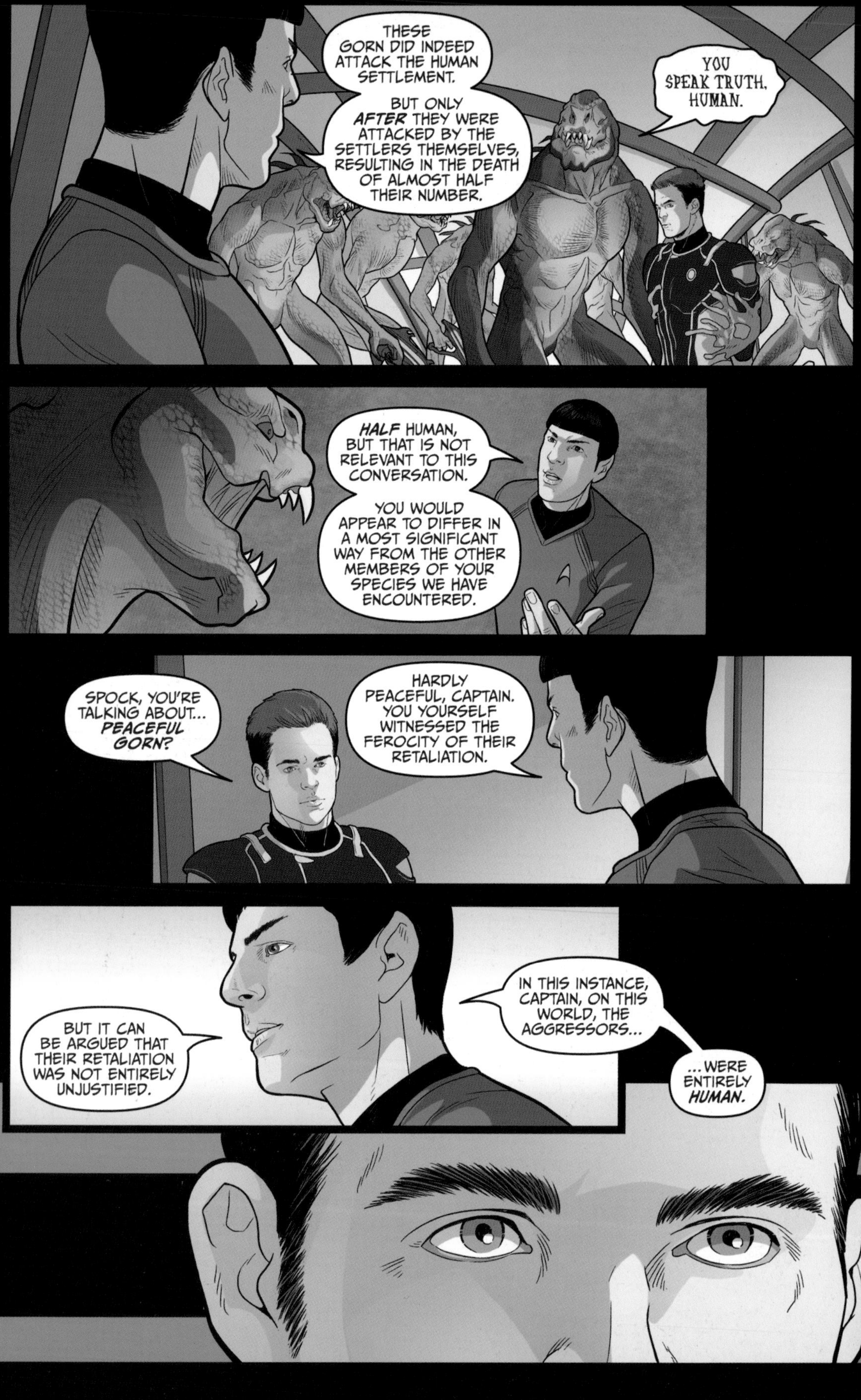
THESE GORN DID INDEED ATTACK THE HUMAN SETTLEMENT.
BUT ONLY *AFTER* THEY WERE ATTACKED BY THE SETTLERS THEMSELVES, RESULTING IN THE DEATH OF ALMOST HALF THEIR NUMBER.
YOU SPEAK TRUTH, HUMAN.
HALF HUMAN, BUT THAT IS NOT RELEVANT TO THIS CONVERSATION.
YOU WOULD APPEAR TO DIFFER IN A MOST SIGNIFICANT WAY FROM THE OTHER MEMBERS OF YOUR SPECIES WE HAVE ENCOUNTERED.
SPOCK, YOU'RE TALKING ABOUT... *PEACEFUL GORN?*
HARDLY PEACEFUL, CAPTAIN. YOU YOURSELF WITNESSED THE FEROCITY OF THEIR RETALIATION.
BUT IT CAN BE ARGUED THAT THEIR RETALIATION WAS NOT ENTIRELY UNJUSTIFIED.
IN THIS INSTANCE, CAPTAIN, ON THIS WORLD, THE AGGRESSORS...
...WERE ENTIRELY *HUMAN.*

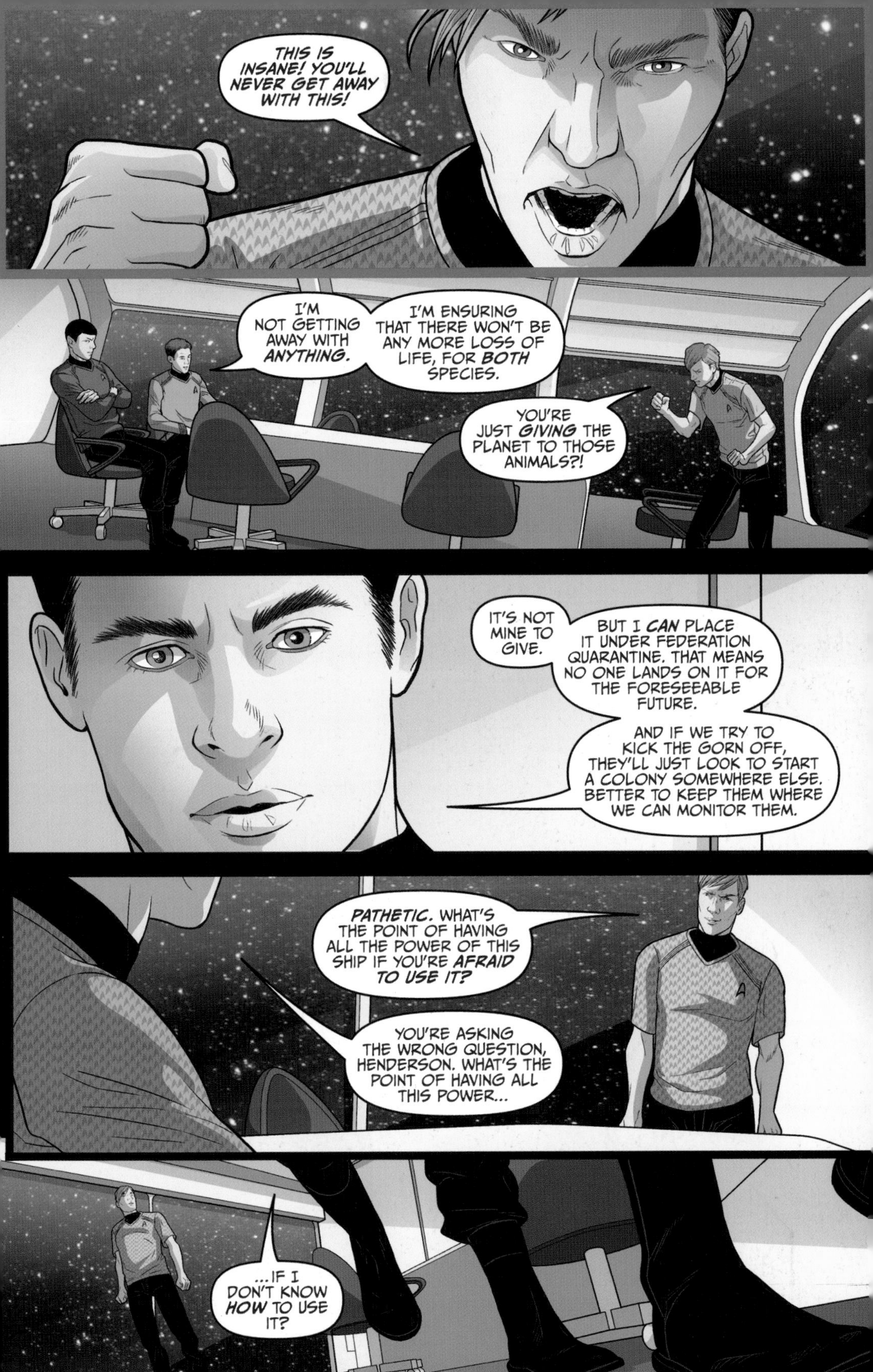
THIS IS INSANE! YOU'LL NEVER GET AWAY WITH THIS!
I'M NOT GETTING AWAY WITH ANYTHING.
I'M ENSURING THAT THERE WON'T BE ANY MORE LOSS OF LIFE, FOR BOTH SPECIES.
YOU'RE JUST GIVING THE PLANET TO THOSE ANIMALS?!
IT'S NOT MINE TO GIVE.
BUT I CAN PLACE IT UNDER FEDERATION QUARANTINE. THAT MEANS NO ONE LANDS ON IT FOR THE FORESEEABLE FUTURE.
AND IF WE TRY TO KICK THE GORN OFF, THEY'LL JUST LOOK TO START A COLONY SOMEWHERE ELSE. BETTER TO KEEP THEM WHERE WE CAN MONITOR THEM.
PATHETIC. WHAT'S THE POINT OF HAVING ALL THE POWER OF THIS SHIP IF YOU'RE AFRAID TO USE IT?
YOU'RE ASKING THE WRONG QUESTION, HENDERSON. WHAT'S THE POINT OF HAVING ALL THIS POWER...
...IF I DON'T KNOW HOW TO USE IT?

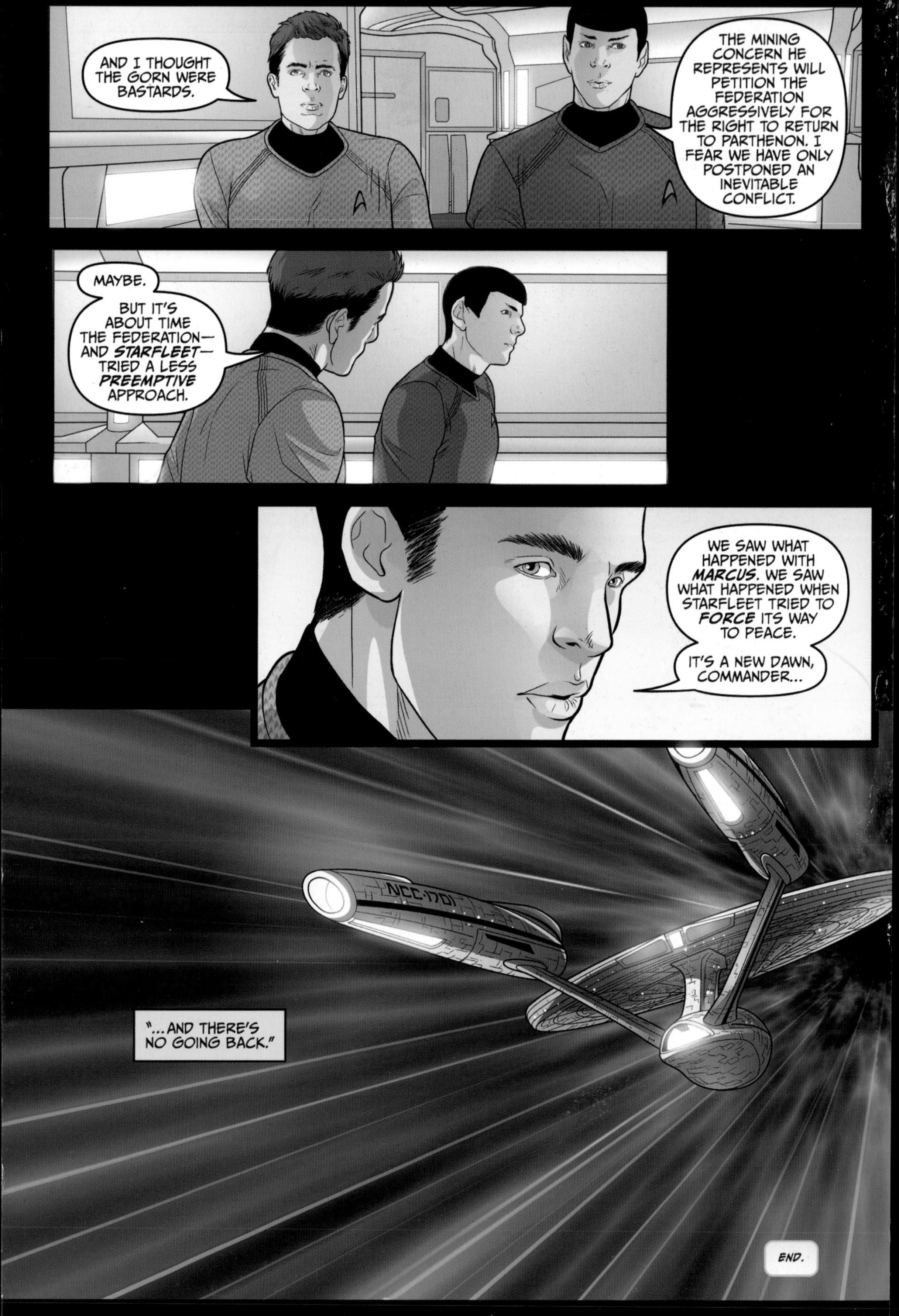

AND I THOUGHT THE GORN WERE BASTARDS.
THE MINING CONCERN HE REPRESENTS WILL PETITION THE FEDERATION AGGRESSIVELY FOR THE RIGHT TO RETURN TO PARTHENON. I FEAR WE HAVE ONLY POSTPONED AN INEVITABLE CONFLICT.
MAYBE.
BUT IT'S ABOUT TIME THE FEDERATION—AND STARFLEET—TRIED A LESS PREEMPTIVE APPROACH.
WE SAW WHAT HAPPENED WITH MARCUS. WE SAW WHAT HAPPENED WHEN STARFLEET TRIED TO FORCE ITS WAY TO PEACE.
IT'S A NEW DAWN, COMMANDER...
NCC-1701
"...AND THERE'S NO GOING BACK."
END.

ART BY **TIM BRADSTREET** COLORS BY **GRANT GOLEASH**

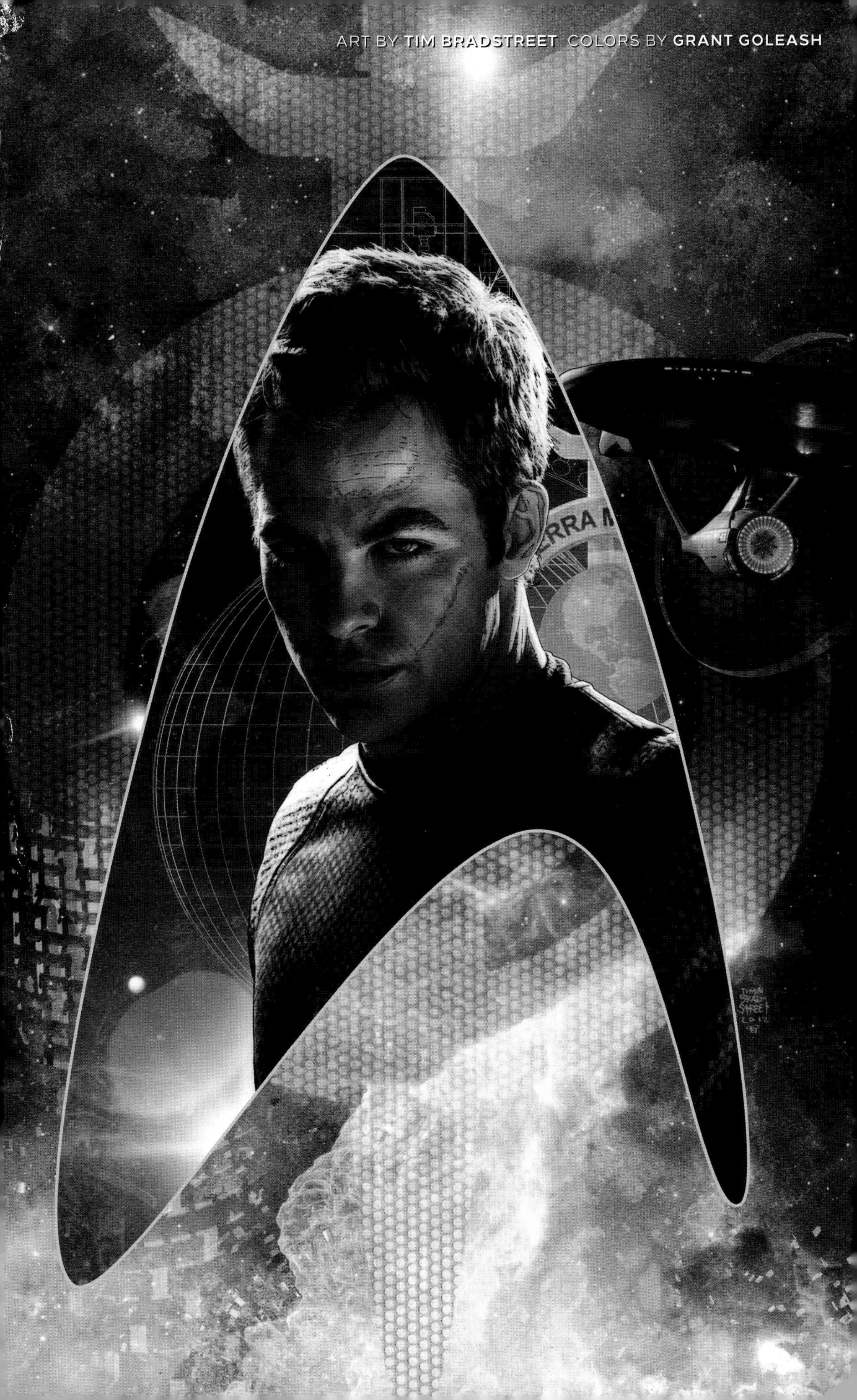
TIM BRAD-STREET 2012

ART BY **TIM BRADSTREET** COLORS BY **GRANT GOLEASH**

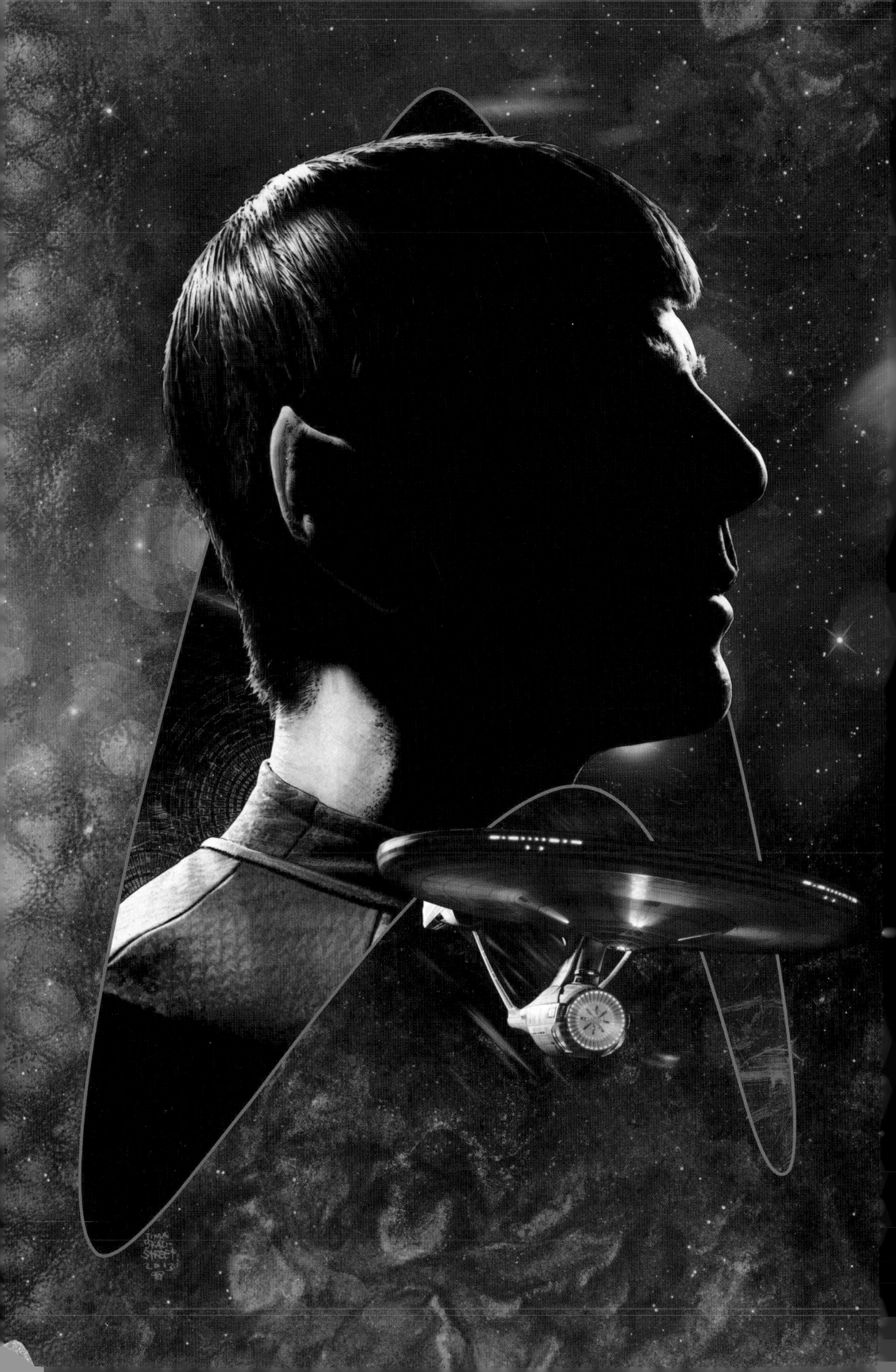

ART BY **TIM BRADSTREET** COLORS BY **GRANT GOLEASH**

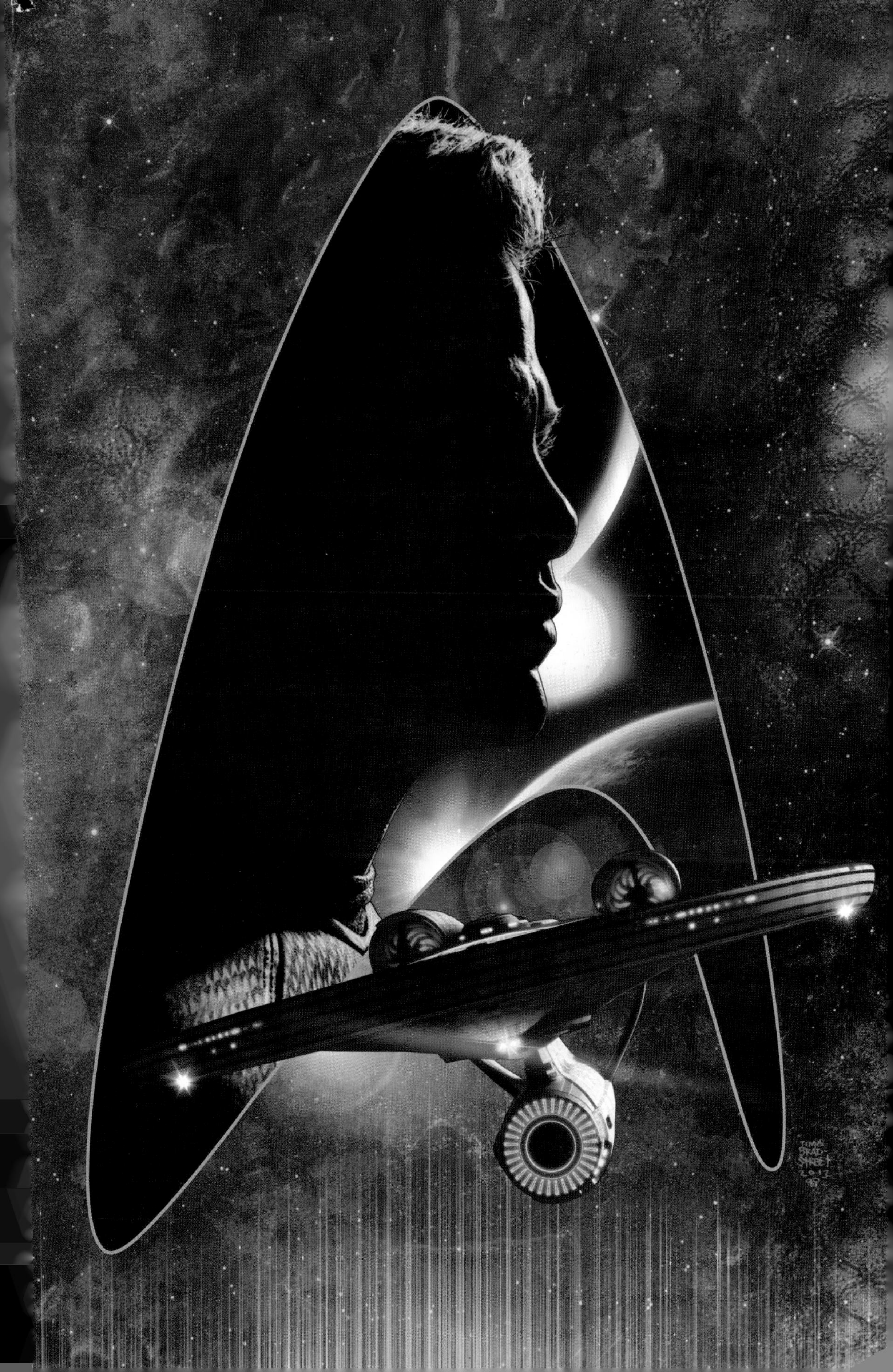

ART BY **GARRIE GASTONNY** COLORS BY **IFANSYAH NOOR**

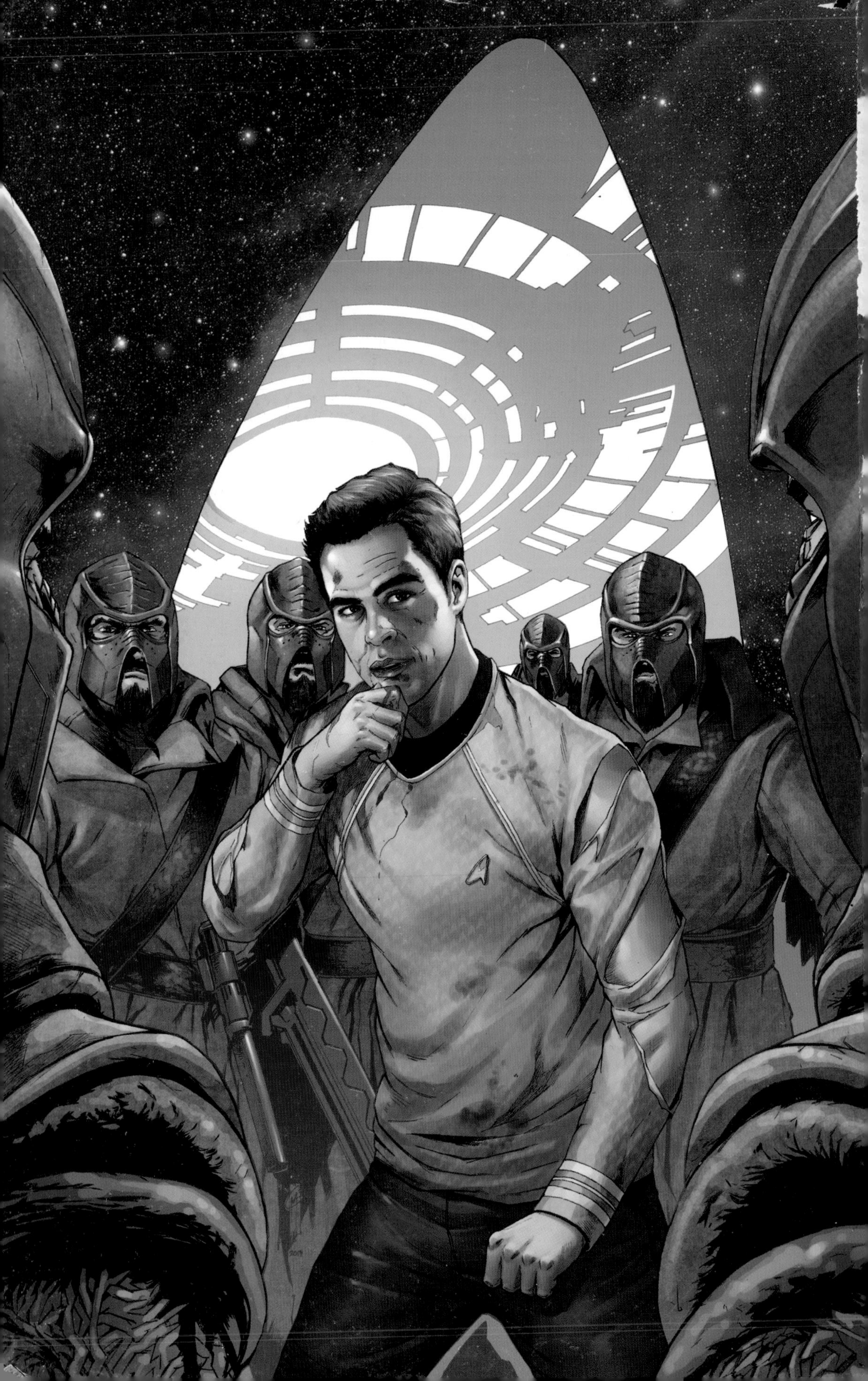